JOHN SILENCE—
PHYSICIAN EXTRAORDINARY

Dr. Silence is an eccentric man of science, philanthropic by nature, who specializes in cases involving psychical afflictions. An authority on the occult after years of rigorous training, John Silence is more interested in curing a home of an ancient haunting than in curing a head of the common cold. Herein are six of his most unusual cases, including the story of the man who seeks to renew childhood memories while travelling through France, but instead stumbles upon a monastery of the dead; and the island camping trip that turns into a shapeshifting nightmare. Six spellbinding tales from the grand master of supernatural fiction.

THE WAVE

Ever since childhood, Tom Kelverdon is haunted by a recurring dream in which a giant wave hovers over him. Strangely, he is aware in the dream that it isn't a wave of water, but something else. There is a sweet smell that accompanies this dream, and a vision of two bright blue eyes. Even as he grows older, Tom never loses this feeling of the Wave—his career as an engineer rides its own wave of success. Now in his 30s, he is reunited with Lettice, whom Tom had fallen in love with as a child, and meets up with her group in Egypt. So begins a strange journey that involves his impulsive cousin Tony—also in love with Lettice—as the three of them re-enact a doomed triangle from Egypt's dim past.

ALSO BY ALGERNON BLACKWOOD

Novels:
Jimbo: A Fantasy (1909)
The Education of Uncle Paul (1909)
The Human Chord (1910)
The Centaur (1911)
A Prisoner in Fairyland (1913)
The Extra Day (1916)
Julius Le Vallon: An Episode (1916)
The Wave: An Egyptian Aftermath (1916)
The Promise of Air (1918)
The Garden of Survival (1918)
The Bright Messenger (1921)

Children's Books:
Sambo and Snitch (1927)
Mr. Cupboard (1928)
Dudley and Gilderoy: A Nonsense (1929)
By Underground (1930)
The Parrot and the - Cat (1931)
The Italian Conjuror (1932)
Maria (of England) in the Rain (1933)
Sergeant Poppett and Policeman James (1934)
The Fruit Stoners (1934)
How the Circus Came to Tea (1936)
The Adventures of Dudley and Gilderoy (1941)

Autobiography:
Episodes Before Thirty (1923)

Original Short Story Collections:
The Empty House and Other Ghost Stories (1906)
The Listener and Other Stories (1907)
John Silence — Physician Extraordinary (1908)
The Lost Valley and Other Stories (1910)
Pan's Garden: A Volume of Nature Stories (1912)
Incredible Adventures (1914)
Ten Minute Stories (1914)
Day and Night Stories (1917)
The Wolves of God and Other Fey Stories, w/Wildred Wilson (1921)
Tongues of Fire and Other Sketches (1924)
Full Circle (1929) [single story]
Shocks (1935)
The Doll and One Other (1946)
The Mysterious House (1987) [single story]
The Magic Mirror: Lost Supernatural and Mystery Stories (1989)
The Face of the Earth & Other Imaginings (2015)

Plays:
Karma: A Reincarnation Play, w/Violet Pearn (1918)
Through the Crack w/Violet Pearn (1925)

JOHN SILENCE—PHYSICIAN EXTRAORDINARY

THE WAVE

Algernon Blackwood

Stark House Press • Eureka California

JOHN SILENCE—PHYSICAN EXTRAORDINARY /
THE WAVE: AN EGYPTIAN AFTERMATH

Published by Stark House Press
1315 H Street
Eureka, CA 95501, USA
griffinskye3@sbcglobal.net
www.starkhousepress.com

JOHN SILENCE—PHYSICAN EXTRAORDINARY
Originally published in 1908 by Eveleigh Nash, London, and in 1914 by
Vaughan & Gomme, New York. "A Victim of Higher Space" originally
published in Occult Review, December 1914; reprinted in *Day and Night
Stories*, 1917.

THE WAVE: AN EGYPTIAN AFTERMATH
Originally published in 1916 by Macmillan, London, and in 1916
by Dutton, New York.

"Introduction" copyright © 2017 by Stefan Dziemianowicz

ISBN: 978-1-944520-25-0

Book design by Mark Shepard, SHEPGRAPHICS.COM
Cover illustration by C. B. Williams

First Stark House Press Edition: September 2017

FIRST EDITION

Contents

INTRODUCTION

By Stefan Dziemianowicz

The odds are pretty good that any reader who picks up this book needs no introduction to its author. Algernon Blackwood (1869–1951) is one of the most celebrated writers in the history of weird fiction. His short tales of the macabre are reprinted perennially in anthologies and collections of his work, and his story "The Willows" is singled out by many critics as the greatest weird tale written in the English language. But many readers who know Blackwood through his ghost and horror stories are unfamiliar with the writer who expressed himself in works of novel length, those larger canvases that allowed him to explore concepts only hinted at in his shorter efforts. This volume provides readers with a unique opportunity to experience the two Blackwoods—who, as one quickly discovers, are the same Blackwood. *John Silence—Physician Extraordinary* is one of the most famous and influential collections of short weird tales published in the twentieth century. *The Wave* is an ambitious experimental novel, written at a point in Blackwood's life when he faced serious challenges to the ecstatic vision he strove to articulate through his writing. Together, these two books provide a context for appreciating Blackwood's achievements as a writer who crafted entertaining stories to serve as vehicles for esoteric ideas and beliefs but who also found awe in mystery in the rhythms of everyday existence.

John Silence—Physician Extraordinary was published on September 16, 1908, when Blackwood was thirty-eight years old and a published writer of fiction for nearly a decade. It was his third collection of short fiction and, like the collection that preceded it, *The Listener and Other Stories* (1907), none of its contents had appeared previously in print. The book features five stories tied together by the presence of John Silence, a "Psychic Doctor" (he resists the term usually applied to him—occult detective—and refers to "occultism" as "that dreadful word") whose casebook the tales represent. A sixth John Silence story dropped from the book, "A Victim of Higher Space," would be collected seven years later in Blackwood's *Ten Minute Stories* and it is the opinion of Blackwood expert Mike Ashley that it was likely the first written, when Blackwood was still working out the particulars of Silence's character and the extent of his personal involvement in his cases.

The concept and character of John Silence had been suggested to Blackwood by his publisher, Eveleigh Nash, as a means for unifying stories on a variety of occult themes that he had been planning to write. In all likelihood, some of the stories were already written and Blackwood had to revise them to accommodate Silence, who is an active character in some and more of an interlocutor or remote observer in others. Although they cohere as a unit, each of the John Silence stories can be appreciated on its own merits, and many readers probably know them through their individual reprintings in anthologies of weird fiction.

The first story, "A Psychical Invasion," provides the reader with what little back story there is to the character of the Doctor. He is a man of independent means who is a doctor by choice. A client praises him for "your wonderful clairvoyant gift and your trained psychic knowledge of the processes by which a personality may be disintegrated and destroyed"—a layman's description of Silence's psychic sensitivity and the sympathy with which he diagnoses maladies that are of the mind and spirit, rather than of the body. He developed his skills through "a long and severe training, at once physical, mental, and spiritual" that led to his disappearance from the world for five years. He only takes cases that interest him or in which he feels he can help the patient, and he charges no fee for his services. Physically, Silence is "sparely built with speaking brown eyes" and "a close beard." He is just past forty years in age, and his features convey both self-confidence and inner tranquility.

As with stories that he had written previous to them, the John Silence adventures feature autobiographical elements drawn from Blackwood's travels and personal experiences. "A Psychical Invasion" concerns a malignant spirit haunting a house that terrorizes its occupant when he becomes sensitized to its presence after dosing himself with *Cannabis indica*. Blackwood would have been very familiar with the methodology for investigating hauntings. Twenty years earlier, he had befriended members of the Society for Psychic Research, an organization devoted to the scientific assessment of psychic phenomena, and he apparently had participated in several haunted house investigations. Blackwood had also experimented with drugs for a very brief time and, aware of their mood-enhancing qualities, he extrapolated from them the heightened state of psychic vibration that has left the house's occupant (as Silence describes it) "cognizant of a much larger world than the one you know normally."

In "A Psychical Invasion" Silence becomes actively involved in neutralizing the haunting, putting himself in personal peril. By contrast, in "Ancient Sorceries," the doctor takes more of an armchair approach. Ashley notes that the story came to Blackwood during his travels through Laon, France, one summer, and it is one of Blackwood's finest weird tales, beguiling the reader with its narrator's growing impression that the small town he has wandered into is home not just to a different and unfamiliar culture—one for which he has an initially inexplicable affinity—but to a species older and more unnatural than the human society that he knows. Assessing the story in his landmark essay "Supernatural Horror in Literature," H. P. Lovecraft praised "Ancient Sorceries" as "perhaps the finest tale in the book" and it's quite possible that Blackwood's story influenced the writing of Lovecraft's own tale of an insular town populated by semi-human beings, "The Shadow Over Innsmouth."

Ashley also proposes that the book's fourth story, "Secret Worship," was likely written around the same time as "Ancient Sorceries," in part because of the passive presence of the doctor, to whom the tale is an adventure related, rather than participated in. The story's German school setting is based on the School of the Moravian Brotherhood at Königsfeld in the Black Forest, which Blackwood attended for a year in 1885. Although it's tempting to consider Blackwood's (near-literal) demonizing of the school's faculty as an act of latent revenge against the strict discipline he encountered while a student there the story is, in fact, a fine example of how attuned Blackwood was to the atmosphere of certain settings and how he could transform experiences that he lived through decades earlier into plot points for his fiction.

To the reader reading the John Silence stories in their sequence in the book, "The Nemesis of Fire" will almost immediately seem different from those that precede it. For one thing, it is narrated by a man named Hubbard who also relates the book's last story, "The Camp of the Dog," and who appears to be a companion and confidential secretary to Silence in the same capacity that Watson is to Sherlock Holmes in Arthur Conan Doyle's stories. Indeed, there is a very Sherlock Holmes-type quality to the story, in which Silence and his assistant travel to an old Manor House to investigate a supernatural peril that has killed the house's previous owner and that now threatens the relative who has taken ownership of the place. More interestingly, this story and its account of a fire elemental that has the power to take possession of the house owner's invalid sister anticipates similar ideas that Blackwood would develop two years later in one of his greatest stories, "The Wendigo."

The most notable aspect of the book's last story, "The Camp of the Dog," is how much of the story Silence is *not* present for. Most of the first half of this tale's account of a wolf-like being stalking Hubbard and the camping party he is part of unfolds with little involvement of the doctor, who is called in like the proverbial marines at the end to solve the mystery of the creature's origins and tie up the loose ends. For this volume, we also include the sixth John Silence story, "A Victim of Higher Space," the story of a man whose advanced perception of "higher space"—what we might call the fourth or fifth dimension—renders him sensitive to expanded consciousness and leaves him vulnerable to slipping inescapably into them. If Ashley is correct in his assertion that this may have been Blackwood's first effort to write a tale of John Silence, some argument could be made that Blackwood eventually refined and transfused some of its ideas into the book's first story, "A Psychical Invasion."

John Silence—Physician Extraordinary proved both a critical and popular success, and it was the first of Blackwood's books to garner an American edition, in 1909. Blackwood's reputation grew with it to the extent that some readers conflated the author with his fictional creation and queried him about their own psychic maladies in the ensuing years. The popularity of John Silence as a character notwithstanding, Blackwood never resurrected him for another story. The reader is left to wonder why, given that Blackwood had forged a template in the last two stories written that could have been used for subsequent adventures involving the doctor. Quite possibly, though, Blackwood saw that template as a potential straitjacket that could limit the extent to which he might explore an idea for a story independent of John Silence's participation, as in "Ancient Sorceries" and "Secret Worship." But it's also quite possible that Blackwood saw his work moving in a different direction. With its series character uniting the individual stories, *John Silence—Physician Extraordinary* can be considered Blackwood's stepping stone to a more ambitious work of fiction at novel length, and in fact *Jimbo: A Fantasy*, his first novel, would be published the following year. From that point on in his writing Blackwood began alternating novels with collections of short fiction.

The Wave, which was first published in 1916, is Blackwood's eighth published novel and one of the most ambitious works of fiction that he ever attempted. At the time he wrote it Blackwood was at a very different place in his life and career than where he had been eight years earlier. For one thing, Europe was two years into World War I, a conflict that many (Blackwood among them) never thought would persist as long as it had. At the war's outbreak Blackwood had sought to serve his country by working as a propagandist, an ambition that carried over into some of his fiction writing. Ultimately, though, the horrors of the war and its destruction of many locales where he experienced the beauty and tranquility that he hoped to convey through his writing devastated Blackwood. The basic idea for *The Wave* had been gestating in his work for several years leading up to its writing and it can be read as one of Blackwood's last attempts to capture the visionary gleam that empowered his best fiction.

Blackwood dedicated his novel to "M. S.-K.," the initials of Maya Stuart-King, a concert violinist who was also the dedicatee of his collection *Pan's Garden* (1912), as well as his novels *A Prisoner of Fairyland* (1913), *The Extra Day* (1915), *Julius LeVallon: An Episode* (1917), and *The Promise of Air* (1918). When Blackwood met Maya around 1910, she was more than a decade into a loveless marriage with the Baron Johann Knoop. Blackwood was smitten with her, and although his love for her would remain unrequited he recognized in her—as did she in him—a spiritual soulmate, one who was to influence the writing of some of his greatest works.

In addition to a home in England, the Knoops kept a sanatorium at Helwan in Egypt, where they lived in the winters and which the wealthy patronized as a spa. Blackwood traveled to Helwan in 1912 to visit the Knoops and he found that Egypt resonated with him spiritually. "Egypt is endless and inexhaustible," he wrote; "some hint of eternity lies there, an awareness of immortality almost." Almost immediately Blackwood was inspired to finish his story "Sand," which he had begun years before but had been unable to finish until his Egyptian sojourn. Other Egyptian-themed stories would follow: "A Descent into Egypt," a tale of a man's absorption spiritually into Egypt's past that many consider to be among Blackwood's finest efforts; and "A Desert Episode," "The Wings of Horus," "By Water," and "An Egyptian Hornet," all written after a return visit to Helwan in 1914.

In fact, "A Desert Episode," with its account of a pair of lovers who merge with eternity in the Egyptian desert, and "The Wings of Horus," about an ill-fated love triangle that unravels under the influence of the Egyptian god Horus, can be read as foretastes of *The Wave*, which Blackwood subtitled *An Egyptian Aftermath*. Blackwood plunges the reader into the thick of the novel's plot with it intriguing first line: "Since childhood days he had been haunted by a Wave." "He" is Tom Kelverton who, at the age of fifteen when the novel opens, has dreamed regularly for years of a wave waiting to break. This wave, we are told, represents both "his earliest recollection of any vividness" and "his first experience of nightmare." The wave is not made of water, but rather of a mass of whirling particles, behind which he senses two pairs of eyes: one of them light-blue eyes, the other a pair of "eastern eyes." Tommy's father, a nerve specialist, is intrigued by what he believes is his son's "unalterable premonition" and gives him access to a cupboard drawer full of Egyptian curios to which the boy is drawn. The spicy perfume emanating from the drawer—what Tommy will refer to as "the Whiff"—becomes a sensory stimulant that puts him in his "wavy" mood whenever he smells it. What Tommy doesn't know is that the drawer also contains a fragment of papyrus from which his father had transcribed the story of a doomed love triangle that occurred in 3,000 b.c., when a Theban general brought home a young Syrian boy from one of his conquests to serve as his wife's slave. The boy and his mistress fall passionately in love with one another and when the cuckolded general has the boy tortured to death his wife leaps to her own death. The general has their bodies thrown into the sea where they are swept under by the same wave. Thousands of years later the mummies of all three are found buried within the same tomb.

All of the foregoing is revealed in the novel's first chapter and it proves pretty much everything the reader will need to know to follow the narrative forward. Blackwood enriches the tale with philosophical speculations that come to the maturing Tommy as he ponders the significance of his dream and the grip it has on him. Blackwood writes, "he read that a wave was a segment of a circle, the perfect form, yet that it never completed itself. The ground on which it broke prevented the achievement of the circle." Also, that "the top of the wave, owing to its curve, was reflected in the under part. Its end, that is, was foretold in its beginning." With the realization that "life itself was a wave that rose, swept, curved," Tommy comes to understand that to seize an object of his moral and spiritual life at the top of that wave is to achieve "success." That object enters Tommy's life in the person of Lettice Aylmer, the daughter of a family acquaintance with whom Tommy shares uncommonly strong affinities. When Lettice enters into a loveless marriage with the Polish Prince Jaretzka, the stage is set for a recapitulation of the love triangle foreordained by the tale from the Egyptian papyrus and the persisting presence of the Wave.

It is tempting to call *The Wave* a novel of reincarnation but that would be an oversimplification of Blackwood's ambitions for the story. Certainly there is the sense of past lives repeated, and even Tommy understands that his haunting by the Wave and its attendant phenomena is "the ghost of some dim memory that brought a forgotten warning in its train—something missed, something to be repeated, something to be faced and learned and—mastered." But in discussing this understanding with his friend Tony Winslowe, Tommy comes the conclusion that existence assumes the form of a spiral: "We're here, I mean, for the purpose of development—whatever one's particular belief may be—and that this development, instead of going forwards in a straight line, has a kind of—spiral movement upwards?" Existence is circular (like the shape the Wave attempts to take), and repetitive, but it moves upward, affording opportunities for improvement and advancement. The life that Tommy knows, and the past life that he seems to remember, are both just circles in a spiral whose endless ascent embodies the eternal.

Separated by eight years and a plethora of Blackwood's personal experiences *John Silence—Physician Extraordinary* and *The Wave* represent two sides of their author's aesthetic approach to the supernatural. In the John Silence stories otherworldly forces are a source of horror to the people at their mercy because they seem to violate the natural order. Not so to John Silence, whose training as a Psychic Doctor has endowed him with the understanding that there are more things in Heaven and Earth than are dreamt of in the philosophies of his patients. The forces that enmesh and bind the characters in *The Wave* are disturbing at first until they come to accept that the inescapable recapitulation in which they are caught up is part of the natural evolutionary process of their spiritual lives. Both books express the vision of a writer whose work has been tagged with many labels—occultist, pantheist, theosophist, etc.—none of which fully express Blackwood's unique gift for conveying the mystical in the mundane and a world of marvels that magical abuts our own ordinary reality.

—Bloomfield, NJ
July 2017

Stefan Dziemianowicz has compiled more than fifty anthologies of horror, mystery, and science fiction and is the co-editor of *Supernatural Literature of the World: An Encyclopedia.*

John Silence—
Physician Extraordinary
by Algernon Blackwood

To M. L. W.
The Original of John Silence
and
My Companion in Many Adventures

CASE I

A PSYCHICAL INVASION

I

"And what is it makes you think I could be of use in this particular case?" asked Dr. John Silence, looking across somewhat sceptically at the Swedish lady in the chair facing him.

"Your sympathetic heart and your knowledge of occultism—"

"Oh, please—that dreadful word!" he interrupted, holding up a finger with a gesture of impatience.

"Well, then," she laughed, "your wonderful clairvoyant gift and your trained psychic knowledge of the processes by which a personality may be disintegrated and destroyed—these strange studies you've been experimenting with all these years—"

"If it's only a case of multiple personality I must really cry off," interrupted the doctor again hastily, a bored expression in his eyes.

"It's not that; now, please, be serious, for I want your help," she said; "and if I choose my words poorly you must be patient with my ignorance. The case I know will interest you, and no one else could deal with it so well. In fact, no ordinary professional man could deal with it at all, for I know of no treatment nor medicine that can restore a lost sense of humour!"

"You begin to interest me with your 'case,'" he replied, and made himself comfortable to listen.

Mrs. Sivendson drew a sigh of contentment as she watched him go to the tube and heard him tell the servant he was not to be disturbed.

"I believe you have read my thoughts already," she said; "your intuitive knowledge of what goes on in other people's minds is positively uncanny."

Her friend shook his head and smiled as he drew his chair up to a convenient position and prepared to listen attentively to what she had to say. He closed his eyes, as he always did when he wished to absorb the real meaning of a recital that might be inadequately expressed, for by this method he found it easier to set himself in tune with the living thoughts that lay behind the broken words.

By his friends John Silence was regarded as an eccentric, because he was rich by accident, and by choice—a doctor. That a man of independent means should devote his time to doctoring, chiefly doctoring folk who could not pay, passed their comprehension entirely. The native nobility of a soul whose first desire was to help those who could not help themselves, puzzled them. After that, it irritated them, and, greatly to his own satisfaction, they left him to his own devices.

Dr. Silence was a free-lance, though, among doctors, having neither consulting-room, bookkeeper, nor professional manner. He took no fees, being at heart a genuine philanthropist, yet at the same time did no harm to his fellow-practitioners, because he only accepted unremunerative cases, and cases that interested him for some very special reason. He argued that the rich could pay, and the very poor could avail themselves of organised charity, but that a very large class of ill-paid, self-respecting workers, often followers of the arts, could not afford the price of a week's comforts merely to be told to travel. And it was these he desired to help: cases often requiring special and patient study—things no doctor can give for a guinea, and that no one would dream of expecting him to give.

But there was another side to his personality and practice, and one with which we are now more directly concerned; for the cases that especially appealed to him were of no ordinary kind, but rather of that intangible, elusive, and difficult nature best described as psychical afflictions; and, though he would have been the last person himself to approve of the title, it was beyond question that he was known more or less generally as the "Psychic Doctor."

In order to grapple with cases of this peculiar kind, he had submitted himself to a long and severe training, at once physical, mental, and spiritual. What precisely this training had been, or where undergone, no one seemed to know, —for he never spoke of it, as, indeed, he betrayed no single other characteristic of the charlatan, —but the fact that it had involved a total disappearance from the world for five years, and that after he returned and began his singular practice no one ever dreamed of applying to him the so easily acquired epithet of quack, spoke much for the seriousness of his strange quest and also for the genuineness of his attainments.

For the modern psychical researcher he felt the calm tolerance of the "man who knows." There was a trace of pity in his voice—contempt he never showed—when he spoke of their methods.

"This classification of results is uninspired work at best," he said once to me, when I had been his confidential assistant for some years. "It leads nowhere, and after a hundred years will lead nowhere. It is playing with the wrong end of a rather dangerous toy. Far better, it would be, to examine the causes, and then the results would so easily slip into place and explain themselves. For the sources are accessible, and open to all who have the courage to lead the life that alone makes practical investigation safe and possible."

And towards the question of clairvoyance, too, his attitude was significantly sane, for he knew how extremely rare the genuine power was, and that what is commonly called clairvoyance is nothing more than a keen power of visualising.

"It connotes a slightly increased sensibility, nothing more," he would say. "The true clairvoyant deplores his power, recognising that it adds a new horror to life, and is in the nature of an affliction. And you will find this always to be the real test."

Thus it was that John Silence, this singularly developed doctor, was able to select his cases with a clear knowledge of the difference between mere hysterical delusion and the kind of psychical affliction that claimed his special powers. It was never necessary for him to resort to the cheap mysteries of divination; for, as I have heard him observe, after the solution of some peculiarly intricate problem—

"Systems of divination, from geomancy down to reading by tea-leaves, are merely so many methods of obscuring the outer vision, in order that the inner vision may become open. Once the method is mastered, no system is necessary at all."

And the words were significant of the methods of this remarkable man, the keynote of whose power lay, perhaps, more than anything else, in the knowledge, first, that thought can act at a distance, and, secondly, that thought is dynamic and can accomplish material results.

"Learn how to *think*," he would have expressed it, "and you have learned to tap power at its source."

To look at—he was now past forty—he was sparely built, with speaking brown eyes in which shone the light of knowledge and self-confidence, while at the same time they made one think of that wondrous gentleness seen most often in the eyes of animals. A close beard concealed the mouth without disguising the grim determination of lips and jaw, and the face somehow conveyed an impression of transparency, almost of light, so delicately were the features refined away. On the fine forehead was that indefinable touch of peace that comes from identifying the mind with what is permanent in the soul, and letting the impermanent slip by without power to wound or distress; while, from his manner, —so gentle, quiet, sympathetic, —few could have guessed the strength of purpose that burned within like a great flame.

"I think I should describe it as a psychical case," continued the Swedish lady, obviously trying to explain herself very intelligently, "and just the kind you like. I mean a case where the cause is hidden deep down in some spiritual distress, and—"

"But the symptoms first, please, my dear Svenska," he interrupted, with a strangely compelling seriousness of manner, "and your deductions afterwards."

She turned round sharply on the edge of her chair and looked him in the face, lowering her voice to prevent her emotion betraying itself too obviously.

"In my opinion there's only one symptom," she half whispered, as though telling something disagreeable—"fear—simply fear."

"Physical fear?"

"I think not; though how can I say? I think it's a horror in the psychical region. It's no ordinary delusion; the man is quite sane; but he lives in mortal terror of something—"

"I don't know what you mean by his 'psychical region,'" said the doctor, with a smile; "though I suppose you wish me to understand that his spiritual, and not his mental, processes are affected. Anyhow, try and tell me briefly and pointedly what you know about the man, his symptoms, his need for help, my peculiar help, that is, and all that seems vital in the case. I promise to listen devotedly."

"I am trying," she continued earnestly, "but must do so in my own words and trust to your intelligence to disentangle as I go along. He is a young author, and lives in a tiny house off Putney Heath somewhere. He writes humorous stories—quite a genre of his own: Pender—you must have heard the name—Felix Pender? Oh, the man had a great gift, and married on the strength of it; his future seemed assured. I say 'had,' for quite suddenly his talent utterly failed him. Worse, it became transformed into its opposite. He can no longer write a line in the old way that was bringing him success—"

Dr. Silence opened his eyes for a second and looked at her.

"He still writes, then? The force has not gone?" he asked briefly, and then closed his eyes again to listen.

"He works like a fury," she went on, "but produces nothing"—she hesitated a moment—"nothing that he can use or sell. His earnings have practically ceased, and he makes a precarious living by book-reviewing and odd jobs—very odd, some of them. Yet, I am certain his talent has not really deserted him finally, but is merely—"

Again Mrs. Sivendson hesitated for the appropriate word.

"In abeyance," he suggested, without opening his eyes.

"Obliterated," she went on, after a moment to weigh the word, "merely obliterated by something else—"

"By some one else?"

"I wish I knew. All I can say is that he is haunted, and temporarily his sense of humour is shrouded—gone—replaced by something dreadful that writes other things. Unless something competent is done, he will simply starve to death. Yet he is afraid to go to a doctor for fear of being pronounced insane; and, anyhow, a man can hardly ask a doctor to take a guinea to restore a vanished sense of humour, can he?"

"Has he tried any one at all—?"

"Not doctors yet. He tried some clergymen and religious people; but they know so little and have so little intelligent sympathy. And most of them are so busy balancing on their own little pedestals—"

John Silence stopped her tirade with a gesture.

"And how is it that you know so much about him?" he asked gently.

"I know Mrs. Pender well—I knew her before she married him—"

"And is she a cause, perhaps?"

"Not in the least. She is devoted; a woman very well educated, though without being really intelligent, and with so little sense of humour herself that she always laughs at the wrong places. But she has nothing to do with the cause of his distress; and, indeed, has chiefly guessed it from observing him, rather than from what little he has told her. And he, you know, is a really lovable fellow, hard-working, patient—altogether worth saving."

Dr. Silence opened his eyes and went over to ring for tea. He did not know very much more about the case of the humorist than when he first sat down to listen; but he realised that no amount of words from his Swedish friend would help to reveal the real facts. A personal interview with the author himself could alone do that.

"All humorists are worth saving," he said with a smile, as she poured out tea. "We can't afford to lose a single one in these strenuous days. I will go and see your friend at the first opportunity."

She thanked him elaborately, effusively, with many words, and he, with much difficulty, kept the conversation thenceforward strictly to the teapot.

And, as a result of this conversation, and a little more he had gathered by means best known to himself and his secretary, he was whizzing in his motor-car one afternoon a few days later up the Putney Hill to have his first interview with Felix Pender, the humorous writer who was the victim of some mysterious malady in his "psychical region" that had obliterated his sense of the comic and threatened to wreck his life and destroy his talent. And his desire to help was probably of equal strength with his desire to know and to investigate.

The motor stopped with a deep purring sound, as though a great black panther lay concealed within its hood, and the doctor—the "psychic doctor," as he was sometimes called—stepped out through the gathering fog, and walked across the tiny garden that held a blackened fir tree and a stunted laurel shrubbery. The house was very small, and it was some time before any one answered the bell. Then, suddenly, a light appeared in the hall, and he saw a pretty little woman standing on the top step begging him to come in. She was dressed in grey, and the gaslight fell on a mass of deliberately brushed light hair. Stuffed, dusty birds, and a shabby array of

African spears, hung on the wall behind her. A hat-rack, with a bronze plate full of very large cards, led his eye swiftly to a dark staircase beyond. Mrs. Pender had round eyes like a child's, and she greeted him with an effusiveness that barely concealed her emotion, yet strove to appear naturally cordial. Evidently she had been looking out for his arrival, and had outrun the servant girl. She was a little breathless.

"I hope you've not been kept waiting—I think it's *most* good of you to come—" she began, and then stopped sharp when she saw his face in the gaslight. There was something in Dr. Silence's look that did not encourage mere talk. He was in earnest now, if ever man was.

"Good evening, Mrs. Pender," he said, with a quiet smile that won confidence, yet deprecated unnecessary words, "the fog delayed me a little. I am glad to see you."

They went into a dingy sitting-room at the back of the house, neatly furnished but depressing. Books stood in a row upon the mantelpiece. The fire had evidently just been lit. It smoked in great puffs into the room.

"Mrs. Sivendson said she thought you might be able to come," ventured the little woman again, looking up engagingly into his face and betraying anxiety and eagerness in every gesture. "But I hardly dared to believe it. I think it is really too good of you. My husband's case is so peculiar that—well, you know, I am quite sure any *ordinary* doctor would say at once the asylum—"

"Isn't he in, then?" asked Dr. Silence gently.

"In the asylum?" she gasped. "Oh dear, no—not yet!"

"In the house, I meant," he laughed.

She gave a great sigh.

"He'll be back any minute now," she replied, obviously relieved to see him laugh; "but the fact is, we didn't expect you so early—I mean, my husband hardly thought you would come at all."

"I am always delighted to come—when I am really wanted, and can be of help," he said quickly; "and, perhaps, it's all for the best that your husband is out, for now that we are alone you can tell me something about his difficulties. So far, you know, I have heard very little."

Her voice trembled as she thanked him, and when he came and took a chair close beside her she actually had difficulty in finding words with which to begin.

"In the first place," she began timidly, and then continuing with a nervous incoherent rush of words, "he will be simply delighted that you've really come, because he said you were the only person he would consent to see at all—the only doctor, I mean. But, of course, he doesn't know how frightened I am, or how much I have noticed. He pretends with me that it's just a nervous breakdown, and I'm sure he doesn't realise all the odd things I've noticed him doing. But the main thing, I suppose—"

"Yes, the main thing, Mrs. Pender," he said, encouragingly, noticing her hesitation.

"—is that he thinks we are not alone in the house. That's the chief thing."

"Tell me more facts—just facts."

"It began last summer when I came back from Ireland; he had been here alone for six weeks, and I thought him looking tired and queer—ragged and scattered about the face, if you know what I mean, and his manner worn out. He said he had been writing hard, but his inspiration had somehow failed him, and he was dissatisfied with his work. His sense of humour was leaving him, or changing into something else, he said. There was something in the house, he declared, that"—she emphasised the words—"prevented his feeling funny."

"Something in the house that prevented his feeling funny," repeated the doctor. "Ah, now we're getting to the heart of it!"

"Yes," she resumed vaguely, "that's what he kept saying."

"And what was it he *did* that you thought strange?" he asked sympathetically. "Be brief, or he may be here before you finish."

"Very small things, but significant it seemed to me. He changed his workroom from the library, as we call it, to the sitting-room. He said all his characters became wrong and terrible in the library; they altered, so that he felt like writing tragedies—vile, debased tragedies, the tragedies of broken souls. But now he says the same of the sitting-room, and he's gone back to the library."

"Ah!"

"You see, there's so little I can tell you," she went on, with increasing speed and countless gestures. "I mean it's only very small things he does and says that are queer. What frightens me is that he assumes there is some one else in the house all the time—some one I never see. He does not actually say so, but on the stairs I've seen him standing aside to let some one pass; I've seen him open a door to let some one in or out; and often in our bedrooms he puts chairs about as though for some one else to sit in. Oh—oh yes, and once or twice," she cried—"once or twice—"

She paused, and looked about her with a startled air.

"Yes?"

"Once or twice," she resumed hurriedly, as though she heard a sound that alarmed her, "I've heard him running—coming in and out of the rooms breathless as if something were after him—"

The door opened while she was still speaking, cutting her words off in the middle, and a man came into the room. He was dark and clean-shaven, sallow rather, with the eyes of imagination, and dark hair growing scantily about the temples. He was dressed in a shabby tweed suit, and wore an untidy flannel collar at the neck. The dominant expression of his face was startled—hunted; an expression that might any moment leap into the dreadful stare of terror and announce a total loss of self-control.

The moment he saw his visitor a smile spread over his worn features, and he advanced to shake hands.

"I hoped you would come; Mrs. Sivendson said you might be able to find time," he said simply. His voice was thin and needy. "I am very glad to see you, Dr. Silence. It is 'Doctor,' is it not?"

"Well, I am entitled to the description," laughed the other, "but I rarely get it. You know, I do not practise as a regular thing; that is, I only take cases that specially interest me, or—"

He did not finish the sentence, for the men exchanged a glance of sympathy that rendered it unnecessary.

"I have heard of your great kindness."

"It's my hobby," said the other quickly, "and my privilege."

"I trust you will still think so when you have heard what I have to tell you," continued the author, a little wearily. He led the way across the hall into the little smoking-room where they could talk freely and undisturbed.

In the smoking-room, the door shut and privacy about them, Pender's attitude changed somewhat, and his manner became very grave. The doctor sat opposite, where he could watch his face. Already, he saw, it looked more haggard. Evidently it cost him much to refer to his trouble at all.

"What I have is, in my belief, a profound spiritual affliction," he began quite bluntly, looking straight into the other's eyes.

"I saw that at once," Dr. Silence said.

"Yes, you saw that, of course; my atmosphere must convey that much to any one with psychic perceptions. Besides which, I feel sure from all I've heard, that you are really a soul-doctor, are you not, more than a healer merely of the body?"

"You think of me too highly," returned the other; "though I prefer cases, as you know, in which the spirit is disturbed first, the body afterwards."

"I understand, yes. Well, I have experienced a curious disturbance in— not in my physical region primarily. I mean my nerves are all right, and my body is all right. I have no delusions exactly, but my spirit is tortured by a calamitous fear which first came upon me in a strange manner."

John Silence leaned forward a moment and took the speaker's hand and held it in his own for a few brief seconds, closing his eyes as he did so. He was not feeling his pulse, or doing any of the things that doctors ordinarily do; he was merely absorbing into himself the main note of the man's mental condition, so as to get completely his own point of view, and thus be able to treat his case with true sympathy. A very close observer might perhaps have noticed that a slight tremor ran through his frame after he had held the hand for a few seconds.

"Tell me quite frankly, Mr. Pender," he said soothingly, releasing the hand, and with deep attention in his manner, "tell me all the steps that led to the beginning of this invasion. I mean tell me what the particular drug was, and why you took it, and how it affected you—"

"Then you know it began with a drug!" cried the author, with undisguised astonishment.

"I only know from what I observe in you, and in its effect upon myself. You are in a surprising psychical condition. Certain portions of your atmosphere are vibrating at a far greater rate than others. This is the effect of a drug, but of no ordinary drug. Allow me to finish, please. If the higher rate of vibration spreads all over, you will become, of course, permanently cognisant of a much larger world than the one you know normally. If, on the other hand, the rapid portion sinks back to the usual rate, you will lose these occasional increased perceptions you now have."

"You amaze me!" exclaimed the author; "for your words exactly describe what I have been feeling "

"I mention this only in passing, and to give you confidence before you approach the account of your real affliction," continued the doctor. "All perception, as you know, is the result of vibrations; and clairvoyance simply means becoming sensitive to an increased scale of vibrations. The awakening of the inner senses we hear so much about means no more than that. Your partial clairvoyance is easily explained. The only thing that puzzles me is how you managed to procure the drug, for it is not easy to get in pure form, and no adulterated tincture could have given you the terrific impetus I see you have acquired. But, please proceed now and tell me your story in your own way."

"This *Cannabis indica*," the author went on, "came into my possession last autumn while my wife was away. I need not explain how I got it, for that has no importance; but it was the genuine fluid extract, and I could not resist the temptation to make an experiment. One of its effects, as you know, is to induce torrential laughter—"

"Yes: sometimes."

"—I am a writer of humorous tales, and I wished to increase my own sense of laughter—to see the ludicrous from an abnormal point of view. I wished to study it a bit, if possible, and—"

"Tell me!"

"I took an experimental dose. I starved for six hours to hasten the effect, locked myself into this room, and gave orders not to be disturbed. Then I swallowed the stuff and waited."

"And the effect?"

"I waited one hour, two, three, four, five hours. Nothing happened. No laughter came, but only a great weariness instead. Nothing in the room or in my thoughts came within a hundred miles of a humorous aspect."

"Always a most uncertain drug," interrupted the doctor. "We make very small use of it on that account."

"At two o'clock in the morning I felt so hungry and tired that I decided to give up the experiment and wait no longer. I drank some milk and went upstairs to bed. I felt flat and disappointed. I fell asleep at once and must have slept for about an hour, when I awoke suddenly with a great noise in my ears. It was the noise of my own laughter! I was simply shaking with merriment. At first I was bewildered and thought I had been laughing in dreams, but a moment later I remembered the drug, and was delighted to think that after all I had got an effect. It had been working all along, only I had miscalculated the time. The only unpleasant thing *then* was an odd feeling that I had not waked naturally, but had been wakened by some one else—deliberately. This came to me as a certainty in the middle of my noisy laughter and distressed me."

"Any impression who it could have been?" asked the doctor, now listening with close attention to every word, very much on the alert.

Pender hesitated and tried to smile. He brushed his hair from his forehead with a nervous gesture.

"You must tell me all your impressions, even your fancies; they are quite as important as your certainties."

"I had a vague idea that it was some one connected with my forgotten dream, some one who had been at me in my sleep, some one of great strength and great ability—of great force—quite an unusual personality— and, I was certain, too—a woman."

"A good woman?" asked John Silence quietly.

Pender started a little at the question and his sallow face flushed; it seemed to surprise him. But he shook his head quickly with an indefinable look of horror.

"Evil," he answered briefly, "appallingly evil, and yet mingled with the sheer wickedness of it was also a certain perverseness—the perversity of the unbalanced mind."

He hesitated a moment and looked up sharply at his interlocutor. A shade of suspicion showed itself in his eyes.

"No," laughed the doctor, "you need not fear that I'm merely humouring you, or think you mad. Far from it. Your story interests me exceedingly and you furnish me unconsciously with a number of clues as you tell it. You see, I possess some knowledge of my own as to these psychic byways."

"I was shaking with such violent laughter," continued the narrator, reassured in a moment, "though with no clear idea what was amusing me, that I had the greatest difficulty in getting up for the matches, and was afraid I should frighten the servants overhead with my explosions. When the gas was lit I found the room empty, of course, and the door locked as usual. Then I half dressed and went out on to the landing, my hilarity better under control, and proceeded to go downstairs. I wished to record my sensations. I stuffed a handkerchief into my mouth so as not to scream aloud and communicate my hysterics to the entire household."

"And the presence of this—this—?"

"It was hanging about me all the time," said Pender, "but for the moment it seemed to have withdrawn. Probably, too, my laughter killed all other emotions."

"And how long did you take getting downstairs?"

"I was just corning to that. I see you know all my 'symptoms' in advance, as it were; for, of course, I thought I should never get to the bottom. Each step seemed to take five minutes, and crossing the narrow hall at the foot of the stairs—well, I could have sworn it was half an hour's journey had not my watch certified that it was a few seconds. Yet I walked fast and tried to push on. It was no good. I walked apparently without advancing, and at that rate it would have taken me a week to get down Putney Hill."

"An experimental dose radically alters the scale of time and space sometimes—"

"But, when at last I got into my study and lit the gas, the change came horridly, and sudden as a flash of lightning. It was like a douche of icy water, and in the middle of this storm of laughter—"

"Yes; what?" asked the doctor, leaning forward and peering into his eyes.

"—I was overwhelmed with terror," said Pender, lowering his reedy voice at the mere recollection of it.

He paused a moment and mopped his forehead. The scared, hunted look in his eyes now dominated the whole face. Yet, all the time, the corners of his mouth hinted of possible laughter as though the recollection of that merriment still amused him. The combination of fear and laughter in his face was very curious, and lent great conviction to his story; it also lent a bizarre expression of horror to his gestures.

"Terror, was it?" repeated the doctor soothingly.

"Yes, terror; for, though the Thing that woke me seemed to have gone, the memory of it still frightened me, and I collapsed into a chair. Then I locked the door and tried to reason with myself, but the drug made my movements so prolonged that it took me five minutes to reach the door, and another five to get back to the chair again. The laughter, too, kept bubbling up inside me—great wholesome laughter that shook me like gusts of wind—so that even my terror almost made me laugh. Oh, but I may tell you, Dr. Silence, it was altogether vile, that mixture of fear and laughter, altogether vile!

"Then, all at once, the things in the room again presented their funny side to me and set me off laughing more furiously than ever. The bookcase was ludicrous, the arm-chair a perfect clown, the way the clock looked at me on the mantelpiece too comic for words; the arrangement of papers and inkstand on the desk tickled me till I roared and shook and held my sides and the tears streamed down my cheeks. And that footstool! Oh, that absurd footstool!"

He lay back in his chair, laughing to himself and holding up his hands at the thought of it, and at the sight of him Dr. Silence laughed, too.

"Go on, please," he said, "I quite understand. I know something myself of the hashish laughter."

The author pulled himself together and resumed, his face growing quickly grave again.

"So, you see, side by side with this extravagant, apparently causeless merriment, there was also an extravagant, apparently causeless terror. The drug produced the laughter, I knew; but what brought in the terror I could not imagine. Everywhere behind the fun lay the fear. It was terror masked by cap and bells; and I became the playground for two opposing emotions, armed and fighting to the death. Gradually, then, the impression grew in me that this fear was caused by the invasion—so you called it just now—of the 'person' who had wakened me: she was utterly evil; inimical to my soul, or at least to all in me that wished for good. There I stood, sweating and trembling, laughing at everything in the room, yet all the while with this white terror mastering my heart. And this creature was putting—putting her—"

He hesitated again, using his handkerchief freely.

"Putting what?"

"—putting ideas into my mind," he went on glancing nervously about the room. "Actually tapping my thought-stream so as to switch off the usual current and inject her own. How mad that sounds! I know it, but it's true. It's the only way I can express it. Moreover, while the operation terrified me, the skill with which it was accomplished filled me afresh with laughter at the clumsiness of men by comparison. Our ignorant, bungling methods of teaching the minds of others, of inculcating ideas, and so on, overwhelmed me with laughter when I understood this superior and diabolical method. Yet my laughter seemed hollow and ghastly, and ideas of evil and tragedy trod close upon the heels of the comic. Oh, doctor, I tell you again, it was unnerving!"

John Silence sat with his head thrust forward to catch every word of the story which the other continued to pour out in nervous, jerky sentences and lowered voice.

"You *saw* nothing—no one—all this time?" he asked.

"Not with my eyes. There was no visual hallucination. But in my mind there began to grow the vivid picture of a woman—large, dark-skinned, with white teeth and masculine features, and one eye—the left—so drooping as to appear almost closed. Oh, such a face—!"

"A face you would recognise again?"

Pender laughed dreadfully.

"I wish I could forget it," he whispered, "I only wish I could forget it!" Then he sat forward in his chair suddenly, and grasped the doctor's hand with an emotional gesture.

"I *must* tell you how grateful I am for your patience and sympathy," he cried, with a tremor in his voice, "and—that you do not think me mad. I have told no one else a quarter of all this, and the mere freedom of speech—the relief of sharing my affliction with another—has helped me already more than I can possibly say."

Dr. Silence pressed his hand and looked steadily into the frightened eyes. His voice was very gentle when he replied.

"Your case, you know, is very singular, but of absorbing interest to me," he said, "for it threatens, not your physical existence but the temple of your psychical existence—the inner life. Your mind would not be permanently affected here and now, in this world; but in the existence after the body is left behind, you might wake up with your spirit so twisted, so distorted, so befouled, that you would be *spiritually insane*—a far more radical condition than merely being insane here."

There came a strange hush over the room, and between the two men sitting there facing one another.

"Do you really mean—Good Lord!" stammered the author as soon as he could find his tongue.

"What I mean in detail will keep till a little later, and I need only say now that I should not have spoken in this way unless I were quite positive of being able to help you. Oh, there's no doubt as to that, believe me. In the first place, I am very familiar with the workings of this extraordinary drug, this drug which has had the chance effect of opening you up to the forces of another region; and, in the second, I have a firm belief in the reality of supersensuous occurrences as well as considerable knowledge of psychic processes acquired by long and painful experiment. The rest is, or should be, merely sympathetic treatment and practical application. The hashish has partially opened another world to you by increasing your rate of psychical vibration, and thus rendering you abnormally sensitive. Ancient forces attached to this house have attacked you. For the moment I am only puzzled as to their precise nature; for were they of an ordinary character, I should myself be psychic enough to feel them. Yet I am conscious of feeling nothing as yet. But now, please continue, Mr. Pender, and tell me the rest of your wonderful story; and when you have finished, I will talk about the means of cure."

Pender shifted his chair a little closer to the friendly doctor and then went on in the same nervous voice with his narrative.

"After making some notes of my impressions I finally got upstairs again to bed. It was four o'clock in the morning. I laughed all the way up—at the grotesque banisters, the droll physiognomy of the staircase window, the burlesque grouping of the furniture, and the memory of that outrageous footstool in the room below; but nothing more happened to alarm or disturb me, and I woke late in the morning after a dreamless sleep, none the worse for my experiment except for a slight headache and a coldness of the extremities due to lowered circulation."

"Fear gone, too?" asked the doctor.

"I seemed to have forgotten it, or at least ascribed it to mere nervousness. Its reality had gone, anyhow for the time, and all that day I wrote and wrote and wrote. My sense of laughter seemed wonderfully quickened and my characters acted without effort out of the heart of true humour. I was exceedingly pleased with this result of my experiment. But when the stenographer had taken her departure and I came to read over the pages she had typed out, I recalled her sudden glances of surprise and the odd way she had looked up at me while I was dictating. I was amazed at what I read and could hardly believe I had uttered it."

"And why?"

"It was so distorted. The words, indeed, were mine so far as I could remember, but the meanings seemed strange. It frightened me. The sense was so altered. At the very places where my characters were intended to tickle the ribs, only curious emotions of sinister amusement resulted. Dreadful innuendoes had managed to creep into the phrases. There was laughter of a kind, but it was bizarre, horrible, distressing; and my attempt at analysis only increased my dismay. The story, as it read then, made me shudder, for by virtue of these slight changes it had come somehow to hold the soul of horror, of horror disguised as merriment. The framework of humour was there, if you understand me, but the characters had turned sinister, and their laughter was evil."

"Can you show me this writing?"

The author shook his head.

"I destroyed it," he whispered. "But, in the end, though of course much perturbed about it, I persuaded myself that it was due to some after-effect of the drug, a sort of reaction that gave a twist to my mind and made me read macabre interpretations into words and situations that did not properly hold them."

"And, meanwhile, did the presence of this person leave you?"

"No; that stayed more or less. When my mind was actively employed I forgot it, but when idle, dreaming, or doing nothing in particular, there she was beside me, influencing my mind horribly—"

"In what way, precisely?" interrupted the doctor.

"Evil, scheming thoughts came to me, visions of crime, hateful pictures of wickedness, and the kind of bad imagination that so far has been foreign, indeed impossible, to my normal nature—"

"The pressure of the Dark Powers upon the personality," murmured the doctor, making a quick note.

"Eh? I didn't quite catch—"

"Pray, go on. I am merely making notes; you shall know their purport fully later."

"Even when my wife returned I was still aware of this Presence in the house; it associated itself with my inner personality in most intimate fashion; and outwardly I always felt oddly constrained to be polite and respectful towards it—to open doors, provide chairs and hold myself carefully deferential when it was about. It became very compelling at last, and, if I failed in any little particular, I seemed to know that it pursued me about the house, from one room to another, haunting my very soul in its inmost abode. It certainly came before my wife so far as my attentions were concerned.

"But, let me first finish the story of my experimental dose, for I took it again the third night, and underwent a very similar experience, delayed like the first in coming, and then carrying me off my feet when it did come with a rush of this false demon-laughter. This time, however, there was a reversal of the changed scale of space and time; it shortened instead of lengthened, so that I dressed and got downstairs in about twenty seconds, and the couple of hours I stayed and worked in the study passed literally like a period of ten minutes."

"That is often true of an overdose," interjected the doctor, "and you may go a mile in a few minutes, or a few yards in a quarter of an hour. It is quite incomprehensible to those who have never experienced it, and is a curious proof that time and space are merely forms of thought."

"This time," Pender went on, talking more and more rapidly in his excitement, "another extraordinary effect came to me, and I experienced a curious changing of the senses, so that I perceived external things through one large main sense-channel instead of through the five divisions known as sight, smell, touch, and so forth. You will, I know, understand me when I tell you that I *heard* sights and *saw* sounds. No language can make this comprehensible, of course, and I can only say, for instance, that the striking of the clock I saw as a visible picture in the air before me. I saw the sounds of the tinkling bell. And in precisely the same way I heard the colours in the room, especially the colours of those books in the shelf behind you. Those red bindings I heard in deep sounds, and the yellow covers of the French bindings next to them made a shrill, piercing note not unlike the chattering of starlings. That brown bookcase muttered, and those green curtains opposite kept up a constant sort of rippling sound like the lower notes of a wood-horn. But I only was conscious of these sounds when I looked steadily at the different objects, and thought about them. The room, you understand, was not full of a chorus of notes; but when I concentrated my mind upon a colour, I heard, as well as saw, it."

"That is a known, though rarely obtained, effect of *Cannabis indica*," observed the doctor. "And it provoked laughter again, did it?"

"Only the muttering of the cupboard-bookcase made me laugh. It was so like a great animal trying to get itself noticed, and made me think of a performing bear—which is full of a kind of pathetic humour, you know. But this mingling of the senses produced no confusion in my brain. On the contrary, I was unusually clear-headed and experienced an intensification of consciousness, and felt marvellously alive and keen-minded.

"Moreover, when I took up a pencil in obedience to an impulse to sketch—a talent not normally mine—I found that I could draw nothing but heads, nothing, in fact, but one head—always the same—the head of a dark-skinned woman, with huge and terrible features and a very drooping left eye; and so well drawn, too, that I was amazed, as you may imagine—"

"And the expression of the face—?"

Pender hesitated a moment for words, casting about with his hands in the air and hunching his shoulders. A perceptible shudder ran over him.

"What I can only describe as—*blackness*," he replied in a low tone; "the face of a dark and evil soul."

"You destroyed that, too?" queried the doctor sharply.

"No; I have kept the drawings," he said, with a laugh, and rose to get them from a drawer in the writing-desk behind him.

"Here is all that remains of the pictures, you see," he added, pushing a number of loose sheets under the doctor's eyes; "nothing but a few scrawly lines. That's all I found the next morning. I had really drawn no heads at all—nothing but those lines and blots and wriggles. The pictures were entirely subjective, and existed only in my mind which constructed them out of a few wild strokes of the pen. Like the altered scale of space and time it was a complete delusion. These all passed, of course, with the passing of the drug's effects. But the other thing did not pass. I mean, the presence of that Dark Soul remained with me. It is here still. It is real. I don't know how I can escape from it."

"It is attached to the house, not to you personally. You must leave the house."

"Yes. Only I cannot afford to leave the house, for my work is my sole means of support, and—well, you see, since this change I cannot even write. They are horrible, these mirthless tales I now write, with their mockery of laughter, their diabolical suggestion. Horrible? I shall go mad if this continues."

He screwed his face up and looked about the room as though he expected to see some haunting shape.

"This influence in this house induced by my experiment, has killed in a flash, in a sudden stroke, the sources of my humour, and though I still go on writing funny tales—I have a certain name you know—my inspiration has dried up, and much of what I write I have to burn—yes, doctor, to burn, before any one sees it."

"As utterly alien to your own mind and personality?"

"Utterly! As though some one else had written it—"

"Ah!"

"And shocking!" He passed his hand over his eyes a moment and let the breath escape softly through his teeth. "Yet most damnably clever in the consummate way the vile suggestions are insinuated under cover of a kind of high drollery. My stenographer left me of course—and I've been afraid to take another—"

John Silence got up and began to walk about the room leisurely without speaking; he appeared to be examining the pictures on the wall and reading the names of the books lying about. Presently he paused on the hearthrug, with his back to the fire, and turned to look his patient quietly in the eyes. Pender's face was grey and drawn; the hunted expression dominated it; the long recital had told upon him.

"Thank you, Mr. Pender," he said, a curious glow showing about his fine, quiet face; "thank you for the sincerity and frankness of your account. But I think now there is nothing further I need ask you." He indulged in a long scrutiny of the author's haggard features drawing purposely the man's eyes to his own and then meeting them with a look of power and confidence calculated to inspire even the feeblest soul with courage. "And, to begin with," he added, smiling pleasantly, "let me assure you without delay that you need have no alarm, for you are no more insane or deluded than I myself am—"

Pender heaved a deep sigh and tried to return the smile.

"—and this is simply a case, so far as I can judge at present, of a very singular psychical invasion, and a very sinister one, too, if you perhaps understand what I mean—"

"It's an odd expression; you used it before, you know," said the author wearily, yet eagerly listening to every word of the diagnosis, and deeply touched by the intelligent sympathy which did not at once indicate the lunatic asylum.

"Possibly," returned the other, "and an odd affliction, too, you'll allow, yet one not unknown to the nations of antiquity, nor to those moderns, perhaps, who recognise the freedom of action under certain pathogenic conditions between this world and another."

"And you think," asked Pender hastily, "that it is all primarily due to the *Cannabis?* There is nothing radically amiss with myself—nothing incurable, or—?"

"Due entirely to the overdose," Dr. Silence replied emphatically, "to the drug's direct action upon your psychical being. It rendered you ultra-sensitive and made you respond to an increased rate of vibration. And, let me tell you, Mr. Pender, that your experiment might have had results far more dire. It has brought you into touch with a somewhat singular class of Invisible, but of one, I think, chiefly human in character. You might, however, just as easily have been drawn out of human range altogether, and the results of such a contingency would have been exceedingly terrible. Indeed, you would not now be here to tell the tale. I need not alarm you on that score, but mention it as a warning you will not misunderstand or underrate after what you have been through.

"You look puzzled. You do not quite gather what I am driving at; and it is not to be expected that you should, for you, I suppose, are the nominal Christian with the nominal Christian's lofty standard of ethics, and his utter ignorance of spiritual possibilities. Beyond a somewhat childish understanding of 'spiritual wickedness in high places,' you probably have no conception of what is possible once you break-down the slender gulf that is mercifully fixed between you and that Outer World. But my studies and training have taken me far outside these orthodox trips, and I have made experiments that I could scarcely speak to you about in language that would be intelligible to you."

He paused a moment to note the breathless interest of Pender's face and manner. Every word he uttered was calculated; he knew exactly the value and effect of the emotions he desired to waken in the heart of the afflicted being before him.

"And from certain knowledge I have gained through various experiences," he continued calmly, "I can diagnose your case as I said before to be one of psychical invasion."

"And the nature of this— er— invasion?" stammered the bewildered writer of humorous tales.

"There is no reason why I should not say at once that I do not yet quite know," replied Dr. Silence. "I may first have to make one or two experiments—"

"On me?" gasped Pender, catching his breath.

"Not exactly," the doctor said, with a grave smile, "but with your assistance, perhaps. I shall want to test the conditions of the house—to ascertain, if possible, the character of the forces, of this strange personality that has been haunting you—"

"At present you have no idea exactly who—what—why—" asked the other in a wild flurry of interest, dread and amazement.

"I have a very good idea, but no proof rather," returned the doctor. "The effects of the drug in altering the scale of time and space, and merging the senses have nothing primarily to do with the invasion. They come to any one who is fool enough to take an experimental dose. It is the other features of your case that are unusual. You see, you are now in touch with certain violent emotions, desires, purposes, still active in this house, that were produced in the past by some powerful and evil personality that lived here. How long ago, or why they still persist so forcibly, I cannot positively say. But I should judge that they are merely forces acting automatically with the momentum of their terrific original impetus."

"Not directed by a living being, a conscious will, you mean?"

"Possibly not—but none the less dangerous on that account, and more difficult to deal with. I cannot explain to you in a few minutes the nature of such things, for you have not made the studies that would enable you to follow me; but I have reason to believe that on the dissolution at death of a human being, its forces may still persist and continue to act in a blind, unconscious fashion. As a rule they speedily dissipate themselves, but in the case of a very powerful personality they may last a long time. And, in some cases—of which I incline to think this is one—these forces may coalesce with certain non-human entities who thus continue their life indefinitely and increase their strength to an unbelievable degree. If the original personality was evil, the beings attracted to the left-over forces will also be evil. In this case, I think there has been an unusual and dreadful aggrandisement of the thoughts and purposes left behind long ago by a woman of consummate wickedness and great personal power of character and intellect. Now, do you begin to see what I am driving at a little?"

Pender stared fixedly at his companion, plain horror showing in his eyes. But he found nothing to say, and the doctor continued—

"In your case, predisposed by the action of the drug, you have experienced the rush of these forces in undiluted strength. They wholly obliterate in you the sense of humour, fancy, imagination, —all that makes for cheerfulness and hope. They seek, though perhaps automatically only, to oust your own thoughts and establish themselves in their place. You are the victim of a psychical invasion. At the same time, you have become clairvoyant in the true sense. You are also a clairvoyant victim."

Pender mopped his face and sighed. He left his chair and went over to the fireplace to warm himself.

"You must think me a quack to talk like this, or a madman," laughed Dr. Silence. "But never mind that. I have come to help you, and I can help you if you will do what I tell you. It is very simple: you must leave this house at once. Oh, never mind the difficulties; we will deal with those together. I can place another house at your disposal, or I would take the lease here off your hands, and later have it pulled down. Your case interests me greatly, and I mean to see you through, so that you have no anxiety, and can drop back into your old groove of work tomorrow! The drug has provided you, and therefore me, with a short-cut to a very interesting experience. I am grateful to you."

The author poked the fire vigorously, emotion rising in him like a tide. He glanced towards the door nervously.

"There is no need to alarm your wife or to tell her the details of our conversation," pursued the other quietly. "Let her know that you will soon be in possession again of your sense of humour and your health, and explain that I am lending you another house for six months. Meanwhile I may have the right to use this house for a night or two for my experiment. Is that understood between us?"

"I can only thank you from the bottom of my heart," stammered Pender, unable to find words to express his gratitude.

Then he hesitated for a moment, searching the doctor's face anxiously.

"And your experiment with the house?" he said at length.

"Of the simplest character, my dear Mr. Pender. Although I am myself an artificially trained psychic, and consequently aware of the presence of discarnate entities as a rule, I have so far felt nothing here at all. This makes me sure that the forces acting here are of an unusual description. What I propose to do is to make an experiment with a view of drawing out this evil, coaxing it from its lair, so to speak, in order that it may *exhaust itself through me* and become dissipated for ever. I have already been inoculated," he added; "I consider myself to be immune."

"Heavens above!" gasped the author, collapsing on to a chair.

"Hell beneath! might be a more appropriate exclamation," the doctor laughed. "But, seriously, Mr. Pender, this is what I propose to do—with your permission."

"Of course, of course," cried the other, "you have my permission and my best wishes for success. I can see no possible objection, but—"

"But what?"

"I pray to Heaven you will not undertake this experiment alone, will you?"

"Oh, dear, no; not alone."

"You will take a companion with good nerves, and reliable in case of disaster, won't you?"

"I shall bring two companions," the doctor said.

"All, that's better. I feel easier. I am sure you must have among your acquaintances men who—"

"I shall not think of bringing men, Mr. Pender."

The other looked up sharply.

"No, or women either; or children."

"I don't understand. Who will you bring, then?"

"Animals," explained the doctor, unable to prevent a smile at his companion's expression of surprise—"two animals, a cat and a dog."

Pender stared as if his eyes would drop out upon the floor, and then led the way without another word into the adjoining room where his wife was awaiting them for tea.

II

A few days later the humorist and his wife, with minds greatly relieved, moved into a small furnished house placed at their free disposal in another part of London; and John Silence, intent upon his approaching experiment, made ready to spend a night in the empty house on the top of Putney Hill. Only two rooms were prepared for occupation: the study on the ground floor and the bedroom immediately above it; all other doors were to be locked, and no servant was to be left in the house. The motor had orders to call for him at nine o'clock the following morning.

And, meanwhile, his secretary had instructions to look up the past history and associations of the place, and learn everything he could concerning the character of former occupants, recent or remote.

The animals, by whose sensitiveness he intended to test any unusual conditions in the atmosphere of the building, Dr. Silence selected with care and judgment. He believed (and had already made curious experiments to prove it) that animals were more often, and more truly, clairvoyant than human beings. Many of them, he felt convinced, possessed powers of perception far superior to that mere keenness of the senses common to all dwellers in the wilds where the senses grow specially alert; they had what he termed "animal clairvoyance," and from his experiments with horses, dogs, cats, and even birds, he had drawn certain deductions, which, however, need not be referred to in detail here.

Cats, in particular, he believed, were almost continuously conscious of a larger field of vision, too detailed even for a photographic camera, and quite beyond the reach of normal human organs. He had, further, observed that while dogs were usually terrified in the presence of such phenomena, cats on the other hand were soothed and satisfied. They welcomed manifestations as something belonging peculiarly to their own region.

He selected his animals, therefore, with wisdom so that they might afford a differing test, each in its own way, and that one should not merely communicate its own excitement to the other. He took a dog and a cat.

The cat he chose, now full grown, had lived with him since kittenhood, a kittenhood of perplexing sweetness and audacious mischief. Wayward it was and fanciful, ever playing its own mysterious games in the corners of the room, jumping at invisible nothings, leaping side-ways into the air and falling with tiny moccasined feet on to another part of the carpet, yet with an air of dignified earnestness which showed that the performance was necessary to its own well-being, and not done merely to impress a stupid human audience. In the middle of elaborate washing it would look up, startled, as though to stare at the approach of some Invisible, cocking its little head sideways and putting out a velvet pad to inspect cautiously. Then it would get absent-minded, and stare with equal intentness in another direction (just to confuse the onlookers), and suddenly go on furiously washing its body again, but in quite a new place. Except for a white patch on its breast it was coal black. And its name was—Smoke.

"Smoke" described its temperament as well as its appearance. Its movements, its individuality, its posing as a little furry mass of concealed mysteries, its elfin-like elusiveness, all combined to justify its name; and a subtle painter might have pictured it as a wisp of floating smoke, the fire below betraying itself at two points only—the glowing eyes.

All its forces ran to intelligence—secret intelligence, the wordless incalculable intuition of the Cat. It was, indeed, *the* cat for the business in hand.

The selection of the dog was not so simple, for the doctor owned many; but after much deliberation he chose a collie, called Flame from his yellow coat. True, it was a trifle old, and stiff in the joints, and even beginning to grow deaf, but, on the other hand, it was a very particular friend of Smoke's, and had fathered it from kittenhood upwards so that a subtle understanding existed between them. It was this that turned the balance in its favour, this and its courage. Moreover, though good-tempered, it was a terrible fighter, and its anger when provoked by a righteous cause was a fury of fire, and irresistible.

It had come to him quite young, straight from the shepherd, with the air of the hills yet in its nostrils, and was then little more than skin and bones and teeth. For a collie it was sturdily built, its nose blunter than most, its yellow hair stiff rather than silky, and it had full eyes, unlike the slit eyes of its breed. Only its master could touch it, for it ignored strangers, and despised their pattings—when any dared to pat it. There was something patriarchal about the old beast. He was in earnest, and went through life with tremendous energy and big things in view, as though he had the reputation of his whole race to uphold. And to watch him fighting against odds was to understand why he was terrible.

In his relations with Smoke he was always absurdly gentle; also he was fatherly; and at the same time betrayed a certain diffidence or shyness. He recognised that Smoke called for strong yet respectful management. The cat's circuitous methods puzzled him, and his elaborate pretences perhaps shocked the dog's liking for direct, undisguised action. Yet, while he failed to comprehend these tortuous feline mysteries, he was never contemptuous or condescending; and he presided over the safety of his furry black friend somewhat as a father, loving, but intuitive, might superintend the vagaries of a wayward and talented child. And, in return, Smoke rewarded him with exhibitions of fascinating and audacious mischief.

And these brief descriptions of their characters are necessary for the proper understanding of what subsequently took place.

With Smoke sleeping in the folds of his fur coat, and the collie lying watchful on the seat opposite, John Silence went down in his motor after dinner on the night of November 15th.

And the fog was so dense that they were obliged to travel at quarter speed the entire way.

It was after ten o'clock when he dismissed the motor and entered the dingy little house with the latchkey provided by Pender. He found the hall gas turned low, and a fire in the study. Books and food had also been placed ready by the servant according to instructions. Coils of fog rushed in after him through the open door and filled the hall and passage with its cold discomfort.

The first thing Dr. Silence did was to lock up Smoke in the study with a saucer of milk before the fire, and then make a search of the house with Flame. The dog ran cheerfully behind him all the way while he tried the doors of the other rooms to make sure they were locked. He nosed about into corners and made little excursions on his own account. His manner was expectant. He knew there must be something unusual about the proceeding, because it was contrary to the habits of his whole life not to be asleep at this hour on the mat in front of the fire. He kept looking up into his master's face, as door after door was tried, with an expression of intelligent sympathy, but at the same time a certain air of disapproval. Yet everything his master did was good in his eyes, and he betrayed as little impatience as possible with all this unnecessary journeying to and fro. If the doctor was pleased to play this sort of game at such an hour of the night, it was surely not for him to object. So he played it, too; and was very busy and earnest about it into the bargain.

After an uneventful search they came down again to the study, and here Dr. Silence discovered Smoke washing his face calmly in front of the fire. The saucer of milk was licked dry and clean; the preliminary examination that cats always make in new surroundings had evidently been satisfactorily concluded. He drew an arm-chair up to the fire, stirred the coals into a blaze, arranged the table and lamp to his satisfaction for reading, and then prepared surreptitiously to watch the animals. He wished to observe them carefully without their being aware of it.

Now, in spite of their respective ages, it was the regular custom of these two to play together every night before sleep. Smoke always made the advances, beginning with grave impudence to pat the dog's tail, and Flame played cumbrously, with condescension. It was his duty, rather than pleasure; he was glad when it was over, and sometimes he was very determined and refused to play at all.

And this night was one of the occasions on which he was firm.

The doctor, looking cautiously over the top of his book, watched the cat begin the performance. It started by gazing with an innocent expression at the dog where he lay with nose on paws and eyes wide open in the middle of the floor. Then it got up and made as though it meant to walk to the door, going deliberately and very softly. Flame's eyes followed it until it was beyond the range of sight, and then the cat turned sharply and began patting his tail tentatively with one paw. The tail moved slightly in reply, and Smoke changed paws and tapped it again. The dog, however, did not rise to play as was his wont, and the cat fell to patting it briskly with both paws. Flame still lay motionless.

This puzzled and bored the cat, and it went round and stared hard into its friend's face to see what was the matter. Perhaps some inarticulate message flashed from the dog's eyes into its own little brain, making it understand that the programme for the night had better not begin with play. Perhaps it only realised that its friend was immovable. But, whatever the reason, its usual persistence thenceforward deserted it, and it made no further attempts at persuasion. Smoke yielded at once to the dog's mood; it sat down where it was and began to wash.

But the washing, the doctor noted, was by no means its real purpose; it only used it to mask something else; it stopped at the most busy and furious moments and began to stare about the room. Its thoughts wandered absurdly. It peered intently at the curtains; at the shadowy corners; at empty space above; leaving its body in curiously awkward positions for whole minutes together. Then it turned sharply and stared with a sudden signal of intelligence at the dog, and Flame at once rose somewhat stiffly to his feet and began to wander aimlessly and restlessly to and fro about the floor. Smoke followed him, padding quietly at his heels. Between them they made what seemed to be a deliberate search of the room.

And, here, as he watched them, noting carefully every detail of the performance over the top of his book, yet making no effort to interfere, it seemed to the doctor that the first beginnings of a faint distress betrayed themselves in the collie, and in the cat the stirrings of a vague excitement.

He observed them closely. The fog was thick in the air, and the tobacco smoke from his pipe added to its density; the furniture at the far end stood mistily, and where the shadows congregated in hanging clouds under the ceiling, it was difficult to see clearly at all; the lamplight only reached to a level of five feet from the floor, above which came layers of comparative darkness, so that the room appeared twice as lofty as it actually was. By means of the lamp and the fire, however, the carpet was everywhere clearly visible.

The animals made their silent tour of the floor, sometimes the dog leading, sometimes the cat; occasionally they looked at one another as though exchanging signals; and once or twice, in spite of the limited space, he lost sight of one or other among the fog and the shadows. Their curiosity, it appeared to him, was something more than the excitement lurking in the unknown territory of a strange room; yet, so far, it was impossible to test this, and he purposely kept his mind quietly receptive lest the smallest mental excitement on his part should communicate itself to the animals and thus destroy the value of their independent behaviour.

They made a very thorough journey, leaving no piece of furniture unexamined, or unsmelt. Flame led the way, walking slowly with lowered head, and Smoke followed demurely at his heels, making a transparent pretence of not being interested, yet missing nothing. And, at length, they returned, the old collie first, and came to rest on the mat before the fire. Flame rested his muzzle on his master's knee, smiling beatifically while he patted the yellow head and spoke his name; and Smoke, coming a little later, pretending he came by chance, looked from the empty saucer to his face, lapped up the milk when it was given him to the last drop, and then sprang upon his knees and curled round for the sleep it had fully earned and intended to enjoy.

Silence descended upon the room. Only the breathing of the dog upon the mat came through the deep stillness, like the pulse of time marking the minutes; and the steady drip, drip of the fog outside upon the windowledges dismally testified to the inclemency of the night beyond. And the soft crashings of the coals as the fire settled down into the grate became less and less audible as the fire sank and the flames resigned their fierceness.

It was now well after eleven o'clock, and Dr. Silence devoted himself again to his book. He read the words on the printed page and took in their meaning superficially, yet without starting into life the correlations of thought and suggestions that should accompany interesting reading. Underneath, all the while, his mental energies were absorbed in watching, listening, waiting for what might come. He was not over-sanguine himself, yet he did not wish to be taken by surprise. Moreover, the animals, his sensitive barometers, had incontinently gone to sleep.

After reading a dozen pages, however, he realised that his mind was really occupied in reviewing the features of Fender's extraordinary story, and that it was no longer necessary to steady his imagination by studying the dull paragraphs detailed in the pages before him. He laid down his book accordingly, and allowed his thoughts to dwell upon the features of the Case. Speculations as to the meaning, however, he rigorously suppressed, knowing that such thoughts would act upon his imagination like wind upon the glowing embers of a fire.

As the night wore on the silence grew deeper and deeper, and only at rare intervals he heard the sound of wheels on the main road a hundred yards away, where the horses went at a walking pace owing to the density of the fog. The echo of pedestrian footsteps no longer reached him, the clamour of occasional voices no longer came down the side street. The night, muffled by fog, shrouded by veils of ultimate mystery, hung about the haunted villa like a doom. Nothing in the house stirred. Stillness, in a thick blanket, lay over the upper storeys. Only the mist in the room grew more dense, he thought, and the damp cold more penetrating. Certainly, from time to time, he shivered.

The collie, now deep in slumber, moved occasionally, —grunted, sighed, or twitched his legs in dreams. Smoke lay on his knees, a pool of warm, black fur, only the closest observation detecting the movement of his sleek sides. It was difficult to distinguish exactly where his head and body joined in that circle of glistening hair; only a black satin nose and a tiny tip of pink tongue betrayed the secret.

Dr. Silence watched him, and felt comfortable. The collie's breathing was soothing. The fire was well built, and would burn for another two hours without attention. He was not conscious of the least nervousness. He particularly wished to remain in his ordinary and normal state of mind, and to force nothing. If sleep came naturally, he would let it come—and even welcome it. The coldness of the room, when the fire died down later, would be sure to wake him again; and it would then be time enough to carry these sleeping barometers up to bed. From various psychic premonitions he knew quite well that the night would not pass without adventure; but he did not wish to force its arrival; and he wished to remain normal, and let the animals remain normal, so that, when it came, it would be unattended by excitement or by any straining of the attention. Many experiments had made him wise. And, for the rest, he had no fear.

Accordingly, after a time, he did fall asleep as he had expected, and the last thing he remembered, before oblivion slipped up over his eyes like soft wool, was the picture of Flame stretching all four legs at once, and sighing noisily as he sought a more comfortable position for his paws and muzzle upon the mat.

It was a good deal later when he became aware that a weight lay upon his chest, and that something was pencilling over his face and mouth. A soft touch on the cheek woke him. Something was patting him.

He sat up with a jerk, and found himself staring straight into a pair of brilliant eyes, half green, half black. Smoke's face lay level with his own; and the cat had climbed up with its front paws upon his chest.

The lamp had burned low and the fire was nearly out, yet Dr. Silence saw in a moment that the cat was in an excited state. It kneaded with its front paws into his chest, shifting from one to the other. He felt them prodding against him. It lifted a leg very carefully and patted his cheek gingerly. Its fur, he saw, was standing ridgewise upon its back; the ears were flattened back somewhat; the tail was switching sharply. The cat, of course, had wakened him with a purpose, and the instant he realised this, he set it upon the arm of the chair and sprang up with a quick turn to face the empty room behind him. By some curious instinct, his arms of their own accord assumed an attitude of defence in front of him, as though to ward off something that threatened his safety. Yet nothing was visible. Only shapes of fog hung about rather heavily in the air, moving slightly to and fro.

His mind was now fully alert, and the last vestiges of sleep gone. He turned the lamp higher and peered about him. Two things he became aware of at once: one, that Smoke, while excited, was *pleasurably* excited; the other, that the collie was no longer visible upon the mat at his feet. He had crept away to the corner of the wall farthest from the window, and lay watching the room with wide-open eyes, in which lurked plainly something of alarm.

Something in the dog's behaviour instantly struck Dr. Silence as unusual, and, calling him by name, he moved across to pat him. Flame got up, wagged his tail, and came over slowly to the rug, uttering a low sound that was half growl, half whine. He was evidently perturbed about something, and his master was proceeding to administer comfort when his attention was suddenly drawn to the antics of his other four-footed companion, the cat.

And what he saw filled him with something like amazement.

Smoke had jumped down from the back of the arm-chair and now occupied the middle of the carpet, where, with tail erect and legs stiff as ram-rods, it was steadily pacing backwards and forwards in a narrow space, uttering, as it did so, those curious little guttural sounds of pleasure that only an animal of the feline species knows how to make expressive of supreme happiness. Its stiffened legs and arched back made it appear larger than usual, and the black visage wore a smile of beatific joy. Its eyes blazed magnificently; it was in an ecstasy.

At the end of every few paces it turned sharply and stalked back again along the same line, padding softly, and purring like a roll of little muffled drums. It behaved precisely as though it were rubbing against the ankles of some one who remained invisible. A thrill ran down the doctor's spine as he stood and stared. His experiment was growing interesting at last.

He called the collie's attention to his friend's performance to see whether he too was aware of anything standing there upon the carpet, and the dog's behaviour was significant and corroborative. He came as far as his master's knees and then stopped dead, refusing to investigate closely. In vain Dr. Silence urged him; he wagged his tail, whined a little, and stood in a half-crouching attitude, staring alternately at the cat and at his master's face. He was, apparently, both puzzled and alarmed, and the whine went deeper and deeper down into his throat till it changed into an ugly snarl of awakening anger.

Then the doctor called to him in a tone of command he had never known to be disregarded; but still the dog, though springing up in response, de-clined to move nearer. He made tentative motions, pranced a little like a dog about to take to water, pretended to bark, and ran to and fro on the carpet. So far there was no actual fear in his manner, but he was uneasy and anxious, and nothing would induce him to go within touching distance of the walking cat. Once he made a complete circuit, but always carefully out of reach; and in the end he returned to his master's legs and rubbed vigorously against him. Flame did not like the performance at all: that much was quite clear.

For several minutes John Silence watched the performance of the cat with profound attention and without interfering. Then he called to the animal by name.

"Smoke, you mysterious beastie, what in the world are you about?" he said, in a coaxing tone.

The cat looked up at him for a moment, smiling in its ecstasy, blinking its eyes, but too happy to pause. He spoke to it again. He called to it sev-eral times, and each time it turned upon him its blazing eyes, drunk with inner delight, opening and shutting its lips, its body large and rigid with excitement. Yet it never for one instant paused in its short journeys to and fro.

He noted exactly what it did: it walked, he saw, the same number of paces each time, some six or seven steps, and then it turned sharply and retraced them. By the pattern of the great roses in the carpet he measured it. It kept to the same direction and the same line. It behaved precisely as though it were rubbing against something solid. Undoubtedly, there was something standing there on that strip of carpet, something invisible to the doctor, something that alarmed the dog, yet caused the cat unspeakable pleasure.

"Smokie!" he called again, "Smokie, you black mystery, what is it excites you so?"

Again the cat looked up at him for a brief second, and then continued its sentry-walk, blissfully happy, intensely preoccupied. And, for an instant, as he watched it, the doctor was aware that a faint uneasiness stirred in the depths of his own being, focusing itself for the moment upon this curious behaviour of the uncanny creature before him.

There rose in him quite a new realisation of the mystery connected with the whole feline tribe, but especially with that common member of it, the domestic cat—their hidden lives, their strange aloofness, their incalculable subtlety. How utterly remote from anything that human beings understood lay the sources of their elusive activities. As he watched the indescribable bearing of the little creature mincing along the strip of carpet under his eyes, coquetting with the powers of darkness, welcoming, maybe, some fearsome visitor, there stirred in his heart a feeling strangely akin to awe. Its indifference to human kind, its serene superiority to the obvious, struck him forcibly with fresh meaning; so remote, so inaccessible seemed the secret purposes of its real life, so alien to the blundering honesty of other animals. Its absolute poise of bearing brought into his mind the opium-eater's words that "no dignity is perfect which does not at some point ally itself with the mysterious"; and he became suddenly aware that the presence of the dog in this foggy, haunted room on the top of Putney Hill was uncommonly welcome to him. He was glad to feel that Flame's dependable personality was with him. The savage growling at his heels was a pleasant sound. He was glad to hear it. That marching cat made him uneasy.

Finding that Smoke paid no further attention to his words, the doctor decided upon action. Would it rub against his leg, too? He would take it by surprise and see.

He stepped quickly forward and placed himself upon the exact strip of carpet where it walked.

But no cat is ever taken by surprise! The moment he occupied the space of the Intruder, setting his feet on the woven roses midway in the line of travel, Smoke suddenly stopped purring and sat down. If lifted up its face with the most innocent stare imaginable of its green eyes. He could have sworn it laughed. It was a perfect child again. In a single second it had resumed its simple, domestic manner; and it gazed at him in such a way that he almost felt Smoke was the normal being, and his was the eccentric behaviour that was being watched. It was consummate, the manner in which it brought about this change so easily and so quickly.

"Superb little actor!" he laughed in spite of himself, and stooped to stroke the shining black back. But, in a flash, as he touched its fur, the cat turned and spat at him viciously, striking at his hand with one paw. Then, with a hurried scutter of feet, it shot like a shadow across the floor and a moment later was calmly sitting over by the window-curtains washing its face as though nothing interested it in the whole world but the cleanness of its cheeks and whiskers.

John Silence straightened himself up and drew a long breath. He realised that the performance was temporarily at an end. The collie, meanwhile, who had watched the whole proceeding with marked disapproval, had now lain down again upon the mat by the fire, no longer growling. It seemed to the doctor just as though something that had entered the room while he slept, alarming the dog, yet bringing happiness to the cat, had now gone out again, leaving all as it was before. Whatever it was that excited its blissful attentions had retreated for the moment.

He realised this intuitively. Smoke evidently realised it, too, for presently he deigned to march back to the fireplace and jump upon his master's knees. Dr. Silence, patient and determined, settled down once more to his book. The animals soon slept; the fire blazed cheerfully; and the cold fog from outside poured into the room through every available chink and crannie.

For a long time silence and peace reigned in the room and Dr. Silence availed himself of the quietness to make careful notes of what had happened. He entered for future use in other cases an exhaustive analysis of what he had observed, especially with regard to the effect upon the two animals. It is impossible here, nor would it be intelligible to the reader unversed in the knowledge of the region known to a scientifically trained psychic like Dr. Silence, to detail these observations. But to him it was clear, up to a certain point—for the rest he must still wait and watch. So far, at least, he realised that while he slept in the chair—that is, while his will was dormant—the room had suffered intrusion from what he recognised as an intensely active Force, and might later be forced to acknowledge as something more than merely a blind force, namely, a distinct personality.

So far it had affected himself scarcely at all, but had acted directly upon the simpler organisms of the animals. It stimulated keenly the centres of the cat's psychic being, inducing a state of instant happiness (intensifying its consciousness probably in the same way a drug or stimulant intensifies that of a human being); whereas it alarmed the less sensitive dog, causing it to feel a vague apprehension and distress.

His own sudden action and exhibition of energy had served to disperse it temporarily, yet he felt convinced—the indications were not lacking even while he sat there making notes—that it still remained near to him, conditionally if not spatially, and was, as it were, gathering force for a second attack.

And, further, he intuitively understood that the relations between the two animals had undergone a subtle change: that the cat had become immeasurably superior, confident, sure of itself in its own peculiar region, whereas Flame had been weakened by an attack he could not comprehend and knew not how to reply to. Though not yet afraid, he was defiant—ready to act against a fear that he felt to be approaching. He was no longer fatherly and protective towards the cat. Smoke held the key to the situation; and both he and the cat knew it.

Thus, as the minutes passed, John Silence sat and waited, keenly on the alert, wondering how soon the attack would be renewed, and at what point it would be diverted from the animals and directed upon himself.

The book lay on the floor beside him, his notes were complete. With one hand on the cat's fur, and the dog's front paws resting against his feet, the three of them dozed comfortably before the hot fire while the night wore on and the silence deepened towards midnight.

It was well after one o'clock in the morning when Dr. Silence turned the lamp out and lighted the candle preparatory to going up to bed. Then Smoke suddenly woke with a loud sharp purr and sat up. It neither stretched, washed nor turned: it listened. And the doctor, watching it, realised that a certain indefinable change had come about that very moment in the room. A swift readjustment of the forces within the four walls had taken place—a new disposition of their personal equations. The balance was destroyed, the former harmony gone. Smoke, most sensitive of barometers, had been the first to feel it, but the dog was not slow to follow suit, for on looking down he noted that Flame was no longer asleep. He was lying with eyes wide open, and that same instant he sat up on his great haunches and began to growl.

Dr. Silence was in the act of taking the matches to re-light the lamp when an audible movement in the room behind him made him pause. Smoke leaped down from his knee and moved forward a few paces across the carpet. Then it stopped and stared fixedly; and the doctor stood up on the rug to watch.

As he rose the sound was repeated, and he discovered that it was not in the room as he first thought, but outside, and that it came from more directions than one. There was a rushing, sweeping noise against the window-panes, and simultaneously a sound of something brushing against the door—out in the hall. Smoke advanced sedately across the carpet, twitching his tail, and sat down within a foot of the door. The influence that had destroyed the harmonious conditions of the room had apparently moved in advance of its cause. Clearly, something was about to happen.

For the first time that night John Silence hesitated; the thought of that dark narrow hall-way, choked with fog, and destitute of human comfort, was unpleasant. He became aware of a faint creeping of his flesh. He knew, of course, that the actual opening of the door was not necessary to the invasion of the room that was about to take place, since neither doors nor windows, nor any other solid barriers could interpose an obstacle to what was seeking entrance. Yet the opening of the door would be significant and symbolic, and he distinctly shrank from it.

But for a moment only. Smoke, turning with a show of impatience, recalled him to his purpose, and he moved past the sitting, watching creature, and deliberately opened the door to its full width.

What subsequently happened, happened in the feeble and flickering light of the solitary candle on the mantlepiece.

Through the opened door he saw the hall, dimly lit and thick with fog. Nothing, of course, was visible—nothing but the hat-stand, the African spears in dark lines upon the wall and the high-backed wooden chair standing grotesquely underneath on the oilcloth floor. For one instant the fog seemed to move and thicken oddly; but he set that down to the score of the imagination. The door had opened upon nothing.

Yet Smoke apparently thought otherwise, and the deep growling of the collie from the mat at the back of the room seemed to confirm his judgment.

For, proud and self-possessed, the cat had again risen to his feet, and having advanced to the door, was now ushering some one slowly into the room. Nothing could have been more evident. He paced from side to side, bowing his little head with great *empressement* and holding his stiffened tail aloft like a flag-staff. He turned this way and that, mincing to and fro, and showing signs of supreme satisfaction. He was in his element. He welcomed the intrusion, and apparently reckoned that his companions, the doctor and the dog, would welcome it likewise.

The Intruder had returned for a second attack.

Dr. Silence moved slowly backwards and took up his position on the hearthrug, keying himself up to a condition of concentrated attention.

He noted that Flame stood beside him, facing the room, with body motionless, and head moving swiftly from side to side with a curious swaying movement. His eyes were wide open, his back rigid, his neck and jaws thrust forward, his legs tense and ready to leap. Savage, ready for attack or defence, yet dreadfully puzzled and perhaps already a little cowed, he stood and stared, the hair on his spine and sides positively bristling outwards as though a wind played through it. In the dim firelight he looked like a great yellow-haired wolf, silent, eyes shooting dark fire, exceedingly formidable. It was Flame, the terrible.

Smoke, meanwhile, advanced from the door towards the middle of the room, adopting the very slow pace of an invisible companion. A few feet away it stopped and began to smile and blink its eyes. There was something deliberately coaxing in its attitude as it stood there undecided on the carpet, clearly wishing to effect some sort of introduction between the Intruder and its canine friend and ally. It assumed its most winning manners, purring, smiling, looking persuasively from one to the other, and making quick tentative steps first in one direction and then in the other. There had always existed such perfect understanding between them in everything. Surely Flame would appreciate Smoke's intention now, and acquiesce.

But the old collie made no advances. He bared his teeth, lifting his lips till the gums showed, and stood stockstill with fixed eyes and heaving sides. The doctor moved a little farther back, watching intently the smallest movement, and it was just then he divined suddenly from the cat's behaviour and attitude that it was not only a single companion it had ushered into the room, but several. It kept crossing over from one to the other, looking up at each in turn. It sought to win over the dog to friendliness with them all. The original Intruder had come back with reinforcements. And at the same time he further realised that the Intruder was something more than a blindly acting force, impersonal though destructive. It was a Personality, and moreover a great personality. And it was accompanied for the purposes of assistance by a host of other personalities, minor in degree, but similar in kind.

He braced himself in the corner against the mantelpiece and waited, his whole being roused to defence, for he was now fully aware that the attack had spread to include himself as well as the animals, and he must be on the alert. He strained his eyes through the foggy atmosphere, trying in vain to see what the cat and dog saw; but the candlelight threw an uncertain and flickering light across the room and his eyes discerned nothing. On the floor Smoke moved softly in front of him like a black shadow, his eyes gleaming as he turned his head, still trying with many insinuating gestures and much purring to bring about the introductions he desired.

But it was all in vain. Flame stood riveted to one spot, motionless as a figure carved in stone.

Some minutes passed, during which only the cat moved, and then there came a sharp change. Flame began to back towards the wall. He moved his head from side to side as he went, sometimes turning to snap at something almost behind him. *They* were advancing upon him, trying to surround him. His distress became very marked from now onwards, and it seemed to the doctor that his anger merged into genuine terror and became overwhelmed by it. The savage growl sounded perilously like a whine, and more than once he tried to dive past his master's legs, as though hunting for a way of escape. He was trying to avoid something that everywhere blocked the way.

This terror of the indomitable fighter impressed the doctor enormously; yet also painfully; stirring his impatience; for he had never before seen the dog show signs of giving in, and it distressed him to witness it. He knew, however, that he was not giving in easily, and understood that it was really impossible for him to gauge the animal's sensations properly at all. What Flame felt, and saw, must be terrible indeed to turn him all at once into a coward. He faced something that made him afraid of more than his life merely. The doctor spoke a few quick words of encouragement to him, and stroked the bristling hair. But without much success. The collie seemed already beyond the reach of comfort such as that, and the collapse of the old dog followed indeed very speedily after this.

And Smoke, meanwhile, remained behind, watching the advance, but not joining in it; sitting, pleased and expectant, considering that all was going well and as it wished. It was kneading on the carpet with its front paws—slowly, laboriously, as though its feet were dipped in treacle. The sound its claws made as they caught in the threads was distinctly audible. It was still smiling, blinking, purring.

Suddenly the collie uttered a poignant short bark and leaped heavily to one side. His bared teeth traced a line of whiteness through the gloom. The next instant he dashed past his master's legs, almost upsetting his balance, and shot out into the room, where he went blundering wildly against walls and furniture. But that bark was significant; the doctor had heard it before and knew what it meant: for it was the cry of the fighter against odds and it meant that the old beast had found his courage again. Possibly it was only the courage of despair, but at any rate the fighting would be terrific. And Dr. Silence understood, too, that he dared not interfere. Flame must fight his own enemies in his own way.

But the cat, too, had heard that dreadful bark; and it, too, had understood. This was more than it had bargained for. Across the dim shadows of that haunted room there must have passed some secret signal of distress between the animals. Smoke stood up and looked swiftly about him. He uttered a piteous meow and trotted smartly away into the greater darkness by the windows. What his object was only those endowed with the spirit-like intelligence of cats might know. But, at any rate, he had at last ranged himself on the side of his friend. And the little beast meant business.

At the same moment the collie managed to gain the door. The doctor saw him rush through into the hall like a flash of yellow light. He shot across the oilcloth, and tore up the stairs, but in another second he appeared again, flying down the steps and landing at the bottom in a tumbling heap, whining, cringing, terrified. The doctor saw him slink back into the room again and crawl round by the wall towards the cat. Was, then, even the staircase occupied? Did *They* stand also in the hall? Was the whole house crowded from floor to ceiling?

The thought came to add to the keen distress he felt at the sight of the collie's discomfiture. And, indeed, his own personal distress had increased in a marked degree during the past minutes, and continued to increase steadily to the climax. He recognised that the drain on his own vitality grew steadily, and that the attack was now directed against himself even more than against the defeated dog, and the too much deceived cat.

It all seemed so rapid and uncalculated after that—the events that took place in this little modern room at the top of Putney Hill between midnight and sunrise—that Dr. Silence was hardly able to follow and remember it all. It came about with such uncanny swiftness and terror; the light was so uncertain; the movements of the black cat so difficult to follow on the dark carpet, and the doctor himself so weary and taken by surprise—that he found it almost impossible to observe accurately, or to recall afterwards precisely what it was he had seen or in what order the incidents had taken place. He never could understand what defect of vision on his part made it seem as though the cat had duplicated itself at first, and then increased indefinitely, so that there were at least a dozen of them darting silently about the floor, leaping softly on to chairs and tables, passing like shadows from the open door to the end of the room, all black as sin, with brilliant green eyes flashing fire in all directions. It was like the reflections from a score of mirrors placed round the walls at different angles. Nor could he make out at the time why the size of the room seemed to have altered, grown much larger, and why it extended away behind him where ordinarily the wall should have been. The snarling of the enraged and terrified collie sounded sometimes so far away; the ceiling seemed to have raised itself so much higher than before, and much of the furniture had changed in appearance and shifted marvellously.

It was all so confused and confusing, as though the little room he knew had become merged and transformed into the dimensions of quite another chamber, that came to him, with its host of cats and its strange distances, in a sort of vision.

But these changes came about a little later, and at a time when his attention was so concentrated upon the proceedings of Smoke and the collie, that he only observed them, as it were, subconsciously. And the excitement, the flickering candlelight, the distress he felt for the collie, and the distorting atmosphere of fog were the poorest possible allies to careful observation.

At first he was only aware that the dog was repeating his short dangerous bark from time to time, snapping viciously at the empty air, a foot or so from the ground. Once, indeed, he sprang upwards and forwards, working furiously with teeth and paws, and with a noise like wolves fighting, but only to dash back the next minute against the wall behind him. Then, after lying still for a bit, he rose to a crouching position as though to spring again, snarling horribly and making short half-circles with lowered head. And Smoke all the while meowed piteously by the window as though trying to draw the attack upon himself.

Then it was that the rush of the whole dreadful business seemed to turn aside from the dog and direct itself upon his own person. The collie had made another spring and fallen back with a crash into the corner, where he made noise enough in his savage rage to waken the dead before he fell to whining and then finally lay still. And directly afterwards the doctor's own distress became intolerably acute. He had made a half movement forward to come to the rescue when a veil that was denser than mere fog seemed to drop down over the scene, draping room, walls, animals and fire in a mist of darkness and folding also about his own mind. Other forms moved silently across the field of vision, forms that he recognised from previous experiments, and welcomed not. Unholy thoughts began to crowd into his brain, sinister suggestions of evil presented themselves seductively. Ice seemed to settle about his heart, and his mind trembled. He began to lose memory—memory of his identity, of where he was, of what he ought to do. The very foundations of his strength were shaken. His will seemed paralysed.

And it was then that the room filled with this horde of cats, all dark as the night, all silent, all with lamping eyes of green fire. The dimensions of the place altered and shifted. He was in a much larger space. The whining of the dog sounded far away, and all about him the cats flew busily to and fro, silently playing their tearing, rushing game of evil, weaving the pattern of their dark purpose upon the floor. He strove hard to collect himself and remember the words of power he had made use of before in similar dread positions where his dangerous practice had sometimes led; but he could recall nothing consecutively; a mist lay over his mind and memory; he felt dazed and his forces scattered. The deeps within were too troubled for healing power to come out of them.

It was glamour, of course, he realised afterwards, the strong glamour thrown upon his imagination by some powerful personality behind the veil; but at the time he was not sufficiently aware of this and, as with all true glamour, was unable to grasp where the true ended and the false began. He was caught momentarily in the same vortex that had sought to lure the cat to destruction through its delight, and threatened utterly to overwhelm the dog through its terror.

There came a sound in the chimney behind him like wind booming and tearing its way down. The windows rattled. The candle flickered and went out. The glacial atmosphere closed round him with the cold of death, and a great rushing sound swept by overhead as though the ceiling had lifted to a great height. He heard the door shut. Far away it sounded. He felt lost, shelterless in the depths of his soul. Yet still he held out and resisted while the climax of the fight came nearer and nearer.... He had stepped into the stream of forces awakened by Pender and he knew that he must withstand them to the end or come to a conclusion that it was not good for a man to come to. Something from the region of utter cold was upon him.

And then quite suddenly, through the confused mists about him, there slowly rose up the Personality that had been all the time directing the battle. Some force entered his being that shook him as the tempest shakes a leaf, and close against his eyes—clean level with his face—he found himself staring into the wreck of a vast dark Countenance, a countenance that was terrible even in its ruin.

For ruined it was, and terrible it was, and the mark of spiritual evil was branded everywhere upon its broken features. Eyes, face and hair rose level with his own, and for a space of time he never could properly measure, or determine, these two, a man and a woman, looked straight into each other's visages and down into each other's hearts.

And John Silence, the soul with the good, unselfish motive, held his own against the dark discarnate woman whose motive was pure evil, and whose soul was on the side of the Dark Powers.

It was the climax that touched the depth of power within him and began to restore him slowly to his own. He was conscious, of course, of effort, and yet it seemed no superhuman one, for he had recognised the character of his opponent's power, and he called upon the good within him to meet and overcome it. The inner forces stirred and trembled in response to his call. They did not at first come readily as was their habit, for under the spell of glamour they had already been diabolically lulled into inactivity, but come they eventually did, rising out of the inner spiritual nature he had learned with so much time and pain to awaken to life. And power and confidence came with them. He began to breathe deeply and regularly, and at the same time to absorb into himself the forces opposed to him, and to *turn them to his own account*. By ceasing to resist, and allowing the deadly stream to pour into him unopposed, he used the very power supplied by his adversary and thus enormously increased his own.

For this spiritual alchemy he had learned. He understood that force ultimately is everywhere one and the same; it is the motive behind that makes it good or evil; and his motive was entirely unselfish. He knew—provided he was not first robbed of self-control—how vicariously to absorb these evil radiations into himself and change them magically into his own good purposes. And, since his motive was pure and his soul fearless, they could not work him harm.

Thus he stood in the main stream of evil unwittingly attracted by Pender, deflecting its course upon himself; and after passing through the purifying filter of his own unselfishness these energies could only add to his store of experience, of knowledge, and therefore of power. And, as his self-control returned to him, he gradually accomplished this purpose, even though trembling while he did so.

Yet the struggle was severe, and in spite of the freezing chill of the air, the perspiration poured down his face. Then, by slow degrees, the dark and dreadful countenance faded, the glamour passed from his soul, the normal proportions returned to walls and ceiling, the forms melted back into the fog, and the whirl of rushing shadow-cats disappeared whence they came.

And with the return of the consciousness of his own identity John Silence was restored to the full control of his own will-power. In a deep, modulated voice he began to utter certain rhythmical sounds that slowly rolled through the air like a rising sea, filling the room with powerful vibratory activities that whelmed all irregularities of lesser vibrations in its own swelling tone. He made certain sigils, gestures and movements at the same time. For several minutes he continued to utter these words, until at length the growing volume dominated the whole room and mastered the manifestation of all that opposed it. For just as he understood the spiritual alchemy that can transmute evil forces by raising them into higher channels, so he knew from long study the occult use of sound, and its direct effect upon the plastic region wherein the powers of spiritual evil work their fell purposes. Harmony was restored first of all to his own soul, and thence to the room and all its occupants.

And, after himself, the first to recognise it was the old dog lying in his corner. Flame began suddenly uttering sounds of pleasure, that "something" between a growl and a grunt that dogs make upon being restored to their master's confidence. Dr. Silence heard the thumping of the collie's tail against the floor. And the grunt and the thumping touched the depth of affection in the man's heart, and gave him some inkling of what agonies the dumb creature had suffered.

Next, from the shadows by the window, a somewhat shrill purring announced the restoration of the cat to its normal state. Smoke was advancing across the carpet. He seemed very pleased with himself, and smiled with an expression of supreme innocence. He was no shadow-cat, but real and full of his usual and perfect self-possession. He marched along, picking his way delicately, but with a stately dignity that suggested his ancestry with the majesty of Egypt. His eyes no longer glared; they shone steadily before him, they radiated, not excitement, but knowledge. Clearly he was anxious to make amends for the mischief to which he had unwittingly lent himself owing to his subtle and electric constitution.

Still uttering his sharp high purrings he marched up to his master and rubbed vigorously against his legs. Then he stood on his hind feet and pawed his knees and stared beseechingly up into his face. He turned his head towards the corner where the collie still lay, thumping his tail feebly and pathetically.

John Silence understood. He bent down and stroked the creature's living fur, noting the line of bright blue sparks that followed the motion of his hand down its back. And then they advanced together towards the corner where the dog was.

Smoke went first and put his nose gently against his friend's muzzle, purring while he rubbed, and uttering little soft sounds of affection in his throat. The doctor lit the candle and brought it over. He saw the collie lying on its side against the wall; it was utterly exhausted, and foam still hung about its jaws. Its tail and eyes responded to the sound of its name, but it was evidently very weak and overcome. Smoke continued to rub against its cheek and nose and eyes, sometimes even standing on its body and kneading into the thick yellow hair. Flame replied from time to time by little licks of the tongue, most of them curiously misdirected.

But Dr. Silence felt intuitively that something disastrous had happened, and his heart was wrung. He stroked the dear body, feeling it over for bruises or broken bones, but finding none. He fed it with what remained of the sandwiches and milk, but the creature clumsily upset the saucer and lost the sandwiches between its paws, so that the doctor had to feed it with his own hand. And all the while Smoke meowed piteously.

Then John Silence began to understand. He went across to the farther side of the room and called aloud to it.

"Flame, old man! come!"

At any other time the dog would have been upon him in an instant, barking and leaping to the shoulder. And even now he got up, though heavily and awkwardly, to his feet. He started to run, wagging his tail more briskly. He collided first with a chair, and then ran straight into a table. Smoke trotted close at his side, trying his very best to guide him. But it was useless. Dr. Silence had to lift him up into his own arms and carry him like a baby. For he was blind.

III

It was a week later when John Silence called to see the author in his new house, and found him well on the way to recovery and already busy again with his writing. The haunted look had left his eyes, and he seemed cheerful and confident.

"Humour restored?" laughed the doctor, as soon as they were comfortably settled in the room overlooking the Park.

"I've had no trouble since I left that dreadful place," returned Pender gratefully; "and thanks to you—"

The doctor stopped him with a gesture.

"Never mind that," he said, "we'll discuss your new plans afterwards, and my scheme for relieving you of the house and helping you settle elsewhere. Of course it must be pulled down, for it's not fit for any sensitive person to live in, and any other tenant might be afflicted in the same way you were. Although, personally, I think the evil has exhausted itself by now."

He told the astonished author something of his experiences in it with the animals.

"I don't pretend to understand," Pender said, when the account was finished, "but I and my wife are intensely relieved to be free of it all. Only I must say I should like to know something of the former history of the house. When we took it six months ago I heard no word against it."

Dr. Silence drew a typewritten paper from his pocket.

"I can satisfy your curiosity to some extent," he said, running his eye over the sheets, and then replacing them in his coat; "for by my secretary's investigations I have been able to check certain information obtained in the hypnotic trance by a 'sensitive' who helps me in such cases. The former occupant who haunted you appears to have been a woman of singularly atrocious life and character who finally suffered death by hanging, after a series of crimes that appalled the whole of England and only came to light by the merest chance. She came to her end in the year 1798, for it was not this particular house she lived in, but a much larger one that then stood upon the site it now occupies, and was then, of course, not in London, but in the country. She was a person of intellect, possessed of a powerful, trained will, and of consummate audacity, and I am convinced availed herself of the resources of the lower magic to attain her ends. This goes far to explain the virulence of the attack upon yourself, and why she is still able to carry on after death the evil practices that formed her main purpose during life."

"You think that after death a soul can still consciously direct—" gasped the author.

"I think, as I told you before, that the forces of a powerful personality may still persist after death in the line of their original momentum," replied the doctor; "and that strong thoughts and purposes can still react upon suitably prepared brains long after their originators have passed away.

"If you knew anything of magic," he pursued, "you would know that thought is dynamic, and that it may call into existence forms and pictures that may well exist for hundreds of years. For, not far removed from the region of our human life is another region where float the waste and drift of all the centuries, the limbo of the shells of the dead; a densely populated region crammed with horror and abomination of all descriptions, and sometimes galvanised into active life again by the will of a trained manipulator, a mind versed in the practices of lower magic. That this woman understood its vile commerce, I am persuaded, and the forces she set going during her life have simply been accumulating ever since, and would have continued to do so had they not been drawn down upon yourself, and afterwards discharged and satisfied through me.

"Anything might have brought down the attack, for, besides drugs, there are certain violent emotions, certain moods of the soul, certain spiritual fevers, if I may so call them, which directly open the inner being to a cognisance of this astral region I have mentioned. In your case it happened to be a peculiarly potent drug that did it.

"But now, tell me," he added, after a pause, handing to the perplexed author a pencil drawing he had made of the dark countenance that had appeared to him during the night on Putney Hill—"tell me if you recognise this face?"

Pender looked at the drawing closely, greatly astonished. He shuddered a little as he looked.

"Undoubtedly," he said, "it is the face I kept trying to draw—dark, with the great mouth and jaw, and the drooping eye. That is the woman."

Dr. Silence then produced from his pocket-book an old-fashioned woodcut of the same person which his secretary had unearthed from the records of the Newgate Calendar. The woodcut and the pencil drawing were two different aspects of the same dreadful visage. The men compared them for some moments in silence.

"It makes me thank God for the limitations of our senses," said Pender quietly, with a sigh; "continuous clairvoyance must be a sore affliction."

"It is indeed," returned John Silence significantly, "and if all the people nowadays who claim to be clairvoyant were really so, the statistics of suicide and lunacy would be considerably higher than they are. It is little wonder," he added, "that your sense of humour was clouded, with the mind-forces of that dead monster trying to use your brain for their dissemination. You have had an interesting adventure, Mr. Felix Pender, and, let me add, a fortunate escape."

The author was about to renew his thanks when there came a sound of scratching at the door, and the doctor sprang up quickly.

"It's time for me to go. I left my dog on the step, but I suppose—"

Before he had time to open the door, it had yielded to the pressure behind it and flew wide open to admit a great yellow-haired collie. The dog, wagging his tail and contorting his whole body with delight, tore across the floor and tried to leap up upon his owner's breast. And there was laughter and happiness in the old eyes; for they were clear again as the day.

CASE II

ANCIENT SORCERIES

There are, it would appear, certain wholly unremarkable persons, with none of the characteristics that invite adventure, who yet once or twice in the course of their smooth lives undergo an experience so strange that the world catches its breath—and looks the other way! And it was cases of this kind, perhaps, more than any other, that fell into the widespread net of John Silence, the psychic doctor, and, appealing to his deep humanity, to his patience, and to his great qualities of spiritual sympathy, led often to the revelation of problems of the strangest complexity, and of the profoundest possible human interest.

Matters that seemed almost too curious and fantastic for belief he loved to trace to their hidden sources. To unravel a tangle in the very soul of things—and to release a suffering human soul in the process—was with him a veritable passion. And the knots he untied were, indeed, after passing strange.

The world, of course, asks for some plausible basis to which it can attach credence—something it can, at least, pretend to explain. The adventurous type it can understand: such people carry about with them an adequate explanation of their exciting lives, and their characters obviously drive them into the circumstances which produce the adventures. It expects nothing else from them, and is satisfied. But dull, ordinary folk have no right to out-of-the-way experiences, and the world having been led to expect otherwise, is disappointed with them, not to say shocked. Its complacent judgment has been rudely disturbed.

"Such a thing happened to *that* man!" it cries—"a commonplace person like that! It is too absurd! There must be something wrong!"

Yet there could be no question that something did actually happen to little Arthur Vezin, something of the curious nature he described to Dr. Silence. Outwardly or inwardly, it happened beyond a doubt, and in spite of the jeers of his few friends who heard the tale, and observed wisely that "such a thing might perhaps have come to Iszard, that crack-brained Iszard, or to that odd fish Minski, but it could never have happened to commonplace little Vezin, who was fore-ordained to live and die according to scale."

But, whatever his method of death was, Vezin certainly did not "live according to scale" so far as this particular event in his otherwise uneventful life was concerned; and to hear him recount it, and watch his pale delicate features change, and hear his voice grow softer and more hushed as he proceeded, was to know the conviction that his halting words perhaps failed sometimes to convey. He lived the thing over again each time he told it. His whole personality became muffled in the recital. It subdued him more than ever, so that the tale became a lengthy apology for an experience that he deprecated. He appeared to excuse himself and ask your pardon for having dared to take part in so fantastic an episode. For little Vezin was a timid, gentle, sensitive soul, rarely able to assert himself, tender to man and beast, and almost constitutionally unable to say No, or to claim many things that should rightly have been his. His whole scheme of life seemed utterly remote from anything more exciting than missing a train or losing an umbrella on an omnibus. And when this curious event came upon him he was already more years beyond forty than his friends suspected or he cared to admit.

John Silence, who heard him speak of his experience more than once, said that he sometimes left out certain details and put in others; yet they were all obviously true. The whole scene was unforgettably cinematographed on to his mind. None of the details were imagined or invented. And when he told the story with them all complete, the effect was undeniable. His appealing brown eyes shone, and much of the charming personality, usually so carefully repressed, came forward and revealed itself. His modesty was always there, of course, but in the telling he forgot the present and allowed himself to appear almost vividly as he lived again in the past of his adventure.

He was on the way home when it happened, crossing northern France from some mountain trip or other where he buried himself solitary-wise every summer. He had nothing but an unregistered bag in the rack, and the train was jammed to suffocation, most of the passengers being unredeemed holiday English. He disliked them, not because they were his fellow-countrymen, but because they were noisy and obtrusive, obliterating with their big limbs and tweed clothing all the quieter tints of the day that brought him satisfaction and enabled him to melt into insignificance and forget that he was anybody. These English clashed about him like a brass band, making him feel vaguely that he ought to be more self-assertive and obstreperous, and that he did not claim insistently enough all kinds of things that he didn't want and that were really valueless, such as corner seats, windows up or down, and so forth.

So that he felt uncomfortable in the train, and wished the journey were over and he was back again living with his unmarried sister in Surbiton.

And when the train stopped for ten panting minutes at the little station in northern France, and he got out to stretch his legs on the platform, and saw to his dismay a further batch of the British Isles debouching from another train, it suddenly seemed impossible to him to continue the journey. Even *his* flabby soul revolted, and the idea of staying a night in the little town and going on next day by a slower, emptier train, flashed into his mind. The guard was already shouting *"en voiture"* and the corridor of his compartment was already packed when the thought came to him. And, for once, he acted with decision and rushed to snatch his bag.

Finding the corridor and steps impassable, he tapped at the window (for he had a corner seat) and begged the Frenchman who sat opposite to hand his luggage out to him, explaining in his wretched French that he intended to break the journey there. And this elderly Frenchman, he declared, gave him a look, half of warning, half of reproach, that to his dying day he could never forget; handed the bag through the window of the moving train; and at the same time poured into his ears a long sentence, spoken rapidly and low, of which he was able to comprehend only the last few words: *"à cause du sommeil et à cause des chats."*

In reply to Dr. Silence, whose singular psychic acuteness at once seized upon this Frenchman as a vital point in the adventure, Vezin admitted that the man had impressed him favourably from the beginning, though without being able to explain why. They had sat facing one another during the four hours of the journey, and though no conversation had passed between them—Vezin was timid about his stuttering French—he confessed that his eyes were being continually drawn to his face, almost, he felt, to rudeness, and that each, by a dozen nameless little politenesses and attentions, had evinced the desire to be kind. The men liked each other and their personalities did not clash, or would not have clashed had they chanced to come to terms of acquaintance. The Frenchman, indeed, seemed to have exercised a silent protective influence over the insignificant little Englishman, and without words or gestures betrayed that he wished him well and would gladly have been of service to him.

"And this sentence that he hurled at you after the bag?" asked John Silence, smiling that peculiarly sympathetic smile that always melted the prejudices of his patient, "were you unable to follow it exactly?"

"It was so quick and low and vehement," explained Vezin, in his small voice, "that I missed practically the whole of it. I only caught the few words at the very end, because he spoke them so clearly, and his face was bent down out of the carriage window so near to mine."

"'*À cause du sommeil et à cause des chats*'?" repeated Dr. Silence, as though half speaking to himself.

"That's it exactly," said Vezin; "which, I take it, means something like 'because of sleep and because of the cats,' doesn't it?"

"Certainly, that's how I should translate it," the doctor observed shortly, evidently not wishing to interrupt more than necessary.

"And the rest of the sentence—all the first part I couldn't understand, I mean—was a warning not to do something—not to stop in the town, or at some particular place in the town, perhaps. That was the impression it made on me."

Then, of course, the train rushed off, and left Vezin standing on the platform alone and rather forlorn.

The little town climbed in straggling fashion up a sharp hill rising out of the plain at the back of the station, and was crowned by the twin towers of the ruined cathedral peeping over the summit. From the station itself it looked uninteresting and modern, but the fact was that the mediaeval position lay out of sight just beyond the crest. And once he reached the top and entered the old streets, he stepped clean out of modern life into a bygone century. The noise and bustle of the crowded train seemed days away. The spirit of this silent hill-town, remote from tourists and motor-cars, dreaming its own quiet life under the autumn sun, rose up and cast its spell upon him. Long before he recognised this spell he acted under it. He walked softly, almost on tiptoe, down the winding narrow streets where the gables all but met over his head, and he entered the doorway of the solitary inn with a deprecating and modest demeanour that was in itself an apology for intruding upon the place and disturbing its dream.

At first, however, Vezin said, he noticed very little of all this. The attempt at analysis came much later. What struck him then was only the delightful contrast of the silence and peace after the dust and noisy rattle of the train. He felt soothed and stroked like a cat.

"Like a cat, you said?" interrupted John Silence, quickly catching him up.

"Yes. At the very start I felt that." He laughed apologetically. "I felt as though the warmth and the stillness and the comfort made me purr. It seemed to be the general mood of the whole place—then."

The inn, a rambling ancient house, the atmosphere of the old coaching days still about it, apparently did not welcome him too warmly. He felt he was only tolerated, he said. But it was cheap and comfortable, and the delicious cup of afternoon tea he ordered at once made him feel really very pleased with himself for leaving the train in this bold, original way. For to him it had seemed bold and original. He felt something of a dog. His room, too, soothed him with its dark panelling and low irregular ceiling, and the long sloping passage that led to it seemed the natural pathway to a real Chamber of Sleep— a little dim cubby hole out of the world where noise could not enter. It looked upon the courtyard at the back. It was all very charming, and made him think of himself as dressed in very soft velvet somehow, and the floors seemed padded, the walls provided with cushions. The sounds of the streets could not penetrate there. It was an atmosphere of absolute rest that surrounded him.

On engaging the two-franc room he had interviewed the only person who seemed to be about that sleepy afternoon, an elderly waiter with Dundreary whiskers and a drowsy courtesy, who had ambled lazily towards him across the stone yard; but on coming downstairs again for a little promenade in the town before dinner he encountered the proprietress herself. She was a large woman whose hands, feet, and features seemed to swim towards him out of a sea of person. They emerged, so to speak. But she had great dark, vivacious eyes that counteracted the bulk of her body, and betrayed the fact that in reality she was both vigorous and alert. When he first caught sight of her she was knitting in a low chair against the sunlight of the wall, and something at once made him see her as a great tabby cat, dozing, yet awake, heavily sleepy, and yet at the same time prepared for instantaneous action. A great mouser on the watch occurred to him.

She took him in with a single comprehensive glance that was polite without being cordial. Her neck, he noticed, was extraordinarily supple in spite of its proportions, for it turned so easily to follow him, and the head it carried bowed so very flexibly.

"But when she looked at me, you know," said Vezin, with that little apologetic smile in his brown eyes, and that faintly deprecating gesture of the shoulders that was characteristic of him, "the odd notion came to me that really she had intended to make quite a different movement, and that with a single bound she could have leaped at me across the width of that stone yard and pounced upon me like some huge cat upon a mouse."

He laughed a little soft laugh, and Dr. Silence made a note in his book without interrupting, while Vezin proceeded in a tone as though he feared he had already told too much and more than we could believe.

"Very soft, yet very active she was, for all her size and mass, and I felt she knew what I was doing even after I had passed and was behind her back. She spoke to me, and her voice was smooth and running. She asked if I had my luggage, and was comfortable in my room, and then added that dinner was at seven o'clock, and that they were very early people in this little country town. Clearly, she intended to convey that late hours were not encouraged."

Evidently, she contrived by voice and manner to give him the impression that here he would be "managed," that everything would be arranged and planned for him, and that he had nothing to do but fall into the groove and obey. No decided action or sharp personal effort would be looked for from him. It was the very reverse of the train. He walked quietly out into the street feeling soothed and peaceful. He realised that he was in a *milieu* that suited him and stroked him the right way. It was so much easier to be obedient. He began to purr again, and to feel that all the town purred with him.

About the streets of that little town he meandered gently, falling deeper and deeper into the spirit of repose that characterised it. With no special aim he wandered up and down, and to and fro. The September sunshine fell slantingly over the roofs. Down winding alleyways, fringed with tumbling gables and open casements, he caught fairylike glimpses of the great plain below, and of the meadows and yellow copses lying like a dream-map in the haze. The spell of the past held very potently here, he felt.

The streets were full of picturesquely garbed men and women, all busy enough, going their respective ways; but no one took any notice of him or turned to stare at his obviously English appearance. He was even able to forget that with his tourist appearance he was a false note in a charming picture, and he melted more and more into the scene, feeling delightfully insignificant and unimportant and unself-conscious. It was like becoming part of a softly coloured dream which he did not even realise to be a dream.

On the eastern side the hill fell away more sharply, and the plain below ran off rather suddenly into a sea of gathering shadows in which the little patches of woodland looked like islands and the stubble fields like deep water. Here he strolled along the old ramparts of ancient fortifications that once had been formidable, but now were only vision-like with their charming mingling of broken grey walls and wayward vine and ivy. From the broad coping on which he sat for a moment, level with the rounded tops of clipped plane trees, he saw the esplanade far below lying in shadow. Here and there a yellow sunbeam crept in and lay upon the fallen yellow leaves, and from the height he looked down and saw that the townsfolk were walking to and fro in the cool of the evening. He could just hear the sound of their slow footfalls, and the murmur of their voices floated up to him through the gaps between the trees. The figures looked like shadows as he caught glimpses of their quiet movements far below.

He sat there for some time pondering, bathed in the waves of murmurs and half-lost echoes that rose to his ears, muffled by the leaves of the plane trees. The whole town, and the little hill out of which it grew as naturally as an ancient wood, seemed to him like a being lying there half asleep on the plain and crooning to itself as it dozed.

And, presently, as he sat lazily melting into its dream, a sound of horns and strings and wood instruments rose to his ears, and the town band began to play at the far end of the crowded terrace below to the accompaniment of a very soft, deep-throated drum. Vezin was very sensitive to music, knew about it intelligently, and had even ventured, unknown to his friends, upon the composition of quiet melodies with low-running chords which he played to himself with the soft pedal when no one was about. And this music floating up through the trees from an invisible and doubtless very picturesque band of the townspeople wholly charmed him. He recognised nothing that they played, and it sounded as though they were simply improvising without a conductor. No definitely marked time ran through the pieces, which ended and began oddly after the fashion of wind through an Æolian harp. It was part of the place and scene, just as the dying sunlight and faintly breathing wind were part of the scene and hour, and the mellow notes of old-fashioned plaintive horns, pierced here and there by the sharper strings, all half smothered by the continuous booming of the deep drum, touched his soul with a curiously potent spell that was almost too engrossing to be quite pleasant.

There was a certain queer sense of bewitchment in it all. The music seemed to him oddly unartificial. It made him think of trees swept by the wind, of night breezes singing among wires and chimney-stacks, or in the rigging of invisible ships; or—and the simile leaped up in his thoughts with a sudden sharpness of suggestion—a chorus of animals, of wild creatures, somewhere in desolate places of the world, crying and singing as animals will, to the moon. He could fancy he heard the wailing, half-human cries of cats upon the tiles at night, rising and falling with weird intervals of sound, and this music, muffled by distance and the trees, made him think of a queer company of these creatures on some roof far away in the sky, uttering their solemn music to one another and the moon in chorus.

It was, he felt at the time, a singular image to occur to him, yet it expressed his sensation pictorially better than anything else. The instruments played such impossibly odd intervals, and the crescendos and diminuendos were so very suggestive of cat-land on the tiles at night, rising swiftly, dropping without warning to deep notes again, and all in such strange confusion of discords and accords. But, at the same time a plaintive sweetness resulted on the whole, and the discords of these half-broken instruments were so singular that they did not distress his musical soul like fiddles out of tune.

He listened a long time, wholly surrendering himself as his character was, and then strolled homewards in the dusk as the air grew chilly.

"There was nothing to alarm?" put in Dr. Silence briefly.

"Absolutely nothing," said Vezin; "but you know it was all so fantastical and charming that my imagination was profoundly impressed. Perhaps, too," he continued, gently explanatory, "it was this stirring of my imagination that caused other impressions; for, as I walked back, the spell of the place began to steal over me in a dozen ways, though all intelligible ways. But there were other things I could not account for in the least, even then."

"Incidents, you mean?"

"Hardly incidents, I think. A lot of vivid sensations crowded themselves upon my mind and I could trace them to no causes. It was just after sunset and the tumbled old buildings traced magical outlines against an opalescent sky of gold and red. The dusk was running down the twisted streets. All round the hill the plain pressed in like a dim sea, its level rising with the darkness. The spell of this kind of scene, you know, can be very moving, and it was so that night. Yet I felt that what came to me had nothing directly to do with the mystery and wonder of the scene."

"Not merely the subtle transformations of the spirit that come with beauty," put in the doctor, noticing his hesitation.

"Exactly," Vezin went on, duly encouraged and no longer so fearful of our smiles at his expense. "The impressions came from somewhere else. For instance, down the busy main street where men and women were bustling home from work, shopping at stalls and barrows, idly gossiping in groups, and all the rest of it, I saw that I aroused no interest and that no one turned to stare at me as a foreigner and stranger. I was utterly ignored, and my presence among them excited no special interest or attention.

"And then, quite suddenly, it dawned upon me with conviction that all the time this indifference and inattention were merely feigned. Everybody as a matter of fact was watching me closely. Every movement I made was known and observed. Ignoring me was all a pretence—an elaborate pretence."

He paused a moment and looked at us to see if we were smiling, and then continued, reassured—

"It is useless to ask me how I noticed this, because I simply cannot explain it. But the discovery gave me something of a shock. Before I got back to the inn, however, another curious thing rose up strongly in my mind and forced my recognition of it as true. And this, too, I may as well say at once, was equally inexplicable to me. I mean I can only give you the fact, as fact it was to me."

The little man left his chair and stood on the mat before the fire. His diffidence lessened from now onwards, as he lost himself again in the magic of the old adventure. His eyes shone a little already as he talked.

"Well," he went on, his soft voice rising somewhat with his excitement, "I was in a shop when it came to me first—though the idea must have been at work for a long time subconsciously to appear in so complete a form all at once. I was buying socks, I think," he laughed, "and struggling with my dreadful French, when it struck me that the woman in the shop did not care two pins whether I bought anything or not. She was indifferent whether she made a sale or did not make a sale. She was only pretending to sell.

"This sounds a very small and fanciful incident to build upon what follows. But really it was not small. I mean it was the spark that lit the line of powder and ran along to the big blaze in my mind.

"For the whole town, I suddenly realised, was something other than I so far saw it. The real activities and interests of the people were elsewhere and otherwise than appeared. Their true lives lay somewhere out of sight behind the scenes. Their busy-ness was but the outward semblance that masked their actual purposes. They bought and sold, and ate and drank, and walked about the streets, yet all the while the main stream of their existence lay somewhere beyond my ken, underground, in secret places. In the shops and at the stalls they did not care whether I purchased their articles or not; at the inn, they were indifferent to my staying or going; their life lay remote from my own, springing from hidden, mysterious sources, coursing out of sight, unknown. It was all a great elaborate pretence, assumed possibly for my benefit, or possibly for purposes of their own. But the main current of their energies ran elsewhere. I almost felt as an unwelcome foreign substance might be expected to feel when it has found its way into the human system and the whole body organises itself to eject it or to absorb it. The town was doing this very thing to me.

"This bizarre notion presented itself forcibly to my mind as I walked home to the inn, and I began busily to wonder wherein the true life of this town could lie and what were the actual interests and activities of its hidden life.

"And, now that my eyes were partly opened, I noticed other things too that puzzled me, first of which, I think, was the extraordinary silence of the whole place. Positively, the town was muffled. Although the streets were paved with cobbles the people moved about silently, softly, with padded feet, like cats. Nothing made noise. All was hushed, subdued, muted. The very voices were quiet, low-pitched like purring. Nothing clamorous, vehement or emphatic seemed able to live in the drowsy atmosphere of soft dreaming that soothed this little hill-town into its sleep. It was like the woman at the inn—an outward repose screening intense inner activity and purpose.

"Yet there was no sign of lethargy or sluggishness anywhere about it. The people were active and alert. Only a magical and uncanny softness lay over them all like a spell."

Vezin passed his hand across his eyes for a moment as though the memory had become very vivid. His voice had run off into a whisper so that we heard the last part with difficulty. He was telling a true thing obviously, yet something that he both liked and hated telling.

"I went back to the inn," he continued presently in a louder voice, "and dined. I felt a new strange world about me. My old world of reality receded. Here, whether I liked it or no, was something new and incomprehensible. I regretted having left the train so impulsively. An adventure was upon me, and I loathed adventures as foreign to my nature. Moreover, this was the beginning apparently of an adventure somewhere deep within me, in a region I could not check or measure, and a feeling of alarm mingled itself with my wonder—alarm for the stability of what I had for forty years recognised as my 'personality.'

"I went upstairs to bed, my mind teeming with thoughts that were unusual to me, and of rather a haunting description. By way of relief I kept thinking of that nice, prosaic noisy train and all those wholesome, blustering passengers. I almost wished I were with them again. But my dreams took me elsewhere. I dreamed of cats, and soft-moving creatures, and the silence of life in a dim muffled world beyond the senses."

II

Vezin stayed on from day to day, indefinitely, much longer than he had intended. He felt in a kind of dazed, somnolent condition. He did nothing in particular, but the place fascinated him and he could not decide to leave. Decisions were always very difficult for him and he sometimes wondered how he had ever brought himself to the point of leaving the train. It seemed as though some one else must have arranged it for him, and once or twice his thoughts ran to the swarthy Frenchman who had sat opposite. If only he could have understood that long sentence ending so strangely with "*à cause du sommeil et à cause des chats.*" He wondered what it all meant.

Meanwhile the hushed softness of the town held him prisoner and he sought in his muddling, gentle way to find out where the mystery lay, and what it was all about. But his limited French and his constitutional hatred of active investigation made it hard for him to buttonhole anybody and ask questions. He was content to observe, and watch, and remain negative.

The weather held on calm and hazy, and this just suited him. He wandered about the town till he knew every street and alley. The people suffered him to come and go without let or hindrance, though it became clearer to him every day that he was never free himself from observation. The town watched him as a cat watches a mouse. And he got no nearer to finding out what they were all so busy with or where the main stream of their activities lay. This remained hidden. The people were as soft and mysterious as cats.

But that he was continually under observation became more evident from day to day.

For instance, when he strolled to the end of the town and entered a little green public garden beneath the ramparts and seated himself upon one of the empty benches in the sun, he was quite alone—at first. Not another seat was occupied; the little park was empty, the paths deserted. Yet, within ten minutes of his coming, there must have been fully twenty persons scattered about him, some strolling aimlessly along the gravel walks, staring at the flowers, and others seated on the wooden benches enjoying the sun like himself. None of them appeared to take any notice of him; yet he understood quite well they had all come there to watch. They kept him under close observation. In the street they had seemed busy enough, hurrying upon various errands; yet these were suddenly all forgotten and they had nothing to do but loll and laze in the sun, their duties unremembered. Five minutes after he left, the garden was again deserted, the seats vacant. But in the crowded street it was the same thing again; he was never alone. He was ever in their thoughts.

By degrees, too, he began to see how it was he was so cleverly watched, yet without the appearance of it. The people did nothing *directly*. They behaved *obliquely*. He laughed in his mind as the thought thus clothed itself in words, but the phrase exactly described it. They looked at him from angles which naturally should have led their sight in another direction altogether. Their movements were oblique, too, so far as these concerned himself. The straight, direct thing was not their way evidently. They did nothing obviously. If he entered a shop to buy, the woman walked instantly away and busied herself with something at the farther end of the counter, though answering at once when he spoke, showing that she knew he was there and that this was only her way of attending to him. It was the fashion of the cat she followed. Even in the dining-room of the inn, the bewhiskered and courteous waiter, lithe and silent in all his movements, never seemed able to come straight to his table for an order or a dish. He came by zigzags, indirectly, vaguely, so that he appeared to be going to another table altogether, and only turned suddenly at the last moment, and was there beside him.

Vezin smiled curiously to himself as he described how he began to realize these things. Other tourists there were none in the hostel, but he recalled the figures of one or two old men, inhabitants, who took their *déjeuner* and dinner there, and remembered how fantastically they entered the room in similar fashion. First, they paused in the doorway, peering about the room, and then, after a temporary inspection, they came in, as it were, sideways, keeping close to the walls so that he wondered which table they were making for, and at the last minute making almost a little quick run to their particular seats. And again he thought of the ways and methods of cats.

Other small incidents, too, impressed him as all part of this queer, soft town with its muffled, indirect life, for the way some of the people appeared and disappeared with extraordinary swiftness puzzled him exceedingly. It may have been all perfectly natural, he knew, yet he could not make it out how the alleys swallowed them up and shot them forth in a second of time when there were no visible doorways or openings near enough to explain the phenomenon. Once he followed two elderly women who, he felt, had been particularly examining him from across the street—quite near the inn this was—and saw them turn the corner a few feet only in front of him. Yet when he sharply followed on their heels he saw nothing but an utterly deserted alley stretching in front of him with no sign of a living thing. And the only opening through which they could have escaped was a porch some fifty yards away, which not the swiftest human runner could have reached in time.

And in just such sudden fashion people appeared, when he never expected them. Once when he heard a great noise of fighting going on behind a low wall, and hurried up to see what was going on, what should he see but a group of girls and women engaged in vociferous conversation which instantly hushed itself to the normal whispering note of the town when his head appeared over the wall. And even then none of them turned to look at him directly, but slunk off with the most unaccountable rapidity into doors and sheds across the yard. And their voices, he thought, had sounded so like, so strangely like, the angry snarling of fighting animals, almost of cats.

The whole spirit of the town, however, continued to evade him as something elusive, protean, screened from the outer world, and at the same time intensely, genuinely vital; and, since he now formed part of its life, this concealment puzzled and irritated him; more—it began rather to frighten him.

Out of the mists that slowly gathered about his ordinary surface thoughts, there rose again the idea that the inhabitants were waiting for him to declare himself, to take an attitude, to do this, or to do that; and that when he had done so they in their turn would at length make some direct response, accepting or rejecting him. Yet the vital matter concerning which his decision was awaited came no nearer to him.

Once or twice he purposely followed little processions or groups of the citizens in order to find out, if possible, on what purpose they were bent; but they always discovered him in time and dwindled away, each individual going his or her own way. It was always the same: he never could learn what their main interest was. The cathedral was ever empty, the old church of St. Martin, at the other end of the town, deserted. They shopped because they had to, and not because they wished to. The booths stood neglected, the stalls unvisited, the little *cafés* desolate. Yet the streets were always full, the townsfolk ever on the bustle.

"Can it be," he thought to himself, yet with a deprecating laugh that he should have dared to think anything so odd, "can it be that these people are people of the twilight, that they live only at night their real life, and come out honestly only with the dusk? That during the day they make a sham though brave pretence, and after the sun is down their true life begins? Have they the souls of night-things, and is the whole blessed town in the hands of the cats?"

The fancy somehow electrified him with little shocks of shrinking and dismay. Yet, though he affected to laugh, he knew that he was beginning to feel more than uneasy, and that strange forces were tugging with a thousand invisible cords at the very centre of his being. Something utterly remote from his ordinary life, something that had not waked for years, began faintly to stir in his soul, sending feelers abroad into his brain and heart, shaping queer thoughts and penetrating even into certain of his minor actions. Something exceedingly vital to himself, to his soul, hung in the balance.

And, always when he returned to the inn about the hour of sunset, he saw the figures of the townsfolk stealing through the dusk from their shop doors, moving sentry-wise to and fro at the corners of the streets, yet always vanishing silently like shadows at his near approach. And as the inn invariably closed its doors at ten o'clock he had never yet found the opportunity he rather half-heartedly sought to see for himself what account the town could give of itself at night.

"—*à cause du sommeil et à cause des chats*"—the words now rang in his ears more and more often, though still as yet without any definite meaning.

Moreover, something made him sleep like the dead.

III

It was, I think, on the fifth day—though in this detail his story sometimes varied—that he made a definite discovery which increased his alarm and brought him up to a rather sharp climax. Before that he had already noticed that a change was going forward and certain subtle transformations being brought about in his character which modified several of his minor habits. And he had affected to ignore them. Here, however, was something he could no longer ignore; and it startled him.

At the best of times he was never very positive, always negative rather, compliant and acquiescent; yet, when necessity arose he was capable of reasonably vigorous action and could take a strongish decision. The discovery he now made that brought him up with such a sharp turn was that this power had positively dwindled to nothing. He found it impossible to make up his mind. For, on this fifth day, he realised that he had stayed long enough in the town and that for reasons he could only vaguely define to himself it was wiser *and safer* that he should leave.

And he found that he could not leave!

This is difficult to describe in words, and it was more by gesture and the expression of his face that he conveyed to Dr. Silence the state of impotence he had reached. All this spying and watching, he said, had as it were spun a net about his feet so that he was trapped and powerless to escape; he felt like a fly that had blundered into the intricacies of a great web; he was caught, imprisoned, and could not get away. It was a distressing sensation. A numbness had crept over his will till it had become almost incapable of decision. The mere thought of vigorous action—action towards escape— began to terrify him. All the currents of his life had turned inwards upon himself, striving to bring to the surface something that lay buried almost beyond reach, determined to force his recognition of something he had long forgotten—forgotten years upon years, centuries almost ago. It seemed as though a window deep within his being would presently open and reveal an entirely new world, yet somehow a world that was not unfamiliar. Beyond that, again, he fancied a great curtain hung; and when that too rolled up he would see still farther into this region and at last understand something of the secret life of these extraordinary people.

"Is this why they wait and watch?" he asked himself with rather a shaking heart, "for the time when I shall join them—or refuse to join them? Does the decision rest with me after all, and not with them?"

And it was at this point that the sinister character of the adventure first really declared itself, and he became genuinely alarmed. The stability of his rather fluid little personality was at stake, he felt, and something in his heart turned coward.

Why otherwise should he have suddenly taken to walking stealthily, silently, making as little sound as possible, for ever looking behind him? Why else should he have moved almost on tiptoe about the passages of the practically deserted inn, and when he was abroad have found himself deliberately taking advantage of what cover presented itself? And why, if he was not afraid, should the wisdom of staying indoors after sundown have suddenly occurred to him as eminently desirable? Why, indeed?

And, when John Silence gently pressed him for an explanation of these things, he admitted apologetically that he had none to give.

"It was simply that I feared something might happen to me unless I kept a sharp look-out. I felt afraid. It was instinctive," was all he could say. "I got the impression that the whole town was after me—wanted me for something; and that if it got me I should lose myself, or at least the Self I knew, in some unfamiliar state of consciousness. But I am not a psychologist, you know," he added meekly, "and I cannot define it better than that."

It was while lounging in the courtyard half an hour before the evening meal that Vezin made this discovery, and he at once went upstairs to his quiet room at the end of the winding passage to think it over alone. In the yard it was empty enough, true, but there was always the possibility that the big woman whom he dreaded would come out of some door, with her pretence of knitting, to sit and watch him. This had happened several times, and he could not endure the sight of her. He still remembered his original fancy, bizarre though it was, that she would spring upon him the moment his back was turned and land with one single crushing leap upon his neck. Of course it was nonsense, but then it haunted him, and once an idea begins to do that it ceases to be nonsense. It has clothed itself in reality.

He went upstairs accordingly. It was dusk, and the oil lamps had not yet been lit in the passages. He stumbled over the uneven surface of the ancient flooring, passing the dim outlines of doors along the corridor—doors that he had never once seen opened—rooms that seemed never occupied. He moved, as his habit now was, stealthily and on tiptoe.

Half-way down the last passage to his own chamber there was a sharp turn, and it was just here, while groping round the walls with outstretched hands, that his fingers touched something that was not wall—something that moved. It was soft and warm in texture, indescribably fragrant, and about the height of his shoulder; and he immediately thought of a furry, sweet-smelling kitten. The next minute he knew it was something quite different.

Instead of investigating, however, —his nerves must have been too overwrought for that, he said, —he shrank back as closely as possible against the wall on the other side. The thing, whatever it was, slipped past him with a sound of rustling and, retreating with light footsteps down the passage behind him, was gone. A breath of warm, scented air was wafted to his nostrils.

Vezin caught his breath for an instant and paused, stockstill, half leaning against the wall—and then almost ran down the remaining distance and entered his room with a rush, locking the door hurriedly behind him. Yet it was not fear that made him run: it was excitement, pleasurable excitement. His nerves were tingling, and a delicious glow made itself felt all over his body. In a flash it came to him that this was just what he had felt twenty-five years ago as a boy when he was in love for the first time. Warm currents of life ran all over him and mounted to his brain in a whirl of soft delight. His mood was suddenly become tender, melting, loving.

The room was quite dark, and he collapsed upon the sofa by the window, wondering what had happened to him and what it all meant. But the only thing he understood clearly in that instant was that something in him had swiftly, magically changed: he no longer wished to leave, or to argue with himself about leaving. The encounter in the passage-way had changed all that. The strange perfume of it still hung about him, bemusing his heart and mind. For he knew that it was a girl who had passed him, a girl's face that his fingers had brushed in the darkness, and he felt in some extraordinary way as though he had been actually kissed by her, kissed full upon the lips.

Trembling, he sat upon the sofa by the window and struggled to collect his thoughts. He was utterly unable to understand how the mere passing of a girl in the darkness of a narrow passage-way could communicate so electric a thrill to his whole being that he still shook with the sweetness of it. Yet, there it was! And he found it as useless to deny as to attempt analysis. Some ancient fire had entered his veins, and now ran coursing through his blood; and that he was forty-five instead of twenty did not matter one little jot. Out of all the inner turmoil and confusion emerged the one salient fact that the mere atmosphere, the merest casual touch, of this girl, unseen, unknown in the darkness, had been sufficient to stir dormant fires in the centre of his heart, and rouse his whole being from a state of feeble sluggishness to one of tearing and tumultuous excitement.

After a time, however, the number of Vezin's years began to assert their cumulative power; he grew calmer, and when a knock came at length upon his door and he heard the waiter's voice suggesting that dinner was nearly over, he pulled himself together and slowly made his way downstairs into the dining-room.

Every one looked up as he entered, for he was very late, but he took his customary seat in the far corner and began to eat. The trepidation was still in his nerves, but the fact that he had passed through the courtyard and hall without catching sight of a petticoat served to calm him a little. He ate so fast that he had almost caught up with the current stage of the table d'hôte, when a slight commotion in the room drew his attention.

His chair was so placed that the door and the greater portion of the long *salle à manger* were behind him, yet it was not necessary to turn round to know that the same person he had passed in the dark passage had now come into the room. He felt the presence long before he heard or saw any one. Then he became aware that the old men, the only other guests, were rising one by one in their places, and exchanging greetings with some one who passed among them from table to table. And when at length he turned with his heart beating furiously to ascertain for himself, he saw the form of a young girl, lithe and slim, moving down the centre of the room and making straight for his own table in the corner. She moved wonderfully, with sinuous grace, like a young panther, and her approach filled him with such delicious bewilderment that he was utterly unable to tell at first what her face was like, or discover what it was about the whole presentment of the creature that filled him anew with trepidation and delight.

"Ah, Ma'mselle est de retour!" he heard the old waiter murmur at his side, and he was just able to take in that she was the daughter of the proprietress, when she was upon him, and he heard her voice. She was addressing him. Something of red lips he saw and laughing white teeth, and stray wisps of fine dark hair about the temples; but all the rest was a dream in which his own emotion rose like a thick cloud before his eyes and prevented his seeing accurately, or knowing exactly what he did. He was aware that she greeted him with a charming little bow; that her beautiful large eyes looked searchingly into his own; that the perfume he had noticed in the dark passage again assailed his nostrils, and that she was bending a little towards him and leaning with one hand on the table at this side. She was quite close to him—that was the chief thing he knew— explaining that she had been asking after the comfort of her mother's guests, and now was introducing herself to the latest arrival—himself.

"M'sieur has already been here a few days," he heard the waiter say; and then her own voice, sweet as singing, replied—

"Ah, but M'sieur is not going to leave us just yet, I hope. My mother is too old to look after the comfort of our guests properly, but now I am here I will remedy all that." She laughed deliciously. "M'sieur shall be well looked after."

Vezin, struggling with his emotion and desire to be polite, half rose to acknowledge the pretty speech, and to stammer some sort of reply, but as he did so his hand by chance touched her own that was resting upon the table, and a shock that was for all the world like a shock of electricity, passed from her skin into his body. His soul wavered and shook deep within him. He caught her eyes fixed upon his own with a look of most curious intentness, and the next moment he knew that he had sat down wordless again on his chair, that the girl was already halfway across the room, and that he was trying to eat his salad with a dessert-spoon and a knife.

Longing for her return, and yet dreading it, he gulped down the remainder of his dinner, and then went at once to his bedroom to be alone with his thoughts. This time the passages were lighted, and he suffered no exciting contretemps; yet the winding corridor was dim with shadows, and the last portion, from the bend of the walls onwards, seemed longer than he had ever known it. It ran downhill like the pathway on a mountain side, and as he tiptoed softly down it he felt that by rights it ought to have led him clean out of the house into the heart of a great forest. The world was singing with him. Strange fancies filled his brain, and once in the room, with the door securely locked, he did not light the candles, but sat by the open window thinking long, long thoughts that came unbidden in troops to his mind.

IV

This part of the story he told to Dr. Silence, without special coaxing, it is true, yet with much stammering embarrassment. He could not in the least understand, he said, how the girl had managed to affect him so profoundly, and even before he had set eyes upon her. For her mere proximity in the darkness had been sufficient to set him on fire. He knew nothing of enchantments, and for years had been a stranger to anything approaching tender relations with any member of the opposite sex, for he was encased in shyness, and realised his overwhelming defects only too well. Yet this bewitching young creature came to him deliberately. Her manner was unmistakable, and she sought him out on every possible occasion. Chaste and sweet she was undoubtedly, yet frankly inviting; and she won him utterly with the first glance of her shining eyes, even if she had not already done so in the dark merely by the magic of her invisible presence.

"You felt she was altogether wholesome and good!" queried the doctor. "You had no reaction of any sort—for instance, of alarm?"

Vezin looked up sharply with one of his inimitable little apologetic smiles. It was some time before he replied. The mere memory of the adventure had suffused his shy face with blushes, and his brown eyes sought the floor again before he answered.

"I don't think I can quite say that," he explained presently. "I acknowledged certain qualms, sitting up in my room afterwards. A conviction grew upon me that there was something about her—how shall I express it?—well, something unholy. It is not impurity in any sense, physical or mental, that I mean, but something quite indefinable that gave me a vague sensation of the creeps. She drew me, and at the same time repelled me, more than—than—"

He hesitated, blushing furiously, and unable to finish the sentence.

"Nothing like it has ever come to me before or since," he concluded, with lame confusion. "I suppose it was, as you suggested just now, something of an enchantment. At any rate, it was strong enough to make me feel that I would stay in that awful little haunted town for years if only I could see her every day, hear her voice, watch her wonderful movements, and sometimes, perhaps, touch her hand."

"Can you explain to me what you felt was the source of her power?" John Silence asked, looking purposely anywhere but at the narrator.

"I am surprised that you should ask me such a question," answered Vezin, with the nearest approach to dignity he could manage. "I think no man can describe to another convincingly wherein lies the magic of the woman who ensnares him. I certainly cannot. I can only say this slip of a girl bewitched me, and the mere knowledge that she was living and sleeping in the same house filled me with an extraordinary sense of delight.

"But there's one thing I can tell you," he went on earnestly, his eyes aglow, "namely, that she seemed to sum up and synthesise in herself all the strange hidden forces that operated so mysteriously in the town and its inhabitants. She had the silken movements of the panther, going smoothly, silently to and fro, and the same indirect, oblique methods as the townsfolk, screening, like them, secret purposes of her own—purposes that I was sure had *me* for their objective. She kept me, to my terror and delight, ceaselessly under observation, yet so carelessly, so consummately, that another man less sensitive, if I may say so"—he made a deprecating gesture—"or less prepared by what had gone before, would never have noticed it at all. She was always still, always reposeful, yet she seemed to be everywhere at once, so that I never could escape from her. I was continually meeting the stare and laughter of her great eyes, in the corners of the rooms, in the passages, calmly looking at me through the windows, or in the busiest parts of the public streets."

Their intimacy, it seems, grew very rapidly after this first encounter which had so violently disturbed the little man's equilibrium. He was naturally very prim, and prim folk live mostly in so small a world that anything violently unusual may shake them clean out of it, and they therefore instinctively distrust originality. But Vezin began to forget his primness after awhile. The girl was always modestly behaved, and as her mother's representative she naturally had to do with the guests in the hotel. It was not out of the way that a spirit of camaraderie should spring up. Besides, she was young, she was charmingly pretty, she was French, and—she obviously liked him.

At the same time, there was something indescribable—a certain indefinable atmosphere of other places, other times—that made him try hard to remain on his guard, and sometimes made him catch his breath with a sudden start. It was all rather like a delirious dream, half delight, half dread, he confided in a whisper to Dr. Silence; and more than once he hardly knew quite what he was doing or saying, as though he were driven forward by impulses he scarcely recognised as his own.

And though the thought of leaving presented itself again and again to his mind, it was each time with less insistence, so that he stayed on from day to day, becoming more and more a part of the sleepy life of this dreamy mediæval town, losing more and more of his recognisable personality. Soon, he felt, the Curtain within would roll up with an awful rush, and he would find himself suddenly admitted into the secret purposes of the hidden life that lay behind it all. Only, by that time, he would have become transformed into an entirely different being.

And, meanwhile, he noticed various little signs of the intention to make his stay attractive to him: flowers in his bedroom, a more comfortable armchair in the corner, and even special little extra dishes on his private table in the dining-room. Conversations, too, with "Mademoiselle Ilsé" became more and more frequent and pleasant, and although they seldom travelled beyond the weather, or the details of the town, the girl, he noticed, was never in a hurry to bring them to an end, and often contrived to interject little odd sentences that he never properly understood, yet felt to be significant.

And it was these stray remarks, full of a meaning that evaded him, that pointed to some hidden purpose of her own and made him feel uneasy. They all had to do, he felt sure, with reasons for his staying on in the town indefinitely.

"And has M'sieur not even yet come to a decision?" she said softly in his ear, sitting beside him in the sunny yard before *déjeuner*, the acquaintance having progressed with significant rapidity. "Because, if it's so difficult, we must all try together to help him!"

The question startled him, following upon his own thoughts. It was spoken with a pretty laugh, and a stray bit of hair across one eye, as she turned and peered at him half roguishly. Possibly he did not quite understand the French of it, for her near presence always confused his small knowledge of the language distressingly. Yet the words, and her manner, and something else that lay behind it all in her mind, frightened him. It gave such point to his feeling that the town was waiting for him to make his mind up on some important matter.

At the same time, her voice, and the fact that she was there so close beside him in her soft dark dress, thrilled him inexpressibly.

"It is true I find it difficult to leave," he stammered, losing his way deliciously in the depths of her eyes, "and especially now that Mademoiselle Ilsé has come."

He was surprised at the success of his sentence, and quite delighted with the little gallantry of it. But at the same time he could have bitten his tongue off for having said it.

"Then after all you like our little town, or you would not be pleased to stay on," she said, ignoring the compliment.

"I am enchanted with it, and enchanted with you," he cried, feeling that his tongue was somehow slipping beyond the control of his brain. And he was on the verge of saying all manner of other things of the wildest description, when the girl sprang lightly up from her chair beside him, and made to go.

"It is *soupe à l'onion* to-day!" she cried, laughing back at him through the sunlight, "and I must go and see about it. Otherwise, you know, M'sieur will not enjoy his dinner, and then, perhaps, he will leave us!"

He watched her cross the courtyard, moving with all the grace and lightness of the feline race, and her simple black dress clothed her, he thought, exactly like the fur of the same supple species. She turned once to laugh at him from the porch with the glass door, and then stopped a moment to speak to her mother, who sat knitting as usual in her corner seat just inside the hall-way.

But how was it, then, that the moment his eye fell upon this ungainly woman, the pair of them appeared suddenly as other than they were? Whence came that transforming dignity and sense of power that enveloped them both as by magic? What was it about that massive woman that made her appear instantly regal, and set her on a throne in some dark and dreadful scenery, wielding a sceptre over the red glare of some tempestuous orgy? And why did this slender stripling of a girl, graceful as a willow, lithe as a young leopard, assume suddenly an air of sinister majesty, and move with flame and smoke about her head, and the darkness of night beneath her feet?

Vezin caught his breath and sat there transfixed. Then, almost simultaneously with its appearance, the queer notion vanished again, and the sunlight of day caught them both, and he heard her laughing to her mother about the *soupe à l'onion*, and saw her glancing back at him over her dear little shoulder with a smile that made him think of a dew-kissed rose bending lightly before summer airs.

And, indeed, the onion soup was particularly excellent that day, because he saw another cover laid at his small table, and, with fluttering heart, heard the waiter murmur by way of explanation that "Ma'mselle Ilsé would honour M'sieur to-day at *déjeuner*, as her custom sometimes is with her mother's guests."

So actually she sat by him all through that delirious meal, talking quietly to him in easy French, seeing that he was well looked after, mixing the salad-dressing, and even helping him with her own hand. And, later in the afternoon, while he was smoking in the courtyard, longing for a sight of her as soon as her duties were done, she came again to his side, and when he rose to meet her, she stood facing him a moment, full of a perplexing sweet shyness before she spoke—

"My mother thinks you ought to know more of the beauties of our little town, and I think so too! Would M'sieur like me to be his guide, perhaps? I can show him everything, for our family has lived here for many generations."

She had him by the hand, indeed, before he could find a single word to express his pleasure, and led him, all unresisting, out into the street, yet in such a way that it seemed perfectly natural she should do so, and without the faintest suggestion of boldness or immodesty. Her face glowed with the pleasure and interest of it, and with her short dress and tumbled hair she looked every bit the charming child of seventeen that she was, innocent and playful, proud of her native town, and alive beyond her years to the sense of its ancient beauty.

So they went over the town together, and she showed him what she considered its chief interest: the tumble-down old house where her forebears had lived; the sombre, aristocratic-looking mansion where her mother's family dwelt for centuries, and the ancient market-place where several hundred years before the witches had been burnt by the score. She kept up a lively running stream of talk about it all, of which he understood not a fiftieth part as he trudged along by her side, cursing his forty-five years and feeling all the yearnings of his early manhood revive and jeer at him. And, as she talked, England and Surbiton seemed very far away indeed, almost in another age of the world's history. Her voice touched something immeasurably old in him, something that slept deep. It lulled the surface parts of his consciousness to sleep, allowing what was far more ancient to awaken. Like the town, with its elaborate pretence of modern active life, the upper layers of his being became dulled, soothed, muffled, and what lay underneath began to stir in its sleep. That big Curtain swayed a little to and fro. Presently it might lift altogether....

He began to understand a little better at last. The mood of the town was reproducing itself in him. In proportion as his ordinary external self became muffled, that inner secret life, that was far more real and vital, asserted itself. And this girl was surely the high-priestess of it all, the chief instrument of its accomplishment. New thoughts, with new interpretations, flooded his mind as she walked beside him through the winding streets, while the picturesque old gabled town, softly coloured in the sunset, had never appeared to him so wholly wonderful and seductive.

And only one curious incident came to disturb and puzzle him, slight in itself, but utterly inexplicable, bringing white terror into the child's face and a scream to her laughing lips. He had merely pointed to a column of blue smoke that rose from the burning autumn leaves and made a picture against the red roofs, and had then run to the wall and called her to his side to watch the flames shooting here and there through the heap of rubbish. Yet, at the sight of it, as though taken by surprise, her face had altered dreadfully, and she had turned and run like the wind, calling out wild sentences to him as she ran, of which he had not understood a single word, except that the fire apparently frightened her, and she wanted to get quickly away from it, and to get him away too.

Yet five minutes later she was as calm and happy again as though nothing had happened to alarm or waken troubled thoughts in her, and they had both forgotten the incident.

They were leaning over the ruined ramparts together listening to the weird music of the band as he had heard it the first day of his arrival. It moved him again profoundly as it had done before, and somehow he managed to find his tongue and his best French. The girl leaned across the stones close beside him. No one was about. Driven by some remorseless engine within he began to stammer something—he hardly knew what—of his strange admiration for her. Almost at the first word she sprang lightly off the wall and came up smiling in front of him, just touching his knees as he sat there. She was hatless as usual, and the sun caught her hair and one side of her cheek and throat.

"Oh, I'm *so* glad!" she cried, clapping her little hands softly in his face, "so very glad, because that means that if you like me you must also like what I do, and what I belong to."

Already he regretted bitterly having lost control of himself. Something in the phrasing of her sentence chilled him. He knew the fear of embarking upon an unknown and dangerous sea.

"You will take part in our real life, I mean," she added softly, with an indescribable coaxing of manner, as though she noticed his shrinking. "You will come back to us."

Already this slip of a child seemed to dominate him; he felt her power coming over him more and more; something emanated from her that stole over his senses and made him aware that her personality, for all its simple grace, held forces that were stately, imposing, august. He saw her again moving through smoke and flame amid broken and tempestuous scenery, alarmingly strong, her terrible mother by her side. Dimly this shone through her smile and appearance of charming innocence.

"You will, I know," she repeated, holding him with her eyes.

They were quite alone up there on the ramparts, and the sensation that she was overmastering him stirred a wild sensuousness in his blood. The mingled abandon and reserve in her attracted him furiously, and all of him that was man rose up and resisted the creeping influence, at the same time acclaiming it with the full delight of his forgotten youth. An irresistible desire came to him to question her, to summon what still remained to him of his own little personality in an effort to retain the right to his normal self.

The girl had grown quiet again, and was now leaning on the broad wall close beside him, gazing out across the darkening plain, her elbows on the coping, motionless as a figure carved in stone. He took his courage in both hands.

"Tell me, Ilsé," he said, unconsciously imitating her own purring softness of voice, yet aware that he was utterly in earnest, "what is the meaning of this town, and what is this real life you speak of? And why is it that the people watch me from morning to night? Tell me what it all means? And, tell me," he added more quickly with passion in his voice, "what you really are—yourself?"

She turned her head and looked at him through half-closed eyelids, her growing inner excitement betraying itself by the faint colour that ran like a shadow across her face.

"It seems to me,"— he faltered oddly under her gaze—"that I have some right to know—"

Suddenly she opened her eyes to the full. "You love me, then?" she asked softly.

"I swear," he cried impetuously, moved as by the force of a rising tide, "I never felt before—I have never known any other girl who—"

"Then you *have* the right to know," she calmly interrupted his confused confession, "for love shares all secrets."

She paused, and a thrill like fire ran swiftly through him. Her words lifted him off the earth, and he felt a radiant happiness, followed almost the same instant in horrible contrast by the thought of death. He became aware that she had turned her eyes upon his own and was speaking again.

"The real life I speak of," she whispered, "is the old, old life within, the life of long ago, the life to which you, too, once belonged, and to which you still belong."

A faint wave of memory troubled the deeps of his soul as her low voice sank into him. What she was saying he knew instinctively to be true, even though he could not as yet understand its full purport. His present life seemed slipping from him as he listened, merging his personality in one that was far older and greater. It was this loss of his present self that brought to him the thought of death.

"You came here," she went on, "with the purpose of seeking it, and the people felt your presence and are waiting to know what you decide, whether you will leave them without having found it, or whether—"

Her eyes remained fixed upon his own, but her face began to change, growing larger and darker with an expression of age.

"It is their thoughts constantly playing about your soul that makes you feel they watch you. They do not watch you with their eyes. The purposes of their inner life are calling to you, seeking to claim you. You were all part of the same life long, long ago, and now they want you back again among them."

Vezin's timid heart sank with dread as he listened; but the girl's eyes held him with a net of joy so that he had no wish to escape. She fascinated him, as it were, clean out of his normal self.

"Alone, however, the people could never have caught and held you," she resumed. "The motive force was not strong enough; it has faded through all these years. But I"—she paused a moment and looked at him with complete confidence in her splendid eyes—"I possess the spell to conquer you and hold you: the spell of old love. I can win you back again and make you live the old life with me, for the force of the ancient tie between us, if I choose to use it, is irresistible. And I do choose to use it. I still want you. And you, dear soul of my dim past"— she pressed closer to him so that her breath passed across his eyes, and her voice positively sang—"I mean to have you, for you love me and are utterly at my mercy."

Vezin heard, and yet did not hear; understood, yet did not understand. He had passed into a condition of exaltation. The world was beneath his feet, made of music and flowers, and he was flying somewhere far above it through the sunshine of pure delight. He was breathless and giddy with the wonder of her words. They intoxicated him. And, still, the terror of it all, the dreadful thought of death, pressed ever behind her sentences. For flames shot through her voice out of black smoke and licked at his soul.

And they communicated with one another, it seemed to him, by a process of swift telepathy, for his French could never have compassed all he said to her. Yet she understood perfectly, and what she said to him was like the recital of verses long since known. And the mingled pain and sweetness of it as he listened were almost more than his little soul could hold.

"Yet I came here wholly by chance—" he heard himself saying.

"No," she cried with passion, "you came here because I called to you. I have called to you for years, and you came with the whole force of the past behind you. You had to come, for I own you, and I claim you."

She rose again and moved closer, looking at him with a certain insolence in the face—the insolence of power.

The sun had set behind the towers of the old cathedral and the darkness rose up from the plain and enveloped them. The music of the band had ceased. The leaves of the plane trees hung motionless, but the chill of the autumn evening rose about them and made Vezin shiver. There was no sound but the sound of their voices and the occasional soft rustle of the girl's dress. He could hear the blood rushing in his ears. He scarcely realised where he was or what he was doing. Some terrible magic of the imagination drew him deeply down into the tombs of his own being, telling him in no unfaltering voice that her words shadowed forth the truth. And this simple little French maid, speaking beside him with so strange authority, he saw curiously alter into quite another being. As he stared into her eyes, the picture in his mind grew and lived, dressing itself vividly to his inner vision with a degree of reality he was compelled to acknowledge. As once before, he saw her tall and stately, moving through wild and broken scenery of forests and mountain caverns, the glare of flames behind her head and clouds of shifting smoke about her feet. Dark leaves encircled her hair, flying loosely in the wind, and her limbs shone through the merest rags of clothing. Others were about her, too, and ardent eyes on all sides cast delirious glances upon her, but her own eyes were always for One only, one whom she held by the hand. For she was leading the dance in some tempestuous orgy to the music of chanting voices, and the dance she led circled about a great and awful Figure on a throne, brooding over the scene through lurid vapours, while innumerable other wild faces and forms crowded furiously about her in the dance. But the one she held by the hand he knew to be himself, and the monstrous shape upon the throne he knew to be her mother.

The vision rose within him, rushing to him down the long years of buried time, crying aloud to him with the voice of memory reawakened.... And then the scene faded away and he saw the clear circle of the girl's eyes gazing steadfastly into his own, and she became once more the pretty little daughter of the innkeeper, and he found his voice again.

"And you," he whispered tremblingly—"you child of visions and enchantment, how is it that you so bewitch me that I loved you even before I saw?"

She drew herself up beside him with an air of rare dignity.

"The call of the Past," she said; "and besides," she added proudly, "in the real life I am a princess—"

"A princess!" he cried.

"—and my mother is a queen!"

At this, little Vezin utterly lost his head. Delight tore at his heart and swept him into sheer ecstasy. To hear that sweet singing voice, and to see those adorable little lips utter such things, upset his balance beyond all hope of control. He took her in his arms and covered her unresisting face with kisses.

But even while he did so, and while the hot passion swept him, he felt that she was soft and loathsome, and that her answering kisses stained his very soul.... And when, presently, she had freed herself and vanished into the darkness, he stood there, leaning against the wall in a state of collapse, creeping with horror from the touch of her yielding body, and inwardly raging at the weakness that he already dimly realised must prove his undoing.

And from the shadows of the old buildings into which she disappeared there rose in the stillness of the night a singular, long-drawn cry, which at first he took for laughter, but which later he was sure he recognised as the almost human wailing of a cat.

V

For a long time Vezin leant there against the wall, alone with his surging thoughts and emotions. He understood at length that he had done the one thing necessary to call down upon him the whole force of this ancient Past. For in those passionate kisses he had acknowledged the tie of olden days, and had revived it. And the memory of that soft impalpable caress in the darkness of the inn corridor came back to him with a shudder. The girl had first mastered him, and then led him to the one act that was necessary for her purpose. He had been waylaid, after the lapse of centuries—caught, and conquered.

Dimly he realised this, and sought to make plans for his escape. But, for the moment at any rate, he was powerless to manage his thoughts or will, for the sweet, fantastic madness of the whole adventure mounted to his brain like a spell, and he gloried in the feeling that he was utterly enchanted and moving in a world so much larger and wilder than the one he had ever been accustomed to.

The moon, pale and enormous, was just rising over the sea-like plain, when at last he rose to go. Her slanting rays drew all the houses into new perspective, so that their roofs, already glistening with dew, seemed to stretch much higher into the sky than usual, and their gables and quaint old towers lay far away in its purple reaches.

The cathedral appeared unreal in a silver mist. He moved softly, keeping to the shadows; but the streets were all deserted and very silent; the doors were closed, the shutters fastened. Not a soul was astir. The hush of night lay over everything; it was like a town of the dead, a churchyard with gigantic and grotesque tombstones.

Wondering where all the busy life of the day had so utterly disappeared to, he made his way to a back door that entered the inn by means of the stables, thinking thus to reach his room unobserved. He reached the courtyard safely and crossed it by keeping close to the shadow of the wall. He sidled down it, mincing along on tiptoe, just as the old men did when they entered the *salle à manger*. He was horrified to find himself doing this instinctively. A strange impulse came to him, catching him somehow in the centre of his body—an impulse to drop upon all fours and run swiftly and silently. He glanced upwards and the idea came to him to leap up upon his window-sill overhead instead of going round by the stairs. This occurred to him as the easiest, and most natural way. It was like the beginning of some horrible transformation of himself into something else. He was fearfully strung up.

The moon was higher now, and the shadows very dark along the side of the street where he moved. He kept among the deepest of them, and reached the porch with the glass doors.

But here there was light; the inmates, unfortunately, were still about. Hoping to slip across the hall unobserved and reach the stairs, he opened the door carefully and stole in. Then he saw that the hall was not empty. A large dark thing lay against the wall on his left. At first he thought it must be household articles. Then it moved, and he thought it was an immense cat, distorted in some way by the play of light and shadow. Then it rose straight up before him and he saw that it was the proprietress.

What she had been doing in this position he could only venture a dreadful guess, but the moment she stood up and faced him he was aware of some terrible dignity clothing her about that instantly recalled the girl's strange saying that she was a queen. Huge and sinister she stood there under the little oil lamp; alone with him in the empty hall. Awe stirred in his heart, and the roots of some ancient fear. He felt that he must bow to her and make some kind of obeisance. The impulse was fierce and irresistible, as of long habit. He glanced quickly about him. There was no one there. Then he deliberately inclined his head toward her. He bowed.

"Enfin! M'sieur s'est done décidé. C'est bien alors. J'en suis contente."

Her words came to him sonorously as through a great open space.

Then the great figure came suddenly across the flagged hall at him and seized his trembling hands. Some overpowering force moved with her and caught him.

"On pourrait faire un p'tit tour ensemble, n'est-ce pas? Nous y allons cette nuit et il faut s'exercer un peu d'avance pour cela. Ilsé, Ilsé, viens done ici. Viens vite!"

And she whirled him round in the opening steps of some dance that seemed oddly and horribly familiar. They made no sound on the stones, this strangely assorted couple. It was all soft and stealthy. And presently, when the air seemed to thicken like smoke, and a red glare as of flame shot through it, he was aware that some one else had joined them and that his hand the mother had released was now tightly held by the daughter. Ilsé had come in answer to the call, and he saw her with leaves of vervain twined in her dark hair, clothed in tattered vestiges of some curious garment, beautiful as the night, and horribly, odiously, loathsomely seductive.

"To the Sabbath! to the Sabbath!" they cried. "On to the Witches' Sabbath!"

Up and down that narrow hall they danced, the women on each side of him, to the wildest measure he had ever imagined, yet which he dimly, dreadfully remembered, till the lamp on the wall flickered and went out, and they were left in total darkness. And the devil woke in his heart with a thousand vile suggestions and made him afraid.

Suddenly they released his hands and he heard the voice of the mother cry that it was time, and they must go. Which way they went he did not pause to see. He only realised that he was free, and he blundered through the darkness till he found the stairs and then tore up them to his room as though all hell was at his heels.

He flung himself on the sofa, with his face in his hands, and groaned. Swiftly reviewing a dozen ways of immediate escape, all equally impossible, he finally decided that the only thing to do for the moment was to sit quiet and wait. He must see what was going to happen. At least in the privacy of his own bedroom he would be fairly safe. The door was locked. He crossed over and softly opened the window which gave upon the courtyard and also permitted a partial view of the hall through the glass doors.

As he did so the hum and murmur of a great activity reached his ears from the streets beyond—the sound of footsteps and voices muffled by distance. He leaned out cautiously and listened. The moonlight was clear and strong now, but his own window was in shadow, the silver disc being still behind the house. It came to him irresistibly that the inhabitants of the town, who a little while before had all been invisible behind closed doors, were now issuing forth, busy upon some secret and unholy errand. He listened intently.

At first everything about him was silent, but soon he became aware of movements going on in the house itself. Rustlings and cheepings came to him across that still, moonlit yard. A concourse of living beings sent the hum of their activity into the night. Things were on the move everywhere.

A biting, pungent odour rose through the air, coming he knew not whence. Presently his eyes became glued to the windows of the opposite wall where the moonshine fell in a soft blaze. The roof overhead, and behind him, was reflected clearly in the panes of glass, and he saw the outlines of dark bodies moving with long footsteps over the tiles and along the coping. They passed swiftly and silently, shaped like immense cats, in an endless procession across the pictured glass, and then appeared to leap down to a lower level where he lost sight of them. He just caught the soft thudding of their leaps. Sometimes their shadows fell upon the white wall opposite, and then he could not make out whether they were the shadows of human beings or of cats. They seemed to change swiftly from one to the other. The transformation looked horribly real, for they leaped like human beings, yet changed swiftly in the air immediately afterwards, and dropped like animals.

The yard, too, beneath him, was now alive with the creeping movements of dark forms all stealthily drawing towards the porch with the glass doors. They kept so closely to the wall that he could not determine their actual shape, but when he saw that they passed on to the great congregation that was gathering in the hall, he understood that these were the creatures whose leaping shadows he had first seen reflected in the windowpanes opposite. They were coming from all parts of the town, reaching the appointed meeting-place across the roofs and tiles, and springing from level to level till they came to the yard.

Then a new sound caught his ear, and he saw that the windows all about him were being softly opened, and that to each window came a face. A moment later figures began dropping hurriedly down into the yard. And these figures, as they lowered themselves down from the windows, were human, he saw; but once safely in the yard they fell upon all fours and changed in the swiftest possible second into—cats—huge, silent cats. They ran in streams to join the main body in the hall beyond.

So, after all, the rooms in the house had not been empty and unoccupied.

Moreover, what he saw no longer filled him with amazement. For he remembered it all. It was familiar. It had all happened before just so, hundreds of times, and he himself had taken part in it and known the wild madness of it all. The outline of the old building changed, the yard grew larger, and he seemed to be staring down upon it from a much greater height through smoky vapours. And, as he looked, half remembering, the old pains of long ago, fierce and sweet, furiously assailed him, and the blood stirred horribly as he heard the Call of the Dance again in his heart and tasted the ancient magic of Ilsé whirling by his side.

Suddenly he started back. A great lithe cat had leaped softly up from the shadows below on to the sill close to his face, and was staring fixedly at him with the eyes of a human. "Come," it seemed to say, "come with us to the Dance! Change as of old! Transform yourself swiftly and come!" Only too well he understood the creature's soundless call.

It was gone again in a flash with scarcely a sound of its padded feet on the stones, and then others dropped by the score down the side of the house, past his very eyes, all changing as they fell and darting away rapidly, softly, towards the gathering point. And again he felt the dreadful desire to do likewise; to murmur the old incantation, and then drop upon hands and knees and run swiftly for the great flying leap into the air. Oh, how the passion of it rose within him like a flood, twisting his very entrails, sending his heart's desire flaming forth into the night for the old, old Dance of the Sorcerers at the Witches' Sabbath! The whirl of the stars was about him; once more he met the magic of the moon. The power of the wind, rushing from precipice and forest, leaping from cliff to cliff across the valleys, tore him away.... He heard the cries of the dancers and their wild laughter, and with this savage girl in his embrace he danced furiously about the dim Throne where sat the Figure with the sceptre of majesty....

Then, suddenly, all became hushed and still, and the fever died down a little in his heart. The calm moonlight flooded a courtyard empty and deserted. They had started. The procession was off into the sky. And he was left behind—alone.

Vezin tiptoed softly across the room and unlocked the door. The murmur from the streets, growing momentarily as he advanced, met his ears. He made his way with the utmost caution down the corridor. At the head of the stairs he paused and listened. Below him, the hall where they had gathered was dark and still, but through opened doors and windows on the far side of the building came the sound of a great throng moving farther and farther into the distance.

He made his way down the creaking wooden stairs, dreading yet longing to meet some straggler who should point the way, but finding no one; across the dark hall, so lately thronged with living, moving things, and out through the opened front doors into the street. He could not believe that he was really left behind, really forgotten, that he had been purposely permitted to escape. It perplexed him.

Nervously he peered about him, and up and down the street; then, seeing nothing, advanced slowly down the pavement.

The whole town, as he went, showed itself empty and deserted, as though a great wind had blown everything alive out of it. The doors and windows of the houses stood open to the night; nothing stirred; moonlight and silence lay over all. The night lay about him like a cloak. The air, soft and cool, caressed his cheek like the touch of a great furry paw. He gained confidence and began to walk quickly, though still keeping to the shadowed side. Nowhere could he discover the faintest sign of the great unholy exodus he knew had just taken place. The moon sailed high over all in a sky cloudless and serene.

Hardly realising where he was going, he crossed the open marketplace and so came to the ramparts, whence he knew a pathway descended to the high road and along which he could make good his escape to one of the other little towns that lay to the northward, and so to the railway.

But first he paused and gazed out over the scene at his feet where the great plain lay like a silver map of some dream country. The still beauty of it entered his heart, increasing his sense of bewilderment and unreality. No air stirred, the leaves of the plane trees stood motionless, the near details were defined with the sharpness of day against dark shadows, and in the distance the fields and woods melted away into haze and shimmering mistiness.

But the breath caught in his throat and he stood stockstill as though transfixed when his gaze passed from the horizon and fell upon the near prospect in the depth of the valley at his feet. The whole lower slopes of the hill, that lay hid from the brightness of the moon, were aglow, and through the glare he saw countless moving forms, shifting thick and fast between the openings of the trees; while overhead, like leaves driven by the wind, he discerned flying shapes that hovered darkly one moment against the sky and then settled down with cries and weird singing through the branches into the region that was aflame.

Spellbound, he stood and stared for a time that he could not measure. And then, moved by one of the terrible impulses that seemed to control the whole adventure, he climbed swiftly upon the top of the broad coping, and balanced a moment where the valley gaped at his feet. But in that very instant, as he stood hovering, a sudden movement among the shadows of the houses caught his eye, and he turned to see the outline of a large animal dart swiftly across the open space behind him, and land with a flying leap upon the top of the wall a little lower down. It ran like the wind to his feet and then rose up beside him upon the ramparts. A shiver seemed to run through the moonlight, and his sight trembled for a second. His heart pulsed fearfully. Ilsé stood beside him, peering into his face.

Some dark substance, he saw, stained the girl's face and skin, shining in the moonlight as she stretched her hands towards him; she was dressed in wretched tattered garments that yet became her mightily; rue and vervain twined about her temples; her eyes glittered with unholy light. He only just controlled the wild impulse to take her in his arms and leap with her from their giddy perch into the valley below.

"See!" she cried, pointing with an arm on which the rags fluttered in the rising wind towards the forest aglow in the distance. "See where they await us! The woods are alive! Already the Great Ones are there, and the dance will soon begin! The salve is here! Anoint yourself and come!"

Though a moment before the sky was clear and cloudless, yet even while she spoke the face of the moon grew dark and the wind began to toss in the crests of the plane trees at his feet. Stray gusts brought the sounds of hoarse singing and crying from the lower slopes of the hill, and the pungent odour he had already noticed about the courtyard of the inn rose about him in the air.

"Transform, transform!" she cried again, her voice rising like a song. "Rub well your skin before you fly. Come! Come with me to the Sabbath, to the madness of its furious delight, to the sweet abandonment of its evil worship! See! the Great Ones are there, and the terrible Sacraments prepared. The Throne is occupied. Anoint and come! Anoint and come!"

She grew to the height of a tree beside him, leaping upon the wall with flaming eyes and hair strewn upon the night. He too began to change swiftly. Her hands touched the skin of his face and neck, streaking him with the burning salve that sent the old magic into his blood with the power before which fades all that is good.

A wild roar came up to his ears from the heart of the wood, and the girl, when she heard it, leaped upon the wall in the frenzy of her wicked joy.

"Satan is there!" she screamed, rushing upon him and striving to draw him with her to the edge of the wall. "Satan has come. The Sacraments call us! Come, with your dear apostate soul, and we will worship and dance till the moon dies and the world is forgotten!"

Just saving himself from the dreadful plunge, Vezin struggled to release himself from her grasp, while the passion tore at his reins and all but mastered him. He shrieked aloud, not knowing what he said, and then he shrieked again. It was the old impulses, the old awful habits instinctively finding voice; for though it seemed to him that he merely shrieked nonsense, the words he uttered really had meaning in them, and were intelligible. It was the ancient call. And it was heard below. It was answered.

The wind whistled at the skirts of his coat as the air round him darkened with many flying forms crowding upwards out of the valley. The crying of hoarse voices smote upon his ears, coming closer. Strokes of wind buffeted him, tearing him this way and that along the crumbling top of the stone wall; and Ilsé clung to him with her long shining arms, smooth and bare, holding him fast about the neck. But not Ilsé alone, for a dozen of them surrounded him, dropping out of the air. The pungent odour of the anointed bodies stifled him, exciting him to the old madness of the Sabbath, the dance of the witches and sorcerers doing honour to the personified Evil of the world.

"Anoint and away! Anoint and away!" they cried in wild chorus about him. "To the Dance that never dies! To the sweet and fearful fantasy of evil!"

Another moment and he would have yielded and gone, for his will turned soft and the flood of passionate memory all but overwhelmed him, when—so can a small thing after the whole course of an adventure—he caught his foot upon a loose stone in the edge of the wall, and then fell with a sudden crash on to the ground below. But he fell towards the houses, in the open space of dust and cobblestones, and fortunately not into the gaping depth of the valley on the farther side.

And they, too, came in a tumbling heap about him, like flies upon a piece of food, but as they fell he was released for a moment from the power of their touch, and in that brief instant of freedom there flashed into his mind the sudden intuition that saved him. Before he could regain his feet he saw them scrabbling awkwardly back upon the wall, as though bat-like they could only fly by dropping from a height, and had no hold upon him in the open. Then, seeing them perched there in a row like cats upon a roof, all dark and singularly shapeless, their eyes like lamps, the sudden memory came back to him of Ilsé's terror at the sight of fire.

Quick as a flash he found his matches and lit the dead leaves that lay under the wall.

Dry and withered, they caught fire at once, and the wind carried the flame in a long line down the length of the wall, licking upwards as it ran; and with shrieks and wailings, the crowded row of forms upon the top melted away into the air on the other side, and were gone with a great rush and whirring of their bodies down into the heart of the haunted valley, leaving Vezin breathless and shaken in the middle of the deserted ground.

"Ilsé!" he called feebly; "Ilsé!" for his heart ached to think that she was really gone to the great Dance without him, and that he had lost the opportunity of its fearful joy. Yet at the same time his relief was so great, and he was so dazed and troubled in mind with the whole thing, that he hardly knew what he was saying, and only cried aloud in the fierce storm of his emotion....

The fire under the wall ran its course, and the moonlight came out again, soft and clear, from its temporary eclipse. With one last shuddering look at the ruined ramparts, and a feeling of horrid wonder for the haunted valley beyond, where the shapes still crowded and flew, he turned his face towards the town and slowly made his way in the direction of the hotel.

And as he went, a great wailing of cries, and a sound of howling, followed him from the gleaming forest below, growing fainter and fainter with the bursts of wind as he disappeared between the houses.

VI

"It may seem rather abrupt to you, this sudden tame ending," said Arthur Vezin, glancing with flushed face and timid eyes at Dr. Silence sitting there with his notebook, "but the fact is—er—from that moment my memory seems to have failed rather. I have no distinct recollection of how I got home or what precisely I did.

"It appears I never went back to the inn at all. I only dimly recollect racing down a long white road in the moonlight, past woods and villages, still and deserted, and then the dawn came up, and I saw the towers of a biggish town and so came to a station.

"But, long before that, I remember pausing somewhere on the road and looking back to where the hill-town of my adventure stood up in the moonlight, and thinking how exactly like a great monstrous cat it lay there upon the plain, its huge front paws lying down the two main streets, and the twin and broken towers of the cathedral marking its torn ears against the sky. That picture stays in my mind with the utmost vividness to this day.

"Another thing remains in my mind from that escape—namely, the sudden sharp reminder that I had not paid my bill, and the decision I made, standing there on the dusty highroad, that the small baggage I had left behind would more than settle for my indebtedness.

"For the rest, I can only tell you that I got coffee and bread at a café on the outskirts of this town I had come to, and soon after found my way to the station and caught a train later in the day. That same evening I reached London."

"And how long altogether," asked John Silence quietly, "do you think you stayed in the town of the adventure?"

Vezin looked up sheepishly.

"I was coming to that," he resumed, with apologetic wrigglings of his body. "In London I found that I was a whole week out in my reckoning of time. I had stayed over a week in the town, and it ought to have been September 15th, —instead of which it was only September 10th!"

"So that, in reality, you had only stayed a night or two in the inn?" queried the doctor.

Vezin hesitated before replying. He shuffled upon the mat.

"I must have gained time somewhere," he said at length—"somewhere or somehow. I certainly had a week to my credit. I can't explain it. I can only give you the fact."

"And this happened to you last year, since when you have never been back to the place?"

"Last autumn, yes," murmured Vezin; "and I have never dared to go back. I think I never want to."

"And, tell me," asked Dr. Silence at length, when he saw that the little man had evidently come to the end of his words and had nothing more to say, "had you ever read up the subject of the old witchcraft practices during the Middle Ages, or been at all interested in the subject?"

"Never!" declared Vezin emphatically. "I had never given a thought to such matters so far as I know—"

"Or to the question of reincarnation, perhaps?"

"Never—before my adventure; but I have since," he replied significantly.

There was, however, something still on the man's mind that he wished to relieve himself of by confession, yet could only with difficulty bring himself to mention; and it was only after the sympathetic tactfulness of the doctor had provided numerous openings that he at length availed himself of one of them, and stammered that he would like to show him the marks he still had on his neck where, he said, the girl had touched him with her anointed hands.

He took off his collar after infinite fumbling hesitation, and lowered his shirt a little for the doctor to see. And there, on the surface of the skin, lay a faint reddish line across the shoulder and extending a little way down the back towards the spine. It certainly indicated exactly the position an arm might have taken in the act of embracing. And on the other side of the neck, slightly higher up, was a similar mark, though not quite so clearly defined.

"That was where she held me that night on the ramparts," he whispered, a strange light coming and going in his eyes.

It was some weeks later when I again found occasion to consult John Silence concerning another extraordinary case that had come under my notice, and we fell to discussing Vezin's story. Since hearing it, the doctor had made investigations on his own account, and one of his secretaries had discovered that Vezin's ancestors had actually lived for generations in the very town where the adventure came to him. Two of them, both women, had been tried and convicted as witches, and had been burned alive at the stake. Moreover, it had not been difficult to prove that the very inn where Vezin stayed was built about 1700 upon the spot where the funeral pyres stood and the executions took place. The town was a sort of headquarters for all the sorcerers and witches of the entire region, and after conviction they were burnt there literally by scores.

"It seems strange," continued the doctor, "that Vezin should have remained ignorant of all this; but, on the other hand, it was not the kind of history that successive generations would have been anxious to keep alive, or to repeat to their children. Therefore I am inclined to think he still knows nothing about it.

"The whole adventure seems to have been a very vivid revival of the memories of an earlier life, caused by coming directly into contact with the living forces still intense enough to hang about the place, and, by a most singular chance, too, with the very souls who had taken part with him in the events of that particular life. For the mother and daughter who impressed him so strangely must have been leading actors, with himself, in the scenes and practices of witchcraft which at that period dominated the imaginations of the whole country.

"One has only to read the histories of the times to know that these witches claimed the power of transforming themselves into various animals, both for the purposes of disguise and also to convey themselves swiftly to the scenes of their imaginary orgies. Lycanthropy, or the power to change themselves into wolves, was everywhere believed in, and the ability to transform themselves into cats by rubbing their bodies with a special salve or ointment provided by Satan himself, found equal credence. The witchcraft trials abound in evidences of such universal beliefs."

Dr. Silence quoted chapter and verse from many writers on the subject, and showed how every detail of Vezin's adventure had a basis in the practices of those dark days.

"But that the entire affair took place subjectively in the man's own consciousness, I have no doubt," he went on, in reply to my questions; "for my secretary who has been to the town to investigate, discovered his signature in the visitors' book, and proved by it that he had arrived on September 8th, and left suddenly without paying his bill. He left two days later, and they still were in possession of his dirty brown bag and some tourist clothes. I paid a few francs in settlement of his debt, and have sent his luggage on to him. The daughter was absent from home, but the proprietress, a large woman very much as he described her, told my secretary that he had seemed a very strange, absentminded kind of gentleman, and after his disappearance she had feared for a long time that he had met with a violent end in the neighbouring forest where he used to roam about alone.

"I should like to have obtained a personal interview with the daughter so as to ascertain how much was subjective and how much actually took place with her as Vezin told it. For her dread of fire and the sight of burning must, of course, have been the intuitive memory of her former painful death at the stake, and have thus explained why he fancied more than once that he saw her through smoke and flame."

"And that mark on his skin, for instance?" I inquired.

"Merely the marks produced by hysterical brooding," he replied, "like the stigmata of the *religieuses,* and the bruises which appear on the bodies of hypnotised subjects who have been told to expect them. This is very common and easily explained. Only it seems curious that these marks should have remained so long in Vezin's case. Usually they disappear quickly."

"Obviously he is still thinking about it all, brooding, and living it all over again," I ventured.

"Probably. And this makes me fear that the end of his trouble is not yet. We shall hear of him again. It is a case, alas! I can do little to alleviate."

Dr. Silence spoke gravely and with sadness in his voice.

"And what do you make of the Frenchman in the train?" I asked further—"the man who warned him against the place, *à cause du sommeil et à cause des chats?* Surely a very singular incident?"

"A very singular incident indeed," he made answer slowly, "and one I can only explain on the basis of a highly improbable coincidence—"

"Namely?"

"That the man was one who had himself stayed in the town and undergone there a similar experience. I should like to find this man and ask him. But the crystal is useless here, for I have no slightest clue to go upon, and I can only conclude that some singular psychic affinity, some force still active in his being out of the same past life, drew him thus to the personality of Vezin, and enabled him to fear what might happen to him, and thus to warn him as he did.

"Yes," he presently continued, half talking to himself, "I suspect in this case that Vezin was swept into the vortex of forces arising out of the intense activities of a past life, and that he lived over again a scene in which he had often played a leading part centuries before. For strong actions set up forces that are so slow to exhaust themselves, they may be said in a sense never to die. In this case they were not vital enough to render the illusion complete, so that the little man found himself caught in a very distressing confusion of the present and the past; yet he was sufficiently sensitive to recognise that it was true, and to fight against the degradation of returning, even in memory, to a former and lower state of development.

"Ah yes!" he continued, crossing the floor to gaze at the darkening sky, and seemingly quite oblivious of my presence, "subliminal up-rushes of memory like this can be exceedingly painful, and sometimes exceedingly dangerous. I only trust that this gentle soul may soon escape from this obsession of a passionate and tempestuous past. But I doubt it, I doubt it."

His voice was hushed with sadness as he spoke, and when he turned back into the room again there was an expression of profound yearning upon his face, the yearning of a soul whose desire to help is sometimes greater than his power.

CASE III

THE NEMESIS OF FIRE

I

By some means which I never could fathom, John Silence always contrived to keep the compartment to himself, and as the train had a clear run of two hours before the first stop, there was ample time to go over the preliminary facts of the case. He had telephoned to me that very morning, and even through the disguise of the miles of wire the thrill of incalculable adventure had sounded in his voice.

"As if it were an ordinary country visit," he called, in reply to my question; "and don't forgot to bring your gun."

"With blank cartridges, I suppose?" for I knew his rigid principles with regard to the taking of life, and guessed that the guns were merely for some obvious purpose of disguise.

Then he thanked me for coming, mentioned the train, snapped down the receiver, and left me, vibrating with the excitement of anticipation, to do my packing. For the honour of accompanying Dr. John Silence on one of his big cases was what many would have considered an empty honour—and risky. Certainly the adventure held all manner of possibilities, and I arrived at Waterloo with the feelings of a man who is about to embark on some dangerous and peculiar mission in which the dangers he expects to run will not be the ordinary dangers to life and limb, but of some secret character difficult to name and still more difficult to cope with.

"The Manor House has a high sound," he told me, as we sat with our feet up and talked, "but I believe it is little more than an overgrown farmhouse in the desolate heather country beyond D—, and its owner, Colonel Wragge, a retired soldier with a taste for books, lives there practically alone, I understand, with an elderly invalid sister. So you need not look forward to a lively visit, unless the case provides some excitement of its own."

"Which is likely?"

By way of reply he handed me a letter marked "Private." It was dated a week ago, and signed "Yours faithfully, Horace Wragge."

"He heard of me, you see, through Captain Anderson," the doctor explained modestly, as though his fame were not almost world-wide; "you remember that Indian obsession case—"

I read the letter. Why it should have been marked private was difficult to understand. It was very brief, direct, and to the point. It referred by way of introduction to Captain Anderson, and then stated quite simply that the writer needed help of a peculiar kind and asked for a personal interview— a morning interview, since it was impossible for him to be absent from the house at night. The letter was dignified even to the point of abruptness, and it is difficult to explain how it managed to convey to me the impression of a strong man, shaken and perplexed. Perhaps the restraint of the wording, and the mystery of the affair had something to do with it; and the reference to the Anderson case, the horror of which lay still vivid in my memory, may have touched the sense of something rather ominous and alarming. But, whatever the cause, there was no doubt that an impression of serious peril rose somehow out of that white paper with the few lines of firm writing, and the spirit of a deep uneasiness ran between the words and reached the mind without any visible form of expression.

"And when you saw him—?" I asked, returning the letter as the train rushed clattering noisily through Clapham Junction.

"I have not seen him," was the reply. "The man's mind was charged to the brim when he wrote that; full of vivid mental pictures. Notice the restraint of it. For the main character of his case psychometry could be depended upon, and the scrap of paper his hand has touched is sufficient to give to another mind—a sensitive and sympathetic mind—clear mental pictures of what is going on. I think I have a very sound general idea of his problem."

"So there may be excitement, after all?"

John Silence waited a moment before he replied.

"Something very serious is amiss there," he said gravely, at length. "Some one—not himself, I gather, —has been meddling with a rather dangerous kind of gunpowder. So—yes, there may be excitement, as you put it."

"And my duties?" I asked, with a decidedly growing interest. "Remember, I am your 'assistant.'"

"Behave like an intelligent confidential secretary. Observe everything, without seeming to. Say nothing—nothing that means anything. Be present at all interviews. I may ask a good deal of you, for if my impressions are correct this is—"

He broke off suddenly.

"But I won't tell you my impressions yet," he resumed after a moment's thought. "Just watch and listen as the case proceeds. Form your own impressions and cultivate your intuitions. We come as ordinary visitors, of course," he added, a twinkle showing for an instant in his eye; "hence, the guns."

Though disappointed not to hear more, I recognised the wisdom of his words and knew how valueless my impressions would be once the powerful suggestion of having heard his own lay behind them. I likewise reflected that intuition joined to a sense of humour was of more use to a man than double the quantity of mere "brains," as such.

Before putting the letter away, however, he handed it back, telling me to place it against my forehead for a few moments and then describe any pictures that came spontaneously into my mind.

"Don't deliberately look for anything. Just imagine you see the inside of the eyelid, and wait for pictures that rise against its dark screen."

I followed his instructions, making my mind as nearly blank as possible. But no visions came. I saw nothing but the lines of light that pass to and fro like the changes of a kaleidoscope across the blackness. A momentary sensation of warmth came and went curiously.

"You see—what?" he asked presently.

"Nothing," I was obliged to admit disappointedly; "nothing but the usual flashes of light one always sees. Only, perhaps, they are more vivid than usual."

He said nothing by way of comment or reply.

"And they group themselves now and then," I continued, with painful candour, for I longed to see the pictures he had spoken of, "group themselves into globes and round balls of fire, and the lines that flash about sometimes look like triangles and crosses—almost like geometrical figures. Nothing more."

I opened my eyes again, and gave him back the letter.

"It makes my head hot," I said, feeling somehow unworthy for not seeing anything of interest. But the look in his eyes arrested my attention at once.

"That sensation of heat is important," he said significantly.

"It was certainly real, and rather uncomfortable," I replied, hoping he would expand and explain. "There was a distinct feeling of warmth—internal warmth somewhere—oppressive in a sense."

"That is interesting," he remarked, putting the letter back in his pocket, and settling himself in the corner with newspapers and books. He vouchsafed nothing more, and I knew the uselessness of trying to make him talk. Following his example I settled likewise with magazines into my corner. But when I closed my eyes again to look for the flashing lights and the sensation of heat, I found nothing but the usual phantasmagoria of the day's events—faces, scenes, memories,—and in due course I fell asleep and then saw nothing at all of any kind.

When we left the train, after six hours' travelling, at a little wayside station standing without trees in a world of sand and heather, the late October shadows had already dropped their sombre veil upon the landscape, and the sun dipped almost out of sight behind the moorland hills. In a high dogcart, behind a fast horse, we were soon rattling across the undulating stretches of an open and bleak country, the keen air stinging our cheeks and the scents of pine and bracken strong about us. Bare hills were faintly visible against the horizon, and the coachman pointed to a bank of distant shadows on our left where he told us the sea lay. Occasional stone farmhouses, standing back from the road among straggling fir trees, and large black barns that seemed to shift past us with a movement of their own in the gloom, were the only signs of humanity and civilisation that we saw, until at the end of a bracing five miles the lights of the lodge gates flared before us and we plunged into a thick grove of pine trees that concealed the Manor House up to the moment of actual arrival.

Colonel Wragge himself met us in the hall. He was the typical army officer who had seen service, real service, and found himself in the process. He was tall and well built, broad in the shoulders, but lean as a greyhound, with grave eyes, rather stern, and a moustache turning grey. I judged him to be about sixty years of age, but his movements showed a suppleness of strength and agility that contradicted the years. The face was full of character and resolution, the face of a man to be depended upon, and the straight grey eyes, it seemed to me, wore a veil of perplexed anxiety that he made no attempt to disguise. The whole appearance of the man at once clothed the adventure with gravity and importance. A matter that gave such a man cause for serious alarm, I felt, must be something real and of genuine moment.

His speech and manner, as he welcomed us, were like his letter, simple and sincere. He had a nature as direct and undeviating as a bullet. Thus, he showed plainly his surprise that Dr. Silence had not come alone.

"My confidential secretary, Mr. Hubbard," the doctor said, introducing me, and the steady gaze and powerful shake of the hand I then received were well calculated, I remember thinking, to drive home the impression that here was a man who was not to be trifled with, and whose perplexity must spring from some very real and tangible cause. And, quite obviously, he was relieved that we had come. His welcome was unmistakably genuine.

He led us at once into a room, half library, half smoking-room, that opened out of the low-ceilinged hall. The Manor House gave the impression of a rambling and glorified farmhouse, solid, ancient, comfortable, and wholly unpretentious. And so it was. Only the heat of the place struck me as unnatural. This room with the blazing fire may have seemed uncomfortably warm after the long drive through the night air; yet it seemed to me that the hall itself, and the whole atmosphere of the house, breathed a warmth that hardly belonged to well-filled grates or the pipes of hot air and water. It was not the heat of the greenhouse; it was an oppressive heat that somehow got into the head and mind. It stirred a curious sense of uneasiness in me, and I caught myself thinking of the sensation of warmth that had emanated from the letter in the train.

I heard him thanking Dr. Silence for having come; there was no preamble, and the exchange of civilities was of the briefest description. Evidently here was a man who, like my companion, loved action rather than talk. His manner was straightforward and direct. I saw him in a flash: puzzled, worried, harassed into a state of alarm by something he could not comprehend; forced to deal with things he would have preferred to despise, yet facing it all with dogged seriousness and making no attempt to conceal that he felt secretly ashamed of his incompetence.

"So I cannot offer you much entertainment beyond that of my own company, and the queer business that has been going on here, and is still going on," he said, with a slight inclination of the head towards me by way of including me in his confidence.

"I think, Colonel Wragge," replied John Silence impressively, "that we shall none of us find the time hangs heavy. I gather we shall have our hands full."

The two men looked at one another for the space of some seconds, and there was an indefinable quality in their silence which for the first time made me admit a swift question into my mind; and I wondered a little at my rashness in coming with so little reflection into a big case of this incalculable doctor. But no answer suggested itself, and to withdraw was, of course, inconceivable. The gates had closed behind me now, and the spirit of the adventure was already besieging my mind with its advance guard of a thousand little hopes and fears.

Explaining that he would wait till after dinner to discuss anything serious, as no reference was ever made before his sister, he led the way upstairs and showed us personally to our rooms; and it was just as I was finishing dressing that a knock came at my door and Dr. Silence entered.

He was always what is called a serious man, so that even in moments of comedy you felt he never lost sight of the profound gravity of life, but as he came across the room to me I caught the expression of his face and understood in a flash that he was now in his most grave and earnest mood. He looked almost troubled. I stopped fumbling with my black tie and stared.

"It is serious," he said, speaking in a low voice, "more so even than I imagined. Colonel Wragge's control over his thoughts concealed a great deal in my psychometrising of the letter. I looked in to warn you to keep yourself well in hand—generally speaking."

"Haunted house?" I asked, conscious of a distinct shiver down my back.

But he smiled gravely at the question.

"Haunted House of Life more likely," he replied, and a look came into his eyes which I had only seen there when a human soul was in the toils and he was thick in the fight of rescue. He was stirred in the deeps.

"Colonel Wragge—or the sister?" I asked hurriedly, for the gong was sounding.

"Neither directly," he said from the door. "Something far older, something very, very remote indeed. This thing has to do with the ages, unless I am mistaken greatly, the ages on which the mists of memory have long lain undisturbed."

He came across the floor very quickly with a finger on his lips, looking at me with a peculiar searchingness of gaze.

"Are you aware yet of anything—odd here?" he asked in a whisper. "Anything you cannot quite define, for instance. Tell me, Hubbard, for I want to know all your impressions. They may help me."

I shook my head, avoiding his gaze, for there was something in the eyes that scared me a little. But he was so in earnest that I set my mind keenly searching.

"Nothing yet," I replied truthfully, wishing I could confess to a real emotion; "nothing but the strange heat of the place."

He gave a little jump forward in my direction.

"The heat again, that's it!" he exclaimed, as though glad of my corroboration. "And how would you describe it, perhaps?" he asked quickly, with a hand on the door knob.

"It doesn't seem like ordinary physical heat," I said, casting about in my thoughts for a definition.

"More a mental heat," he interrupted, "a glowing of thought and desire, a sort of feverish warmth of the spirit. Isn't that it?"

I admitted that he had exactly described my sensations.

"Good!" he said, as he opened the door, and with an indescribable gesture that combined a warning to be ready with a sign of praise for my correct intuition, he was gone.

I hurried after him, and found the two men waiting for me in front of the fire.

"I ought to warn you," our host was saying as I came in, "that my sister, whom you will meet at dinner, is not aware of the real object of your visit. She is under the impression that we are interested in the same line of study—folklore—and that your researches have led to my seeking acquaintance. She comes to dinner in her chair, you know. It will be a great pleasure to her to meet you both. We have few visitors."

So that on entering the dining-room we were prepared to find Miss Wragge already at her place, seated in a sort of bath-chair. She was a vivacious and charming old lady, with smiling expression and bright eyes, and she chatted all through dinner with unfailing spontaneity. She had that face, unlined and fresh, that some people carry through life from the cradle to the grave; her smooth plump cheeks were all pink and white, and her hair, still dark, was divided into two glossy and sleek halves on either side of a careful parting. She wore gold-rimmed glasses, and at her throat was a large scarab of green jasper that made a very handsome brooch.

Her brother and Dr. Silence talked little, so that most of the conversation was carried on between herself and me, and she told me a great deal about the history of the old house, most of which I fear I listened to with but half an ear.

"And when Cromwell stayed here," she babbled on, "he occupied the very rooms upstairs that used to be mine. But my brother thinks it safer for me to sleep on the ground floor now in case of fire."

And this sentence has stayed in my memory only because of the sudden way her brother interrupted her and instantly led the conversation on to another topic. The passing reference to fire seemed to have disturbed him, and thenceforward he directed the talk himself.

It was difficult to believe that this lively and animated old lady, sitting beside me and taking so eager an interest in the affairs of life, was practically, we understood, without the use of her lower limbs, and that her whole existence for years had been passed between the sofa, the bed, and the bath-chair in which she chatted so naturally at the dinner-table. She made no allusion to her affliction until the dessert was reached, and then, touching a bell, she made us a witty little speech about leaving us "like time, on noise-less feet," and was wheeled out of the room by the butler and carried off to her apartments at the other end of the house.

And the rest of us were not long in following suit, for Dr. Silence and myself were quite as eager to learn the nature of our errand as our host was to impart it to us. He led us down a long flagged passage to a room at the very end of the house, a room provided with double doors, and windows, I saw, heavily shuttered. Books lined the walls on every side, and a large desk in the bow window was piled up with volumes, some open, some shut, some showing scraps of paper stuck between the leaves, and all smothered in a general cataract of untidy foolscap and loose-half sheets.

"My study and workroom," explained Colonel Wragge, with a delightful touch of innocent pride, as though he were a very serious scholar. He placed arm-chairs for us round the fire. "Here," he added significantly, "we shall be safe from interruption and can talk securely."

During dinner the manner of the doctor had been all that was natural and spontaneous, though it was impossible for me, knowing him as I did, not to be aware that he was subconsciously very keenly alert and already receiving upon the ultra-sensitive surface of his mind various and vivid impressions; and there was now something in the gravity of his face, as well as in the significant tone of Colonel Wragge's speech, and something, too, in the fact that we three were shut away in this private chamber about to listen to things probably strange, and certainly mysterious—something in all this that touched my imagination sharply and sent an undeniable thrill along my nerves. Taking the chair indicated by my host, I lit my cigar and waited for the opening of the attack, fully conscious that we were now too far gone in the adventure to admit of withdrawal, and wondering a little anxiously where it was going to lead.

What I expected precisely, it is hard to say. Nothing definite, perhaps. Only the sudden change was dramatic. A few hours before the prosaic atmosphere of Piccadilly was about me, and now I was sitting in a secret chamber of this remote old building waiting to hear an account of things that held possibly the genuine heart of terror. I thought of the dreary moors and hills outside, and the dark pine copses soughing in the wind of night; I remembered my companion's singular words up in my bedroom before dinner; and then I turned and noted carefully the stern countenance of the Colonel as he faced us and lit his big black cigar before speaking.

The threshold of an adventure, I reflected as I waited for the first words, is always the most thrilling moment—until the climax comes.

But Colonel Wragge hesitated—mentally—a long time before he began. He talked briefly of our journey, the weather, the country, and other comparatively trivial topics, while he sought about in his mind for an appropriate entry into the subject that was uppermost in the thoughts of all of us. The fact was he found it a difficult matter to speak of at all, and it was Dr. Silence who finally showed him the way over the hedge.

"Mr. Hubbard will take a few notes when you are ready—you won't object," he suggested; "I can give my undivided attention in this way."

"By all means," turning to reach some of the loose sheets on the writing table, and glancing at me. He still hesitated a little, I thought. "The fact is," he said apologetically, "I wondered if it was quite fair to trouble you so soon. The daylight might suit you better to hear what I have to tell. Your sleep, I mean, might be less disturbed, perhaps."

"I appreciate your thoughtfulness," John Silence replied with his gentle smile, taking command as it were from that moment, "but really we are both quite immune. There is nothing, I think, that could prevent either of us sleeping, except—an outbreak of fire, or some such very physical disturbance."

Colonel Wragge raised his eyes and looked fixedly at him. This reference to an outbreak of fire I felt sure was made with a purpose. It certainly had the desired effect of removing from our host's manner the last signs of hesitancy.

"Forgive me," he said. "Of course, I know nothing of your methods in matters of this kind—so, perhaps, you would like me to begin at once and give you an outline of the situation?"

Dr. Silence bowed his agreement. "I can then take my precautions accordingly," he added calmly.

The soldier looked up for a moment as though he did not quite gather the meaning of these words; but he made no further comment and turned at once to tackle a subject on which he evidently talked with diffidence and unwillingness.

"It's all so utterly out of my line of things," he began, puffing out clouds of cigar smoke between his words, "and there's so little to tell with any real evidence behind it, that it's almost impossible to make a consecutive story for you. It's the total cumulative effect that is so—so disquieting." He chose his words with care, as though determined not to travel one hair's breadth beyond the truth.

"I came into this place twenty years ago when my elder brother died," he continued, "but could not afford to live here then. My sister, whom you met at dinner, kept house for him till the end, and during all these years, while I was seeing service abroad, she had an eye to the place—for we never got a satisfactory tenant—and saw that it was not allowed to go to ruin. I myself took possession, however, only a year ago.

"My brother," he went on, after a perceptible pause, "spent much of his time away, too. He was a great traveller, and filled the house with stuff he brought home from all over the world. The laundry—a small detached building beyond the servants' quarters—he turned into a regular little museum. The curios and things I have cleared away—they collected dust and were always getting broken—but the laundry-house you shall see tomorrow."

Colonel Wragge spoke with such deliberation and with so many pauses that this beginning took him a long time. But at this point he came to a full stop altogether. Evidently there was something he wished to say that cost him considerable effort. At length he looked up steadily into my companion's face.

"May I ask you—that is, if you won't think it strange," he said, and a sort of hush came over his voice and manner, "whether you have noticed anything at all unusual—anything queer, since you came into the house?"

Dr. Silence answered without a moment's hesitation.

"I have," he said. "There is a curious sensation of heat in the place."

"Ah!" exclaimed the other, with a slight start. "You *have* noticed it. This unaccountable heat—"

"But its cause, I gather, is not in the house itself—but outside," I was astonished to hear the doctor add.

Colonel Wragge rose from his chair and turned to unhook a framed map that hung upon the wall. I got the impression that the movement was made with the deliberate purpose of concealing his face.

"Your diagnosis, I believe, is amazingly accurate," he said after a moment, turning round with the map in his hands. "Though, of course, I can have no idea how you should guess—"

John Silence shrugged his shoulders expressively. "Merely my impression," he said. "If you pay attention to impressions, and do not allow them to be confused by deductions of the intellect, you will often find them surprisingly, uncannily, accurate."

Colonel Wragge resumed his seat and laid the map upon his knees. His face was very thoughtful as he plunged abruptly again into his story.

"On coming into possession," he said, looking us alternately in the face, "I found a crop of stories of the most extraordinary and impossible kind I had ever heard—stories which at first I treated with amused indifference, but later was forced to regard seriously, if only to keep my servants. These stories I thought I traced to the fact of my brother's death—and, in a way, I think so still."

He leant forward and handed the map to Dr. Silence.

"It's an old plan of the estate," he explained, "but accurate enough for our purpose, and I wish you would note the position of the plantations marked upon it, especially those near the house. That one," indicating the spot with his finger, "is called the Twelve Acre Plantation. It was just there, on the side nearest the house, that my brother and the head keeper met their deaths."

He spoke as a man forced to recognise facts that he deplored, and would have preferred to leave untouched—things he personally would rather have treated with ridicule if possible. It made his words peculiarly dignified and impressive, and I listened with an increasing uneasiness as to the sort of help the doctor would look to me for later. It seemed as though I were a spectator of some drama of mystery in which any moment I might be summoned to play a part.

"It was twenty years ago," continued the Colonel, "but there was much talk about it at the time, unfortunately, and you may, perhaps, have heard of the affair. Stride, the keeper, was a passionate, hot-tempered man but I regret to say, so was my brother, and quarrels between them seem to have been frequent."

"I do not recall the affair," said the doctor. "May I ask what was the cause of death?" Something in his voice made me prick up my ears for the reply.

"The keeper, it was said, from suffocation. And at the inquest the doctors averred that both men had been dead the same length of time when found."

"And your brother?" asked John Silence, noticing the omission, and listening intently.

"Equally mysterious," said our host, speaking in a low voice with effort. "But there was one distressing feature I think I ought to mention. For those who saw the face—I did not see it myself—and though Stride carried a gun its chambers were undischarged—" He stammered and hesitated with confusion. Again that sense of terror moved between his words. He stuck.

"Yes," said the chief listener sympathetically.

"My brother's face, they said, looked as though it had been scorched. It had been swept, as it were, by something that burned—blasted. It was, I am told, quite dreadful. The bodies were found lying side by side, faces downwards, both pointing away from the wood, as though they had been in the act of running, and not more than a dozen yards from its edge."

Dr. Silence made no comment. He appeared to be studying the map attentively.

"I did not see the face myself," repeated the other, his manner somehow expressing the sense of awe he contrived to keep out of his voice, "but my sister unfortunately did, and her present state I believe to be entirely due to the shock it gave to her nerves. She never can be brought to refer to it, naturally, and I am even inclined to think that the memory has mercifully been permitted to vanish from her mind. But she spoke of it at the time as a face swept by flame—blasted."

John Silence looked up from his contemplation of the map, but with the air of one who wished to listen, not to speak, and presently Colonel Wragge went on with his account. He stood on the mat, his broad shoulders hiding most of the mantelpiece.

"They all centred about this particular plantation, these stories. That was to be expected, for the people here are as superstitious as Irish peasantry, and though I made one or two examples among them to stop the foolish talk, it had no effect, and new versions came to my ears every week. You may imagine how little good dismissals did, when I tell you that the servants dismissed themselves. It was not the house servants, but the men who worked on the estate outside. The keepers gave notice one after another, none of them with any reason I could accept; the foresters refused to enter the wood, and the beaters to beat in it. Word flew all over the countryside that Twelve Acre Plantation was a place to be avoided, day or night.

"There came a point," the Colonel went on, now well in his swing, "when I felt compelled to make investigations on my own account. I could not kill the thing by ignoring it; so I collected and analysed the stories at first hand. For this Twelve Acre Wood, you will see by the map, comes rather near home. Its lower end, if you will look, almost touches the end of the back lawn, as I will show you tomorrow, and its dense growth of pines forms the chief protection the house enjoys from the east winds that blow up from the sea. And in olden days, before my brother interfered with it and frightened all the game away, it was one of the best pheasant coverts on the whole estate."

"And what form, if I may ask, did this interference take?" asked Dr. Silence.

"In detail, I cannot tell you, for I do not know—except that I understand it was the subject of his frequent differences with the head keeper; but during the last two years of his life, when he gave up travelling and settled down here, he took a special interest in this wood, and for some unaccountable reason began to build a low stone wall around it. This wall was never finished, but you shall see the ruins tomorrow in the daylight."

"And the result of your investigations—these stories, I mean?" the doctor broke in, anxious to keep him to the main issues.

"Yes, I'm coming to that," he said slowly, "but the wood first, for this wood out of which they grew like mushrooms has nothing in any way peculiar about it. It is very thickly grown, and rises to a clearer part in the centre, a sort of mound where there is a circle of large boulders—old Druid stones, I'm told. At another place there's a small pond. There's nothing distinctive about it that I could mention—just an ordinary pine-wood, a very ordinary pine-wood—only the trees are a bit twisted in the trunks, some of 'em, and very dense. Nothing more.

"And the stories? Well, none of them had anything to do with my poor brother, or the keeper, as you might have expected; and they were all odd—such odd things, I mean, to invent or imagine. I never could make out how these people got such notions into their heads."

He paused a moment to relight his cigar.

"There's no regular path through it," he resumed, puffing vigorously, "but the fields round it are constantly used, and one of the gardeners whose cottage lies over that way declared he often saw moving lights in it at night, and luminous shapes like globes of fire over the tops of the trees, skimming and floating, and making a soft hissing sound—most of 'em said that, in fact—and another man saw shapes flitting in and out among the trees, things that were neither men nor animals, and all faintly luminous. No one ever pretended to see human forms—always queer, huge things they could not properly describe. Sometimes the whole wood was lit up, and one fellow—he's still here and you shall see him—has a most circumstantial yarn about having seen great stars lying on the ground round the edge of the wood at regular intervals "

"What kind of stars?" put in John Silence sharply, in a sudden way that made me start.

"Oh, I don't know quite; ordinary stars, I think he said, only very large, and apparently blazing as though the ground was alight. He was too terrified to go close and examine, and he has never seen them since."

He stooped and stirred the fire into a welcome blaze—welcome for its blaze of light rather than for its heat. In the room there was already a strange pervading sensation of warmth that was oppressive in its effect and far from comforting.

"Of course," he went on, straightening up again on the mat, "this was all commonplace enough—this seeing lights and figures at night. Most of these fellows drink, and imagination and terror between them may account for almost anything. But others saw things in broad daylight. One of the woodmen, a sober, respectable man, took the shortcut home to his midday meal, and swore he was followed the whole length of the wood by something that never showed itself, but dodged from tree to tree, always keeping out of sight, yet solid enough to make the branches sway and the twigs snap on the ground. And it made a noise, he declared—but really"— the speaker stopped and gave a short laugh—"it's too absurd—"

"*Please!*" insisted the doctor; "for it is these small details that give me the best clues always."

"—it made a crackling noise, he said, like a bonfire. Those were his very words: like the crackling of a bonfire," finished the soldier, with a repetition of his short laugh.

"Most interesting," Dr. Silence observed gravely. "Please omit nothing."

"Yes," he went on, "and it was soon after that the fires began—the fires in the wood. They started mysteriously burning in the patches of coarse white grass that cover the more open parts of the plantation. No one ever actually saw them start, but many, myself among the number, have seen them burning and smouldering. They are always small and circular in shape, and for all the world like a picnic fire. The head keeper has a dozen explanations, from sparks flying out of the house chimneys to the sunlight focusing through a dewdrop, but none of them, I must admit, convince me as being in the least likely or probable. They are most singular, I consider, most singular, these mysterious fires, and I am glad to say that they come only at rather long intervals and never seem to spread.

"But the keeper had other queer stories as well, and about things that are verifiable. He declared that no life ever willingly entered the plantation; more, that no life existed in it at all. No birds nested in the trees, or flew into their shade. He set countless traps, but never caught so much as a rabbit or a weasel. Animals avoided it, and more than once he had picked up dead creatures round the edges that bore no obvious signs of how they had met their death.

"Moreover, he told me one extraordinary tale about his retriever chasing some invisible creature across the field one day when he was out with his gun. The dog suddenly pointed at something in the field at his feet, and then gave chase, yelping like a mad thing. It followed its imaginary quarry to the borders of the wood, and then went in—a thing he had never known it to do before. The moment it crossed the edge—it is darkish in there even in daylight—it began fighting in the most frenzied and terrific fashion. It made him afraid to interfere, he said. And at last, when the dog came out, hanging its tail down and panting, he found something like white hair stuck to its jaws, and brought it to show me. I tell you these details because—"

"They are important, believe me," the doctor stopped him. "And you have it still, this hair?" he asked.

"It disappeared in the oddest way," the Colonel explained. "It was curious looking stuff, something like asbestos, and I sent it to be analysed by the local chemist. But either the man got wind of its origin, or else he didn't like the look of it for some reason, because he returned it to me and said it was neither animal, vegetable, nor mineral, so far as he could make out, and he didn't wish to have anything to do with it. I put it away in paper, but a week later, on opening the package—it was gone! Oh, the stories are simply endless. I could tell you hundreds all on the same lines."

"And personal experiences of your own, Colonel Wragge?" asked John Silence earnestly, his manner showing the greatest possible interest and sympathy.

The soldier gave an almost imperceptible start. He looked distinctly uncomfortable.

"Nothing, I think," he said slowly, "nothing—er—I should like to rely on. I mean nothing I have the right to speak of, perhaps—yet."

His mouth closed with a snap. Dr. Silence, after waiting a little to see if he would add to his reply, did not seek to press him on the point.

"Well," he resumed presently, and as though he would speak contemptuously, yet dared not, "this sort of thing has gone on at intervals ever since. It spreads like wildfire, of course, mysterious chatter of this kind, and people began trespassing all over the estate, coming to see the wood, and making themselves a general nuisance. Notices of man-traps and spring-guns only seemed to increase their persistence; and—think of it," he snorted, "some local Research Society actually wrote and asked permission for one of their members to spend a night in the wood! Bolder fools, who didn't write for leave, came and took away bits of bark from the trees and gave them to clairvoyants, who invented in their turn a further batch of tales. There was simply no end to it all."

"Most distressing and annoying, I can well believe," interposed the doctor.

"Then suddenly, the phenomena ceased as mysteriously as they had begun, and the interest flagged. The tales stopped. People got interested in something else. It all seemed to die out. This was last July. I can tell you exactly, for I've kept a diary more or less of what happened."

"Ah!"

"But now, quite recently, within the past three weeks, it has all revived again with a rush—with a kind of furious attack, so to speak. It has really become unbearable. You may imagine what it means, and the general state of affairs, when I say that the possibility of leaving has occurred to me."

"Incendiarism?" suggested Dr. Silence, half under his breath, but not so low that Colonel Wragge did not hear him.

"By Jove, sir, you take the very words out of my mouth!" exclaimed the astonished man, glancing from the doctor to me and from me to the doctor, and rattling the money in his pocket as though some explanation of my friend's divining powers were to be found that way.

"It's only that you are thinking very vividly," the doctor said quietly, "and your thoughts form pictures in my mind before you utter them. It's merely a little elementary thought-reading."

His intention, I saw, was not to perplex the good man, but to impress him with his powers so as to ensure obedience later.

"Good Lord! I had no idea—" He did not finish the sentence, and dived again abruptly into his narrative.

"I did not see anything myself, I must admit, but the stories of independent eye-witnesses were to the effect that lines of light, like streams of thin fire, moved through the wood and sometimes were seen to shoot out precisely as flames might shoot out—in the direction of this house. There," he explained, in a louder voice that made me jump, pointing with a thick finger to the map, "where the westerly fringe of the plantation comes up to the end of the lower lawn at the back of the house—where it links on to those dark patches, which are laurel shrubberies, running right up to the back premises—that's where these lights were seen. They passed from the wood to the shrubberies, and in this way reached the house itself. Like silent rockets, one man described them, rapid as lightning and exceedingly bright."

"And this evidence you spoke of?"

"They actually reached the sides of the house. They've left a mark of scorching on the walls—the walls of the laundry building at the other end. You shall see 'em tomorrow." He pointed to the map to indicate the spot, and then straightened himself and glared about the room as though he had said something no one could believe and expected contradiction.

"Scorched—just as the faces were," the doctor murmured, looking significantly at me.

"Scorched—yes," repeated the Colonel, failing to catch the rest of the sentence in his excitement.

There was a prolonged silence in the room, in which I heard the gurgling of the oil in the lamp and the click of the coals and the heavy breathing of our host. The most unwelcome sensations were creeping about my spine, and I wondered whether my companion would scorn me utterly if I asked to sleep on the sofa in his room. It was eleven o'clock, I saw by the clock on the mantelpiece. We had crossed the dividing line and were now well in the movement of the adventure. The fight between my interest and my dread became acute. But, even if turning back had been possible, I think the interest would have easily gained the day.

"I have enemies, of course," I heard the Colonel's rough voice break into the pause presently, "and have discharged a number of servants—"

"It's not that," put in John Silence briefly.

"You think not? In a sense I am glad, and yet—there are some things that can be met and dealt with—"

He left the sentence unfinished, and looked down at the floor with an expression of grim severity that betrayed a momentary glimpse of character. This fighting man loathed and abhorred the thought of an enemy he could not see and come to grips with. Presently he moved over and sat down in the chair between us. Something like a sigh escaped him. Dr. Silence said nothing.

"My sister, of course, is kept in ignorance, as far as possible, of all this," he said disconnectedly, and as if talking to himself. "But even if she knew she would find matter-of-fact explanations. I only wish I could. I'm sure they exist."

There came then an interval in the conversation that was very significant. It did not seem a real pause, or the silence real silence, for both men continued to think so rapidly and strongly that one almost imagined their thoughts clothed themselves in words in the air of the room. I was more than a little keyed up with the strange excitement of all I had heard, but what stimulated my nerves more than anything else was the obvious fact that the doctor was clearly upon the trail of discovery. In his mind at that moment, I believe, he had already solved the nature of this perplexing psychical problem. His face was like a mask, and he employed the absolute minimum of gesture and words. All his energies were directed inwards, and by those incalculable methods and processes he had mastered with such infinite patience and study, I felt sure he was already in touch with the forces behind these singular phenomena and laying his deep plans for bringing them into the open, and then effectively dealing with them.

Colonel Wragge meanwhile grew more and more fidgety. From time to time he turned towards my companion, as though about to speak, yet always changing his mind at the last moment. Once he went over and opened the door suddenly, apparently to see if any one were listening at the keyhole, for he disappeared a moment between the two doors, and I then heard him open the outer one. He stood there for some seconds and made a noise as though he were sniffing the air like a dog. Then he closed both doors cautiously and came back to the fireplace. A strange excitement seemed growing upon him. Evidently he was trying to make up his mind to say something that he found it difficult to say. And John Silence, as I rightly judged, was waiting patiently for him to choose his own opportunity and his own way of saying it. At last he turned and faced us, squaring his great shoulders, and stiffening perceptibly.

Dr. Silence looked up sympathetically.

"Your own experiences help me most," he observed quietly.

"The fact is," the Colonel said, speaking very low, "this past week there have been outbreaks of fire in the house itself. Three separate outbreaks—and all—in my sister's room."

"Yes," the doctor said, as if this was just what he had expected to hear.

"Utterly unaccountable—all of them," added the other, and then sat down. I began to understand something of the reason of his excitement. He was realising at last that the "natural" explanation he had held to all along was becoming impossible, and he hated it. It made him angry.

"Fortunately," he went on, "she was out each time and does not know. But I have made her sleep now in a room on the ground floor."

"A wise precaution," the doctor said simply. He asked one or two questions. The fires had started in the curtains—once by the window and once by the bed. The third time smoke had been discovered by the maid coming from the cupboard, and it was found that Miss Wragge's clothes hanging on the hooks were smouldering. The doctor listened attentively, but made no comment.

"And now can you tell me," he said presently, "what your own feeling about it is—your general impression?"

"It sounds foolish to say so," replied the soldier, after a moment's hesitation, "but I feel exactly as I have often felt on active service in my Indian campaigns: just as if the house and all in it were in a state of siege; as though a concealed enemy were encamped about us—in ambush somewhere." He uttered a soft nervous laugh. "As if the next sign of smoke would precipitate a panic—a dreadful panic."

The picture came before me of the night shadowing the house, and the twisted pine trees he had described crowding about it, concealing some powerful enemy; and, glancing at the resolute face and figure of the old soldier, forced at length to his confession, I understood something of all he had been through before he sought the assistance of John Silence.

"And tomorrow, unless I am mistaken, is full moon," said the doctor suddenly, watching the other's face for the effect of his apparently careless words.

Colonel Wragge gave an uncontrollable start, and his face for the first time showed unmistakable pallor.

"What in the world—?" he began, his lip quivering.

"Only that I am beginning to see light in this extraordinary affair," returned the other calmly, "and, if my theory is correct, each month when the moon is at the full should witness an increase in the activity of the phenomena."

"I don't see the connection," Colonel Wragge answered almost savagely, "but I am bound to say my diary bears you out." He wore the most puzzled expression I have ever seen upon an honest face, but he abhorred this additional corroboration of an explanation that perplexed him.

"I confess," he repeated, "I cannot see the connection."

"Why should you?" said the doctor, with his first laugh that evening. He got up and hung the map upon the wall again. "But I do—because these things are my special study—and let me add that I have yet to come across a problem that is not natural, and has not a natural explanation. It's merely a question of how much one knows—and admits."

Colonel Wragge eyed him with a new and curious respect in his face. But his feelings were soothed. Moreover, the doctor's laugh and change of manner came as a relief to all, and broke the spell of grave suspense that had held us so long. We all rose and stretched our limbs, and took little walks about the room.

"I am glad, Dr. Silence, if you will allow me to say so, that you are here," he said simply, "very glad indeed. And now I fear I have kept you both up very late," with a glance to include me, "for you must be tired, and ready for your beds. I have told you all there is to tell," he added, "and tomorrow you must feel perfectly free to take any steps you think necessary."

The end was abrupt, yet natural, for there was nothing more to say, and neither of these men talked for mere talking's sake.

Out in the cold and chilly hall he lit our candles and took us upstairs. The house was at rest and still, every one asleep. We moved softly. Through the windows on the stairs we saw the moonlight falling across the lawn, throwing deep shadows. The nearer pine trees were just visible in the distance, a wall of impenetrable blackness.

Our host came for a moment to our rooms to see that we had everything. He pointed to a coil of strong rope lying beside the window, fastened to the wall by means of an iron ring. Evidently it had been recently put in.

"I don't think we shall need it," Dr. Silence said, with a smile.

"I trust not," replied our host gravely. "I sleep quite close to you across the landing," he whispered, pointing to his door, "and if you—if you want anything in the night you will know where to find me."

He wished us pleasant dreams and disappeared down the passage into his room, shading the candle with his big muscular hand from the draughts.

John Silence stopped me a moment before I went.

"You know what it is?" I asked, with an excitement that even overcame my weariness.

"Yes," he said, "I'm almost sure. And you?"

"Not the smallest notion."

He looked disappointed, but not half as disappointed as I felt.

"Egypt," he whispered, "Egypt!"

II

Nothing happened to disturb me in the night—nothing, that is, except a nightmare in which Colonel Wragge chased me amid thin streaks of fire, and his sister always prevented my escape by suddenly rising up out of the ground in her chair—dead. The deep baying of dogs woke me once, just before the dawn, it must have been, for I saw the window frame against the sky; there was a flash of lightning, too, I thought, as I turned over in bed. And it was warm, for October oppressively warm.

It was after eleven o'clock when our host suggested going out with the guns, these, we understood, being a somewhat thin disguise for our true purpose. Personally, I was glad to be in the open air, for the atmosphere of the house was heavy with presentiment. The sense of impending disaster hung over all. Fear stalked the passages, and lurked in the corners of every room. It was a house haunted, but really haunted; not by some vague shadow of the dead, but by a definite though incalculable influence that was actively alive, and dangerous. At the least smell of smoke the entire household quivered. An odour of burning, I was convinced, would paralyse all the inmates. For the servants, though professedly ignorant by the master's unspoken orders, yet shared the common dread; and the hideous uncertainty, joined with this display of so spiteful and calculated a spirit of malignity, provided a kind of black doom that draped not only the walls, but also the minds of the people living within them.

Only the bright and cheerful vision of old Miss Wragge being pushed about the house in her noiseless chair, chatting and nodding briskly to every one she met, prevented us from giving way entirely to the depression which governed the majority. The sight of her was like a gleam of sunshine through the depths of some ill-omened wood, and just as we went out I saw her being wheeled along by her attendant into the sunshine of the back lawn, and caught her cheery smile as she turned her head and wished us good sport.

The morning was October at its best. Sunshine glistened on the dew-drenched grass and on leaves turned golden-red. The dainty messengers of coming hoar-frost were already in the air, a search for permanent winter quarters. From the wide moors that everywhere swept up against the sky, like a purple sea splashed by the occasional grey of rocky clefts, there stole down the cool and perfumed wind of the west. And the keen taste of the sea ran through all like a master-flavour, borne over the spaces perhaps by the seagulls that cried and circled high in the air.

But our host took little interest in this sparkling beauty, and had no thought of showing off the scenery of his property. His mind was other-wise intent, and, for that matter, so were our own.

"Those bleak moors and hills stretch unbroken for hours," he said, with a sweep of the hand; "and over there, some four miles," pointing in an-other direction, "lies S— Bay, a long, swampy inlet of the sea, haunted by myriads of seabirds. On the other side of the house are the plantations and pine-woods. I thought we would get the dogs and go first to the Twelve Acre Wood I told you about last night. It's quite near."

We found the dogs in the stable, and I recalled the deep baying of the night when a fine bloodhound and two great Danes leaped out to greet us. Singular companions for guns, I thought to myself, as we struck out across the fields and the great creatures bounded and ran beside us, nose to ground.

The conversation was scanty. John Silence's grave face did not encour-age talk. He wore the expression I knew well—that look of earnest solic-itude which meant that his whole being was deeply absorbed and preoc-cupied. Frightened, I had never seen him, but anxious often—it always moved me to witness it—and he was anxious now.

"On the way back you shall see the laundry building," Colonel Wragge observed shortly, for he, too, found little to say. "We shall attract less at-tention then."

Yet not all the crisp beauty of the morning seemed able to dispel the feel-ings of uneasy dread that gathered increasingly about our minds as we went.

In a very few minutes a clump of pine trees concealed the house from view, and we found ourselves on the outskirts of a densely grown planta-tion of conifers. Colonel Wragge stopped abruptly, and, producing a map from his pocket, explained once more very briefly its position with regard to the house. He showed how it ran up almost to the walls of the laundry building—though at the moment beyond our actual view—and pointed to the windows of his sister's bedroom where the fires had been. The room, now empty, looked straight on to the wood. Then, glancing nervously about him, and calling the dogs to heel, he proposed that we should enter the plantation and make as thorough examination of it as we thought worth while. The dogs, he added, might perhaps be persuaded to accompany us a little way—and he pointed to where they cowered at his feet—but he doubted it. "Neither voice nor whip will get them very far, I'm afraid," he said. "I know by experience."

"If you have no objection," replied Dr. Silence, with decision, and speaking almost for the first time, "we will make our examination alone—Mr. Hubbard and myself. It will be best so."

His tone was absolutely final, and the Colonel acquiesced so politely that even a less intuitive man than myself must have seen that he was genuinely relieved.

"You doubtless have good reasons," he said.

"Merely that I wish to obtain my impressions uncoloured. This delicate clue I am working on might be so easily blurred by the thought-currents of another mind with strongly preconceived ideas."

"Perfectly. I understand," rejoined the soldier, though with an expression of countenance that plainly contradicted his words. "Then I will wait here with the dogs; and we'll have a look at the laundry on our way home."

I turned once to look back as we clambered over the low stone wall built by the late owner, and saw his straight, soldierly figure standing in the sunlit field watching us with a curiously intent look on his face. There was something to me incongruous, yet distinctly pathetic, in the man's efforts to meet all far-fetched explanations of the mystery with contempt, and at the same time in his stolid, unswerving investigation of it all. He nodded at me and made a gesture of farewell with his hand. That picture of him, standing in the sunshine with his big dogs, steadily watching us, remains with me to this day.

Dr. Silence led the way in among the twisted trunks, planted closely together in serried ranks, and I followed sharp at his heels. The moment we were out of sight he turned and put down his gun against the roots of a big tree, and I did likewise.

"We shall hardly want these cumbersome weapons of murder," he observed, with a passing smile.

"You are sure of your clue, then?" I asked at once, bursting with curiosity, yet fearing to betray it lest he should think me unworthy. His own methods were so absolutely simple and untheatrical.

"I am sure of my clue," he answered gravely. "And I think we have come just in time. You shall know in due course. For the present—be content to follow and observe. And think, steadily. The support of your mind will help me."

His voice had that quiet mastery in it which leads men to face death with a sort of happiness and pride. I would have followed him anywhere at that moment. At the same time his words conveyed a sense of dread seriousness. I caught the thrill of his confidence; but also, in this broad light of day, I felt the measure of alarm that lay behind.

"You still have no strong impressions?" he asked. "Nothing happened in the night, for instance? No vivid dreamings?"

He looked closely for my answer, I was aware.

"I slept almost an unbroken sleep. I was tremendously tired, you know, and, but for the oppressive heat—"

"Good! You still notice the heat, then," he said to himself, rather than expecting an answer. "And the lightning?" he added, "that lightning out of a clear sky—that flashing—did you notice *that?*"

I answered truly that I thought I had seen a flash during a moment of wakefulness, and he then drew my attention to certain facts before moving on.

"You remember the sensation of warmth when you put the letter to your forehead in the train; the heat generally in the house last evening, and, as you now mention, in the night. You heard, too, the Colonel's stories about the appearances of fire in this wood and in the house itself, and the way his brother and the gamekeeper came to their deaths twenty years ago."

I nodded, wondering what in the world it all meant.

"And you get no clue from these facts?" he asked, a trifle surprised.

I searched every corner of my mind and imagination for some inkling of his meaning, but was obliged to admit that I understood nothing so far.

"Never mind, you will later. And now," he added, "we will go over the wood and see what we can find."

His words explained to me something of his method. We were to keep our minds alert and report to each other the least fancy that crossed the picture-gallery of our thoughts. Then, just as we started, he turned again to me with a final warning.

"And, for your safety," he said earnestly, "imagine *now*—and for that matter, imagine always until we leave this place—imagine with the utmost keenness, that you are surrounded by a shell that protects you. Picture yourself inside a protective envelope, and build it up with the most intense imagination you can evoke. Pour the whole force of your thought and will into it. Believe vividly all through this adventure that such a shell, constructed of your thought, will and imagination, surrounds you completely, and that nothing can pierce it to attack."

He spoke with dramatic conviction, gazing hard at me as though to enforce his meaning, and then moved forward and began to pick his way over the rough, tussocky ground into the wood. And meanwhile, knowing the efficacy of his prescription, I adopted it to the best of my ability.

The trees at once closed about us like the night. Their branches met overhead in a continuous tangle, their stems crept closer and closer, the brambly undergrowth thickened and multiplied. We tore our trousers, scratched our hands, and our eyes filled with fine dust that made it most difficult to avoid the clinging, prickly network of branches and creepers. Coarse white grass that caught our feet like string grew here and there in patches. It crowned the lumps of peaty growth that stuck up like human heads, fantastically dressed, thrusting up at us out of the ground with crests of dead hair. We stumbled and floundered among them. It was hard going, and I could well conceive it impossible to find a way at all in the night-time. We jumped, when possible, from tussock to tussock, and it seemed as though we were springing among heads on a battlefield, and that this dead white grass concealed eyes that turned to stare as we passed.

Here and there the sunlight shot in with vivid spots of white light, dazzling the sight, but only making the surrounding gloom deeper by contrast. And on two occasions we passed dark circular places in the grass where fires had eaten their mark and left a ring of ashes. Dr. Silence pointed to them, but without comment and without pausing, and the sight of them woke in me a singular realisation of the dread that lay so far only just out of sight in this adventure.

It was exhausting work, and heavy going. We kept close together. The warmth, too, was extraordinary. Yet it did not seem the warmth of the body due to violent exertion, but rather an inner heat of the mind that laid glowing hands of fire upon the heart and set the brain in a kind of steady blaze. When my companion found himself too far in advance, he waited for me to come up. The place had evidently been untouched by hand of man, keeper, forester or sportsman, for many a year; and my thoughts, as we advanced painfully, were not unlike the state of the wood itself—dark, confused, full of a haunting wonder and the shadow of fear.

By this time all signs of the open field behind us were hid. No single gleam penetrated. We might have been groping in the heart of some primeval forest. Then, suddenly, the brambles and tussocks and stringlike grass came to an end; the trees opened out; and the ground began to slope upwards towards a large central mound. We had reached the middle of the plantation, and before us stood the broken Druid stones our host had mentioned. We walked easily up the little hill, between the sparser stems, and, resting upon one of the ivy-covered boulders, looked round upon a comparatively open space, as large, perhaps, as a small London Square.

Thinking of the ceremonies and sacrifices this rough circle of prehistoric monoliths might have witnessed, I looked up into my companion's face with an unspoken question. But he read my thought and shook his head.

"Our mystery has nothing to do with these dead symbols," he said, "but with something perhaps even more ancient, and of another country altogether."

"Egypt?" I said half under my breath, hopelessly puzzled, but recalling his words in my bedroom.

He nodded. Mentally I still floundered, but he seemed intensely preoccupied and it was no time for asking questions; so while his words circled unintelligibly in my mind I looked round at the scene before me, glad of the opportunity to recover breath and some measure of composure. But hardly had I time to notice the twisted and contorted shapes of many of the pine trees close at hand when Dr. Silence leaned over and touched me on the shoulder. He pointed down the slope. And the look I saw in his eyes keyed up every nerve in my body to its utmost pitch.

A thin, almost imperceptible column of blue smoke was rising among the trees some twenty yards away at the foot of the mound. It curled up and up, and disappeared from sight among the tangled branches overhead. It was scarcely thicker than the smoke from a small brand of burning wood.

"Protect yourself! Imagine your shell strongly," whispered the doctor sharply, "and follow me closely."

He rose at once and moved swiftly down the slope towards the smoke, and I followed, afraid to remain alone. I heard the soft crunching of our steps on the pine needles. Over his shoulder I watched the thin blue spiral, without once taking my eyes off it. I hardly know how to describe the peculiar sense of vague horror inspired in me by the sight of that streak of smoke pencilling its way upwards among the dark trees. And the sensation of increasing heat as we approached was phenomenal. It was like walking towards a glowing yet invisible fire.

As we drew nearer his pace slackened. Then he stopped and pointed, and I saw a small circle of burnt grass upon the ground. The tussocks were blackened and smouldering, and from the centre rose this line of smoke, pale, blue, steady. Then I noticed a movement of the atmosphere beside us, as if the warm air were rising and the cooler air rushing in to take its place: a little centre of wind in the stillness. Overhead the boughs stirred and trembled where the smoke disappeared. Otherwise, not a tree sighed, not a sound made itself heard. The wood was still as a graveyard. A horrible idea came to me that the course of nature was about to change without warning, *had* changed a little already, that the sky would drop, or the surface of the earth crash inwards like a broken bubble. Something, certainly, reached up to the citadel of my reason, causing its throne to shake.

John Silence moved forward again. I could not see his face, but his attitude was plainly one of resolution, of muscles and mind ready for vigorous action. We were within ten feet of the blackened circle when the smoke of a sudden ceased to rise, and vanished. The tail of the column disappeared in the air above, and at the same instant it seemed to me that the sensation of heat passed from my face, and the motion of the wind was gone. The calm spirit of the fresh October day resumed command.

Side by side we advanced and examined the place. The grass was smouldering, the ground still hot. The circle of burned earth was a foot to a foot and a half in diameter. It looked like an ordinary picnic fireplace. I bent down cautiously to look, but in a second I sprang back with an involuntary cry of alarm, for, as the doctor stamped on the ashes to prevent them spreading, a sound of hissing rose from the spot as though he had kicked a living creature. This hissing was faintly audible in the air. It moved past us, away towards the thicker portion of the wood in the direction of our field, and in a second Dr. Silence had left the fire and started in pursuit.

And then began the most extraordinary hunt of invisibility I can ever conceive.

He went fast even at the beginning, and, of course, it was perfectly obvious that he was following something. To judge by the poise of his head he kept his eyes steadily at a certain level—just above the height of a man— and the consequence was he stumbled a good deal over the roughness of the ground. The hissing sound had stopped. There was no sound of any kind, and what he saw to follow was utterly beyond me. I only know, that in mortal dread of being left behind, and with a biting curiosity to see whatever there was to be seen, I followed as quickly as I could, and even then barely succeeded in keeping up with him.

And, as we went, the whole mad jumble of the Colonel's stories ran through my brain, touching a sense of frightened laughter that was only held in check by the sight of this earnest, hurrying figure before me. For John Silence at work inspired me with a kind of awe. He looked so diminutive among these giant twisted trees, while yet I knew that his purpose and his knowledge were so great, and even in hurry he was dignified. The fancy that we were playing some queer, exaggerated game together met the fact that we were two men dancing upon the brink of some possible tragedy, and the mingling of the two emotions in my mind was both grotesque and terrifying.

He never turned in his mad chase, but pushed rapidly on, while I panted after him like a figure in some unreasoning nightmare. And, as I ran, it came upon me that he had been aware all the time, in his quiet, internal way, of many things that he had kept for his own secret consideration; he had been watching, waiting, planning from the very moment we entered the shade of the wood. By some inner, concentrated process of mind, dynamic if not actually magical, he had been in direct contact with the source of the whole adventure, the very essence of the real mystery. And now the forces were

moving to a climax. Something was about to happen, something important, something possibly dreadful. Every nerve, every sense, every significant gesture of the plunging figure before me proclaimed the fact just as
surely as the skies, the winds, and the face of the earth tell the birds the time
to migrate and warn the animals that danger lurks and they must move.

In a few moments we reached the foot of the mound and entered the tangled undergrowth that lay between us and the sunlight of the field. Here
the difficulties of fast travelling increased a hundredfold. There were
brambles to dodge, low boughs to dive under, and countless tree trunks
closing up to make a direct path impossible. Yet Dr. Silence never seemed
to falter or hesitate. He went, diving, jumping, dodging, ducking, but ever
in the same main direction, following a clean trail. Twice I tripped and fell,
and both times, when I picked myself up again, I saw him ahead of me,
still forcing a way like a dog after its quarry. And sometimes, like a dog,
he stopped and pointed—human pointing it was, psychic pointing, —and
each time he stopped to point I heard that faint high hissing in the air beyond us. The instinct of an infallible dowser possessed him, and he made
no mistakes.

At length, abruptly, I caught up with him, and found that we stood at
the edge of the shallow pond Colonel Wragge had mentioned in his account
the night before. It was long and narrow, filled with dark brown water, in
which the trees were dimly reflected. Not a ripple stirred its surface.

"Watch!" he cried out, as I came up. "It's going to cross. It's bound to
betray itself. The water is its natural enemy, and we shall see the direction."

And, even as he spoke, a thin line like the track of a water-spider, shot
swiftly across the shiny surface; there was a ghost of steam in the air above;
and immediately I became aware of an odour of burning.

Dr. Silence turned and shot a glance at me that made me think of lightning. I began to shake all over.

"Quick!" he cried with excitement, "to the trail again! We must run
around. It's going to the house!"

The alarm in his voice quite terrified me. Without a false step I dashed
round the slippery banks and dived again at his heels into the sea of bushes
and tree trunks. We were now in the thick of the very dense belt that ran
around the outer edge of the plantation, and the field was near; yet so dark
was the tangle that it was some time before the first shafts of white sunlight became visible. The doctor now ran in zigzags. He was following
something that dodged and doubled quite wonderfully, yet had begun, I
fancied, to move more slowly than before.

"Quick!" he cried. "In the light we shall lose it!"

I still saw nothing, heard nothing, caught no suggestion of a trail; yet this
man, guided by some interior divining that seemed infallible, made no false

turns, though how he failed to crash headlong into the trees has remained a mystery to me ever since. And then, with a sudden rush, we found ourselves on the skirts of the wood with the open field lying in bright sunshine before our eyes.

"Too late!" I heard him cry, a note of anguish in his voice. "It's out—and, by God, it's making for the house!"

I saw the Colonel standing in the field with his dogs where we had left him. He was bending double, peering into the wood where he heard us running, and he straightened up like a bent whip released. John Silence dashed passed, calling him to follow.

"We shall lose the trail in the light," I heard him cry as he ran. "But quick! We may yet get there in time!"

That wild rush across the open field, with the dogs at our heels, leaping and barking, and the elderly Colonel behind us running as though for his life, shall I ever forget it? Though I had only vague ideas of the meaning of it all, I put my best foot forward, and, being the youngest of the three, I reached the house an easy first. I drew up, panting, and turned to wait for the others. But, as I turned, something moving a little distance away caught my eye, and in that moment I swear I experienced the most overwhelming and singular shock of surprise and terror I have ever known, or can conceive as possible.

For the front door was open, and the waist of the house being narrow, I could see through the hall into the dining-room beyond, and so out on to the back lawn, and there I saw no less a sight than the figure of Miss Wragge—running. Even at that distance it was plain that she had seen me, and was coming fast towards me, running with the frantic gait of a terror-stricken woman. She had recovered the use of her legs.

Her face was a livid grey, as of death itself, but the general expression was one of laughter, for her mouth was gaping, and her eyes, always bright, shone with the light of a wild merriment that seemed the merriment of a child, yet was singularly ghastly. And that very second, as she fled past me into her brother's arms behind, I smelt again most unmistakably the odour of burning, and to this day the smell of smoke and fire can come very near to turning me sick with the memory of what I had seen.

Fast on her heels, too, came the terrified attendant, more mistress of herself, and able to speak—which the old lady could not do—but with a face almost, if not quite, as fearful.

"We were down by the bushes in the sun,"—she gasped and screamed in reply to Colonel Wragge's distracted questionings, —"I was wheeling the chair as usual when she shrieked and leaped—I don't know exactly—I was too frightened to see—Oh, my God! she jumped clean out of the chair—*and ran!* There was a blast of hot air from the wood, and she hid her face and jumped. She didn't make a sound—she didn't cry out, or make a sound. She just ran."

But the nightmare horror of it all reached the breaking point a few minutes later, and while I was still standing in the hall temporarily bereft of speech and movement; for while the doctor, the Colonel and the attendant were half-way up the staircase, helping the fainting woman to the privacy of her room, and all in a confused group of dark figures, there sounded a voice behind me, and I turned to see the butler, his face dripping with perspiration, his eyes starting out of his head.

"The laundry's on fire!" he cried; "the laundry building's a-caught!"

I remember his odd expression "a-caught," and wanting to laugh, but finding my face rigid and inflexible.

"The devil's about again, s'help me Gawd!" he cried, in a voice thin with terror, running about in circles.

And then the group on the stairs scattered as at the sound of a shot, and the Colonel and Dr. Silence came down three steps at a time, leaving the afflicted Miss Wragge to the care of her single attendant.

We were out across the front lawn in a moment and round the corner of the house, the Colonel leading, Silence and I at his heels, and the portly butler puffing some distance in the rear, getting more and more mixed in his addresses to God and the devil; and the moment we passed the stables and came into view of the laundry building, we saw a wicked-looking volume of smoke pouring out of the narrow windows, and the frightened women-servants and grooms running hither and thither, calling aloud as they ran.

The arrival of the master restored order instantly, and this retired soldier, poor thinker perhaps, but capable man of action, had the matter in hand from the start. He issued orders like a martinet, and, almost before I could realise it, there were streaming buckets on the scene and a line of men and women formed between the building and the stable pump.

"Inside," I heard John Silence cry, and the Colonel followed him through the door, while I was just quick enough at their heels to hear him add, "the smoke's the worst part of it. There's no fire yet, I think."

And, true enough, there was no fire. The interior was thick with smoke, but it speedily cleared and not a single bucket was used upon the floor or walls. The air was stifling, the heat fearful.

"There's precious little to burn in here; it's all stone," the Colonel exclaimed, coughing. But the doctor was pointing to the wooden covers of the great cauldron in which the clothes were washed, and we saw that these were smouldering and charred. And when we sprinkled half a bucket of water on them the surrounding bricks hissed and fizzed and sent up clouds of steam. Through the open door and windows this passed out with the rest of the smoke, and we three stood there on the brick floor staring at the spot and wondering, each in our own fashion, how in the name of natural law the place could have caught fire or smoked at all. And each was silent—myself from sheer incapacity and befuddlement, the Colonel from the quiet pluck that faces all things yet speaks little, and John Silence from the intense mental grappling with this latest manifestation of a profound problem that called for concentration of thought rather than for any words.

There was really nothing to say. The facts were indisputable. Colonel Wragge was the first to utter.

"My sister," he said briefly, and moved off. In the yard I heard him sending the frightened servants about their business in an excellently matter-of-fact voice, scolding some one roundly for making such a big fire and letting the flues get over-heated, and paying no heed to the stammering reply that no fire had been lit there for several days. Then he dispatched a groom on horseback for the local doctor.

Then Dr. Silence turned and looked at me. The absolute control he possessed, not only over the outward expression of emotion by gesture, change of colour, light in the eyes, and so forth, but also, as I well knew, over its very birth in his heart, the masklike face of the dead he could assume at will, made it extremely difficult to know at any given moment what was at work in his inner consciousness. But now, when he turned and looked at me, there was no sphinx-expression there, but rather the keen triumphant face of a man who had solved a dangerous and complicated problem, and saw his way to a clean victory.

"*Now* do you guess?" he asked quietly, as though it were the simplest matter in the world, and ignorance were impossible.

I could only stare stupidly and remain silent. He glanced down at the charred cauldron-lids, and traced a figure in the air with his finger. But I was too excited, or too mortified, or still too dazed, perhaps, to see what it was he outlined, or what it was he meant to convey. I could only go on staring and shaking my puzzled head.

"A fire-elemental," he cried, "a fire-elemental of the most powerful and malignant kind—"

"A what?" thundered the voice of Colonel Wragge behind us, having returned suddenly and overheard.

"It's a fire-elemental," repeated Dr. Silence more calmly, but with a note of triumph in his voice he could not keep out, "and a fire-elemental enraged."

The light began to dawn in my mind at last. But the Colonel—who had never heard the term before, and was besides feeling considerably worked up for a plain man with all this mystery he knew not how to grapple with—

the Colonel stood, with the most dumfoundered look ever seen on a human countenance, and continued to roar, and stammer, and stare.

"And why," he began, savage with the desire to find something visible he could fight—"why, in the name of all the blazes—?" and then stopped as John Silence moved up and took his arm.

"There, my dear Colonel Wragge," he said gently, "you touch the heart of the whole thing. You ask 'Why.' That is precisely our problem." He held the soldier's eyes firmly with his own. "And that, too, I think, we shall soon know. Come and let us talk over a plan of action—that room with the double doors, perhaps."

The word "action" calmed him a little, and he led the way, without further speech, back into the house, and down the long stone passage to the room where we had heard his stories on the night of our arrival. I understood from the doctor's glance that my presence would not make the interview easier for our host, and I went upstairs to my own room—shaking.

But in the solitude of my room the vivid memories of the last hour revived so mercilessly that I began to feel I should never in my whole life lose the dreadful picture of Miss Wragge running—that dreadful human climax after all the non-human mystery in the wood—and I was not sorry when a servant knocked at my door and said that Colonel Wragge would be glad if I would join them in the little smoking-room.

"I think it is better you should be present," was all Colonel Wragge said as I entered the room. I took the chair with my back to the window. There was still an hour before lunch, though I imagine that the usual divisions of the day hardly found a place in the thoughts of any one of us.

The atmosphere of the room was what I might call electric. The Colonel was positively bristling; he stood with his back to the fire, fingering an unlit black cigar, his face flushed, his being obviously roused and ready for action. He hated this mystery. It was poisonous to his nature, and he longed to meet something face to face—something he could gauge and fight. Dr. Silence, I noticed at once, was sitting before the map of the estate which was spread upon a table. I knew by his expression the state of his mind. He was in the thick of it all, knew it, delighted in it, and was working at high pressure. He recognised my presence with a lifted eyelid, and the flash of the eye, contrasted with his stillness and composure, told me volumes.

"I was about to explain to our host briefly what seems to me afoot in all this business," he said without looking up, "when he asked that you should join us so that we can all work together." And, while signifying my assent, I caught myself wondering what quality it was in the calm speech of this undemonstrative man that was so full of power, so charged with the strange, virile personality behind it and that seemed to inspire us with his own confidence as by a process of radiation.

"Mr. Hubbard," he went on gravely, turning to the soldier, "knows something of my methods, and in more than one—er—interesting situation has proved of assistance. What we want now"—and here he suddenly got up and took his place on the mat beside the Colonel, and looked hard at him—"is men who have self-control, who are sure of themselves, whose minds at the critical moment will emit positive forces, instead of the wavering and uncertain currents due to negative feelings—due, for instance, to fear."

He looked at us each in turn. Colonel Wragge moved his feet farther apart, and squared his shoulders; and I felt guilty but said nothing, conscious that my latent store of courage was being deliberately hauled to the front. He was winding me up like a clock.

"So that, in what is yet to come," continued our leader, "each of us will contribute his share of power, and ensure success for my plan."

"I'm not afraid of anything I can *see*," said the Colonel bluntly.

"I'm ready," I heard myself say, as it were automatically, "for anything," and then added, feeling the declaration was lamely insufficient, "and everything."

Dr. Silence left the mat and began walking to and fro about the room, both hands plunged deep into the pockets of his shooting-jacket. Tremendous vitality streamed from him. I never took my eyes off the small, moving figure; small yes, —and yet somehow making me think of a giant plotting the destruction of worlds. And his manner was gentle, as always, soothing almost, and his words uttered quietly without emphasis or emotion. Most of what he said was addressed, though not too obviously, to the Colonel.

"The violence of this sudden attack," he said softly, pacing to and fro beneath the bookcase at the end of the room, "is due, of course, partly to the fact that tonight the moon is at the full"—here he glanced at me for a moment—"and partly to the fact that we have all been so deliberately concentrating upon the matter. Our thinking, our investigation, has stirred it into unusual activity. I mean that the intelligent force behind these manifestations has realised that some one is busied about its destruction. And it is now on the defensive: more, it is aggressive."

"But 'it'—what is 'it'?" began the soldier, fuming. "What, in the name of all that's dreadful, *is* a fire-elemental?"

"I cannot give you at this moment," replied Dr. Silence, turning to him, but undisturbed by the interruption, "a lecture on the nature and history of magic, but can only say that an Elemental is the active force behind the elements, — whether earth, air, water, or *fire*, —it is impersonal in its essential nature, but can be focused, personified, ensouled, so to say, by those who know how—by magicians, if you will—for certain purposes of their own, much in the same way that steam and electricity can be harnessed by the practical man of this century.

"Alone, these blind elemental energies can accomplish little, but governed and directed by the trained will of a powerful manipulator they may become potent activities for good or evil. They are the basis of all magic, and it is the motive behind them that constitutes the magic 'black' or 'white'; they can be the vehicles of curses or of blessings, for a curse is nothing more than the thought of a violent will perpetuated. And in such cases—cases like this—the conscious, directing will of the mind that is using the elemental stands always behind the phenomena—"

"You think that my brother—!" broke in the Colonel, aghast.

"Has nothing whatever to do with it—directly. The fire-elemental that has here been tormenting you and your household was sent upon its mission long before you, or your family, or your ancestors, or even the nation you belong to—unless I am much mistaken—was even in existence. We will come to that a little later; after the experiment I propose to make we shall be more positive. At present I can only say we have to deal now, not only with the phenomenon of Attacking Fire merely, but with the vindictive and enraged intelligence that is directing it from behind the scenes—vindictive and enraged,"—he repeated the words.

"That explains—" began Colonel Wragge, seeking furiously for words he could not find quickly enough.

"Much," said John Silence, with a gesture to restrain him.

He stopped a moment in the middle of his walk, and a deep silence came down over the little room. Through the windows the sunlight seemed less bright, the long line of dark hills less friendly, making me think of a vast wave towering to heaven and about to break and overwhelm us. Something formidable had crept into the world about us. For, undoubtedly, there was a disquieting thought, holding terror as well as awe, in the picture his words conjured up: the conception of a human will reaching its deathless hand, spiteful and destructive, down through the ages, to strike the living and afflict the innocent.

"But what *is* its object?" burst out the soldier, unable to restrain himself longer in the silence. "Why does it come from that plantation? And why should it attack us, or any one in particular?" Questions began to pour from him in a stream.

"All in good time," the doctor answered quietly, having let him run on for several minutes. "But I must first discover positively what, or who, it is that directs this particular fire-elemental. And, to do that, we must first"—he spoke with slow deliberation—"seek to capture—to confine by visibility—to limit its sphere in a concrete form."

"Good heavens almighty!" exclaimed the soldier, mixing his words in his unfeigned surprise.

"Quite so," pursued the other calmly; "for in so doing I think we can release it from the purpose that binds it, restore it to its normal condition of latent fire, and also"—he lowered his voice perceptibly—"also discover the face and form of the Being that ensouls it."

"The man behind the gun!" cried the Colonel, beginning to understand something, and leaning forward so as not to miss a single syllable.

"I mean that in the last resort, before it returns to the womb of potential fire, it will probably assume the face and figure of its Director, of the man of magical knowledge who originally bound it with his incantations and sent it forth upon its mission of centuries."

The soldier sat down and gasped openly in his face, breathing hard; but it was a very subdued voice that framed the question.

"And how do you propose to make it visible? How capture and confine it? What d'ye mean, Dr. John Silence?"

"By furnishing it with the materials for a form. By the process of materialisation simply. Once limited by dimensions, it will become slow, heavy, visible. We can then dissipate it. Invisible fire, you see, is dangerous and incalculable; locked up in a form we can perhaps manage it. We must betray it—to its death."

"And this material?" we asked in the same breath, although I think I had already guessed.

"Not pleasant, but effective," came the quiet reply; "the exhalations of freshly spilled blood."

"Not human blood!" cried Colonel Wragge, starting up from his chair with a voice like an explosion. I thought his eyes would start from their sockets.

The face of Dr. Silence relaxed in spite of himself, and his spontaneous little laugh brought a welcome though momentary relief.

"The days of human sacrifice, I hope, will never come again," he explained. "Animal blood will answer the purpose, and we can make the experiment as pleasant as possible. Only, the blood must be freshly spilled and strong with the vital emanations that attract this peculiar class of elemental creature. Perhaps—perhaps if some pig on the estate is ready for the market—"

He turned to hide a smile; but the passing touch of comedy found no echo in the mind of our host, who did not understand how to change quickly from one emotion to another. Clearly he was debating many things laboriously in his honest brain. But, in the end, the earnestness and scientific disinterestedness of the doctor, whose influence over him was already very great, won the day, and he presently looked up more calmly, and observed shortly that he thought perhaps the matter could be arranged.

"There are other and pleasanter methods," Dr. Silence went on to explain, "but they require time and preparation, and things have gone much too far, in my opinion, to admit of delay. And the process need cause you no distress: we sit round the bowl and await results. Nothing more. The emanations of blood—which, as Levi says, is the first incarnation of the universal fluid—furnish the materials out of which the creatures of discarnate life, spirits if you prefer, can fashion themselves a temporary appearance. The process is old, and lies at the root of all blood sacrifice. It was known to the priests of Baal, and it is known to the modern ecstasy dancers who cut themselves to produce objective phantoms who dance with them. And the least gifted clairvoyant could tell you that the forms to be seen in the vicinity of slaughter-houses, or hovering above the deserted battlefields, are—well, simply beyond all description. I do not mean," he added, noticing the uneasy fidgeting of his host, "that anything in our laundry-experiment need appear to terrify us, for this case seems a comparatively simple one, and it is only the vindictive character of the intelligence directing this fire-elemental that causes anxiety and makes for personal danger."

"It is curious," said the Colonel, with a sudden rush of words, drawing a deep breath, and as though speaking of things distasteful to him, "that during my years among the Hill Tribes of Northern India I came across—personally came across—instances of the sacrifices of blood to certain deities being stopped suddenly, and all manner of disasters happening until they were resumed. Fires broke out in the huts, and even on the clothes, of the natives—and—and I admit I have read, in the course of my studies,"—he made a gesture toward his books and heavily laden table, —"of the Yezidis of Syria evoking phantoms by means of cutting their bodies with knives during their whirling dances—enormous globes of fire which turned into monstrous and terrible forms—and I remember an account somewhere, too, how the emaciated forms and pallid countenances of the spectres, that appeared to the Emperor Julian, claimed to be the true Immortals, and told him to renew the sacrifices of blood 'for the fumes of which, since the establishment of Christianity, they had been pining'— that these were in reality the phantoms evoked by the rites of blood."

Both Dr. Silence and myself listened in amazement, for this sudden speech was so unexpected, and betrayed so much more knowledge than we had either of us suspected in the old soldier.

"Then perhaps you have read, too," said the doctor, "how the Cosmic Deities of savage races, elemental in their nature, have been kept alive through many ages by these blood rites?"

"No," he answered; "that is new to me."

"In any case," Dr. Silence added, "I am glad you are not wholly unfamiliar with the subject, for you will now bring more sympathy, and therefore more help, to our experiment. For, of course, in this case, we only want the blood to tempt the creature from its lair and enclose it in a form—"

"I quite understand. And I only hesitated just now," he went on, his words coming much more slowly, as though he felt he had already said too much, "because I wished to be quite sure it was no mere curiosity, but an actual sense of necessity that dictated this horrible experiment."

"It is your safety, and that of your household, and of your sister, that is at stake," replied the doctor. "Once I have *seen*, I hope to discover whence this elemental comes, and what its real purpose is."

Colonel Wragge signified his assent with a bow.

"And the moon will help us," the other said, "for it will be full in the early hours of the morning, and this kind of elemental-being is always most active at the period of full moon. Hence, you see, the clue furnished by your diary."

So it was finally settled. Colonel Wragge would provide the materials for the experiment, and we were to meet at midnight. How he would contrive at that hour—but that was his business. I only know we both realised that he would keep his word, and whether a pig died at midnight, or at noon, was after all perhaps only a question of the sleep and personal comfort of the executioner.

"Tonight, then, in the laundry," said Dr. Silence finally, to clinch the plan; "we three alone—and at midnight, when the household is asleep and we shall be free from disturbance."

He exchanged significant glances with our host, who, at that moment, was called away by the announcement that the family doctor had arrived, and was ready to see him in his sister's room.

For the remainder of the afternoon John Silence disappeared. I had my suspicions that he made a secret visit to the plantation and also to the laundry building; but, in any case, we saw nothing of him, and he kept strictly to himself. He was preparing for the night, I felt sure, but the nature of his preparations I could only guess. There was movement in his room, I heard, and an odour like incense hung about the door, and knowing that he regarded rites as the vehicles of energies, my guesses were probably not far wrong.

Colonel Wragge, too, remained absent the greater part of the afternoon, and, deeply afflicted, had scarcely left his sister's bedside, but in response to my inquiry when we met for a moment at tea-time, he told me that although she had moments of attempted speech, her talk was quite incoherent and hysterical, and she was still quite unable to explain the nature of what she had seen. The doctor, he said, feared she had recovered the use of her limbs, only to lose that of her memory, and perhaps even of her mind.

"Then the recovery of her legs, I trust, may be permanent, at any rate,"

I ventured, finding it difficult to know what sympathy to offer. And he replied with a curious short laugh, "Oh yes; about that there can be no doubt whatever."

And it was due merely to the chance of my overhearing a fragment of conversation—unwillingly, of course—that a little further light was thrown upon the state in which the old lady actually lay. For, as I came out of my room, it happened that Colonel Wragge and the doctor were going downstairs together, and their words floated up to my ears before I could make my presence known by so much as a cough.

"Then you must find a way," the doctor was saying with decision; "for I cannot insist too strongly upon that—and at all costs she must be kept quiet. These attempts to go out must be prevented—if necessary, by force. This desire to visit some wood or other she keeps talking about is, of course, hysterical in nature. It cannot be permitted for a moment."

"It shall not be permitted," I heard the soldier reply, as they reached the hall below.

"It has impressed her mind for some reason—" the doctor went on, by way evidently of soothing explanation, and then the distance made it impossible for me to hear more.

At dinner Dr. Silence was still absent, on the public plea of a headache, and though food was sent to his room, I am inclined to believe he did not touch it, but spent the entire time fasting.

We retired early, desiring that the household should do likewise, and I must confess that at ten o'clock when I bid my host a temporary goodnight, and sought my room to make what mental preparation I could, I realised in no very pleasant fashion that it was a singular and formidable assignation, this midnight meeting in the laundry building, and that there were moments in every adventure of life when a wise man, and one who knew his own limitations, owed it to his dignity to withdraw discreetly. And, but for the character of our leader, I probably should have then and there offered the best excuse I could think of, and have allowed myself quietly to fall asleep and wait for an exciting story in the morning of what had happened. But with a man like John Silence, such a lapse was out of the question, and I sat before my fire counting the minutes and doing everything I could think of to fortify my resolution and fasten my will at the point where I could be reasonably sure that my self-control would hold against all attacks of men, devils, or elementals.

III

At a quarter before midnight, clad in a heavy ulster, and with slippered feet, I crept cautiously from my room and stole down the passage to the top of the stairs. Outside the doctor's door I waited a moment to listen. All was still; the house in utter darkness; no gleam of light beneath any door; only, down the length of the corridor, from the direction of the sick-room, came faint sounds of laughter and incoherent talk that were not things to reassure a mind already half a-tremble, and I made haste to reach the hall and let myself out through the front door into the night.

The air was keen and frosty, perfumed with night smells, and exquisitely fresh; all the million candles of the sky were alight, and a faint breeze rose and fell with far-away sighings in the tops of the pine trees. My blood leaped for a moment in the spaciousness of the night, for the splendid stars brought courage; but the next instant, as I turned the corner of the house, moving stealthily down the gravel drive, my spirits sank again ominously. For, yonder, over the funereal plumes of the Twelve Acre Plantation, I saw the broken, yellow disc of the half-moon just rising in the east, staring down like some vast Being come to watch upon the progress of our doom. Seen through the distorting vapours of the earth's atmosphere, her face looked weirdly unfamiliar, her usual expression of benignant vacancy somehow a-twist. I slipped along by the shadows of the wall, keeping my eyes upon the ground.

The laundry-house, as already described, stood detached from the other offices, with laurel shrubberies crowding thickly behind it, and the kitchen-garden so close on the other side that the strong smells of soil and growing things came across almost heavily. The shadows of the haunted plantation, hugely lengthened by the rising moon behind them, reached to the very walls and covered the stone tiles of the roof with a dark pall. So keenly were my senses alert at this moment that I believe I could fill a chapter with the endless small details of the impression I received—shadows, odour, shapes, sounds—in the space of the few seconds I stood and waited before the closed wooden door.

Then I became aware of some one moving towards me through the moonlight, and the figure of John Silence, without overcoat and bare-headed, came quickly and without noise to join me. His eyes, I saw at once, were wonderfully bright, and so marked was the shining pallor of his face that I could hardly tell when he passed from the moonlight into the shade.

He passed without a word, beckoning me to follow, and then pushed the door open, and went in.

The chill air of the place met us like that of an underground vault; and the brick floor and whitewashed walls, streaked with damp and smoke, threw back the cold in our faces. Directly opposite gaped the black throat of the huge open fireplace, the ashes of wood fires still piled and scattered about the hearth, and on either side of the projecting chimney-column were the deep recesses holding the big twin cauldrons for boiling clothes. Upon the lids of these cauldrons stood the two little oil lamps, shaded red, which gave all the light there was, and immediately in front of the fireplace there was a small circular table with three chairs set about it. Overhead, the narrow slit windows, high up the walls, pointed to a dim network of wooden rafters half lost among the shadows, and then came the dark vault of the roof. Cheerless and unalluring, for all the red light, it certainly was, reminding me of some unused conventicle, bare of pews or pulpit, ugly and severe, and I was forcibly struck by the contrast between the normal uses to which the place was ordinarily put, and the strange and mediæval purpose which had brought us under its roof tonight.

Possibly an involuntary shudder ran over me, for my companion turned with a confident look to reassure me, and he was so completely master of himself that I at once absorbed from his abundance, and felt the chinks of my failing courage beginning to close up. To meet his eye in the presence of danger was like finding a mental railing that guided and supported thought along the giddy edges of alarm.

"I am quite ready," I whispered, turning to listen for approaching footsteps.

He nodded, still keeping his eyes on mine. Our whispers sounded hollow as they echoed overhead among the rafters.

"I'm glad you are here," he said. "Not all would have the courage. Keep your thoughts controlled, and imagine the protective shell round you—round your *inner* being."

"I'm all right," I repeated, cursing my chattering teeth.

He took my hand and shook it, and the contact seemed to shake into me something of his supreme confidence. The eyes and hands of a strong man can touch the soul. I think he guessed my thought, for a passing smile flashed about the corners of his mouth.

"You will feel more comfortable," he said, in a low tone, "when the chain is complete. The Colonel we can count on, of course. Remember, though," he added warningly, "he may perhaps become controlled—possessed—when the thing comes, because he won't know how to resist. And to explain the business to such a man—!" He shrugged his shoulders expressively. "But it will only be temporary, and I will see that no harm comes to him."

He glanced round at the arrangements with approval.

"Red light," he said, indicating the shaded lamps, "has the lowest rate of vibration. Materialisations are dissipated by strong light—won't form, or hold together—in rapid vibrations."

I was not sure that I approved altogether of this dim light, for in complete darkness there is something protective—the knowledge that one cannot be seen, probably—which a half-light destroys, but I remembered the warning to keep my thoughts steady, and forbore to give them expression.

There was a step outside, and the figure of Colonel Wragge stood in the doorway. Though entering on tiptoe, he made considerable noise and clatter, for his free movements were impeded by the burden he carried, and we saw a large yellowish bowl held out at arms' length from his body, the mouth covered with a white cloth. His face, I noted, was rigidly composed. He, too, was master of himself. And, as I thought of this old soldier moving through the long series of alarms, worn with watching and wearied with assault, unenlightened yet undismayed, even down to the dreadful shock of his sister's terror, and still showing the dogged pluck that persists in the face of defeat, I understood what Dr. Silence meant when he described him as a man "to be counted on."

I think there was nothing beyond this rigidity of his stern features, and a certain greyness of the complexion, to betray the turmoil of the emotions that were doubtless going on within; and the quality of these two men, each in his own way, so keyed me up that, by the time the door was shut and we had exchanged silent greetings, all the latent courage I possessed was well to the fore, and I felt as sure of myself as I knew I ever could feel.

Colonel Wragge set the bowl carefully in the centre of the table.

"Midnight," he said shortly, glancing at his watch, and we all three moved to our chairs.

There, in the middle of that cold and silent place, we sat, with the vile bowl before us, and a thin, hardly perceptible steam rising through the damp air from the surface of the white cloth and disappearing upwards the moment it passed beyond the zone of red light and entered the deep shadows thrown forward by the projecting wall of chimney.

The doctor had indicated our respective places, and I found myself seated with my back to the door and opposite the black hearth. The Colonel was on my left, and Dr. Silence on my right, both half facing me, the latter more in shadow than the former. We thus divided the little table into even sections, and sitting back in our chairs we awaited events in silence.

For something like an hour I do not think there was even the faintest sound within those four walls and under the canopy of that vaulted roof. Our slippers made no scratching on the gritty floor, and our breathing was suppressed almost to nothing; even the rustle of our clothes as we shifted from time to time upon our seats was inaudible. Silence smothered us absolutely—the silence of night, of listening, the silence of a haunted expectancy. The very gurgling of the lamps was too soft to be heard, and if light itself had sound, I do not think we should have noticed the silvery tread of the moonlight as it entered the high narrow windows and threw upon the floor the slender traces of its pallid footsteps.

Colonel Wragge and the doctor, and myself too for that matter, sat thus like figures of stone, without speech and without gesture. My eyes passed in ceaseless journeys from the bowl to their faces, and from their faces to the bowl. They might have been masks, however, for all the signs of life they gave; and the light steaming from the horrid contents beneath the white cloth had long ceased to be visible.

Then presently, as the moon rose higher, the wind rose with it. It sighed, like the lightest of passing wings, over the roof; it crept most softly round the walls; it made the brick floor like ice beneath our feet. With it I saw mentally the desolate moorland flowing like a sea about the old house, the treeless expanse of lonely hills, the nearer copses, sombre and mysterious in the night. *The* plantation, too, in particular I saw, and imagined I heard the mournful whisperings that must now be a-stirring among its tree-tops as the breeze played down between the twisted stems. In the depth of the room behind us the shafts of moonlight met and crossed in a growing network.

It was after an hour of this wearing and unbroken attention, and I should judge about one o'clock in the morning, when the baying of the dogs in the stableyard first began, and I saw John Silence move suddenly in his chair and sit up in an attitude of attention. Every force in my being instantly leaped into the keenest vigilance. Colonel Wragge moved too, though slowly, and without raising his eyes from the table before him.

The doctor stretched his arm out and took the white cloth from the bowl.

It was perhaps imagination that persuaded me the red glare of the lamps grew fainter and the air over the table before us thickened. I had been expecting something for so long that the movement of my companions, and the lifting of the cloth, may easily have caused the momentary delusion that something hovered in the air before my face, touching the skin of my cheeks with a silken run. But it was certainly not a delusion that the Colonel looked up at the same moment and glanced over his shoulder, as though his eyes followed the movements of something to and fro about the room, and that he then buttoned his overcoat more tightly about him and his eyes sought my own face first, and then the doctor's. And it was no delusion that his face seemed somehow to have turned dark, become spread as it were with a shadowy blackness. I saw his lips tighten and his expression grow hard and stern, and it came to me then with a rush that, of course, this man had told us but a part of the experiences he had been through in the house, and that there was much more he had never been able to bring himself to reveal at all. I felt sure of it. The way he turned and stared about him betrayed a familiarity with other things than those he had described to us. It was not merely a sight of fire he looked for; it was a sight of something alive, intelligent, something able to evade his searching; it was a *person*. It was the watch for the ancient Being who sought to obsess him.

And the way in which Dr. Silence answered his look— though it was only by a glance of subtlest sympathy—confirmed my impression.

"We may be ready now," I heard him say in a whisper, and I understood that his words were intended as a steadying warning, and braced myself mentally to the utmost of my power.

Yet long before Colonel Wragge had turned to stare about the room, and long before the doctor had confirmed my impression that things were at last beginning to stir, I had become aware in most singular fashion that the place held more than our three selves. With the rising of the wind this increase to our numbers had first taken place. The baying of the hounds almost seemed to have signalled it. I cannot say how it may be possible to realise that an empty place has suddenly become—not empty, when the new arrival is nothing that appeals to any one of the senses; for this recognition of an "invisible," as of the change in the balance of personal forces in a human group, is indefinable and beyond proof. Yet it is unmistakable. And I knew perfectly well at what given moment the atmosphere within these four walls became charged with the presence of other living beings besides ourselves. And, on reflection, I am convinced that both my companions knew it too.

"Watch the light," said the doctor under his breath, and then I knew too that it was no fancy of my own that had turned the air darker, and the way he turned to examine the face of our host sent an electric thrill of wonder and expectancy shivering along every nerve in my body.

Yet it was no kind of terror that I experienced, but rather a sort of mental dizziness, and a sensation as of being suspended in some remote and dreadful altitude where things might happen, indeed were about to happen, that had never before happened within the ken of man. Horror may have formed an ingredient, but it was not chiefly horror, and in no sense ghostly horror.

Uncommon thoughts kept beating on my brain like tiny hammers, soft yet persistent, seeking admission; their unbidden tide began to wash along the far fringes of my mind, the currents of unwonted sensations to rise over the remote frontiers of my consciousness. I was aware of thoughts, and the fantasies of thoughts, that I never knew before existed. Portions of my being stirred that had never stirred before, and things ancient and inexplicable rose to the surface and beckoned me to follow. I felt as though I were about to fly off, at some immense tangent, into an outer space hitherto unknown even in dreams. And so singular was the result produced upon me that I was uncommonly glad to anchor my mind, as well as my eyes, upon the masterful personality of the doctor at my side, for there, I realised, I could draw always upon the forces of sanity and safety.

With a vigorous effort of will I returned to the scene before me, and tried to focus my attention, with steadier thoughts, upon the table, and upon the silent figures seated round it. And then I saw that certain changes had come about in the place where we sat.

The patches of moonlight on the floor, I noted, had become curiously shaded; the faces of my companions opposite were not so clearly visible as before; and the forehead and cheeks of Colonel Wragge were glistening with perspiration. I realised further, that an extraordinary change had come about in the temperature of the atmosphere. The increased warmth had a painful effect, not alone on Colonel Wragge, but upon all of us. It was oppressive and unnatural. We gasped figuratively as well as actually.

"You are the first to feel it," said Dr. Silence in low tones, looking across at him. "You are in more intimate touch, of course—"

The Colonel was trembling, and appeared to be in considerable distress. His knees shook, so that the shuffling of his slippered feet became audible. He inclined his head to show that he had heard, but made no other reply. I think, even then, he was sore put to it to keep himself in hand. I knew what he was struggling against. As Dr. Silence had warned me, he was about to be obsessed, and was savagely, though vainly, resisting.

But, meanwhile, a curious and whirling sense of exhilaration began to come over me. The increasing heat was delightful, bringing a sensation of intense activity, of thoughts pouring through the mind at high speed, of vivid pictures in the brain, of fierce desires and lightning energies alive in every part of the body. I was conscious of no physical distress, such as the Colonel felt, but only of a vague feeling that it might all grow suddenly too intense—that I might be consumed—that my personality as well as my body, might become resolved into the flame of pure spirit. I began to live at a speed too intense to last. It was as if a thousand ecstasies besieged me—

"Steady!" whispered the voice of John Silence in my ear, and I looked up with a start to see that the Colonel had risen from his chair. The doctor rose too. I followed suit, and for the first time saw down into the bowl. To my amazement and horror I saw that the contents were troubled. The blood was astir with movement.

The rest of the experiment was witnessed by us standing. It came, too, with a curious suddenness. There was no more dreaming, for me at any rate.

I shall never forget the figure of Colonel Wragge standing there beside me, upright and unshaken, squarely planted on his feet, looking about him, puzzled beyond belief, yet full of a fighting anger. Framed by the white walls, the red glow of the lamps upon his streaming cheeks, his eyes glowing against the deathly pallor of his skin, breathing hard and making convulsive efforts of hands and body to keep himself under control, his whole being roused to the point of savage fighting, yet with nothing visible to get at anywhere—he stood there, immovable against odds. And the strange contrast of the pale skin and the burning face I had never seen before, or wish to see again.

But what has left an even sharper impression on my memory was the blackness that then began crawling over his face, obliterating the features, concealing their human outline, and hiding him inch by inch from view. This was my first realisation that the process of materialisation was at work. His visage became shrouded. I moved from one side to the other to keep him in view, and it was only then I understood that, properly speaking, the blackness was not upon the countenance of Colonel Wragge, but that something had inserted itself between me and him, thus screening his face with the effect of a dark veil. Something that apparently rose through the floor was passing slowly into the air above the table and above the bowl. The blood in the bowl, moreover, was considerably less than before.

And, with this change in the air before us, there came at the same time a further change, I thought, in the face of the soldier. One-half was turned towards the red lamps, while the other caught the pale illumination of the moonlight falling aslant from the high windows, so that it was difficult to estimate this change with accuracy of detail. But it seemed to me that, while the features—eyes, nose, mouth—remained the same, the life informing them had undergone some profound transformation. The signature of a new power had crept into the face and left its traces there—an expression dark, and in some unexplained way, terrible.

Then suddenly he opened his mouth and spoke, and the sound of this changed voice, deep and musical though it was, made me cold and set my heart beating with uncomfortable rapidity. The Being, as he had dreaded, was already in control of his brain, using his mouth.

"I see a blackness like the blackness of Egypt before my face," said the tones of this unknown voice that seemed half his own and half another's. "And out of this darkness they come, they come."

I gave a dreadful start. The doctor turned to look at me for an instant, and then turned to centre his attention upon the figure of our host, and I understood in some intuitive fashion that he was there to watch over the strangest contest man ever saw—to watch over and, if necessary, to protect.

"He is being controlled—possessed," he whispered to me through the shadows. His face wore a wonderful expression, half triumph, half admiration.

Even as Colonel Wragge spoke, it seemed to me that this visible darkness began to increase, pouring up thickly out of the ground by the hearth, rising up in sheets and veils, shrouding our eyes and faces. It stole up from below—an awful blackness that seemed to drink in all the radiations of light in the building, leaving nothing but the ghost of a radiance in their place. Then, out of this rising sea of shadows, issued a pale and spectral light that gradually spread itself about us, and from the heart of this light I saw the shapes of fire crowd and gather. And these were not human shapes, or the shapes of anything I recognised as alive in the world, but outlines of fire that traced globes, triangles, crosses, and the luminous bodies of various geometrical figures. They grew bright, faded, and then grew bright again with an effect almost of pulsation. They passed swiftly to and fro through the air, rising and falling, and particularly in the immediate neighbourhood of the Colonel, often gathering about his head and shoulders, and even appearing to settle upon him like giant insects of flame. They were accompanied, moreover, by a faint sound of hissing—the same sound we had heard that afternoon in the plantation.

"The fire-elementals that precede their master," the doctor said in an undertone. "Be ready."

And while this weird display of the shapes of fire alternately flashed and faded, and the hissing echoed faintly among the dim rafters overhead, we heard the awful voice issue at intervals from the lips of the afflicted soldier. It was a voice of power, splendid in some way I cannot describe, and with a certain sense of majesty in its cadences, and, as I listened to it with quickly beating heart, I could fancy it was some ancient voice of Time itself, echoing down immense corridors of stone, from the depths of vast temples, from the very heart of mountain tombs.

"I have seen my divine Father, Osiris," thundered the great tones. "I have scattered the gloom of the night. I have burst through the earth, and am one with the starry Deities!"

Something grand came into the soldier's face. He was staring fixedly before him, as though seeing nothing.

"Watch," whispered Dr. Silence in my ear, and his whisper seemed to come from very far away.

Again the mouth opened and the awesome voice issued forth.

"Thoth," it boomed, "has loosened the bandages of Set which fettered my mouth. I have taken my place in the great winds of heaven."

I heard the little wind of night, with its mournful voice of ages, sighing round the walls and over the roof.

"Listen!" came from the doctor at my side, and the thunder of the voice continued—

"I have hidden myself with you, O ye stars that never diminish. I remember my name—in—the—House—of—Fire!"

The voice ceased and the sound died away. Something about the face and figure of Colonel Wragge relaxed, I thought. The terrible look passed from his face. The Being that obsessed him was gone.

"The great Ritual," said Dr. Silence aside to me, very low, "the Book of the Dead. Now it's leaving him. Soon the blood will fashion it a body."

Colonel Wragge, who had stood absolutely motionless all this time, suddenly swayed, so that I thought he was going to fall, —and, but for the quick support of the doctor's arm, he probably would have fallen, for he staggered as in the beginning of collapse.

"I am drunk with the wine of Osiris," he cried, —and it was half with his own voice this time—"but Horus, the Eternal Watcher, is about my path—for—safety." The voice dwindled and failed, dying away into something almost like a cry of distress.

"Now, watch closely," said Dr. Silence, speaking loud, "for after the cry will come the Fire!"

I began to tremble involuntarily; an awful change had come without warning into the air; my legs grew weak as paper beneath my weight and I had to support myself by leaning on the table. Colonel Wragge, I saw, was also leaning forward with a kind of droop. The shapes of fire had vanished all, but his face was lit by the red lamps and the pale, shifting moonlight rose behind him like mist.

We were both gazing at the bowl, now almost empty; the Colonel stooped so low I feared every minute he would lose his balance and drop into it; and the shadow, that had so long been in process of forming, now at length began to assume material outline in the air before us.

Then John Silence moved forward quickly. He took his place between us and the shadow. Erect, formidable, absolute master of the situation, I saw him stand there, his face calm and almost smiling, and fire in his eyes. His protective influence was astounding and incalculable. Even the abhorrent dread I felt at the sight of the creature growing into life and substance before us, lessened in some way so that I was able to keep my eyes fixed on the air above the bowl without too vivid a terror.

But as it took shape, rising out of nothing as it were, and growing momentarily more defined in outline, a period of utter and wonderful silence settled down upon the building and all it contained. A hush of ages, like the sudden centre of peace at the heart of the travelling cyclone, descended through the night, and out of this hush, as out of the emanations of the steaming blood, issued the form of the ancient being who had first sent the elemental of fire upon its mission. It grew and darkened and so-lidified before our eyes. It rose from just beyond the table so that the lower portions remained invisible, but I saw the outline limn itself upon the air, as though slowly revealed by the rising of a curtain. It apparently had not then quite concentrated to the normal proportions, but was spread out on all sides into space, huge, though rapidly condensing, for I saw the colossal shoulders, the neck, the lower portion of the dark jaws, the terrible mouth, and then the teeth and lips—and, as the veil seemed to lift further upon the tremendous face—I saw the nose and cheek bones. In another moment I should have looked straight into the eyes—

But what Dr. Silence did at that moment was so unexpected, and took me so by surprise, that I have never yet properly understood its nature, and he has never yet seen fit to explain in detail to me. He uttered some sound that had a note of command in it—and, in so doing, stepped forward and intervened between me and the face. The figure, just nearing completeness, he therefore hid from my sight—and I have always thought purposely hid from my sight.

"The fire!" he cried out. "The fire! Beware!"

There was a sudden roar as of flame from the very mouth of the pit, and for the space of a single second all grew light as day. A blinding flash passed across my face, and there was heat for an instant that seemed to shrivel skin, and flesh, and bone. Then came steps, and I heard Colonel Wragge utter a great cry, wilder than any human cry I have ever known. The heat sucked all the breath out of my lungs with a rush, and the blaze of light, as it vanished, swept my vision with it into enveloping darkness.

When I recovered the use of my senses a few moments later I saw that Colonel Wragge with a face of death, its whiteness strangely stained, had moved closer to me. Dr. Silence stood beside him, an expression of triumph and success in his eyes. The next minute the soldier tried to clutch me with his hand. Then he reeled, staggered, and, unable to save himself, fell with a great crash upon the brick floor.

After the sheet of flame, a wind raged round the building as though it would lift the roof off, but then passed as suddenly as it came. And in the intense calm that followed I saw that the form had vanished, and the doctor was stooping over Colonel Wragge upon the floor, trying to lift him to a sitting position.

"Light," he said quietly, "more light. Take the shades off."

Colonel Wragge sat up and the glare of the unshaded lamps fell upon his face. It was grey and drawn, still running heat, and there was a look in the eyes and about the corners of the mouth that seemed in this short space of time to have added years to its age. At the same time, the expression of effort and anxiety had left it. It showed relief.

"Gone!" he said, looking up at the doctor in a dazed fashion, and struggling to his feet. "Thank God! it's gone at last." He stared round the laundry as though to find out where he was. "Did it control me—take possession of me? Did I talk nonsense?" he asked bluntly. "After the heat came, I remember nothing—"

"You'll feel yourself again in a few minutes," the doctor said. To my infinite horror I saw that he was surreptitiously wiping sundry dark stains from the face. "Our experiment has been a success and—"

He gave me a swift glance to hide the bowl, standing between me and our host while I hurriedly stuffed it down under the lid of the nearest cauldron.

"—and none of us the worse for it," he finished.

"And fires?" he asked, still dazed, "there'll be no more fires?"

"It is dissipated—partly, at any rate," replied Dr. Silence cautiously. "And the man behind the gun," he went on, only half realising what he was saying, I think; "have you discovered *that?*"

"A form materialised," said the doctor briefly. "I know for certain now what the directing intelligence was behind it all."

Colonel Wragge pulled himself together and got upon his feet. The words conveyed no clear meaning to him yet. But his memory was returning gradually, and he was trying to piece together the fragments into a connected whole. He shivered a little, for the place had grown suddenly chilly. The air was empty again, lifeless.

"You feel all right again now," Dr. Silence said, in the tone of a man stating a fact rather than asking a question.

"Thanks to you—both, yes." He drew a deep breath, and mopped his face, and even attempted a smile. He made me think of a man coming from the battlefield with the stains of fighting still upon him, but scornful of his wounds. Then he turned gravely towards the doctor with a question in his eyes. Memory had returned and he was himself again.

"Precisely what I expected," the doctor said calmly; "a fire-elemental sent upon its mission in the days of Thebes, centuries before Christ, and tonight, for the first time all these thousands of years, released from the spell that originally bound it."

We stared at him in amazement, Colonel Wragge opening his lips for words that refused to shape themselves.

"And, if we dig," he continued significantly, pointing to the floor where the blackness had poured up, "we shall find some underground connection—a tunnel most likely—leading to the Twelve Acre Wood. It was made by—your predecessor."

"A tunnel made by my brother!" gasped the soldier. "Then my sister should know—she lived here with him—" He stopped suddenly.

John Silence inclined his head slowly. "I think so," he said quietly. "Your brother, no doubt, was as much tormented as you have been," he continued after a pause in which Colonel Wragge seemed deeply preoccupied with his thoughts, "and tried to find peace by burying it in the wood, and surrounding the wood then, like a large magic circle, with the enchantments of the old formulæ. So the stars the man saw blazing—"

"But burying *what?*" asked the soldier faintly, stepping backwards towards the support of the wall.

Dr. Silence regarded us both intently for a moment before he replied. I think he weighed in his mind whether to tell us now, or when the investigation was absolutely complete.

"The mummy," he said softly, after a moment; "the mummy that your brother took from its resting place of centuries, and brought home—here."

Colonel Wragge dropped down upon the nearest chair, hanging breathlessly on every word. He was far too amazed for speech.

"The mummy of some important person—a priest most likely—protected from disturbance and desecration by the ceremonial magic of the time. For they understood how to attach to the mummy, to lock up with it in the tomb, an elemental force that would direct itself even after ages upon any one who dared to molest it. In this case it was an elemental of fire."

Dr. Silence crossed the floor and turned out the lamps one by one. He had nothing more to say for the moment. Following his example, I folded the table together and took up the chairs, and our host, still dazed and silent, mechanically obeyed him and moved to the door.

We removed all traces of the experiment, taking the empty bowl back to the house concealed beneath an ulster.

The air was cool and fragrant as we walked to the house, the stars beginning to fade overhead and a fresh wind of early morning blowing up out of the east where the sky was already hinting of the coming day. It was after five o'clock.

Stealthily we entered the front hall and locked the door, and as we went on tiptoe upstairs to our rooms, the Colonel, peering at us over his candle as he nodded good-night, whispered that if we were ready the digging should be begun that very day.

Then I saw him steal along to his sister's room and disappear.

IV

But not even the mysterious references to the mummy, or the prospect of a revelation by digging, were able to hinder the reaction that followed the intense excitement of the past twelve hours, and I slept the sleep of the dead, dreamless and undisturbed. A touch on the shoulder woke me, and I saw Dr. Silence standing beside the bed, dressed to go out.

"Come," he said, "it's tea-time. You've slept the best part of a dozen hours."

I sprang up and made a hurried toilet, while my companion sat and talked. He looked fresh and rested, and his manner was even quieter than usual.

"Colonel Wragge has provided spades and pickaxes. We're going out to unearth this mummy at once," he said; "and there's no reason we should not get away by the morning train."

"I'm ready to go tonight, if you are," I said honestly.

But Dr. Silence shook his head.

"I must see this through to the end," he said gravely, and in a tone that made me think he still anticipated serious things, perhaps. He went on talking while I dressed.

"This case is really typical of all stories of mummy-haunting, and none of them are cases to trifle with," he explained, "for the mummies of important people—kings, priests, magicians—were laid away with profoundly significant ceremonial, and were very effectively protected, as you have seen, against desecration, and especially against destruction.

"The general belief," he went on, anticipating my questions, "held, of course, that the perpetuity of the mummy guaranteed that of its Ka, —the owner's spirit, —but it is not improbable that the magical embalming was also used to retard reincarnation, the preservation of the body preventing the return of the spirit to the toil and discipline of earth-life; and, in any case, they knew how to attach powerful guardian-forces to keep off trespassers. And any one who dared to remove the mummy, or especially to unwind it—well," he added, with meaning, "you have seen—and you *will* see."

I caught his face in the mirror while I struggled with my collar. It was deeply serious. There could be no question that he spoke of what he believed and knew.

"The traveller-brother who brought it here must have been haunted too," he continued, "for he tried to banish it by burial in the wood, making a magic circle to enclose it. Something of genuine ceremonial he must have known, for the stars the man saw were of course the remains of the still flaming pentagrams he traced at intervals in the circle. Only he did not know enough, or possibly was ignorant that the mummy's guardian was a fire-force. Fire cannot be enclosed by fire, though, as you saw, it can be released by it."

"Then that awful figure in the laundry?" I asked, thrilled to find him so communicative.

"Undoubtedly the actual Ka of the mummy operating always behind its agent, the elemental, and most likely thousands of years old."

"And Miss Wragge—?" I ventured once more.

"Ah, Miss Wragge," he repeated with increased gravity, "Miss Wragge—"

A knock at the door brought a servant with word that tea was ready, and the Colonel had sent to ask if we were coming down. The thread was broken. Dr. Silence moved to the door and signed to me to follow. But his manner told me that in any case no real answer would have been forthcoming to my question.

"And the place to dig in," I asked, unable to restrain my curiosity, "will you find it by some process of divination or—?"

He paused at the door and looked back at me, and with that he left me to finish my dressing.

It was growing dark when the three of us silently made our way to the Twelve Acre Plantation; the sky was overcast, and a black wind came out of the east. Gloom hung about the old house and the air seemed full of sighings. We found the tools ready laid at the edge of the wood, and each shouldering his piece, we followed our leader at once in among the trees. He went straight forward for some twenty yards and then stopped. At his feet lay the blackened circle of one of the burned places. It was just discernible against the surrounding white grass.

"There are three of these," he said, "and they all lie in a line with one another. Any one of them will tap the tunnel that connects the laundry— the former Museum—with the chamber where the mummy now lies buried."

He at once cleared away the burnt grass and began to dig; we all began to dig. While I used the pick, the others shovelled vigorously. No one spoke. Colonel Wragge worked the hardest of the three. The soil was light and sandy, and there were only a few snake-like roots and occasional loose stones to delay us. The pick made short work of these. And meanwhile the darkness settled about us and the biting wind swept roaring through the trees overhead.

Then, quite suddenly, without a cry, Colonel Wragge disappeared up to his neck.

"The tunnel!" cried the doctor, helping to drag him out, red, breathless, and covered with sand and perspiration. "Now, let me lead the way." And he slipped down nimbly into the hole, so that a moment later we heard his voice, muffled by sand and distance, rising up to us.

"Hubbard, you come next, and then Colonel Wragge—if he wishes," we heard.

"I'll follow you, of course," he said, looking at me as I scrambled in.

The hole was bigger now, and I got down on all-fours in a channel not much bigger than a large sewer-pipe and found myself in total darkness. A minute later a heavy thud, followed by a cataract of loose sand, announced the arrival of the Colonel.

"Catch hold of my heel," called Dr. Silence, "and Colonel Wragge can take yours."

In this slow, laborious fashion we wormed our way along a tunnel that had been roughly dug out of the shifting sand, and was shored up clumsily by means of wooden pillars and posts. Any moment, it seemed to me, we might be buried alive. We could not see an inch before our eyes, but had to grope our way feeling the pillars and the walls. It was difficult to breathe, and the Colonel behind me made but slow progress, for the cramped position of our bodies was very severe.

We had travelled in this way for ten minutes, and gone perhaps as much as ten yards, when I lost my grasp of the doctor's heel.

"Ah!" I heard his voice, sounding above me somewhere. He was standing up in a clear space, and the next moment I was standing beside him. Colonel Wragge came heavily after, and he too rose up and stood. Then Dr. Silence produced his candles and we heard preparations for striking matches.

Yet even before there was light, an indefinable sensation of awe came over us all. In this hole in the sand, some three feet under ground, we stood side by side, cramped and huddled, struck suddenly with an overwhelming apprehension of something ancient, something formidable, something incalculably wonderful, that touched in each one of us a sense of the sublime and the terrible even before we could see an inch before our faces. I know not how to express in language this singular emotion that caught us here in utter darkness, touching no sense directly, it seemed, yet with the recognition that before us in the blackness of this underground night there lay something that was mighty with the mightiness of long past ages.

I felt Colonel Wragge press in closely to my side, and I understood the pressure and welcomed it. No human touch, to me at least, has ever been more eloquent.

Then the match flared, a thousand shadows fled on black wings, and I saw John Silence fumbling with the candle, his face lit up grotesquely by the flickering light below it.

I had dreaded this light, yet when it came there was apparently nothing to explain the profound sensations of dread that preceded it. We stood in a small vaulted chamber in the sand, the sides and roof shored with bars of wood, and the ground laid roughly with what seemed to be tiles. It was six feet high, so that we could all stand comfortably, and may have been ten feet long by eight feet wide. Upon the wooden pillars at the side I saw that Egyptian hieroglyphics had been rudely traced by burning.

Dr. Silence lit three candles and handed one to each of us. He placed a fourth in the sand against the wall on his right, and another to mark the entrance to the tunnel. We stood and stared about us, instinctively holding our breath.

"Empty, by God!" exclaimed Colonel Wragge. His voice trembled with excitement. And then, as his eyes rested on the ground, he added, "And footsteps—look—footsteps in the sand!"

Dr. Silence said nothing. He stooped down and began to make a search of the chamber, and as he moved, my eyes followed his crouching figure and noted the queer distorted shadows that poured over the walls and ceiling after him. Here and there thin trickles of loose sand ran fizzing down the sides. The atmosphere, heavily charged with faint yet pungent odours, lay utterly still, and the flames of the candles might have been painted on the air for all the movement they betrayed.

And, as I watched, it was almost necessary to persuade myself forcibly that I was only standing upright with difficulty in this little sand-hole of a modern garden in the south of England, for it seemed to me that I stood, as in vision, at the entrance of some vast rock-hewn Temple far, far down the river of Time. The illusion was powerful, and persisted. Granite columns, that rose to heaven, piled themselves about me, majestically up-rearing, and a roof like the sky itself spread above a line of colossal figures that moved in shadowy procession along endless and stupendous aisles. This huge and splendid fantasy, borne I knew not whence, possessed me so vividly that I was actually obliged to concentrate my attention upon the small stooping figure of the doctor, as he groped about the walls, in order to keep the eye of imagination on the scene before me.

But the limited space rendered a long search out of the question, and his footsteps, instead of shuffling through loose sand, presently struck something of a different quality that gave forth a hollow and resounding echo. He stooped to examine more closely.

He was standing exactly in the centre of the little chamber when this happened, and he at once began scraping away the sand with his feet. In less than a minute a smooth surface became visible—the surface of a wooden covering. The next thing I saw was that he had raised it and was peering down into a space below. Instantly, a strong odour of nitre and bitumen, mingled with the strange perfume of unknown and powdered aromatics, rose up from the uncovered space and filled the vault, stinging the throat and making the eyes water and smart.

"The mummy!" whispered Dr. Silence, looking up into our faces over his candle; and as he said the word I felt the soldier lurch against me, and heard his breathing in my very ear.

"The mummy!" he repeated under his breath, as we pressed forward to look.

It is difficult to say exactly why the sight should have stirred in me so prodigious an emotion of wonder and veneration, for I have had not a little to do with mummies, have unwound scores of them, and even experimented magically with not a few. But there was something in the sight of that grey and silent figure, lying in its modern box of lead and wood at the bottom of this sandy grave, swathed in the bandages of centuries and wrapped in the perfumed linen that the priests of Egypt had prayed over with their mighty enchantments thousands of years before—something in the sight of it lying there and breathing its own spice-laden atmosphere even in the darkness of its exile in this remote land, something that pierced to the very core of my being and touched that root of awe which slumbers in every man near the birth of tears and the passion of true worship.

I remember turning quickly from the Colonel, lest he should see my emotion, yet fail to understand its cause, turn and clutch John Silence by the arm, and then fall trembling to see that he, too, had lowered his head and was hiding his face in his hands.

A kind of whirling storm came over me, rising out of I know not what utter deeps of memory, and in a whiteness of vision I heard the magical old chauntings from the Book of the Dead, and saw the Gods pass by in dim procession, the mighty, immemorial Beings who were yet themselves only the personified attributes of the true Gods, the God with the Eyes of Fire, the God with the Face of Smoke. I saw again Anubis, the dog-faced deity, and the children of Horus, eternal watcher of the ages, as they swathed Osiris, the first mummy of the world, in the scented and mystic bands, and I tasted again something of the ecstasy of the justified soul as it embarked in the golden Boat of Ra, and journeyed onwards to rest in the fields of the blessed.

And then, as Dr. Silence, with infinite reverence, stooped and touched the still face, so dreadfully staring with its painted eyes, there rose again to our nostrils wave upon wave of this perfume of thousands of years, and time fled backwards like a thing of naught, showing me in haunted panorama the most wonderful dream of the whole world.

A gentle hissing became audible in the air, and the doctor moved quickly backwards. It came close to our faces and then seemed to play about the walls and ceiling.

"The last of the Fire—still waiting for its full accomplishment," he muttered; but I heard both words and hissing as things far away, for I was still busy with the journey of the soul through the Seven Halls of Death, listening for echoes of the grandest ritual ever known to men.

The earthen plates covered with hieroglyphics still lay beside the mummy, and round it, carefully arranged at the points of the compass, stood the four jars with the heads of the hawk, the jackal, the cynocephalus, and man, the jars in which were placed the hair, the nail parings, the heart, and other special portions of the body. Even the amulets, the mirror, the blue clay statues of the Ka, and the lamp with seven wicks were there. Only the sacred scarabæus was missing.

"Not only has it been torn from its ancient resting-place," I heard Dr. Silence saying in a solemn voice as he looked at Colonel Wragge with fixed gaze, "but it has been partially unwound,"—he pointed to the wrappings of the breast, —"and—the scarabæus has been removed from the throat."

The hissing, that was like the hissing of an invisible flame, had ceased; only from time to time we heard it as though it passed backwards and forwards in the tunnel; and we stood looking into each other's faces without speaking.

Presently Colonel Wragge made a great effort and braced himself. I heard the sound catch in his throat before the words actually became audible.

"My sister," he said, very low. And then there followed a long pause, broken at length by John Silence.

"It must be replaced," he said significantly.

"I knew nothing," the soldier said, forcing himself to speak the words he hated saying. "Absolutely nothing."

"It must be returned," repeated the other, "if it is not now too late. For I fear—I fear—"

Colonel Wragge made a movement of assent with his head.

"It shall be," he said.

The place was still as the grave.

I do not know what it was then that made us all three turn round with so sudden a start, for there was no sound audible to my ears, at least.

The doctor was on the point of replacing the lid over the mummy, when he straightened up as if he had been shot.

"There's something coming," said Colonel Wragge under his breath, and the doctor's eyes, peering down the small opening of the tunnel, showed me the true direction.

A distant shuffling noise became distinctly audible coming from a point about half-way down the tunnel we had so laboriously penetrated.

"It's the sand falling in," I said, though I knew it was foolish.

"No," said the Colonel calmly, in a voice that seemed to have the ring of iron, "I've heard it for some time past. It is something alive—and it is coming nearer."

He stared about him with a look of resolution that made his face almost noble. The horror in his heart was overmastering, yet he stood there prepared for anything that might come.

"There's no other way out," John Silence said.

He leaned the lid against the sand, and waited. I knew by the masklike expression of his face, the pallor, and the steadiness of the eyes, that he anticipated something that might be very terrible—appalling.

The Colonel and myself stood on either side of the opening. I still held my candle and was ashamed of the way it shook, dripping the grease all over me; but the soldier had set his into the sand just behind his feet.

Thoughts of being buried alive, of being smothered like rats in a trap, of being caught and done to death by some invisible and merciless force we could not grapple with, rushed into my mind. Then I thought of fire—of suffocation—of being roasted alive. The perspiration began to pour from my face.

"Steady!" came the voice of Dr. Silence to me through the vault.

For five minutes, that seemed fifty, we stood waiting, looking from each other's faces to the mummy, and from the mummy to the hole, and all the time the shuffling sound, soft and stealthy, came gradually nearer. The tension, for me at least, was very near the breaking point when at last the cause of the disturbance reached the edge. It was hidden for a moment just behind the broken rim of soil. A jet of sand, shaken by the close vibration, trickled down on to the ground; I have never in my life seen anything fall with such laborious leisure. The next second, uttering a cry of curious quality, it came into view.

And it was far more distressingly horrible than anything I had anticipated.

For the sight of some Egyptian monster, some god of the tombs, or even of some demon of fire, I think I was already half prepared; but when, instead, I saw the white visage of Miss Wragge framed in that round opening of sand, followed by her body crawling on all-fours, her eyes bulging and reflecting the yellow glare of the candles, my first instinct was to turn and run like a frantic animal seeking a way of escape.

But Dr. Silence, who seemed no whit surprised, caught my arm and steadied me, and we both saw the Colonel then drop upon his knees and come thus to a level with his sister. For more than a whole minute, as though struck in stone, the two faces gazed silently at each other: hers, for all the dreadful emotion in it, more like a gargoyle than anything human; and his, white and blank with an expression that was beyond either astonishment or alarm. She looked up; he looked down. It was a picture in a nightmare, and the candle, stuck in the sand close to the hole, threw upon it the glare of impromptu footlights.

Then John Silence moved forward and spoke in a voice that was very low, yet perfectly calm and natural.

"I am glad you have come," he said. "You are the one person whose presence at this moment is most required. And I hope that you may yet be in time to appease the anger of the Fire, and to bring peace again to your household, and," he added lower still so that no one heard it but myself, "safety to yourself."

And while her brother stumbled backwards, crushing a candle into the sand in his awkwardness, the old lady crawled farther into the vaulted chamber and slowly rose upon her feet.

At the sight of the wrapped figure of the mummy I was fully prepared to see her scream and faint, but on the contrary, to my complete amazement, she merely bowed her head and dropped quietly upon her knees. Then, after a pause of more than a minute, she raised her eyes to the roof and her lips began to mutter as in prayer. Her right hand, meanwhile, which had been fumbling for some time at her throat suddenly came away, and before the gaze of all of us she held it out, palm upwards, over the grey and ancient figure outstretched below. And in it we beheld glistening the green jasper of the stolen scarabæus.

Her brother, leaning heavily against the wall behind, uttered a sound that was half cry, half exclamation, but John Silence, standing directly in front of her, merely fixed his eyes on her and pointed downwards to the staring face below.

"Replace it," he said sternly, "where it belongs."

Miss Wragge was kneeling at the feet of the mummy when this happened. We three men all had our eyes riveted on what followed. Only the reader who by some remote chance may have witnessed a line of mummies, freshly laid from their tombs upon the sand, slowly stir and bend as the heat of the Egyptian sun warms their ancient bodies into the semblance of life, can form any conception of the ultimate horror we experienced when the silent figure before us moved in its grave of lead and sand. Slowly, before our eyes, it writhed, and, with a faint rustling of the immemorial cerements, rose up, and, through sightless and bandaged eyes, stared across the yellow candle-light at the woman who had violated it,

I tried to move—her brother tried to move—but the sand seemed to hold our feet. I tried to cry—her brother tried to cry—but the sand seemed to fill our lungs and throat. We could only stare—and, even so, the sand seemed to rise like a desert storm and cloud our vision....

And when I managed at length to open my eyes again, the mummy was lying once more upon its back, motionless, the shrunken and painted face upturned towards the ceiling, and the old lady had tumbled forward and was lying in the semblance of death with her head and arms upon its crumbling body.

But upon the wrappings of the throat I saw the green jasper of the sacred scarabæus shining again like a living eye.

Colonel Wragge and the doctor recovered themselves long before I did, and I found myself helping them clumsily and unintelligently to raise the frail body of the old lady, while John Silence carefully replaced the covering over the grave and scraped back the sand with his foot, while he issued brief directions.

I heard his voice as in a dream; but the journey back along that cramped tunnel, weighted by a dead woman, blinded with sand, suffocated with heat, was in no sense a dream. It took us the best part of half an hour to reach the open air. And, even then, we had to wait a considerable time for the appearance of Dr. Silence. We carried her undiscovered into the house and up to her own room.

"The mummy will cause no further disturbance," I heard Dr. Silence say to our host later that evening as we prepared to drive for the night train, "provided always," he added significantly, "that you, and yours, cause *it* no disturbance."

It was in a dream, too, that we left.

"You did not see her face, I know," he said to me as we wrapped our rugs about us in the empty compartment. And when I shook my head, quite unable to explain the instinct that had come to me not to look, he turned toward me, his face pale, and genuinely sad.

"Scorched and blasted," he whispered.

CASE IV

SECRET WORSHIP

Harris, the silk merchant, was in South Germany on his way home from a business trip when the idea came to him suddenly that he would take the mountain railway from Strassbourg and run down to revisit his old school after an interval of something more than thirty years. And it was to this chance impulse of the junior partner in Harris Brothers of St. Paul's Churchyard that John Silence owed one of the most curious cases of his whole experience, for at that very moment he happened to be tramping these same mountains with a holiday knapsack, and from different points of the compass the two men were actually converging towards the same inn.

Now, deep down in the heart that for thirty years had been concerned chiefly with the profitable buying and selling of silk, this school had left the imprint of its peculiar influence, and, though perhaps unknown to Harris, had strongly coloured the whole of his subsequent existence. It belonged to the deeply religious life of a small Protestant community (which it is unnecessary to specify), and his father had sent him there at the age of fifteen, partly because he would learn the German requisite for the conduct of the silk business, and partly because the discipline was strict, and discipline was what his soul and body needed just then more than anything else.

The life, indeed, had proved exceedingly severe, and young Harris benefited accordingly; for though corporal punishment was unknown, there was a system of mental and spiritual correction which somehow made the soul stand proudly erect to receive it, while it struck at the very root of the fault and taught the boy that his character was being cleaned and strengthened, and that he was not merely being tortured in a kind of personal revenge.

That was over thirty years ago, when he was a dreamy and impressionable youth of fifteen; and now, as the train climbed slowly up the winding mountain gorges, his mind travelled back somewhat lovingly over the intervening period, and forgotten details rose vividly again before him out of the shadows. The life there had been very wonderful, it seemed to him, in that remote mountain village, protected from the tumults of the world by the love and worship of the devout Brotherhood that ministered to the needs of some hundred boys from every country in Europe. Sharply the scenes came back to him. He smelt again the long stone corridors, the hot pinewood rooms, where the sultry hours of summer study were passed with bees droning through open windows in the sunshine, and German characters struggling in the mind with dreams of English lawns—and then the sudden awful cry of the master in German—

"Harris, stand up! You sleep!"

And he recalled the dreadful standing motionless for an hour, book in hand, while the knees felt like wax and the head grew heavier than a cannon-ball.

The very smell of the cooking came back to him—the daily Sauerkraut, the watery chocolate on Sundays, the flavour of the stringy meat served twice a week at *Mittagessen*; and he smiled to think again of the half-rations that was the punishment for speaking English. The very odour of the milk-bowls, —the hot sweet aroma that rose from the soaking peasant-bread at the six-o'clock breakfast, —came back to him pungently, and he saw the huge *Speisesaal* with the hundred boys in their school uniform, all eating sleepily in silence, gulping down the coarse bread and scalding milk in terror of the bell that would presently cut them short—and, at the far end where the masters sat, he saw the narrow slit windows with the vistas of enticing field and forest beyond.

And this, in turn, made him think of the great barnlike room on the top floor where all slept together in wooden cots, and he heard in memory the clamour of the cruel bell that woke them on winter mornings at five o'-clock and summoned them to the stone-flagged *Waschkammer*, where boys and masters alike, after scanty and icy washing, dressed in complete silence.

From this his mind passed swiftly, with vivid picture-thoughts, to other things, and with a passing shiver he remembered how the loneliness of never being alone had eaten into him, and how everything—work, meals, sleep, walks, leisure—was done with his "division" of twenty other boys and under the eyes of at least two masters. The only solitude possible was by asking for half an hour's practice in the cell-like music rooms, and Harris smiled to himself as he recalled the zeal of his violin studies.

Then, as the train puffed laboriously through the great pine forests that cover these mountains with a giant carpet of velvet, he found the pleasanter layers of memory giving up their dead, and he recalled with admiration the kindness of the masters, whom all addressed as Brother, and marvelled afresh at their devotion in burying themselves for years in such a place, only to leave it, in most cases, for the still rougher life of missionaries in the wild places of the world.

He thought once more of the still, religious atmosphere that hung over the little forest community like a veil, barring the distressful world; of the picturesque ceremonies at Easter, Christmas, and New Year; of the numerous feast-days and charming little festivals. The *Beschehr-Fest*, in particular, came back to him,—the feast of gifts at Christmas,—when the entire community paired off and gave presents, many of which had taken weeks to make or the savings of many days to purchase. And then he saw the midnight ceremony in the church at New Year, with the shining face of the *Prediger* in the pulpit,—the village preacher who, on the last night of the old year, saw in the empty gallery beyond the organ loft the faces of all who were to die in the ensuing twelve months, and who at last recognised himself among them, and, in the very middle of his sermon, passed into a state of rapt ecstasy and burst into a torrent of praise.

Thickly the memories crowded upon him. The picture of the small village dreaming its unselfish life on the mountain-tops, clean, wholesome, simple, searching vigorously for its God, and training hundreds of boys in the grand way, rose up in his mind with all the power of an obsession. He felt once more the old mystical enthusiasm, deeper than the sea and more wonderful than the stars; he heard again the winds sighing from leagues of forest over the red roofs in the moonlight; he heard the Brothers' voices talking of the things beyond this life as though they had actually experienced them in the body; and, as he sat in the jolting train, a spirit of unutterable longing passed over his seared and tired soul, stirring in the depths of him a sea of emotions that he thought had long since frozen into immobility.

And the contrast pained him, —the idealistic dreamer then, the man of business now, —so that a spirit of unworldly peace and beauty known only to the soul in meditation laid its feathered finger upon his heart, moving strangely the surface of the waters.

Harris shivered a little and looked out of the window of his empty carriage. The train had long passed Hornberg, and far below the streams tumbled in white foam down the limestone rocks. In front of him, dome upon dome of wooded mountain stood against the sky. It was October, and the air was cool and sharp, woodsmoke and damp moss exquisitely mingled in it with the subtle odours of the pines. Overhead, between the tips of the highest firs, he saw the first stars peeping, and the sky was a clean, pale amethyst that seemed exactly the colour all these memories clothed themselves with in his mind.

He leaned back in his corner and sighed. He was a heavy man, and he had not known sentiment for years; he was a big man, and it took much to move him, literally and figuratively; he was a man in whom the dreams of God that haunt the soul in youth, though overlaid by the scum that gathers in the fight for money, had not, as with the majority, utterly died the death.

He came back into this little neglected pocket of the years, where so much fine gold had collected and lain undisturbed, with all his semi-spiritual emotions aquiver; and, as he watched the mountain-tops come nearer, and smelt the forgotten odours of his boyhood, something melted on the surface of his soul and left him sensitive to a degree he had not known since, thirty years before, he had lived here with his dreams, his conflicts, and his youthful suffering.

A thrill ran through him as the train stopped with a jolt at a tiny station and he saw the name in large black lettering on the grey stone building, and below it, the number of metres it stood above the level of the sea.

"The highest point on the line!" he exclaimed. "How well I remember it—Sommerau—Summer Meadow. The very next station is mine!"

And, as the train ran downhill with brakes on and steam shut off, he put his head out of the window and one by one saw the old familiar landmarks in the dusk. They stared at him like dead faces in a dream. Queer, sharp feelings, half poignant, half sweet, stirred in his heart.

"There's the hot, white road we walked along so often with the two Brüder always at our heels," he thought; "and there, by Jove, is the turn through the forest to '*Die Galgen*,' the stone gallows where they hanged the witches in olden days!"

He smiled a little as the train slid past.

"And there's the copse where the Lilies of the Valley powdered the ground in spring; and, I swear,"—he put his head out with a sudden impulse—"if that's not the very clearing where Calame, the French boy, chased the swallow-tail with me, and Bruder Pagel gave us half-rations for leaving the road without permission, and for shouting in our mother tongues!" And he laughed again as the memories came back with a rush, flooding his mind with vivid detail.

The train stopped, and he stood on the grey gravel platform like a man in a dream. It seemed half a century since he last waited there with corded wooden boxes, and got into the train for Strassbourg and home after the two years' exile. Time dropped from him like an old garment and he felt a boy again. Only, things looked so much smaller than his memory of them; shrunk and dwindled they looked, and the distances seemed on a curiously smaller scale.

He made his way across the road to the little Gasthaus, and, as he went, faces and figures of former schoolfellows, —German, Swiss, Italian, French, Russian, —slipped out of the shadowy woods and silently accompanied him. They flitted by his side, raising their eyes questioningly, sadly, to his. But their names he had forgotten. Some of the Brothers, too, came with them, and most of these he remembered by name—Bruder Röst, Bruder Pagel, Bruder Schliemann, and the bearded face of the old preacher who had seen himself in the haunted gallery of those about to die—Bruder Gysin. The dark forest lay all about him like a sea that any moment might rush with velvet waves upon the scene and sweep all the faces away. The air was cool and wonderfully fragrant, but with every perfumed breath came also a pallid memory....

Yet, in spite of the underlying sadness inseparable from such an experience, it was all very interesting, and held a pleasure peculiarly its own, so that Harris engaged his room and ordered supper feeling well pleased with himself, and intending to walk up to the old school that very evening. It stood in the centre of the community's village, some four miles distant through the forest, and he now recollected for the first time that this little Protestant settlement dwelt isolated in a section of the country that was otherwise Catholic. Crucifixes and shrines surrounded the clearing like the sentries of a beleaguering army. Once beyond the square of the village, with its few acres of field and orchard, the forest crowded up in solid phalanxes, and beyond the rim of trees began the country that was ruled by the priests of another faith. He vaguely remembered, too, that the Catholics had showed sometimes a certain hostility towards the little Protestant oasis that flourished so quietly and benignly in their midst. He had quite forgotten this. How trumpery it all seemed now with his wide experience of life and his knowledge of other countries and the great outside world. It was like stepping back, not thirty years, but three hundred.

There were only two others besides himself at supper. One of them, a bearded, middle-aged man in tweeds, sat by himself at the far end, and Harris kept out of his way because he was English. He feared he might be in business, possibly even in the silk business, and that he would perhaps talk on the subject. The other traveller, however, was a Catholic priest. He was a little man who ate his salad with a knife, yet so gently that it was almost inoffensive, and it was the sight of "the cloth" that recalled his memory of the old antagonism. Harris mentioned by way of conversation the object of his sentimental journey, and the priest looked up sharply at him with raised eyebrows and an expression of surprise and suspicion that somehow piqued him. He ascribed it to his difference of belief.

"Yes," went on the silk merchant, pleased to talk of what his mind was so full, "and it was a curious experience for an English boy to be dropped down into a school of a hundred foreigners. I well remember the loneliness and intolerable Heimweh of it at first." His German was very fluent.

The priest opposite looked up from his cold veal and potato salad and smiled. It was a nice face. He explained quietly that he did not belong here, but was making a tour of the parishes of Württemberg and Baden.

"It was a strict life," added Harris. "We English, I remember, used to call it *Gefängnisleben*—prison life!"

The face of the other, for some unaccountable reason, darkened. After a slight pause, and more by way of politeness than because he wished to continue the subject, he said quietly—

"It was a flourishing school in those days, of course. Afterwards, I have heard—" He shrugged his shoulders slightly, and the odd look—it almost seemed a look of alarm—came back into his eyes. The sentence remained unfinished.

Something in the tone of the man seemed to his listener uncalled for— in a sense reproachful, singular. Harris bridled in spite of himself. "It has changed?" he asked. "I can hardly believe—"

"You have not heard, then?" observed the priest gently, making a gesture as though to cross himself, yet not actually completing it. "You have not heard what happened there before it was abandoned—?"

It was very childish, of course, and perhaps he was overtired and overwrought in some way, but the words and manner of the little priest seemed to him so offensive—so disproportionately offensive—that he hardly noticed the concluding sentence. He recalled the old bitterness and the old antagonism, and for a moment he almost lost his temper.

"Nonsense," he interrupted with a forced laugh, "*Unsinn!* You must forgive me, sir, for contradicting you. But I was a pupil there myself. I was at school there. There was no place like it. I cannot believe that anything serious could have happened to—to take away its character. The devotion of the Brothers would be difficult to equal anywhere—"

He broke off suddenly, realising that his voice had been raised unduly and that the man at the far end of the table might understand German; and at the same moment he looked up and saw that this individual's eyes were fixed upon his face intently. They were peculiarly bright. Also they were rather wonderful eyes, and the way they met his own served in some way he could not understand to convey both a reproach and a warning. The whole face of the stranger, indeed, made a vivid impression upon him, for it was a face, he now noticed for the first time, in whose presence one would not willingly have said or done anything unworthy. Harris could not explain to himself how it was he had not become conscious sooner of its presence.

But he could have bitten off his tongue for having so far forgotten himself. The little priest lapsed into silence. Only once he said, looking up and speaking in a low voice that was not intended to be overheard, but that evidently *was* overheard, "You will find it different." Presently he rose and left the table with a polite bow that included both the others.

And, after him, from the far end rose also the figure in the tweed suit, leaving Harris by himself.

He sat on for a bit in the darkening room, sipping his coffee and smoking his fifteen-pfennig cigar, till the girl came in to light the oil lamps. He felt vexed with himself for his lapse from good manners, yet hardly able to account for it. Most likely, he reflected, he had been annoyed because the priest had unintentionally changed the pleasant character of his dream by introducing a jarring note. Later he must seek an opportunity to make amends. At present, however, he was too impatient for his walk to the school, and he took his stick and hat and passed out into the open air.

And, as he crossed before the Gasthaus, he noticed that the priest and the man in the tweed suit were engaged already in such deep conversation that they hardly noticed him as he passed and raised his hat.

He started off briskly, well remembering the way, and hoping to reach the village in time to have a word with one of the Brüder. They might even ask him in for a cup of coffee. He felt sure of his welcome, and the old memories were in full possession once more. The hour of return was a matter of no consequence whatever.

It was then just after seven o'clock, and the October evening was drawing in with chill airs from the recesses of the forest. The road plunged straight from the railway clearing into its depths, and in a very few minutes the trees engulfed him and the clack of his boots fell dead and echoless against the serried stems of a million firs. It was very black; one trunk was hardly distinguishable from another. He walked smartly, swinging his holly stick. Once or twice he passed a peasant on his way to bed, and the guttural "Gruss Got," unheard for so long, emphasised the passage of time, while yet making it seem as nothing. A fresh group of pictures crowded his mind. Again the figures of former schoolfellows flitted out of the forest and kept pace by his side, whispering of the doings of long ago. One reverie stepped hard upon the heels of another. Every turn in the road, every clearing of the forest, he knew, and each in turn brought forgotten associations to life. He enjoyed himself thoroughly.

He marched on and on. There was powdered gold in the sky till the moon rose, and then a wind of faint silver spread silently between the earth and stars. He saw the tips of the fir trees shimmer, and heard them whisper as the breeze turned their needles towards the light. The mountain air was indescribably sweet. The road shone like the foam of a river through the gloom. White moths flitted here and there like silent thoughts across his path, and a hundred smells greeted him from the forest caverns across the years.

Then, when he least expected it, the trees fell away abruptly on both sides, and he stood on the edge of the village clearing.

He walked faster. There lay the familiar outlines of the houses, sheeted with silver; there stood the trees in the little central square with the fountain and small green lawns; there loomed the shape of the church next to the Gasthof der Brüdergemeinde; and just beyond, dimly rising into the sky, he saw with a sudden thrill the mass of the huge school building, blocked castlelike with deep shadows in the moonlight, standing square and formidable to face him after the silences of more than a quarter of a century.

He passed quickly down the deserted village street and stopped close beneath its shadow, staring up at the walls that had once held him prisoner for two years—two unbroken years of discipline and homesickness. Memories and emotions surged through his mind; for the most vivid sensations of his youth had focused about this spot, and it was here he had first begun to live and learn values. Not a single footstep broke the silence, though lights glimmered here and there through cottage windows; but when he looked up at the high walls of the school, draped now in shadow, he easily imagined that well-known faces crowded to the windows to greet him—closed windows that really reflected only moonlight and the gleam of stars.

This, then, was the old school building, standing foursquare to the world, with its shuttered windows, its lofty, tiled roof, and the spiked lightning-conductors pointing like black and taloned fingers from the corners.

For a long time he stood and stared. Then, presently, he came to himself again, and realised to his joy that a light still shone in the windows of the *Bruderstube.*

He turned from the road and passed through the iron railings; then climbed the twelve stone steps and stood facing the black wooden door with the heavy bars of iron, a door he had once loathed and dreaded with the hatred and passion of an imprisoned soul, but now looked upon tenderly with a sort of boyish delight.

Almost timorously he pulled the rope and listened with a tremor of excitement to the clanging of the bell deep within the building. And the long-forgotten sound brought the past before him with such a vivid sense of reality that he positively shivered. It was like the magic bell in the fairy-tale that rolls back the curtain of Time and summons the figures from the shadows of the dead. He had never felt so sentimental in his life. It was like being young again. And, at the same time, he began to bulk rather large in his own eyes with a certain spurious importance. He was a big man from the world of strife and action. In this little place of peaceful dreams would he, perhaps, not cut something of a figure?

"I'll try once more," he thought after a long pause, seizing the iron bell-rope, and was just about to pull it when a step sounded on the stone passage within, and the huge door slowly swung open.

A tall man with a rather severe cast of countenance stood facing him in silence.

"I must apologise—it is somewhat late," he began a trifle pompously, "but the fact is I am an old pupil. I have only just arrived and really could not restrain myself." His German seemed not quite so fluent as usual. "My interest is so great. I was here in '70."

The other opened the door wider and at once bowed him in with a smile of genuine welcome.

"I am Bruder Kalkmann," he said quietly in a deep voice. "I myself was a master here about that time. It is a great pleasure always to welcome a former pupil." He looked at him very keenly for a few seconds, and then added, "I think, too, it is splendid of you to come—very splendid."

"It is a very great pleasure," Harris replied, delighted with his reception.

The dimly lighted corridor with its flooring of grey stone, and the familiar sound of a German voice echoing through it, —with the peculiar intonation the Brothers always used in speaking, —all combined to lift him bodily, as it were, into the dream-atmosphere of long-forgotten days. He stepped gladly into the building and the door shut with the familiar thunder that completed the reconstruction of the past. He almost felt the old sense of imprisonment, of aching nostalgia, of having lost his liberty.

Harris sighed involuntarily and turned towards his host, who returned his smile faintly and then led the way down the corridor.

"The boys have retired," he explained, "and, as you remember, we keep early hours here. But, at least, you will join us for a little while in the *Bruderstube* and enjoy a cup of coffee." This was precisely what the silk merchant had hoped, and he accepted with an alacrity that he intended to be tempered by graciousness. "And tomorrow," continued the Bruder, "you must come and spend a whole day with us. You may even find acquaintances, for several pupils of your day have come back here as masters."

For one brief second there passed into the man's eyes a look that made the visitor start. But it vanished as quickly as it came. It was impossible to define. Harris convinced himself it was the effect of a shadow cast by the lamp they had just passed on the wall. He dismissed it from his mind.

"You are very kind, I'm sure," he said politely. "It is perhaps a greater pleasure to me than you can imagine to see the place again. Ah,"—he stopped short opposite a door with the upper half of glass and peered in—"surely there is one of the music rooms where I used to practise the violin. How it comes back to me after all these years!"

Bruder Kalkmann stopped indulgently, smiling, to allow his guest a moment's inspection.

"You still have the boys' orchestra? I remember I used to play *'zweite Geige'* in it. Bruder Schliemann conducted at the piano. Dear me, I can see him now with his long black hair and—and—" He stopped abruptly. Again the odd, dark look passed over the stern face of his companion. For an instant it seemed curiously familiar.

"We still keep up the pupils' orchestra," he said, "but Bruder Schliemann, I am sorry to say—" he hesitated an instant, and then added, "Bruder Schliemann is dead."

"Indeed, indeed," said Harris quickly. "I am sorry to hear it." He was conscious of a faint feeling of distress, but whether it arose from the news of his old music teacher's death, or—from something else—he could not quite determine. He gazed down the corridor that lost itself among shadows. In the street and village everything had seemed so much smaller than he remembered, but here, inside the school building, everything seemed so much bigger. The corridor was loftier and longer, more spacious and vast, than the mental picture he had preserved. His thoughts wandered dreamily for an instant.

He glanced up and saw the face of the Bruder watching him with a smile of patient indulgence.

"Your memories possess you," he observed gently, and the stern look passed into something almost pitying.

"You are right," returned the man of silk, "they do. This was the most wonderful period of my whole life in a sense. At the time I hated it—" He hesitated, not wishing to hurt the Brother's feelings.

"According to English ideas it seemed strict, of course," the other said persuasively, so that he went on.

"—Yes, partly that; and partly the ceaseless nostalgia, and the solitude which came from never being really alone. In English schools the boys enjoy peculiar freedom, you know."

Bruder Kalkmann, he saw, was listening intently.

"But it produced one result that I have never wholly lost," he continued self-consciously, "and am grateful for."

"*Ach! Wie so, denn?*"

"The constant inner pain threw me headlong into your religious life, so that the whole force of my being seemed to project itself towards the search for a deeper satisfaction—a real resting-place for the soul. During my two years here I yearned for God in my boyish way as perhaps I have never yearned for anything since. Moreover, I have never quite lost that sense of peace and inward joy which accompanied the search. I can never quite forget this school and the deep things it taught me."

He paused at the end of his long speech, and a brief silence fell between them. He feared he had said too much, or expressed himself clumsily in the foreign language, and when Bruder Kalkmann laid a hand upon his shoulder, he gave a little involuntary start.

"So that my memories perhaps do possess me rather strongly," he added apologetically; "and this long corridor, these rooms, that barred and gloomy front door, all touch chords that—that—" His German failed him and he glanced at his companion with an explanatory smile and gesture. But the Brother had removed the hand from his shoulder and was standing with his back to him, looking down the passage.

"Naturally, naturally so," he said hastily without turning round. "*Es ist doch selbstverständlich.* We shall all understand."

Then he turned suddenly, and Harris saw that his face had turned most oddly and disagreeably sinister. It may only have been the shadows again playing their tricks with the wretched oil lamps on the wall, for the dark expression passed instantly as they retraced their steps down the corridor, but the Englishman somehow got the impression that he had said something to give offence, something that was not quite to the other's taste. Opposite the door of the *Bruderstube* they stopped. Harris realised that it was late and he had possibly stayed talking too long. He made a tentative effort to leave, but his companion would not hear of it.

"You must have a cup of coffee with us," he said firmly as though he meant it, "and my colleagues will be delighted to see you. Some of them will remember you, perhaps."

The sound of voices came pleasantly through the door, men's voices talking together. Bruder Kalkmann turned the handle and they entered a room ablaze with light and full of people.

"Ah, —but your name?" he whispered, bending down to catch the reply; "you have not told me your name yet."

"Harris," said the Englishman quickly as they went in. He felt nervous as he crossed the threshold, but ascribed the momentary trepidation to the fact that he was breaking the strictest rule of the whole establishment, which forbade a boy under severest penalties to come near this holy of holies where the masters took their brief leisure.

"Ah, yes, of course—Harris," repeated the other as though he remembered it. "Come in, Herr Harris, come in, please. Your visit will be immensely appreciated. It is really very fine, very wonderful of you to have come in this way."

The door closed behind them and, in the sudden light which made his sight swim for a moment, the exaggeration of the language escaped his attention. He heard the voice of Bruder Kalkmann introducing him. He spoke very loud, indeed, unnecessarily, —absurdly loud, Harris thought.

"Brothers," he announced, "it is my pleasure and privilege to introduce to you Herr Harris from England. He has just arrived to make us a little visit, and I have already expressed to him on behalf of us all the satisfaction we feel that he is here. He was, as you remember, a pupil in the year '70."

It was a very formal, a very German introduction, but Harris rather liked it. It made him feel important and he appreciated the tact that made it almost seem as though he had been expected.

The black forms rose and bowed; Harris bowed; Kalkmann bowed. Every one was very polite and very courtly. The room swam with moving figures; the light dazzled him after the gloom of the corridor, there was thick cigar smoke in the atmosphere. He took the chair that was offered to him between two of the Brothers, and sat down, feeling vaguely that his perceptions were not quite as keen and accurate as usual. He felt a trifle dazed perhaps, and the spell of the past came strongly over him, confusing the immediate present and making everything dwindle oddly to the dimensions of long ago. He seemed to pass under the mastery of a great mood that was a composite reproduction of all the moods of his forgotten boyhood.

Then he pulled himself together with a sharp effort and entered into the conversation that had begun again to buzz round him. Moreover, he entered into it with keen pleasure, for the Brothers—there were perhaps a dozen of them in the little room—treated him with a charm of manner that speedily made him feel one of themselves. This, again, was a very subtle delight to him. He felt that he had stepped out of the greedy, vulgar, self-seeking world, the world of silk and markets and profit-making—stepped into the cleaner atmosphere where spiritual ideals were paramount and life was simple and devoted. It all charmed him inexpressibly, so that he realised—yes, in a sense—the degradation of his twenty years' absorption in business. This keen atmosphere under the stars where men thought only of their souls, and of the souls of others, was too rarefied for the world he was now associated with. He found himself making comparisons to his own disadvantage, —comparisons with the mystical little dreamer that had stepped thirty years before from the stern peace of this devout community, and the man of the world that he had since become, —and the contrast made him shiver with a keen regret and something like self-contempt.

He glanced round at the other faces floating towards him through tobacco smoke—this acrid cigar smoke he remembered so well: how keen they were, how strong, placid, touched with the nobility of great aims and unselfish purposes. At one or two he looked particularly. He hardly knew why. They rather fascinated him. There was something so very stern and uncompromising about them, and something, too, oddly, subtly, familiar, that yet just eluded him. But whenever their eyes met his own they held undeniable welcome in them; and some held more—a kind of perplexed admiration, he thought, something that was between esteem and deference. This note of respect in all the faces was very flattering to his vanity.

Coffee was served presently, made by a black-haired Brother who sat in the corner by the piano and bore a marked resemblance to Bruder Schliemann, the musical director of thirty years ago. Harris exchanged bows with him when he took the cup from his white hands, which he noticed were like the hands of a woman. He lit a cigar, offered to him by his neighbour, with whom he was chatting delightfully, and who, in the glare of the lighted match, reminded him sharply for a moment of Bruder Pagel, his former room-master.

"*Es ist wirklich merkwürdig*," he said, "how many resemblances I see, or imagine. It is really very curious!"

"Yes," replied the other, peering at him over his coffee cup, "the spell of the place is wonderfully strong. I can well understand that the old faces rise before your mind's eye—almost to the exclusion of ourselves perhaps."

They both laughed presently. It was soothing to find his mood understood and appreciated. And they passed on to talk of the mountain village, its isolation, its remoteness from worldly life, its peculiar fitness for meditation and worship, and for spiritual development—of a certain kind.

"And your coming back in this way, Herr Harris, has pleased us all so much," joined in the Bruder on his left. "We esteem you for it most highly. We honour you for it."

Harris made a deprecating gesture. "I fear, for my part, it is only a very selfish pleasure," he said a trifle unctuously.

"Not all would have had the courage," added the one who resembled Bruder Pagel.

"You mean," said Harris, a little puzzled, "the disturbing memories—?"

Bruder Pagel looked at him steadily, with unmistakable admiration and respect. "I mean that most men hold so strongly to life, and can give up so little for their beliefs," he said gravely.

The Englishman felt slightly uncomfortable. These worthy men really made too much of his sentimental journey. Besides, the talk was getting a little out of his depth. He hardly followed it.

"The worldly life still has *some* charms for me," he replied smilingly, as though to indicate that sainthood was not yet quite within his grasp.

"All the more, then, must we honour you for so freely coming," said the Brother on his left; "so unconditionally!"

A pause followed, and the silk merchant felt relieved when the conversation took a more general turn, although he noted that it never travelled very far from the subject of his visit and the wonderful situation of the lonely village for men who wished to develop their spiritual powers and practise the rites of a high worship. Others joined in, complimenting him on his knowledge of the language, making him feel utterly at his ease, yet at the same time a little uncomfortable by the excess of their admiration. After all, it was such a very small thing to do, this sentimental journey.

The time passed along quickly; the coffee was excellent, the cigars soft and of the nutty flavour he loved. At length, fearing to outstay his welcome, he rose reluctantly to take his leave. But the others would not hear of it. It was not often a former pupil returned to visit them in this simple, unaffected way. The night was young. If necessary they could even find him a corner in the great *Schlafzimmer* upstairs. He was easily persuaded to stay a little longer. Somehow he had become the centre of the little party. He felt pleased, flattered, honoured.

"And perhaps Bruder Schliemann will play something for us—now."

It was Kalkmann speaking, and Harris started visibly as he heard the name, and saw the black-haired man by the piano turn with a smile. For Schliemann was the name of his old music director, who was dead. Could this be his son? They were so exactly alike.

"If Bruder Meyer has not put his Amati to bed, I will accompany him," said the musician suggestively, looking across at a man whom Harris had not yet noticed, and who, he now saw, was the very image of a former master of that name.

Meyer rose and excused himself with a little bow, and the Englishman quickly observed that he had a peculiar gesture as though his neck had a false join on to the body just below the collar and feared it might break.

Meyer of old had this trick of movement. He remembered how the boys used to copy it.

He glanced sharply from face to face, feeling as though some silent, unseen process were changing everything about him. All the faces seemed oddly familiar. Pagel, the Brother he had been talking with, was of course the image of Pagel, his former room-master, and Kalkmann, he now realised for the first time, was the very twin of another master whose name he had quite forgotten, but whom he used to dislike intensely in the old days. And, through the smoke, peering at him from the corners of the room, he saw that all the Brothers about him had the faces he had known and lived with long ago—Röst, Fluheim, Meinert, Rigel, Gysin.

He stared hard, suddenly grown more alert, and everywhere saw, or fancied he saw, strange likenesses, ghostly resemblances, —more, the identical faces of years ago. There was something queer about it all, something not quite right, something that made him feel uneasy. He shook himself, mentally and actually, blowing the smoke from before his eyes with a long breath, and as he did so he noticed to his dismay that every one was fixedly staring. They were watching him.

This brought him to his senses. As an Englishman, and a foreigner, he did not wish to be rude, or to do anything to make himself foolishly conspicuous and spoil the harmony of the evening. He was a guest, and a privileged guest at that. Besides, the music had already begun. Bruder Schliemann's long white fingers were caressing the keys to some purpose.

He subsided into his chair and smoked with half-closed eyes that yet saw everything.

But the shudder had established itself in his being, and, whether he would or not, it kept repeating itself. As a town, far up some inland river, feels the pressure of the distant sea, so he became aware that mighty forces from somewhere beyond his ken were urging themselves up against his soul in this smoky little room. He began to feel exceedingly ill at ease.

And as the music filled the air his mind began to clear. Like a lifted veil there rose up something that had hitherto obscured his vision. The words of the priest at the railway inn flashed across his brain unbidden: "You will find it different." And also, though why he could not tell, he saw mentally the strong, rather wonderful eyes of that other guest at the supper-table, the man who had overheard his conversation, and had later got into earnest talk with the priest. He took out his watch and stole a glance at it. Two hours had slipped by. It was already eleven o'clock.

Schliemann, meanwhile, utterly absorbed in his music, was playing a solemn measure. The piano sang marvellously. The power of a great conviction, the simplicity of great art, the vital spiritual message of a soul that had found itself—all this, and more, were in the chords, and yet somehow the music was what can only be described as impure—atrociously and di-abolically impure. And the piece itself, although Harris did not recognise it as anything familiar, was surely the music of a Mass—huge, majestic, sombre? It stalked through the smoky room with slow power, like the passage of something that was mighty, yet profoundly intimate, and as it went there stirred into each and every face about him the signature of the enormous forces of which it was the audible symbol. The countenances round him turned sinister, but not idly, negatively sinister: they grew dark with purpose. He suddenly recalled the face of Bruder Kalkmann in the corridor earlier in the evening. The motives of their secret souls rose to the eyes, and mouths, and foreheads, and hung there for all to see like the black banners of an assembly of ill-starred and fallen creatures. Demons—was the horrible word that flashed through his brain like a sheet of fire.

When this sudden discovery leaped out upon him, for a moment he lost his self-control. Without waiting to think and weigh his extraordinary impression, he did a very foolish but a very natural thing. Feeling himself irresistibly driven by the sudden stress to some kind of action, he sprang to his feet—and screamed! To his own utter amazement he stood up and shrieked aloud!

But no one stirred. No one, apparently, took the slightest notice of his absurdly wild behaviour. It was almost as if no one but himself had heard the scream at all—as though the music had drowned it and swallowed it up—as though after all perhaps he had not really screamed as loudly as he imagined, or had not screamed at all.

Then, as he glanced at the motionless, dark faces before him, something of utter cold passed into his being, touching his very soul.... All emotion cooled suddenly, leaving him like a receding tide. He sat down again, ashamed, mortified, angry with himself for behaving like a fool and a boy. And the music, meanwhile, continued to issue from the white and snake-like fingers of Bruder Schliemann, as poisoned wine might issue from the weirdly fashioned necks of antique phials.

And, with the rest of them, Harris drank it in.

Forcing himself to believe that he had been the victim of some kind of illusory perception, he vigorously restrained his feelings. Then the music presently ceased, and every one applauded and began to talk at once, laughing, changing seats, complimenting the player, and behaving naturally and easily as though nothing out of the way had happened. The faces appeared normal once more. The Brothers crowded round their visitor, and he joined in their talk and even heard himself thanking the gifted musician.

But, at the same time, he found himself edging towards the door, nearer and nearer, changing his chair when possible, and joining the groups that stood closest to the way of escape.

"I must thank you all *tausendmal* for my little reception and the great pleasure—the very great honour you have done me," he began in decided tones at length, "but I fear I have trespassed far too long already on your hospitality. Moreover, I have some distance to walk to my inn."

A chorus of voices greeted his words. They would not hear of his going, —at least not without first partaking of refreshment. They produced pumpernickel from one cupboard, and rye-bread and sausage from another, and all began to talk again and eat. More coffee was made, fresh cigars lighted, and Bruder Meyer took out his violin and began to tune it softly.

"There is always a bed upstairs if Herr Harris will accept it," said one. "And it is difficult to find the way out now, for all the doors are locked," laughed another loudly.

"Let us take our simple pleasures as they come," cried a third. "Bruder Harris will understand how we appreciate the honour of this last visit of his."

They made a dozen excuses. They all laughed, as though the politeness of their words was but formal, and veiled thinly—more and more thinly— a very different meaning.

"And the hour of midnight draws near," added Bruder Kalkmann with a charming smile, but in a voice that sounded to the Englishman like the grating of iron hinges.

Their German seemed to him more and more difficult to understand. He noted that they called him "Bruder" too, classing him as one of themselves.

And then suddenly he had a flash of keener perception, and realised with a creeping of his flesh that he had all along misinterpreted—grossly misinterpreted all they had been saying. They had talked about the beauty of the place, its isolation and remoteness from the world, its peculiar fitness for certain kinds of spiritual development and worship—yet hardly, he now grasped, in the sense in which he had taken the words. They had meant something different. Their spiritual powers, their desire for loneliness, their passion for worship, were not the powers, the solitude, or the worship that he meant and understood. He was playing a part in some horrible masquerade; he was among men who cloaked their lives with religion in order to follow their real purposes unseen of men.

What did it all mean? How had he blundered into so equivocal a situation? Had he blundered into it at all? Had he not rather been led into it, deliberately led? His thoughts grew dreadfully confused, and his confidence in himself began to fade. And why, he suddenly thought again, were they so impressed by the mere fact of his coming to revisit his old school? What was it they so admired and wondered at in his simple act? Why did they set such store upon his having the courage to come, to "give himself so freely," "unconditionally" as one of them had expressed it with such a mockery of exaggeration?

Fear stirred in his heart most horribly, and he found no answer to any of his questionings. Only one thing he now understood quite clearly: it was their purpose to keep him here. They did not intend that he should go. And from this moment he realised that they were sinister, formidable and, in some way he had yet to discover, inimical to himself, inimical to his life. And the phrase one of them had used a moment ago—"this *last* visit of his"—rose before his eyes in letters of flame.

Harris was not a man of action, and had never known in all the course of his career what it meant to be in a situation of real danger. He was not necessarily a coward, though, perhaps, a man of untried nerve. He realised at last plainly that he was in a very awkward predicament indeed, and that he had to deal with men who were utterly in earnest. What their intentions were he only vaguely guessed. His mind, indeed, was too confused for definite ratiocination, and he was only able to follow blindly the strongest instincts that moved in him. It never occurred to him that the Brothers might all be mad, or that he himself might have temporarily lost his senses and be suffering under some terrible delusion. In fact, nothing occurred to him—he realised nothing—except that he meant to escape—and the quicker the better. A tremendous revulsion of feeling set in and overpowered him.

Accordingly, without further protest for the moment, he ate his pumpernickel and drank his coffee, talking meanwhile as naturally and pleasantly as he could, and when a suitable interval had passed, he rose to his feet and announced once more that he must now take his leave. He spoke very quietly, but very decidedly. No one hearing him could doubt that he meant what he said. He had got very close to the door by this time.

"I regret," he said, using his best German, and speaking to a hushed room, "that our pleasant evening must come to an end, but it is now time for me to wish you all good-night." And then, as no one said anything, he added, though with a trifle less assurance, "And I thank you all most sincerely for your hospitality."

"On the contrary," replied Kalkmann instantly, rising from his chair and ignoring the hand the Englishman had stretched out to him, "it is we who have to thank you; and we do so most gratefully and sincerely."

And at the same moment at least half a dozen of the Brothers took up their position between himself and the door.

"You are very good to say so," Harris replied as firmly as he could manage, noticing this movement out of the corner of his eye, "but really I had no conception that—my little chance visit could have afforded you so much pleasure." He moved another step nearer the door, but Bruder Schliemann came across the room quickly and stood in front of him. His attitude was uncompromising. A dark and terrible expression had come into his face.

"But it was *not* by chance that you came, Bruder Harris," he said so that all the room could hear; "surely we have not misunderstood your presence here?" He raised his black eyebrows.

"No, no," the Englishman hastened to reply, "I was—I am delighted to be here. I told you what pleasure it gave me to find myself among you. Do not misunderstand me, I beg." His voice faltered a little, and he had difficulty in finding the words. More and more, too, he had difficulty in understanding *their* words.

"Of course," interposed Bruder Kalkmann in his iron bass, "we have not misunderstood. You have come back in the spirit of true and unselfish devotion. You offer yourself freely, and we all appreciate it. It is your willingness and nobility that have so completely won our veneration and respect." A faint murmur of applause ran round the room. "What we all delight in—what our great Master will especially delight in—is the value of your spontaneous and voluntary—"

He used a word Harris did not understand. He said "*Opfer.*" The bewildered Englishman searched his brain for the translation, and searched in vain. For the life of him he could not remember what it meant. But the word, for all his inability to translate it, touched his soul with ice. It was worse, far worse, than anything he had imagined. He felt like a lost, helpless creature, and all power to fight sank out of him from that moment.

"It is magnificent to be such a willing—" added Schliemann, sidling up to him with a dreadful leer on his face. He made use of the same word— "*Opfer.*"

"God! What could it all mean?" "Offer himself!" "True spirit of devotion!" "Willing," "unselfish," "magnificent!" *Opfer, Opfer, Opfer!* What in the name of heaven did it mean, that strange, mysterious word that struck such terror into his heart?

He made a valiant effort to keep his presence of mind and hold his nerves steady. Turning, he saw that Kalkmann's face was a dead white. Kalkmann! He understood that well enough. *Kalkmann* meant "Man of Chalk": he knew that. But what did "*Opfer*" mean? That was the real key to the situation. Words poured through his disordered mind in an endless stream— unusual, rare words he had perhaps heard but once in his life—while "*Opfer,*" a word in common use, entirely escaped him. What an extraordinary mockery it all was!

Then Kalkmann, pale as death, but his face hard as iron, spoke a few low words that he did not catch, and the Brothers standing by the walls at once turned the lamps down so that the room became dim. In the half light he could only just discern their faces and movements.

"It is time," he heard Kalkmann's remorseless voice continue just behind him. "The hour of midnight is at hand. Let us prepare. He comes! He comes; Bruder Asmodelius comes!" His voice rose to a chant.

And the sound of that name, for some extraordinary reason, was terrible—utterly terrible; so that Harris shook from head to foot as he heard it. Its utterance filled the air like soft thunder, and a hush came over the whole room. Forces rose all about him, transforming the normal into the horrible, and the spirit of craven fear ran through all his being, bringing him to the verge of collapse.

Asmodelius! Asmodelius! The name was appalling. For he understood at last to whom it referred and the meaning that lay between its great syllables. At the same instant, too, he suddenly understood the meaning of that unremembered word. The import of the word *"Opfer"* flashed upon his soul like a message of death.

He thought of making a wild effort to reach the door, but the weakness of his trembling knees, and the row of black figures that stood between, dissuaded him at once. He would have screamed for help, but remembering the emptiness of the vast building, and the loneliness of the situation, he understood that no help could come that way, and he kept his lips closed. He stood still and did nothing. But he knew now what was coming.

Two of the Brothers approached and took him gently by the arm.

"Bruder Asmodelius accepts you," they whispered; "are you ready?"

Then he found his tongue and tried to speak. "But what have I to do with this Bruder Asm—Asmo—?" he stammered, a desperate rush of words crowding vainly behind the halting tongue.

The name refused to pass his lips. He could not pronounce it as they did. He could not pronounce it at all. His sense of helplessness then entered the acute stage, for this inability to speak the name produced a fresh sense of quite horrible confusion in his mind, and he became extraordinarily agitated.

"I came here for a friendly visit," he tried to say with a great effort, but, to his intense dismay, he heard his voice saying something quite different, and actually making use of that very word they had all used: "I came here as a willing *Opfer*," he heard his own voice say, "and *I am quite ready.*"

He was lost beyond all recall now! Not alone his mind, but the very muscles of his body had passed out of control. He felt that he was hovering on the confines of a phantom or demon-world, — a world in which the name they had spoken constituted the Master-name, the word of ultimate power.

What followed he heard and saw as in a nightmare.

"In the half light that veils all truth, let us prepare to worship and adore," chanted Schliemann, who had preceded him to the end of the room.

"In the mists that protect our faces before the Black Throne, let us make ready the willing victim," echoed Kalkmann in his great bass.

They raised their faces, listening expectantly, as a roaring sound, like the passing of mighty projectiles, filled the air, far, far away, very wonderful, very forbidding. The walls of the room trembled.

"He comes! He comes! He comes!" chanted the Brothers in chorus.

The sound of roaring died away, and an atmosphere of still and utter cold established itself over all. Then Kalkmann, dark and unutterably stern, turned in the dim light and faced the rest.

"Asmodelius, our *Hauptbruder*, is about us," he cried in a voice that even while it shook was yet a voice of iron; "Asmodelius is about us. Make ready."

There followed a pause in which no one stirred or spoke. A tall Brother approached the Englishman; but Kalkmann held up his hand.

"Let the eyes remain uncovered," he said, "in honour of so freely giving himself." And to his horror Harris then realised for the first time that his hands were already fastened to his sides.

The Brother retreated again silently, and in the pause that followed all the figures about him dropped to their knees, leaving him standing alone, and as they dropped, in voices hushed with mingled reverence and awe, they cried, softly, odiously, appallingly, the name of the Being whom they momentarily expected to appear.

Then, at the end of the room, where the windows seemed to have disappeared so that he saw the stars, there rose into view far up against the night sky, grand and terrible, the outline of a man. A kind of grey glory enveloped it so that it resembled a steel-cased statue, immense, imposing, horrific in its distant splendour; while, at the same time, the face was so spiritually mighty, yet so proudly, so austerely sad, that Harris felt as he stared, that the sight was more than his eyes could meet, and that in another moment the power of vision would fail him altogether, and he must sink into utter nothingness.

So remote and inaccessible hung this figure that it was impossible to gauge anything as to its size, yet at the same time so strangely close, that when the grey radiance from its mightily broken visage, august and mournful, beat down upon his soul, pulsing like some dark star with the powers of spiritual evil, he felt almost as though he were looking into a face no farther removed from him in space than the face of any one of the Brothers who stood by his side.

And then the room filled and trembled with sounds that Harris understood full well were the failing voices of others who had preceded him in a long series down the years. There came first a plain, sharp cry, as of a man in the last anguish, choking for his breath, and yet, with the very final expiration of it, breathing the name of the Worship—of the dark Being who rejoiced to hear it. The cries of the strangled; the short, running gasp of the suffocated; and the smothered gurgling of the tightened throat, all these, and more, echoed back and forth between the walls, the very walls in which he now stood a prisoner, a sacrificial victim. The cries, too, not alone of the broken bodies, but—far worse—of beaten, broken souls. And as the ghastly chorus rose and fell, there came also the faces of the lost and unhappy creatures to whom they belonged, and, against that curtain of pale grey light, he saw float past him in the air, an array of white and piteous human countenances that seemed to beckon and gibber at him as though he were already one of themselves.

Slowly, too, as the voices rose, and the pallid crew sailed past, that giant form of grey descended from the sky and approached the room that contained the worshippers and their prisoner. Hands rose and sank about him in the darkness, and he felt that he was being draped in other garments than his own; a circlet of ice seemed to run about his head, while round the waist, enclosing the fastened arms, he felt a girdle tightly drawn. At last, about his very throat, there ran a soft and silken touch which, better than if there had been full light, and a mirror held to his face, he understood to be the cord of sacrifice—and of death.

At this moment the Brothers, still prostrate upon the floor, began again their mournful, yet impassioned chanting, and as they did so a strange thing happened. For, apparently without moving or altering its position, the huge Figure seemed, at once and suddenly, to be inside the room, almost beside him, and to fill the space around him to the exclusion of all else.

He was now beyond all ordinary sensations of fear, only a drab feeling as of death—the death of the soul—stirred in his heart. His thoughts no longer even beat vainly for escape. The end was near, and he knew it.

The dreadfully chanting voices rose about him in a wave: "We worship! We adore! We offer!" The sounds filled his ears and hammered, almost meaningless, upon his brain.

Then the majestic grey face turned slowly downwards upon him, and his very soul passed outwards and seemed to become absorbed in the sea of those anguished eyes. At the same moment a dozen hands forced him to his knees, and in the air before him he saw the arm of Kalkmann upraised, and felt the pressure about his throat grow strong.

It was in this awful moment, when he had given up all hope, and the help of gods or men seemed beyond question, that a strange thing happened. For before his fading and terrified vision there slid, as in a dream of light, —yet without apparent rhyme or reason—wholly unbidden and unexplained, —the face of that other man at the supper table of the railway inn. And the sight, even mentally, of that strong, wholesome, vigorous English face, inspired him suddenly with a new courage.

It was but a flash of fading vision before he sank into a dark and terrible death, yet, in some inexplicable way, the sight of that face stirred in him unconquerable hope and the certainty of deliverance. It was a face of power, a face, he now realised, of simple goodness such as might have been seen by men of old on the shores of Galilee; a face, by heaven, that could conquer even the devils of outer space.

And, in his despair and abandonment, he called upon it, and called with no uncertain accents. He found his voice in this overwhelming moment to some purpose; though the words he actually used, and whether they were in German or English, he could never remember. Their effect, nevertheless, was instantaneous. The Brothers understood, and that grey Figure of evil understood.

For a second the confusion was terrific. There came a great shattering sound. It seemed that the very earth trembled. But all Harris remembered afterwards was that voices rose about him in the clamour of terrified alarm—

"A man of power is among us! A man of God!"

The vast sound was repeated—the rushing through space as of huge projectiles—and he sank to the floor of the room, unconscious. The entire scene had vanished, vanished like smoke over the roof of a cottage when the wind blows.

And, by his side, sat down a slight un-German figure, —the figure of the stranger at the inn, —the man who had the "rather wonderful eyes."

When Harris came to himself he felt cold. He was lying under the open sky, and the cool air of field and forest was blowing upon his face. He sat up and looked about him. The memory of the late scene was still horribly in his mind, but no vestige of it remained. No walls or ceiling enclosed him; he was no longer in a room at all. There were no lamps turned low, no cigar smoke, no black forms of sinister worshippers, no tremendous grey Figure hovering beyond the windows.

Open space was about him, and he was lying on a pile of bricks and mortar, his clothes soaked with dew, and the kind stars shining brightly overhead. He was lying, bruised and shaken, among the heaped-up debris of a ruined building.

He stood up and stared about him. There, in the shadowy distance, lay the surrounding forest, and here, close at hand, stood the outline of the village buildings. But, underfoot, beyond question, lay nothing but the broken heaps of stones that betokened a building long since crumbled to dust. Then he saw that the stones were blackened, and that great wooden beams, half burnt, half rotten, made lines through the general débris. He stood, then, among the ruins of a burnt and shattered building, the weeds and nettles proving conclusively that it had lain thus for many years.

The moon had already set behind the encircling forest, but the stars that spangled the heavens threw enough light to enable him to make quite sure of what he saw. Harris, the silk merchant, stood among these broken and burnt stones and shivered.

Then he suddenly became aware that out of the gloom a figure had risen and stood beside him. Peering at him, he thought he recognised the face of the stranger at the railway inn.

"Are *you* real?" he asked in a voice he hardly recognised as his own.

"More than real—I'm friendly," replied the stranger; "I followed you up here from the inn."

Harris stood and stared for several minutes without adding anything. His teeth chattered. The least sound made him start; but the simple words in his own language, and the tone in which they were uttered, comforted him inconceivably.

"You're English too, thank God," he said inconsequently. "These German devils—" He broke off and put a hand to his eyes. "But what's become of them all—and the room—and—and—" The hand travelled down to his throat and moved nervously round his neck. He drew a long, long breath of relief. "Did I dream everything—everything?" he said distractedly.

He stared wildly about him, and the stranger moved forward and took his arm. "Come," he said soothingly, yet with a trace of command in the voice, "we will move away from here. The high-road, or even the woods will be more to your taste, for we are standing now on one of the most haunted—and most terribly haunted—spots of the whole world."

He guided his companion's stumbling footsteps over the broken masonry until they reached the path, the nettles stinging their hands, and Harris feeling his way like a man in a dream. Passing through the twisted iron railing they reached the path, and thence made their way to the road, shining white in the night. Once safely out of the ruins, Harris collected himself and turned to look back.

"But, how is it possible?" he exclaimed, his voice still shaking. "How can it be possible? When I came in here I saw the building in the moonlight. They opened the door. I saw the figures and heard the voices and touched, yes touched their very hands, and saw their damned black faces, saw them far more plainly than I see you now." He was deeply bewildered. The glamour was still upon his eyes with a degree of reality stronger than the reality even of normal life. "Was I so utterly deluded?"

Then suddenly the words of the stranger, which he had only half heard or understood, returned to him.

"Haunted?" he asked, looking hard at him; "haunted, did you say?" He paused in the roadway and stared into the darkness where the building of the old school had first appeared to him. But the stranger hurried him forward.

"We shall talk more safely farther on," he said. "I followed you from the inn the moment I realised where you had gone. When I found you it was eleven o'clock—"

"Eleven o'clock," said Harris, remembering with a shudder.

"—I saw you drop. I watched over you–till you recovered consciousness of your own accord, and now—now I am here to guide you safely back to the inn. I have broken the spell—the glamour—"

"I owe you a great deal, sir," interrupted Harris again, beginning to understand something of the stranger's kindness, "but I don't understand it all. I feel dazed and shaken." His teeth still chattered, and spells of violent shivering passed over him from head to foot. He found that he was clinging to the other's arm. In this way they passed beyond the deserted and crumbling village and gained the highroad that led homewards through the forest.

"That school building has long been in ruins," said the man at his side presently; "it was burnt down by order of the Elders of the community at least ten years ago. The village has been uninhabited ever since. But the simulacra of certain ghastly events that took place under that roof in past days still continue. And the 'shells' of the chief participants still enact there the dreadful deeds that led to its final destruction, and to the desertion of the whole settlement. They were devil-worshippers!"

Harris listened with beads of perspiration on his forehead that did not come alone from their leisurely pace through the cool night. Although he had seen this man but once before in his life, and had never before exchanged so much as a word with him, he felt a degree of confidence and a subtle sense of safety and well-being in his presence that were the most healing influences he could possibly have wished after the experience he had been through. For all that, he still felt as if he were walking in a dream, and though he heard every word that fell from his companion's lips, it was only the next day that the full import of all he said became fully clear to him. The presence of this quiet stranger, the man with the wonderful eyes which he felt now, rather than saw, applied a soothing anodyne to his shattered spirit that healed him through and through. And this healing influence, distilled from the dark figure at his side, satisfied his first imperative need, so that he almost forgot to realise how strange and opportune it was that the man should be there at all.

It somehow never occurred to him to ask his name, or to feel any undue wonder that one passing tourist should take so much trouble on behalf of another. He just walked by his side, listening to his quiet words, and allowing himself to enjoy the very wonderful experience after his recent ordeal, of being helped, strengthened, blessed. Only once, remembering vaguely something of his reading of years ago, he turned to the man beside him, after some more than usually remarkable words, and heard himself, almost involuntarily it seemed, putting the question: "Then are you a Rosicrucian, sir, perhaps?" But the stranger had ignored the words, or possibly not heard them, for he continued with his talk as though unconscious of any interruption, and Harris became aware that another somewhat unusual picture had taken possession of his mind, as they walked there side by side through the cool reaches of the forest, and that he had found his imagination suddenly charged with the childhood memory of Jacob wrestling with an angel, —wrestling all night with a being of superior quality whose strength eventually became his own.

"It was your abrupt conversation with the priest at supper that first put me upon the track of this remarkable occurrence," he heard the man's quiet voice beside him in the darkness, "and it was from him I learned after you left the story of the devil-worship that became secretly established in the heart of this simple and devout little community."

"Devil-worship! Here—!" Harris stammered, aghast.

"Yes—here;—conducted secretly for years by a group of Brothers before unexplained disappearances in the neighbourhood led to its discovery. For where could they have found a safer place in the whole wide world for their ghastly traffic and perverted powers than here, in the very precincts—under cover of the very shadow of saintliness and holy living?"

"Awful, awful!" whispered the silk merchant, "and when I tell you the words they used to me—"

"I know it all," the stranger said quietly. "I saw and heard everything. My plan first was to wait till the end and then to take steps for their destruction, but in the interest of your personal safety,"—he spoke with the utmost gravity and conviction, —"in the interest of the safety of your soul, I made my presence known when I did, and before the conclusion had been reached—"

"My safety! The danger, then, was real. They were alive and—" Words failed him. He stopped in the road and turned towards his companion, the shining of whose eyes he could just make out in the gloom.

"It was a concourse of the shells of violent men, spiritually developed but evil men, seeking after death—the death of the body—to prolong their vile and unnatural existence. And had they accomplished their object you, in turn, at the death of your body, would have passed into their power and helped to swell their dreadful purposes."

Harris made no reply. He was trying hard to concentrate his mind upon the sweet and common things of life. He even thought of silk and St. Paul's Churchyard and the faces of his partners in business.

"For you came all prepared to be caught," he heard the other's voice like some one talking to him from a distance; "your deeply introspective mood had already reconstructed the past so vividly, so intensely, that you were *en rapport* at once with any forces of those days that chanced still to be lingering. And they swept you up all unresistingly."

Harris tightened his hold upon the stranger's arm as he heard. At the moment he had room for one emotion only. It did not seem to him odd that this stranger should have such intimate knowledge of his mind.

"It is, alas, chiefly the evil emotions that are able to leave their photographs upon surrounding scenes and objects," the other added, "and who ever heard of a place haunted by a noble deed, or of beautiful and lovely ghosts revisiting the glimpses of the moon? It is unfortunate. But the wicked passions of men's hearts alone seem strong enough to leave pictures that persist; the good are ever too lukewarm."

The stranger sighed as he spoke. But Harris, exhausted and shaken as he was to the very core, paced by his side, only half listening. He moved as in a dream still. It was very wonderful to him, this walk home under the stars in the early hours of the October morning, the peaceful forest all about them, mist rising here and there over the small clearings, and the sound of water from a hundred little invisible streams filling in the pauses of the talk. In after life he always looked back to it as something magical and impossible, something that had seemed too beautiful, too curiously beautiful, to have been quite true. And, though at the time he heard and understood but a quarter of what the stranger said, it came back to him afterwards, staying with him till the end of his days, and always with a curious, haunting sense of unreality, as though he had enjoyed a wonderful dream of which he could recall only faint and exquisite portions.

But the horror of the earlier experience was effectually dispelled; and when they reached the railway inn, somewhere about three o'clock in the morning, Harris shook the stranger's hand gratefully, effusively, meeting the look of those rather wonderful eyes with a full heart, and went up to his room, thinking in a hazy, dream-like way of the words with which the stranger had brought their conversation to an end as they left the confines of the forest—

"And if thought and emotion can persist in this way so long after the brain that sent them forth has crumbled into dust, how vitally important it must be to control their very birth in the heart, and guard them with the keenest possible restraint."

But Harris, the silk merchant, slept better than might have been expected, and with a soundness that carried him half-way through the day. And when he came downstairs and learned that the stranger had already taken his departure, he realised with keen regret that he had never once thought of asking his name.

"Yes, he signed the visitors' book," said the girl in reply to his question.

And he turned over the blotted pages and found there, the last entry, in a very delicate and individual handwriting—

"*John Silence*, London."

CASE V

THE CAMP OF THE DOG

I

Islands of all shapes and sizes troop northward from Stockholm by the hundred, and the little steamer that threads their intricate mazes in summer leaves the traveller in a somewhat bewildered state as regards the points of the compass when it reaches the end of its journey at Waxholm. But it is only after Waxholm that the true islands begin, so to speak, to run wild, and start up the coast on their tangled course of a hundred miles of deserted loveliness, and it was in the very heart of this delightful confusion that we pitched our tents for a summer holiday. A veritable wilderness of islands lay about us: from the mere round button of a rock that bore a single fir, to the mountainous stretch of a square mile, densely wooded, and bounded by precipitous cliffs; so close together often that a strip of water ran between no wider than a country lane, or, again, so far that an expanse stretched like the open sea for miles.

Although the larger islands boasted farms and fishing stations, the majority were uninhabited. Carpeted with moss and heather, their coast-lines showed a series of ravines and clefts and little sandy bays, with a growth of splendid pine-woods that came down to the water's edge and led the eye through unknown depths of shadow and mystery into the very heart of primitive forest.

The particular islands to which we had camping rights by virtue of paying a nominal sum to a Stockholm merchant lay together in a picturesque group far beyond the reach of the steamer, one being a mere reef with a fringe of fairy-like birches, and two others, cliff-bound monsters rising with wooded heads out of the sea. The fourth, which we selected because it enclosed a little lagoon suitable for anchorage, bathing, night-lines, and whatnot, shall have what description is necessary as the story proceeds; but, so far as paying rent was concerned, we might equally well have pitched our tents on any one of a hundred others that clustered about us as thickly as a swarm of bees.

It was in the blaze of an evening in July, the air clear as crystal, the sea a cobalt blue, when we left the steamer on the borders of civilisation and sailed away with maps, compasses, and provisions for the little group of dots in the Skägård that were to be our home for the next two months. The dinghy and my Canadian canoe trailed behind us, with tents and dunnage carefully piled aboard, and when the point of cliff intervened to hide the steamer and the Waxholm hotel we realised for the first time that the horror of trains and houses was far behind us, the fever of men and cities, the weariness of streets and confined spaces. The wilderness opened up on all sides into endless blue reaches, and the map and compasses were so frequently called into requisition that we went astray more often than not and progress was enchantingly slow. It took us, for instance, two whole days to find our crescent-shaped home, and the camps we made on the way were so fascinating that we left them with difficulty and regret, for each island seemed more desirable than the one before it, and over all lay the spell of haunting peace, remoteness from the turmoil of the world, and the freedom of open and desolate spaces.

And so many of these spots of world-beauty have I sought out and dwelt in, that in my mind remains only a composite memory of their faces, a true map of heaven, as it were, from which this particular one stands forth with unusual sharpness because of the strange things that happened there, and also, I think, because anything in which John Silence played a part has a habit of fixing itself in the mind with a living and lasting quality of vividness.

For the moment, however, Dr. Silence was not of the party. Some private case in the interior of Hungary claimed his attention, and it was not till later—the 15th of August, to be exact—that I had arranged to meet him in Berlin and then return to London together for our harvest of winter work. All the members of our party, however, were known to him more or less well, and on this third day as we sailed through the narrow opening into the lagoon and saw the circular ridge of trees in a gold and crimson sunset before us, his last words to me when we parted in London for some unaccountable reason came back very sharply to my memory, and recalled the curious impression of prophecy with which I had first heard them:

"Enjoy your holiday and store up all the force you can," he had said as the train slipped out of Victoria; "and we will meet in Berlin on the 15th—unless you should send for me sooner."

And now suddenly the words returned to me so clearly that it seemed I almost heard his voice in my ear: "Unless you should send for me sooner";

and returned, moreover, with a significance I was wholly at a loss to understand that touched somewhere in the depths of my mind a vague sense of apprehension that they had all along been intended in the nature of a prophecy.

In the lagoon, then, the wind failed us this July evening, as was only natural behind the shelter of the belt of woods, and we took to the oars, all breathless with the beauty of this first sight of our island home, yet all talking in somewhat hushed voices of the best place to land, the depth of water, the safest place to anchor, to put up the tents in, the most sheltered spot for the camp-fires, and a dozen things of importance that crop up when a home in the wilderness has actually to be made.

And during this busy sunset hour of unloading before the dark, the souls of my companions adopted the trick of presenting themselves very vividly anew before my mind, and introducing themselves afresh.

In reality, I suppose, our party was in no sense singular. In the conventional life at home they certainly seemed ordinary enough, but suddenly, as we passed through these gates of the wilderness, I saw them more sharply than before, with characters stripped of the atmosphere of men and cities. A complete change of setting often furnishes a startlingly new view of people hitherto held for well-known; they present another facet of their personalities. I seemed to see my own party almost as new people—people I had not known properly hitherto, people who would drop all disguises and henceforth reveal themselves as they really were. And each one seemed to say: "Now you will see me as I am. You will see me here in this primitive life of the wilderness without clothes. All my masks and veils I have left behind in the abodes of men. So, look out for surprises!"

The Reverend Timothy Maloney helped me to put up the tents, long practice making the process easy, and while he drove in pegs and tightened ropes, his coat off, his flannel collar flying open without a tie, it was impossible to avoid the conclusion that he was cut out for the life of a pioneer rather than the church. He was fifty years of age, muscular, blue-eyed and hearty, and he took his share of the work, and more, without shirking. The way he handled the axe in cutting down saplings for the tent-poles was a delight to see, and his eye in judging the level was unfailing.

Bullied as a young man into a lucrative family living, he had in turn bullied his mind into some semblance of orthodox beliefs, doing the honours of the little country church with an energy that made one think of a coal-heaver tending china; and it was only in the past few years that he had resigned the living and taken instead to cramming young men for their examinations. This suited him better. It enabled him, too, to indulge his passion for spells of "wild life," and to spend the summer months of most years under canvas in one part of the world or another where he could take his young men with him and combine "reading" with open air.

His wife usually accompanied him, and there was no doubt she enjoyed the trips, for she possessed, though in less degree, the same joy of the wilderness that was his own distinguishing characteristic. The only difference was that while he regarded it as the real life, she regarded it as an interlude. While he camped out with his heart and mind, she played at camping out with her clothes and body. None the less, she made a splendid companion, and to watch her busy cooking dinner over the fire we had built among the stones was to understand that her heart was in the business for the moment and that she was happy even with the detail.

Mrs. Maloney at home, knitting in the sun and believing that the world was made in six days, was one woman; but Mrs. Maloney, standing with bare arms over the smoke of a wood fire under the pine trees, was another; and Peter Sangree, the Canadian pupil, with his pale skin, and his loose, though not ungainly figure, stood beside her in very unfavourable contrast as he scraped potatoes and sliced bacon with slender white fingers that seemed better suited to hold a pen than a knife. She ordered him about like a slave, and he obeyed, too, with willing pleasure, for in spite of his general appearance of debility he was as happy to be in camp as any of them.

But more than any other member of the party, Joan Maloney, the daughter, was the one who seemed a natural and genuine part of the landscape, who belonged to it all just in the same way that the trees and the moss and the grey rocks running out into the water belonged to it. For she was obviously in her right and natural setting, a creature of the wilds, a gipsy in her own home.

To any one with a discerning eye this would have been more or less apparent, but to me, who had known her during all the twenty-two years of her life and was familiar with the ins and outs of her primitive, utterly unmodern type, it was strikingly clear. To see her there made it impossible to imagine her again in civilisation. I lost all recollection of how she looked in a town. The memory somehow evaporated. This slim creature before me, flitting to and fro with the grace of the woodland life, swift, supple, adroit, on her knees blowing the fire, or stirring the frying-pan through a veil of smoke, suddenly seemed the only way I had ever really seen her. Here she was at home; in London she became some one concealed by clothes, an artificial doll overdressed and moving by clockwork, only a portion of her alive. Here she was alive all over.

I forget altogether how she was dressed, just as I forget how any particular tree was dressed, or how the markings ran on any one of the boulders that lay about the Camp. She looked just as wild and natural and untamed as everything else that went to make up the scene, and more than that I cannot say.

Pretty, she was decidedly not. She was thin, skinny, dark-haired, and possessed of great physical strength in the form of endurance. She had, too, something of the force and vigorous purpose of a man, tempestuous sometimes and wild to passionate, frightening her mother, and puzzling her easy-going father with her storms of waywardness, while at the same time she stirred his admiration by her violence. A pagan of the pagans she was besides, and with some haunting suggestion of old-world pagan beauty about her dark face and eyes. Altogether an odd and difficult character, but with a generosity and high courage that made her very lovable.

In town life she always seemed to me to feel cramped, bored, a devil in a cage, in her eyes a hunted expression as though any moment she dreaded to be caught. But up in these spacious solitudes all this disappeared. Away from the limitations that plagued and stung her, she would show at her best, and as I watched her moving about the Camp I repeatedly found myself thinking of a wild creature that had just obtained its freedom and was trying its muscles.

Peter Sangree, of course, at once went down before her. But she was so obviously beyond his reach, and besides so well able to take care of herself, that I think her parents gave the matter but little thought, and he himself worshipped at a respectful distance, keeping admirable control of his passion in all respects save one; for at his age the eyes are difficult to master, and the yearning, almost the devouring, expression often visible in them was probably there unknown even to himself. He, better than any one else, understood that he had fallen in love with something most hard of attainment, something that drew him to the very edge of life, and almost beyond it. It, no doubt, was a secret and terrible joy to him, this passionate worship from afar; only I think he suffered more than any one guessed, and that his want of vitality was due in large measure to the constant stream of unsatisfied yearning that poured for ever from his soul and body. Moreover, it seemed to me, who now saw them for the first time together, that there was an unnamable something—an elusive quality of some kind—that marked them as belonging to the same world, and that although the girl ignored him she was secretly, and perhaps unknown to herself, drawn by some attribute very deep in her own nature to some quality equally deep in his.

This, then, was the party when we first settled down into our two months' camp on the island in the Baltic Sea. Other figures flitted from time to time across the scene, and sometimes one reading man, sometimes another, came to join us and spend his four hours a day in the clergyman's tent, but they came for short periods only, and they went without leaving much trace in my memory, and certainly they played no important part in what subsequently happened.

The weather favoured us that night, so that by sunset the tents were up, the boats unloaded, a store of wood collected and chopped into lengths, and the candle-lanterns hung round ready for lighting on the trees. Sangree, too, had picked deep mattresses of balsam boughs for the women's beds, and had cleared little paths of brushwood from their tents to the central fireplace. All was prepared for bad weather. It was a cosy supper and a well-cooked one that we sat down to and ate under the stars, and, according to the clergyman, the only meal fit to eat we had seen since we left London a week before.

The deep stillness, after that roar of steamers, trains, and tourists, held something that thrilled, for as we lay round the fire there was no sound but the faint sighing of the pines and the soft lapping of the waves along the shore and against the sides of the boat in the lagoon. The ghostly outline of her white sails was just visible through the trees, idly rocking to and fro in her calm anchorage, her sheets flapping gently against the mast. Beyond lay the dim blue shapes of other islands floating in the night, and from all the great spaces about us came the murmur of the sea and the soft breathing of great woods. The odours of the wilderness—smells of wind and earth, of trees and water, clean, vigorous, and mighty—were the true odours of a virgin world unspoilt by men, more penetrating and more subtly intoxicating than any other perfume in the whole world. Oh!—and dangerously strong, too, no doubt, for some natures!

"Ahhh!" breathed out the clergyman after supper, with an indescribable gesture of satisfaction and relief. "Here there is freedom, and room for body and mind to turn in. Here one can work and rest and play. Here one can be alive and absorb something of the earth-forces that never get within touching distance in the cities. By George, I shall make a permanent camp here and come when it is time to die!"

The good man was merely giving vent to his delight at being under canvas. He said the same thing every year, and he said it often. But it more or less expressed the superficial feelings of us all. And when, a little later, he turned to compliment his wife on the fried potatoes, and discovered that she was snoring, with her back against a tree, he grunted with content at the sight and put a ground-sheet over her feet, as if it were the most natural thing in the world for her to fall asleep after dinner, and then moved back to his own corner, smoking his pipe with great satisfaction.

And I, smoking mine too, lay and fought against the most delicious sleep imaginable, while my eyes wandered from the fire to the stars peeping through the branches, and then back again to the group about me. The Rev. Timothy soon let his pipe go out, and succumbed as his wife had done, for he had worked hard and eaten well. Sangree, also smoking, leaned against a tree with his gaze fixed on the girl, a depth of yearning in his face that he could not hide, and that really distressed me for him. And Joan herself, with wide staring eyes, alert, full of the new forces of the place, evidently keyed up by the magic of finding herself among all the things her soul recognised as "home," sat rigid by the fire, her thoughts roaming through the spaces, the blood stirring about her heart. She was as unconscious of the Canadian's gaze as she was that her parents both slept. She looked to me more like a tree, or something that had grown out of the island, than a living girl of the century; and when I spoke across to her in a whisper and suggested a tour of investigation, she started and looked up at me as though she heard a voice in her dreams.

Sangree leaped up and joined us, and without waking the others we three went over the ridge of the island and made our way down to the shore behind. The water lay like a lake before us still coloured by the sunset. The air was keen and scented, wafting the smell of the wooded islands that hung about us in the darkening air. Very small waves tumbled softly on the sand. The sea was sown with stars, and everywhere breathed and pulsed the beauty of the northern summer night. I confess I speedily lost consciousness of the human presences beside me, and I have little doubt Joan did too. Only Sangree felt otherwise, I suppose, for presently we heard him sighing; and I can well imagine that he absorbed the whole wonder and passion of the scene into his aching heart, to swell the pain there that was more searching even than the pain at the sight of such matchless and incomprehensible beauty.

The splash of a fish jumping broke the spell.

"I wish we had the canoe now," remarked Joan; "we could paddle out to the other islands."

"Of course," I said; "wait here and I'll go across for it," and was turning to feel my way back through the darkness when she stopped me in a voice that meant what it said.

"No; Mr. Sangree will get it. We will wait here and cooee to guide him."

The Canadian was off in a moment, for she had only to hint of her wishes and he obeyed.

"Keep out from shore in case of rocks," I cried out as he went, "and turn to the right out of the lagoon. That's the shortest way round by the map."

My voice travelled across the still waters and woke echoes in the distant islands that came back to us like people calling out of space. It was only thirty or forty yards over the ridge and down the other side to the lagoon where the boats lay, but it was a good mile to coast round the shore in the dark to where we stood and waited. We heard him stumbling away among the boulders, and then the sounds suddenly ceased as he topped the ridge and went down past the fire on the other side.

"I didn't want to be left alone with him," the girl said presently in a low voice. "I'm always afraid he's going to say or do something—" She hesitated a moment, looking quickly over her shoulder towards the ridge where he had just disappeared—"something that might lead to unpleasantness."

She stopped abruptly.

"*You* frightened, Joan!" I exclaimed, with genuine surprise. "This is a new light on your wicked character. I thought the human being who could frighten you did not exist." Then I suddenly realised she was talking seriously—looking to me for help of some kind—and at once I dropped the teasing attitude.

"He's very far gone, I think, Joan," I added gravely. "You must be kind to him, whatever else you may feel. He's exceedingly fond of you."

"I know, but I can't help it," she whispered, lest her voice should carry in the stillness; "there's something about him that—that makes me feel creepy and half afraid."

"But, poor man, it's not his fault if he is delicate and sometimes looks like death," I laughed gently, by way of defending what I felt to be a very innocent member of my sex.

"Oh, but it's not that I mean," she answered quickly; "it's something I feel about him, something in his soul, something he hardly knows himself, but that may come out if we are much together. It draws me, I feel, tremendously. It stirs what is wild in me—deep down—oh, very deep down, —yet at the same time makes me feel afraid."

"I suppose his thoughts are always playing about you," I said, "but he's nice-minded and—"

"Yes, yes," she interrupted impatiently, "I can trust myself absolutely with him. He's gentle and singularly pure-minded. But there's something else that—" She stopped again sharply to listen. Then she came up close beside me in the darkness, whispering—

"You know, Mr. Hubbard, sometimes my intuitions warn me a little too strongly to be ignored. Oh, yes, you needn't tell me again that it's difficult to distinguish between fancy and intuition. I know all that. But I also know that there's something deep down in that man's soul that calls to something deep down in mine. And at present it frightens me. Because I cannot make out what it is; and I know, I *know*, he'll do something some day that—that will shake my life to the very bottom." She laughed a little at the strangeness of her own description.

I turned to look at her more closely, but the darkness was too great to show her face. There was an intensity, almost of suppressed passion, in her voice that took me completely by surprise.

"Nonsense, Joan," I said, a little severely; "you know him well. He's been with your father for months now."

"But that was in London; and up here it's different—I mean, I feel that it may be different. Life in a place like this blows away the restraints of the artificial life at home. I know, oh, I know what I'm saying. I feel all untied in a place like this; the rigidity of one's nature begins to melt and flow. Surely *you* must understand what I mean!"

"Of course I understand," I replied, yet not wishing to encourage her in her present line of thought, "and it's a grand experience—for a short time. But you're overtired to-night, Joan, like the rest of us. A few days in this air will set you above all fears of the kind you mention."

Then, after a moment's silence, I added, feeling I should estrange her confidence altogether if I blundered any more and treated her like a child—

"I think, perhaps, the true explanation is that you pity him for loving you, and at the same time you feel the repulsion of the healthy, vigorous animal for what is weak and timid. If he came up boldly and took you by the throat and shouted that he would force you to love him—well, then you would feel no fear at all. You would know exactly how to deal with him. Isn't it, perhaps, something of that kind?"

The girl made no reply, and when I took her hand I felt that it trembled a little and was cold.

"It's not his love that I'm afraid of," she said hurriedly, for at this moment we heard the dip of a paddle in the water, "it's something in his very soul that terrifies me in a way I have never been terrified before, —yet fascinates me. In town I was hardly conscious of his presence. But the moment we got away from civilisation, it began to come. He seems so—so *real* up here. I dread being alone with him. It makes me feel that something must burst and tear its way out—that he would do something—or I should do something—I don't know exactly what I mean, probably, —but that I should let myself go and scream—"

"Joan!"

"Don't be alarmed," she laughed shortly; "I shan't do anything silly, but I wanted to tell you my feelings in case I needed your help. When I have intuitions as strong as this they are never wrong, only I don't know yet what it means exactly."

"You must hold out for the month, at any rate," I said in as matter-of-fact a voice as I could manage, for her manner had somehow changed my surprise to a subtle sense of alarm. "Sangree only stays the month, you know. And, anyhow, you are such an odd creature yourself that you should feel generously towards other odd creatures," I ended lamely, with a forced laugh.

She gave my hand a sudden pressure. "I'm glad I've told you at any rate," she said quickly under her breath, for the canoe was now gliding up silently like a ghost to our feet, "and I'm glad you're here, too," she added as we moved down towards the water to meet it.

I made Sangree change into the bows and got into the steering seat myself, putting the girl between us so that I could watch them both by keeping their outlines against the sea and stars. For the intuitions of certain folk—women and children usually, I confess—I have always felt a great respect that has more often than not been justified by experience; and now the curious emotion stirred in me by the girl's words remained somewhat vividly in my consciousness. I explained it in some measure by the fact that the girl, tired out by the fatigue of many days' travel, had suffered a vigorous reaction of some kind from the strong, desolate scenery, and further, perhaps, that she had been treated to my own experience of seeing the members of the party in a new light—the Canadian, being partly a stranger, more vividly than the rest of us. But, at the same time, I felt it was quite possible that she had sensed some subtle link between his personality and her own, some quality that she had hitherto ignored and that the routine of town life had kept buried out of sight. The only thing that seemed difficult to explain was the fear she had spoken of, and this I hoped the wholesome effects of camp-life and exercise would sweep away naturally in the course of time.

We made the tour of the island without speaking. It was all too beautiful for speech. The trees crowded down to the shore to hear us pass. We saw their fine dark heads, bowed low with splendid dignity to watch us, forgetting for a moment that the stars were caught in the needled network of their hair. Against the sky in the west, where still lingered the sunset gold, we saw the wild toss of the horizon, shaggy with forest and cliff, gripping the heart like the motive in a symphony, and sending the sense of beauty all a-shiver through the mind—all these surrounding islands standing above the water like low clouds, and like them seeming to post along silently into the engulfing night. We heard the musical drip-drip of the paddle, and the little wash of our waves on the shore, and then suddenly we found ourselves at the opening of the lagoon again, having made the complete circuit of our home.

The Reverend Timothy had awakened from sleep and was singing to himself; and the sound of his voice as we glided down the fifty yards of enclosed water was pleasant to hear and undeniably wholesome. We saw the glow of the fire up among the trees on the ridge, and his shadow moving about as he threw on more wood.

"There you are!" he called aloud. "Good again! Been setting the night-lines, eh? Capital! And your mother's still fast asleep, Joan."

His cheery laugh floated across the water; he had not been in the least disturbed by our absence, for old campers are not easily alarmed.

"Now, remember," he went on, after we had told our little tale of travel by the fire, and Mrs. Maloney had asked for the fourth time exactly where her tent was and whether the door faced east or south, "every one takes their turn at cooking breakfast, and one of the men is always out at sunrise to catch it first. Hubbard, I'll toss you which you do in the morning and which I do!" He lost the toss. "Then I'll catch it," I said, laughing at his discomfiture, for I knew he loathed stirring porridge. "And mind you don't burn it as you did every blessed time last year on the Volga," I added by way of reminder.

Mrs. Maloney's fifth interruption about the door of her tent, and her further pointed observation that it was past nine o'clock, set us lighting lanterns and putting the fire out for safety.

But before we separated for the night the clergyman had a time-honoured little ritual of his own to go through that no one had the heart to deny him. He always did this. It was a relic of his pulpit habits. He glanced briefly from one to the other of us, his face grave and earnest, his hands lifted to the stars and his eyes all closed and puckered up beneath a momentary frown. Then he offered up a short, almost inaudible prayer, thanking Heaven for our safe arrival, begging for good weather, no illness or accidents, plenty of fish, and strong sailing winds.

And then, unexpectedly—no one knew why exactly—he ended up with an abrupt request that nothing from the kingdom of darkness should be allowed to afflict our peace, and no evil thing come near to disturb us in the night-time.

And while he uttered these last surprising words, so strangely unlike his usual ending, it chanced that I looked up and let my eyes wander round the group assembled about the dying fire. And it certainly seemed to me that Sangree's face underwent a sudden and visible alteration. He was staring at Joan, and as he stared the change ran over it like a shadow and was gone. I started in spite of myself, for something oddly concentrated, potent, collected, had come into the expression usually so scattered and feeble. But it was all swift as a passing meteor, and when I looked a second time his face was normal and he was looking among the trees.

And Joan, luckily, had not observed him, her head being bowed and her eyes tightly closed while her father prayed.

"The girl has a vivid imagination indeed," I thought, half laughing, as I lit the lanterns, "if her thoughts can put a glamour upon mine in this way"; and yet somehow, when we said good-night, I took occasion to give her a few vigorous words of encouragement, and went to her tent to make sure I could find it quickly in the night in case anything happened. In her quick way the girl understood and thanked me, and the last thing I heard as I moved off to the men's quarters was Mrs. Maloney crying that there were beetles in her tent, and Joan's laughter as she went to help her turn them out.

Half an hour later the island was silent as the grave, but for the mournful voices of the wind as it sighed up from the sea. Like white sentries stood the three tents of the men on one side of the ridge, and on the other side, half hidden by some birches, whose leaves just shivered as the breeze caught them, the women's tents, patches of ghostly grey, gathered more closely together for mutual shelter and protection. Something like fifty yards of broken ground, grey rock, moss and lichen, lay between, and over all lay the curtain of the night and the great whispering winds from the forests of Scandinavia.

And the very last thing, just before floating away on that mighty wave that carries one so softly off into the deeps of forgetfulness, I again heard the voice of John Silence as the train moved out of Victoria Station; and by some subtle connection that met me on the very threshold of consciousness there rose in my mind simultaneously the memory of the girl's half-given confidence, and of her distress. As by some wizardry of approaching dreams they seemed in that instant to be related; but before I could analyse the why and the wherefore, both sank away out of sight again, and I was off beyond recall.

"Unless you should send for me sooner."

II

Whether Mrs. Maloney's tent door opened south or east I think she never discovered, for it is quite certain she always slept with the flap tightly fastened; I only know that my own little "five by seven, all silk" faced due east, because next morning the sun, pouring in as only the wilderness sun knows how to pour, woke me early, and a moment later, with a short run over soft moss and a flying dive from the granite ledge, I was swimming in the most sparkling water imaginable.

It was barely four o'clock, and the sun came down a long vista of blue islands that led out to the open sea and Finland. Nearer by rose the wooded domes of our own property, still capped and wreathed with smoky trails of fast-melting mist, and looking as fresh as though it was the morning of Mrs. Maloney's Sixth Day and they had just issued, clean and brilliant, from the hands of the great Architect.

In the open spaces the ground was drenched with dew, and from the sea a cool salt wind stole in among the trees and set the branches trembling in an atmosphere of shimmering silver. The tents shone white where the sun caught them in patches. Below lay the lagoon, still dreaming of the summer night; in the open the fish were jumping busily, sending musical ripples towards the shore; and in the air hung the magic of dawn—silent, incommunicable.

I lit the fire, so that an hour later the clergyman should find good ashes to stir his porridge over, and then set forth upon an examination of the island, but hardly had I gone a dozen yards when I saw a figure standing a little in front of me where the sunlight fell in a pool among the trees.

It was Joan. She had already been up an hour, she told me, and had bathed before the last stars had left the sky. I saw at once that the new spirit of this solitary region had entered into her, banishing the fears of the night, for her face was like the face of a happy denizen of the wilderness, and her eyes stainless and shining. Her feet were bare, and drops of dew she had shaken from the branches hung in her loose-flying hair. Obviously she had come into her own.

"I've been all over the island," she announced laughingly, "and there are two things wanting."

"You're a good judge, Joan. What are they?"

"There's no animal life, and there's no—water."

"They go together," I said. "Animals don't bother with a rock like this unless there's a spring on it."

And as she led me from place to place, happy and excited, leaping adroitly from rock to rock, I was glad to note that my first impressions were correct. She made no reference to our conversation of the night before. The new spirit had driven out the old. There was no room in her heart for fear or anxiety, and Nature had everything her own way.

The island, we found, was some three-quarters of a mile from point to point, built in a circle, or wide horseshoe, with an opening of twenty feet at the mouth of the lagoon. Pine-trees grew thickly all over, but here and there were patches of silver birch, scrub oak, and considerable colonies of wild raspberry and gooseberry bushes. The two ends of the horseshoe formed bare slabs of smooth granite running into the sea and forming dangerous reefs just below the surface, but the rest of the island rose in a forty-foot ridge and sloped down steeply to the sea on either side, being nowhere more than a hundred yards wide.

The outer shore-line was much indented with numberless coves and bays and sandy beaches, with here and there caves and precipitous little cliffs against which the sea broke in spray and thunder. But the inner shore, the shore of the lagoon, was low and regular, and so well protected by the wall of trees along the ridge that no storm could ever send more than a passing ripple along its sandy marges. Eternal shelter reigned there.

On one of the other islands, a few hundred yards away—for the rest of the party slept late this first morning, and we took to the canoe—we discovered a spring of fresh water untainted by the brackish flavour of the Baltic, and having thus solved the most important problem of the Camp, we next proceeded to deal with the second—fish. And in half an hour we reeled in and turned homewards, for we had no means of storage, and to clean more fish than may be stored or eaten in a day is no wise occupation for experienced campers.

And as we landed towards six o'clock we heard the clergyman singing as usual and saw his wife and Sangree shaking out their blankets in the sun, and dressed in a fashion that finally dispelled all memories of streets and civilisation.

"The Little People lit the fire for me," cried Maloney, looking natural and at home in his ancient flannel suit and breaking off in the middle of his singing, "so I've got the porridge going—and this time it's *not* burnt."

We reported the discovery of water and held up the fish.

"Good! Good again!" he cried. "We'll have the first decent breakfast we've had this year. Sangree'll clean 'em in no time, and the Bo'sun's Mate—"

"Will fry them to a turn," laughed the voice of Mrs. Maloney, appearing on the scene in a tight blue jersey and sandals, and catching up the frying-pan. Her husband always called her the Bo'sun's Mate in Camp, because it was her duty, among others, to pipe all hands to meals.

"And as for you, Joan," went on the happy man, "you look like the spirit of the island, with moss in your hair and wind in your eyes, and sun and stars mixed in your face." He looked at her with delighted admiration. "Here, Sangree, take these twelve, there's a good fellow, they're the biggest; and we'll have 'em in butter in less time than you can say Baltic island!"

I watched the Canadian as he slowly moved off to the cleaning pail. His eyes were drinking in the girl's beauty, and a wave of passionate, almost feverish, joy passed over his face, expressive of the ecstasy of true worship more than anything else. Perhaps he was thinking that he still had three weeks to come with that vision always before his eyes; perhaps he was thinking of his dreams in the night. I cannot say. But I noticed the curious mingling of yearning and happiness in his eyes, and the strength of the impression touched my curiosity. Something in his face held my gaze for a second, something to do with its intensity. That so timid, so gentle a personality should conceal so virile a passion almost seemed to require explanation.

But the impression was momentary, for that first breakfast in Camp permitted no divided attentions, and I dare swear that the porridge, the tea, the Swedish "flatbread," and the fried fish flavoured with points of frizzled bacon, were better than any meal eaten elsewhere that day in the whole world.

The first clear day in a new camp is always a furiously busy one, and we soon dropped into the routine upon which in large measure the real comfort of every one depends. About the cooking-fire, greatly improved with stones from the shore, we built a high stockade consisting of upright poles thickly twined with branches, the roof lined with moss and lichen and weighted with rocks, and round the interior we made low wooden seats so that we could lie round the fire even in rain and eat our meals in peace. Paths, too, outlined themselves from tent to tent, from the bathing places and the landing stage, and a fair division of the island was decided upon between the quarters of the men and the women. Wood was stacked, awkward trees and boulders removed, hammocks slung, and tents strengthened. In a word, Camp was established, and duties were assigned and accepted as though we expected to live on this Baltic island for years to come and the smallest detail of the Community life was important.

Moreover, as the Camp came into being, this sense of a community developed, proving that we were a definite whole, and not merely separate human beings living for a while in tents upon a desert island. Each fell willingly into the routine. Sangree, as by natural selection, took upon himself the cleaning of the fish and the cutting of the wood into lengths sufficient for a day's use. And he did it well. The pan of water was never without a fish, cleaned and scaled, ready to fry for whoever was hungry; the nightly fire never died down for lack of material to throw on without going farther afield to search.

And Timothy, once reverend, caught the fish and chopped down the trees. He also assumed responsibility for the condition of the boat, and did it so thoroughly that nothing in the little cutter was ever found wanting. And when, for any reason, his presence was in demand, the first place to look for him was—in the boat, and there, too, he was usually found, tinkering away with sheets, sails, or rudder and singing as he tinkered.

"Nor was the "reading" neglected; for most mornings there came a sound of droning voices from the white tent by the raspberry bushes, which signified that Sangree, the tutor, and whatever other man chanced to be in the party at the time, were hard at it with history or the classics.

And while Mrs. Maloney, also by natural selection, took charge of the larder and the kitchen, the mending and general supervision of the rough comforts, she also made herself peculiarly mistress of the megaphone which summoned to meals and carried her voice easily from one end of the island to the other; and in her hours of leisure she daubed the surrounding scenery on to a sketching block with all the honesty and devotion of her determined but unreceptive soul.

Joan, meanwhile, Joan, elusive creature of the wilds, became I know not exactly what. She did plenty of work in the Camp, yet seemed to have no very precise duties. She was everywhere and anywhere. Sometimes she slept in her tent, sometimes under the stars with a blanket. She knew every inch of the island and kept turning up in places where she was least expected—for ever wandering about, reading her books in sheltered corners, making little fires on sunless days to "worship by to the gods," as she put it, ever finding new pools to dive and bathe in, and swimming day and night in the warm and waveless lagoon like a fish in a huge tank. She went bare-legged and bare-footed, with her hair down and her skirts caught up to the knees, and if ever a human being turned into a jolly savage within the compass of a single week, Joan Maloney was certainly that human being. She ran wild.

So completely, too, was she possessed by the strong spirit of the place that the little human fear she had yielded to so strangely on our arrival seemed to have been utterly dispossessed. As I hoped and expected, she made no reference to our conversation of the first evening. Sangree bothered her with no special attentions, and after all they were very little together. His behaviour was perfect in that respect, and I, for my part, hardly gave the matter another thought. Joan was ever a prey to vivid fancies of one kind or another, and this was one of them. Mercifully for the happiness of all concerned, it had melted away before the spirit of busy, active life and deep content that reigned over the island. Every one was intensely alive, and peace was upon all.

Meanwhile the effect of the camp-life began to tell. Always a searching test of character, its results, sooner or later, are infallible, for it acts upon the soul as swiftly and surely as the hypo bath upon the negative of a photograph. A readjustment of the personal forces takes place quickly; some parts of the personality go to sleep, others wake up: but the first sweeping change that the primitive life brings about is that the artificial portions of the character shed themselves one after another like dead skins. Attitudes and poses that seemed genuine in the city drop away. The mind, like the body, grows quickly hard, simple, uncomplex. And in a camp as primitive and close to nature as ours was, these effects became speedily visible.

Some folk, of course, who talk glibly about the simple life when it is safely out of reach, betray themselves in camp by for ever peering about for the artificial excitements of civilisation which they miss. Some get bored at once; some grow slovenly; some reveal the animal in most unexpected fashion; and some, the select few, find themselves in very short order and are happy.

And, in our little party, we could flatter ourselves that we all belonged to the last category, so far as the general effect was concerned. Only there were certain other changes as well, varying with each individual, and all interesting to note.

It was only after the first week or two that these changes became marked, although this is the proper place, I think, to speak of them. For, having myself no other duty than to enjoy a well-earned holiday, I used to load my canoe with blankets and provisions and journey forth on exploration trips among the islands of several days together; and it was on my return from the first of these—when I rediscovered the party, so to speak— that these changes first presented themselves vividly to me, and in one particular instance produced a rather curious impression.

In a word, then, while every one had grown wilder, naturally wilder, Sangree, it seemed to me, had grown much wilder, and what I can only call unnaturally wilder. He made me think of a savage.

To begin with, he had changed immensely in mere physical appearance, and the full brown cheeks, the brighter eyes of absolute health, and the general air of vigour and robustness that had come to replace his customary lassitude and timidity, had worked such an improvement that I hardly knew him for the same man. His voice, too, was deeper and his manner bespoke for the first time a greater measure of confidence in himself. He now had some claims to be called nice-looking, or at least to a certain air of virility that would not lessen his value in the eyes of the opposite sex.

All this, of course, was natural enough, and most welcome. But, altogether apart from this physical change, which no doubt had also been going forward in the rest of us, there was a subtle note in his personality that came to me with a degree of surprise that almost amounted to shock.

And two things—as he came down to welcome me and pull up the canoe—leaped up in my mind unbidden, as though connected in some way I could not at the moment divine—first, the curious judgment formed of him by Joan; and secondly, that fugitive expression I had caught in his face while Maloney was offering up his strange prayer for special protection from Heaven.

The delicacy of manner and feature—to call it by no milder term—which had always been a distinguishing characteristic of the man, had been replaced by something far more vigorous and decided, that yet utterly eluded analysis. The change which impressed me so oddly was not easy to name. The others—singing Maloney, the bustling Bo'sun's Mate, and Joan, that fascinating half-breed of undine and salamander—all showed the effects of a life so close to nature; but in their case the change was perfectly natural and what was to be expected, whereas with Peter Sangree, the Canadian, it was something unusual and unexpected.

It is impossible to explain how he managed gradually to convey to my mind the impression that something in him had turned savage, yet this, more or less, is the impression that he did convey. It was not that he seemed really less civilised, or that his character had undergone any definite alteration, but rather that something in him, hitherto dormant, had awakened to life. Some quality, latent till now—so far, at least, as we were concerned, who, after all, knew him but slightly—had stirred into activity and risen to the surface of his being.

And while, for the moment, this seemed as far as I could get, it was but natural that my mind should continue the intuitive process and acknowledge that John Silence, owing to his peculiar faculties, and the girl, owing to her singularly receptive temperament, might each in a different way have divined this latent quality in his soul, and feared its manifestation later.

On looking back to this painful adventure, too, it now seems equally natural that the same process, carried to its logical conclusion, should have wakened some deep instinct in me that, wholly without direction from my will, set itself sharply and persistently upon the watch from that very moment. Thenceforward the personality of Sangree was never far from my thoughts, and I was for ever analysing and searching for the explanation that took so long in coming.

"I declare, Hubbard, you're tanned like an aboriginal, and you look like one, too," laughed Maloney.

"And I can return the compliment," was my reply, as we all gathered round a brew of tea to exchange news and compare notes.

And later, at supper, it amused me to observe that the distinguished tutor, once clergyman, did not eat his food quite as "nicely" as he did at home—he devoured it; that Mrs. Maloney ate more, and, to say the least, with less delay, than was her custom in the select atmosphere of her English dining-room; and that while Joan attacked her tin plateful with genuine avidity, Sangree, the Canadian, bit and gnawed at his, laughing and talking and complimenting the cook all the while, and making me think with secret amusement of a starved animal at its first meal. While, from their remarks about myself, I judged that I had changed and grown wild as much as the rest of them.

In this and in a hundred other little ways the change showed, ways difficult to define in detail, but all proving—not the coarsening effect of leading the primitive life, but, let us say, the more direct and unvarnished methods that became prevalent. For all day long we were in the bath of the elements—wind, water, sun—and just as the body became insensible to cold and shed unnecessary clothing, the mind grew straightforward and shed many of the disguises required by the conventions of civilisation.

And in each, according to temperament and character, there stirred the life-instincts that were natural, untamed, and, in a sense—savage.

III

So it came about that I stayed with our island party, putting off my second exploring trip from day to day, and I think that this far-fetched instinct to watch Sangree was really the cause of my postponement.

For another ten days the life of the Camp pursued its even and delightful way, blessed by perfect summer weather, a good harvest of fish, fine winds for sailing, and calm, starry nights. Maloney's selfish prayer had been favourably received. Nothing came to disturb or perplex. There was not even the prowling of night animals to vex the rest of Mrs. Maloney; for in previous camps it had often been her peculiar affliction that she heard the porcupines scratching against the canvas, or the squirrels dropping fir-cones in the early morning with a sound of miniature thunder upon the roof of her tent. But on this island there was not even a squirrel or a mouse. I think two toads and a small and harmless snake were the only living creatures that had been discovered during the whole of the first fortnight. And these two toads in all probability were not two toads, but one toad.

Then, suddenly, came the terror that changed the whole aspect of the place—the devastating terror.

It came, at first, gently, but from the very start it made me realise the unpleasant loneliness of our situation, our remote isolation in this wilderness of sea and rock, and how the islands in this tideless Baltic ocean lay about us like the advance guard of a vast besieging army. Its entry, as I say, was gentle, hardly noticeable, in fact, to most of us: singularly undramatic it certainly was. But, then, in actual life this is often the way the dreadful climaxes move upon us, leaving the heart undisturbed almost to the last minute, and then overwhelming it with a sudden rush of horror. For it was the custom at breakfast to listen patiently while each in turn related the trivial adventures of the night—how they slept, whether the wind shook their tent, whether the spider on the ridge pole had moved, whether they had heard the toad, and so forth—and on this particular morning Joan, in the middle of a little pause, made a truly novel announcement:

"In the night I heard the howling of a dog," she said, and then flushed up to the roots of her hair when we burst out laughing. For the idea of there being a dog on this forsaken island that was only able to support a snake and two toads was distinctly ludicrous, and I remember Maloney, half-way through his burnt porridge, capping the announcement by declaring that he had heard a "Baltic turtle" in the lagoon, and his wife's expression of frantic alarm before the laughter undeceived her.

But the next morning Joan repeated the story with additional and convincing detail.

"Sounds of whining and growling woke me," she said, "and I distinctly heard sniffing under my tent, and the scratching of paws."

"Oh, Timothy! Can it be a porcupine?" exclaimed the Bo'sun's Mate with distress, forgetting that Sweden was not Canada.

But the girl's voice had sounded to me in quite another key, and looking up I saw that her father and Sangree were staring at her hard. They, too, understood that she was in earnest, and had been struck by the serious note in her voice.

"Rubbish, Joan! You are always dreaming something or other wild," her father said a little impatiently.

"There's not an animal of any size on the whole island," added Sangree with a puzzled expression. He never took his eyes from her face.

"But there's nothing to prevent one swimming over," I put in briskly, for somehow a sense of uneasiness that was not pleasant had woven itself into the talk and pauses. "A deer, for instance, might easily land in the night and take a look round—"

"Or a bear!" gasped the Bo'sun's Mate, with a look so portentous that we all welcomed the laugh.

But Joan did not laugh. Instead, she sprang up and called to us to follow.

"There," she said, pointing to the ground by her tent on the side farthest from her mother's; "there are the marks close to my head. You can see for yourselves."

We saw plainly. The moss and lichen—for earth there was hardly any— had been scratched up by paws. An animal about the size of a large dog it must have been, to judge by the marks. We stood and stared in a row.

"Close to my head," repeated the girl, looking round at us. Her face, I noticed, was very pale, and her lip seemed to quiver for an instant. Then she gave a sudden gulp—and burst into a flood of tears.

The whole thing had come about in the brief space of a few minutes, and with a curious sense of inevitableness, moreover, as though it had all been carefully planned from all time and nothing could have stopped it. It had all been rehearsed before—had actually happened before, as the strange feeling sometimes has it; it seemed like the opening movement in some ominous drama, and that I knew exactly what would happen next. Something of great moment was impending.

For this sinister sensation of coming disaster made itself felt from the very beginning, and an atmosphere of gloom and dismay pervaded the entire Camp from that moment forward.

I drew Sangree to one side and moved away, while Maloney took the distressed girl into her tent, and his wife followed them, energetic and greatly flustered.

For thus, in undramatic fashion, it was that the terror I have spoken of first attempted the invasion of our Camp, and, trivial and unimportant though it seemed, every little detail of this opening scene is photographed upon my mind with merciless accuracy and precision. It happened exactly as described. This was exactly the language used. I see it written before me in black and white. I see, too, the faces of all concerned with the sudden ugly signature of alarm where before had been peace. The terror had stretched out, so to speak, a first tentative feeler toward us and had touched the hearts of each with a horrid directness. And from this moment the Camp changed.

Sangree in particular was visibly upset. He could not bear to see the girl distressed, and to hear her actually cry was almost more than he could stand. The feeling that he had no right to protect her hurt him keenly, and I could see that he was itching to do something to help, and liked him for it. His expression said plainly that he would tear in a thousand pieces anything that dared to injure a hair of her head.

We lit our pipes and strolled over in silence to the men's quarters, and it was his odd Canadian expression "Gee whiz!" that drew my attention to a further discovery.

"The brute's been scratching round my tent too," he cried, as he pointed to similar marks by the door and I stooped down to examine them. We both stared in amazement for several minutes without speaking.

"Only I sleep like the dead," he added, straightening up again, "and so heard nothing, I suppose."

We traced the paw-marks from the mouth of his tent in a direct line across to the girl's, but nowhere else about the Camp was there a sign of the strange visitor. The deer, dog, or whatever it was that had twice favoured us with a visit in the night, had confined its attentions to these two tents. And, after all, there was really nothing out of the way about these visits of an unknown animal, for although our own island was destitute of life, we were in the heart of a wilderness, and the mainland and larger islands must be swarming with all kinds of four-footed creatures, and no very prolonged swimming was necessary to reach us. In any other country it would not have caused a moment's interest—interest of the kind we felt, that is. In our Canadian camps the bears were for ever grunting about among the provision bags at night, porcupines scratching unceasingly, and chipmunks scuttling over everything.

"My daughter is overtired, and that's the truth of it," explained Maloney presently when he rejoined us and had examined in turn the other paw-marks. "She's been overdoing it lately, and camp-life, you know, always means a great excitement to her. It's natural enough. If we take no notice she'll be all right." He paused to borrow my tobacco pouch and fill his pipe, and the blundering way he filled it and spilled the precious weed on the ground visibly belied the calm of his easy language. "You might take her out for a bit of fishing, Hubbard, like a good chap; she's hardly up to the long day in the cutter. Show her some of the other islands in your canoe, perhaps. Eh?"

And by lunch-time the cloud had passed away as suddenly, and as suspiciously, as it had come.

But in the canoe, on our way home, having till then purposely ignored the subject uppermost in our minds, she suddenly spoke to me in a way that again touched the note of sinister alarm—the note that kept on sounding and sounding until finally John Silence came with his great vibrating presence and relieved it; yes, and even after he came, too, for a while.

"I'm ashamed to ask it," she said abruptly, as she steered me home, her sleeves rolled up, her hair blowing in the wind, "and ashamed of my silly tears too, because I really can't make out what caused them; but, Mr. Hubbard, I want you to promise me not to go off for your long expeditions—just yet. I beg it of you." She was so in earnest that she forgot the canoe, and the wind caught it sideways and made us roll dangerously. "I have tried hard not to ask this," she added, bringing the canoe round again, "but I simply can't help myself."

It was a good deal to ask, and I suppose my hesitation was plain; for she went on before I could reply, and her beseeching expression and intensity of manner impressed me very forcibly.

"For another two weeks only—"

"Mr. Sangree leaves in a fortnight," I said, seeing at once what she was driving at, but wondering if it was best to encourage her or not.

"If I knew you were to be on the island till then," she said, her face alternately pale and blushing, and her voice trembling a little, "I should feel so much happier."

I looked at her steadily, waiting for her to finish.

"And safer," she added almost in a whisper; "especially—at night, I mean."

"Safer, Joan?" I repeated, thinking I had never seen her eyes so soft and tender. She nodded her head, keeping her gaze fixed on my face.

It was really difficult to refuse, whatever my thoughts and judgment may have been, and somehow I understood that she spoke with good reason, though for the life of me I could not have put it into words.

"Happier—and safer," she said gravely, the canoe giving a dangerous lurch as she leaned forward in her seat to catch my answer. Perhaps, after all, the wisest way was to grant her request and make light of it, easing her anxiety without too much encouraging its cause.

"All right, Joan, you queer creature; I promise," and the instant look of relief in her face, and the smile that came back like sunlight to her eyes, made me feel that, unknown to myself and the world, I was capable of considerable sacrifice after all.

"But, you know, there's nothing to be afraid of," I added sharply; and she looked up in my face with the smile women use when they know we are talking idly, yet do not wish to tell us so.

"*You* don't feel afraid, I know," she observed quietly.

"Of course not; why should I?"

"So, if you will just humour me this once I—I will never ask anything foolish of you again as long as I live," she said gratefully.

"You have my promise," was all I could find to say.

She headed the nose of the canoe for the lagoon lying a quarter of a mile ahead, and paddled swiftly; but a minute or two later she paused again and stared hard at me with the dripping paddle across the thwarts.

"You've not heard anything at night yourself, have you?" she asked.

"I never hear anything at night," I replied shortly, "from the moment I lie down till the moment I get up."

"That dismal howling, for instance," she went on, determined to get it out, "far away at first and then getting closer, and stopping just outside the Camp?"

"Certainly not."

"Because, sometimes I think I almost dreamed it."

"Most likely you did," was my unsympathetic response.

"And you don't think father has heard it either, then?"

"No. He would have told me if he had."

This seemed to relieve her mind a little. "I know mother hasn't," she added, as if speaking to herself, "for she hears nothing—ever."

It was two nights after this conversation that I woke out of deep sleep and heard sounds of screaming. The voice was really horrible, breaking the peace and silence with its shrill clamour. In less than ten seconds I was half dressed and out of my tent. The screaming had stopped abruptly, but I knew the general direction, and ran as fast as the darkness would allow over to the women's quarters, and on getting close I heard sounds of suppressed weeping. It was Joan's voice. And just as I came up I saw Mrs. Maloney, marvellously attired, fumbling with a lantern. Other voices became audible in the same moment behind me, and Timothy Maloney arrived, breathless, less than half dressed, and carrying another lantern that had gone out on the way from being banged against a tree. Dawn was just breaking, and a chill wind blew in from the sea. Heavy black clouds drove low overhead.

The scene of confusion may be better imagined than described. Questions in frightened voices filled the air against this background of suppressed weeping. Briefly—Joan's silk tent had been torn, and the girl was in a state bordering upon hysterics. Somewhat reassured by our noisy presence, however, —for she was plucky at heart, —she pulled herself together and tried to explain what had happened; and her broken words, told there on the edge of night and morning upon this wild island ridge, were oddly thrilling and distressingly convincing.

"Something touched me and I woke," she said simply, but in a voice still hushed and broken with the terror of it, "something pushing against the tent; I felt it through the canvas. There was the same sniffing and scratching as before, and I felt the tent give a little as when wind shakes it. I heard breathing—very loud, very heavy breathing—and then came a sudden great tearing blow, and the canvas ripped open close to my face."

She had instantly dashed out through the open flap and screamed at the top of her voice, thinking the creature had actually got into the tent. But nothing was visible, she declared, and she heard not the faintest sound of an animal making off under cover of the darkness. The brief account seemed to exercise a paralysing effect upon us all as we listened to it. I can see the dishevelled group to this day, the wind blowing the women's hair, and Maloney craning his head forward to listen, and his wife, open-mouthed and gasping, leaning against a pine tree.

"Come over to the stockade and we'll get the fire going," I said; "that's the first thing," for we were all shaking with the cold in our scanty garments. And at that moment Sangree arrived wrapped in a blanket and carrying his gun; he was still drunken with sleep.

"The dog again," Maloney explained briefly, forestalling his questions; "been at Joan's tent. Torn it, by Gad! this time. It's time we did something." He went on mumbling confusedly to himself.

Sangree gripped his gun and looked about swiftly in the darkness. I saw his eyes aflame in the glare of the flickering lanterns. He made a movement as though to start out and hunt—and kill. Then his glance fell on the girl crouching on the ground, her face hidden in her hands, and there leaped into his features an expression of savage anger that transformed them. He could have faced a dozen lions with a walking-stick at that moment, and again I liked him for the strength of his anger, his self-control, and his hopeless devotion.

But I stopped him going off on a blind and useless chase.

"Come and help me start the fire, Sangree," I said, anxious also to relieve the girl of our presence; and a few minutes later the ashes, still growing from the night's fire, had kindled the fresh wood, and there was a blaze that warmed us well while it also lit up the surrounding trees within a radius of twenty yards.

"I heard nothing," he whispered; "what in the world do you think it is? It surely can't be only a dog!"

"We'll find that out later," I said, as the others came up to the grateful warmth; "the first thing is to make as big a fire as we can."

Joan was calmer now, and her mother had put on some warmer, and less miraculous, garments. And while they stood talking in low voices Maloney and I slipped off to examine the tent. There was little enough to see, but that little was unmistakable. Some animal had scratched up the ground at the head of the tent, and with a great blow of a powerful paw—a paw clearly provided with good claws—had struck the silk and torn it open. There was a hole large enough to pass a fist and arm through.

"It can't be far away," Maloney said excitedly. "We'll organise a hunt at once; this very minute."

We hurried back to the fire, Maloney talking boisterously about his proposed hunt. "There's nothing like prompt action to dispel alarm," he whispered in my ear; and then turned to the rest of us.

"We'll hunt the island from end to end at once," he said, with excitement; "that's what we'll do. The beast can't be far away. And the Bo'sun's Mate and Joan must come too, because they can't be left alone. Hubbard, you take the right shore, and you, Sangree, the left, and I'll go in the middle with the women. In this way we can stretch clean across the ridge, and nothing bigger than a rabbit can possibly escape us." He was extraordinarily excited, I thought. Anything affecting Joan, of course, stirred him prodigiously. "Get your guns and we'll start the drive at once," he cried. He lit another lantern and handed one each to his wife and Joan, and while I ran to fetch my gun I heard him singing to himself with the excitement of it all.

Meanwhile the dawn had come on quickly. It made the flickering lanterns look pale. The wind, too, was rising, and I heard the trees moaning overhead and the waves breaking with increasing clamour on the shore. In the lagoon the boat dipped and splashed, and the sparks from the fire were carried aloft in a stream and scattered far and wide.

We made our way to the extreme end of the island, measured our distances carefully, and then began to advance. None of us spoke. Sangree and I, with cocked guns, watched the shore lines, and all within easy touch and speaking distance. It was a slow and blundering drive, and there were many false alarms, but after the best part of half an hour we stood on the farther end, having made the complete tour, and without putting up so much as a squirrel. Certainly there was no living creature on that island but ourselves.

"*I* know what it is!" cried Maloney, looking out over the dim expanse of grey sea, and speaking with the air of a man making a discovery; "it's a dog from one of the farms on the larger islands" —he pointed seawards where the archipelago thickened—" and it's escaped and turned wild. Our fires and voices attracted it, and it's probably half starved as well as savage, poor brute!"

No one said anything in reply, and he began to sing again very low to himself.

The point where we stood—a huddled, shivering group—faced the wider channels that led to the open sea and Finland. The grey dawn had broken in earnest at last, and we could see the racing waves with their angry crests of white. The surrounding islands showed up as dark masses in the distance, and in the east, almost as Maloney spoke, the sun came up with a rush in a stormy and magnificent sky of red and gold. Against this splashed and gorgeous background black clouds, shaped like fantastic and legendary animals, filed past swiftly in a tearing stream, and to this day I have only to close my eyes to see again that vivid and hurrying procession in the air. All about us the pines made black splashes against the sky. It was an angry sunrise. Rain, indeed, had already begun to fall in big drops.

We turned, as by a common instinct, and, without speech, made our way back slowly to the stockade, Maloney humming snatches of his songs, Sangree in front with his gun, prepared to shoot at a moment's notice, and the women floundering in the rear with myself and the extinguished lanterns.

Yet it was only a dog!

Really, it was most singular when one came to reflect soberly upon it all. Events, say the occultists, have souls, or at least that agglomerate life due to the emotions and thoughts of all concerned in them, so that cities, and even whole countries, have great astral shapes which may become visible to the eye of vision; and certainly here, the soul of this drive—this vain, blundering, futile drive—stood somewhere between ourselves and— laughed.

All of us heard that laugh, and all of us tried hard to smother the sound, or at least to ignore it. Every one talked at once, loudly, and with exaggerated decision, obviously trying to say something plausible against heavy odds, striving to explain naturally that an animal might so easily conceal itself from us, or swim away before we had time to light upon its trail. For we all spoke of that "trail" as though it really existed, and we had more to go upon than the mere marks of paws about the tents of Joan and the Canadian. Indeed, but for these, and the torn tent, I think it would, of course, have been possible to ignore the existence of this beast intruder altogether.

And it was here, under this angry dawn, as we stood in the shelter of the stockade from the pouring rain, weary yet so strangely excited—it was here, out of this confusion of voices and explanations, that—very stealthily— the ghost of something horrible slipped in and stood among us. It made all our explanations seem childish and untrue; the false relation was instantly exposed. Eyes exchanged quick, anxious glances, questioning, expressive of dismay. There was a sense of wonder, of poignant distress, and of trepidation. Alarm stood waiting at our elbows. We shivered.

Then, suddenly, as we looked into each other's faces, came the long, unwelcome pause in which this new arrival established itself in our hearts.

And, without further speech, or attempt at explanation, Maloney moved off abruptly to mix the porridge for an early breakfast; Sangree to clean the fish; myself to chop wood and tend the fire; Joan and her mother to change their wet garments; and, most significant of all, to prepare her mother's tent for its future complement of two.

Each went to his duty, but hurriedly, awkwardly, silently; and this new arrival, this shape of terror and distress stalked, viewless, by the side of each.

"If only I could have traced that dog," I think was the thought in the minds of all.

But in Camp, where every one realises how important the individual contribution is to the comfort and well-being of all, the mind speedily recovers tone and pulls itself together.

During the day, a day of heavy and ceaseless rain, we kept more or less to our tents, and though there were signs of mysterious conferences between the three members of the Maloney family, I think that most of us slept a good deal and stayed alone with his thoughts. Certainly, I did, because when Maloney came to say that his wife invited us all to a special "tea" in her tent, he had to shake me awake before I realised that he was there at all.

And by supper-time we were more or less even-minded again, and almost jolly. I only noticed that there was an undercurrent of what is best described as "jumpiness," and that the merest snapping of a twig, or plop of a fish in the lagoon, was sufficient to make us start and look over our shoulders. Pauses were rare in our talk, and the fire was never for one instant allowed to get low. The wind and rain had ceased, but the dripping of the branches still kept up an excellent imitation of a downpour. In particular, Maloney was vigilant and alert, telling us a series of tales in which the wholesome humorous element was especially strong. He lingered, too, behind with me after Sangree had gone to bed, and while I mixed myself a glass of hot Swedish punch, he did a thing I had never known him do before—he mixed one for himself, and then asked me to light him over to his tent. We said nothing on the way, but I felt that he was glad of my companionship.

I returned alone to the stockade, and for a long time after that kept the fire blazing, and sat up smoking and thinking. I hardly knew why; but sleep was far from me for one thing, and for another, an idea was taking form in my mind that required the comfort of tobacco and a bright fire for its growth. I lay against a corner of the stockade seat, listening to the wind whispering and to the ceaseless drip-drip of the trees. The night, otherwise, was very still, and the sea quiet as a lake. I remember that I was conscious, peculiarly conscious, of this host of desolate islands crowding about us in the darkness, and that we were the one little spot of humanity in a rather wonderful kind of wilderness.

But this, I think, was the only symptom that came to warn me of highly strung nerves, and it certainly was not sufficiently alarming to destroy my peace of mind. One thing, however, did come to disturb my peace, for just as I finally made ready to go, and had kicked the embers of the fire into a last effort, I fancied I saw, peering at me round the farther end of the stockade wall, a dark and shadowy mass that might have been—that strongly resembled, in fact—the body of a large animal. Two glowing eyes shone for an instant in the middle of it. But the next second I saw that it was merely a projecting mass of moss and lichen in the wall of our stockade, and the eyes were a couple of wandering sparks from the dying ashes I had kicked. It was easy enough, too, to imagine I saw an animal moving here and there between the trees, as I picked my way stealthily to my tent. Of course, the shadows tricked me.

And though it was after one o'clock, Maloney's light was still burning, for I saw his tent shining white among the pines.

It was, however, in the short space between consciousness and sleep— that time when the body is low and the voices of the submerged region tell sometimes true—that the idea which had been all this while maturing reached the point of an actual decision, and I suddenly realised that I had resolved to send word to Dr. Silence. For, with a sudden wonder that I had hitherto been so blind, the unwelcome conviction dawned upon me all at once that some dreadful thing was lurking about us on this island, and that the safety of at least one of us was threatened by something monstrous and unclean that was too horrible to contemplate. And, again remembering those last words of his as the train moved out of the platform, I understood that Dr. Silence would hold himself in readiness to come.

"Unless you should send for me sooner," he had said.

I found myself suddenly wide awake. It is impossible to say what woke me, but it was no gradual process, seeing that I jumped from deep sleep to absolute alertness in a single instant. I had evidently slept for an hour and more, for the night had cleared, stars crowded the sky, and a pallid half-moon just sinking into the sea threw a spectral light between the trees.

I went outside to sniff the air, and stood upright. A curious impression that something was astir in the Camp came over me, and when I glanced across at Sangree's tent, some twenty feet away, I saw that it was moving. He too, then, was awake and restless, for I saw the canvas sides bulge this way and that as he moved within.

Then the flap pushed forward. He was coming out, like myself, to sniff the air; and I was not surprised, for its sweetness after the rain was intoxicating. And he came on all fours, just as I had done. I saw a head thrust round the edge of the tent.

And then I saw that it was not Sangree at all. It was an animal. And the same instant I realised something else too—it was *the* animal; and its whole presentment for some unaccountable reason was unutterably malefic.

A cry I was quite unable to suppress escaped me, and the creature turned on the instant and stared at me with baleful eyes. I could have dropped on the spot, for the strength all ran out of my body with a rush. Something about it touched in me the living terror that grips and paralyses. If the mind requires but the tenth of a second to form an impression, I must have stood there stockstill for several seconds while I seized the ropes for support and stared. Many and vivid impressions flashed through my mind, but not one of them resulted in action, because I was in instant dread that the beast any moment would leap in my direction and be upon me. Instead, however, after what seemed a vast period, it slowly turned its eyes from my face, uttered a low whining sound, and came out altogether into the open.

Then, for the first time, I saw it in its entirety and noted two things: it was about the size of a large dog, but at the same time it was utterly unlike any animal that I had ever seen. Also, that the quality that had impressed me first as being malefic was really only its singular and original strangeness. Foolish as it may sound, and impossible as it is for me to adduce proof, I can only say that the animal seemed to me then to be—not real.

But all this passed through my mind in a flash, almost subconsciously, and before I had time to check my impressions, or even properly verify them, I made an involuntary movement, catching the tight rope in my hand so that it twanged like a banjo string, and in that instant the creature turned the corner of Sangree's tent and was gone into the darkness.

Then, of course, my senses in some measure returned to me, and I realised only one thing: it had been inside his tent!

I dashed out, reached the door in half a dozen strides, and looked in. The Canadian, thank God! lay upon his bed of branches. His arm was stretched outside, across the blankets, the fist tightly clenched, and the body had an appearance of unusual rigidity that was alarming. On his face there was an expression of effort, almost of painful effort, so far as the uncertain light permitted me to see, and his sleep seemed to be very profound. He looked, I thought, so stiff, so unnaturally stiff, and in some indefinable way, too, he looked smaller—shrunken.

I called to him to wake, but called many times in vain. Then I decided to shake him, and had already moved forward to do so vigorously when there came a sound of footsteps padding softly behind me, and I felt a stream of hot breath burn my neck as I stooped. I turned sharply. The tent door was darkened and something silently swept in. I felt a rough and shaggy body push past me, and knew that the animal had returned. It seemed to leap forward between me and Sangree—in fact, to leap upon Sangree, for its dark body hid him momentarily from view, and in that moment my soul turned sick and coward with a horror that rose from the very dregs and depths of life, and gripped my existence at its central source.

The creature seemed somehow to melt away into him, almost as though it belonged to him and were a part of himself, but in the same instant— that instant of extraordinary confusion and terror in my mind—it seemed to pass over and behind him, and, in some utterly unaccountable fashion, it was gone. And the Canadian woke and sat up with a start.

"Quick! You fool!" I cried, in my excitement, "the beast has been in your tent, here at your very throat while you sleep like the dead. Up, man! Get your gun! Only this second it disappeared over there behind your head. Quick! or Joan—!"

And somehow the fact that he was there, wide-awake now, to corroborate me, brought the additional conviction to my own mind that this was no animal, but some perplexing and dreadful form of life that drew upon my deeper knowledge, that much reading had perhaps assented to, but that had never yet come within actual range of my senses.

He was up in a flash, and out. He was trembling, and very white. We searched hurriedly, feverishly, but found only the traces of paw-marks passing from the door of his own tent across the moss to the women's. And the sight of the tracks about Mrs. Maloney's tent, where Joan now slept, set him in a perfect fury.

"Do you know what it is, Hubbard, this beast?" he hissed under his breath at me; "it's a damned wolf, that's what it is—a wolf lost among the islands, and starving to death—desperate. So help me God, I believe it's that!"

He talked a lot of rubbish in his excitement. He declared he would sleep by day and sit up every night until he killed it. Again his rage touched my admiration; but I got him away before he made enough noise to wake the whole Camp.

"I have a better plan than that," I said, watching his face closely. "I don't think this is anything we can deal with. I'm going to send for the only man I know who can help. We'll go to Waxholm this very morning and get a telegram through."

Sangree stared at me with a curious expression as the fury died out of his face and a new look of alarm took its place.

"John Silence," I said, "will know—"

"You think it's something—of that sort?" he stammered.

"I am sure of it."

There was a moment's pause. "That's worse, far worse than anything material," he said, turning visibly paler. He looked from my face to the sky, and then added with sudden resolution, "Come; the wind's rising. Let's get off at once. From there you can telephone to Stockholm and get a telegram sent without delay."

I sent him down to get the boat ready, and seized the opportunity myself to run and wake Maloney. He was sleeping very lightly, and sprang up the moment I put my head inside his tent. I told him briefly what I had seen, and he showed so little surprise that I caught myself wondering for the first time whether he himself had seen more going on than he had deemed wise to communicate to the rest of us.

He agreed to my plan without a moment's hesitation, and my last words to him were to let his wife and daughter think that the great psychic doctor was coming merely as a chance visitor, and not with any professional interest.

So, with frying-pan, provisions, and blankets aboard, Sangree and I sailed out of the lagoon fifteen minutes later, and headed with a good breeze for the direction of Waxholm and the borders of civilisation.

IV

Although nothing John Silence did ever took me, properly speaking, by surprise, it was certainly unexpected to find a letter from Stockholm waiting for me. "I have finished my Hungary business," he wrote, "and am here for ten days. Do not hesitate to send if you need me. If you telephone any morning from Waxholm I can catch the afternoon steamer."

My years of intercourse with him were full of "coincidences" of this description, and although he never sought to explain them by claiming any magical system of communication with my mind, I have never doubted that there actually existed some secret telepathic method by which he knew my circumstances and gauged the degree of my need. And that this power was independent of time in the sense that it saw into the future, always seemed to me equally apparent.

Sangree was as much relieved as I was, and within an hour of sunset that very evening we met him on the arrival of the little coasting steamer, and carried him off in the dinghy to the camp we had prepared on a neighbouring island, meaning to start for home early next morning.

"Now," he said, when supper was over and we were smoking round the fire, "let me hear your story." He glanced from one to the other, smiling.

"You tell it, Mr. Hubbard," Sangree interrupted abruptly, and went off a little way to wash the dishes, yet not so far as to be out of earshot. And while he splashed with the hot water, and scraped the tin plates with sand and moss, my voice, unbroken by a single question from Dr. Silence, ran on for the next half-hour with the best account I could give of what had happened.

My listener lay on the other side of the fire, his face half hidden by a big sombrero; sometimes he glanced up questioningly when a point needed elaboration, but he uttered no single word till I had reached the end, and his manner all through the recital was grave and attentive. Overhead, the wash of the wind in the pine branches filled in the pauses; the darkness settled down over the sea, and the stars came out in thousands, and by the time I finished the moon had risen to flood the scene with silver. Yet, by his face and eyes, I knew quite well that the doctor was listening to something he had expected to hear, even if he had not actually anticipated all the details.

"You did well to send for me," he said very low, with a significant glance at me when I finished; "very well," —and for one swift second his eye took in Sangree, —"for what we have to deal with here is nothing more than a werewolf—rare enough, I am glad to say, but often very sad, and sometimes very terrible."

I jumped as though I had been shot, but the next second was heartily ashamed of my want of control; for this brief remark, confirming as it did my own worst suspicions, did more to convince me of the gravity of the adventure than any number of questions or explanations. It seemed to draw close the circle about us, shutting a door somewhere that locked us in with the animal and the horror, and turning the key. Whatever it was had now to be faced and dealt with.

"No one has been actually injured so far?" he asked aloud, but in a matter-of-fact tone that lent reality to grim possibilities.

"Good heavens, no!" cried the Canadian, throwing down his dish-cloths and coming forward into the circle of firelight. "Surely there can be no question of this poor starved beast injuring anybody, can there?"

His hair straggled untidily over his forehead, and there was a gleam in his eyes that was not all reflection from the fire. His words made me turn sharply. We all laughed a little short, forced laugh.

"I trust not, indeed," Dr. Silence said quietly. "But what makes you think the creature is starved?" He asked the question with his eyes straight on the other's face. The prompt question explained to me why I had started, and I waited with just a tremor of excitement for the reply.

Sangree hesitated a moment, as though the question took him by surprise. But he met the doctor's gaze unflinchingly across the fire, and with complete honesty.

"Really," he faltered, with a little shrug of the shoulders, "I can hardly tell you. The phrase seemed to come out of its own accord. I have felt from the beginning that it was in pain and—starved, though why I felt this never occurred to me till you asked."

"You really know very little about it, then?" said the other, with a sudden gentleness in his voice.

"No more than that," Sangree replied, looking at him with a puzzled expression that was unmistakably genuine. "In fact, nothing at all, really," he added, by way of further explanation.

"I am glad of that," I heard the doctor murmur under his breath, but so low that I only just caught the words, and Sangree missed them altogether, as evidently he was meant to do.

"And now," he cried, getting on his feet and shaking himself with a characteristic gesture, as though to shake out the horror and the mystery, "let us leave the problem till to-morrow and enjoy this wind and sea and stars. I've been living lately in the atmosphere of many people, and feel that I want to wash and be clean. I propose a swim and then bed. Who'll second me?" And two minutes later we were all diving from the boat into cool, deep water, that reflected a thousand moons as the waves broke away from us in countless ripples.

We slept in blankets under the open sky, Sangree and I taking the outside places, and were up before sunrise to catch the dawn wind. Helped by this early start we were half-way home by noon, and then the wind shifted to a few points behind us so that we fairly ran. In and out among a thousand islands, down narrow channels where we lost the wind, out into open spaces where we had to take in a reef, racing along under a hot and cloudless sky, we flew through the very heart of the bewildering and lonely scenery.

"A real wilderness," cried Dr. Silence from his seat in the bows where he held the jib sheet. His hat was off, his hair tumbled in the wind, and his lean brown face gave him the touch of an Oriental. Presently he changed places with Sangree, and came down to talk with me by the tiller.

"A wonderful region, all this world of islands," he said, waving his hand to the scenery rushing past us, "but doesn't it strike you there's something lacking?"

"It's—hard," I answered, after a moment's reflection. "It has a superficial, glittering prettiness, without—" I hesitated to find the word I wanted.

John Silence nodded his head with approval.

"Exactly," he said. "The picturesqueness of stage scenery that is not real, not alive. It's like a landscape by a clever painter, yet without true imagination. Soulless—that's the word you wanted."

"Something like that," I answered, watching the gusts of wind on the sails. "Not dead so much, as without soul. That's it."

"Of course," he went on, in a voice calculated, it seemed to me, not to reach our companion in the bows, "to live long in a place like this—long and alone—might bring about a strange result in some men."

I suddenly realised he was talking with a purpose and pricked up my ears.

"There's no life here. These islands are mere dead rocks pushed up from below the sea—not living land; and there's nothing really alive on them. Even the sea, this tideless, brackish sea, neither salt water nor fresh, is dead. It's all a pretty image of life without the real heart and soul of life. To a man with too strong desires who came here and lived close to nature, strange things might happen."

"Let her out a bit," I shouted to Sangree, who was coming aft. "The wind's gusty and we've got hardly any ballast."

He went back to the bows, and Dr. Silence continued—

"Here, I mean, a long sojourn would lead to deterioration, to degeneration. The place is utterly unsoftened by human influences, by any humanising associations of history, good or had. This landscape has never awakened into life; it's still dreaming in its primitive sleep."

"In time," I put in, "you mean a man living here might become brutal?"

"The passions would run wild, selfishness become supreme, the instincts coarsen and turn savage probably."

"But—"

"In other places just as wild, parts of Italy for instance, where there are other moderating influences, it could not happen. The character might grow wild, savage too in a sense, but with a human wildness one could understand and deal with. But here, in a hard place like this, it might be otherwise." He spoke slowly, weighing his words carefully.

I looked at him with many questions in my eyes, and a precautionary cry to Sangree to stay in the fore part of the boat, out of earshot.

"First of all there would come callousness to pain, and indifference to the rights of others. Then the soul would turn savage, not from passionate human causes, or with enthusiasm, but by deadening down into a kind of cold, primitive, emotionless savagery—by turning, like the landscape, soulless."

"And a man with strong desires, you say, might change?"

"Without being aware of it, yes; he might turn savage, his instincts and desires turn animal. And if"—he lowered his voice and turned for a moment towards the bows, and then continued in his most weighty manner—"owing to delicate health or other predisposing causes, his Double—you know what I mean, of course—his etheric Body of Desire, or astral body, as some term it—that part in which the emotions, passions and desires reside—if this, I say, were for some constitutional reason loosely joined to his physical organism, there might well take place an occasional projection—"

Sangree came aft with a sudden rush, his face aflame, but whether with wind or sun, or with what he had heard, I cannot say. In my surprise I let the tiller slip and the cutter gave a great plunge as she came sharply into the wind and flung us all together in a heap on the bottom. Sangree said nothing, but while he scrambled up and made the jib sheet fast my companion found a moment to add to his unfinished sentence the words, too low for any ear but mine—

"Entirely unknown to himself, however."

We righted the boat and laughed, and then Sangree produced the map and explained exactly where we were. Far away on the horizon, across an open stretch of water, lay a blue cluster of islands with our crescent-shaped home among them and the safe anchorage of the lagoon. An hour with this wind would get us there comfortably, and while Dr. Silence and Sangree fell into conversation, I sat and pondered over the strange suggestions that had just been put into my mind concerning the "Double," and the possible form it might assume when dissociated temporarily from the physical body.

The whole way home these two chatted, and John Silence was as gentle and sympathetic as a woman. I did not hear much of their talk, for the wind grew occasionally to the force of a hurricane and the sails and tiller absorbed my attention; but I could see that Sangree was pleased and happy, and was pouring out intimate revelations to his companion in the way that most people did—when John Silence wished them to do so.

But it was quite suddenly, while I sat all intent upon wind and sails, that the true meaning of Sangree's remark about the animal flared up in me with its full import. For his admission that he knew it was in pain and starved was in reality nothing more or less than a revelation of his deeper self. It was in the nature of a confession. He was speaking of something that he knew positively, something that was beyond question or argument, something that had to do directly with himself. "Poor starved beast" he had called it in words that had "come out of their own accord," and there had not been the slightest evidence of any desire to conceal or explain away.

He had spoken instinctively—from his heart, and as though about his own self.

And half an hour before sunset we raced through the narrow opening of the lagoon and saw the smoke of the dinner-fire blowing here and there among the trees, and the figures of Joan and the Bo'sun's Mate running down to meet us at the landing-stage.

V

Everything changed from the moment John Silence set foot on that island; it was like the effect produced by calling in some big doctor, some great arbiter of life and death, for consultation. The sense of gravity increased a hundredfold. Even inanimate objects took upon themselves a subtle alteration, for the setting of the adventure—this deserted bit of sea with its hundreds of uninhabited islands—somehow turned sombre. An element that was mysterious, and in a sense disheartening, crept unbidden into the severity of grey rock and dark pine forest and took the sparkle from the sunshine and the sea.

I, at least, was keenly aware of the change, for my whole being shifted, as it were, a degree higher, becoming keyed up and alert. The figures from the background of the stage moved forward a little into the light—nearer to the inevitable action. In a word this man's arrival intensified the whole affair.

And, looking back down the years to the time when all this happened, it is clear to me that he had a pretty sharp idea of the meaning of it from the very beginning. How much he knew beforehand by his strange divining powers, it is impossible to say, but from the moment he came upon the scene and caught within himself the note of what was going on amongst us, he undoubtedly held the true solution of the puzzle and had no need to ask questions. And this certitude it was that set him in such an atmosphere of power and made us all look to him instinctively; for he took no tentative steps, made no false moves, and while the rest of us floundered he moved straight to the climax. He was indeed a true diviner of souls.

I can now read into his behaviour a good deal that puzzled me at the time, for though I had dimly guessed the solution, I had no idea how he would deal with it. And the conversations I can reproduce almost verbatim, for, according to my invariable habit, I kept full notes of all he said.

To Mrs. Maloney, foolish and dazed; to Joan, alarmed, yet plucky; and to the clergyman, moved by his daughter's distress below his usual shallow emotions, he gave the best possible treatment in the best possible way, yet all so easily and simply as to make it appear naturally spontaneous. For he dominated the Bo'sun's Mate, taking the measure of her ignorance with infinite patience; he keyed up Joan, stirring her courage and interest to the highest point for her own safety; and the Reverend Timothy he soothed and comforted, while obtaining his implicit obedience, by taking him into his confidence, and leading him gradually to a comprehension of the issue that was bound to follow.

And Sangree—here his wisdom was most wisely calculated—he neglected outwardly because inwardly he was the object of his unceasing and most concentrated attention. Under the guise of apparent indifference his mind kept the Canadian under constant observation.

There was a restless feeling in the Camp that evening and none of us lingered round the fire after supper as usual. Sangree and I busied ourselves with patching up the torn tent for our guest and with finding heavy stones to hold the ropes, for Dr. Silence insisted on having it pitched on the highest point of the island ridge, just where it was most rocky and there was no earth for pegs. The place, moreover, was midway between the men's and women's tents, and, of course, commanded the most comprehensive view of the Camp.

"So that if your dog comes," he said simply, "I may be able to catch him as he passes across."

The wind had gone down with the sun and an unusual warmth lay over the island that made sleep heavy, and in the morning we assembled at a late breakfast, rubbing our eyes and yawning. The cool north wind had given way to the warm southern air that sometimes came up with haze and moisture across the Baltic, bringing with it the relaxing sensations that produced enervation and listlessness.

And this may have been the reason why at first I failed to notice that anything unusual was about, and why I was less alert than normally; for it was not till after breakfast that the silence of our little party struck me and I discovered that Joan had not yet put in an appearance. And then, in a flash, the last heaviness of sleep vanished and I saw that Maloney was white and troubled and his wife could not hold a plate without trembling.

A desire to ask questions was stopped in me by a swift glance from Dr. Silence, and I suddenly understood in some vague way that they were waiting till Sangree should have gone. How this idea came to me I cannot determine, but the soundness of the intuition was soon proved, for the moment he moved off to his tent, Maloney looked up at me and began to speak in a low voice.

"You slept through it all," he half whispered.

"Through what?" I asked, suddenly thrilled with the knowledge that something dreadful had happened.

"We didn't wake you for fear of getting the whole Camp up," he went on, meaning, by the Camp, I supposed, Sangree. "It was just before dawn when the screams woke me."

"The dog again?" I asked, with a curious sinking of the heart.

"Got right into the tent," he went on, speaking passionately but very low, "and woke my wife by scrambling all over her. Then she realised that Joan was struggling beside her. And, by God! the beast had torn her arm; scratched all down the arm she was, and bleeding."

"Joan injured?" I gasped.

"Merely scratched—this time," put in John Silence, speaking for the first time; "suffering more from shock and fright than actual wounds."

"Isn't it a mercy the doctor was here?" said Mrs. Maloney, looking as if she would never know calmness again. "I think we should both have been killed."

"It has been a most merciful escape," Maloney said, his pulpit voice struggling with his emotion. "But, of course, we cannot risk another—we must strike Camp and get away at once—"

"Only poor Mr. Sangree must not know what has happened. He is so attached to Joan and would he so terribly upset," added the Bo'sun's Mate distractedly, looking all about in her terror.

"It is perhaps advisable that Mr. Sangree should not know what has occurred," Dr. Silence said with quiet authority, "but I think, for the safety of all concerned, it will be better not to leave the island just now." He spoke with great decision and Maloney looked up and followed his words closely.

"If you will agree to stay here a few days longer, I have no doubt we can put an end to the attentions of your strange visitor, and incidentally have the opportunity of observing a most singular and interesting phenomenon—"

"What!" gasped Mrs. Maloney, "a phenomenon?—you mean that you know what it is?"

"I am quite certain I know what it is," he replied very low, for we heard the footsteps of Sangree approaching, "though I am not so certain yet as to the best means of dealing with it. But in any case it is not wise to leave precipitately—"

"Oh, Timothy, does he think it's a devil—?" cried the Bo'sun's Mate in a voice that even the Canadian must have heard.

"In my opinion," continued John Silence, looking across at me and the clergyman, "it is a case of modern lycanthropy with other complications that may—" He left the sentence unfinished, for Mrs. Maloney got up with a jump and fled to her tent fearful she might hear a worse thing, and at that moment Sangree turned the corner of the stockade and came into view.

"There are footmarks all round the mouth of my tent," he said with excitement. "The animal has been here again in the night. Dr. Silence, you really must come and see them for yourself. They're as plain on the moss as tracks in snow."

But later in the day, while Sangree went off in the canoe to fish the pools near the larger islands, and Joan still lay, bandaged and resting, in her tent, Dr. Silence called me and the tutor and proposed a walk to the granite slabs at the far end. Mrs. Maloney sat on a stump near her daughter, and busied herself energetically with alternate nursing and painting.

"We'll leave you in charge," the doctor said with a smile that was meant to be encouraging, "and when you want us for lunch, or anything, the megaphone will always bring us back in time."

For, though the very air was charged with strange emotions, every one talked quietly and naturally as with a definite desire to counteract unnecessary excitement.

"I'll keep watch," said the plucky Bo'sun's Mate, "and meanwhile I find comfort in my work." She was busy with the sketch she had begun on the day after our arrival. "For even a tree," she added proudly, pointing to her little easel, "is a symbol of the divine, and the thought makes me feel safer." We glanced for a moment at a daub which was more like the symptom of a disease than a symbol of the divine—and then took the path round the lagoon.

At the far end we made a little fire and lay round it in the shadow of a big boulder. Maloney stopped his humming suddenly and turned to his companion.

"And what do you make of it all?" he asked abruptly.

"In the first place," replied John Silence, making himself comfortable against the rock, "it is of human origin, this animal; it is undoubted lycanthropy."

His words had the effect precisely of a bombshell. Maloney listened as though he had been struck.

"You puzzle me utterly," he said, sitting up closer and staring at him.

"Perhaps," replied the other, "but if you'll listen to me for a few moments you may be less puzzled at the end—or more. It depends how much you know. Let me go further and say that you have underestimated, or miscalculated, the effect of this primitive wild life upon all of you."

"In what way?" asked the clergyman, bristling a trifle.

"It is strong medicine for any town-dweller, and for some of you it has been too strong. One of you has gone wild." He uttered these last words with great emphasis.

"Gone savage," he added, looking from one to the other. Neither of us found anything to reply.

"To say that the brute has awakened in a man is not a mere metaphor always," he went on presently.

"Of course not!"

"But, in the sense I mean, may have a very literal and terrible significance," pursued Dr. Silence. "Ancient instincts that no one dreamed of, least of all their possessor, may leap forth—"

"Atavism can hardly explain a roaming animal with teeth and claws and sanguinary instincts," interrupted Maloney with impatience.

"The term is of your own choice," continued the doctor equably, "not mine, and it is a good example of a word that indicates a result while it conceals the process; but the explanation of this beast that haunts your island and attacks your daughter is of far deeper significance than mere atavistic tendencies, or throwing back to animal origin, which I suppose is the thought in your mind."

"You spoke just now of lycanthropy," said Maloney, looking bewildered and anxious to keep to plain facts evidently; "I think I have come across the word, but really—really—it can have no actual significance today, can it? These superstitions of mediæval times can hardly—"

He looked round at me with his jolly red face, and the expression of astonishment and dismay on it would have made me shout with laughter at any other time. Laughter, however, was never farther from my mind than at this moment when I listened to Dr. Silence as he carefully suggested to the clergyman the very explanation that had gradually been forcing itself upon my own mind.

"However mediæval ideas may have exaggerated the idea is not of much importance to us now," he said quietly, "when we are face to face with a modern example of what, I take it, has always been a profound fact. For the moment let us leave the name of any one in particular out of the matter and consider certain possibilities."

We all agreed with that at any rate. There was no need to speak of Sangree, or of any one else, until we knew a little more.

"The fundamental fact in this most curious case," he went on, "is that the 'Double' of a man—"

"You mean the astral body? I've heard of that, of course," broke in Maloney with a snort of triumph.

"No doubt," said the other, smiling, "no doubt you have;—that this Double, or fluidic body of a man, as I was saying, has the power under certain conditions of projecting itself and becoming visible to others. Certain training will accomplish this, and certain drugs likewise; illnesses, too, that ravage the body may produce temporarily the result that death produces permanently, and let loose this counterpart of a human being and render it visible to the sight of others.

"Every one, of course, knows this more or less today; but it is not so generally known, and probably believed by none who have not witnessed it, that this fluidic body can, under certain conditions, assume other forms than human, and that such other forms may be determined by the dominating thought and wish of the owner. For this Double, or astral body as you call it, is really the seat of the passions, emotions and desires in the psychical economy. It is the Passion Body; and, in projecting itself, it can often assume a form that gives expression to the overmastering desire that moulds it; for it is composed of such tenuous matter that it lends itself readily to the moulding by thought and wish."

"I follow you perfectly," said Maloney, looking as if he would much rather be chopping firewood elsewhere and singing.

"And there are some persons so constituted," the doctor went on with increasing seriousness, "that the fluid body in them is but loosely associated with the physical, persons of poor health as a rule, yet often of strong desires and passions; and in these persons it is easy for the Double to dissociate itself during deep sleep from their system, and, driven forth by some consuming desire, to assume an animal form and seek the fulfilment of that desire."

There, in broad daylight, I saw Maloney deliberately creep closer to the fire and heap the wood on. We gathered in to the heat, and to each other, and listened to Dr. Silence's voice as it mingled with the swish and whirr of the wind about us, and the falling of the little waves.

"For instance, to take a concrete example," he resumed; "suppose some young man, with the delicate constitution I have spoken of, forms an overpowering attachment to a young woman, yet perceives that it is not welcomed, and is man enough to repress its outward manifestations. In such a case, supposing his Double be easily projected, the very repression of his love in the daytime would add to the intense force of his desire when released in deep sleep from the control of his will, and his fluidic body might issue forth in monstrous or animal shape and become actually visible to others. And, if his devotion were dog-like in its fidelity, yet concealing the fires of a fierce passion beneath, it might well assume the form of a creature that seemed to be half dog, half wolf— "

"A werewolf, you mean?" cried Maloney, pale to the lips as he listened.

John Silence held up a restraining hand. "A werewolf," he said, "is a true psychical fact of profound significance, however absurdly it may have been exaggerated by the imaginations of a superstitious peasantry in the days of unenlightenment, for a werewolf is nothing but the savage, and possibly sanguinary, instincts of a passionate man scouring the world in his fluidic body, his passion body, his body of desire. As in the case at hand, he may not know it—"

"It is not necessarily deliberate, then?" Maloney put in quickly, with relief.

"It is hardly ever deliberate. It is the desires released in sleep from the control of the will finding a vent. In all savage races it has been recognised and dreaded, this phenomenon styled 'Wehr Wolf,' but today it is rare. And it is becoming rarer still, for the world grows tame and civilised, emotions have become refined, desires lukewarm, and few men have savagery enough left in them to generate impulses of such intense force, and certainly not to project them in animal form."

"By Gad!" exclaimed the clergyman breathlessly, and with increasing excitement, "then I feel I must tell you—what has been given to me in confidence—that Sangree has in him an admixture of savage blood—of Red Indian ancestry—"

"Let us stick to our supposition of a man as described," the doctor stopped him calmly, "and let us imagine that he has in him this admixture of savage blood; and further, that he is wholly unaware of his dreadful physical and psychical infirmity; and that he suddenly finds himself leading the primitive life together with the object of his desires; with the result that the strain of the untamed wild-man in his blood—"

"Red Indian, for instance," from Maloney.

"Red Indian, perfectly," agreed the doctor; "the result, I say, that this savage strain in him is awakened and leaps into passionate life. What then?"

He looked hard at Timothy Maloney, and the clergyman looked hard at him.

"The wild life such as you lead here on this island, for instance, might quickly awaken his savage instincts—his buried instincts—and with profoundly disquieting results."

"You mean his Subtle Body, as you call it, might issue forth automatically in deep sleep and seek the object of its desire?" I said, corning to Maloney's aid, who was finding it more and more difficult to get words.

"Precisely; —yet the desire of the man remaining utterly unmalefic—pure and wholesome in every sense—"

"Ah!" I heard the clergyman gasp.

"The lover's desire for union run wild, run savage, tearing its way out in primitive, untamed fashion, I mean," continued the doctor, striving to make himself clear to a mind bounded by conventional thought and knowledge; "for the desire to possess, remember, may easily become importunate, and, embodied in this animal form of the Subtle Body which acts as its vehicle, may go forth to tear in pieces all that obstructs, to reach to the very heart of the loved object and seize it. *Au fond,* it is nothing more than the aspiration for union, as I said—the splendid and perfectly clean desire to absorb utterly into itself—"

He paused a moment and looked into Maloney's eyes.

"To bathe in the very heart's blood of the one desired," he added with grave emphasis.

The fire spurted and crackled and made me start, but Maloney found relief in a genuine shudder, and I saw him turn his head and look about him from the sea to the trees. The wind dropped just at that moment and the doctor's words rang sharply through the stillness.

"Then it might even kill?" stammered the clergyman presently in a hushed voice, and with a little forced laugh by way of protest that sounded quite ghastly.

"In the last resort it might kill," repeated Dr. Silence. Then, after another pause, during which he was clearly debating how much or how little it was wise to give to his audience, he continued: "And if the Double does not succeed in getting back to its physical body, that physical body would wake an imbecile—an idiot—or perhaps never wake at all."

Maloney sat up and found his tongue.

"You mean that if this fluid animal thing, or whatever it is, should be prevented getting back, the man might never wake again?" he asked, with shaking voice.

"He might be dead," replied the other calmly. The tremor of a positive sensation shivered in the air about us.

"Then isn't that the best way to cure the fool—the brute—?" thundered the clergyman, half rising to his feet.

"Certainly it would be an easy and undiscoverable form of murder," was the stern reply, spoken as calmly as though it were a remark about the weather.

Maloney collapsed visibly, and I gathered the wood over the fire and coaxed up a blaze.

"The greater part of the man's life—of his vital forces—goes out with this Double," Dr. Silence resumed, after a moment's consideration, "and a considerable portion of the actual material of his physical body. So the physical body that remains behind is depleted, not only of force, but of matter. You would see it small, shrunken, dropped together, just like the body of a materialising medium at a séance. Moreover, any mark or injury inflicted upon this Double will be found exactly reproduced by the phenomenon of repercussion upon the shrunken physical body lying in its trance—"

"An injury inflicted upon the one you say would be reproduced also on the other?" repeated Maloney, his excitement growing again.

"Undoubtedly," replied the other quietly; "for there exists all the time a continuous connection between the physical body and the Double—a connection of matter, though of exceedingly attenuated, possibly of etheric, matter. The wound *travels*, so to speak, from one to the other, and if this connection were broken the result would be death."

"Death," repeated Maloney to himself, "death!" He looked anxiously at our faces, his thoughts evidently beginning to clear.

"And this solidity?" he asked presently, after a general pause; "this tearing of tents and flesh; this howling, and the marks of paws? You mean that the Double—?"

"Has sufficient material drawn from the depleted body to produce physical results? Certainly!" the doctor took him up. "Although to explain at this moment such problems as the passage of matter through matter would be as difficult as to explain how the thought of a mother can actually break the bones of the child unborn."

Dr. Silence pointed out to sea, and Maloney, looking wildly about him, turned with a violent start. I saw a canoe, with Sangree in the stern-seat, slowly coming into view round the farther point. His hat was off, and his tanned face for the first time appeared to me—to us all, I think—as though it were the face of some one else. He looked like a wild man. Then he stood up in the canoe to make a cast with the rod, and he looked for all the world like an Indian. I recalled the expression of his face as I had seen it once or twice, notably on that occasion of the evening prayer, and an involuntary shudder ran down my spine.

At that very instant he turned and saw us where we lay, and his face broke into a smile, so that his teeth showed white in the sun. He looked in his element, and exceedingly attractive. He called out something about his fish, and soon after passed out of sight into the lagoon.

For a time none of us said a word.

"And the cure?" ventured Maloney at length.

"Is not to quench this savage force," replied Dr. Silence, "but to steer it better, and to provide other outlets. This is the solution of all these problems of accumulated force, for this force is the raw material of usefulness, and should be increased and cherished, not by separating it from the body by death, but by raising it to higher channels. The best and quickest cure of all," he went on, speaking very gently and with a hand upon the clergyman's arm, "is to lead it towards its object, provided that object is not unalterably hostile—to let it find rest where—"

He stopped abruptly, and the eyes of the two men met in a single glance of comprehension.

"Joan?" Maloney exclaimed, under his breath.

"Joan!" replied John Silence.

We all went to bed early. The day had been unusually warm, and after sunset a curious hush descended on the island. Nothing was audible but that faint, ghostly singing which is inseparable from a pinewood even on the stillest day—a low, searching sound, as though the wind had hair and trailed it o'er the world.

With the sudden cooling of the atmosphere a sea fog began to form. It appeared in isolated patches over the water, and then these patches slid together and a white wall advanced upon us. Not a breath of air stirred; the firs stood like flat metal outlines; the sea became as oil. The whole scene lay as though held motionless by some huge weight in the air; and the flames from our fire—the largest we had ever made—rose upwards, straight as a church steeple.

As I followed the rest of our party tent-wards, having kicked the embers of the fire into safety, the advance guard of the fog was creeping slowly among the trees, like white arms feeling their way. Mingled with the smoke was the odour of moss and soil and bark, and the peculiar flavour of the Baltic, half salt, half brackish, like the smell of an estuary at low water.

It is difficult to say why it seemed to me that this deep stillness masked an intense activity; perhaps in every mood lies the suggestion of its opposite, so that I became aware of the contrast of furious energy, for it was like moving through the deep pause before a thunderstorm, and I trod gently lest by breaking a twig or moving a stone I might set the whole scene into some sort of tumultuous movement. Actually, no doubt, it was nothing more than a result of overstrung nerves.

There was no more question of undressing and going to bed than there was of undressing and going to bathe. Some sense in me was alert and expectant. I sat in my tent and waited. And at the end of half an hour or so my waiting was justified, for the canvas suddenly shivered, and some one tripped over the ropes that held it to the earth. John Silence came in.

The effect of his quiet entry was singular and prophetic: it was just as though the energy lying behind all this stillness had pressed forward to the edge of action. This, no doubt, was merely the quickening of my own mind, and had no other justification; for the presence of John Silence always suggested the near possibility of vigorous action, and as a matter of fact, he came in with nothing more than a nod and a significant gesture.

He sat down on a corner of my ground-sheet, and I pushed the blanket over so that he could cover his legs. He drew the flap of the tent after him and settled down, but hardly had he done so when the canvas shook a second time, and in blundered Maloney.

"Sitting in the dark?" he said self-consciously, pushing his head inside, and hanging up his lantern on the ridge-pole nail. "I just looked in for a smoke. I suppose—"

He glanced round, caught the eye of Dr. Silence, and stopped. He put his pipe back into his pocket and began to hum softly—that under-breath humming of a nondescript melody I knew so well and had come to hate.

Dr. Silence leaned forward, opened the lantern and blew the light out. "Speak low," he said, "and don't strike matches. Listen for sounds and movements about the Camp, and be ready to follow me at a moment's notice." There was light enough to distinguish our faces easily, and I saw Maloney glance again hurriedly at both of us.

"Is the Camp asleep?" the doctor asked presently, whispering. "Sangree is," replied the clergyman, in a voice equally low. "I can't answer for the women; I think they're sitting up."

"That's for the best." And then he added: "I wish the fog would thin a bit and let the moon through; later—we may want it."

"It is lifting now, I think," Maloney whispered back. "It's over the tops of the trees already."

I cannot say what it was in this commonplace exchange of remarks that thrilled. Probably Maloney's swift acquiescence in the doctor's mood had something to do with it; for his quick obedience certainly impressed me a good deal. But, even without that slight evidence, it was clear that each recognised the gravity of the occasion, and understood that sleep was impossible and sentry duty was the order of the night.

"Report to me," repeated John Silence once again, "the least sound, and do nothing precipitately."

He shifted across to the mouth of the tent and raised the flap, fastening it against the pole so that he could see out. Maloney stopped humming and began to force the breath through his teeth with a kind of faint hissing, treating us to a medley of church hymns and popular songs of the day.

Then the tent trembled as though some one had touched it.

"That's the wind rising," whispered the clergyman, and pulled the flap open as far as it would go. A waft of cold damp air entered and made us shiver, and with it came a sound of the sea as the first wave washed its way softly along the shores.

"It's got round to the north," he added, and following his voice came a long-drawn whisper that rose from the whole island as the trees sent forth a sighing response. "The fog'll move a bit now. I can make out a lane across the sea already."

"Hush!" said Dr. Silence, for Maloney's voice had risen above a whisper, and we settled down again to another long period of watching and waiting, broken only by the occasional rubbing of shoulders against the canvas as we shifted our positions, and the increasing noise of waves on the outer coast-line of the island. And over all whirred the murmur of wind sweeping the tops of the trees like a great harp, and the faint tapping on the tent as drops fell from the branches with a sharp pinging sound.

We had sat for something over an hour in this way, and Maloney and I were finding it increasingly hard to keep awake, when suddenly Dr. Silence rose to his feet and peered out. The next minute he was gone.

Relieved of the dominating presence, the clergyman thrust his face close into mine. "I don't much care for this waiting game," he whispered, "but Silence wouldn't hear of my sitting up with the others; he said it would prevent anything happening if I did."

"He knows," I answered shortly.

"No doubt in the world about that," he whispered back; "it's this 'Double' business, as he calls it, or else it's obsession as the Bible describes it. But it's bad, whichever it is, and I've got my Winchester outside ready cocked, and I brought this too." He shoved a pocket Bible under my nose. At one time in his life it had been his inseparable companion.

"One's useless and the other's dangerous," I replied under my breath, conscious of a keen desire to laugh, and leaving him to choose. "Safety lies in following our leader—"

"I'm not thinking of myself," he interrupted sharply; "only, if anything happens to Joan tonight I'm going to shoot first—and pray afterwards!"

Maloney put the book back into his hip-pocket, and peered out of the doorway. "What is he up to now, in the devil's name, I wonder!" he added; "going round Sangree's tent and making gestures. How weird he looks disappearing in and out of the fog."

"Just trust him and wait," I said quickly, for the doctor was already on his way back. "Remember, he has the knowledge, and knows what he's about. I've been with him through worse cases than this."

Maloney moved back as Dr. Silence darkened the doorway and stooped to enter.

"His sleep is very deep," he whispered, seating himself by the door again. "He's in a cataleptic condition, and the Double may be released any minute now. But I've taken steps to imprison it in the tent, and it can't get out till I permit it. Be on the watch for signs of movement." Then he looked hard at Maloney. "But no violence, or shooting, remember, Mr. Maloney, unless you want a murder on your hands. Anything done to the Double acts by repercussion upon the physical body. You had better take out the cartridges at once."

His voice was stern. The clergyman went out, and I heard him emptying the magazine of his rifle. When he returned he sat nearer the door than before, and from that moment until we left the tent he never once took his eyes from the figure of Dr. Silence, silhouetted there against sky and canvas.

And, meanwhile, the wind came steadily over the sea and opened the mist into lanes and clearings, driving it about like a living thing.

It must have been well after midnight when a low booming sound drew my attention; but at first the sense of hearing was so strained that it was impossible exactly to locate it, and I imagined it was the thunder of big guns far out at sea carried to us by the rising wind. Then Maloney, catching hold of my arm and leaning forward, somehow brought the true relation, and I realised the next second that it was only a few feet away.

"Sangree's tent," he exclaimed in a loud and startled whisper.

I craned my head round the corner, but at first the effect of the fog was so confusing that every patch of white driving about before the wind looked like a moving tent and it was some seconds before I discovered the one patch that held steady. Then I saw that it was shaking all over, and the sides, flapping as much as the tightness of the ropes allowed, were the cause of the booming sound we had heard. Something alive was tearing frantically about inside, banging against the stretched canvas in a way that made me think of a great moth dashing against the walls and ceiling of a room. The tent bulged and rocked.

"It's trying to get out, by Jupiter!" muttered the clergyman, rising to his feet and turning to the side where the unloaded rifle lay. I sprang up too, hardly knowing what purpose was in my mind, but anxious to be prepared for anything. John Silence, however, was before us both, and his figure slipped past and blocked the doorway of the tent. And there was some quality in his voice next minute when he began to speak that brought our minds instantly to a state of calm obedience.

"First—the women's tent," he said low, looking sharply at Maloney, "and if I need your help, I'll call."

The clergyman needed no second bidding. He dived past me and was out in a moment. He was labouring evidently under intense excitement. I watched him picking his way silently over the slippery ground, giving the moving tent a wide berth, and presently disappearing among the floating shapes of fog.

Dr. Silence turned to me. "You heard those footsteps about half an hour ago?" he asked significantly.

"I heard nothing."

"They were extraordinarily soft—almost the soundless tread of a wild creature. But now, follow me closely," he added, "for we must waste no time if I am to save this poor man from his affliction and lead his were-wolf Double to its rest. And, unless I am much mistaken"—he peered at me through the darkness, whispering with the utmost distinctness—"Joan and Sangree are absolutely made for one another. And I think she knows it too—just as well as he does."

My head swam a little as I listened, but at the same time something cleared in my brain and I saw that he was right. Yet it was all so weird and incredible, so remote from the commonplace facts of life as commonplace people know them; and more than once it flashed upon me that the whole scene—people, words, tents, and all the rest of it—were delusions created by the intense excitement of my own mind somehow, and that suddenly the sea-fog would clear off and the world become normal again.

The cold air from the sea stung our cheeks sharply as we left the close atmosphere of the little crowded tent. The sighing of the trees, the waves breaking below on the rocks, and the lines and patches of mist driving about us seemed to create the momentary illusion that the whole island had broken loose and was floating out to sea like a mighty raft.

The doctor moved just ahead of me, quickly and silently; he was making straight for the Canadian's tent where the sides still boomed and shook as the creature of sinister life raced and tore about impatiently within. A little distance from the door he paused and held up a hand to stop me. We were, perhaps, a dozen feet away.

"Before I release it, you shall see for yourself," he said, "that the reality of the werewolf is beyond all question. The matter of which it is composed is, of course, exceedingly attenuated, but you are partially clairvoyant—and even if it is not dense enough for normal sight you will see something."

He added a little more I could not catch. The fact was that the curiously strong vibrating atmosphere surrounding his person somewhat confused my senses. It was the result, of course, of his intense concentration of mind and forces, and pervaded the entire Camp and all the persons in it. And as I watched the canvas shake and heard it boom and flap I heartily welcomed it. For it was also protective.

At the back of Sangree's tent stood a thin group of pine trees, but in front and at the sides the ground was comparatively clear. The flap was wide open and any ordinary animal would have been out and away without the least trouble. Dr. Silence led me up to within a few feet, evidently careful not to advance beyond a certain limit, and then stooped down and signalled to me to do the same. And looking over his shoulder I saw the interior lit faintly by the spectral light reflected from the fog, and the dim blot upon the balsam boughs and blankets signifying Sangree; while over him, and round him, and up and down him, flew the dark mass of "something" on four legs, with pointed muzzle and sharp ears plainly visible against the tent sides, and the occasional gleam of fiery eyes and white fangs.

I held my breath and kept utterly still, inwardly and outwardly, for fear, I suppose, that the creature would become conscious of my presence; but the distress I felt went far deeper than the mere sense of personal safety, or the fact of watching something so incredibly active and real. I became keenly aware of the dreadful psychic calamity it involved. The realisation that Sangree lay confined in that narrow space with this species of monstrous projection of himself—that he was wrapped there in the cataleptic sleep, all unconscious that this thing was masquerading with his own life and energies—added a distressing touch of horror to the scene. In all the cases of John Silence—and they were many and often terrible—no other psychic affliction has ever, before or since, impressed me so convincingly with the pathetic impermanence of the human personality, with its fluid nature, and with the alarming possibilities of its transformations.

"Come," he whispered, after we had watched for some minutes the frantic efforts to escape from the circle of thought and will that held it prisoner, "come a little farther away while I release it."

We moved back a dozen yards or so. It was like a scene in some impossible play, or in some ghastly and oppressive nightmare from which I should presently awake to find the blankets all heaped up upon my chest.

By some method undoubtedly mental, but which, in my confusion and excitement, I failed to understand, the doctor accomplished his purpose, and the next minute I heard him say sharply under his breath, "It's out! Now watch!"

At this very moment a sudden gust from the sea blew aside the mist, so that a lane opened to the sky, and the moon, ghastly and unnatural as the effect of stage limelight, dropped down in a momentary gleam upon the door of Sangree's tent, and I perceived that something had moved forward from the interior darkness and stood clearly defined upon the threshold. And, at the same moment, the tent ceased its shuddering and held still.

There, in the doorway, stood an animal, with neck and muzzle thrust forward, its head poking into the night, its whole body poised in that attitude of intense rigidity that precedes the spring into freedom, the running leap of attack. It seemed to be about the size of a calf, leaner than a mastiff, yet more squat than a wolf, and I can swear that I saw the fur ridged sharply upon its back. Then its upper lip slowly lifted, and I saw the whiteness of its teeth.

Surely no human being ever stared as hard as I did in those next few minutes. Yet, the harder I stared the clearer appeared the amazing and monstrous apparition. For, after all, it was Sangree—and yet it was not Sangree. It was the head and face of an animal, and yet it was the face of Sangree: the face of a wild dog, a wolf, and yet his face. The eyes were sharper, narrower, more fiery, yet they were his eyes—his eyes run wild; the teeth were longer, whiter, more pointed—yet they were his teeth, his teeth grown cruel; the expression was flaming, terrible, exultant—yet it was his expression carried to the border of savagery—his expression as I had already surprised it more than once, only dominant now, fully released from human constraint, with the mad yearning of a hungry and importunate soul. It was the soul of Sangree, the long suppressed, deeply loving Sangree, expressed in its single and intense desire—pure utterly and utterly wonderful.

Yet, at the same time, came the feeling that it was all an illusion. I suddenly remembered the extraordinary changes the human face can undergo in circular insanity, when it changes from melancholia to elation; and I recalled the effect of hascheesh, which shows the human countenance in the form of the bird or animal to which in character it most approximates; and for a moment I attributed this mingling of Sangree's face with a wolf to some kind of similar delusion of the senses. I was mad, deluded, dreaming! The excitement of the day, and this dim light of stars and bewildering mist combined to trick me. I had been amazingly imposed upon by some false wizardry of the senses. It was all absurd and fantastic; it would pass.

And then, sounding across this sea of mental confusion like a bell through a fog, came the voice of John Silence bringing me back to a consciousness of the reality of it all—

"Sangree—in his Double!"

And when I looked again more calmly, I plainly saw that it was indeed the face of the Canadian, but his face turned animal, yet mingled with the brute expression a curiously pathetic look like the soul seen sometimes in the yearning eyes of a dog, —the face of an animal shot with vivid streaks of the human.

The doctor called to him softly under his breath—

"Sangree! Sangree, you poor afflicted creature! Do you know me? Can you understand what it is you're doing in your 'Body of Desire'?"

For the first time since its appearance the creature moved. Its ears twitched and it shifted the weight of its body on to the hind legs. Then, lifting its head and muzzle to the sky, it opened its long jaws and gave vent to a dismal and prolonged howling.

But, when I heard that howling rise to heaven, the breath caught and strangled in my throat and it seemed that my heart missed a beat; for, though the sound was entirely animal, it was at the same time entirely human. But, more than that, it was the cry I had so often heard in the Western States of America where the Indians still fight and hunt and struggle— it was the cry of the Redskin!

"The Indian blood!" whispered John Silence, when I caught his arm for support; "the ancestral cry."

And that poignant, beseeching cry, that broken human voice, mingling with the savage howl of the brute beast, pierced straight to my very heart and touched there something that no music, no voice, passionate or tender, of man, woman or child has ever stirred before or since for one second into life. It echoed away among the fog and the trees and lost itself somewhere out over the hidden sea. And some part of myself—something that was far more than the mere act of intense listening—went out with it, and for several minutes I lost consciousness of my surroundings and felt utterly absorbed in the pain of another stricken fellow-creature.

Again the voice of John Silence recalled me to myself.

"Hark!" he said aloud. "Hark!"

His tone galvanised me afresh. We stood listening side by side.

Far across the island, faintly sounding through the trees and brushwood, came a similar, answering cry. Shrill, yet wonderfully musical, shaking the heart with a singular wild sweetness that defies description, we heard it rise and fall upon the night air.

"It's across the lagoon," Dr. Silence cried, but this time in full tones that paid no tribute to caution. "It's Joan! She's answering him!"

Again the wonderful cry rose and fell, and that same instant the animal lowered its head, and, muzzle to earth, set off on a swift easy canter that took it off into the mist and out of our sight like a thing of wind and vision.

The doctor made a quick dash to the door of Sangree's tent, and, following close at his heels, I peered in and caught a momentary glimpse of the small, shrunken body lying upon the branches but half covered by the blankets—the cage from which most of the life, and not a little of the actual corporeal substance, had escaped into that other form of life and energy, the body of passion and desire.

By another of those swift, incalculable processes which at this stage of my apprenticeship I failed often to grasp, Dr. Silence reclosed the circle about the tent and body.

"Now it cannot return till I permit it," he said, and the next second was off at full speed into the woods, with myself close behind him. I had already had some experience of my companion's ability to run swiftly through a dense wood, and I now had the further proof of his power almost to see in the dark. For, once we left the open space about the tents, the trees seemed to absorb all the remaining vestiges of light, and I understood that special sensibility that is said to develop in the blind—the sense of obstacles.

And twice as we ran we heard the sound of that dismal howling drawing nearer and nearer to the answering faint cry from the point of the island whither we were going.

Then, suddenly, the trees fell away, and we emerged, hot and breathless, upon the rocky point where the granite slabs ran bare into the sea. It was like passing into the clearness of open day. And there, sharply defined against sea and sky, stood the figure of a human being. It was Joan.

I at once saw that there was something about her appearance that was singular and unusual, but it was only when we had moved quite close that I recognised what caused it. For while the lips wore a smile that lit the whole face with a happiness I had never seen there before, the eyes themselves were fixed in a steady, sightless stare as though they were lifeless and made of glass.

I made an impulsive forward movement, but Dr. Silence instantly dragged me back.

"No," he cried, "don't wake her!"

"What do you mean?" I replied aloud, struggling in his grasp.

"She's asleep. It's somnambulistic. The shock might injure her permanently."

I turned and peered closely into his face. He was absolutely calm. I began to understand a little more, catching, I suppose, something of his strong thinking.

"Walking in her sleep, you mean?"

He nodded. "She's on her way to meet him. From the very beginning he must have drawn her—irresistibly."

"But the torn tent and the wounded flesh?"

"When she did not sleep deep enough to enter the somnambulistic trance he missed her—he went instinctively and in all innocence to seek her out—with the result, of course, that she woke and was terrified—"

"Then in their heart of hearts they love?" I asked finally.

John Silence smiled his inscrutable smile. "Profoundly," he answered, "and as simply as only primitive souls can love. If only they both come to realise it in their normal waking states his Double will cease these nocturnal excursions. He will be cured, and at rest."

The words had hardly left his lips when there was a sound of rustling branches on our left, and the very next instant the dense brushwood parted where it was darkest and out rushed the swift form of an animal at full gallop. The noise of feet was scarcely audible, but in that utter stillness I heard the heavy panting breath and caught the swish of the low bushes against its sides. It went straight towards Joan—and as it went the girl lifted her head and turned to meet it. And the same instant a canoe that had been creeping silently and unobserved round the inner shore of the lagoon, emerged from the shadows and defined itself upon the water with a figure at the middle thwart. It was Maloney.

It was only afterwards I realised that we were invisible to him where we stood against the dark background of trees; the figures of Joan and the animal he saw plainly, but not Dr. Silence and myself standing just beyond them. He stood up in the canoe and pointed with his right arm. I saw something gleam in his hand.

"Stand aside, Joan girl, or you'll get hit," he shouted, his voice ringing horribly through the deep stillness, and the same instant a pistol-shot cracked out with a burst of flame and smoke, and the figure of the animal, with one tremendous leap into the air, fell back in the shadows and disappeared like a shape of night and fog. Instantly, then, Joan opened her eyes, looked in a dazed fashion about her, and pressing both hands against her heart, fell with a sharp cry into my arms that were just in time to catch her.

And an answering cry sounded across the lagoon—thin, wailing, piteous. It came from Sangree's tent.

"Fool!" cried Dr. Silence, "you've wounded him!" and before we could move or realise quite what it meant, he was in the canoe and half-way across the lagoon.

Some kind of similar abuse came in a torrent from my lips, too—though I cannot remember the actual words—as I cursed the man for his disobedience and tried to make the girl comfortable on the ground. But the clergyman was more practical. He was spreading his coat over her and dashing water on her face.

"It's not Joan I've killed at any rate," I heard him mutter as she turned and opened her eyes and smiled faintly up in his face. "I swear the bullet went straight."

Joan stared at him; she was still dazed and bewildered, and still imagined herself with the companion of her trance. The strange lucidity of the somnambulist still hung over her brain and mind, though outwardly she appeared troubled and confused.

"Where has he gone to? He disappeared so suddenly, crying that he was hurt," she asked, looking at her father as though she did not recognise him. "And if they've done anything to him—they have done it to me too—for he is more to me than—"

Her words grew vaguer and vaguer as she returned slowly to her normal waking state, and now she stopped altogether, as though suddenly aware that she had been surprised into telling secrets. But all the way back, as we carried her carefully through the trees, the girl smiled and murmured Sangree's name and asked if he was injured, until it finally became clear to me that the wild soul of the one had called to the wild soul of the other and in the secret depths of their beings the call had been heard and understood. John Silence was right. In the abyss of her heart, too deep at first for recognition, the girl loved him, and had loved him from the very beginning. Once her normal waking consciousness recognised the fact they would leap together like twin flames, and his affliction would be at an end; his intense desire would be satisfied; he would be cured.

And in Sangree's tent Dr. Silence and I sat up for the remainder of the night—this wonderful and haunted night that had shown us such strange glimpses of a new heaven and a new hell—for the Canadian tossed upon his balsam boughs with high fever in his blood, and upon each cheek a dark and curious contusion showed, throbbing with severe pain although the skin was not broken and there was no outward and visible sign of blood.

"Maloney shot straight, you see," whispered Dr. Silence to me after the clergyman had gone to his tent, and had put Joan to sleep beside her mother, who, by the way, had never once awakened. "The bullet must have passed clean through the face, for both cheeks are stained. He'll wear these marks all his life—smaller, but always there. They're the most curious scars in the world, these scars transferred by repercussion from an injured Double. They'll remain visible until just before his death, and then with the withdrawal of the subtle body they will disappear finally."

His words mingled in my dazed mind with the sighs of the troubled sleeper and the crying of the wind about the tent. Nothing seemed to paralyse my powers of realisation so much as these twin stains of mysterious significance upon the face before me.

It was odd, too, how speedily and easily the Camp resigned itself again to sleep and quietness, as though a stage curtain had suddenly dropped down upon the action and concealed it; and nothing contributed so vividly to the feeling that I had been a spectator of some kind of visionary drama as the dramatic nature of the change in the girl's attitude.

Yet, as a matter of fact, the change had not been so sudden and revolutionary as appeared. Underneath, in those remoter regions of consciousness where the emotions, unknown to their owners, do secretly mature, and owe thence their abrupt revelation to some abrupt psychological climax, there can be no doubt that Joan's love for the Canadian had been growing steadily and irresistibly all the time. It had now rushed to the surface so that she recognised it; that was all.

And it has always seemed to me that the presence of John Silence, so potent, so quietly efficacious, produced an effect, if one may say so, of a psychic forcing-house, and hastened incalculably the bringing together of these two "wild" lovers. In that sudden awakening had occurred the very psychological climax required to reveal the passionate emotion accumulated below. The deeper knowledge had leaped across and transferred itself to her ordinary consciousness, and in that shock the collision of the personalities had shaken them to the depths and shown her the truth beyond all possibility of doubt.

"He's sleeping quietly now," the doctor said, interrupting my reflections. "If you will watch alone for a bit I'll go to Maloney's tent and help him to arrange his thoughts." He smiled in anticipation of that "arrangement." "He'll never quite understand how a wound on the Double can transfer itself to the physical body, but at least I can persuade him that the less he talks and 'explains' tomorrow, the sooner the forces will run their natural course now to peace and quietness."

He went away softly, and with the removal of his presence Sangree, sleeping heavily, turned over and groaned with the pain of his broken head.

And it was in the still hour just before the dawn, when all the islands were hushed, the wind and sea still dreaming, and the stars visible through clearing mists, that a figure crept silently over the ridge and reached the door of the tent where I dozed beside the sufferer, before I was aware of its presence. The flap was cautiously lifted a few inches and in looked—Joan.

That same instant Sangree woke and sat up on his bed of branches. He recognised her before I could say a word, and uttered a low cry. It was pain and joy mingled, and this time all human. And the girl too was no longer walking in her sleep, but fully aware of what she was doing. I was only just able to prevent him springing from his blankets.

"Joan, Joan!" he cried, and in a flash she answered him, "I'm here—I'm with you always now," and had pushed past me into the tent and flung herself upon his breast.

"I knew you would come to me in the end," I heard him whisper.

"It was all too big for me to understand at first," she murmured, "and for a long time I was frightened—"

"But not now!" he cried louder; "you don't feel afraid now of—of anything that's in me—"

"I fear nothing," she cried, "nothing, nothing!"

I led her outside again. She looked steadily into my face with eyes shining and her whole being transformed. In some intuitive way, surviving probably from the somnambulism, she knew or guessed as much as I knew.

"You must talk tomorrow with John Silence," I said gently, leading her towards her own tent. "He understands everything."

I left her at the door, and as I went back softly to take up my place of sentry again with the Canadian, I saw the first streaks of dawn lighting up the far rim of the sea behind the distant islands.

And, as though to emphasise the eternal closeness of comedy to tragedy, two small details rose out of the scene and impressed me so vividly that I remember them to this very day. For in the tent where I had just left Joan, all aquiver with her new happiness, there rose plainly to my ears the grotesque sounds of the Bo'sun's Mate heavily snoring, oblivious of all things in heaven or hell; and from Maloney's tent, so still was the night, where I looked across and saw the lantern's glow, there came to me, through the trees, the monotonous rising and falling of a human voice that was beyond question the sound of a man praying to his God.

Extra John Silence story from *Day and Night Stories*

CASE VI

A VICTIM OF HIGHER SPACE

"There's a hextraordinary gentleman to see you, sir," said the new man.

"Why 'extraordinary'?" asked Dr. Silence, drawing the tips of his thin fingers through his brown beard. His eyes twinkled pleasantly. "Why 'extraordinary,' Barker?" he repeated encouragingly, noticing the perplexed expression in the man's eyes.

"He's so—so thin, sir. I could hardly see 'im at all—at first. He was inside the house before I could ask the name," he added, remembering strict orders.

"And who brought him here?"

"He come alone, sir, in a closed cab. He pushed by me before I could say a word—making no noise not what I could hear. He seemed to move so soft like—"

The man stopped short with obvious embarrassment, as though he had already said enough to jeopardise his new situation, but trying hard to show that he remembered the instructions and warnings he had received with regard to the admission of strangers not properly accredited.

"And where is the gentleman now?" asked Dr. Silence, turning away to conceal his amusement.

"I really couldn't exactly say, sir. I left him standing in the 'all—"

The doctor looked up sharply. "But why in the hall, Barker? Why not in the waiting-room?" He fixed his piercing though kindly eyes on the man's face. "Did he frighten you ?" he asked quickly.

"I think he did, sir, if I may say so. I seemed to lose sight of him, as it were—" The man stammered, evidently convinced by now that he had earned his dismissal. "He come in so funny, just like a cold wind," he added boldly, setting his heels at attention and looking his master full in the face.

The doctor made an internal note of the man's halting description; he was pleased that the slight signs of psychic intuition which had induced him to engage Barker had not entirely failed at the first trial. Dr. Silence sought for this qualification in all his assistants, from secretary to serving man, and if it surrounded him with a somewhat singular crew, the drawbacks were more than compensated for on the whole by their occasional flashes of insight.

"So the gentleman made you feel queer, did he?"

"That was it, I think, sir," repeated the man stolidly.

"And he brings no kind of introduction to me—no letter or anything?" asked the doctor, with feigned surprise, as though he knew what was coming.

The man fumbled, both in mind and pockets, and finally produced an envelope.

"I beg pardon, sir," he said, greatly flustered; "the gentleman handed me this for you."

It was a note from a discerning friend, who had never yet sent him a case that was not vitally interesting from one point or another.

"Please see the bearer of this note," the brief message ran, "though I doubt if even you can do much to help him."

John Silence paused a moment, so as to gather from the mind of the writer all that lay behind the brief words of the letter. Then he looked up at his servant with a graver expression than he had yet worn.

"Go back and find this gentleman," he said, "and show him into the green study. Do not reply to his question, or speak more than actually necessary; but think kind, helpful, sympathetic thoughts as strongly as you can, Barker. You remember what I told you about the importance of *thinking*, when I engaged you. Put curiosity out of your mind, and think gently, sympathetically, affectionately, if you can."

He smiled, and Barker, who had recovered his composure in the doctor's presence, bowed silently and went out.

There were two different reception-rooms in Dr. Silence's house. One (intended for persons who imagined they needed spiritual assistance when really they were only candidates for the asylum) had padded walls, and was well supplied with various concealed contrivances by means of which sudden violence could be instantly met and overcome. It was, however, rarely used. The other, intended for the reception of genuine cases of spiritual distress and out-of-the-way afflictions of a psychic nature, was entirely draped and furnished in a soothing deep green, calculated to induce calmness and repose of mind. And this room was the one in which Dr. Silence interviewed the majority of his "queer" cases, and the one into which he had directed Barker to show his present caller.

To begin with, the arm-chair in which the patient was always directed to sit, was nailed to the floor, since its immovability tended to impart this same excellent characteristic to the occupant. Patients invariably grew excited when talking about themselves, and their excitement tended to confuse their thoughts and to exaggerate their language. The inflexibility of the chair helped to counteract this. After repeated endeavours to drag it forward, or push it back, they ended by resigning themselves to sitting quietly. And with the futility of fidgeting there followed a calmer state of mind.

Upon the floor, and at intervals in the wall immediately behind, were certain tiny green buttons, practically unnoticeable, which on being pressed permitted a soothing and persuasive narcotic to rise invisibly about the occupant of the chair. The effect upon the excitable patient was rapid, admirable, and harmless. The green study was further provided with a secret spy-hole; for John Silence liked when possible to observe his patient's face before it had assumed that mask the features of the human countenance invariably wear in the presence of another person. A man sitting alone wears a psychic expression; and this expression is the man himself. It disappears the moment another person joins him. And Dr. Silence often learned more from a few moments' secret observation of a face than from hours of conversation with its owner afterwards.

A very light, almost a dancing, step followed Barker's heavy tread towards the green room, and a moment afterwards the man came in and announced that the gentleman was waiting. He was still pale and his manner nervous.

"Never mind, Barker," the doctor said kindly; "if you were not psychic the man would have had no effect upon you at all. You only need training and development. And when you have learned to interpret these feelings and sensations better, you will feel no fear, but only a great sympathy."

"Yes, sir; thank you, sir!" And Barker bowed and made his escape, while Dr. Silence, an amused smile lurking about the corners of his mouth, made his way noiselessly down the passage and put his eye to the spy-hole in the door of the green study.

This spy-hole was so placed that it commanded a view of almost the entire room, and, looking through it, the doctor saw a hat, gloves, and umbrella lying on a chair by the table, but searched at first in vain for their owner.

The windows were both closed and a brisk fire burned in the grate. There were various signs—signs intelligible at least to a keenly intuitive soul—that the room was occupied, yet so far as human beings were concerned, it was empty, utterly empty. No one sat in the chairs; no one stood on the mat before the fire; there was no sign even that a patient was anywhere close against the wall, examining the Böcklin reproductions—as patients so often did when they thought they were alone—and therefore rather difficult to see from the spy-hole. Ordinarily speaking, there was no one in the room. It was undeniable.

Yet Dr. Silence was quite well aware that a human being was in the room. His psychic apparatus never failed in letting him know the proximity of an incarnate or discarnate being. Even in the dark he could tell that. And he now knew positively that his patient—the patient who had alarmed Barker, and had then tripped down the corridor with that dancing footstep—was somewhere concealed within the four walls commanded by his spy-hole. He also realised—and this was most unusual—that this individual whom he desired to watch knew that he was being watched. And, further, that the stranger himself was also watching! In fact, that it was he, the doctor, who was being observed—and by an observer as keen and trained as himself.

An inkling of the true state of the case began to dawn upon him, and he was on the verge of entering—indeed, his hand already touched the door-knob—when his eye, still glued to the spy-hole, detected a slight movement. Directly opposite, between him and the fireplace, something stirred. He watched very attentively and made certain that he was not mistaken. An object on the mantelpiece—it was a blue vase—disappeared from view. It passed out of sight together with the portion of the marble mantelpiece on which it rested. Next, that part of the fire and grate and brass fender immediately below it vanished entirely, as though a slice had been taken clean out of them.

Dr. Silence then understood that something between him and these objects was slowly coming into being, something that concealed them and obstructed his vision by inserting itself in the line of sight between them and himself.

He quietly awaited further results before going in. First he saw a thin perpendicular line tracing itself from just above the height of the clock and continuing downwards till it reached the woolly fire-mat. This line grew wider, broadened, grew solid. It was no shadow; it was something substantial. It defined itself more and more. Then suddenly, at the top of the line, and about on a level with the face of the clock, he saw a round luminous disc gazing steadily at him. It was a human eye, looking straight into his own, pressed there against the spy-hole. And it was bright with intelligence. Dr. Silence held his breath for a moment—and stared back at it.

Then, like some one moving out of deep shadow into light, he saw the figure of a man come sliding sideways into view, a whitish face following the eye, and the perpendicular line he had first observed broadening out and developing into the complete figure of a human being. It was the patient. He had apparently been standing there in front of the fire all the time. A second eye had followed the first, and both of them stared steadily at the spy-hole, sharply concentrated, yet with a sly twinkle of humour and amusement that made it impossible for the doctor to maintain his position any longer.

He opened the door and went in quickly. As he did so he noticed for the first time the sound of a German band coming in gaily through the open ventilators. In some intuitive, unaccountable fashion the music connected itself with the patient he was about to interview. This sort of prevision was not unfamiliar to him. It always explained itself later.

The man, he saw, was of middle age and of very ordinary appearance; so ordinary, in fact, that he was difficult to describe—his only peculiarity being his extreme thinness. Pleasant—that is, good—vibrations issued from his atmosphere and met Dr. Silence as he advanced to greet him, yet vibrations alive with currents and discharges betraying the perturbed and disordered condition of his mind and brain. There was evidently something wholly out of the usual in the state of his thoughts. Yet, though strange, it was not altogether distressing; it was not the impression that the broken and violent atmosphere of the insane produces upon the mind. Dr. Silence realised in a flash that here was a case of absorbing interest that might require all his powers to handle properly.

"I was watching you through my little peep-hole—as you saw," he began, with a pleasant smile, advancing to shake hands. "I find it of the greatest assistance sometimes—"

But the patient interrupted him at once. His voice was hurried and had odd, shrill changes in it, breaking from high to low in unexpected fashion. One moment it thundered, the next it almost squeaked.

"I understand without explanation," he broke in rapidly. "You get the true note of a man in this way—when he thinks himself unobserved. I quite agree. Only, in my case, I fear, you saw very little. My case, as you of course grasp, Dr. Silence, is extremely peculiar, uncomfortably peculiar. Indeed, unless Sir William had positively assured me—"

"My friend has sent you to me," the doctor interrupted gravely, with a gentle note of authority, "and that is quite sufficient. Pray, be seated, Mr.—"

"Mudge—Racine Mudge," returned the other.

"Take this comfortable one, Mr. Mudge," leading him to the fixed chair, "and tell me your condition in your own way and at your own pace. My whole day is at your service if you require it."

Mr. Mudge moved towards the chair in question and then hesitated.

"You will promise me not to use the narcotic buttons," he said, before sitting down. "I do not need them. Also I ought to mention that anything you think of vividly will reach my mind. That is apparently part of my peculiar case." He sat down with a sigh and arranged his thin legs and body into a position of comfort. Evidently he was very sensitive to the thoughts of others, for the picture of the green buttons had only entered the doctor's mind for a second, yet the other had instantly snapped it up. Dr. Silence noticed, too, that Mr. Mudge held on tightly with both hands to the arms of the chair.

"I'm rather glad the chair is nailed to the floor," he remarked, as he settled himself more comfortably. "It suits me admirably. The fact is—and this is my case in a nutshell—which is all that a doctor of your marvellous development requires—the fact is, Dr. Silence, I am a victim of Higher

Space. That's what's the matter with me—Higher Space!"

The two looked at each other for a space in silence, the little patient holding tightly to the arms of the chair which "suited him admirably," and looking up with staring eyes, his atmosphere positively trembling with the waves of some unknown activity; while the doctor smiled kindly and sympathetically, and put his whole person as far as possible into the mental condition of the other.

"Higher Space," repeated Mr. Mudge, "that's what it is. Now, do you think you can help me with *that?*"

There was a pause during which the men's eyes steadily searched down below the surface of their respective personalities. Then Dr. Silence spoke.

"I am quite sure I can help," he answered quietly; "sympathy must always help, and suffering always owns my sympathy. I see you have suffered cruelly. You must tell me all about your case, and when I hear the gradual steps by which you reached this strange condition, I have no doubt I can be of assistance to you."

He drew a chair up beside his interlocutor and laid a hand on his shoulder for a moment. His whole being radiated kindness, intelligence, desire to help.

"For instance," he went on, "I feel sure it was the result of no mere chance that you became familiar with the terrors of what you term Higher Space; for Higher Space is no mere external measurement. It is, of course, a spiritual state, a spiritual condition, an inner development, and one that we must recognise as abnormal, since it is beyond the reach of the world at the present stage of evolution. Higher Space is a mythical state."

"Oh!" cried the other, rubbing his birdlike hands with pleasure, "the relief it is to be to talk to some one who can understand! Of course what you say is the utter truth. And you are right that no mere chance led me to my present condition, but, on the other hand, prolonged and deliberate study. Yet chance in a sense now governs it. I mean, my entering the condition of Higher Space seems to depend upon the chance of this and that circumstance. For instance, the mere sound of that German band sent me off. Not that all music will do so, but certain sounds, certain vibrations, at once key me up to the requisite pitch, and off I go. Wagner's music always does it, and that band must have been playing a stray bit of Wagner. But I'll come to all that later. Only, first, I must ask you to send away your man from the spy-hole."

John Silence looked up with a start, for Mr. Mudge's back was to the door, and there was no mirror. He saw the brown eye of Barker glued to the little circle of glass, and he crossed the room without a word and snapped down the black shutter provided for the purpose, and then heard Barker shuffle away along the passage.

"Now," continued the little man in the chair, "I can begin. You have managed to put me completely at my ease, and I feel I may tell you my whole case without shame or reserve. You will understand. But you must be patient with me if I go into details that are already familiar to you—details of Higher Space, I mean—and if I seem stupid when I have to describe things that transcend the power of language and are really therefore indescribable."

"My dear friend," put in the other calmly, "that goes without saying. To know Higher Space is an experience that defies description, and one is obliged to make use of more or less intelligible symbols. But, pray, proceed. Your vivid thoughts will tell me more than your halting words."

An immense sigh of relief proceeded from the little figure half lost in the depths of the chair. Such intelligent sympathy meeting him half-way was a new experience to him, and it touched his heart at once. He leaned back, relaxing his tight hold of the arms, and began in his thin, scale-like voice.

"My mother was a Frenchwoman, and my father an Essex bargeman," he said abruptly. "Hence my name—Racine and Mudge. My father died before I ever saw him. My mother inherited money from her Bordeaux relations, and when she died soon after, I was left alone with wealth and a strange freedom. I had no guardian, trustees, sisters, brothers, or any connection in the world to look after me. I grew up, therefore, utterly without education. This much was to my advantage; I learned none of that deceitful rubbish taught in schools, and so had nothing to unlearn when I awakened to my true love—mathematics, higher mathematics and higher geometry. These, however, I seemed to know instinctively. It was like the memory of what I had deeply studied before; the principles were in my blood, and I simply raced through the ordinary stages, and beyond, and then did the same with geometry. Afterwards, when I read the books on these subjects, I understood how swift and undeviating the knowledge had come back to me. It was simply memory. It was simply *re-collecting* the memories of what I had known before in a previous existence and required no books to teach me."

In his growing excitement, Mr. Mudge attempted to drag the chair forward a little nearer to his listener, and then smiled faintly as he resigned himself instantly again to its immovability, and plunged anew into the recital of his singular "disease."

"The audacious speculations of Bolyai, the amazing theories of Gauss—that through a point more than one line could be drawn parallel to a given line; the possibility that the angles of a triangle are together *greater* than two right angles, if drawn upon immense curvatures—the breathless intuitions of Beltrami and Lobatchewsky—all these I hurried through, and emerged, panting but unsatisfied, upon the verge of my—my new world, my Higher Space possibilities—in a word, my disease!

"How I got there," he resumed after a brief pause, during which he appeared to be listening intently for an approaching sound, "is more than I can put intelligibly into words. I can only hope to leave your mind with an intuitive comprehension of the possibility of what I say.

"Here, however, came a change. At this point I was no longer absorbing the fruits of studies I had made before; it was the beginning of new efforts to learn for the first time, and I had to go slowly and laboriously through terrible work. Here I sought for the theories and speculations of others. But books were few and far between, and with the exception of one man—a 'dreamer,' the world called him—whose audacity and piercing intuition amazed and delighted me beyond description, I found no one to guide or help.

"You, of course, Dr. Silence, understand something of what I am driving at with these stammering words, though you cannot perhaps yet guess what depths of pain my new knowledge brought me to, nor why an acquaintance with a new development of space should prove a source of misery and terror."

Mr. Racine Mudge, remembering that the chair would not move, did the next best thing he could in his desire to draw nearer to the attentive man facing him, and sat forward upon the very edge of the cushions, crossing his legs and gesticulating with both hands as though he saw into this region of new space he was attempting to describe, and might any moment tumble into it bodily from the edge of the chair and disappear from view. John Silence, separated from him by three paces, sat with his eyes fixed upon the thin white face opposite, noting every word and every gesture with deep attention.

"This room we now sit in, Dr. Silence, has one side open to space—to Higher Space. A closed box only *seems* closed. There is a way in and out of a soap bubble without breaking the skin."

"You tell me no new thing," the doctor interposed gently.

"Hence, if Higher Space exists and our world borders upon it and lies partially in it, it follows necessarily that we see only portions of all objects. We never see their true and complete shape. We see their three measurements, but not their fourth. The new direction is concealed from us, and when I hold this book and move my hand all round it I have not really made a complete circuit. We only perceive those portions of any object which exist in our three dimensions; the rest escapes us. But, once we learn to see in Higher Space, and objects will appear as they actually are. Only they will thus be hardly recognisable!

"Now, you may begin to grasp something of what I am coming to."

"I am beginning to understand something of what you must have suffered," observed the doctor soothingly, "for I have made similar experiments myself, and only stopped just in time—"

"You are the one man in all the world who can hear and understand, *and* sympathise," exclaimed Mr. Mudge, grasping his hand and holding it tightly while he spoke. The nailed chair prevented further excitability.

"Well," he resumed, after a moment's pause, "I procured the implements and the coloured blocks for practical experiment, and I followed the instructions carefully till I had arrived at a working conception of four-dimensional space. The tessaract, the figure whose boundaries are cubes, I knew by heart. That is to say, I knew it and saw it mentally, for my eye, of course, could never take in a new measurement, or my hands and feet handle it.

"So, at least, I thought," he added, making a wry face. "I had reached the stage, you see, when I could *imagine* in a new dimension. I was able to conceive the shape of that new figure which is intrinsically different to all we know—the shape of the tessaract. I could perceive in four dimensions. When, therefore, I looked at a cube I could see all its sides at once. Its top was not foreshortened, nor its farther side and base invisible. I saw the whole thing out flat, so to speak. And this Tessaract was bounded by cubes! Moreover, I also saw its content—its insides."

"You were not yourself able to enter this new world," interrupted Dr. Silence.

"Not then. I was only able to conceive intuitively what it was like and how exactly it must look. Later, when I slipped in there and saw objects in their entirety, unlimited by the paucity of our poor three measurements, I very nearly lost my life. For, you see, space does not stop at a single new dimension, a fourth. It extends in all possible new ones, and we must conceive it as containing any number of new dimensions. In other words, there is no space at all, but only a spiritual condition. But, meanwhile, I had come to grasp the strange fact that the objects in our normal world appear to us only partially."

Mr. Mudge moved farther forward till he was balanced dangerously on the very edge of the chair. "From this starting point," he resumed, "I began my studies and experiments, and continued them for years. I had money, and I was without friends. I lived in solitude and experimented. My intellect, of course, had little part in the work, for intellectually it was all unthinkable. Never was the limitation of mere reason more plainly demonstrated. It was mystically, intuitively, spiritually that I began to advance. And what I learnt, and knew, and did is all impossible to put into language, since it all describes experiences transcending the experiences of men. It is only some of the results—what you would call the symptoms of my disease—that I can give you, and even these must often appear absurd contradictions and impossible paradoxes.

"I can only tell you, Dr. Silence"—his manner became exceedingly impressive—"that I reached sometimes a point of view whence all the great puzzle of the world became plain to me, and I understood what they call in the Yoga books 'The Great Heresy of Separateness'; why all great teachers have urged the necessity of man loving his neighbour as himself; how men are all really *one*; and why the utter loss of self is necessary to salvation and the discovery of the true life of the soul."

He paused a moment and drew breath.

"Your speculations have been my own long ago," the doctor said quietly. "I fully realise the force of your words. Men are doubtless not separate at all—in the sense they imagine— "

"All this about the very much Higher Space I only dimly, very dimly, conceived, of course," the other went on, raising his voice again by jerks; "but what did happen to me was the humbler accident of—the simpler disaster—oh, dear, how shall I put it—?"

He stammered and showed visible signs of distress. "It was simply this," he resumed with a sudden rush of words, "that, accidentally, as the result of my years of experiment, I one day slipped bodily into the next world, the world of four dimensions, yet without knowing precisely how I got there, or how I could get back again. I discovered, that is, that my ordinary three-dimensional body was but an expression—a projection—of my higher four-dimensional body!

"Now you understand what I meant much earlier in our talk when I spoke of chance. I cannot control my entrance or exit. Certain people, certain human atmospheres, certain wandering forces, thoughts, desires even—the radiations of certain combinations of colour, and above all, the vibrations of certain kinds of music, will suddenly throw me into a state of what I can only describe as an intense and terrific inner vibration—and behold I am off! Off in the direction at right angles to all our known directions! Off in the direction the cube takes when it begins to trace the outlines of the new figure! Off into my breathless and semi-divine Higher Space! Off, *inside myself*, into the world of four dimensions!"

He gasped and dropped back into the depths of the immovable chair.

"And there," he whispered, his voice issuing from among the cushions, "there I have to stay until these vibrations subside, or until they do something which I cannot find words to describe properly or intelligibly to you—and then, behold, I am back again. First, that is, I disappear. Then I reappear."

"Just so," exclaimed Dr. Silence, "and that is why a few—"

"Why a few moments ago," interrupted Mr. Mudge, taking the words out of his mouth, "you found me gone, and then saw me return. The music of that wretched German band sent me off. Your intense thinking about me brought me back—when the band had stopped its Wagner. I saw you approach the peep-hole and I saw Barker's intention of doing so later. For me no interiors are hidden. I see inside. When in that state the content of your mind, as of your body, is open to me as the day. Oh, dear, oh, dear, oh, dear!"

Mr. Mudge stopped and again mopped his brow. A light trembling ran over the surface of his small body like wind over grass. He still held tightly to the arms of the chair.

"At first," he presently resumed, "my new experiences were so vividly interesting that I felt no alarm. There was no room for it. The alarm came a little later."

"Then you actually penetrated far enough into that state to experience yourself as a normal portion of it?" asked the doctor, leaning forward, deeply interested.

Mr. Mudge nodded a perspiring face in reply.

"I did," he whispered, "undoubtedly I did. I am coming to all that. It began first at night, when I realised that sleep brought no loss of consciousness—"

"The spirit, of course, can never sleep. Only the body becomes unconscious," interposed John Silence. "Yes, we know that—theoretically. At night, of course, the spirit is active elsewhere, and we have no memory of where and how, simply because the brain stays behind and receives no record. But I found that, while remaining conscious, I also retained memory. I had attained to the state of continuous consciousness, for at night I regularly, with the first approaches of drowsiness, entered *nolens volens* the four-dimensional world.

"For a time this happened regularly, and I could not control it; though later I found a way to regulate it better. Apparently sleep is unnecessary in the higher—the four-dimensional—body. Yes, perhaps. But I should infinitely have preferred dull sleep to the knowledge. For, unable to control my movements, I wandered to and fro, attracted, owing to my partial development and premature arrival, to parts of this new world that alarmed me more and more. It was the awful waste and drift of a monstrous world, so utterly different to all we know and see that I cannot even hint at the nature of the sights and objects and beings in it. More than that, I cannot even remember them. I cannot now picture them to myself even, but can recall only the *memory of the impression* they made upon me, the horror and devastating terror of it all. To be in several places at once, for instance—"

"Perfectly," interrupted John Silence, noticing the increase of the other's excitement, "I understand exactly. But now, please, tell me a little more of this alarm you experienced, and how it affected you."

"It's not the disappearing and reappearing *per se* that I mind," continued Mr. Mudge, "so much as certain other things. It's seeing people and objects in their weird entirety, in their true and complete shapes, that is so distressing. It introduces me to a world of monsters. Horses, dogs, cats, all of which I loved; people, trees, children; all that I have considered beautiful in life—everything, from a human face to a cathedral—appear to me in a different shape and aspect to all I have known before. I cannot perhaps convince you why this should be terrible, but I assure you that it is so. To hear the human voice proceeding from this novel appearance which I scarcely recognise as a human body is ghastly, simply ghastly. To see inside everything and everybody is a form of insight peculiarly distressing. To be so confused in geography as to find myself one moment at the North Pole, and the next at Clapham Junction—or possibly at both places simultaneously—is absurdly terrifying. Your imagination will readily furnish other details without my multiplying my experiences now. But you have no idea what it all means, and how I suffer."

Mr. Mudge paused in his panting account and lay back in his chair. He still held tightly to the arms as though they could keep him in the world of sanity and three measurements, and only now and again released his left hand in order to mop his face. He looked very thin and white and oddly unsubstantial, and he stared about him as though he saw into this other space he had been talking about.

John Silence, too, felt warm. He had listened to every word and had made many notes. The presence of this man had an exhilarating effect upon him. It seemed as if Mr. Racine Mudge still carried about with him something of that breathless Higher-Space condition he had been describing. At any rate, Dr. Silence had himself advanced sufficiently far along the legitimate paths of spiritual and psychic transformations to realise that the visions of this extraordinary little person had a basis of truth for their origin.

After a pause that prolonged itself into minutes, he crossed the room and unlocked a drawer in a bookcase, taking out a small book with a red cover. It had a lock to it, and he produced a key out of his pocket and proceeded to open the covers. The bright eyes of Mr. Mudge never left him for a single second.

"It almost seems a pity," he said at length, "to cure you, Mr. Mudge. You are on the way to discovery of great things. Though you may lose your life in the process—that is, your life here in the world of three dimensions— you would lose thereby nothing of great value—you will pardon my apparent rudeness, I know—and you might gain what is infinitely greater. Your suffering, of course, lies in the fact that you alternate between the two worlds and are never wholly in one or the other. Also, I rather imagine, though I cannot be certain of this from any personal experiments, that you have here and there penetrated even into space of more than four dimensions, and have hence experienced the terror you speak of."

The perspiring son of the Essex bargeman and the woman of Normandy bent his head several times in assent, but uttered no word in reply.

"Some strange psychic predisposition, dating no doubt from one of your former lives, has favoured the development of your 'disease'; and the fact that you had no normal training at school or college, no leading by the poor intellect into the culs-de-sac falsely called knowledge, has further caused your exceedingly rapid movement along the lines of direct inner experience. None of the knowledge you have foreshadowed has come to you through the senses, of course."

Mr. Mudge, sitting in his immovable chair, began to tremble slightly. A wind again seemed to pass over his surface and again to set it curiously in motion like a field of grass.

"You are merely talking to gain time," he said hurriedly, in a shaking voice. "This thinking aloud delays us. I see ahead what you are coming to, only please be quick, for something is going to happen. A band is again coming down the street, and if it plays—if it plays Wagner—I shall be off in a twinkling."

"Precisely. I will be quick. I was leading up to the point of how to effect your cure. The way is this: You must simply learn to *block the entrances*."

"True, true, utterly true!" exclaimed the little man, dodging about nervously in the depths of the chair. "But how, in the name of space, is that to be done?"

"By concentration. They are all within you, these entrances, although outer cases such as colour, music and other things lead you towards them. These external things you cannot hope to destroy, but once the entrances are blocked, they will lead you only to bricked walls and closed channels. You will no longer be able to find the way."

"Quick, quick!" cried the bobbing figure in the chair. "How is this concentration to be effected?"

"This little book," continued Dr. Silence calmly, "will explain to you the way." He tapped the cover. "Let me now read out to you certain simple instructions, composed, as I see you divine, entirely from my own personal experiences in the same direction. Follow these instructions and you will no longer enter the state of Higher Space. The entrances will be blocked effectively."

Mr. Mudge sat bolt upright in his chair to listen, and John Silence cleared his throat and began to read slowly in a very distinct voice.

But before he had uttered a dozen words, something happened. A sound of street music entered the room through the open ventilators, for a band had begun to play in the stable mews at the back of the house—the

March from *Tannhäuser*. Odd as it may seem that a German band should twice within the space of an hour enter the same mews and play Wagner, it was nevertheless the fact.

Mr. Racine Mudge heard it. He uttered a sharp, squeaking cry and twisted his arms with nervous energy round the chair. A piteous look that was not far from tears spread over his white face. Grey shadows followed it—the grey of fear. He began to struggle convulsively.

"Hold me fast! Catch me! For God's sake, keep me here! I'm on the rush already. Oh, it's frightful!" he cried in tones of anguish, his voice as thin as a reed.

Dr. Silence made a plunge forward to seize him, but in a flash, before he could cover the space between them, Mr. Racine Mudge, screaming and struggling, seemed to shoot past him into invisibility. He disappeared like an arrow from a bow propelled at infinite speed, and his voice no longer sounded in the external air, but seemed in some curious way to make it-self heard somewhere within the depths of the doctor's own being. It was almost like a faint singing cry in his head, like a voice of dream, a voice of vision and unreality.

"Alcohol, alcohol!" it cried, "give me alcohol! It's the quickest way. Al-cohol, before I'm out of reach!"

The doctor, accustomed to rapid decisions and even more rapid action, remembered that a brandy flask stood upon the mantelpiece, and in less than a second he had seized it and was holding it out towards the space above the chair recently occupied by the visible Mudge. Then, before his very eyes, and long ere he could unscrew the metal stopper, he saw the con-tents of the closed glass phial sink and lessen as though some one were drinking violently and greedily of the liquor within.

"Thanks! Enough! It deadens the vibrations!" cried the faint voice in his interior, as he withdrew the flask and set it back upon the mantelpiece. He understood that in Mudge's present condition one side of the flask was open to space and he could drink without removing the stopper. He could hardly have had a more interesting proof of what he had been hearing de-scribed at such length.

But the next moment—the very same moment it almost seemed—the German band stopped midway in its tune—and there was Mr. Mudge back in his chair again, gasping and panting!

"Quick!" he shrieked, "stop that band! Send it away! Catch hold of me! Block the entrances! Block the entrances! Give me the red book! Oh, oh, oh-h-h-h!!!"

The music had begun again. It was merely a temporary interruption. The *Tannhäuser* March started again, this time at a tremendous pace that made it sound like a rapid two-step as though the instruments played against time.

But the brief interruption gave Dr. Silence a moment in which to collect his scattering thoughts, and before the band had got through half a bar, he had flung forward upon the chair and held Mr. Racine Mudge, the struggling little victim of Higher Space, in a grip of iron. His arms went all round his diminutive person, taking in a good part of the chair at the same time. He was not a big man, yet he seemed to smother Mudge completely.

Yet, even as he did so, and felt the wriggling form underneath him, it began to melt and slip away like air or water. The wood of the arm-chair somehow disentangled itself from between his own arms and those of Mudge. The phenomenon known as the passage of matter through matter took place. The little man seemed actually to get mixed up in his own being. Dr. Silence could just see his face beneath him. It puckered and grew dark as though from some great internal effort. He heard the thin, reedy voice cry in his ear to "Block the entrances, block the entrances!" and then—but how in the world describe what is indescribable?

John Silence half rose up to watch. Racine Mudge, his face distorted beyond all recognition, was making a marvellous inward movement, as though doubling back upon himself. He turned funnel-wise like water in a whirling vortex, and then appeared to break up somewhat as a reflection breaks up and divides in a distorting convex mirror. He went neither forward nor backwards, neither to the right nor the left, neither up nor down. But he went. He went utterly. He simply flashed away out of sight like a vanishing projectile.

All but one leg! Dr. Silence just had the time and the presence of mind to seize upon the left ankle and boot as it disappeared, and to this he held on for several seconds like grim death. Yet all the time he knew it was a foolish and useless thing to do.

The foot was in his grasp one moment, and the next it seemed—this was the only way he could describe it—inside his own skin and bones, and at the same time outside his hand and all round it. It seemed mixed up in some amazing way with his own flesh and blood. Then it was gone, and he was tightly grasping a draught of heated air.

"Gone! gone! gone!" cried a thick, whispering voice, somewhere deep within his own consciousness. "Lost! lost! lost!" it repeated, growing fainter and fainter till at length it vanished into nothing and the last signs of Mr. Racine Mudge vanished with it.

John Silence locked his red book and replaced it in the cabinet, which he fastened with a click, and when Barker answered the bell he inquired if Mr. Mudge had left a card upon the table. It appeared that he had, and when the servant returned with it, Dr. Silence read the address and made a note of it. It was in North London.

"Mr. Mudge has gone," he said quietly to Barker, noticing his expression of alarm.

"He's not taken his 'at with him, sir."

"Mr. Mudge requires no hat where he is now," continued the doctor, stooping to poke the fire. "But he may return for it—"

"And the humbrella, sir."

"And the umbrella."

"He didn't go out *my* way, sir, if you please," stuttered the amazed servant, his curiosity overcoming his nervousness.

"Mr. Mudge has his own way of coming and going, and prefers it. If he returns by the door at any time remember to bring him instantly to me, and be kind and gentle with him and ask no questions. Also, remember, Barker, to think pleasantly, sympathetically, affectionately of him while he is away. Mr. Mudge is a very suffering gentleman."

Barker bowed and went out of the room backwards, gasping and feeling round the inside of his collar with three very hot fingers of one hand.

It was two days later when he brought in a telegram to the study. Dr. Silence opened it, and read as follows :

"Bombay. Just slipped out again. All safe. Have blocked entrances. Thousand thanks. Address Cooks, London.—MUDGE."

Dr. Silence looked up and saw Barker staring at him bewilderingly. It occurred to him that somehow he knew the contents of the telegram.

"Make a parcel of Mr. Mudge's things," he said briefly, "and address them Thomas Cook & Sons, Ludgate Circus. And send them there exactly a month from to-day and marked 'To be called for.'"

"Yes, sir," said Barker, leaving the room with a deep sigh and a hurried glance at the waste-paper basket where his master had dropped the pink paper.

THE END

The Wave
An Egyptian Aftermath
by Algernon Blackwood

To M. S.-K.
Egypt's Forgetful and Unwilling Child

Part I

CHAPTER I

Since childhood days he had been haunted by a Wave. It appeared with the very dawn of thought, and was his earliest recollection of any vividness. It was also his first experience of nightmare: a wave of an odd, dun color, almost tawny, that rose behind him, advanced, curled over in the act of toppling, and then stood still. It threatened, but it did not fall. It paused, hovering in a position contrary to nature; it waited.

Something prevented; it was not meant to fall; the right moment had not yet arrived.

If only it would fall! It swept across the skyline in a huge, long curve far overhead, hanging dreadfully suspended. Beneath his feet he felt the roots of it withdrawing; he shuffled furiously and made violent efforts; but the suction undermined him where he stood. The ground yielded and dropped away. He only sank in deeper. His entire weight became that of a feather against the gigantic tension of the mass that any moment, it seemed, must lift him in its rising curve, bend, break, and twist him, then fling him crashing forward to his smothering fate.

Yet the moment never came. The Wave hung balanced between him and the sky, poised in mid-air. It did not fall. And the torture of that infinite pause contained the essence of the nightmare.

The Wave invariably came up behind him, stealthily, from what seemed interminable distance. He never met it. It overtook him from the rear. The horizon hid it till it rose.

There were stages in its history, moreover, and in the effect it produced upon his early mind. Usually he woke up the moment he realized it was there. For it invariably announced its presence. He heard no sound, but knew that it was coming—there was a feeling in the atmosphere not unlike the heavy brooding that precedes a thunderstorm, only so different from anything he had yet known in life, that his heart sank into his boots. He looked up. There, above his head was the huge, curved monster, hanging in mid-air. The mood had justified itself. He called it the "wavy feeling." He was never wrong about it.

The second stage was reached when, instead of trying to escape shorewards, where there were tufts of coarse grass upon a sandy bank, he turned and faced the thing. He looked straight into the main under-body of the poised billow. He saw the opaque mass out of which this line rose up and curved. He stared against the dull, dun-colored parent body whence it came—the sea. Terrified yet fascinated, he examined it in detail, as a man about to be executed might examine the grain of the wooden block close against his eyes. A little higher, some dozen feet above the level of his head, it became transparent; sunlight shot through the glassy curve. He saw what appeared to be streaks and bubbles and transverse lines of foam that yet did not shine quite as water shines. It moved suddenly; it curled a little towards the crest; it was about to topple over, to break—yet did not break.

About this time he noticed another thing: there was a curious faint sweetness in the air beneath the bend of it, a delicate and indescribable odor that was almost perfume. It was sweet; it choked him. He called it, in his boyish way, a whiff. The "whiff" and the "wavy feeling" impressed themselves so vividly upon his mind that if ever he met them in his ordinary life—out of dream that is—he was sure that he would know them. In another sense he felt he knew them already. They were familiar.

But another stage went further than all the others put together. It amounted to a discovery. He was perhaps ten years old at this time, for he was still addressed as "Tommy," and it was not till the age of fifteen that his solid type of character made "Tom" seem more appropriate. He had just told the dream to his mother for the hundredth time, and she, after listening with sympathy, had made her ever-green suggestion—"If you dream of water, Tommy, it means you're thirsty in your sleep,"—when he turned and stared straight into her eyes with such intentness that she gave an involuntary start.

"But, mother, it *isn't* water!"

"Well, darling, if it isn't water, what is it, then?" She asked the question quietly enough, but she felt, apparently, something of the queer dismay that her boy felt too. It seemed the mother-sense was touched. The instinct to protect her offspring stirred uneasily in her heart. She repeated the question, interested in the old, familiar dream for the first time since she heard it several years before: "If it isn't water, Tommy, what is it? What can it be?" His eyes, his voice, his manner—something she could not properly name—had startled her.

But Tommy noticed her slight perturbation, and knowing that a boy of his age did not frighten his mother without reason, or even with it, turned his eyes aside and answered:

"I couldn't tell. There wasn't time. You see, I woke up then."

"How curious, Tommy," she rejoined. "A wave is a wave, isn't it?"

And he answered thoughtfully: "Yes, mother; but there are lots of things besides water, aren't there?"

She assented with a nod, and a searching look at him which he purposely avoided. The subject dropped; no more was said; yet somehow from that moment his mother knew that this idea of a wave, whether it was nightmare or only dream, had to do with her boy's life in a way that touched the protective thing in her, almost to the point of positive defense. She could not explain it; she did not like it; instinct warned her—that was all she knew. And Tommy said no more. The truth was, indeed, that he did not know himself of what the wave was composed. He could not have told his mother even had he considered it permissible. He would have loved to speculate and talk about it with her, but, having divined her nervousness, he knew he must not feed it. No boy should do such a thing.

Moreover, the interest he felt in the Wave was of such a deep enormous character—the adjectives were his own—that he could not talk about it lightly. Unless to some one who showed genuine interest, he could not even mention it. To his brothers and sister, both older and younger than himself, he never spoke of it at all. It had to do with something so fundamental in him that it was sacred. The realization of it, moreover, came and went, and often remained buried for weeks together; months passed without a hint of it; the nightmare disappeared. Then, suddenly, the feeling would surge over him, perhaps just as he was getting into bed, or saying his prayers, or thinking of quite other things. In the middle of a discussion with his brother about their air-guns and the water-rat they hadn't hit—up would steal the "wavy" feeling with its dim, familiar menace. It stole in across his brother's excited words about the size and speed of the rat; interest in sport entirely vanished; he stared at Tim, not hearing a word he said; he dived into bed; he had to be alone with the great mood of wonder and terror that was rising. The approach was unmistakable; he cuddled beneath the sheets, fighting-angry if Tim tried to win him back to the original interest. The dream was coming; and, sure enough, a little later in his sleep, it came.

For, even at this stage of his development he recognized instinctively this special quality about it—that it could not, was not meant to be avoided. It was inevitable and right. It hurt, yet he must face it. It was as necessary to his well-being as having a tooth out. Nor did he ever seek to dodge it. His character was not the kind that flinched. The one thing he did ask was—to understand. Some day, he felt, this full understanding would come.

There arrived then a new and startling development in this curious obsession, the very night, Tommy claims, that there had been the fuss about the gun and water-rat, on the day before the conversation with his mother. His brother had plagued him to come out from beneath the sheets and go on with the discussion, and Tommy, furious at being disturbed in the "wavy" mood he both loved and dreaded, had felt himself roused uncommonly. He silenced Tim easily enough with a smashing blow from a pillow, then, with a more determined effort than usual, buried himself to face the advent of the Wave. He fell asleep in the attempt, but the attempt bore fruit. He felt the great thing coming up behind him; he turned; he saw it with greater distinctness than ever before; almost he discovered of what it was composed.

That it was *not* water established itself finally in his mind; but more—he got very close to deciding its exact composition. He stared hard into the threatening mass of it; there was a certain transparency about the substance, yet this transparency was not clear enough for water: there were particles, and these particles went drifting by the thousand, by the million, through the mass of it. They rose and fell, they swept along, they were very minute indeed, they whirled. They glistened, shimmered, flashed. He made a guess; he was just on the point of guessing right, in fact, when he saw another thing that for the moment obliterated all his faculties. There was both cold and heat in the sensation, fear and delight. It transfixed him. He saw eyes.

Steady, behind the millions of minute particles that whirled and drifted, he distinctly saw a pair of eyes of light-blue color, and hardly had he registered this new discovery, when another pair, but of quite different kind, became visible beyond the first pair—dark, with a fringe of long, thick lashes. They were—he decided afterwards—what is called eastern eyes, and they smiled into his own through half-closed lids. He thinks he made out a face that was dimly sketched behind them, but the whirling particles glinted and shimmered in such a confusing way that he could not swear to this. Of one thing only, or rather of two, did he feel quite positive: that the dark eyes were those of a woman, and that they were kind and beautiful and true: but that the pale-blue eyes were false, unkind, and treacherous, and that the face to which they belonged, although he could not see it, was a man's. Dimly his boyish heart was aware of happiness and suffering. The heat and cold he felt, the joy and terror, were half explained. He stared. The whirling particles drifted up and hid them. He woke.

That day, however, the "wavy" feeling hovered over him more or less continuously. The impression of the night held sway over all he did and thought. There was a kind of guidance in it somewhere. He obeyed this guidance as by an instinct he could not, dared not disregard, and towards dusk it led him into the quiet room overlooking the small Gardens at the back of the house, his father's study. The room was empty; he approached the big mahogany cupboard; he opened one of the deep drawers where he knew his father kept gold and private things, and birthday or Christmas presents. But there was no dishonorable intention in him anywhere; indeed, he hardly knew exactly why he did this thing. The drawer, though moving easily, was heavy; he pulled hard; it slid out with a rush; and at that moment a stern voice sounded in the room behind him: "What are you doing at my eastern drawer?"

Tommy, one hand still on the knob, turned as if he had been struck. He gazed at his father, but without a trace of guilt upon his face.

"I wanted to see, Daddy."

"I'll show you," said the stern-faced man, yet with kindness and humor in the tone. "It's full of wonderful things. I've nothing secret from you, but another time you'd better ask first—Tommy."

"I wanted to see," faltered the boy. "I don't know why I did it. I just had a feeling. It's the first time—*really*."

The man watched him searchingly a moment, but without appearing to do so. A look of interest and understanding, wholly missed by the culprit, stole into his fine gray eyes. He smiled, then drew Tommy towards him, and gave him a kiss on the top of his curly head. He also smacked him playfully. "Curiosity," he said with pretended disapproval, "is divine, and at your age it is right that you should feel curiosity about everything in the world. But another time just ask me—and I'll show you all I possess." He lifted his son in his arms, so that for the first time the boy could overlook the contents of the opened drawer. "So you just had a feeling, eh—?" he continued, when Tommy wriggled in his arms, uttered a curious exclamation, and half collapsed. He seemed upon the verge of tears. An ordinary father must have held him guilty there and then. The boy cried out excitedly:

"The whiff! Oh, Daddy, it's my whiff!"

The tears, no longer to be denied, came freely then; after them came confession too, and confused though it was, the man made something approaching sense out of the jumbled utterance. It was not mere patient kindness on his part, for an older person would have seen that genuine interest lay behind the half-playful, half-serious cross-examination. He watched the boy's eager, excited face out of the corner of his eyes; he put discerning questions to him; he assisted his faltering replies; and he obtained in the end the entire story of the dream, the eyes, the wavy feeling and the whiff. How much coherent meaning he discovered in it all is hard to say, or whether the story he managed to disentangle held together. There was this strange deep feeling in the boy, this strong emotion, this odd conviction amounting to an obsession; and so far as could be discovered, it was not traceable to any definite cause that Tommy could name—a fright, a shock, a vivid impression of one kind or another upon a sensitive young imagination. It lay so deeply in his being that its roots were utterly concealed; but it was real.

Dr. Kelverdon established the existence in his eldest boy of an unalterable premonition, and, being a famous nerve specialist, and a disciple of Freud into the bargain, he believed that a premonition has a cause, however primitive, however carefully concealed that cause may be. He put the boy to bed himself and tucked him up, told Tim that if he teased his brother too much he would smack him with his best Burmese slipper which had tiny nails in it, and then whispered into Tommy's ear as he cuddled down, happy and comforted, among the blankets: "Don't make a special effort to dream, my boy, but if you do dream, try to remember it next morning, and tell me exactly what you see and feel." He used the Freudian method.

Then, going down to his study again, he looked at the open drawer and sniffed the faint perfume of things—chiefly from Egypt—that lay inside it. But there was nothing of special interest in the drawer: indeed, it was one he had not touched for years. He went over one by one a few of the articles, collected from various points of travel long ago. There were bead necklaces from Memphis, some trash from a mummy of doubtful authenticity, including several amulets and a crumbling fragment of old papyrus, and, among all this, a tiny packet of incense mixed from a recipe said to have been found in a Theban tomb. All these, jumbled together in pieces of tissue paper, had lain undisturbed since the day he wrapped them up some dozen years before—indeed he heard the dry rattle of the falling sand as he undid the tissue paper. But a strong perfume rose from the parcel to his nostrils. "That's what Tommy means by his whiff," he said to himself. "That's Tommy's whiff beyond all question. I wonder how he got it first?"

He remembered, then, that he had made a note of the story connected with the incense, and after some rummaging, he found the envelope, and read the account jotted down at the time. He had meant to hand it over to a literary friend—the tale was so poignantly human—then had forgotten all about it. The papyrus, dating over 3,000 B.C. had many gaps. The Egyptologist had admittedly filled in considerable blanks in the afflicting story:

"A victorious Theban General, Prince of the blood, brought back a Syrian youth from one of his foreign conquests and presented him to his young wife who, first mothered him for his beauty, then made him her personal slave, and ended by caring deeply for him. The slave, in return, loved her with passionate adoration he was unable to conceal. As a Lady of the Court, her quasi-adoption of the youth caused comment. Her husband ordered his dismissal. But she still made his welfare her especial object, finding frequent reasons for their meeting. One day, however, her husband caught them together, though their meeting was in innocence. He half strangled the youth, till the blood poured down upon his own hands, then had him flogged and sent away to On the City of the Sun.

"The Syrian found his way back again, vengeance in his fiery blood. The clandestine yet innocent meetings were renewed. Rank was forgotten. They met among the sand-dunes in the desert behind the city where a pleasure tent among a grove of palms provided shelter, and the slave losing his head, urged the Princess to fly with him. Yet the wife, true to her profligate and brutal husband, refused his plea, saying she could only give a mother's love, a mother's care. This he rejected bitterly, accusing her of trifling with him. He grew bolder and more insistent. To divert her husband's violent suspicions she became purposely cruel, even ordering him punishments. But the slave misinterpreted. Finally, warning him that if caught he would be killed, she devised a plan to convince him of her sincerity. Hiding him behind the curtains of her tent, she pleaded with her husband for the youth's recall, swearing that she meant no wrong. But the soldier, in his fury, abused and struck her, and the slave, unable to contain himself, rushed out of his hiding-place and stabbed him, though not mortally. He was condemned to death by torture. She was to be chief witness against him.

"Meanwhile, having extracted a promise from her husband that the torture should not be carried to the point of death, she conveyed word to the victim that he should endure bravely, knowing that he would not die. She now realized that she loved. She promised to fly with him.

"The sentence was duly carried out, the slave only half believing in her truth. It was a public holiday in Thebes. She was compelled to see the punishment inflicted before the crowd. There were a thousand drums. A sandstorm hid the sun.

"Seated beside her husband on a terrace above the Nile, she watched the torture—then knew she had been tricked. But the Syrian did not know; he believed her false. As he expired, casting his last glance of anguish and reproach at her, she rose, leaped the parapet, flung herself into the river, and was drowned. The husband had their bodies thrown into the sea, unburied. The same wave took them both. Later, however, they were recovered by influential friends; they were embalmed, and secretly laid to rest in his ancestral Tomb in the Valley of the Kings among the Theban Hills. In due course, the husband, unwittingly, was buried with them.

"Nearly five thousand years later all three mummies were discovered lying side by side, their story inscribed upon a papyrus inside the great sarcophagus."

Dr. Kelverdon glanced through the story he had forgotten, then tore it into little pieces and threw them into the fire-place. For a moment longer, however, he stood beside the open drawer, reflectingly. Had he ever told the tale to Tommy? No; it was hardly likely; indeed it was impossible. The boy was not born even when first he heard it. To his wife, then? Less likely still. He could not remember, anyhow. The faint suggestion in his mind— a story communicated pre-natally—was not worth following up. He dismissed the matter from his thoughts. He closed the drawer and turned away. The little packet of incense, however, taken from the Tomb, he did not destroy. "I'll give it to Tommy," he decided. "Its whiff may possibly stimulate him into explanation!"

CHAPTER II

As a result of having told everything to his father, Tommy's nightmare, however, largely ceased to trouble him. He had found the relief of expression, which is confession, and had laid upon the older mind the burden of his terror. Once a month, once a week, or even daily if he wanted to, he could repeat the expression as the need for it accumulated, and the load which decency forbade being laid upon his mother, the stern-faced man could carry easily for him.

The comfortable sensation that forgiveness is the completion of confession invaded his awakening mind, and had he been older this thin end of a religious wedge might have persuaded him to join what his mother called that "vast conspiracy." But even at this early stage there was something stalwart and self-reliant in his cast of character that resisted the cunning sophistry; vicarious relief woke resentment in him; he meant to face his troubles alone. So far as he knew, he had not sinned, yet the Wave, the Whiff, the Eyes were symptoms of some fate that threatened him, a premonition of something coming that he must meet with his own strength, something that he could only deal with effectively alone, since it was deserved and just. One day the Wave would fall; his father could not help him then. This instinct in him remained unassailable. He even began to look forward to the time when it should come—to have done with it and get it over, conquering or conquered.

The premonition, that is, while remaining an obsession as before, transferred itself from his inner to his outer life. The nightmare, therefore, ceased. The menacing interest, however, held unchanged. Though the name had not hitherto occurred to him, he became a fatalist. "It's got to come; I've got to meet it. I will."

"Well, Tommy," his father would ask from time to time, "been dreaming anything lately?"

"Nothing, Daddy. It's all stopped."

"Wave, eyes and whiff all forgotten, eh?"

Tommy shook his head. "They're still there," he answered slowly, "but—." He seemed unable to complete the sentence. His father helped him at a venture.

"But they can't catch you—is that it?"

The boy looked up with a dogged expression in his big gray eyes. "I'm ready for them," he replied. And his father laughed and said "Of course. That's half the battle."

He gave him a present then—one of the packets of tissue-paper, and Tommy took it in triumph to his room. He opened it in private, but the contents seemed to him without especial interest. Only the Whiff was, somehow, sweet and precious, and he kept the packet in a drawer apart where the fossils and catapult and air-gun ammunition could not interfere with it, hiding the key so that Tim and the servants could not find it. And on rare occasions, when the rest of the household was asleep, he performed a little ritual of his own that, for a boy of eight, was distinctly singular.

When the room was dark, lit in winter by the dying fire, or in summer by the stars, he would creep out of bed, make quite sure that Tim was asleep, stand on a chair to reach the key from the top of the big cupboard, and carefully unlock the drawer. He had oiled the wood with butter, so that it was silent. The tissue-paper gleamed dimly pink; the Whiff came out to meet him. He lifted the packet, soft and crackling, and set it on the window-sill; he did not open it; its contents had no interest for him, it was the perfume he was after. And the moment the perfume reached his nostrils there came a trembling over him that he could not understand. He both loved and dreaded it. This manly, wholesome-minded, plucky little boy, the basis of whose steady character was common sense, became the prey of a strange, unreasonable fantasy. A faintness stole upon him; he lost the sense of kneeling on a solid chair; something immense and irresistible came piling up behind him; there was nothing firm he could push against to save himself; he began shuffling with his bare feet, struggling to escape from something that was coming, something that would probably overwhelm him yet must positively be faced and battled with. The Wave was rising. It was the wavy feeling.

He did not turn to look, because he knew quite well there was nothing in the room but beds, a fender, furniture, vague shadows and his brother Tim. That kind of childish fear had no place in what he felt. But the Wave was piled and curving over none the less; it hung between him and the shadowed ceiling, above the roof of the house, it came from beyond the world, far overhead against the crowding stars. It would not break, for the time had not yet come. But it was there. It waited. He knelt beneath its mighty shadow of advance; it was still arrested, poised above his eager life, competent to engulf him when the time arrived. The sweep of its curved mass was mountainous. He knelt inside this curve, small, helpless, but not too afraid to fight. The perfume stole about him. The Whiff was in his nostrils. There was a strange, rich pain—oddly remote, yet oddly poignant....

And it was with this perfume that the ritual chiefly had to do. He loved the extraordinary sensations that came with it, and tried to probe their meaning in his boyish way. Meaning there was, but it escaped him. The sweetness clouded something in his brain, and made his muscles weak; it robbed him of that resistance which is fighting strength. It was this battle that he loved, this sense of shoving against something that might so easily crush and finish him. There was a way to beat it, a way to win—could he but discover it. As yet he could not. Victory, he felt, lay more in yielding and going-with than in violent resistance.

And, meanwhile, in an ecstasy of this half yielding, half resisting, he lent himself fully to the over-mastering tide. He was conscious of attraction and repulsion, something that enticed, yet thrust him backwards. Some final test of manhood, character, value, lay in the way he faced it. The strange, rich pain stole marvelously into his blood and nerves. His heart beat faster. There was this exquisite seduction that contained delicious danger. It rose upon him out of some inner depth he could not possibly get at. He trembled with mingled terror and delight. And it invariably ended with a kind of inexpressible yearning that choked him, crumpled him inwardly, as he described it, brought the moisture, hot and smarting, into his burning eyes, and—each time to his bitter shame—left his cheeks wet with scalding tears.

He cried silently, there was no heaving, gulping, audible sobbing; just a relieving gush of heartfelt tears that took away the strange, rich pain and brought the singular ritual to a finish. He replaced the tissue-paper, blotted with his tears; locked the drawer carefully; hid the key on the top of the cupboard again, and tumbled back into bed.

Downstairs, meanwhile, a conversation was in progress concerning the welfare of the growing hero.

"I'm glad that dream has left him anyhow. It used to frighten me rather. I did not like it," observed his mother.

"He doesn't speak to you about it any more?" the father asked.

For months, she told him, Tommy had not mentioned it. They went on to discuss his future together. The other children presented fewer problems, but Tommy, apparently, felt no particular call to any profession.

"It will come with a jump," the doctor inclined to think. "He's been on the level for some time now. Suddenly he'll grow up and declare his mighty mind."

Father liked humor in the gravest talk; indeed the weightier the subject, the more he valued a humorous light upon it. The best judgment, he held, was shaped by humor, sense of proportion lost without it. His wife, however, thought "it a pity." Grave things she liked grave.

"There's something very deep in Tommy," she observed as though he were developing a hidden malady.

"Hum," agreed her husband. "His subconscious content is unusual, both in kind and quantity." His eyes twinkled. "It's possible he may turn out an artist, or a preacher. If the former, I'll bet his output will be original; and, as for the latter"—he paused a second—"he's too logical and too fearless to be orthodox. Already he thinks things out for himself."

"I should like to see him in the Church, though," said Mother. "He would do a lot of good. But he is uncompromising, rather."

"His honesty certainly is against him," sighed his father. "What do you think he asked me the other day?"

"I'm sure I don't know, John." The answer completed itself with the unspoken: "He never asks *me* anything now."

"He came straight up to me and said, 'Father, is it good to feel pain? To let it come, I mean, or try to dodge it?'"

"Had he hurt himself?" the woman asked quickly. It seemed she winced.

"Not physically. He had been feeling something inside. He wanted to know how 'a man' should meet the case."

"And what did you tell him, dear?"

"That pain was usually a sign of growth, to be understood, accepted, faced. That most pain was cured in that way—"

"He didn't tell you what had hurt him?" she interrupted.

"Oh, I didn't ask him. He'd have shut up like a clam. Tommy likes to deal with things alone in his own way. He just wanted to know if his way was—well, my way."

There fell a pause between them; then Mother, without looking up, inquired, "Have you noticed Lettice lately? She's here a good deal now."

But her husband only smiled, making no direct reply. "Tommy will have a hard time of it when he falls in love," he remarked presently. "He'll know the real thing and won't stand any nonsense—just as I did." Whereupon his wife informed him that if he was not careful he would simply ruin the boy—and the brief conversation died away of its own accord. As she was leaving the room, a little later, unsatisfied but unaggressive, he asked her: "Have you left the picture books, my dear?"; and she pointed to an ominous heap upon the table in the window, with the remark that Jane had "unearthed every book that Tommy had set eyes upon since he was three. You'll find everything that's ever interested him," she added as she went out, "every picture, that is—and I suppose it is the pictures that you want."

For an hour and a half the great specialist turned pages without ceasing; well-thumbed pages, torn, crumpled, blotted, painted pages; it was easy to discover the boy's favorite pictures; and all were commonplace enough, the sort that any normal, adventure-loving boy would find delightful. But nothing of special significance resulted from the search; nothing that might account for the recurrent nightmare; nothing in the way of eyes or wave. He had already questioned Jane as to what stories she told him, and which among them he liked best. "Hunting or travel or collecting," Jane had answered, and it was about "collecting that he asks most questions. What kind of collecting, sir? Oh, treasure or rare beetles mostly, and sometimes—just bones."

"Bones! What kind of bones?"

"The villin's, sir," explained the frightened Jane. "He always likes the villin to get lost, and for the jackals to pick his bones in the desert—"

"Any particular desert?"

"No, sir; just desert."

"Ah—just desert! Any old desert, eh?"

"I think so, sir—as long as it *is* desert."

Dr. Kelverdon put the woman at her ease with the humorous smile that made all the household love—and respect—him; then asked another question, as if casually: Had she ever told him a story in which a wave or a pair of eyes were in any way conspicuous?

"No, never, sir," replied the honest Jane, after careful reflection; "nor I wouldn't," she added, "because my father he was drowned in a tidal wave, and as for eyes, I know that's wrong for children, and I wouldn't tell Master Tommy such a thing for all the world—"

"Because?" inquired the doctor kindly, seeing her hesitation.

"I'd be frightening myself, sir, and he'd make such fun of me," she finally confessed.

No, it was clear that the nurse was not responsible for the vivid impression in Tommy's mind which bore fruit in so strange a complex of emotions. Nor were other lines of inquiry more successful. There was a cause, of course, but it would remain unascertainable unless some clue offered itself by chance. Both the doctor and the father in him were pledged to a persistent search that was prolonged over several months, but without result. The most perplexing element in the problem seemed to him the whiff. The association of terror with a wave needed little explanation; the introduction of the eyes, however, was puzzling, unless some story of a drowning man was possibly the clue; but the addition of a definite odor, an eastern odor, moreover, with which the boy could hardly have become yet acquainted,—this combination of the three accounted for the peculiar interest in the doctor's mind.

Of one thing alone did he feel reasonably certain: the impression had been printed upon the deepest part of Tommy's being, the very deepest; it arose from those unplumbed profundities—though a scientist, he considered them unfathomable—of character and temperament whence emerge the most primitive of instincts; the generative and creative instinct; choice of a mate; natural likes and dislikes; the bed-rock of the nature. A girl was in it somewhere, somehow....

Midnight had sounded from the stable clock in the mews when he stole up into the boys' room and cautiously approached the yellow iron bed where Tommy lay. The reflection of a street electric light just edged his face. He was sound asleep—with tear-stains marked clearly on the cheek not pressed into the pillow. Dr. Kelverdon paused a moment, looked round the room, shading the candle with one hand. He saw no photographs, no pictures anywhere. Then he sniffed. There was a faint and delicate perfume in the air. He recognized it. He stood there, thinking deeply.

"Lettice Aylmer," he said to himself presently as he went softly out again to seek his own bed; "I'll try Lettice. It's just possible.... Next time I see her I'll have a little talk." For he suddenly remembered that Lettice Aylmer, his daughter's friend and playmate, had very large and beautiful dark eyes.

CHAPTER III

Lettice Aylmer, daughter of the Irish Member of Parliament, did not provide the little talk that he anticipated, however, because she went back to her Finishing School abroad. Dr. Kelverdon was sorry when he heard it. So was Tommy. She was to be away a year at least. "I must remember to have a word with her when she comes back," thought the father, and made a note of it in his diary twelve months ahead. "Three hundred and sixty-five days," thought Tommy, and made a private calendar of his own.

It seemed an endless, zodiacal kind of period; he counted the days, a sheet of foolscap paper for each month, and at the bottom of each sheet two columns showing the balance of days gone and days to come. Tuesday, when he had first seen her, was underlined, and each Tuesday had a number attached to it, giving the total number of weeks since that wonderful occasion. But Saturdays were printed. On Saturday Lettice had spoken to him: she had smiled; and the words were "Don't forget me, Tommy!" And Tommy, looking straight into her great dark eyes, that seemed to him more tender even than his mother's, had stammered a reply that he meant with literal honesty: "I won't—never..."; and she was gone... to France... across the sea.

She took his soul away with her, leaving him behind to pore over his father's big atlas and learn French sentences by heart. It seemed the only way. Life had begun, and he must be prepared. Also, his career was chosen. For Lettice had said another thing—one other thing. When Mary, his sister, introduced him: "This is Tommy," Lettice looked down and asked: "Are you going to be an engineer?" adding proudly, "My brother is." Before he could answer she was scampering away with Mary, the dark hair flying in a cloud, the bright bow upon it twinkling like a star in heaven—and Tommy, hating his ridiculous boyish name with an intense hatred, stood there trembling, but aware that the die was cast—he was going to be an engineer.

Trembling, yes; for he felt dazed and helpless, caught in a mist of fire and gold, the furniture whirling round him, and something singing wildly in his heart. Two things, each containing in them the essence of genuine shock, had fallen upon him: shock, because there was impetus in them as of a blow. They had been coming; they had reached him. There was no doubt or question possible. He staggered from the impact. Joy and terror touched him; at one and the same moment he felt the enticement and the shrinking of his dream.... He longed to seize her and prevent her ever going away, yet also he wanted to push her from him as though she somehow caused him pain.

For, on the two occasions when speech had taken place between himself and Lettice the dream had transferred itself boldly into his objective life— yet not entirely. Two characteristics only had been thus transferred. When his sister first came into the hall with "This is Tommy," the wavy feeling had already preceded her by a definite interval that was perhaps a second by the watch. He was aware of it behind him, curved and risen—not curving, rising—from the open fireplace, but also from the woods behind the house, from the whole of the country right back to the coast, from across the world, it seemed, towering overhead against the wintry sky. And when Lettice smiled and asked that question of childish admiration about being an engineer—he was already shuffling furiously with his feet upon the Indian rug. She was gone again, luckily, he hoped, before the ridiculous pantomime was noticeable.

He saw her once or twice. He was invariably speechless when she came into his presence, and his silence and awkwardness made him appear at great disadvantage. He seemed intentionally rude. Nervous self-consciousness caused him to bridle over nothing. Even to answer her was a torture. He dreaded a snub appallingly, and bridled in anticipation. Furious with himself for his inability to use each precious opportunity, he pretended he didn't care. The consequence was that when she once spoke to him sweetly, he was too overpowered to respond as he might have done. That she had not even noticed his anguished attitude never occurred to him.

"We're always friends, aren't we, Tommy?"

"Rather," he blurted, before he could regain his composure for a longer sentence.

"And always will be, won't we?"

"Rather," he repeated, cursing himself later for thinking of nothing better to say. Then, just as she flew off in that dancing way of hers, he found his tongue. Out of the jumbled mass of phrases in his head three words got loose and offered themselves: "We'll always be!" he flung at her retreating figure of intolerable beauty. And she turned her head over her shoulder, waved her hand without stopping her career, and shouted "Rather!"

That was the Tuesday in his calendar. But on Saturday, the printed Saturday following it, the second characteristic of his dream announced itself: he recognized the Eyes! Why he had not recognized them on the Tuesday lay beyond explanation; he only knew it was so. And afterwards, when he tried to think it over, it struck him that she had scampered out of the hall with peculiar speed and hurry; had made her escape without the extra word or two the occasion naturally demanded—almost as though she, too, felt something that uneasily surprised her.

Tommy wondered about it till his head spun round. She, too, had received an impact that was shock. He was as thorough about it as an instinctive scientist. He also registered this further fact—that the dream-details had not entirely reproduced themselves in the affair. There was no trace of the Whiff or of the other pair of Eyes. Some day the three would come together; but then....

The main thing, however, undoubtedly was this: Lettice felt something too: she was aware of feelings similar to his own. He was too honest to assume that she felt exactly what he felt; he only knew that her eyes betrayed familiar intimacy when she said "Don't forget me, Tommy," and that when she rushed out of the hall with that unnecessary abruptness, it was because—well, he could only transfer to her some degree of the "wavy" feeling in himself.

And he fell in love with abandonment and a delicious, infinite yearning. From that moment he thought of himself as Tom instead of Tommy.

It was an entire, sweeping love that left no atom or corner of his being untouched. Lettice was real; she hid below the horizon of distant France, yet could not, did not, hide from him. She also waited.

He knew the difference between real and unreal people. The latter wavered about his life and were uncertain; sometimes he liked them, sometimes he did not; but the former—remained fixed quantities: he could not alter towards them. Even at this stage he knew when a person came into his life to stay, or merely to pass out again. Lettice, though seen but twice, belonged to this first category. His feeling for her had the Wave in it; it gathered weight and mass; it was irresistible. From the dim, invisible foundations of his life it came, out of the foundations of the world, out of that inexhaustible sea-foundation that lay below everything. It was real; it was not to be avoided. He knew. He persuaded himself that she knew too.

And it was then, realizing for the first time the searching pain of being separated from something that seemed part of his being by natural right, he spoke to his father and asked if pain should be avoided. This conversation has been already sufficiently recorded; but he asked other things as well. From being so long on the level he had made a sudden jump that his father had foretold; he grew up; his mind began to think; he had peered into certain books; he analyzed. Out of the nonsense of his speculative reflections the doctor pounced on certain points that puzzled him completely. Probing for the repressed elements in the boy's psychic life that caused the triple complex of Wave and Eyes and Whiff, he only saw the cause receding further and further from his grasp until it finally lost itself in ultimate obscurity. The disciple of Freud was baffled hopelessly....

Tom, meanwhile, bathed in a sea of new sensations. Distance held meaning for him, separation was a kind of keen starvation. He made discoveries—watched the moon rise, heard the wind, and knew the stars shone over the meadows below the house—things that before had been merely commonplace. He pictured these details as they might occur in France, and once when he saw a Swallow Tail butterfly, knowing that the few English specimens were said to have crossed the Channel, he had a touch of ecstasy, as though the proud insect brought him a message from the fields below the Finishing School. Also he read French books and found the language difficult but exquisite. All sweet and lovely things came from France, and at school he attempted violent friendships with three French boys and the Foreign Language masters, friendships that were not appreciated because they were not understood. But he made progress with the language, and it stood him in good stead in his examinations. He was aiming now at an Engineering College. He passed in— eventually—brilliantly enough.

Before that satisfactory moment, however, he knew difficult times. His inner life was in a splendid tumult. From the books he purloined he read a good many facts concerning waves and wave-formation. He learned, among other things, that all sensory impressions reached the nerves by impact of force in various wave-lengths; heat, light and sound broke upon the skin and eyes and ears in vibrations of aether or air that advanced in steady series of wavy formations which, though not quite similar to his dream-wave, were akin to it. Sensation, which is life, was thus linked on to his deepest, earliest memory.

A wave, however, instantly rejoined the parent stock and formed again. And perhaps it was the repetition of the wave—its forming again and breaking again—that impressed him most. For he imagined his impulses, emotions, tendencies, all taking this wave-form, sweeping his moods up to a certain point, then dropping back into his center—the Sea, he called it—which held steady below all temporary fluctuations—only to form once more and happen all over again.

With his moral and spiritual life it was similar: a wind came, wind of desire, wind of yearning, wind of hope, and he felt his strength accumulating, rising, bending with power upon the object that he had in view. To take that object exactly at the top of the wave was to achieve success; to miss that moment was to act with a receding and diminishing power, to dissipate himself in foam and spray before he could retire for a second rise. He saw existence as a wave. Life itself was a wave that rose, swept, curved, and finally—must break.

He merely visualized these feelings into pictures; he did not think them out, nor get them into words. The wave became symbolic to him of all life's energies. It was the way in which all sensation expressed itself. Lettice was the high-water mark on shore he longed to reach and sweep back into his own tumultuous being. In that great underneath, the Sea, they belonged eternally together....

One thing, however, troubled him exceedingly: he read that a wave was a segment of a circle, the perfect form, yet that it never completed itself. The ground on which it broke prevented the achievement of the circle. That, he felt, was a pity, and might be serious; there was always that sinister retirement for another effort that yet never did, and never could, result in complete achievement. He watched the waves a good deal on the shore, when occasion offered in the holidays—they came from France!— and made a discovery on his own account that was not mentioned in any of the books. And it was this: that the top of the wave, owing to its curve, was reflected in the under part. Its end, that is, was foretold in its beginning.

There was a want of scientific accuracy here, a confusion of time and space, perhaps, yet he noticed the idea and registered the thrill. At the moment when the wave was poised to fall its crest shone reflected in the base from which it rose.

But the more he watched the waves on the shore, the more puzzled he became. They seemed merely a movement of the sea itself. They endlessly repeated themselves. They had no true, separate existence until they— broke. Nor could he determine whether the crest or the base was the beginning, for the two ran along together, and what was above one minute was below the minute after. Which part started first he never could decide. The head kept chasing the tail in an effort to join up. Only when a wave broke and fell was it really—a wave. It had to "happen" to earn its name.

There were ripples too. These indicated the direction of the parent wave upon whose side they happened, but not its purpose. Moods were ripples: they varied the surface of life but did not influence its general direction.

His own life followed a similar behavior; he was full of ripples that were forever trying to complete themselves by happening in acts. But the main Wave was the thing—end and beginning sweeping along together, both at the same time somehow. That is, he knew the end and could foretell it. It rose from the great "beneath" which was the sea in him. It must topple over in the end and complete itself. He knew it would; he knew it would hurt; he knew also that he would not shirk it when it came. For it was a repetition somehow.

"I jolly well mean to enjoy the smash," he felt. "I know one pair of Eyes already; there's only the Whiff and the other Eyes to come. The moment I find them, I'll go bang into it." He experienced a delicious shiver at the prospect.

One thing, however, remained uncertain: the stuff the Wave was made of. Once he discovered that, he would discover also—*where* the smash would come.

CHAPTER IV

"Can a chap feel things coming?" he asked his father. He was perhaps fifteen or sixteen then. "I mean, when you feel them coming, does that mean they *must* come?"

His father listened warily. There had been many similar questions lately.

"You can feel ordinary things coming," he replied; "things due to association of ideas."

Tom looked up. "Associations?" he queried uncertainly.

"If you feel hungry," explained the doctor, "you know that dinner's coming; you associate the hunger with the idea of eating. You recognize them because you've felt them both together before."

"They *ought* to come, then?"

"Dinner does come—ordinarily speaking. You've learned to expect it from the hunger. You could, of course, prevent it coming," he added dryly, "only that would be bad for you. You need it."

Tom reflected a moment with a puckered face. His father waited for him to ask more, hoping he would. The boy felt the sympathy and invitation.

"*Before*," he repeated, picking out the word with sudden emphasis, his mind evidently breaking against a problem. "But if I felt hungry for something I *hadn't* had before—?"

"In that case you wouldn't call it hunger. You wouldn't know what to call it. You'd feel a longing of some kind and would wonder what it meant."

Tom's next words surprised him considerably. They came promptly, but with slow and thoughtful emphasis.

"So that if I know what I want, and call it dinner, or pain, or—love, or something," he exclaimed, "it means that I've had it *before*? And that's why I know it." The last five words were not a question but a statement of fact apparently.

The doctor pretended not to notice the variants of dinner. At least he did not draw attention to them.

"Not necessarily," he answered. "The things you feel you want may be the things that everybody wants—things common to the race. Such wants are naturally in your blood; you feel them because your parents, your grandparents, and all humanity in turn behind your own particular family have always wanted them."

"They come out of the sea, you mean?"

"That's very well expressed, Tom. They come out of the sea of human nature, which is everywhere the same, yes."

The compliment seemed to annoy the boy.

"Of course," he said bluntly. "But—if it hurts?" The words were sharply emphasized.

"Association of ideas again. Toothache suggests the pincers. You want to get rid of the pain, but the pain has to get worse before it can get better. You know that, so you face it gladly—to get it over."

"You face it, yes," said Tom. "It makes you better in the end."

It suddenly dawned upon him that his learned father knew nothing, nothing at least that could help him. He knew only what other people knew. He turned then, and asked the ridiculous question that lay at the back of his mind all the time. It cost him an effort, for his father would certainly deem it foolish.

"Can a thing happen before it really happens?"

Dr. Kelverdon may or may not have thought the question foolish; his face was hidden a moment as he bent down to put the Indian rug straight with his hand. There was no impatience in the movement, nor was there mockery in his expression, when he resumed his normal position. He had gained an appreciable interval of time—some fifteen seconds. "Tom, you've got good ideas in that head of yours," he said calmly; "but what is it that you mean exactly?"

Tom was quite ready to amplify. He knew what he meant:

"If I *know* something is going to happen, doesn't that mean that it has already happened—and that I remember it?"

"You're a psychologist as well as engineer, Tom," was the approving reply. "It's like this, you see: an emotion, with desire in it, can predict the fulfilment of that desire. In great hunger you imagine you're eating all sorts of good things."

"But that's looking forward," the boy pounced on the mistake. "It's not remembering."

"That *is* the difficulty," explained his father; "to decide whether you're anticipating only—or actually remembering."

"I see," Tom said politely.

All this analysis concealed merely: it did not reveal. The thing itself dived deeper out of sight with every phrase. *He* knew quite well the difference between anticipating and remembering. With the latter there was the sensation of having been through it. Each time he remembered seeing Lettice the sensation was the same, but when he looked forward to seeing her *again* the sensation varied with his mood.

"For instance, Tom—between ourselves this—we're going to send Mary to that Finishing School in France where Lettice is." The doctor, it seemed, spoke carelessly while he gathered his papers together with a view to going out. He did not look at the boy; he said it walking about the room. "Mary will look forward to it so much and think about it that when she gets there it will seem a little familiar to her, as if—almost as if she remembered it."

"Thank you, father; I see, yes," murmured Tom. But in his mind a voice said so distinctly "Rot!" that he was half afraid the word was audible.

"You see the difficulty, eh? And the difference?"

"Rather," exclaimed the boy with decision.

And thereupon, without the slightest warning, he looked out of the window and asked certain other questions. Evidently they cost him effort; his will forced them out. Since his back was turned he did not see his father's understanding smile, but neither did the latter see the lad's crimson cheeks, though possibly he divined them.

"Father—is Miss Aylmer older than me?"

"Ask Mary, Tom. She'll know. Or, stay—I'll ask her for you—if you like."

"Oh, that's all right. I just wanted to know," with an assumed indifference that only just concealed the tremor in the voice.

"I suppose," came a moment later, "a Member of Parliament is a grander thing than a doctor, is it?"

"That depends," replied his father, "upon the man himself. Some M.P.'s vote as they're told, and never open their mouths in the House. Some doctors, again—"

But the boy interrupted him. He quite understood the point.

"It's fine to be an engineer, though, isn't it?" he asked. "It's a real profession?"

"The world couldn't get along without them, or the Government either. It's a most important profession indeed."

Tom, playing idly with the swinging tassel of the window-blind, asked one more question. His voice and manner were admirably under control, but there was a gulp, and his father heard and noted it.

"Shall I have—shall I be rich enough—to marry—some day?"

Dr. Kelverdon crossed the room and put his hand on his son's shoulder, but did not try to make him show his face. "Yes," he said quietly, "you will, my boy—when the time comes." He paused a moment, then added: "But money will not make you a distinguished man, whereas if you become a famous engineer, you'll have money of your own and—any nice girl would be proud to have you."

"I see," said Tom, tying the strings of the tassel into knots, then untying them again with a visible excess of energy—and the conversation came somewhat abruptly to an end. He was aware of the invitation to talk further about Lettice Aylmer, but he resisted and declined it. What was the use? He knew his own mind already about that.

Yet, strictly speaking, Tom was not imaginative. It was as if an instinct taught him. More and more, the Wave, with its accompanying details of Eyes and Whiff, seemed to him the ghost of some dim memory that brought a forgotten warning in its train—something missed, something to be repeated, something to be faced and learned and—mastered....

His father, meanwhile, went forth upon his rounds that day, much preoccupied about the character of his eldest boy. He felt a particular interest in the peculiar obsession that he knew overshadowed the young, growing life. It puzzled him; he found no clue to it; in his thought he was aware of a faint uneasiness, although he did not give it a definite name—something akin to what the mother felt. Admitting he was baffled, he fell back, however, upon such generalities as prenatal influence, ancestral, racial, and so eventually dismissed it from his active mind.

Tom, meanwhile, for his part, also went along his steep, predestined path. The nightmare had entirely deserted him, he now rarely dreamed; and his outer life shaped bravely, as with a boy of will, honesty, and healthy ambition might be expected. Neither wavy feeling, eyes, nor whiff obtruded themselves: they left him alone and waited: he never forgot them, but he did not seek them out. Things once firmly realized remained in his consciousness; he knew that his life was rising like a wave, that all his energies worked in the form of waves, his moods and wishes, his passions, emotions, yearnings—all expressed themselves by means of this unalterable formula, yet all contributed filially to the one big important Wave whose climax would be reached only when it fell. He distinguished between Wave and Ripples. He, therefore, did not trouble himself with imaginary details; he did not search; he waited. This steady strength was his. His firm, square jaw and the fearless eyes of gray beneath the shock of straight dark hair told plainly enough the kind of stuff behind them. No one at school took unnecessary liberties with Tom Kelverdon.

But, having discovered one pair of Eyes, he did not let them go. In his earnest, dull, inflexible way he loved their owner with a belief in her truth and loyalty that admitted of no slightest question. Had his mother divined the strength and value of his passion, she would surely have asked herself with painful misgiving: "Is she—*can* she be—worthy of my boy?" But his mother guessed it as little as any one else; even the doctor had forgotten those early signs of its existence; and Tom was not the kind to make unnecessary confidences, nor to need sympathy in any matter he was sure about.

There was down now upon his upper lip, for he was close upon seventeen and the Entrance Examination was rising to the crest of its particular minor wave, yet during the two years' interval nothing—no single fact—had occurred to justify his faith or to confirm its amazing certainty within his heart. Mary, his sister, had not gone after all to the Finishing School in France; other girl friends came to spend the holidays with her; the Irish member of Parliament had either died or sunk into another kind of oblivion; the paths of the Kelverdons and the Aylmer family had gone apart; and the name of Lettice no longer thrilled the air across the tea-table, nor chance reports of her doings filled the London house with sudden light.

Yet for Tom she existed more potently than ever. His yearning never lessened; he was sure she remembered him as he remembered her; he persuaded himself that she thought about him; she doubtless knew that he was going to be an engineer. He had cut a thread from the carpet in the hall—from the exact spot her flying foot had touched that Tuesday when she scampered off from him—and kept it in the drawer beside the Eastern packet that enshrined the Whiff. Occasionally he took it out and touched it, fingered it, even caressed it; the thread and the perfume belonged together; the ritual of the childish years altered a little—worship raised it to a higher level.

He saw her with her hair done up now, long skirts, and a softer expression in the tender, faithful eyes; the tomboy in her had disappeared; she gazed at him with admiration. The face was oddly real, it came very close to his own; once or twice, indeed, their cheeks almost touched: "almost," because he withdrew instantly, uneasily aware that he had gone too far—not that the intimacy was unwelcome, but that it was somehow premature. And the instant he drew back, a kind of lightning distance came between them; he saw her eyes across an immense and curious interval, though whether of time or space he could not tell. There was strange heat and radiance in it—as of some blazing atmosphere that was not England.

The eyes, moreover, held a new expression when this happened—pity. And with this pity came also pain: the strange, rich pain broke over all the other happier feelings in him and swamped them utterly....

But at that point instinct failed him; he could not understand why she should pity him, why pain should come to him through her, nor why it was necessary for him to feel and face it. He only felt sure of one thing—that it was essential to the formation of the Wave which was his life. The Wave must "happen," or he would miss an important object of his being—and she would somehow miss it too. The Wave would one day fall, but when it fell she would be with him, by his side, under the mighty curve, involved in the crash and tumult—with himself.

CHAPTER V

Then, without any warning, he received a second shock—it fell upon him from the blue and came direct from Lettice.

The occasion was a tennis party in the garden by the sea where the family had come to spend the summer holidays. Tom was already at College, doing brilliantly, and rapidly growing up. The August afternoon was very hot; no wind ruffled the quiet blue-green water; there were no waves; the leaves of the privet hedge upon the side of the cliffs were motionless. A couple of Chalk-Blues danced round and round each other as though a wire connected them, and Tom, walking in to tea with his partner after a victorious game, found himself watching the butterflies and making a remark about them—a chance observation merely to fill an empty pause. He felt as little interest in the insects as he did in his partner, an uncommonly pretty, sunburned girl, whose bare arms and hatless light hair became her admirably. She, however, approved of the remark and by no means despised the opportunity to linger a moment by the side of her companion. They stood together, perhaps a dozen seconds, watching the capricious scraps of color rise, float over the privet hedge on balanced wings, dip abruptly down and vanish on the further side below the cliff. The girl said something—an intentional something that was meant to be heard and answered: but no answer was forthcoming. She repeated the remark with emphasis; then, as still no answer came, she laughed brightly to make his silence appear natural.

But Tom had no word to say. He had not noticed the maneuver of the girl, nor the maneuver of the two Chalk-Blues; neither had he heard the words, although conscious that she spoke. For in that brief instant when the insects floated over the hedge, his eyes had wandered beyond them to the sea, and on the sea, far off against the cloudless horizon, he had seen— the Wave.

Thinking it over afterwards, however, he realized that it was not actually a wave he saw, for the surface of the blue-green sea was smooth as the tennis lawn itself: it was the sudden appearance of the "wavy feeling" that made him *think* he saw the old, familiar outline of his early dream. He had objectified his emotion. His father perhaps would have called it association of ideas.

Abruptly, out of nothing obvious, the feeling rose and mastered him: and, after its quiescence—its absence—for so long an interval, this revival without hint or warning of any kind was disconcerting. The feeling was vivid and unmistakable. The joy and terror swept him as of old. He braced himself. Almost—he began shuffling with his feet....

"Tea's waiting for you," his mother's voice floated to his ears across the lawn, as he turned with an effort from the sea and made towards the group about the tables. The Wave, he knew, was coming up behind him, growing, rising, curving high against the evening sky. Beside him walked the sunburned girl, wondering doubtless at his silence, but happy enough, it seemed, in her own interpretation of its cause. Scarcely aware of her presence, however, Tom was searching almost fiercely in his thoughts, searching for the clue. He knew there was a clue, he felt sure of it; the "wavy feeling" had not come with this overwhelming suddenness without a reason. Something had brought it back. But what? Was there any recent factor in his life that might explain it? He stole a swift glance at the girl beside him: had she, perhaps, to do with it? They had played tennis together for the first time that afternoon: he had never seen her before, was not even quite sure what her name was; to him, so far, she was only "a very pretty girl who played a ripping game." Had this girl to do with it?

Feeling his questioning look, she glanced up at him and smiled. "You're very absent-minded," she observed with mischief in her manner. "You took so many of my balls, it's tired you out!" She had beautiful blue eyes, and her voice, he noticed for the first time, was very pleasant. Her figure was slim, her ankles neat, she had nice, even teeth. But, even as he registered the charming details, he knew quite well that he registered them, one and all, as belonging merely to a member of the sex, and not to this girl in particular. For all he cared, she might follow the two Chalk-Blues and disappear below the edge of the cliff into the sea. This "pretty girl" left him as untroubled as she found him. The wavy feeling was not brought by her.

He drank his tea, keeping his back to the sea, and as the talk was lively, his silence was not noticed. The Wave, meanwhile, he knew, had come up closer. It towered above him. Its presence would shortly be explained. Then, suddenly, in the middle of a discussion as to partners for the games to follow, a further detail presented itself—also apparently out of nothing. He smelt the Whiff. He knew then that the Wave was poised immediately above his head, and that he stood underneath its threatening great curve. The clue, therefore, was at hand.

And at this moment his father came into view, moving across the lawn towards them from the French window. No one guessed how Tom welcomed the slight diversion, for the movement was already in his legs and in another moment must have set his feet upon that dreadful shuffling. As from a distance, he heard the formal talk and introductions, his father's statement that he had won his round of golf with "the Dean," praise of the weather, and something or other about the strange stillness of the sea—but then, with a sudden, hollow crash against his very ear, the appalling words: "... broke his mashie into splinters, yes. And, by the by, the Dean knows the Aylmers. They were staying here earlier in the summer, he told me. Lettice, the girl,—Mary's friend, you remember—is going to be married this week...."

Tom clutched the back of the wicker-chair in front of him. The sun went out. An icy air passed up his spine. The blood drained from his face. The tennis courts, and the group of white figures moving towards them, swung up into the sky. He gripped the chair till the rods of wicker pressed through the flesh into the bone. For a moment he felt that the sensation of actual sickness was more than he could master; his legs bent like paper beneath his weight.

"*You* remember Lettice, Tom, don't you?" his father was saying somewhere in mid-air above him.

"Yes, rather." Apparently he said these words; the air at any rate went through his teeth and lips, and the same minute, with a superhuman effort that only just escaped a stagger, he moved away towards the tennis courts. His feet carried him, that is, across the lawn, where some figures dressed in white were calling his name loudly; his legs went automatically. "Hold steady!" he remembers saying somewhere deep inside him. "Don't make an ass of yourself"; whereupon another voice—or was it still his own?—joined in quickly, "She's gone from me, Lettice has gone. She's dead." And the words, for the first time in his life, had meaning: for the first time in his life, rather, he realized what their meaning was. The Wave had fallen. Moreover—this also for the first time in the history of the Wave—there was something audible. He heard a Sound.

Shivering in the hot summer sunshine, as though icy water drenched him, he knew the same instant that he was wrong about the falling: the Wave, indeed, had curled lower over him than ever before, had even toppled — but it had not broken. As a whole, it had not broken. It was a smaller wave, upon the parent side, that had formed and fallen. The sound he heard was the soft crash of this lesser wave that grew out of the greater mass of the original monster, broke upon the rising volume of it, and returned into the greater body. It was a ripple only. The shock and terror he felt were a foretaste of what the final smothering crash would be. Yet the Sound he had heard was not the sound of water. There was a sharp, odd rattling in it that he had never consciously heard before. And it was—dry.

He reached the group of figures on the tennis-courts: he played: a violent energy had replaced the sudden physical weakness. His skill, it seemed, astonished everybody; he drove and smashed and volleyed with a reck-lessness that was always accurate: but when, at the end of the amazing game, he heard voices praising him, as from a distance, he knew only that there was a taste of gall and ashes in his mouth, and that he had but one desire—to get to his room alone and open the drawer. Even to himself he would not admit that he wished for the relief of tears. He put it, rather, that he must see and feel the one real thing that still connected him with Let-tice—the thread of carpet she had trodden on. That—and the "whiff"—alone could comfort him.

The comedy, that is, of all big events lay in it; no one must see, no one must know: no one must guess the existence of this sweet, rich pain that ravaged the heart in him until from very numbness it ceased aching. He double-locked the bedroom door. He had waited till darkness folded away the staring day, till the long dinner was over, and the drawn-out evening afterwards. None, fortunately, had noticed the change in his de-meanor, his silence, his absentmindedness when spoken to, his want of ap-petite. "She is going to be married... this week," were the only words he heard; they kept ringing in his brain. To his immense relief the family had not referred to it again.

And at last he had said good-night and was in his room—alone. The drawer was open. The morsel of green thread lay in his hand. The faint eastern perfume floated on the air. "I am not a sentimental ass," he said to himself aloud, but in a low, steady tone. "She touched it, therefore it has part of her life about it still." Three years and a half ago! He examined the diary too; lived over in thought every detail of their so slight acquaintance together; they were few enough; he remembered every one.... Prolonging the backward effort, he reviewed the history of the Wave. His mind stretched back to his earliest recollections of the nightmare. He faced the situation, tried to force its inner meaning from it, but without success.

He did not linger uselessly upon any detail, nor did he return upon his traces as a sentimental youth might do, prolonging the vanished sweetness of recollection in order to taste the pain more vividly. He merely "read up," so to speak, the history of the Wave to get a bird's-eye view of it. And in the end he obtained a certain satisfaction from the process—a certain strength. That is to say, he did not understand, but he accepted. "Lettice has gone from me—but she hasn't gone for good." The deep reflection of hours condensed itself into this.

Whatever might happen "temporarily," the girl was loyal and true: and she was—his. It never once occurred to him to blame or chide her. All that she did sincerely, she had a right to do. They were in the "underneath" to-gether forever and ever. They were in the sea.

The pain, nevertheless, was acute and agonizing; the temporary separation of "France" was nothing compared to this temporary separation of her marrying. There were alternate intervals of numbness and of acute sensation; for each time thought and feeling collapsed from the long strain of their own tension, the relief that followed proved false and vain. Up sprang the aching pain again, the hungry longing, the dull, sweet yearning—and the whole sensation started afresh as at the first, yet with a vividness that increased with each new realization of it. "Wish I could cry it out," he thought. "I wouldn't be a bit ashamed to cry." But he had no tears to spill....

Midnight passed towards the small hours of the morning, and the small hours slipped on towards the dawn before he put away the parcel of tissue-paper, closed the drawer and locked it. And when at length he dropped exhausted into bed, the eastern sky was already tinged with the crimson of another summer's day. He dreaded it, and closed his eyes. It had tennis parties and engagements in its wearisome, long hours of heat and utter emptiness....

Just before actual sleep took him, however, he was aware of one other singular reflection. It rose of its own accord out of that moment's calm when thought and feeling sank away and deliberate effort ceased: the fact namely that, with the arrival of the Sound, all his five senses had been now affected. His entire being, through the only channels of perception it possessed, had responded to the existence of the Wave and all it might portend. Here was no case of a single sense being tricked by some illusion: all five supported each other, taste being, of course, a modification of smell.

And the strange reflection brought to his aching mind and weary body a measure of relief. The Wave was real: being real, it was also well worth facing when it—fell.

CHAPTER VI

Between twenty and thirty a man rises through years reckless of power and spendthrift of easy promises. The wave of life is rising, and every force tends upwards in a steady rush. At thirty comes a pause upon the level, but with thirty-five there are signs of the droop downhill. Age is first realized when, instead of looking forward only, he surprises thought in the act of looking—behind.

Of the physical, at any rate, this is true; for the mental and emotional wave is still ripening towards its higher curve, while the spiritual crest hangs hiding in the sky far overhead, beckoning beyond towards unvistaed reaches.

Tom Kelverdon climbed through these crowded years with the usual scars and bruises, but steadily, and without the shame of any considerable disaster. His father's influence having procured him an opening in an engineering firm of the first importance, his own talent and application maintained the original momentum bravely. He justified his choice of a profession. Also, staring eagerly into life's marvelous shop-window, he entered, hand in pocket, and made the customary purchases of the enchantress behind the counter. If worthless, well,—everybody bought them; the things had been consummately advertised; he paid his money, found out their value, threw them away or kept them accordingly. A certain good taste made his choice not too foolish: and there was this wholesome soundness in him, that he rarely repeated a purchase that had furnished him cheap goods. Slowly he began to find himself.

From learning what it meant to be well thrashed by a boy he loathed, and to apply a similar treatment himself—he passed on to the pleasure of being told he had nice eyes, that his voice was pleasant, his presence interesting. He fell in love—and out again. But he went straight. Moreover, beyond a given point in any affair of the heart he seemed unable to advance: some secret, inner tension held him back. While believing he loved various adorable girls the years offered him, he found it impossible to open his lips and tell them so. And the mysterious instinct invariably justified itself: they faded, one and all, soon after separation. There was no wave in them; they were ripples only....

And, meanwhile, as the years rushed up towards the crest of thirty, he did well in his profession, worked for the firm in many lands, obtained the confidence of his principals, and proved his steady judgment if not his brilliance. He became, too, a good, if generous, judge of other men, seeing all sorts, both good and bad, and in every kind of situation that proves character. His nature found excuses too easily, perhaps, for the unworthy ones. It is not a bad plan, wiser companions hinted, to realize that a man has dark behavior in him, while yet believing that he need not necessarily prove it. The other view has something childlike in it; Tom Kelverdon kept, possibly, this simpler attitude alive in him, trusting overmuch, because suspicion was abhorrent to his soul. The man of ideals had never become the man of the world. Some high, gentle instinct had preserved him from the infliction that so often results in this regrettable conversion. Slow to dislike, he saw the best in everybody. "Not a bad fellow," he would say of some one quite obviously detestable. "I admit his face and voice and manner are against him; but that's not his fault exactly. He didn't make himself, you know."

The idea of a tide in the affairs of men is obvious, familiar enough. Nations rise and fall, equally with the fortunes of a family. History repeats itself, so does the tree, the rose: and if a man live long enough he recovers the state of early childhood. There is repetition everywhere. But while some think evolution moves in a straight line forward, others speculate fancifully that it has a spiral twist upwards. At any given moment, that is, the soul looks down upon a passage made before—but from a point a little higher. Without living through events already experienced, it literally lives them over; it sees them mapped out below, and with the bird's-eye view it understands them.

And in regard to his memory of Lettice Aylmer—the fact that he was still waiting for her and she for him—this was somewhat the fanciful conception that lodged itself, subconsciously perhaps, in the mind of Tom Kelverdon, grown now to man's estate. He was dimly aware of a curious familiarity with his present situation, a sense of repetition—yet with a difference. Something he had experienced before was coming to him again. It was waiting for him. Its wave was rising. When it happened before it had not happened properly somehow—had left a sense of defeat, of dissatisfaction behind. He had taken it, perhaps, at the period of receding momentum, and so had failed towards it. This time he meant to face it. His own phrase, as has been seen, was simple: "I'll let it all come." It was something his character needed. Deep down within him hid this attitude, and with the passage of the years it remained—but remained an attitude merely.

But the attitude, being subconscious in him, developed into a definite point of view that came, more and more, to influence the way he felt towards life in general. Life was too active to allow of much introspection, yet whenever pauses came—pauses in thought and feeling, still backwaters in which he lay without positive direction—there banked up, unchanging in the background, stood the enduring thing: his love for Lettice Aylmer. And this background was "the sea" of his boyhood days, the "underneath" in which they remained unalterably together. There, too, hid the four signs that haunted his impressionable youth: the Wave, the other Eyes, the Whiff, the Sound. In due course, and at their appointed time, they could combine and "happen" in his outward life. The Wave would—fall.

Meanwhile his sense of humor had long ago persuaded him that, so far as any claim upon the girl existed, or that she reciprocated his own deep passion, his love-dream was of questionable security. The man in him that built bridges and cut tunnels laughed at it; the man that devised these first in imagination, however, believed in it, and waited. Behind thought and reason, suspected of none with whom he daily came in contact, and surprised only by himself when he floated in these silent, tideless backwaters— it persisted with an amazing conviction that seemed deathless. In these calm deeps of his being, securely anchored, hid what he called the "spiral" attitude. The thing that was coming, a tragedy whereof that childish nightmare was both a memory and a premonition, clung and haunted still with its sense of dim familiarity. Something he had known before would eventually repeat itself. But—with a difference; that he would see it from above—from a higher curve of the ascending spiral.

There lay the enticing wonder of the situation. With his present English temperament, stolid rather, he would meet it differently, treat it otherwise, learn and understand. He would see it from another—higher—point of view. He would know great pain, yet some part of him would look on, compare, accept the pain—and smile. The words that offered themselves were that he had "suffered blindly," but suffered with fierce and bitter resentment, savagely, even with murder in his heart ; suffered, moreover, somehow or other, at the hands of Lettice Aylmer.

Lettice, of course,—he clung to it absurdly still—was true and loyal to him, though married to another. Her name was changed. But Lettice Aylmer was not changed. And this mad assurance, though he kept it deliberately from his conscious thoughts, persisted with the rest of the curious business, for nothing, apparently, could destroy it in him. It was part of the situation, as he called it, part of the "sea," out of which would rise eventually—the Wave.

Outwardly, meanwhile, much had happened to him, each experience contributing its modifying touch to the character as he realized it, instead of merely knowing that it came to others. His sister married; Tim, following his father's trade, became a doctor with a provincial practise, buried in the country. His father died suddenly while he was away in Canada, busy with a prairie railway across the wheat fields of Assiniboia. He met the usual disillusions in a series, savored and mastered them more or less in turn.

He was in England when his mother died; and, while his other experiences were ripples only, her going had the wave in it. The enormous mother-tie came also out of the "sea"; its dislocation was a shock of fundamental kind, and he felt it in the foundations of his life. It was one of the things he could not quite realize. He still felt her always close and near. He had just been made a junior partner in the firm; the love and pride in her eyes, before they faded from the world of partnerships, were unmistakable: "Of course," she murmured, her thin hand clinging to his own, "they had to do it... if only your father knew..." and she was gone. The wave of her life sank back into the sea whence it arose. And her going somehow strengthened him, added to his own foundations, as though her wave had merged in his.

With her departure, he felt vaguely the desire to settle down, to marry. Unconsciously he caught himself thinking of women in a new light, appraising them as possible wives. It was a dangerous attitude rather; for a man then seeks to persuade himself that such and such a woman may do, instead of awaiting the inevitable draw of love which alone can justify a life-long union.

In Tom's case, however, as with the smaller fires of his younger days, he never came to a decision, much less to a positive confession. His immense idealism concerning women preserved him from being caught by mere outward beauty. While aware that Lettice was an impossible dream of boyhood, he yet clung to an ideal she somehow foreshadowed and typified. He never relinquished this standard of his dream; a mysterious woman waited for him somewhere, a woman with all the fairy qualities he had built about her personality; a woman he could not possibly mistake when at last he met her. Only he did not meet her. He waited.

And so it was, as time passed onwards, that he found himself standing upon the little level platform of his life at a stage nearer to thirty-five than thirty, conscious that a pause surrounded him. There was a lull. The rush of the years slowed down. He looked about him. He looked—back.

CHAPTER VII

The particular moment when this happened, suitable, too, in a chance, odd way, was upon a mountain ridge in winter, a level platform of icy snow to which he had climbed with some hotel acquaintances on a ski-ing expedition. It was on the Polish side of the Hohe Tatra. Why, at this special moment, pausing for breath and admiring the immense wintry scene about him, he should have realized that he reached a similar position in his life, is hard to say. There is always a particular moment when big changes claim attention. They have been coming slowly; but at a given moment they announce themselves. Tom associated that icy ridge above Zakopané with a pause in the rushing of the years: "I'm getting on towards middle age; the first swift climb—impetuous youth—lies now behind me." The physical parallel doubtless suggested it; he had felt his legs and wind a trifle less willing, perhaps; there was still a steep, laborious slope of snow beyond; he discovered that he was no longer twenty-five.

He drew breath and watched the rest of the party as they slowly came nearer in the track he had made through the deep snow below. Each man made this track in his turn, it was hard work, his share was done. "Nagorsky will tackle the next bit," he thought with relief, watching a young Pole of twenty-three in the ascending line, and glancing at the summit beyond where the run home was to begin. And then the wonder of the white silent scene invaded him, the exhilarating thrill of the vast wintry heights swept over him, he forgot the toil, he regained his wind and felt his muscles taut and vigorous once more. It was pleasant, standing upon this level ridge, to inspect the long ascent below, and to know the heavy yet enjoyable exertion was nearly over.

But he had felt—older. That ridge remained in his memory as the occasion of its first realization; a door opened behind him; he looked back. He envied the other's twenty-three years. It is curious that, about thirty, a man feels he is getting old, whereas at forty he feels himself young again. At thirty he judges by the standard of eighteen, at the later age by that of sixty. But this particular occasion remained vivid for another reason—it was accompanied by a strange sensation he had almost forgotten; and so long an interval had elapsed since its last manifestation that for a moment a kind of confusion dropped upon him, as from the cloudless sky. Something was gathering behind him, something was about to fall. He recognized the familiar feeling that he knew of old, the subterranean thrill, the rich, sweet pain, the power, the reality. It was the wavy feeling.

Balanced on his ski, the seal-skin strips gripping the icy ridge securely, he turned instinctively to seek the reason, if any were visible, of the abrupt revival. His mind, helped by the stimulating air and sunshine, worked swiftly. The odd confusion clouded his faculties still, as in a dream state, but he pierced it in several directions simultaneously.

Was it that, envying another's youth, he had reentered imaginatively his own youthful feelings? He looked down at the rest of the party climbing towards him. And doing so, he picked out the slim figure of Nagorsky's sister, a girl whose winter costume became her marvelously, and whom the happy intimacy of the hotel life had made so desirable that an expedition without her seemed a lost, blank day. Unless she was of the party there was no sunshine. He watched her now, looking adorable in her big gauntlet gloves, her short skirt, her tasseled cap of black and gold, a fairy figure on the big snowfield, filling the world with sunshine—and knew abruptly that she meant to him just exactly—nothing. The intensity of the wavy feeling reduced her to an unreality.

It was not she who brought the great emotion.

The confusion in him deepened. Another scale of measurement appeared. The crowded intervening years now seemed but a pause, a brief delay; he had run down a side track and returned. *He* had not grown older. Seen by the grand scale to which the Wave and "sea" belonged, he had scarcely moved from the old starting-point, where, far away in some unassailable recess of life, still waiting for him, stood—Lettice Aylmer.

Turning his eyes, then, from the approaching climbers, he glanced at the steep slope above him, and saw—as once before on the English coast—something that took his breath away and made his muscles weak. He stared at it. It looked down at him.

Five hundred feet above, outlined against the sky of crystal clearness, ran a colossal wave of solid snow. At the highest point it was, of course, a cornice, but towards the east, whence came the prevailing weather, the wind had so manipulated the mass that it formed a curling billow, twenty or thirty feet in depth, leaping over in the very act of breaking, yet arrested just before it fell. It hung waiting in mid-air, perfectly molded, a wave but a wave of snow.

It swung along the ridge for half a mile and more: it seemed to fill the sky; it rose out of the sea of eternal snow below it, poised between the earth and heavens. In the hollow beneath its curve lay purple shadows the eye could not pierce. And the similarity to the earlier episode struck him vividly; in each case Nature assisted with a visible wave as by way of counterpart; each time, too, there was a girl—as though some significance of sex hid in the "wavy feeling." He was profoundly puzzled.

The same second, in this wintry world where movement, sound, and perfume have no place, there stole to his nostrils across the desolate ranges another detail. It was more intimate in its appeal even than the wavy feeling, yet was part of it. He recognized the Whiff. And the joint attack, both by its suddenness and by its intensity, overwhelmed him. Only the Sound was lacking, but that, too, he felt, was on the way. Already a sharp instinctive movement was running down his legs. He began to shuffle on his ski....

A chorus of voices, as from far away, broke round him, disturbing the intense stillness; and he knew that the others had reached the ridge. With a violent effort he mastered the ridiculous movement of his disobedient legs, but what really saved him from embarrassing notice was the breathless state of his companions, and the fact that his action looked after all quite natural—he seemed merely rubbing his ski along the snow to clean their under-surface.

Exclamations in French, English, Polish rose on all sides, as the view into the deep opposing valley caught the eye, and a shower of questions all delivered at once, drew attention from himself. What scenery, what a sky, what masses of untrodden snow! Should they lunch on the ridge or continue to the summit? What were the names of all these peaks, and was the Danube visible? How lucky there was no wind, and how they pitied the people who stayed behind in the hotels! Sweaters and woolen waistcoats emerged from half-a-dozen knapsacks, cooking apparatus was produced, one chose a spot to make a fire, while another broke the dead branches from a stunted pine, and in five minutes had made a blaze behind a little wall of piled-up snow. The Polish girl came up and asked Tom for his Zeiss glasses, examined the soaring slope beyond, then obediently put on the extra sweater he held out for her. He hardly saw her face, and certainly did not notice the expression in her eyes. All took off their ski and plunged them upright in the nearest drift. The sun blazed everywhere, the snow crystals sparkled. They settled down for lunch, a small dark clot of busy life upon the vast expanse of desolate snow ... and anything unusual about Tom Kelverdon, muffled to the throat against the freezing cold, his eyes, moreover, concealed by green snow spectacles, was certainly not noticed.

Another party, besides, was discovered climbing upwards along their own laborious track: in the absorbing business of satisfying big appetites, tending the fire, and speculating who these other skiers might be, Tom's silence caused no comment. His self-control, for the rest, was soon recovered. But his interest in the expedition had oddly waned; he was still searching furiously in his thoughts for an explanation of the unexpected "attack," waiting for the Sound, but chiefly wondering why his boyhood's nightmare had never revealed that the Wave was of snow instead of water—and, at the same time, oddly convinced that he had moved but *one* stage nearer to its final elucidation. That it was solid he had already discovered, but that it was actually of snow left a curious doubt in him.

Of all this he was thinking as he devoured his eggs and sandwiches, something still trembling in him, nerves keenly sensitive, but not *quite* persuaded that this wave of snow was the sufficient cause of what he had just experienced—when at length the other climbers, moving swiftly, came close enough to be inspected. The customary remarks and criticisms passed from mouth to mouth, with warnings to lower voices since sound carried too easily in the rarefied air. One of the party was soon recognized as the hotel doctor, and the other, first set down as a Norwegian owing to his light hair, shining hatless in the sunlight, proved on closer approach to be an Englishman—both men evidently experienced and accomplished "runners."

In any other place the two parties would hardly have spoken, settling down into opposing camps of hostile silence; but in the lonely winter mountains human relationship becomes more natural; the time of day was quickly passed, and details of the route exchanged; the doctor and his friend mingled easily with the first arrivals; all agreed spontaneously to take the run home together; and finally, when names were produced with laughing introductions, the Englishman—by one of those coincidences people pretend to think strange, but that actually ought to occur more often than they do—turned out to be known to Tom, and after considerable explanations was proved to be more than that—a cousin.

Welcoming the diversion, making the most of it in fact, Kelverdon presented Anthony Winslowe to his Polish companions with a certain zeal to which the new arrival responded with equal pleasure. The light-haired, blue-eyed Englishman, young and skilful on his ski, formed a distinct addition to the party. He was tall, with a slight stoop about the shoulders that suggested study; he was gay and very easy-going too. It was "Tom" and

"Tony" before lunch was over; they recalled their private school, a fight, an eternal friendship vowed after it, and the twenty intervening years melted as though they had not been.

"Of course," Tom said, proud of his new-found cousin, "and I've read your bird books, what's more. By Jove, you're quite an authority on natural history, aren't you?"

The other modestly denied any fame, but the girls, especially Nagorsky's sister, piqued by Tom's want of notice, pressed for details in their pretty broken English. It became a merry and familiar party, as the way is with easy foreigners, particularly when they meet in such wild and unconventional surroundings. Winslowe had lantern slides in his trunk: that night he promised to show them: they chattered and paid compliments and laughed, Tony explaining that he was on his way to Egypt to study the bird-life along the Nile. Natural history was his passion; he talked delightfully; he made the bird and animal life seem real and interesting; there was imagination, humor, lightness in him. There was a fascination, too, not due to looks alone. It was in his atmosphere, what is currently, perhaps, called magnetism.

"No animals *here* for you," said a girl, pointing to the world of white death about them.

"There's something better," he said quickly in quite decent Polish. "We're all in the animal kingdom, you know." And he glanced with a bow of admiration at the speaker, whom the others instantly began to tease. It was Irena, Nagorsky's sister; she flushed and laughed. "We thought," she said, "you were Norwegian, because of your light hair, and the way you moved on your ski."

"A great compliment," he rejoined, "but I saw you long ago on the ridge, and I knew at once that you were—Polish."

The girl returned his bow. "The largest compliment," she answered gaily, "I had ever in my life."

Tom had only arrived two days before, bringing a letter of introduction to the doctor, and that night he changed his hotel, joining his new friends and his cousin at the Grand. An obvious flirtation, possibly something more, sprung up spontaneously between him and the Polish girl, but Kelverdon welcomed it and felt no jealousy. "Not trespassing, old chap, am I?" Tony asked jokingly, having divined on the mountains that the girl was piqued. "On the contrary," was the honest assurance given frankly, "I'm relieved. A delightful girl, though, isn't she? And fascinatingly pretty!"

For the existence of Nagorsky's sister had become suddenly to him of no importance whatsoever. It was strange enough, but the vivid recurrence of long-forgotten symbols that afternoon upon the heights had restored to him something he had curiously forgotten, something he had shamefully neglected, almost, it seemed, had been in danger of losing altogether. It came back upon him now. He clung desperately to it as to a real, a vital, a necessary thing. It was a genuine relief that the relationship between him and the girl might be ended thus. In any case, he reflected, it would have "ended thus" a little later—like all the others. No trace or sign of envy stayed in him. Irena and Tony, anyhow, seemed admirably suited to one another; he noticed on the long run home how naturally they came together. And even his own indifference would not bring her back to him. He felt quite pleased and satisfied. He had a long talk with Tony before going to bed. He felt drawn to him. There was a spontaneous innate sympathy between them.

They had many other talks together, and Tom liked his interesting, brilliant cousin. A week passed; dances, ski-ing trips, skating, and the usual program of wintry enjoyments filled the time too quickly; companionship became intimacy; all sat at the same table: Tony became a general favorite. He had just that combination of reserve and abandon which—provided something genuine lies behind—attracts the majority of people who, being dull, have neither. Most are reserved, through emptiness, or else abandoned—also through emptiness. Tony Winslowe, full of experience and ideas, vivid experience and original ideas, combined the two in rarest equipoise. It was spontaneous, and not calculated in him. There was a stimulating quality in his personality. Like those tiny, exciting Japanese tales that lead to the edge of a precipice, then end with unexpected abruptness that is their purpose, he led all who liked him to the brink of a delightful revelation—then paused, stopped, vanished. And all did like him. He was light and gay, for all the depth in him. Something of the child peeped out. He won Tom Kelverdon's confidence without an effort. He also won the affectionate confidence of the Polish girl.

"You're not married, Tony, are you?" Tom asked him.

"Married!" Tony answered with a flush—he flushed so easily when teased—"I love my wild life and animals far too much." He stammered slightly. Then he looked up quickly into his cousin's eyes with frankness. Tom, without knowing why, almost felt ashamed of having asked it. "I—I never can go beyond a certain point," he said, "with girls. Something always holds me back. Odd—isn't it?" He hesitated. Then this flashed from him: "Bees never sip the last, the sweetest drop of honey from the rose, you know. The sunset always leaves one golden cloud adrift—eh?" So there was poetry in him too!

And Tom, simpler, as well as more rigidly molded, felt a curious touch of passionate sympathy as he heard it. His heart went out to the other suddenly with a burst of confidence. Some barrier melted in him and disappeared. For the first time in his life he knew the inclination, even the desire, to speak of things hidden deep within his heart. His cousin would understand.

And Tony's sudden, wistful silence invited the confession. They had already been talking of their forgotten youthful days together. The ground was well prepared. They had even talked of his sister, Mary, and her marriage. Tony remembered her distinctly. He spoke of it, leaning forward and putting a hand on his cousin's knee. Tom noticed vaguely the size of the palm, the wrist, the fingers—they seemed disproportionate. They were ugly hands. But it was subconscious notice. His mind was on another thing.

"I say," Tom began with a sudden plunge, "you know a lot about birds and natural history—biology too, I suppose. Have you ever heard of the spiral movement?"

"Spinal, did you say?" queried the other, turning the stem of his glass and looking up.

"No—*spiral*," Tom repeated, laughing dryly in spite of himself. "I mean the idea—that evolution, whether individually in men and animals, or with nations—historically, that is—is not in a straight line ahead, but moves upwards—in a spiral?"

"It's in the air," replied Tony vaguely, yet somehow as if he knew a great deal more about it. "The movement of the race, you mean?"

"And of the individual too. We're here, I mean, for the purpose of development—whatever one's particular belief may be—and that this development, instead of going forwards in a straight line, has a kind of—spiral movement—upwards?"

Tony looked wonderfully wise. "I've heard of it," he said. "The spiral movement, as you say, is full of suggestion. It's common among plants. But I don't think science, biology, at any rate, takes much account of it."

Tom interrupted eagerly, and with a certain grave enthusiasm that evidently intrigued his companion. "I mean—a movement that is always upwards, always getting higher, and always looking down upon what has gone before. That, if it's true, a soul can look back—look down upon what it has been through before, but from a higher point—do you see?"

Tony emptied his glass and then lit a cigarette. "I see right enough," he said at length, quick and facile to appropriate any and every idea he came across, yet obviously astonished by his companion's sudden seriousness. "Only the other day I read that humanity, for instance, is just now above the superstitious period—of the Middle Ages, say—going over it again— but that the recrudescence everywhere of psychic interests—fortune-telling, palmistry, magic, and the rest—has become quasi-scientific. It's going through the same period, but seeks to explain and understand. It's above it—one stage or so. Is that what you mean, perhaps?"

Tom drew in his horns, though for the life of him he could not say why. Tony appropriated his own idea too easily somehow—had almost read his thoughts. Vaguely he resented it. Tony had stolen from him—offended against some schoolboy *meum* and *tuum* standard.

"That's it—the idea, at any rate," he said, wondering why confidence had frozen in him. "Interesting, rather, isn't it?"

And then abruptly he found that he was staring at his cousin's hands, spread on the table, palm downwards. He had been staring at them for some time, but unconsciously. Now he saw them. And there was something about them that he did not like. Absurd as it seemed, his change of mood had to do with those big, ungainly hands, tanned a deep brown-black by the sun. A faint shiver ran through him. He looked away.

"Extraordinary," Tony went chattering on. "It explains these new, wild dances perhaps. Anything more spiral and twisty than these modern gyrations I never saw!" He turned it off in his light, amusing way, yet as though quite familiar with the deeper aspects of the question—if he cared. "And what the body does," he added, "the mind has already done a little time before!"

He laughed, but whether he was in earnest, or merely playing with the idea, was uncertain. What had stopped Tom was, perhaps, that they were not in the same key together; Tom had used a word he rarely cared to use—soul—it had cost him a certain effort—but his cousin had not responded. That, and the hands, explained his change of mood. For the first time it occurred to his honest, simple mind that Tony was of other stuff, perhaps, than he had thought. That remark about the bees and sunset jarred a little. The lightness suggested insincerity almost.

He shook the notion off, for it was disagreeable, ungenerous as well. This was holiday-time, and serious discussion was out of place. The airy lightness in his cousin was just suited to the conditions of a winter-sport hotel; it was what made him so attractive to all and sundry; so easy to get on with. Yet Tom would have liked to confide in him, to have told him more, asked further questions and heard the answers; stranger still, he would have liked to lead from the spiral to the wave, to his own wavy feeling, and, further even—almost to speak of Lettice and his boyhood nightmare. He had never met a man in regard to whom he felt so forthcoming in this way. Tony surely had seriousness and depth in him; this irresponsibility was on the surface only.... There was a queer confusion in his mind—several incongruous things trying to combine....

"I knew a princess once—the widow of a Russian," Tony was saying. He had been talking on, gayly, lightly, for some time, but Tom, busy with these reflections, had not listened properly. He now looked up sharply, something suddenly alert in him. "They're all princes in Russia," Tony laughed. "It means less than Count in France or *von* in Germany." He stopped and drained his glass. "But you know," he went on, his thoughts half elsewhere, it seemed, "it's bad for a country when titles are too common, it lowers the aristocratic ideal. In the Caucasus—Batoum for instance—every Georgian is a noble, your hotel porter a prince." He broke off abruptly, as though reminded of something. "Of course!" he exclaimed, "I was going to tell you about the Russian woman I knew who had something of that idea of yours." He stopped, as his eye caught his cousin's empty glass. "Let's have another," he said, beckoning to the waitress, "it's very light stuff, this beer. These long ski-trips give one an endless thirst, don't they?"

Tom didn't know whether he said yes or no. "What idea?" he asked quickly. "What do you mean exactly?" A curious feeling of familiarity stirred in him. This conversation had happened before.

"Eh?" Tony glanced up as though he had again forgotten what he was going to say. "Oh, yes," he went on, "the Russian woman, the Princess I met in Egypt. She talked a bit like that once... I remember now."

"Like what?" Tom felt a sudden, breathless curiosity in him: he was afraid the other would change his mind, or pass to something else, or forget what he was going to say. It would prove another Japanese tale—disappear before it satisfied.

But Tony went on at last, noticing, perhaps, his cousin's interest.

"I was up at Edfu after birds," he said, "and she had a *dehabieh* on the river. Some friends took me there to tea, or something. It was nothing particular. Only it occurred to me just now when you talked of spirals and things."

"You talked about the spiral?" Tom asked. "Talked with *her* about it, I mean?" He was slow, almost stupid compared to the other who seemed to flash lightly and quickly over a dozen ideas at once. But there was this real, natural sympathy between them both again. It seemed he knew exactly what his cousin was going to say.

Tony, blowing the foam off his beer glass, proceeded to quench his wholesome thirst. "Not exactly," he said at length, "but we talked, I remember, along that line. I was explaining about the flight of birds—that all wild animal life moves in a spontaneous sort of natural rhythm—with an unconscious grace, I mean, we've lost because we think too much. Birds, in particular, rise and fall with a swoop, the simplest, freest movement in the world—like a wave—"

"Yes?" interrupted Tom, leaning over the table a little and nearly upsetting his untouched glass. "I like that idea. It's true."

"And—oh, that all the forces known to science move in a similar way— by wave-form, don't you see? Something like that it was." He took another draught of the nectar his day's exertions had certainly earned.

"*She* said that?" asked Tom, watching his cousin's face buried in the enormous mug.

Tony set it down with a sigh of intense satisfaction. "*I* said it," he exclaimed with a frank egoism. "You're too tired after all your falls this afternoon to listen properly. *I* was the teacher on that occasion, she the adoring listener! But if you want to know what she said too, I'll tell you."

Tom waited; he raised his glass, pretending to drink; if he showed too much interest, the other might swerve off again to something else. He knew what was coming, yet could not have actually foretold it. He recognized it only the instant afterwards.

"She talked about water," Tony went on, as though he had difficulty in recalling what she really had said, "and I think she had water on the brain," he added lightly. "The Nile had bewitched her probably; it affects most of 'em out there, the women, that is. She said life moved in a stream—that she moved down a stream, or something, and that only things going down the stream with her were real. Anything on the banks—stationary, that is—was not real. Oh, she said a lot. I've really forgotten now—it was a year or two ago—but I remember her mentioning shells and the spiral twist of shells. In fact," he added, as if there was no more to tell, "I suppose that's what made me think of her just now—your mentioning the spiral movement."

The door of the room, half *café* and half bar, where the peasants sat at wooden tables about them, opened, and the pretty head of Irena Nagorsky appeared. A burst of music came in with her. "We dance," she said, a note of reproach as well as invitation in her voice—then vanished. Tony, leaving his beer unfinished, laughed at his cousin and went after her. "My last night," he said cheerily. "Must be gay and jolly. I'm off to Trieste to-morrow for Alexandria. See you later, Tom—unless you're coming to dance too."

But, though they saw each other many a time again that evening, there was no further conversation. Next day the party broke up, Tom returning to the Water Works his firm was constructing outside Warsaw, and Tony taking the train for Budapesth *en route* for Trieste and Egypt. He urged Tom to follow him as soon as his work was finished, gave the Turf Club, Cairo, as his permanent address where letters would always reach him sooner or later, waved his hat to the assembled group upon the platform, and was gone. The last detail of him visible was the hand that held the waving hat. It looked bigger, darker, thought Tom, than ever. It was almost disfiguring. It stirred a hint of dislike in him. He turned his eyes away.

But Tom Kelverdon remembered that last night in the hotel for another reason too. In the small hours of the morning he woke up, hearing a sound close beside him in the room. He listened a moment, then turned on the light above the bed. The sound, of an unusual and peculiar character, continued faintly. But it was not actually in the room as he first supposed. It was outside.

More than ten years had passed since he had heard that sound. He had expected it that day on the mountains when the wavy feeling and the Whiff had come to him. Sooner or later he felt positive he would hear it. He heard it now. It had merely been delayed, postponed. Something gathering slowly and steadily behind his life was drawing nearer—had come already very close. He heard the dry, rattling Sound that was associated with the Wave and with the Whiff. In it, too, was a vague familiarity.

And then he realized that the wind was rising. A frozen pine-branch, stiff with little icicles, was rattling and scraping faintly outside the wooden framework of the double windows. It was the icy branch that made the dry, rattling sound. He listened intently; the sound was repeated at certain intervals, then ceased, as the wind died down. And he turned over and fell asleep again, aware that what he had heard was an imitation only, but an imitation strangely accurate—of a reality. Similarly, the wave of snow was but an imitation of a reality to come. This reality lay waiting still beyond him. One day—one day soon—he would know it face to face. The Wave, he felt, was rising behind his life, and his life was rising with it towards a climax. On the little level platform where the years had landed him for a temporary pause, he began to shuffle with his feet in dream. And something deeper than his mind—looked back....

The instinct, or by whatever name he called that positive, interior affirmation, proved curiously right. Life rose with the sweep and power of a wave, bearing him with it towards various climaxes. His powers, such as they were, seemed all in the ascendant. He passed from that level platform as with an upward rush, all his enterprises, all his energies, all that he wanted and tried to do, surging forward towards the crest of successful accomplishment.

And a dozen times at least he caught himself asking mentally for his cousin Tony; wishing he had confided in him more, revealed more of this curious business to him, exchanged sympathies with him about it all. A kind of yearning rose in him for his vanished friend. Almost he had missed an opportunity. Tony would have understood and helped to clear things up; to no other man of his acquaintance could he have felt similarly. But Tony was now out of reach in Egypt, chasing his birds among the temples of the haunted Nile, already, doubtless, the center of a circle of new friends and acquaintances who found him as attractive and fascinating as the little Zakopané group had found him. Tony must keep.

Tom Kelverdon, meanwhile, his brief holiday over, returned to his work at Warsaw, and brought it to a successful conclusion with a rapidity no one had foreseen, and he himself had least of all expected. The power of the rising wave was in all he did. He could not fail. Out of the success grew other contracts, highly profitable to his firm. Some energy that overcame all obstacles, some clarity of judgment that selected unerringly the best ways and means, some skill and wisdom in him that made all his powers work in unison till they became irresistible, declared themselves, yet naturally and without adventitious aid. He seemed to have found himself anew. He felt pleased and satisfied with himself: always self-confident, as a man of ability ought to be, he now felt proud; and, though conceit had never been his failing, this new-born assurance moved distinctly towards pride. In a moment of impulsive pleasure he wrote to Tony, at the Turf Club, Cairo, and told him of his success.... The senior partner, his father's old friend, wrote and asked his advice upon certain new proposals the firm had in view; it was a question of big docks to be constructed at Salonica, and something to do with a barrage on the Nile as well—there were several juicy contracts to choose between, it seemed,—and Sir William proposed a meeting in Switzerland, on his way out to the Near East; he would break the journey before crossing the Simplon for Milan and Trieste. The final telegram said Montreux, and Kelverdon hurried to Vienna, and caught the night express to Lausanne by way of Bâle.

And at Montreux further evidence that the wave of life was rising then declared itself, when Sir William, having discussed the various propositions with him, listening with attention, even with deference, to Kelverdon's opinion, told him quietly that his brother's retirement left a vacancy in the firm which—he and his co-directors hoped confidently—Kelverdon might fill with benefit to all concerned. A senior partnership was offered to him before he was thirty-five! Sir William left the same night for his steamer, and Tom was to wait at Montreux, perhaps a month, perhaps six weeks, until a personal inspection of the several sites enable the final decision to be made; he was then to follow and take charge of the work itself.

Tom was immensely pleased. He wrote to his married sister in her Surrey vicarage, told her the news with a modesty he did not really feel, and sent her a handsome cheque by way of atonement for his bursting pride.

For simple natures, devoid of a saving introspection and self-criticism, upon becoming unexpectedly successful, easily develop an honest, yet none the less corroding pride. Tom felt himself rather a desirable person suddenly; by no means negligible at any rate; pleased and satisfied with himself, if not yet over-weeningly so. His native confidence took this exaggerated turn and twist. His star was in the ascendant, a man to be counted with...

The hidden weakness rose—as all else in him was rising—with the Wave. But he did not call it pride, because he did not recognize it. It was akin, perhaps, to that fatuous complacency of the bigoted religionist who, thinking he has discovered absolute truth, looks down from his narrow cell upon the rest of the world with a contemptuous pity that, in itself, is but the ignorance of crass self-delusion. Tom felt very sure of himself. For a rising wave drags up with it the mud and rubbish that have hitherto lain hidden out of sight in the ground below it. Only with the fall do these undesirable elements return to their proper place again—where they belong and are of value. Sense of proportion is recovered only with perspective, and Tom Kelverdon, rising too rapidly began to see himself in disproportionate relation to the rest of life. In his solid, perhaps stolid, way he considered himself a Personality—indispensable to no small portion of the world about him.

PART II

CHAPTER VIII

It was towards the end of March, and spring was flowing down almost visibly from the heights behind the town. April stood on tiptoe in the woods, finger on lip, ready to dance out between the sunshine and the rain.

Above four thousand feet the snows of winter still clung thickly, but the lower slopes were clear, men and women already working busily among the dull brown vineyards. The early mist cleared off by ten o'clock, letting through floods of sunshine that drenched the world, sparkled above the streets crowded with foreigners from many lands, and lay basking with an appearance of July upon the still, blue lake. The clear brilliance of the light had a quality of crystal. Sea-gulls fluttered along the shores, tame as ducks and eager to be fed. They lent to this inland lake an atmosphere of the sea, and Kelverdon found himself thinking of some southern port, Marseilles, Trieste, Toulon.

In the morning he watched the graceful fishing-boats set forth, and at night, when only the glitter of the lamps painted the gleaming water for a little distance, he saw the swans, their heads tucked back impossibly into the center of their backs, scarcely moving on the unruffled surface as they slept into the night. The first sounds he heard soon after dawn through his wide-opened windows were the whanging strokes of their powerful wings flying low across the misty water; they flew in twos and threes, coming from their nests now building in the marshes beyond Villeneuve. This, and the screaming of the gulls, usually woke him. The summits of Savoy, on the southern shore, wore pink and gold upon their heavy snows; the sharp air nipped; far in the west a few stars peeped before they faded; and in the distance he heard the faint, drum-like mutter of a paddle-steamer, reminding him that he was in a tourist center after all, and that this was busy, little, organized Switzerland.

But sometimes it was the beating strokes of the invisible paddle-steamer that woke him, for it seemed somehow a continuation of dreams he could never properly remember. That he had been dreaming busily every night of late he knew as surely as that he instantly forgot these dreams. That muffled drum-like thud, coming nearer and nearer towards him out of the quiet distance, had some connection—undecipherable as yet—with the curious, dry, rattling sound belonging to the Wave. The two were so dissimilar, however, that he was unable to discover any theory that could harmonize them. Nor, for that matter, did he seek it. He merely registered a mental note, as it were, in passing. The beating and the rattling were associated.

He chose a small and quiet hotel, as his liking was, and made himself comfortable, for he might have six weeks to wait for Sir William's telegram, or even longer, if, as seemed likely, the summons came by post. And Montreux was a pleasant place in early spring, before the heat and glare of summer scorched the people out of it towards the heights. He took long walks towards the snow-line beyond Les Avants and Les Pléiades, where presently the carpets of narcissus would smother the fields with white as though winter had returned and flung, instead of crystal flakes, a hundred showers of white feathers upon the ground. He discovered paths that led into the whispering woods of pine and chestnut. The young larches wore feathery green upon their crests, primroses shone on slopes where the grass was still pale and dead, snowdrops peeped out beside the wooden fences, and here and there, shining out of the brown decay of last year's leaves and thick ground-ivy, he found hepaticas. He had never felt the spring so marvelous before; it rose in a wave of color out of the sweet brown earth.

Though outwardly nothing of moment seemed to fill his days, inwardly he was aware of big events—maturing. There was this sense of approach, of preparation, of gathering. How insipid external events were after all, compared to the mass, the importance of interior changes! A change of heart, an altered point of view, a decision taken—these were the big events of life.

Yet it was a pleasant thing to be a senior partner. Here by the quiet lake, stroking himself complacently, he felt that life was very active, very significant, as he wondered what the choice would be. He rather hoped for Egypt, on the whole. He could look up Tony and the birds. They could go after duck and snipe together along the Nile. He would, moreover, be quite an important man out there. Pride and vanity rose with the Wave in him, but unobserved. For the Wave was in this too.

One afternoon, late, he returned from a long scramble among icy rocks about the Dent de Jaman, changed his clothes, and sat with a cigarette beside the open window, watching the throng of people underneath. In a steady stream they moved along the front of the lake, their voices rising through the air, their feet producing a dull murmur as of water. The lake was still as glass; gulls asleep on it and patches, and here and there a swan, looking like a bundle of dry white paper, floated idly. Off-shore lay several fishing-boats, becalmed; and far beyond them, a rowing-skiff broke the surface into two lines of widening ripples. They seemed floating in midair against the evening glow. The Savoy Alps formed a deep blue rampart, and the serrated battlements of the Dent du Midi, full in the blaze of sunset, blocked the Rhone Valley far away with its formidable barricade.

He watched the glow of approaching sunset with keen enjoyment; he sat back, listening to the people's voices, the gentle lap of the little waves; and the pleasant lassitude that follows upon hard physical exertion combined with the even pleasanter stimulus of the tea to produce a state of absolute contentment with the world....

Through the murmur of feet and voices, then, and from far across the water, stole out another sound that introduced into his peaceful mood an element of vague disquiet. He moved nearer to the window and looked out. The steamer, however, was invisible; the sea of shining haze towards Geneva hid it still: he could not see its outline. But he heard the echoless mutter of the paddlewheels, and he knew that it was coming nearer. Yet at first it did not disturb him so much as that, for a moment, he heard no other sound: the voices, the tread of feet, the screaming of the gulls all died away, leaving this single, distant beating audible alone—as though the entire scenery combined to utter it. And, though no ordinary echo answered it, there seemed—or did he fancy it?—a faint, interior response within himself. The blood in his veins went pulsing in rhythmic unison with this remote hammering upon the water.

He leaned forward in his chair, watching the people, listening intently, almost as though he expected something to happen, when immediately below him chance left a temporary gap in the stream of pedestrians, and in this gap—for a second merely—a figure stood sharply defined, cut off from the throng, set by itself, alone. His eyes fixed instantly upon its appearance, movements, attitude. Before he could think or reason he heard himself exclaim aloud:

"Why—it's—"

He stopped. The rest of the sentence remained unspoken. The words rushed down again. He swallowed, and with a gulp he ended—as though the other pedestrians all were men—

"—a woman!"

The next thing he knew was that the cigarette was burning his fingers—

had been burning them for several seconds. The figure melted back into the crowd. The throng closed around her. His eyes searched uselessly; no space, no gap was visible; the stream of people was continuous once more. Almost, it seemed, he had not really seen her—had merely thought her— up against the background of his mind.

For ten minutes, longer perhaps, he sat by that open window with eyes fastened on the moving crowd. His heart was beating oddly; his breath came rapidly. "She'll pass by presently again," he thought; "she'll come back!" He looked alternately to the right and to the left, until, finally, the sinking sun blazed too directly in his eyes for him to see at all. The glare blurred everybody into a smudged line of golden color, and the faces became a series of artificial suns that mocked him.

He did, then, an unusual thing—out of rhythm with his normal self,— he acted on impulse. Kicking his slippers off, he quickly put on a pair of boots, took his hat and stick, and went downstairs. There was no reflection in him; he did not pause and ask himself a single question: he ran to join the throng of people, moved up and down with them, in and out, passing and re-passing the same groups over and over again, but seeing no sign of the particular figure he sought so eagerly. She was dressed in black, he knew, with a black fur boa round her neck: she was slim and rather tall; more than that he could not say. But the poise and attitude, the way the head sat on the shoulders, the tilt upwards of the chin—he was as positive of recognizing these as if he had seen her close instead of a hundred yards away.

The sun was down behind the Jura Mountains before he gave up the search. Sunset slipped insensibly into dusk. The throng thinned out quickly at the first sign of chill. A dozen times he experienced the thrill—his heart suddenly arrested—of seeing her, but on each occasion it proved to be some one else. Every second woman seemed to be dressed in black that afternoon, a loose black boa round the neck. His eyes ached with the strain, the change of focus, the question that burned behind and in them, the joy— the strange rich pain.

But half, at least, of these dull people, he remembered, were birds of passage only; to-morrow or the next day they would take the train. He said to himself a dozen times, "Once more to the end and back again!" For she, too, might be a bird of passage, leaving to-morrow or the next day, leaving that very night, perhaps. The thought afflicted, goaded him. And on getting back to the hotel he searched the *Liste des Etrangers* as eagerly as he had searched the crowded front—and as uselessly, since he did not even know what name he hoped to find.

But later that evening a change came over him. He surprised some sense of humor: catching it in the act, he also surprised himself a little—smiling at himself. The laughter, however, was significant. For it was just that rest-less interval after dinner when he knew not what to do with the hours un-til bed-time: whether to sit in his room and think and read, or to visit the principal hotels in the hope of chance discovery. He was even considering this wild-goose chase to himself, when suddenly he realized that his course of procedure was entirely the wrong one.

This thing was going to happen anyhow, it was inevitable: but—it would happen in its own time and way, and nothing he might do could hurry it. To hunt in this violent manner was to delay its coming. To behave as usual was the proper way. It was then he smiled.

He crossed the hall instead, and put his head in at the door of the little Lounge. Some Polish people, with whom he had a bowing acquaintance, were in there smoking. He had seen them enter, and the Lounge was so small that he could hardly sit in their presence without some effort at con-versation. And, feeling in no mood for this, he put his head past the edge of the glass door, glanced round carelessly, as though looking for some one—then drew sharply back. For his heart stopped dead an instant, then beat furiously, like a piston suddenly released. On the sofa, talking calmly to the Polish people, was—the figure. He recognized her instantly.

Her back was turned; he did not see her face. There was a vast excite-ment in him that seemed beyond control. He seemed unable to make up his mind. He walked round and round the little hall examining intently the notices upon the walls. The excitement grew into tumult, as though the meeting involved something of immense importance—to his inmost self—his soul. It was difficult to account for. Then a voice behind him said, "There is a concert to-night. Radwan is playing Chopin. There are tick-ets in the Bureau still—if Monsieur cares to go." He thanked the speaker without turning to show his face: while another voice said passionately within him, "I was wrong; she is slim, but she is not so tall as I thought." And a minute later, without remembering how he got there, he was in his room upstairs, the door shut safely after him, standing before the mirror and staring into his own eyes. Apparently the instinct to see what he looked like operated automatically. For he now remembered—realized—another thing. Facing the door of the Lounge was a mirror, and their eyes had met. He had gazed for an instant straight into the kind and beautiful Eyes he had first seen twenty years ago—in the Wave.

His behavior then became more normal. He did the little, obvious things that any man would do. He took a clothes-brush and brushed his coat; he pulled his waist-coat down, straightened his black tie and smoothed his hair, poked his hanging watch-chain back into its pocket. Then, drawing a deep breath, and compressing his lips, he opened the door and went downstairs. He even remembered to turn off the electric light according to hotel instructions. "It's perfectly all right," he thought, as he reached the top of the stairs. "Why shouldn't I? There's nothing unusual about it." He did not take the lift, he preferred action. Reaching the *salon* floor, he heard voices in the hall below. She was already leaving therefore, the brief visit over. He quickened his pace. There was not the slightest notion in him what he meant to say. It merely struck him that—idiotically—he had stayed longer in his bedroom than he realized: too long; he might have missed his chance. The thought urged him forward more rapidly again.

In the hall—he seemed to be there without any interval of time—he saw her going out; the swinging doors were closing just behind her. The Polish friends, having said good-by, were already rising past him in the lift. A minute later he was in the street. He realized that, because he felt the cool night air upon his cheeks. He was beside her—looking down into her face.

"May I see you back—home—to your hotel?" he heard himself saying. And then the queer voice—it *must* have been his own—added abruptly, as though it was all he really had to say: "You haven't forgotten me really. I'm Tommy—Tom Kelverdon."

Her reply, her gesture, what she did and showed of herself in a word, was as queer as in a dream, yet so natural that it simply could not have been otherwise: "Tom Kelverdon! So it is! Fancy—*you* being here!" Then: "Thank you very much. And suppose we walk; it's only a few minutes— and quite dry."

How trivial and commonplace, yet how wonderful!

He remembers that she said something to a coachman who immediately drove off, that she moved beside him on this Montreux pavement, that they went up-hill a little, and that, very soon, a brilliant door of glass blazed in front of them, that she had said, "How strange that we should meet again like this. Do come and see me—any day—just telephone. I'm staying some weeks probably,"—and he found himself standing in the middle of the road, then walking wildly at a rapid pace downhill—he knew not whither, that he was hot and breathless, that stars were shining, and swans, like bundles of white newspaper, were asleep on the lake, and—that he had found her.

He had walked and talked with Lettice. He bumped into more than one irate pedestrian before he realized it; they knew it better than he did, apparently. "It was Lettice Aylmer, Lettice..." he kept saying to himself. "I've found her. She shook hands with me. That was her voice, her touch, her perfume. She's here—here in little Montreux—for several weeks. After all these years! Can it be true—really true at last? She said I might telephone— might go and see her. She's glad to see me—again."

How often he paced the entire length of the deserted front beside the lake he did not count: it must have been many times, for the hotel door, which

closed at midnight, was locked and the night-porter let him in. He went
to bed—if there was rose in the eastern sky and upon the summits of the
Dent du Midi, he did not notice it. He dropped into a half-sleep in which
thought continued but not wearingly. The excitement of his nerves relaxed,
soothed and mothered by something far greater than his senses, stronger
than his rushing blood. This greater Rhythm took charge of him most comfortably. He fell back into the mighty arms of something that was rising
irresistibly—something inevitable and—half-familiar. It had long been
gathering; there was no need to ask a thousand questions, no need to fight
it anywhere. From the moment when he glanced idly into the Lounge, he
had been aware of it. It had driven him downstairs without reflection, as
it had driven him also uphill till the blazing door was reached. He smelt
it, heard it, saw it, touched it. It was the Wave.

Time certainly proved its unreality that night; the hours seemed both endless and absurdly brief. His mind flew round and round in a circle, lingering
over every detail of the short interview with a tumultuous pleasure that hid
pain very thinly. He felt afraid, felt himself on the brink of plunging headlong into a gigantic whirlpool. Yet he wanted to plunge.... He would.... He
had to.... It was irresistible.

He reviewed the scene, holding each detail forcibly still, until the last delight had been sucked out of it. At first he remembered next to nothing—
a blur, a haze, the houses flying past him, no feeling of pavement under his
feet, but only her voice saying nothing in particular, her touch, as he sometimes drew involuntarily against her arm, her eyes shining up at him. For
her eyes remained the chief impression perhaps—so kind, so true, so very
sweet and frank—soft Irish eyes with something mysterious and semi-east-
ern in them. The conversation seemed to have entirely escaped recovery.

Then, one by one, he remembered things that she had said. Sentences offered themselves of their own accord. He flung himself upon them, trying
to keep tight hold of their first meaning—before he filled them with significance of his own. It was a desperate business altogether; emotion distorted her simple words so quickly. "I was thinking of you only to-day. I
had the feeling you were here. Curious, wasn't it?" He distinctly remembered her saying this. And then another sentence: "I should have known
you anywhere; though, of course, you've changed a lot. But I knew your
eyes. Eyes don't change much, do they?" The meanings he read into these
simple phrases filled an hour at least; he lost entirely their simple first significance. But this last remark brought up another in its train. As the tram
went past them she had raised her voice a little and looked up into his
face—it was just then they had cannonaded. People who like one another
always cannonade, he reflected. And her remark—"Ah, it comes back to
me. You're so very like your sister, Mary. I've seen her several times since

the days in Cavendish Square. There's a strong family likeness."

He disliked the last part of the sentence. Mary, besides, had mentioned nothing; her rare letters made no reference to it. The schooldays' friendship had evaporated perhaps. This sent his thoughts back upon the early trail of those distant months when Lettice was at a Finishing School in France and he had kept that tragic Calendar....

Another sentence interrupted them: "I had, oddly enough, been thinking of you this very afternoon. I knew you the moment you put your head in at the door, but, for the life of me, I couldn't get the name. All I got was 'Tommy!'" And only his sense of humor prevented the obvious rejoinder, "I wish you would always call me that." It struck him sharply. Such talk could have no part in a meeting of this kind; the idea of flirtation was impossible, not even thought of. Yet twice she had said "I was thinking of you only to-day!"

But other things came back as well. It was strange how much they had really said to each other in those few brief minutes. Next day he retraced the way and discovered that, even walking quickly, it took him a good half hour; yet they had walked slowly, even leisurely. But, try as he would, he was unable to force deeper meanings into these other remarks that he recalled. She was evidently pleased to see him, that at least was certain, for she had asked him to come and see her, and she meant it. He remembered his reply, "I'll come to-morrow—may I?" and then abruptly realized for the first time that the Plunge was taken. He felt himself committed, sink or swim. The Wave already had lifted him off his feet.

And it was on this his whirling thoughts came down to rest at last, and sleep crept over him—just as dawn was breaking. He felt himself in the "sea" with Lettice, there was nothing he could do, no course to choose, no decision to be made. Though married, she was somehow free—he felt it in her attitude. That sense of fatalism known in boyhood took charge of him. The Wave was rising towards the moment when it must invariably break and fall, and every impulse in him rising in it without a shade of denial or resistance. It would hurt—the fall and break would cause atrocious pain. But it was somewhere necessary to him. No atom of him held back or hesitated. For there was joy beyond it somehow—an intense and lasting joy, like the joy that belongs to growth and development after accepted suffering.

Vaguely—not put into definite words—it was this he felt, when at length sleep took him. Yet just before he slept he remembered two other little details—and smiled to himself as they rose before his sleepy mind, yet not understanding exactly why he smiled: for he did not yet know her name— and there was, of course, a husband.

CHAPTER IX

This resumption of a childhood's acquaintance that, by one at least, had been imaginatively coaxed into a relationship of ideal character, at once took on a standing of its own. It started as from a new beginning.

Tom Kelverdon did not forget the childhood part, but he neglected it at first. It was as if he met now for the first time—a woman who charmed him beyond anything known before; he longed for her; that he had longed for her subconsciously these twenty years slipped somehow or other out of memory. With it slipped also those strange corroborative details that imagination had clung to so tenaciously during the interval. The Whiff, the Sound, the other pair of Eyes, the shuffling feet, the joy that cloaked the singular prophecy of pain—all these, if not entirely forgotten, ceased to intrude themselves. Even when looking into her clear, dark eyes, he no longer quite realized them as the "eastern eyes" of his dim, dim dream; they belonged to a woman, and a married woman, whom he desired with body, heart and soul. Calm introspection was impossible, he could only feel, and feel intensely. He could not fuse this girl and woman into one continuous picture: each was a fragment of some much older, larger picture. But this larger canvas he could never visualize successfully. It was colored, radiant, gorgeous; it blazed as with gold, a gold of sun and stars. But the strain of effort caused rupture instantly. The vaster memory escaped him. He was conscious of reserve.

The comedy of telephoning to a name he did not know was obviated next morning by the arrival of a note: Dear Tom Kelverdon," it began, and was signed "Yours, Lettice Jaretzka." It invited him to come up for *dejeuner* in her hotel. He went. The luncheon led naturally to a walk together afterwards, and then to other luncheons and other walks, to evening rows upon the lake, and to excursions into the surrounding country.... They had tea together in the lower mountain inns, picked flowers, photographed one another, laughed, talked and sat side by side at concerts or in the little Montreux cinema theater. It was all as easy and natural as any innocent companionship well could be—because it was so deep. The foundations were of such solid strength that nothing on the surface trembled.... Madame de Jaretzka was well known in the hotel—she came annually, it seemed, about this time and made a lengthy stay—but no breath of anything untoward could ever be connected with her. He, too, was accepted by one and all, no glances came their way. He was her friend: that was apparently enough. And though he desired her, body, heart and soul, he was quick to realize that the first named in the trio had no rôle to play. Something in her, something of attitude and atmosphere, rendered it inconceivable. The reserve he was conscious of lay very deep in him; it lay in her too. There was a fence, a barrier he must not, could not pass—both recognized it. Being a man, romance for him drew some tendril doubtless from the creative physical, but the shade of passing disappointment, if it existed, was renounced as instantly as recognized. Yet he was not aware at first of any incompleteness in her. He felt only a bigger thing. There was something in this simple woman that bore him to the stars.

For simple she undoubtedly was, not in the way of shallowness, but because her nature seemed at harmony with itself: uncomplex, natural, frank and open, and with an unconventional carelessness that did no evil for the reason that she thought and meant none. She could do things that must have made an ordinary worldly woman the center of incessant talk and scandal. There was, indeed, an extraordinary innocence about her that perturbed the judgment, somewhat baffling it. Whereas with many women it might have roused the suspicion of being a pose, an affectation, with her, Tom felt, it was a genuine innocence, beyond words delightful and refreshing. And it arose, he soon discovered, from the fact that, being good and true herself, she thought everybody else was also good and true. This he realized before two days' intercourse had made it seem as if they had been together always and were made for one another. Something bigger and higher than he had ever felt before stirred in him for this woman, whom he thought of now invariably as Madame de Jaretzka, rather than as Lettice of his younger dream. If she woke something nobler in him that had slept, he did not label it as such: nor, if a portion of his younger dream was fulfilling itself before his eyes, in a finer set of terms, did he think it out and set it down in definite words. There was this intense and intimate familiarity between them both, but somehow he did not call it by these names. He just thought her wonderful—and longed for her. The reserve began to trouble him....

"It's sweet," she said, "when real people come together—find each other."

"Again," he added. "You left that out. For *I've* never forgotten—all these years."

She laughed. "Well, I'll tell you the truth," she confessed frankly. "I hadn't forgotten either; I often thought of you and wondered—"

"What I was like now?"

"What you were doing, where you were," she said. "I always knew what you were like. But I often wondered how far on you had got."

"You had no news of me?"

"None. But I always believed you'd do something big in the world."

Something in her voice or manner made it wholly natural for him to tell her of his boyhood love. He mentioned the Wave and wavy feeling, the nightmare too, but when he tried to go beyond that, something checked him; he felt a sudden shyness. It "sounds so silly," was his thought. "But I always know a real person," he said aloud, "anybody who's going to be real in my life; they always arrive on a wave, as it were. My wavy feeling announces them." And the interest with which she responded prevented his regretting having made his confession.

"It's an instinct, I think," she agreed, "and instincts are meant to be listened to. I've had something similar, though with me it's not a wave." Her voice grew slower, she made a pause; when he looked up—her eyes were gazing across the lake as though in a moment of sudden absent-mindedness.... "And what's yours?" he asked, wondering why his heart was beating as though something painful was to be disclosed.

"I see a stream," she went on slowly, still gazing away from him across the expanse of shining water, "a flowing stream—with faces on it. They float down with the current. And when I see one I know it's somebody real—real to me. The unreal faces are always on the bank. I pass them by."

"You've seen mine?" he asked, unable to hide the eagerness. "My face?"

"Often, yes," she told him simply. "I dream it usually, I think: but it's quite vivid."

"And is that all? You just see the faces floating down with the current?"

"There's one other thing," she answered, "if you'll promise not to laugh."

"Oh, I won't laugh," he assured her. "I'm awfully interested. It's no funnier than my Wave, anyhow."

"They're faces I have to save," she said. "Somehow I'm meant to rescue them." In what way she did not know. "Just keep them above water, I suppose!" And the smile in her face gave place to a graver look. The stream of faces was real to her in the way his Wave was real. There was meaning in it. "Only three weeks ago," she added, "I saw you like that." He asked where it was, and she told him Warsaw. They compared notes; they had been in the town together, it turned out. Their outer paths had been converging for some time, then.

"Why—did you leave?" he asked suddenly. He wanted to ask why she was there at all, but something stopped him.

"I usually come here," she said quietly, "about this time. It's restful. There's peace in these quiet hills above the town, and the lake is soothing. I get strength and courage here."

He glanced at her with astonishment a moment. Behind the simple language another meaning flashed. There was a look in the eyes, a hint in the voice that betrayed her.... He waited, but she said no more. Not that she wished to conceal, but that she did not wish to speak of something. Warsaw meant pain for her, she came here to rest, to recuperate after a time of stress and struggle, he felt. And looking at the face he recognized for the first time that behind its quiet strength there lay deep pain and sadness, yet accepted pain and sadness conquered, a suffering she had turned to sweetness. Without a particle of proof, he yet felt sure of this. And an immense respect woke in him. He saw her saving, rescuing others, regardless of herself: he felt the floating faces real; the stream was life—her life.... And, side by side with the deep respect, the bigger, higher impulse stirred in him again. Name it he could not: it just came: it stole into him like some rare and exquisite new fragrance, and it came from her.... He saw her far above him, stooping down from a higher level to reach him with her little hand.... He knew a yearning, to climb up to her—a sudden and searching yearning in his soul. "She's come back to fetch me," ran across his mind before he realized it; and suddenly his heart became so light that he thought he had never felt such happiness before. Then, before he realized it, he heard himself saying aloud—from his heart:

"You do me an awful lot of good—really you do. I feel better and happier when I'm with you. I feel—" He broke off, aware that he was talking rather foolishly. Yet the boyish utterance was honest; she did not think it foolish apparently. For she replied at once, and without a sign of lightness:

"Do I? Then I mustn't leave you, Tom!"

"Never!" he exclaimed impetuously.

"Until I've saved you." And this time she did not laugh.

She was still looking away from him across the water, and the tone was quiet and unaccented. But the words rang like a clarion in his mind. He turned; she turned too: their eyes met in a brief but penetrating gaze. And for an instant he caught an expression that frightened him, though he could not understand its meaning. Her beauty struck him like a sheet of fire— all over. He saw gold about her like the soft fire of the southern stars. With any other woman, at any other time, he would—but the thought utterly denied itself before it was half completed even. It sank back as though ashamed. There was something in her that made it ugly, out of rhythm, undesirable, and undesired. She would not respond—she would not understand.

In its place another blazed up with that strange, big yearning at the back of it, and though he gazed at her as a man gazes at a woman he needs and asks for, her quiet eyes did not lower or turn aside. The cheaper feeling, "I'm not worthy of you," took in his case a stronger form: "I'll be better, bigger, for you." And then, so gently it might have been a mother's action, she put her hand on his with firm pressure, and left it lying there a moment before she withdrew it again. Her long white glove, still fastened about the wrist, was flung back so that it left the palm and fingers bare, and the touch of the soft skin upon his own was marvelous; yet he did not attempt to seize it, he made no movement in return. He kept control of himself in a way he did not understand. He just sat and looked into her face. There was an entire absence of response from her—in one sense. Something poured from her eyes into his very soul, but something beautiful, uplifting. This new yearning emotion rose through him like a wave, bearing him upwards.... At the same time he was vaguely aware of a lack as well... of something incomplete and unawakened....

"Thank you—for saying that," he was murmuring; "I shall never forget it;" and though the suppressed passion changed the tone and made it tremble even, he held himself as rigid as a statue. It was she who moved. She leaned nearer to him. Like a flower the wind bends on its graceful stalk, her face floated very softly against his own. She kissed him. It was all very swift and sudden. But, though exquisite, it was not a woman's kiss.... The same instant she was sitting straight again, gazing across the blue lake below her.

"You're still a boy," she said, with a little innocent laugh, "still a wonderful, big boy."

"Your boy," he returned. "I always have been."

There was deep, deep joy in his heart, it lifted him above the world—with her. Yet with the joy there was this faint touch of disappointment too.

"But, I say—isn't it awfully strange?" he went on, words failing him absurdly. "It's very wonderful, this friendship. It's so natural." Then he began to flush and stammer.

In an even tone of voice she answered: "It's wonderful, Tom, but it's not strange." And again he was vaguely aware that something which might have made her words yet more convincing was not there.

"But I've got that curious feeling—I could swear it's all happened before." He moved closer as he spoke; her dress was actually against his coat, but he could not touch her. Something made it impossible, wrong, a false, even a petty thing. It would have taken away the kiss. "Have *you?*" he asked abruptly, with an intensity that seemed to startle her, "have you got that feeling of familiarity too?"

And for a moment in the middle of their talk they both, for some reason, grew very thoughtful....

"It had to be—perhaps," she answered simply a little later. "We are both real, so I suppose—yes, it *has* to be."

There was the definite feeling that both spoke of a bigger thing that neither quite understood. Their eyes searched, but their hearts searched too. There was a gap in her that somehow must be filled, Tom felt.... They stared long at one another. He was close upon the missing thing—when suddenly she withdrew her eyes. And with that, as though a wave had swept them together and passed on, the conversation abruptly changed its key. They fell to talking of other things. The man in him was again aware of disappointment.

The change was quite natural, nothing forced or awkward about it. The significance had gone its way, but the results remained. They were in the "sea" together. It "had to be." As from the beginning of the world they belonged to one another, each for the other—real. There was nothing about it of a text-book "love affair," absolutely nothing. Deeper far than a passional relationship, guiltless of any fruit of mere propinquity, the foundations of the sudden intimacy were as ancient as immovable. The inevitable touch lay in it. And Tom knew this partly confirmed, at any rate, by the emotion in him when she said "my boy," for the term woke no annoyance, conveyed no lightness. Yet there was a flavor of disappointment in it somewhere—something of necessary value that he missed in her.... To a man in love it must have sounded superior, contemptuous: whereas to him it sounded merely true. He was her boy. This mother-touch was in her. To care, to cherish, somehow even to rescue, she had come to find him out—again. She had come *back*.... It was thus, at first, he felt it. From somewhere above, beyond the place where he now stood in life, she had "come back, come down, to fetch him." She was further on than he was. He longed to stand beside her. Until he did... this gap in her must prevent absolute union. On both sides it was not entirely natural as yet.... Thought grew confused in him.

And, though he could not understand, he accepted it as inevitable. The joy, moreover, was so urgent and uprising, that it smothered a delicate whisper that yet came with it—that the process involved also—pain. Though aware, from time to time, of this vague uneasiness, he easily brushed it aside. It was the merest gossamer thread of warning that with each recurrent appearance became more tenuous, until finally it ceased to make its presence felt at all....

In the entire affair of this sudden intercourse he felt the Wave, yet the Wave though steadily rising, ceased to make its presence too consciously known; the Whiff, the Sound, the Eyes seemed equally forgotten: that is, he did not realize them. He was living now, and introspection was a waste of time, living too intensely to reflect or analyze. He felt swept onwards upon a tide that was greater than he could manage, for instead of swimming consciously, he was borne and carried with it. There was certainly no attempt to stem. Life was rising. It rushed him forwards too deliciously to think....

He began asking himself the old eternal question: "Do I love? Am I in love—at last, then?"... Some time passed, however, before he realized that he loved, and it was in a sudden, curious way that this realization came. Two little words conveyed the truth—some days later as they were at tea on the verandah of her hotel, watching the sunset behind the blue line of the Jura Mountains. He had been talking about himself, his engineering prospects—rather proudly—his partnership and the letter he expected daily from Sir William. "I hope it will be Assouan," he said, "I've never been in Egypt. I'm awfully keen to see it." She said she hoped so too. She knew Egypt well: it enchanted, even enthralled her: "familiar as though I'd lived there all my life. A change comes over me, I become a different person— and a much older one; not physically," she explained with a curious shy gaze at him, "but in the sense that I feel a longer pedigree behind me." She gave the little laugh that so often accompanied her significant remarks. "I always think of the Nile as the 'stream' where I see the floating faces."

They went on chatting for some minutes about it. Tom asked if she had met his cousin out there; yes, she remembered vaguely a Mr. Winslowe coming to tea on her *dahabieh* once, but it was only when he described Tony more closely that she recalled him positively. "He interested me," she said then: "he talked wildly, but rather picturesquely about what he called the 'spiral movement of life,' or something." "He goes after birds," Tom mentioned. "Of course," she replied, "I remember distinctly now. It was something about the flight of birds that introduced the spiral part of it. He had a good deal in him, that man," she added, "but he hid it behind a lot of nonsense—almost purposely, I felt."

"That's Tony all over," Tom assented, "but he's a rare good sort and I'm awfully fond of him. He's 'real' in our sense too, I think."

She said then very slowly, as though her thoughts were far away in Egypt at the moment: "Yes, I think he is. I've seen *his* face too."

"Floating down, you mean—or on the bank?"

"Floating," she answered. "I'm sure I have."

Tom laughed happily. "Then you've got him to rescue too," he said. "But, remember, if we're both drowning, I come first."

She looked into his face and smiled her answer, touching his fingers with her hand. And again it was not a woman's touch.

"He was in Warsaw too a few weeks ago," Tom went on. "So we were all three there together. Rather odd, you know. He was ski-ing with me in the Carpathians," and he described their meeting at Zakopané after the long interval since boyhood. "He told me about you in Egypt, too, now I come to think of it. He mentioned the *dahabieh*, but called you a Russian— yes, I remember now—and a Russian Princess into the bargain. Evidently you made less impression on Tony than—"

It was then he stopped as though he had been struck. The idle conversation changed. He heard her interrupting words from a curious distance.

They fell like particles of ice upon his heart.

"Polish, of course, not Russian." she mentioned casually, "but the rest is right, though I never use the title. My husband, in his own country, is a Prince, you see."

Something reeled in him, then instantly righted itself. For a moment he felt as though the freedom of their intercourse had received a shock that blighted it. The words, "my husband," struck chill and ominous into his heart. The recovery, however—almost simultaneous— showed him that both the freedom and the intercourse were right and unashamed. She gave him nothing that belonged to any other: she was loyal and true to that other as she was loyal and true to himself. Their relationship was high above mere passional intrigue; it could exist—in the way she knew it, felt it—side by side with that other one, before that other one's very eyes, if need be.... He saw it true: he saw it innocent as daylight.... For what he felt was somehow this: the woman in her was not his, but more than that—it was not anyone's. It still lay dormant....

If there was a momentary confusion in his own mind, there was none, he felt positive, in hers. The two words that struck him such a blow, she uttered as lightly, innocently, as the rest of the talk between them. Indeed, had that other—even in thought Tom preferred the paraphrase—been present, she would have introduced them to each other then and there. He heard her saying the little phrases even: "My husband," and, "This is Tom Kelverdon whom I've loved since childhood."

Nothing brought more home to him the high innocence, the purity and sweetness of this woman than the reflections that flung after one another in his mind as he realized that his hope of her being a widow was not justified, and at the same moment that he desired exclusive possession of her— that he was definitely in love.

That she was unaware of any discovery, even if she divined the storm in him at all, was clear from the way she went on speaking. For, while all this flashed through his mind, she added quietly: "He is in Warsaw now. He— lives there. I go to him for part of every year." To which Tom heard his voice reply something as natural and commonplace as "Yes—I see."

Of the hundred pregnant questions that presented themselves, he did not ask a single one: not that he lacked the courage so much as that he felt the right was—not yet—his. Moreover, behind her quiet words he divined a tragedy. The suffering that had become sweetness in her face was half explained, but the full revelation of it belonged to "that other" and to herself alone. It had been their secret, he remembered, for at least fifteen years.

CHAPTER X

Yet, knowing himself in love, he was able to set his house in order. Confusion disappeared. With the method and thoroughness of his character he looked things in the face and put them where they belonged. Even to wake up to an untidy room was an affliction. He might arrive in a hotel at midnight, but he could not sleep until his trunks were empty and everything in its place. In such outer details the intensity of his nature showed itself: it was the intensity, indeed, that compelled the orderliness.

And the morning after this conversation, he woke up to an ordered mind—thoughts and emotions in their proper places where he could see and lay his hand upon them. The strength and weakness of his temperament betrayed themselves plainly here, for the security that pedantic order brought precluded the perspective of a larger vision. This careful labeling enclosed him within somewhat rigid fences. To insist upon this precise ticketing had its perilous corollary; the entire view—perspective, proportion—was lost sight of.

"I'm in love: she's beautiful, body, mind and soul. She's high above me, but I'll climb up to where she is." This was his morning thought, and the thought that accompanied him all day long and every day until the moment came to separate again.... She's a married woman but her husband has no claim on her." Somehow he was positive of that; the husband had forfeited all claim to her; details he did not know; but she was free; she did no wrong.

In imagination he furnished plausible details from sensational experiences life had shown him. These may have been right or wrong; possibly the husband had ill-treated, then deserted her; they were separated possibly, though—she had told him this—there were no children to complicate the situation. He made his guesses....

There was a duty, however, that she would not, did not neglect: in fulfilment of its claim she went to Warsaw every year. What it was, of course, he did not know; but this thought and the emotions caused by it, he put away into their proper places; he asked no questions of her; the matter did not concern him really. The shock experienced the day before was the shock of realizing that—he loved. Those two significant words had suddenly shown it to him. The order of his life was changed. "She is essential to me; I am essential to her." But "She's all the world to me" involved equally "I'm all the world to her." The sense of his own importance was enormously increased. The Wave surged upwards with a sudden leap....

There was one thing lacking in this love, perhaps, though he hardly noticed it—the element of surprise. Ever since childhood he had suspected this would happen. The love was predestined, and in so far seemed a deliberate affair, pedestrian, almost calm. This sense of the inevitable robbed it of that amazing unearthly glamour which steals upon those who love for the first time, taking them deliciously by surprise. He saw her beautiful, and probably she was, but her beauty was familiar to him. He had come up with the childhood dream, and in coming up with it he recognized it. It seemed thus somewhat.... But her mind and soul were beautiful too, only these were more beautiful than he had dreamed. In that lay surprise and wonder too. There was genuine magic here, discovery and exhilarating novelty. He had not caught up with *that*. The love as a whole, however, was expected, natural. It was inevitable. The familiarity, alone, remained strange, a flavor of the uncanny about it almost—yet certainly real.

And these things also he tried to face and label, though with less success. To bring order into them was beyond his powers. She had outstripped him somehow in her soul, but had come back to fetch him—also to get something for herself she lacked. The rest was oddly familiar: it had happened before. It was about to happen now again, but on a higher level; only before it could happen completely he must overtake her. The spiral idea lay in it somewhere. But the Wave contained and drove it.... His mind was not supple; analogy, that spiritual solvent, did not help him. Yet the fact remained that he somehow visualized the thing in picture form; a rising wave bore them charging up the spiral curve to a point whence they both looked down upon a passage they had made before. She was always a little in front of him, beyond him. But when the Wave finally broke they would rush together—become one... there would be pain, but joy would follow.

And during all their subsequent, happy days of companionship this one thing alone marred his supreme contentment—this sense of elusiveness, that while he held her she yet slipped between his fingers and escaped. He loved; but whereas to most men love brings a feeling of finality and rest, as of a search divinely ended, to Tom came the feeling that his search was merely resumed, or, indeed, had only just begun. He had not come into full possession of this woman: he had only found her.... She was deep; her deceptive simplicity hid surprises from him; much—and it was the greater part—he could not understand. Only when he came up with that would possession be complete. Not that she said or did a single thing that suggested this; she was not elusive of set purpose; she was entirely guiltless of any desire to hold back a fraction of herself, and to conceal was as foreign to her nature as to play with him; but that some part of her hung high above his reach and that he, knowing this, admitted a subtle pain behind the joy. "I can't get at her—quite," he put it to himself. "Some part of her is not mine yet—doesn't belong to me."

He thought chiefly, that is, of his own possible disabilities rather than of hers.

"I often wonder why we've come together like this," he said once, as they lay in the shade of a larch wood above Corvaux and looked towards the snowy summits of Savoy. "What brought us together, I mean? There's something mysterious about it to me—"

"God," she said quietly. "You needed me. You've been lonely. But you'll never be lonely again."

Her introduction of the Deity into a conversation did not displease. Fate or any similar word could have taken its place; she merely conveyed her sense that their coming together was right and inevitable. Moreover, now that she said it, he recognized the fact of loneliness—that he always had been lonely, but that it was no longer possible. He felt like a boy and spoke like a boy. She had come to look after, care for him. She asked nothing for herself. The thought gave him a sharp and sudden pang.

"But my love means a lot to you, doesn't it?" he asked tenderly. "I mean, you need me too?"

"Everything, Tom," she told him softly. He was conscious of the mother in her, as though the mother overshadowed the woman. But while he loved it, the tinge of resentment still remained.

"You couldn't do without me, could you?" He took the hand she placed upon his knee and looked up into her quiet eyes. "You'd be lonely too if—I went?"

For a moment she gazed down at him and did not answer; he was aware of both the pain and sweetness in her face; an interval of thoughtfulness again descended on them both: then a great tenderness came welling up into her eyes as she answered slowly: "You couldn't go, Tom. You couldn't leave me ever."

Her hand was on his shoulder, almost about his neck as she said it, and he came in closer, and before he knew what he was doing his face was buried in her lap. Her hand stroked his hair. Twenty-five years dropped from him—he was a child again, a little boy, and she, in some gigantic, half-impersonal sense he could not understand, was mothering him. No foolish feeling of shame came with it; the mood was too sudden for analysis, it passed away swiftly too; but he knew, for a brief second, all the sensations of a restless and dissatisfied boy who needed above all else—comfort: the comfort that only an inexhaustible mother-love could give.... And this love poured from her in a flood. Till now he had never known it, nor known the need of it. And because it had been curiously lacking he suddenly wondered how he had done without it. A strange sense of tears rose in his heart. He felt pain and tragedy somewhere. For there was another thing he wanted from her too.... Through the sparkle of his joy peeped out that familiar, strange, rich pain, but so swiftly he hardly recognized it. It withdrew again. It vanished.

"But *you* couldn't leave me, either, could you?" he asked, sitting erect again. He made a movement as though to draw her head down upon his shoulder in the protective way of a man who loves, but—he could not do it. It was curious. She did nothing to prevent, only somehow the position would be a false one. She did not need him in that way. He was not yet big enough to protect. It was she who protected him. And when she answered the same second, the familiar sentence flashed across his mind again: "She has come back to fetch me."

"I shall never, never leave you, Tom. We're together for always. I know it absolutely." The girl of seventeen, the unawakened woman who was desired, the mother who thought not of herself,—all three spoke in those quiet words; but with them, too, he was aware of this elusive other thing he could not name. Perhaps her eyes conveyed it, perhaps the pain and sweetness in the little face so close above his own. She was bending over him. He looked up. And over his heart rushed again that intolerable yearning—the yearning to stand where she stood, far, far beyond him, yet with it the certainty that pain must attend the effort. Until that pain, that effort were accomplished, she could not entirely belong to him. He had to win her yet. Yet also he had to teach *her* something... Meanwhile, in the act of protecting, mothering him she must use pain, as to a learning child. Their love would gain completeness only thus.

Yet in words he could not approach it; he knew not how to.

"It's a strange relationship," he stammered, concealing as he thought the deep emotions that perplexed him. "The world would misunderstand it utterly." She smiled, nodding her head. "I wish—" he added, "I mean it comes to me sometimes—that you don't need me quite as I need you. You're my whole life, you know—now."

"You're growing imaginative, Tom," she teased him, smilingly. Then, catching the earnest expression in his face, she added: "My life has been very full, you see, and I've always had to stand alone. There's been so much for me to do that I've had no time to feel loneliness perhaps."

"Rescuing the other floating faces!"

A slight tinge of a new emotion slipped through his mind, something he had never felt before, yet so faint he could not even recapture it, much less wonder whether it were jealousy or envy. It rose from the depths; it vanished into him again.... Besides, he saw that she was smiling; the teasing mood that so often baffled him was upon her; he heard her give that passing laugh that almost "kept him guessing," as the Americans say, whether she was in play or earnest.

"It's worth doing, anyhow—rescuing the floating faces," she said: "worth living for." And she half closed her eyes so that he saw her as a girl again. He saw her as she had been even before he knew her, as he used to see her in his dream. It was the dream-eyes that peered at him through long, thick lashes. They looked down at him. He felt caught away to some remote, strange place and time. He was aware of gold, of color, of a hotter blood, a fiercer sunlight....

And the sense of familiarity became suddenly very real; he knew what she was going to say, how he would answer, why they had come together. It all flashed near, yet still just beyond his reach. He almost understood. They had been side by side like this before, not in this actual place, but somewhere—somewhere that he knew intimately. Her eyes had looked down into his own precisely so, long, long ago, yet at the same time strangely near. There was a perfume, a little ghostly perfume—it was the Whiff. It was gone instantly, but he had tasted it.... A veil drew up.... He saw, he knew, he remembered—almost.... Another second and he would capture the meaning of it all. Another moment and it would reveal itself— then, suddenly, the whole sensation vanished. He had missed it by the minutest fraction in the world, yet missed it utterly. It left him confused and baffled.

The veil was down again, and he was talking with Madame Jaretzka, the Lettice Aylmer of his boyhood days. Such moments of the *déjà-vu* leave bewilderment behind them, like the effect of sudden change of focus in the eye; and with the bewilderment a sense of insecurity as well.

"Yes," he said half dreamily, "and you've rescued a lot already, haven't you?" as though he still followed in speech the direction of the vanished emotion.

"You know that, Tom?" she inquired, raising her eyelids, thus finally restoring the normal.

He stammered rather: "I have the feeling—that you're always doing good to some one somewhere. There's something"—he searched for a word— "impersonal about you—almost." And he knew the word was nearly right, though found by chance. It included "un-physical," the word he did not like to use. He did not want an angel's love; the spiritual, to him, rose from the physical, and was not apart from it. He was not in heaven yet, and had no wish to be. He was on earth; and everything of value—love, above all— must spring from earth, or else remain incomplete, insecure, ineffective even.

And again a tiny dart of pain shot through him. Yet he was glad he said it, for it was true. He liked to face what hurt him. To face it was to get it over....

But she was laughing again gently to herself, though certainly not at him.

"What were you thinking about so long?" she asked. "You've been silent for several minutes and your thoughts were far away." And as he did not reply immediately, she went on: "If you go to Assouan you mustn't fall into reveries like that or you'll leave holes in the dam, or whatever your engineering work is—*Tom!*"

She spoke the name with a sudden emphasis that startled him. It was a call.

"Yes," he said, looking up at her. He was emerging from a dream.

"Come back to me. I don't like your going away in that strange way—forgetting me."

"Ah, I like that. Say it again," he returned, a deeper note in his voice.

"You *were* away—weren't you?"

"Perhaps," he said slowly. "I can't say quite. I was thinking of you, wherever I was." He went on, holding her eyes with a steady gaze: "A curious feeling came over me like—like heat and light. You seemed so familiar to me all of a sudden that I felt I had known you ages and ages. I was trying to make out where—it was—"

She dropped her eyelids again and peered at him, but no longer smiling. There was a sterner expression in her face. The lips curved a moment in a new strange way. The air seemed to waver an instant between them. She peered down at him as through a mist....

"There—like that!" he exclaimed passionately. "Only I wish you wouldn't. There's something I don't like about it. It hurts"—and the same minute felt ashamed, as though he had said a foolish thing. It had come out in spite of himself.

"Then I won't, Tom—if you'll promise not to go away again. I was thinking of Egypt for a second—I don't know why."

But he did not laugh with her; his face kept the graver expression still.

"It changes you—rather oddly," he said quietly, "that lowering of the eyelids. I can't say why exactly, but it makes you look—eastern." Again he had said a foolish thing. A kind of spell seemed over him.

"Irish eyes!" he heard her saying. "They sometimes look like that, I'm told. But you promise, don't you?"

"Of course, I promise," he answered bluntly enough because he meant it. "I can never go away from you because"—he turned and looked very hard at her a moment—"because there's something in you I need in my very soul," he went on earnestly, "yet that always escapes me. I can't get hold of—all of you."

And though she refused his very earnest mood, she answered with obvious sincerity at once. "That's as it should be, Tom. A man tires of a woman the moment he gets to the end of her." She gave her little laugh and touched his hand. "Perhaps that's what I'm meant to teach you. When you know all of me—"

"I shall never know all of you," said Tom.

"You never will," she replied with meaning, "for I don't even know it all myself." And as she said it, he thought he had never seen anything so beautiful in all the world before, for the breeze caught her long gauzy veil of blue and tossed it across her face so that the eyes seemed gazing at him from a distance, but a distance that had height in it. He felt her above him, beyond him, on this height, a height he must climb before he could know complete possession.

"By Jove!" he thought, "isn't it rising just!" For the Wave was under them tremendously.

April meanwhile had slipped into May, and their daily companionship had become the most natural thing in the world, when the telegram arrived that threatened to interrupt the delightful intercourse. But it was not the telegram Tom expected. Neither Greece nor Egypt claimed his talents yet, for the contracts both at Assouan and Salonica were postponed until the autumn, and the routine of a senior partner's life in London was to be his immediate fate. He brought her the news at once: they discussed it together in all its details and as intimately as though it affected their joint lives similarly. His first thought was to run and talk it over with her; hers, how the change might influence their intercourse, their present and their future. Their relationship was now established in this solid, natural way. He told her everything as a son might tell his mother: she asked questions, counseled, made suggestions as a woman whose loving care considered his welfare and his happiness before all else.

However, it brought no threatened interruption after all—involved, indeed, less of separation than if he had been called away as they expected: for though he must go to London that same week, she would shortly follow him. "And if you go to Egypt in the autumn, Tom"—she smiled at the way they influenced the future nearer to the heart's desire—"I may go with you. I could make my arrangements accordingly—take my holiday out there earlier instead of here as usual in the spring."

The days passed quickly; her first duty was to return to Warsaw; she would then follow him to London and help him with his flat. No man could choose furniture and carpets and curtains properly. They discussed the details with the enthusiasm of children: she would come up several times a week from her bungalow in Kent and make sure that his wall-papers did not clash with the general scheme. Brown was his color, he told her, and always had been. It was the dominant shade of her eyes as well. He made her promise to stand in the rooms with her eyes opened very wide so that there could be no mistake, and they laughed over the picture happily.

She came to the train, and although he declared vehemently that he disliked "being seen off," he was secretly delighted. "One says such silly things merely because one feels one must say something. And those silly things remain in the memory out of all proportion to their value." But she insisted. "Good-bys are always serious to me, Tom. One never knows. I want to see you to the very last minute." She had this way of making him feel little things significant with Fate. But another little thing also was in store for him. As the train moved slowly out he noticed some letters in her hand; and one of them was addressed to Warsaw. The name leaped up and stung him—Jaretzka. A spasm of pain shot through him. She was leaving in the morning, he knew....

"Write to me from Warsaw," he said. "Take care! We're moving!"

"I'll write every day, my dearest Tom, my boy. You won't forget me. I shall see you in a fortnight."

He let go the little hand he held till the last possible minute. The bells drowned her final words. She stood there waving her hand with the unposted letters in them, till the station pillars intervened and hid her from him.

And this time no "silly last things" had been said that could "stay in the memory out of all proportion to their value." It was something he had noticed on the envelope that stayed—not the husband's name, but a word in the address, a peculiar Polish word he happened to know:—"Tworki"—the name of the principal *maison de santé* that stood just outside the city of Warsaw....

Half an hour, perhaps an hour, he sat smoking in his narrow sleeping compartment, thinking with a kind of intense confusion out of which no order came.... At Pontarlier he had to get out for the Customs formalities. It was midnight. The stars were bright. The keen spring air from the wooded Jura mountains had a curious effect, for he returned to his carriage feeling sleepy, the throng of pictures drowned into calmness by one master-thought that reduced their confusion into order. He looked back over the past weeks and realized their intensity. He had lived. There was a change in him, the change of growth, development. He loved. There was now a woman who was his entire world, essential to him. He was essential to her too. And the importance of this ousted all lesser things, even the senior partnership. This was the master-thought—that he now lived for her. He was "real" even as she was "real," each to the other *real*. The Wave had lifted him to a level never reached before. And it was rising still....

He fell asleep on this, to dream of a mighty stream that swept them together irresistibly towards some climax that he never could quite see. She floated near to save him. She floated down. Her little hands were stretched.

It was a gorgeous and stupendous dream—a dream of rising life itself—
rising till it would curve and break and fall, and the inevitable thing
would happen that would bring her finally into his hungry arms, complete,
mother and woman, a spiritual love securely founded on the sweet and
wholesome earth....

CHAPTER XI

During the brief separation of a fortnight Tom was too busy in London
to allow himself much reflection. Absence, once the first keen sense of loss
is over, is apt to bring reaction. The self makes an automatic effort to regain the normal life it led before the new emotion dislocated the long-ac-
customed routine. It tries to run back again along the line of least resistance that habit has made smooth and easy. If the reaction continues to
assert its claim, the new emotion is proved thereby a delusion. The test lies
there.

In Tom's case, however, the reaction was a feeble reminder merely that
he had once lived—without her. It took the form of regret for all the best
years of his life he had endured—how, he could not think—without this
tender, loving woman at his side. That is, he recognized that his love was
real and had changed his outlook fundamentally. He could never do without her from this moment onwards. She, equally, needed him. He would
never leave her.... Further than that, for the present, he did not allow himself to think. Having divined something of her tragedy, he accepted the definite limitations. Speculations concerning another he looked on as beside
the point. As far as possible he denied himself the indulgence in them. But
another thing he felt as well—the right to claim her, whether he exercised
that right or not.

Concerning his relationship with her, however, he did not deny specula-
tion, though somehow this time the perspective was too vast for him to
manage quite. There was a strange distance in it: he lost himself in remoteness. In either direction it ran into mists that were interminable, as
though veils and curtains lifted endlessly, melting into shadowy reaches beyond that baffled all inquiry. The horizons of his life had grown so huge.
This woman had introduced him to a scale of living that he could only gaze
at with wondering amazement and delight, too large as yet to conform to
the order that his nature sought. He could not properly find himself.

"It feels almost as if I've loved her before like this—yet somehow not
enough. That's what I've got to learn," was the kind of thought that came
to him, at odd moments only. The situation seemed so curiously familiar,
yet only half familiar. They were certainly made for one another, and the

tie between them had this deep touch of the inevitable about it that refused to go. That notion of the soul's advance in a spiral cropped up in his mind again. He saw her both coming nearer and retreating—as a moving figure against high light leaves the spectator uncertain whether it is advancing or retiring. He would have liked to talk to Tony all about it, for Tony would be sympathetic. He wanted a confidant and turned instinctively to his cousin.... *She* already understood more than he did, though perhaps not consciously, and therein lay the secret of her odd elusiveness. Yet, in another sense, his possession was incomplete because a part of her still lay unawakened. "I must love her more and more and more," he told himself. But, at the same time, he took it for granted that he was indispensable to her, as she was to him.

These flashes of perception, deeper than anything he had experienced in life hitherto, came occasionally while he waited in London for her return; and though puzzled—his straightforward nature disliked all mystery—he noted them with uncommon interest. Nothing, however, could prevent the rise upwards of the Wave that bore the situation on its breast. The affair swept him onwards; it was not to be checked or hindered. He resigned direction to its elemental tide.

The faint uneasiness, also, recurred from time to time, especially now that he was alone again. He attributed it to the unsatisfied desire in his heart, the knowledge that as yet he had no exclusive possession, and did not really own her; the sense of insecurity unsettled him, the feeling that she was open to capture by any one—"who understands and appreciates her better than I do," was the way he phrased it sometimes. He was troubled and uneasy because so much of her lay unresponsive to his touch—not needing him. While he was climbing up to reach her, another, with a stronger claim, might step in—step back—and seize her.

It made him smile a little even while he thought of it, for her truth and constancy were beyond all question. And then, suddenly, he traced the uneasiness to its source. There *was* "another" who had first claim upon her—who had it once, at any rate. Though at present some cloud obscured and negatived that claim, the cloud might lift, the situation change, the claim become paramount again, as once it surely had been paramount. And, disquieting though the possibility was, Tom was pleased with himself—he was so naïve and simple towards life for having discerned it clearly. He recognized the risk and thus felt half prepared in advance.... In another way it satisfied him too. With this dream-like suggestion that it all had happened before—he had always felt that a further detail was lacking to complete the scene he half remembered. Something, as yet, was wanting. And, this item needed to make the strange repetition of the scene fulfil itself precisely, the presence of "another."

Their intercourse, meanwhile, proved beyond words delightful during the following weeks, when, after her return from Warsaw, she kept her word and helped him in the prosaic business of furnishing his flat and settling down, as in a hundred other details of his daily life as well. All that they did and said together confirmed their dear relationship and established it beyond reproach. There was no question of anything false, illicit, requiring concealment: nothing to hide and no one to evade. In their own minds their innocence was so sure, indeed, that it was not once alluded to between them. It was impossible to look at her and doubt: nor could the most cynical suspect Tom Kelverdon of an undesirable intrigue with the wife of another man. His acquaintance, moreover, were not of the kind that harbored the usual "worldly" thoughts, he went little into society, whereas the comparatively few Londoners she knew were almost entirely—he discovered it by degrees—people whose welfare in one way or another she had earnestly at heart. It was a marvel to him, indeed, how she never wearied of helping ungrateful folk, for the wish to be of service seemed ingrained in her. Her first thought on making new acquaintances was always what she could do for them, not with money necessarily, but by "seeing" them in their proper *milieu* and planning to bring about the conditions they needed in order to realize themselves fully. Failure, discontent, unhappiness were due to wrong conditions more than to radical fault in the people themselves; once they "found themselves," the rest would follow. It amounted to a genius in her.

It seemed the artist instinct that sought this unselfish end rather than any religious tendency. She felt it ugly to see people at issue with their surroundings. Her religion was humanity, and had no dogmas. Even Tony Winslowe, now in England again, came in for his share of this sweet fashioning energy in her; much to his own bewilderment and to Tom's amusement....

The summer passed towards early autumn and London emptied, but it made no difference to them. Tom had urgent work to do and was absorbed in it, never forgetting for a moment that he was now a Partner in the Firm. He spent frequent week-ends at Madame Jaretzka's Kentish bungalow, where she had for companion at the moment an Irish cousin who, as Tom easily guessed, was also a dependant. This cousin had been invited with her child, Molly, for the summer holidays, and these summer holidays had run on into three months at least.

A tall, thin, angular woman, of uncertain manners and capricious temperament, Mrs. Haughstone had perhaps lived so long upon another's bounty that she had come to take her good fortune for granted, and permitted herself freely two cardinal indulgences—grumbling and jealousy. Having married unwisely, in order to better herself rather than because she loved, her shiftless husband had disgraced himself with an adventuress governess, leaving her with three children and something below £150 a year. Madame Jaretzka had stepped in to bring them together again: she provided schooling abroad, holidays, doctors, clothes and all she could devise by way of helping them "find themselves" again, and so turning their broken lives to good account. With the husband, sly, lazy, devoid of both pride and honesty, she could do little, and she was quite aware that he and his wife put their heads together to increase the flow of "necessaries" she generously supplied.

It was a sordid, commonplace story, sordidly treated by the soured and vindictive wife, whose eventual aims upon her savior's purse were too obvious to be mistaken. Even Tom perceived the fact without delay. He also perceived, behind the flattering tongue, an acid and suspicious jealousy that regarded new friends with ill-disguised alarm. Mrs. Haughstone thought of herself and her children before all else. She mistook the impersonal attitude of her benefactress for credulous weakness. A new friend was hostile to her shameless ambitions and disliked accordingly.... Tom scented an enemy the first time he met her. To him she expressed her disapproval of Tony, and *vice versa*, while to her hostess she professed she liked them both—"but": the "but" implying that men were selfish and ambitious creatures who thought only of their own advantage.

His country visits, therefore, were not made happier by the presence in the cottage of this woman and her child, but the manner in which the benefactress met the situation justified the respect he had felt first months before. It increased his love and admiration. Madame Jaretzka behaved unusually. That she grasped the position there could be no doubt, but her manner of dealing with it was unique. For when Mrs. Haughstone grumbled, Madame Jaretzka gave her more, and when Mrs. Haughstone yielded to jealousy, Madame Jaretzka smiled and said no word. She won her victories with further generosity.

"Another face that has to be rescued?" Tom permitted himself to say once, after an unfortunate scene in which his hostess had been subtly accused of favoritism to another child in the house. He could hardly suppress the annoyance and impatience that he felt.

"Oh, I never thought about it in that way," she answered with her little laugh, quite unruffled by what had happened. "The best way is to help them to—see themselves. Then they try to cure themselves." She laughed again, as though she had said a childish thing instead of something distinctly wise. "I can't *cure* them," she added. "I can only help."

Tom looked at her. "Help others to see themselves—as they are," he repeated slowly. "So that's how you do it, is it?" He reflected a moment. "That's being impersonal. You rouse no opposition that way. It's good."

"Is it?" she replied, as though guiltless of any conscious plan. "It seems the natural thing to do."

Then, as he was evidently preparing for discussion in his honest and laborious way, she stopped him with a look, smiling, sighing, and holding up her little finger warningly. He understood. Analysis and argument she avoided always; they obscured the essential thing; here was the intuitive method of grasping the solution the instant the problem was stated. Detailed examination exhausted her merely. And Tom obeyed that look, that threatening finger. In little things he invariably yielded, while in big things he remained firm, even obstinate, though without realizing it.

Her head inclined gracefully, acknowledging her victory. "That's one reason I love you, Tom," she told him as reward: "you're a boy on the surface and a man inside."

Tom saw beauty flash about her as she said it; emotion rose through him in a sudden tumult; he would have seized her, kissed her, crumpled her little self against his heart and held her there, but for the tantalizing truth that the thing he wanted would have escaped him in the very act. The loveliness he yearned for, craved, was not open to physical attack; it was a loveliness of the spirit, a bird, a star, a wild flower on some high pinnacle near the snow: to obtain it he must climb to where it soared above the earth— rise up to her.

He laughed and took her little finger in both hands. He felt awkward, big and clumsy, a giant trying to catch an elusive butterfly. "You turn us all round *that!*" he declared. "You turn her," nodding towards the door, "and me," kissing the tip quickly, "and Tony too. Only she and Tony don't know you twiddle them—and I do."

She let him kiss her hand, but when he drew nearer, trying to set his lips upon the arm her summer dress left bare, she put up her face instead and kissed him lightly on the cheek. Her free hand made a caressing gesture across his neck and shoulder, as she stood on tiptoe to reach him. The mother in her, not the woman, caressed him dearly. It was wonderful; but the surge of mingled emotions clouded something in his brain, and a string of words came tumbling out in a fire of joy and pain. "You're a queen and a conqueror," he said, longing to seize her, yet holding himself back strongly. "Somewhere I'm your helpless slave, but somewhere I'm your master." The protective sense came up in him. "It's too delicious! I'm in a dream! Lettice," he whispered, "it's my Wave! The Wave is behind it! It's behind us both!"

For an instant she half closed her eyelids in the way she knew both pleased and frightened him. Invariably this gave her the advantage. He felt her above him when she looked like this, he kneeling with hands outstretched, yearning to be raised to where she stood. "You're a baby, a poet and a man rolled into a dear big boy," she said quickly, moving towards the door away from him. "And now I must go and get my garden hat, for it's time to meet Tony and Moyra at the train, and as you have so much surplus energy to-day we'll walk through the woods instead of going in the motor." She waved her hand and vanished behind the door. He heard the patter of her feet as she ran upstairs.

He went to the open window, lit his pipe, leaned out with his head among the climbing roses, and thought of many things. Great joy was in him, but behind it, far down where he could not reach it quite, hid a gnawing pain that was obscure uneasiness. Pictures came floating across his mind, rising and falling, sometimes rushing hurriedly; he saw things and faces mixed, his own and hers chief among them. Her little finger pointed to a star. He sighed, he wondered, he half prayed. Would he ever understand, rise to her level, possess her for his very own? She seemed so far beyond him. It was only part of her he touched.

The faces fluttered and looked into his own, one among them an imagined face—the husband's. It was a face with light blue eyes, moreover. He saw Tony's too, frank, laughing, irresponsible, and the face of the Irish girl who was Tony's latest passion. Tony could settle down to no one for long. Tom remembered suddenly his remark at Zakopané months ago, that the bee never sipped the last drop of honey from the flower.... His thoughts tumbled and flew in many directions, yet all at once. Life seemed very full and marvelous; it had never seemed so intense before; it bore him onwards, upwards, forwards, with a rush beyond all possible control and guidance. He acknowledged a rather delicious sense of helplessness. The Wave was everywhere behind and under him. It was sweeping him along.

Then thought returned to Tony and the Irish girl who were coming down for the Sunday, and he smiled to himself as he recalled his cousin's ardent admiration at a theater party a few nights ago in town. Tony had something that naturally attracted women, dominating them too easily. Was he heartless a little in the business? Would he never, like Tom, settle down with one? His thought passed to the latest capture: there were signs, indeed, that here Tony was caught at last.

For Tom, Tony, and Madame Jaretzka formed an understanding trio, and there were few expeditions, town or country, of which the lively bird-enthusiast did not form an active member. Tony took it all very lightly, unaware of any serious intention behind the pleasant invitations. Tom was amused by it. He looked forward to his cousin's visit now. He was feeling the need of a confidant, and Tony might so admirably fill the rôle. It was curious, a little: Tom often felt that he wanted to confide in Tony, yet somehow or other the confidences were never actually made. There was something in Tony that invited that free, purging confidence which is a need of every human being. It was so easy to tell things, difficult things, to this careless, sympathetic being; yet Tom never passed the frontier into definite revelation. At the last moment he invariably held back.

Thought passed to his hostess, already maneuvering to help Tony "find himself." It amused Tom, even while he gave his willing assistance; for Tony was of evasive, slippery material, like a fluid that, pressed in one given direction, resists and runs away into several others. "He scatters himself too much," she remarked, "and it's a pity; there's waste." Tom laughed, thinking of his episodic love affairs. "I didn't mean that," she added, smiling with him; "I meant generally. He's full of talent and knowledge. His power over women is natural, but it comes of mere brilliance. If all that were concentrated instead, he would do something real; he might be extraordinarily effective in life. Yes, Tom, I mean it." But Tom, though he smiled, agreed with her, feeling rather flattered that she liked his cousin.

"But he breaks too many hearts," he said lightly, thinking of his last conquest, and then added, hardly knowing why he said it, "By the by, did you ever notice his hands?"

The way she quickly looked up at him proved that she divined his meaning. But the glance had a flash of something that escaped him.

"You're very observant, Tommy," she said evasively. It seemed impossible for her to say a disparaging thing of anybody. She invariably picked out and emphasized the best. "You don't admire them?"

"Do *you*, Lettice?"

She paused for an imperceptible second, then smiled. "I rather like big rough hands in a man—perhaps," she said without any particular interest, "though—in a way—they frighten me sometimes. Tony's are ugly, but there's power in them." And she placed her own small gloved hand upon his arm. "He's rather irresponsible, I know," she added gently, "but he'll grow out of that in time. He's beginning to improve already."

"You see, he's got no mother," Tom observed.

"No wife either—yet," she added with a laugh.

"Or work," put in Tom, with a touch of self-praise, and thinking of his own position in the world. Her interest in Tony had the effect of making himself seem worthier, more important. This fine woman, who judged people from so high a standpoint, had picked out—himself! He had an absurd yet delightful feeling as though Tony was their child, and the perfectly natural way she took him under her mothering wing stirred an admiring pity in him.

Then as they walked together through the fragrant pine-woods to the station, an incident at a recent theater party rose before his memory. Tony and his Amanda had been with them. The incident in question had left a singular impression on his mind, though why it emerged now, as they wandered through the quiet wood, he could not tell. It had occurred a week or two ago. He now saw it again—in a tenth of the time it takes to tell:

The scene was laid in ancient Egypt, and while the play was commonplace, the elaborate production—scenery, dresses, atmosphere—were good. But Tom, unable to feel interest in the trivial and badly acted story, had felt interest in another thing he could not name. There was a subtle charm, a delicate glamour about it as of immensely old romance, but some lost romance of very far away. Yet, whether this charm was due to the stage effects or to themselves, sitting there in the stalls together, escaped him. For in some singular way, the party, his hostess certainly, seemed to interpenetrate the play itself. She, above all, and Tony vaguely, seemed inseparable from what he gazed at, heard and felt.

Continually, he caught himself thinking how delightful it was to know himself next to Madame Jaretzka, so close that he shared her atmosphere, her perfume, touched her even: that their minds were engaged intimately together watching the same scene; and also, that on her other side, sat Tony, affectionate, whimsical, fascinating Tony, whom they were trying to help "find himself"; and that he, again, was next to a girl he liked. The harmonious feeling of the four was pleasurable to Tom. He felt himself, moreover, an important and indispensable item in its composition. It was vague; he did not attempt to analyze it as self-flattery, as vanity, as pride—he was aware, merely, that he felt very pleased with himself and so with everybody else. It was gratifying to sit at the head of the group; everybody could see how beautiful *she* was; the dream of exclusive ownership stole over him more definitely than ever before. "She's chosen *me!* She needs me—a woman like that!"

The audience, the lights, the color, the music influenced him. It seemed he caught something from the crude human passion that was being ranted on the stage and transferred it unconsciously into his relations with the party he belonged to, but, above all, into his relationship with her—and with another. But he refused to let his mind dwell upon that other. He found himself thinking instead of the divine tenderness that was in her, yet at the same time of her elusiveness and the curious pain it caused him. Whence came, he wondered, the sweet and cruel flavor? It seemed like a memory of something suffered long ago, the sweetness in it true and exquisite, the cruelty an error on his own part somehow. The old hint of uneasiness, the strange, rich pain he had known in boyhood, stole faintly over him; its first and immediate effect heightening the sense of dim, old-world romance already present....

And he had turned cautiously to look at her. She was leaning forward a little as though the play absorbed her, and the attitude startled him. It caused him almost a definite shock. The face had pain in it.

She was not aware that he stared: her attention was fastened upon the stage; but the eyes were fixed, the little mouth was fixed as well, the lips compressed; and all her features wore this expression of curious pain. There was sternness in them, something almost hard. He watched her for some minutes, surprised and fascinated. It came over him that he almost knew what that was in her mind. Another moment and he would discover it— when, past her profile, he caught his cousin's eyes peering across at him. Tony had felt the direction of his glance and had looked round: and Tony— mischievously—winked!

The spell was broken. In that instant, however, through the heated air of the crowded stalls already weighted with sickly artificial perfumes, there reached him faintly, as from very far away, another and a subtler perfume, something of elusive fragrance in it. It was very poignant, instinct as with forgotten associations. It was the Whiff. It came, it went; but it was unmistakable. And he connected it, as by some instantaneous certitude, with the play—with Egypt.

"What do you think of it, Lettice?" he had whispered, nodding towards the stage.

She turned with a start. She came back. The expression of pain flashed instantly away. She had evidently not been thinking of the performance. "It's not much, Tom, is it? But I like the scenery. It makes me feel strange somewhere—the change that comes over me in Egypt. We'll be there together—some day." She leaned over with her lips against his ear.

And there was significance in the commonplace words, he thought—a significance her whisper did not realize, and certainly did not intend.

"All three of us," he rejoined before he knew what he meant exactly.

And she nodded hurriedly. Either she agreed, or else she had not heard him. He did not insist, he did not repeat, he sat there wondering why on earth he said the thing. A touch of pain pricked him like an insect's sting, but a pain he could not account for. His blood, at the same time, leaped as she bent her face so near to his own. He felt his heart swell as he looked into her eyes. Her beauty astonished him; in this twilight of the theater it glowed and burned like a veiled star. He fancied—it was the trick of the half-light, of course—she had grown darker and that a dusky flush lay on her cheeks.

"What were you thinking about?" he whispered lower again, changing the sentence slightly. And, as he asked it, he saw Tony still watching him, two seats away. It annoyed him; he drew his head back a little so that her face concealed him.

"I don't know," she whispered back; "nothing in particular." She put her gloved hand stealthily towards him and touched his knee. The gesture, he felt, was intended to supplement the words. For the first time in his life he did not quite believe her. The thought was odious, but not to be denied. It merely flashed across him, however. He forgot it instantly.

"Seems oddly familiar somehow," he said, "doesn't it?"

Again she nodded, smiling, as she gazed for a moment first into one eye, then into the other, then turned away to watch the stage. And abruptly, as she did so, the entire feeling vanished, the mood evaporated, her expression was normal once more, and he fixed his attention on the stupid play.

He turned his interest into other channels; he would take his party on to supper. He did so. Yet an impression remained—the impression that the Wave had come nearer, higher, that it was rising and gaining impetus, accumulating mass, momentum, power. The gay supper could not dissipate that, nor could the happy ten minutes in a taxi, when he drove her to her door, decrease or weaken it. She was very tired. They spoke little, he remembered; she gave him a gentle touch as the cab drew up, and the few things she said had entirely to do with his comfort in his flat. He felt in that touch and in those tender questions the mother only. The woman, it suddenly occurred to him, had gone elsewhere. He had never had it, never even claimed it. A deep sense of loneliness touched him for a moment....

Why the scene came back to him now as they walked slowly through the summery pine-wood he knew not. He caught himself thinking vividly of Egypt suddenly, of being in Egypt with her—and with another. But on that other he refused to let thought linger. Of set purpose he chose Tony in that other's place. He saw it in a picture: he and she together helping Tony, she and Tony equally helping him. It passed before him merely, a glowing colored picture set in high light against the heavy background of these English fir-woods and the Kentish sky. Whether it came towards him or retreated, he could not say. It was very brief, instantaneous almost. The memory of the play, with its numerous attendant correlations, rose up, then vanished.

"Give me your arm, Tom, you mighty giant: these pine-needles are so slippery." He felt her hand creep in and rest upon his muscles, and a glow of boyish pride came with it. In her summer dress of white, her big garden hat and flowing violet veil, she looked adorable. He liked the long white gauntlet gloves. The shadows of the trees became her well: against the thick dark trunks she seemed slim and dainty as a flower that the breeze bent over towards him. "You're so horribly big and strong," she said, and her eyes, full of expression, glanced up at him. He watched her little feet in the neat, white shoes peep out in turn as they walked along; her fingers pressed his arm. He tried to take her parasol, but she prevented him, saying it was her only weapon of defense against a giant, "and there is a gi-

ant in this forest, though only a baby one perhaps!" He felt the mother in
her pour over him in a flood of tenderness that blessed and soothed and
comforted. It was as if a divine and healing power streamed from her into
him.

"And what *were* you thinking about, Tom?" she inquired teasingly. "You
haven't said a word for a whole five minutes!"

"I was thinking of Egypt," he answered with truth.

She looked up quickly.

"I'm to go out in December," he went on. "I told you. It was decided at
our last Board Meeting."

She said she remembered. "But it's funny," she added, "because I was
thinking of Egypt too just then—thinking of the Nile, my river with the
floating faces."

The week-end visit was typical of many others; Mrs. Haughstone, seeing safety in numbers possibly, was pleasant on the surface, Molly deflecting
most of her poisoned darts towards herself; while Tom and Tony shared
the society of their unconventional hostess with boyish enjoyment. Tom
modified the air of ownership he indulged when alone with her, and no one
need have noticed that there was anything more between them than a
hearty, understanding friendship. Tony, for instance, may have guessed the
true situation, or, again, he may not; for he said no word, nor showed the
smallest hint by word, by gesture, or by silence—most significant betrayal
of all—that he was aware of any special tie. Though a keen observer, he
gave no sign. "She's an interesting woman, Tom," he remarked lightly, yet
with enthusiasm once, "and a rare good hostess—a woman in a thousand,
I declare. We make a famous trio. As you've got that Assouan job we'll have
some fun next winter in Egypt, eh?"

And Tom, pleased and secretly flattered by the admiration, tried to make
his confidences. Unless Tony had liked her this would have been impossible. But they formed such a natural, happy trio together, giving the lie to
the hoary proverb, that Tom felt it was permissible to speak of her to his
sympathetic cousin. Already they had laughingly discussed the half-forgotten acquaintanceship begun in the *dahabieh* on the Nile, Tony making
a neat apology by declaring to her, "Beautiful women blind me so,
Madame Jaretzka, that I invariably forget all lesser details. And that's why
I told Tom you were a Russian."

On this particular occasion, too, it was made easier because Tony had
asked his cousin's opinion about the Irish girl, invited for his special benefit. "I was never so disappointed in my life," he said in his convincing yet
airy way. "She looked so wonderful the other night. It was the evening
dress, I suppose. You should always see a girl first in the daytime; the day-

light self is the real self." And Tom, amused by the irresponsible attitude towards the sex, replied that the right woman looked herself in any dress because it was as much a part of her as her own skin. "Yes," said Tony, "it's the thing inside the skin that counts, of course; you're right; the rest is only a passing glamour. But friendship with a woman is the best of all, for friendship grows insensibly into the best kind of love. It's a delightful feeling," he added sympathetically, "that kind of friendship. Independent of what they wear!"

He enjoyed his pun and laughed. "I say, Tom," he went on suddenly with a certain inconsequence, "have you ever met the Prince—Madame Jaretzka's husband—by the way? I wonder what he's like." He looked up carelessly and raised his eyebrows.

"No," replied Tom in a quiet tone, "but I—exp—hope to some day."

"I think he ran away and left her, or something," continued the other. "He's dead, anyhow, to all intents and purposes. But I've been wondering lately. I'll be bound there was ill-treatment. She looks so sad sometimes. The other night at the theater I was watching her—"

"That Egyptian play?" broke in Tom.

"Yes; it was bad enough to make any one look sad, wasn't it? But it was curious all the same—"

"I didn't mean the badness."

"Nor did I. It was odd. There was atmosphere in spite of everything."

"I thought you were too occupied to notice the performance," Tom hinted.

Tony laughed good naturedly. "I was a bit taken up, I admit," he said. "But there was something curious all the same. I kept seeing you and our hostess on the stage—"

"In Egypt!"

"In a way, yes." He hesitated.

"Odd," said his cousin briefly.

"Very. It seemed—there was some one else who ought to have been there as well as you two. Only he never came on."

Tom made no comment. Was this thought-transference, he wondered?

The natural sympathy between them furnished the requisite conditions certainly.

"He never came on," continued Tony, "and I had the queer feeling that he was being kept off on purpose, that he was busy with something else, but that the moment he came on the play would get good and interesting— real. Something would happen. And it was then I noticed Madame Jaretzka—"

"And me, too, I suppose," Tom put in, half amused, half serious. There was an excited yet uneasy feeling in him.

"Chiefly her, I think. And she looked so sad,—it struck me suddenly. D'you know, Tom," he went on more earnestly, "it was really quite curious. I got the feeling that we three were watching that play together from above it somewhere, looking down on it—sort of from a height above—"

"Above," exclaimed his cousin. There was surprise in him—surprise at himself. That faint uneasiness increased. He realized that to confide in Tony was impossible. But why?

"H'm," Tony went on in a reflective way as if half to himself. "I may have seen it before and forgotten it." Then he looked up at his cousin. "And what's more—that we three, as we watched it, knew the same thing together—knew that we were waiting for another chap to come on, and that when he came the silly piece would turn suddenly interesting, dramatic in a true sense, only tragedy instead of comedy. Did *you*, Tom?" he asked abruptly, screwing tip his eyes and looking quite serious a moment.

Tom had no answer ready, but his cousin left no time for answering.

"And the fact is," he continued, lowering his voice, "I had the feeling the other chap we were waiting for was *him*."

Tom was too interested to smile at the grammar. "You mean—her husband?" he said quietly. He did not like the turn the talk had taken; it pleased him to talk of her, but he disliked to bring the absent husband in. There was trouble in him as he listened.

"Possibly it was," he added a trifle stiffly. Then ashamed of his feeling towards his imaginative cousin, he changed his manner quickly. He went up and stood behind him by the open window. "Tony, old boy, we're together somehow in this thing," he began impulsively; "I'm sure of it." Then the words stuck. "If ever I want your help—"

"Rather, Tom," said the other with enthusiasm, yet puzzled, turning with an earnest expression in his frank blue eyes. In another moment, like two boys swearing eternal friendship they would have shaken hands. Tom again felt the impulse to make the confidences that desire for sympathy prompted, and again realized that it was difficult, yet that he would accomplish it. Indeed, he was on the point of doing so, relieving his mind of the childhood story, the accumulated details of Wave and Whiff and Sound and Eyes, the singular Montreux meeting, the strange medley of joy and uneasiness as well, all in fact without reserve—when a voice from the lawn came floating into the room and broke the spell. It lifted him sharply to another plane. He felt glad suddenly that he had not spoken—afterwards, he felt very glad. It was not right in regard to her, he realized.

"You're never ready, you boys," their hostess was saying, "and Miss Monnigan declares that men always wait to be fetched. The lunch-baskets are all in, and the motor's waiting."

"We didn't want to be in the way," cried Tony gaily, ever ready with an answer first. "We're both so big and clumsy. But we'll make the fire in the woods and do the work that requires mere strength without skill all right." He leaped out of the window to join them, while Tom went by the door to fetch his cap and overcoat. Turning an instant he saw the three figures on the lawn standing in the sunlight, Madame Jaretzka with a loose, rough motor-coat over her white dress, a rose at her throat and the long blue veil he loved wound round her hair and face. He saw her eyes look up at Tony and heard her chiding him. "You've been talking mischief in there together," she was saying laughingly, giving him a searching glance in play, though the tone had meaning in it. "We were talking of you," swore Tony, "and you," he added, turning by way of polite after-thought to the girl. And one of his big hands he laid for a moment upon Madame Jaretzka's arm.

Tom turned sharply and hurried on into the hall. The first thought in his mind was how tender and gentle Madame Jaretzka looked standing in the sunshine, her eyes turned up at Tony. His second thought was vaguer; he felt glad that Tony admired and liked her so. The third was vaguer still: Tony didn't really care for the girl a bit and was only amusing himself with her, but Madame Jaretzka would protect her and see that no harm came of it. She could protect the whole world. That was her genius.

In a moment these three thoughts flashed through him, but while the last two vanished as quickly as they came, the first lingered like sunlight in him. It remained and grew and filled his heart, and all that day it kept close by him—her love, her comfort, her mothering compassion.

And Tom felt glad for some reason that his confidences to Tony after all had been interrupted and prevented. They remained thus interrupted and prevented until the end, even when the "other" came upon the scene, and above all while that "other" stayed. It all seemed curiously inevitable.

CHAPTER XII

The last few weeks of September they were much alone together, for Mrs. Haughstone had gone back to her husband's tiny house at Kew, Molly to the Dresden school, and Tony somewhere into space—northern Russia, he said, to watch the birds beginning to leave.

Meanwhile, with deepening of friendship, and experiences whose ordinariness was raised into significance because this woman shared them with him, Tom saw the summer fade in England and usher in the longer evenings. Light and heat waned from the sighing year; winds, charged with the memory of roses, took the paling skies; the swallows whispered together of the southern tour. New stars swam into their autumnal places, and the

Milky Way came majestically to its own. He watched the curve of it on moonless nights, pouring its grand river across the heavens. And in the heart of its soft brilliance he saw Cygnus, cruciform and shining, immersed in the white foam of the arching wave.

He noticed these things now, as once long ago, in early boyhood, because a time of separation was at hand. His yearning now was akin to his yearning then—it left a chasm in his soul that beauty alone could help to fill. At fifteen he was thirty-five, as now at thirty-five he was fifteen again.

Lettice was not, indeed, at a Finishing School across the Channel, but she was shortly going to Warsaw to spend October with her husband, and in November she was to sail for Egypt from Trieste. Tom was to follow in December, so a separation of three months was close at hand. "But a necessary separation," she said, one evening as they motored home beneath the stars, "is always bearable and strengthening; we shall both be occupied with things that must—I mean, things we ought to do. It's the needless separations that are hard to bear." He replied that it would be wonderful meeting again and pretending they were strangers. He tried to share her mood, her point of view with honesty. "Yes," she answered, "only that wouldn't be quite true, because you and I can never be separated—really. The curve of the earth may hide us from each other's sight like that"—and she pointed to the sinking moon, "but we feel the pull just the same."

They leaned back among the cushions, sharing the mysterious beauty of the night-sky in their hearts. They lowered their voices as though the hush upon the world demanded it. The little things they said seemed suddenly to possess a significance they could not account for quite and yet admitted.

He told her that the Milky Way was at its best these coming months, and that Cygnus would be always visible on clear nights. "We'll look at that and remember," he said half playfully. "The astronomers say the Milky Way is the very ground-plan of the Universe. So we all come out of it. And you're Cygnus." She called him sentimental, and he admitted that perhaps he was. "I don't like this separation," he said bluntly. In his mind he was thinking that the Milky Way had his wave in it, and that its wondrous arch, like his life and hers, rose out of the "sea" below the world. In that sea no separation was possible.

"But it's not that that makes you suddenly poetic, Tom. It's something else."

"Is it?" he answered. A whisper of pain went past him across the night. He felt something coming; he was convinced she felt it too. But he could not name it.

"The Milky Way is a stream as well as a wave. You say it rises in the autumn—?" She leaned nearer to him a little.

"But it's seen at its best a little later—in the winter, I believe."

"We shall be in Egypt then," she mentioned. He could have sworn she would say those very words.

"Egypt," he repeated slowly. "Yes—in Egypt."

And a little shiver came over him, so slight, so quickly gone again, that he hoped it was imperceptible. Yet she had noticed it.

"Why, Tom, don't you like the idea?"

"I wonder—" he began, then changed the sentence—"I wonder what it will be like. I have an enormous desire to see it—I know that."

He heard her laugh under her breath a little. What came over them both in that moment he couldn't say. There was a sense of tumult in him somewhere, a hint of pain, of menace too. Her laughter, slight as it was, jarred upon him. She was not feeling quite what he felt—this flashed, then vanished.

"You don't sound enthusiastic," she said calmly.

"I am, though. Only—I had a feeling—" He broke off. The truth was he couldn't describe that feeling even to himself.

"Tom, dear, my dear one—" she began, then stopped. She also stopped an impulsive movement towards him. She drew back her sentence and her arms. And Tom, aware of a rising passion in him he might be unable to control, turned his face away a moment. Something clutched at his heart as with cruel pincers. A chill followed close upon the shiver. He felt a moment of keen shame, yet knew not exactly why he felt it.

"I am a sentimental ass!" he exclaimed abruptly with a natural laugh. His voice was tender. He turned again to her. "I believe I've never properly grown up." And before he could restrain himself he drew her towards him, seized her hand and kissed it like a boy. It was that kiss, combined with her blocked sentence and uncompleted gesture, rather than any more passionate expression of their love for one another, that he remembered throughout the empty months to follow.

But there was another reason, too, why he remembered it. For she wore a silk dress, and the arm against his ear produced a momentary rustling that brought back the noise in the Zakopané bedroom when the frozen branch had scraped the outside wall. And with the Sound, absent now so long, the old strange uneasiness revived acutely. For that caressing gesture, that kiss, that phrase of love that blocked its own final utterance brought back the strange rich pain.

In the act of giving them, even while he felt her touch and held her within his arms—she evaded him and went far away into another place where he could not follow her. And he knew for the first time a singular emotion that seemed like a faint, distant jealousy that stirred in him, yet a spiritual jealousy... and of some one he had never even seen.

They lingered a moment in the garden to enjoy the quiet stars and see the moon go down below the pinewood. The tense mood of half an hour ago in the motor car had evaporated of its own accord apparently.

A conversation that followed emphasized this elusive emotion in him, because it somehow increased the remoteness of the part of her he could not claim. She mentioned that she was taking Mrs. Haughstone with her to Egypt in November; it again exasperated him; such unselfishness he could not understand. The invitation came, moreover, upon what Tom felt was a climax of shameless behavior. For Madame Jaretzka had helped the family with money that, to save their pride, was to be considered lent. The husband had written gushing letters of thanks and promises that—Tom had seen these letters—could hardly have deceived a schoolgirl. Yet a recent legacy, which rendered a part repayment possible, had been purposely concealed, with the result that yet more money had been "lent" to tide them over nonexistent or invented difficulties.

And now, on the top of this, Madame Jaretzka not only refused to divulge that the legacy was known to her, but even proposed an expensive two months' holiday to the woman who was tricking her.

Tom objected strongly for two reasons; he thought it foolish kindness, and he did not want her.

"You're too good to the woman, far too good," he said. But his annoyance was only increased by the firmness of the attitude that met him. "No, Tom; you're wrong. They'll find out in time that I know, and see themselves as they are."

"You forgive everything to everybody," he observed critically. "It's too much."

She turned round upon him. Her attitude was a rebuke, and feeling rebuked, he did not like it. For though she did not quote "until seventy times seven," she lived it.

"When she sees herself sly and treacherous like that, she'll understand," came the answer, "she'll get her own forgiveness."

"Her own forgiveness!"

"The only real kind. If I forgive, it doesn't alter her. But if she understands and feels shame and makes up her mind not to repeat—that's forgiving herself. She really changes then."

Tom gasped inwardly. This was a level of behavior where he found the air somewhat rarefied. He saw the truth of it, but had no answer ready.

"Remorse and regret," she went on, "only make one ineffective in the present. It's looking backwards, instead of looking forwards."

He felt something very big in her as she said it, holding his eyes firmly with her own. To have the love of such a woman was, indeed, a joy and wonder. It was a keen happiness to feel that he, Tom Kelverdon, had obtained it. His admiration for himself, and his deep, admiring love for her rose side by side. He did not recognize the flattery of self in this attitude. The simplicity in her baffled him.

"I could forgive *you* anything, Lettice!" he cried.

"Could you?" she said gently. "If so, you really love me."

It was not the doubt in her voice that overwhelmed him then; she never indulged in hints. It was a doubt in himself, not that he loved her, but that his love was not yet big enough, unselfish enough, sufficiently large and deep to be worthy of this exquisite soul beside him. Perhaps it was realizing he could not yet possess her spirit that made him seize the precious little body that contained it. Nothing could stop him. He took her in his arms and held her till she became breathless. The passionate moment expressed real spiritual yearning. And she knew it. She did not struggle, yet neither did she respond. They stood upon different levels somehow.

"There'll be nothing left to love," she gasped, "if you do that often!" She released herself quietly, tidying her hair and putting her hat straight while she smiled at him. Her dark veil had caught in his tie-pin. She disentangled it, her hands touching his mouth as she did so. He kissed them gently, bending his head down with an air of repentance.

"My God, Lettice—you're precious to me!" he stammered.

But even as he said it, even while he still felt her soft cheeks against his lips, her frail unresisting figure within his arms, there came this pang of sudden pain that was so acute it frightened him. There was something impersonal in her attitude that alarmed him. What was it? He was helpless to understand it. The excitement in his blood obscured inner perception.... Such tempestuous moments were rare enough between them, and when they came he felt that she endured them rather than responded. He was aware of a touch of shame in himself. But this pain? Even while he held her it seemed again that she escaped him because of the heights she lived on, yet, partly, too, because of the innocence which had not yet eaten of the tree of knowledge...

Was that, then, the lack in her? Had she yet to learn that the spiritual dare not be divorced wholly from the physical and that the divine blending of the two in purity of heart alone brings safety?

She slipped from his encircling arms and—rose. He struggled after her. But that air he could not breathe. She was too far above him. She had to stoop to meet the passionate man in him that sought to seize and hold her. She had—the earlier phrase returned—come back to fetch him. He did not really love yet as he ought to love. He loved himself—in her; selfishly somehow, somewhere. But this thought he did not capture wholly. It cast a shadow merely and was gone.

Somewhere, too, there was jealous resentment in him. He could not feel himself indispensable to a woman who occupied a pinnacle.

His cocksureness wavered a little before the sharp attack. Pang after pang stung him shrewdly, stung his pride, his confidence, his vanity, shaking the platform on which he stood till each separate plank trembled and the sense of security grew less.

But the confusion in his heart and mind bewildered him. It was all so strange and incomprehensible; he could not understand it. He knew she was true and loyal, her purity beyond reproach, her elusiveness not calculated or intended, yet that somewhere, somehow she could do without him, and that if he left her she—almost—would have neither remorse nor regret. She would just accept it and—forgive....

And he thought suddenly with an intense bitterness that amazed him— of the husband. The thought of that "other" who had yet to come afflicted him desperately. When he met those light-blue eyes of the Wave he would surely know them...! He felt again the desire to seek counsel and advice from another, some one of his own sex, a sympathetic and understanding soul like Tony. The turmoil in him was beyond elucidation: thoughts and emotions of nameless kind combined to produce a fluid state of insecurity he could not explain. As usual, however, there emerged finally the solid fact which seemed now the keynote of his character; at least, he invariably fell back upon it for support against these occasional storms: "She has singled me out; she can't really do without me; we're necessary to each other; I'm safe." The rest he dismissed as half realized only and therefore not quite real. His position with her was unique, of course, something the world could not possibly understand, and, while resenting what he called the "impersonal" attitude in her, he yet knew that it was precisely this impersonal attitude that justified their love. Their love, in fine, was proved spiritual thereby. They were in the "sea" together. Invariably in the end he blamed himself.

The rising Wave, it seemed, was bringing up from day to day new, unexpected qualities from the depths within him, just as it brings up mud and gravel from the ground-bed of the shore. He felt it driving him forward with increasing speed and power. With an irresistible momentum that left him helpless, it was hurrying him along towards the moment when it would lower its crest again towards the earth—and break.

He knew now where the smothering crash would come, where he would finally meet the singular details of his boyhood's premonition face to face,— the Sound, the Whiff, the other pair of Eyes. They awaited him—in Egypt. In Egypt, at last, he would find the entire series, recognize each item. He would also discover the nature of the wave that was neither of water nor of snow....

Yet, strange to say, when he actually met the pair of light-blue eyes, he did not recognize them. He encountered the face to which they belonged, but was not warned. While fulfilling its prophecy, the premonition failed, of course, to operate.

For premonitions are a delicate matter, losing their power in the act of justifying themselves. To prevent their fulfilment were to stultify their existence. Between a spiritual warning and its material consummation there is but a friable and gossamer alliance. Had he recognized, he might possibly have prevented; whereas the deeper part of him unconsciously invited and said, Come.

And so, not recognizing the arrival of the other pair of eyes, Tom, when he met them, knew himself attracted instead of repelled. Far from being warned, he knew himself drawn towards their owner by natural sympathy, as towards some one whose deep intrusion into his inner life was necessary to its fuller realization—the tumultuous breaking of the rapidly accumulating Wave.

PART III

CHAPTER XIII

The weeks that followed seemed both brief and long to Tom. The separation he felt keenly, though as a breathing spell the interval was even welcome in a measure. Since the days at Montreux he had been living intensely, swept along by a movement he could not control: now he could pause and think a moment. He tried to get the bird's-eye view in which alone details are seen in their accurate relations and proportions. There was much that perplexed his plain, straightforward nature. But the more he thought, the more puzzled he became, and in the end he resigned himself happily to the great flow of life that was sweeping him along. He was distinctly conscious of being "swept along." What was going to happen, would happen. He wondered, watched and waited. The idea of Egypt, meanwhile, thrilled him with a curious anticipation each time he thought of it. And he thought of it a good deal.

He received letters from Warsaw, but they told nothing of her life there: she referred vaguely to duties whose afflicting nature he half guessed now; and the rest was filled with loving solicitude for his welfare. Even through the post she mothered him absurdly. He felt his life now based upon her. Her love was indispensable to him.

The last letters—from Vienna and Trieste—were full of a tenderness most comforting, and he felt relief that she had "finished with Warsaw," as he put it. His own last letter was timed to catch her steamer. "You have all my love," he wrote, "but you can give what you can spare to Tony, as he's in Egypt by now, and tell him I shall be out a month from to-day. Everything goes well here. I'm to have full charge of the work at Assouan. The Firm has put everything in my hands, but there won't be much to do at first, and I shall be with you at Luxor a great deal. I'm looking forward to Egypt too—immensely. I believe all sorts of wonderful things are going to happen to us there."

He was very pleased with himself, and very pleased with her, and very pleased with everything. The wave of his life was rising still triumphantly.

He kept her Warsaw letters and re-read them frequently. She wrote admirably. Mrs. Haughstone, it seemed, complained about everything, from the cabin and hotel room "which, she declares, are never so good as my own," to her position as an invited guest, "which she accepts as though she favored me by coming, thinking herself both chaperone and indispensable companion. How little some people realize that no one is ever really indispensable." And the first letter from Egypt told him to come out quickly and "help me keep her in her place, as only a man can do. Tony wonders why you're so long about it." It pleased him very much, and as the time approached for leaving, his spirits rose; indeed, he reached Marseilles much in the mood of a happy, confident boy who has passed all exams, and is off upon a holiday most thoroughly deserved.

There had been time for three or four letters from Luxor, and he read them in the train as he hurried along from Geneva towards the south, leaving the snowy Jura hills behind him. "Those are the blue mountains we watched from Montreux together in the spring," he said to himself, looking out of the window. "Soon, in Egypt, we shall watch the Desert and the Nile instead." And, remembering that dream-like, happy time of their earliest acquaintance, his heart beat in delighted anticipation. He could think of nothing else but her. Those Montreux days seemed years ago instead of a brief six months. What a lot he had to tell her, how much they would have to talk about. Life, indeed, was rich and full. He was a lucky man; yet—he deserved it all. Belief and confidence in himself increased. He gazed out of the window, thinking happily as the scenery rushed by.... Then he came back to the letters and read them over yet once again; he almost knew them now by heart; he opened his bag and read the Warsaw letters too. Then, putting them all away, he lay back in his corner and tried to sleep. The express train seemed so slow, but the steamer would seem slower still.... Thoughts and memories passed idly through his brain, grew mingled and confused; his eyes were closed; he fell into a doze: he almost slept—when something rose into his drowsy mind and made him suddenly wakeful.

What was it? He didn't know. It had vanished as soon as it appeared. But the drowsy mood had passed, the desire to sleep was gone. There was impatience in him, the keen wish to be in Egypt—immediately. He cursed the slow means of travel, longed to be out there, on the spot, with her and Tony. Her last letters had been full of descriptions of the place and people, of Tony and his numerous friends, his kindness in introducing her to the most interesting among them, their picnics together on the Nile and in the Desert, visits to the famous sites of tomb and temple, in particular of an all-night bivouac somewhere and the sunrise over the Theban hills…. Tom, as he read it all, felt this keen impatience to be sharing it with them; he was out of it; oh, how he would enjoy it all when he got there! The words "Theban hills" called up a vivid and stimulating picture in particular.

But it was not this that chased the drowsy mood and made him wakeful. It was the letters themselves, something he had not noticed hitherto, something that had escaped him as he first read them one by one. Indefinable, it hid between the lines. Only on reading the series as a whole was it noticeable at all. He wondered. He asked himself vague questions.

Opening his bag again, he went through the letters in the order of their arrival; then put them back inside the elastic ring with a sensation of relief and a happy sigh. He had discovered the faint, elusive impression that had made him wakeful, but in discovering it had satisfied himself that it was imagination—caused by the increasing impatience of his impetuous heart. For it had seemed to him that he was aware of a change, though so slight as to be scarcely perceptible, and certainly not traceable to actual words or sentences. It struck him that the Warsaw letters felt the separation more keenly, more poignantly, than the Egyptian letters. This seemed due rather to omissions in the latter than to anything else that he could name, for while the Warsaw letters spoke frequently of the separation, of her longing to see him close, those from Luxor omitted all such phrases. There were pleas in plenty for his health, his comfort, his welfare and success—the Mother found full scope—but no direct expression of her need for him. This, briefly, was the notion he had caught faintly from "between the lines."

But, having run it to earth, he easily explained it too. At Warsaw she was unhappy; whereas now, in Egypt, their reunion was almost within sight: she felt happier, too, her unpleasant duties over. It was all natural enough. "What a sentimental donkey a man is when he's in love!" he exclaimed with a self-indulgent smile of pleased forgiveness; "but the fact is—when she's not by me to explain—I could imagine anything!" And he fell at length into the doze his excited fancy had postponed.

After leaving Marseilles his impatience grew with the slowness of the steamer. The voyage of four days seemed interminable. The sea and sky took on a deeper blue, the air turned softer, the sweetness of the south became more marked. His exhilaration increased with every hour, the desire to reach his destination increasing with it. There was an intensity about his feelings he could not entirely account for. The longing to see Egypt merged with the longing to see Lettice. But the two were separate. The latter was impatient happiness, while the former struck a slower note—respect and wonder that contained a hint of awe.

Somewhere in this anticipatory excitement, too, hid drama. And his first glimpse of the marvelous old land did prove dramatic in a sense. For when a passenger drew his attention to the white Alexandrian harbor floating on the shining blue, he caught his breath a moment and his heart gave a sudden unexpected leap. He saw the low-lying coast, a palm, a mosque, a minaret; he saw the sandy lip of—Africa.

That shimmering line of blue and gold was Egypt.... He had known it would look exactly thus, exactly as he saw it. The same instant his heart contracted a little.... He leaned motionless upon the rail and watched the coast-line coming nearer, ever nearer. It rose out of the burning haze of blue and gold that hung motionless between the water and the air. Bathed in the drenching sunlight, the fringe of the great thirsty Desert seemed to drink the sea....

His entry was accompanied by mingled emotions and sensations. That Lettice stood waiting for him somewhere behind the blaze of light contributed much; yet the thrill owned a more complex origin, it seemed. To any one not entirely callous to the stab of strange romance and stranger beauty, the first sight of Egypt must always be an event, and Tom, by no means thus insensitive, felt it vividly. He was aware of something not wholly unfamiliar. The invitation was so strong, it seemed to entice as with an attraction that was almost summons. As the ship drew nearer, and thoughts of landing filled his mind, he felt no opposition, no resistance, no difficulty, as with other countries. There was no hint of friction any-where. He seemed instantly at home. Egypt not merely enticed—she pulled him in.

"Here I am at last!" whispered a voice, as he watched the noisy throng of Arabs, Nubians, Soudanese upon the crowded wharf. He delighted in the color, the gleaming eyes, bronze skins, the white caftans with their red and yellow sashes. The phantasmal amber light that filled the huge, still heavens lit something similar in his mind and thoughts. Only the train, with its luxurious restaurant car, its shutters to keep out the dust and heat, appeared incongruous. He lost the power to think this or that. He could only feel, and feel intensely. His feet touched Egypt, and a deep glow of inner happiness possessed him. He was not disappointed anywhere, though as yet he had seen nothing but a steamer quay. Then he sent a telegram to Let-tice: "Arrived safely. Reach Luxor eight o'clock to-morrow morning"; and, having slid through the Delta country with the flaming sunset, he had his first glimpse of the lordly Pyramids as the train drew into Cairo. Dim and immense he saw them across the swift-falling dusk, shadowy as forgotten centuries that cannot die. Though too distant to feel their menace, he yet knew them towering over him, mysterious, colossal, unintelligible, the sentinels of a gateway he had passed.

Such was the first touch of Egypt on his soul. It was as big and magical as he had known it would be. The magnificence and the glamour both were there. Europe already lay forgotten far behind him, non-existent. Some one tapped him on the shoulder, whispered a password, he was—in.

He dined in Cairo and took the night-train on to Luxor, the white, luxurious *wagon lit* again striking an incongruous note. For he had stepped from a platform into space, a space that floated suns and constellations. About him was that sense of the illimitable which broods everywhere in Egypt, in sand and sky, in sun and stars; it absorbed him easily, small human speck in a toy train with electric lights and modern comforts! An emotion difficult to seize gripped his heart, as he slid deeper and deeper into the land towards Lettice.... For Lettice also was involved in this. With happiness, yet somehow, too, with tears, he thought of her waiting for him now, expecting him, perhaps reading his telegram for the twentieth time. Through a mist of blue and gold she seemed to beckon to him across the shimmer of the endless yellow sands. He saw the little finger he had kissed. The dear face smiled. But there was a change upon it somewhere, though a change too subtle to be precisely named. The eyelids were half closed, and in the smile was power; the beckoning finger conveyed a gesture that was new—command. It seemed to point; it had a motion downwards; about her aspect was some flavor of authority almost royal, borrowed, doubtless, from the regal gold and purple of the sky's magnificence.

Oddly, again, his heart contracted as this changed aspect of her, due to heightened imagination, rose before the inner eye. A sensation of uncertainty and question slipped in with it, though whence he knew not. A hint of insecurity assailed his soul—almost a sense of inferiority in himself. It even flashed across him that he was under orders. It was inexplicable.... A restlessness in his blood prevented sleep.... He drew the blind up and looked out.

There was no moon. The night was drowned in stars. The train rushed south towards Thebes along the green thread of the Nile; the Lybian desert keeping pace with it, immense and desolate, death gnawing eternally at the narrow strip of life.... And again he knew the feeling at he had stepped from a platform into space. Egypt lay spread *below* him. He fell towards it, plunging, and as he fell, looked down—upon something vaguely familiar and half known.... An underlying sadness, inexplicable but significant, crept in upon his thoughts.

They rushed past Bedrashein, a straggling Arab village where once great Memphis owned eighteen miles of frontage on the stately river; he saw the low mud huts, the groves of date-palms that now marked the vanished splendor. They slid by in their hundreds, the spectral desert gleaming like snow between the openings. The huge pyramids of Sakkhâra loomed against the faint western afterglow. He saw the shaft of strange green light they call zodiacal.

And the sadness in him deepened inexplicably—that strange Egyptian sadness which ever underlies the brilliance.... The watchful stars looked down with sixty hundred centuries between them and a forgotten glory that dreamed now among a thousand sandy tombs. For the silent landscape flying past him like a dream woke emotions both sweet and painful that he could not understand—sweet to poignancy, exquisitely painful.

Perhaps it was natural enough, natural, too, that he should transfer these in some dim measure to the woman now waiting for him among the ruins of many-gated Thebes. The ancient city, dreaming still beside the storied river, assumed an appearance half fabulous in his thoughts. Egypt had wakened imagination in his soul. The change he fancied in Lettice was due, doubtless, to the transforming magic that mingled an actual present with a haunted past. Possibly this was some portion of the truth.... And yet, while the mood possessed him, some joy, some inner sheath, as it were, of anticipated happiness slipped off him into the encroaching yellow sand— as though he surrendered, not so much the actual happiness, as his right to it. A second's helplessness crept over him; another Self that was inferior peeped up and sighed and whispered.... He was aware of hidden touches that stabbed him into uneasiness, disquiet, almost pain.... Some outer tissue was stripped from his normal being, leaving him naked to the tang of extremely delicate shafts, buried so long that interpretation failed him.

The curious sensation, luckily, did not last; but this hint of a familiarity that seemed both sweet and dangerous, made it astonishingly convincing at the time. Some aspect of vanity, of confidence in himself distinctly weakened....

It passed with the spectral palm trees as the train sped further south. He finally dismissed it as the result of fatigue, excitement and anticipation too prolonged.... Yes, he dismissed it. At any rate it passed. It sank out of sight and was forgotten. It had become, perhaps, an integral portion of his being. Possibly, it had always been so, and had been merely waiting to emerge....

But such intangible and elusive emotions were so new to him that he could not pretend to deal with them. There is a stimulus as of ether about the Egyptian climate that gets into the mind, it is said, and stirs unwonted dreams and fantasies. The climate becomes mental. His stolid temperament was, perhaps, pricked thus half unintelligibly. He could not understand it. He drew the blind down. But before turning out the light, he read over once again the note of welcome Lettice had sent to meet him at the steamer. It was brief, but infinitely precious. The thought of her love sponged all lesser feelings completely from his mind, and he fell asleep thinking only of their approaching meeting, and of his marvelous deep joy.

CHAPTER XIV

On reaching Luxor at eight o'clock in the morning, to his keen delight an Arab servant met him with an unexpected invitation. He had meant to go first to his hotel, but Lettice willed otherwise, everything thought out beforehand in her loving way. He drove accordingly to her house on the outskirts of the town towards Karnak, changed and bathed in a room where he recognized with supreme joy a hundred familiar touches that seemed transplanted from the Brown Flat at home—and found her at nine o'clock waiting for him on the verandah. Breakfast was laid in the shady garden just beyond.

It was ideal as a dream. She stood there dressed in white, wearing a big sun-hat with little roses, sparkling, radiant, a graceful fairy figure from the heart of spring. "Here's the inevitable fly-whisk, Tom," was the first thing she said, and as naturally as though they had parted a few hours before, "it's to keep the flies away, and to keep you at your distance too!" And his first remark, escaping him impulsively in place of a hundred other things he had meant to say, was, "You look different; you've changed. Lettice, you're far more lovely than I knew. I've never seen you look like that before!" He felt his entire being go out to her in a consuming flame. "You look perfectly divine." Sheer admiration took his breath away. "I believe you're Isis herself," he laughed in his delight, "come back into her own!"

"Then you must be Osiris, Tom!" her happy voice responded, "new risen from his sandy tomb!"

There was no time for private conversation, for Mrs. Haughstone appeared just then and inquired politely after his health and journey. "The flies are awful," she mentioned, "but Lettice always insists on having breakfast out of doors. I hope you'll be able to stand it." And she continued to flutter her horse-hair whisk as though she would have liked to sweep Egypt itself from the face of the map. "No wonder the Israelites were glad to leave. There's sand in everything you eat and flies on everything you see." Yet she said it with what passed in her case for good nature; she, too, was evidently enjoying herself in Egypt.

Tom said that flies and sand would not trouble him with such gorgeous sunlight to compensate, and that anyhow they were better than soot and fogs in London.

"You'll be tired of the sun before a week is over," she replied, "and long to see a cloud or feel a drop of rain." She followed his eyes which seemed unable to leave the face and figure of his hostess. "But it all agrees wonderfully with my cousin. Don't you find her looking well? She's quite changed into another person, *I* think," the tone suggesting that it was not altogether a change that she herself approved of. "We're all different here, a little. Even Mr. Winslowe's improved enormously. He's steadier and wiser than he used to be." And Tom, laughing, said he hoped he would improve, too, himself.

The comforting hot coffee, the delicious rolls, the cool iced fruit, and, above all, Lettice beside him at last in the pleasant shade, gave Tom such high spirits that the woman's disagreeable personality produced no effect. Through the gate in the stone wall at the end of the garden, beneath masses of drooping bougainvillæa, the Nile dreamed past in a sheet of golden haze; the Theban hills, dipped in the crystal azure of the sky, rose stern and desolate upon the horizon; the air, at this early hour, was fresh and keen. He felt himself in some enchanted garden of the ancient world with a radiant goddess for companion.... There was a sound of singing from the river below—the song of the Nile boatman that has not changed these thousand years; a quaint piping melody floated in from the street outside; from the further shore came the dull beating of a native tom-tom; and the still, burning atmosphere held the mystery of wonder in suspension. Her beauty, at last, had found its perfect setting.

"I never saw your eyes so wonderful—so soft and brilliant," he whispered as soon as they were alone. "You're very happy." He paused, looking at her. "That's me, isn't it? Lettice, say it is at once." He was very playful in his joy; but he longed eagerly to hear her admit that his coming meant as much to her as it meant to him.

"I suppose it must be," she replied, "but it's the climate too. This keen dry air and the sunshine bring all one's power out. There's something magical in it. You forget the years and feel young—against the background of this old land a life-time seems like an afternoon, merely. And the nights—oh, Tom, the stars are too, too marvelous." She spoke with a kind of exuberance that seemed new in her.

"They must be," he rejoined, as he gazed exultantly, "for they're all in you, sun, air, and stars. You're a perfect revelation to me of what a woman—"

"Am I?" she interrupted, fluttering her whisk between her chair and his. "But now, dear Tom, my headstrong boy, tell me how you are and all about yourself, your plans, and everything else in the world besides." He told her what he could, answered all her questions, declared he and she were going to have the time of their lives, and behaved generally, as she told him, like a boy out of school. He admitted it. "But I'm hungry, Lettice, awfully hungry." He kept reminding her that he had been starving for two long months; surely she was starving too. He longed to hear her confess it with a sigh of happy relief. "My arms and lips are hungry," he went on incorrigibly, "but I'm tired, too, from traveling. I feel like putting my head on your breast and going sound asleep." "My boy," she said tenderly, "you shall." She responded instantly to that. "You always were a baby and I'm here to take care of you." He seized her hand and kissed it before she could draw it away. "You must be careful, Tom. Everything has eyes in Egypt; the Arabs move like ghosts." She glanced towards the windows. "And the gossip is unbelievable." She was quiet again now, and very gentle; it struck him how calm and sweet she was towards him, yet that there was a delightful happy excitement underneath that she only just controlled. He was aware of something wild in her just out of sight—a kind of mental effervescence, almost intoxication she deliberately suppressed.

"And so are you—unbelievable," he exclaimed impetuously; "unbelievably beautiful. This is your country with a vengeance, Lettice. You're like an Egyptian queen—a princess of the sun!"

He gazed critically at her till she lowered her eyes. He realized that, actually, they were not visible from the house and that the garden trees were thick about them; but he also received a faint impression that she did not want, did not intend, to allow quite the same intimacy as before. It just flashed across him with a hint of disappointment, then was gone. His boyish admiration, perhaps, annoyed her. He had felt for a second that her excuse of the windows and the gossip was not the entire truth. The merest shadow of a thought it was. He noticed her eyes fixed intently upon him. The same minute, then, she rose quietly and rustled over to his chair, kissed him on the cheek quickly, and sat down again. "There!" she said playfully as though she had guessed his thoughts, "I've done the awful thing; now you'll be reasonable, perhaps!" And whether or not she had divined his mood, she instantly dispelled it—for the moment....

They talked about a hundred things, moving their chairs as the blazing sunshine found them out, till finally they sat with cushions on the steps of stone that led down to the river beneath the flaming bougainvillæa. He felt the strange touch of Egypt all about them, that touch of eternity that floats in the very air, a hint of something deathless and sublime that whispers in the sunshine. Already he was aware of the long fading stretch of years behind. He thought of Egypt as two vast hands that held him, one of tawny gold and one of turquoise blue—the desert and the sky. In the hollow of those great hands, he lay with Lettice—two tiny atoms of sand....

He watched her every movement, every gesture, noted the slightest inflection of her voice, was aware that five years at least had dropped from her, that her complexion had grown softer, a shade darker, too, from the sun; but, above all, that there was a new expression, a new light certainly, soft and brilliant, in her eyes. It seemed, briefly put, that she had blossomed somehow into a fuller expression of herself. An overflowing vitality, masked behind her calmness, betrayed itself in every word and glance and gesture. There was an exuberance he called joy, but it was, somehow, a new, an unexpected joy.

She was, of course, aware of his untiring scrutiny; and presently, in a lull, keeping her eyes on the river below them, she spoke of it. "You find me a little changed, Tom, don't you? I warned you that Egypt had a certain effect on me. It inflames the heart and—"

"But a very wonderful effect," he broke in with admiration. "You're different in a way—yes—but you haven't changed—not towards me, I mean." He wanted to say a great deal more, but could not find the words; he divined that something had happened to her, in Warsaw probably, and he longed to question her about the "other" who was her husband, but he could not, of course, allow himself to do so. An intuitive feeling came to him that the claim upon her of this other was more remote than formerly. His dread had certainly lessened. The claims upon her of this "other" seemed no longer—dangerous.... He wondered.... There was a certain confusion in his mind.

"You got my letter at Alexandria?" she interrupted his reflections. He thanked her with enthusiasm, trying to remember what it said—but without success. It struck him suddenly that there was very little in it after all, and he mentioned this with a reproachful smile. "That's my restraint," she replied. "You always liked restraint. Besides, I wasn't sure it would reach you." She laughed and blew a kiss towards him. She made a curious gesture he had never seen her make before. It seemed unlike her. More and more, he registered a difference in her, as if side by side with the increase of spontaneous vitality, there ran another mood, another aspect, almost another point of view. It was not towards him, yet it affected him. There seemed a certain new lightness, even irresponsibility in her; she was more worldly, more human, not more ordinary by any means, but less "impersonal." He remembered her singular words: "It inflames the heart." He wondered—a little uneasily. There seemed a new touch of wonder about her that made him aware of something commonplace, almost inferior, in himself....

At the same time he felt another thing—a breath of coldness touched him somewhere, though he could not trace its origin to anything she did or said.

Was it perhaps in what she left unsaid, undone? He longed to hear her confess how she had missed him, how thrilled she was that he had come: but she did not say these passionately desired things, and when he teased her about it, she showed a slight impatience almost: "Tom, you know I never talk like that. Anything sentimental I abhor. But I live it. Can't you see?" His ungenerous fancies vanished then at once; at a word, a smile, a glance of the expressive eyes, he instantly forgot all else.

"But I am different in Egypt," she warned him playfully again, half closing her eyelids as she said it. "I wonder if you'll like me—quite as well."

"More," he replied ardently, "a thousand times more. I feel it already. There's mischief in you," he went on watching the half-closed eyes, "a touch of magic too, but very human magic. I love it." And then he whispered, "I think you're more within my reach."

"Am I?" She looked bewitching, a being of light and air.

"Everybody will fall in love with you at sight." He laughed happily, aware of an enchantment that fascinated him more and more, but when he suddenly went over to her chair, she stopped him with decision. "Don't, Tom, please don't. Tony'll be here any minute now. It would be unpleasant if he saw you behaving wildly like this! He wouldn't understand."

He drew back. "Oh, Tony's coming—then I must be careful!" He laughed, but he was disappointed and he showed it: it was their first day together, and eager though he was to see his cousin, he felt it might well have been postponed a little. He said so.

"One must be natural, Tom," she told him in reply; "it's always the best way. This isn't London or Montreux, you see, and—"

"Lettice, I understand," he interrupted, a trifle ashamed of himself. "You're quite right." He tried to look pleased and satisfied, but the truth was he felt suddenly—stupid. "And we've got lots of time—three months or more ahead of us, haven't we?" She gave him an expressive, tender look with which he had to be contented for the moment.

"And by the by, how is old Tony, and who is his latest?" he inquired carelessly.

"Very excited at your coming, Tom. You'll think him improved, I hope. I believe *I'm* his latest," she added, tilting her chin with a delicious pretense at mischief. And the gesture again surprised him. It was new. He thought it foreign to her. There seemed a flavor of impatience, of audacity, almost of challenge in it.

"Finding himself at last. That's good. Then you've been fishing to some purpose."

"Fishing?"

"Rescuing floating faces."

She pouted at him. "I'm not a saint, Tom. You know I never was. Saints are very inspiring to read about, but you couldn't live with one—or love one. Could you, now?"

He gave an inward start she did not notice. The same instant he was aware that it was her happy excitement that made her talk in this exaggerated way. That was why it sounded so unnatural. He forgot it instantly.

They laughed and chatted as happily as two children—Tom felt a boy again—until Mrs. Haughstone appeared, marching down the river-bank with an enormous white umbrella over her head, and the talk became general. Tom said he would go to his hotel and return for lunch; he wanted to telephone to Assouan. He asked where Tony was staying. "But he knew I was at the Winter Palace," he exclaimed when she mentioned the Savoy. "He found some people there he wanted to avoid," she explained, "so moved down to the Savoy."

Tom said he would do the same; it was much nearer to her house, for one thing: "You'll keep him for lunch, won't you?" he said as he went off. "I'll try," she promised, "but he's so busy with his numerous friends as usual that I can't be sure of him. He has more engagements here than in London,"—whereupon Mrs. Haughstone added, "Oh, he'll stay, Mr. Kelverdon. I'm sure he'll stay. We lunch at one o'clock, remember."

And in his room at the hotel Tom found a dozen signs of tenderness and care that increased his happiness; there were touches everywhere of her loving thought for comfort and well-being—flowers, his favorite soap, some cigarettes, one of her own deck-chairs, books, and even a big box of crystallized dates as though he was a baby or a little boy. It all touched him deeply; no other woman in the world could possibly have thought out such clear reminders, much less have carried them into effect. There was even a writing-pad and a penholder with the special nib he liked. He laughed. But her care for him in such trivial things was exquisite because it showed she claimed the right to do them.

His heart brimmed over as he saw them. It was impossible to give up any room, even a hotel room, into which she had put her sweet and mothering personality. He could do without Tony's presence and companionship, rather than resign a room she had thus prepared for him. He engaged it permanently therefore. Then, telephoning to Assouan, he decided to take the night train and see what had to be done there. It all sounded most satisfactory; he foresaw much free time ahead of him; occasional trips to the work would meet the case at present....

Happier than ever, he returned to a lunch in the open air with her and Tony, and it was the gayest, merriest meal he had ever known. Mrs. Haughstone retired to sleep through the hotter hours of the afternoon, leaving the trio to amuse themselves in freedom. And though they never left the shady garden by the Nile, they amused themselves so well that tea was over and it was time for Tom to get ready for his train before he realized it. Tony and Madame Jaretzka drove him to his hotel, and afterwards to the station, sitting in the compartment with him until the train was actually moving. He watched them standing on the platform together, waving their hands. He waved his own. "I'll be back to-morrow or the next day," he cried. Emotions and sensations were somewhat tangled in him, but happiness certainly was uppermost.

"Don't forget," he heard Tony shout.... And her eyes were on his own until the trees on the platform hid her from his sight behind their long deep shadows.

CHAPTER XV

The first excitement of arrival over, he drew breath as it were and looked about him. Egypt delighted and amazed him, surpassing his expectations. Its effect upon him was instantaneous and profound. The decisive note sounded at Alexandria continued in his ears. Egypt drew him in with golden, powerful arms. In every detail it was strange, yet with the strangeness of a pre-determined welcome. It was not strange to *him*. The thrill of welcome made him feel at home. He had come back....

Here, at Assouan, he was aware of Africa, mystic, half-monstrous continent, lying with its heat and wonder just beyond the horizon. He saw the Southern Cross, pitched low above the sandy rim... Yet Africa had no call for him. It left him without a thrill, an uninviting, undesirable land. It was Egypt that made the intimate and personal appeal, as of a deeply loved and half-familiar place. It seemed to gather him in against its mighty heart. He lay in some niche of comforting warm sand against the ancient mass that claimed him, tucked in by the wonder and the mystery, protected, even mothered. It was an oddly stimulated imagination that supplied the picture—and made him smile. He snuggled down deeper and deeper into this figurative warm bed of sand the ages had preordained. He felt secure and sheltered—as though the wonder and the mystery veiled something that menaced joy in him, something that concealed a notion of attack. Almost there seemed a whisper in the wind, a watchful and unclosing eye behind the dazzling sunshine: "Surrender yourself to me, and I will care for you. I will protect you against... yourself.... Beware!" This peculiar excitement in his blood was somehow precisely what he had expected; the wonder and the thrill were natural and right. He had known that Egypt would mesmerize his soul exactly in this way. He had, it seemed, anticipated both the exhilaration and the terror. He thought much about it all, and each time Egypt looked him in the face, he saw Lettice too. They were inseparably connected, as it were. He saw her brilliant eyes peering past the great tawny visage. Together they bade him pause and listen.... The wind brought up its faint, elusive whisper: "Wait.... We have not done with you.... Wait and listen! Watch...!"

Before his mind's eye the mighty land lay like a map, a blazing garden of intenser life that the desolation ill concealed. Europe seemed infinitely remote, the life he had been accustomed to unreal, of tepid interest, while the intimate appeal that Egypt made grew more insistent every hour of the day. It was Luxor, however, that called him peremptorily—Luxor where all that was dearest to him in life now awaited his return. He yearned for Luxor; Thebes drew him like a living magnet. Lettice was in Thebes, and Thebes also seemed the heart of ancient Egypt, its center and its climax. "Come back to us," whispered the sweet desert wind; "we are waiting...." In Thebes seemed the focus of the strange Egyptian spell.

At all hours of the day and night, here in Assouan, it caught him, asking forever the great unanswerable questions. In the pauses of his strenuous work, in the watches of the night, when he heard the little owls and the weird barking of the prowling jackals; in the noon-tide heat, and in the cold glimmer of the quiet stars, he was never unconscious of its haunting presence, he was never beyond its influence. He was never quite alone....

What did it mean? And why did this hint of danger, of pain, of loneliness lurk behind the exhilaration and the peace? Wherein lay the essence of the enchantment this singular Egyptian glamour laid upon his very soul?

In his laborious way, Tom worked at the disentanglement, but without much success. One curious thought, however, persisted with a strange enough significance. It rose, in a sense, unbidden. It was not his brain that discovered it. It just "came."

For he was thinking of other wonderful countries he had known. He remembered Japan and India, both surpassing Egypt in color, sunshine, gorgeous pageantry, and certainly equaling it in historical association and the rest. Yet, for him, these old lands had no spell, no glamour comparable to what he now experienced. The mind contains them, understands them easily. They are continuous with their past. The traveler drops in and sees them as they always have been. They are still, so to speak, going on comfortably as before. There is no shock of dislocation. They have not died.

Whereas Egypt has left the world; Egypt is dead; there is no link with present things. Both heart and mind are aware of this deep vacuum they vainly strive to fill. That ancient civilization, both marvelous and somewhere monstrous, breaking with beauty, burning with aspiration, mysterious and vital—all has vanished as completely as though it had not been. The prodigious ruins hint, but cannot utter. No reconstruction from tomb or temple can recall a great dream the world has lost. It is forgotten, swept away, there is no clue. Egypt has left the world....

Yet, as he thought about it in his uninspired way, it seemed that some part of him still beat in sympathy with the pulse of the forgotten dream. Egypt indeed was dead, yet sometimes—she came back.... She came to revisit her soft stars and moon, her great temples and her mighty tombs. She stole back into the sunshine and the sand; her broken, ruined heart at Thebes received her. He saw her as a spirit, a persistent, living presence, a stupendous Ghost....

And the idea, having offered itself, remained. Both he and Lettice somehow were associated with it, and with this elusive notion of return. They, too, were entangled in the glamour and the spell. They, too, had stolen back as from some immemorial lost dream to revisit the scenes of an intenser yet forgotten life. And Thebes was its center; the secretive and forbidding Theban Hills, with their desolate myriad sepulchers, its focus and its climax....

Assouan detained him only a couple of days. He had capable lieutenants; there was delay, moreover, in the arrival of certain material; he could always be summoned quickly by telephone. He sent home his report and took the express train back to Luxor and to—her.

He had been too occupied, too tired at night, to do more than write a fond, short letter, then go to sleep; the heat was considerable; he realized that he was in Africa; the scenery fascinated him, the enormous tawny desert, the cataracts of golden yellow sand, the magical old river. The wonder of Philae, with its Osirian shrine and island sanctuary, caught him as it has caught most other humans. After the sheer bulk of the pyramids and temples, Philae bursts into the heart with almost lyrical sweetness. But his heart was fast in Thebes, and not all the enchantment of this desert paradise could seduce him. Moreover, one detail he disliked: the ubiquitous earthenware tom-tom that sounded day and night... he heard its sullen beating in his dreams.

Yet of one thing he was ever chiefly conscious—that he was impatient to be with Lettice, that his heart hungered without ceasing, that she meant more to him than ever. Her new beauty astonished him, there was a subtle charm in her presence he had not felt in London, her fresh spontaneous gaiety filled him with keen delight. And all this was his. His arrival gave her such joy that she could not even speak of it; yet he was the cause of it. It made him feel almost shy.

He received one characteristic letter from her. "Come back as quickly as you can," she wrote. "Tony has gone down the river after his birds, and I feel lonely. Telegraph, and come to dinner or breakfast according to your train. I'll meet you if possible. You must come here for all your meals as

I'm sure the hotel food is poor and the drinking water unsafe. This is open house, remember, for you both." And there was a delicious P.S. "Mind you only drink filtered water, and avoid the hotel salads because the water hasn't been boiled." He kissed the letter. He laughed. Her tender thought for him almost brought the tears into his eyes. It was the tenderness of his own mother who was dead.

He reached Luxor in the evening, and to his delight she was on the platform; long before the train stopped he recognized her figure, the wide sun-hat with the little roses, the white serge skirt and jacket of knitted yellow silk to keep the evening chill away. They drove straight to her house; the sun was down behind the rocky hills and the Nile lay in a dream of burnished gold; the little owls were calling; there was singing among the native boatmen on the water; they saw the fields of brilliant green with the sands beyond, and the keen air from the desert wafted down the street of what once was great-hundred-gated Thebes. A strangely delicate perfume hung about the ancient city. Tom turned to look at the woman beside him in the narrow-seated carriage, and felt as if he were driving through a dream.

"I can stay a week or ten days at least," he said at last. "Is old Tony back?"

Yes, he had just arrived and telephoned to ask if he might come to dinner. "And look, Tom, you can just see the heads of the Colossi rising out of the haze,"—she pointed quickly—"I thought we would go and show them you to-morrow. We might all take our tea and eat it in the clover. You've seen nothing of Egypt yet." She spoke rapidly, eagerly, full of her little plan.

"All?" he repeated doubtfully.

"Yes, wouldn't you like it?"

"Oh, rather," he said, wondering why he did not say another thing that rose for a moment in his mind.

"You must see everything," she went on spontaneously, "and a dragoman's a bore. Tony's a far better guide. He knows old Egypt as well as he knows his old birds." She laughed. "It's too ridiculous—his enthusiasm: he's been dying to explain it all to you as he did to me, and he does it exactly like a museum guide who is a scholar and a poet too. And he is a poet, you know. I'd never noticed it before."

"Splendid," said Tom. He was thinking several things at once, among them that the perfumed air reminded him of something he could not quite recall. It seemed far away and yet familiar. "I'm a rare listener too," he added.

"The King's Valley you really must do alone together," she went on, "I can't face it a second time—the heat, the gloom of it—it oppressed and frightened me a little. Those terrible grim hills—they're full of death, those Theban hills."

"Tony took you?" he asked.

She nodded. "We did the whole thing," she added, "every single Tomb. I was exhausted. I think we all were—except Tony." The eager look in her face had gone. Her voice betrayed a certain effort. A darkness floated over it, like the shadow of a passing cloud.

"All of you!" he exclaimed, as though it were important. "No bird-man ever feels tired." He seemed to think a moment. There was a tiny pause. The carriage was close to the house now, driving up with a flourish, and Tony and Mrs. Haughstone, an incongruous couple, were visible standing against the luminous orange sky beside the river. Tom pointed to them with a chuckle. "All right," he exclaimed, with a gesture as though he came to a decision suddenly, "it shall be the Colossi tomorrow. There are two of them, aren't there—only two?"

"Two, yes, the Twin Colossi, they call them," she replied, joining in his chuckle at the silhouetted figures in the sunset.

"Two," he repeated with emphasis, "not three." But either she did not notice or else she did not hear. She was leaning forward waving her hand to her other guests upon the bank.

There followed then the happiest week that Tom had ever known, for there was no incident to mar it, nor a single word or act that cast the slightest shadow. His dread of the "other" who was to come apparently had left him, the faint uneasiness he had felt so often seemed gone. He even forgot to think about it. Lettice he had never seen so gay, so full of enterprise, so radiant. She sparkled as though she had recovered her girlhood suddenly. With Tony in particular she had incessant battles, and Tom listened to their conversations with amusement, for on no single subject were they able to agree, yet neither seemed to get the best of it. Tom felt unable to keep pace with their more nimble minds....

Tony was certainly improved in many ways, more serious than he had showed himself before, and extraordinarily full of entertaining knowledge into the bargain. Birds and the lore of ancient Egypt, it appeared, were merely two of his pet hobbies; and he talked in such amusing fashion that he kept Tom in roars of laughter, while stimulating Madame Jaretzka to vehement contradictions. They were much alone, and profited by it. The numerous engagements Lettice had mentioned gave no sign. Tony certainly was a brilliant companion as well as an instructive cicerone. There was more in him than Tom had divined before. His clever humor was a great asset in the longer expeditions. "Tony, I'm tired and hot; please come and talk to me: I want refreshing" was never addressed to Tom, for instance, whose good nature could not take the place of wit. Each of the three, as it were, supplied what the other lacked; it was not surprising they got on well together. Tom, however, though always happy provided Lettice was of the party, envied his cousin's fluid temperament and facile gifts—even in the smallest things. Tony, for instance, would mimic Mrs. Haughstone's attitude of having done her hostess a kindness in coming out to Egypt: "I couldn't do it *again*, dear Lettice, even for *you*"—the way Tony said and acted it had a touch of inspiration.

Mrs. Haughstone herself, meanwhile, within the limits of her angular personality, Tom found also considerably improved. Egypt had changed her too. He forgave her much because she was afraid of the sun, so left them often alone. She showed unselfishness, too, even kindness, on more than one occasion. Tom was aware of a nicer side in her; in spite of her jealousy and criticism, she was genuinely careful of her hostess's reputation amid the scandal-loving atmosphere of Egyptian hotel life. It amused him to see how she arrogated to herself the place of chaperone, yet Tom saw true solicitude in it, the attitude of a woman who knew the world towards one who was too trustful. He figured her always holding up a warning finger, and Lettice always laughingly disregarding her advice.

Her warnings to Lettice to be more circumspect were, at any rate, by no means always wrong. Though not particularly observant as a rule, he caught more than once the tail-end of conversations between them in which advice, evidently, had been proffered and laughed aside. But, since it did not concern him, he paid little attention, merely aware that there existed this difference of view. One such occasion, however, Tom had good cause to remember, because it gave him a piece of knowledge he had long desired to possess, yet had never felt within his rights to ask for. Yet it merely gave details of something he already knew.

He entered the room, coming straight from a morning's work at his own hotel, and found them engaged hammer and tongs upon some dispute regarding "conduct." Tony, who had been rowing Madame Jaretzka down the river, had made his escape. Madame Jaretzka effected hers as Tom came in, throwing him a look of comical relief across her shoulder. He was alone with the Irish cousin. "After all, she is a married woman," remarked Mrs. Haughstone, still somewhat indignant from the little battle.

She addressed the words to him as he was the only person within earshot. It seemed natural enough, he thought.

"Yes," said Tom politely. "I suppose she is."

And it was then, quite unexpectedly, that the woman spoke to him as though he knew as much as she did. He ought, perhaps, to have stopped her, but the temptation was too great. He learned the facts concerning Warsaw and the—husband. That the Prince had ill-treated her consistently during the first five years of their married life could certainly not justify her freedom, but that he had lost his reason incurably, no longer even recognized her, that her presence was discouraged by the doctors, since it increased the violence of his attacks, and that his malady was hopeless and could end only in his death—all this, while adding to the wonder of her faithful pilgrimages, did assuredly at the same time set her free.... The effect upon his mind may be imagined; it deepened his love, increased his admiration, for it explained the suffering in the face she had turned to sweetness, while also justifying her conduct towards himself. With a single final blow, moreover, it killed the dread Tom had been haunted by so long—that this was that "other" who must one day take her from him, obedient to a bigger claim.

This knowledge, as though surreptitiously obtained, Tom locked within his breast until the day when she herself should choose to share it with him.

He remembered another little conversation too when, similarly, he disturbed them in discussion: this time it was Mrs. Haughstone who was called away.

"Behaving badly, Lettice, is she? Scolding you again?"

"Not at all. Only she sees the bad in every one and I see the good. She disapproves of Tony rather."

"Then she will be less often deceived than you," he replied laughingly. The reference to Tony had escaped him; his slow mind was on the general proposition.

"Perhaps. But you can only make people better by believing that they *are* better," she went on with conviction—when Mrs. Haughstone joined them and took up her parable again:

"My cousin behaves like a child," she said with amusing severity. "She doesn't understand the world. But the world is hard upon grown-ups who behave like children. Lettice thinks everybody good. Her innocence gets her misjudged. And it's a pity."

"I'll keep an eye on her," Tom said solemnly, "and we'll begin this very afternoon."

"Do, Mr. Kelverdon, I'm glad to hear it." And as she said it, he noticed another expression on her face as she glanced down the drive where Tony, dressed in gray flannels and singing to himself, was seen sauntering towards them. She wore an enigmatic smile by no means pleasant. It gave him a moment's twinge. He turned from her to Lettice by way of relief. She was waving her white-gloved hand, her eyes were shining, her little face was radiant—and Tom's happiness came back upon him in a rising flood again as he watched her beauty.... He thought that Egypt was the most marvelous place he had ever known. Even Tony looked enchanted—almost handsome. But Lettice looked divine. He felt more and more that the woman in her blossomed into life before his very eyes. His content was absolute.

CHAPTER XVI

With Tony as guide they took their fill of wonder. The principal expeditions were made alone, introducing Tom to the marvels of ancient Egypt which they already knew. On the sturdiest donkey Thebes could furnish, he raced his cousin across the burning sands, Madame Jaretzka following in a sand-cart, her blue veil streaming in the cool north wind. They played like children, defying the tide of mystery that this haunted land pours against the modern human soul, while yet the wonder and the mystery added to their enjoyment, deepening their happiness by contrast.

They ate their *al fresco* luncheons gaily, seated by hoary tombs that opened into the desolate hills; kings, priests, princesses, dead six thousand years, listening in caverns underground to their careless talk. Yet their gaiety had a hush in it, a significance behind the sentences; for even their lightest moments touched ever upon the borders of an awfulness that was sublime, and all that they said or did gained this hint of deeper value—that it was set against a background of the infinite, the deathless.

It was impossible to forget that this was Egypt, the deposit of immemorial secrets, the store-house of stupendous vanished dreams.

"There was a majesty, after all, about their strange old gods," said Tony one afternoon as they emerged from the stifling darkness of a forgotten kingly tomb into the sunlight. "They seem to thunder still—below the ground—subconsciously." He was ever ready with the latest modern catchword. He flung himself down upon the sand, shaded from the glare by a recumbent column of granite exquisitely carved, then abandoned of the ages. "They touch something in one even to-day—something superb. Human worship hasn't changed so fundamentally after all."

"A sort of ghostly deathlessness," agreed Lettice, making a bed of sand beside him. "I think that's what one feels."

Tony looked up. He glanced alertly at her. A question flashed a moment in his eyes, then passed unspoken.

"Perhaps," Tony went on in a more flippant tone, "even the dullest has to acknowledge the sublime in their conceptions. Isis! Why, the very name is a poem in a single word. Anubis, Nepthys, Horus—there's poetry in them all. They seem to sing themselves into the heart, as Petrie might have said—but didn't."

"The names *are* rather splendid," Tom put in, as he unpacked the kettle and spirit-lamp for tea. "One can't forget them either."

There was a moment's silence, then Tony spoke again. He had lost his flippant tone. He addressed his remark to Lettice. Tom was aware that she was somehow waiting for it.

"Their deathlessness! Yes, you're right." He turned an instant to look at the colossal structure behind them, whence the imposing figures of a broken Pharaoh and his Queen stared to the east across the shoulder of some granite Deity that had refused to crumble for three thousand years. "Their deathlessness," he repeated, lowering his voice, "it's really startling."

He looked about him. It was amazing how his little words, his gesture, his very atmosphere created a spontaneous expectancy—as though Thoth might stride sublimely up across the sand, or even Ra himself come blazing with extended wings and awful disk of fire.

Tom felt the touch of the unearthly as he watched and listened. Lettice— he was certain of it—shivered. He moved nearer and spread a rug across her feet.

"Don't, Tom, please! I'm hot enough already." Her tone had a childish exasperation in it—as though he interrupted some mood that gave her pleasure. She turned her eyes to Tony, but Tony was busily opening sandwich packets with hands that—Tom thought—shared one quality at least of the stone effigies they had been discussing—size. And he laughed. The spell was broken. They fell hungrily upon their desert meal....

Yet, it was odd how Tony had expressed precisely what Tom had himself been vaguely feeling, though unable to find the language for his fancy—odd, too, that apparently all three of them had felt the same dim thing. No one among them was "religious," nor, strictly speaking, imaginative; poetical least of all, in the regenerative, creative sense. Not one of the trio, that is, could have seized imaginatively the conception of an alien deity and made it live. Yet Tony's idle mood or idler words had done this very thing—and all three acknowledged it in their various ways. The flavor of a remote familiarity was manifest in each one of them—collectively as well.

Another time they sat by night in ruined Karnak, watching the silver moonlight bring out another world among the mighty pylons. It painted the empty and enormous aisles with crowding processions of lost ages. Speaking in whispers, they saw the stars peep down between the soaring forest of old stone; the cold desert wind brought with it a sadness, a mournful retrospect too vast to realize, the tragedy that such splendor left but a lifeless skeleton behind, a gigantic, soul-less ruin. That such great prophecies remained unfulfilled was somewhere both terrible and melancholy. The immortal strength of these Egyptian stones conveyed a grandeur almost sinister. The huge dumb beauty seemed menacing, even ominous; they sat closer; they felt dwarfed uncomfortably, their selves reduced to insignificance, almost threatened. Even Tony sobered as they talked in lowered voices, seated in the shadow of the towering columns, their feet resting on the sand.

"I'm sure we've sat here before just like this, the three of us," he said in a lowered voice; "it all seems like a dream to me."

Madame Jaretzka, who was between them, made no answer, and Tom, leaning forward, caught his cousin's eye beyond her.... The scene in the London theater flashed across his mind. He felt very happy, very close to them both, extraordinarily at one with them, the woman he loved best in all the world, the man who was his greatest friend. He felt truth, not foolishness, in Tony's otherwise commonplace remarks that followed: "I could swear I'd known you both before—here in Egypt."

Madame Jaretzka moved a little, shuffling further back so that she could lean against the great curved pillar. It brought them closer together still. She said no word, however.

"There's certainly a curious sympathy between the three of us," murmured Tom, who usually felt out of his depth in similar talks, leaving his companions to carry it further while he listened merely. "It's hard to believe that we meet for the first time now."

He sat close to her, fingering her gauzy veil that brushed his face. There was a pause, and then Madame Jaretzka said, turning to Tony, "*We* met here first anyhow, didn't we? Two winters ago, before I met Tom—"

But Tony said he meant something far older than that, much longer ago. "You and Tom knew each other as children, you told me once. Tom and I were boys together too... but... "

His voice died away in Tom's ears; her answers also were inaudible as she kept her head turned towards Tony: his thoughts, besides, were caught away a moment to the days in Montreux and in London.... He fell into a reverie that lasted possibly a minute, possibly several minutes. The conversation between them left him somehow out of it; he had little to contribute; they had an understanding, as it were, on certain subjects that neglected him. His mind accordingly left them. He followed his own thoughts dreamily... far away... past the deep black shadows and out into the soft blaze of moonlight that showered upon the distant Theban hills.... He remembered the curious emotions that had marked his entry into Egypt. He thought of a change in Lettice, at present still undefined. He wondered what it was about her now that lent to her gentle spirit a touch of authority, of worldly authority almost, that he dared not fail to recognize—as though she had the right to it. The flavor of uneasiness stole back. It occurred to him suddenly that he felt no longer quite at home with her *alone* as of old. Some one watched him: some one watched them both....

It was as though for the first time he realized distance—a new distance creeping in upon their relationship somewhere....

A slight shiver brought him back. The wind came moaning down the monstrous, yawning aisles against them. The overpowering effect of so much grandeur had become intolerable. "Ugh! I'm cold," he exclaimed abruptly. "I vote we move a bit. I think—*I'll* move anyhow."

Madame Jaretzka turned to him with a definite start; she straightened herself against the huge sandstone column. The moonlight touched her. It clothed her in gold and silver, the gold of the sand, the silver of the moon. She looked ethereal, ghostly, a figure of air and distance. She seemed to belong to her surroundings—another person somehow—faintly Egyptian almost.

"I thought you were asleep, Tom," she said softly.

She had been in the middle of an animated, though whispered talk with Tony. She peered at him, with a little smile that lifted her lip oddly.

"I was far away somewhere," he returned, peering at her closely. "I forgot all about you both. I thought, for a moment, I was quite—alone."

He saw her start again. A significance he hardly intended had crept into his tone. Her face moved back into the shadow quickly, beside Tony.

She teased Tom for his want of manners, then fell to caring for his comfort. "It's icy," she said, "and you're in flannels. The sudden chill of these Egyptian nights is really treacherous," and she took the rug from her lap and put it round his shoulders. As she did so the strange appearance he had noted increased about her.

And Tom got up abruptly. "No, Lettice dear, thank you; I think I'll move a bit." He had said "Lettice dear" without realizing it, and before his cousin too. "I'll take a turn and then come back for you. You stay here with Tony," and he moved off somewhat briskly.

Then, instantly, the other two rose up like one person, following him to where the carriage waited....

"They're frightening rather, don't you think—these ancient places?" she said presently, as they drove along past palms and flat-topped houses of the felaheen. "There's something watching and listening all the time."

Tom made no answer. He felt suddenly unsure of something—almost unsure of himself, it seemed.

"One feels a bit lost," he said slowly after a bit, "and lonely. It's the size, I think."

"Perhaps," she rejoined, peering at him with half-lowered eyelids, "and the silence." She broke off, then added, "You can hear your thoughts too clearly."

Tom was sitting back amid a bundle of rugs she had wrapped him in; Tony, beside her, on the front seat, seemed in a gentle doze. They drove the rest of the way in silence, dropping Tony first at the Savoy, then going on to Tom's hotel. She insisted, although her own house was in the opposite direction. "And you're to take a hot whisky when you get into bed, remember, and don't get up to-morrow if you feel a chill." She gave him orders for his health and comfort as though he were her son. Tom noticed it, told her she was divinely precious to him, and promised faithfully to obey.

"What do you think about Tony?" he asked suddenly, when they had driven alone for several minutes. "I mean, what impression does he make on you? How do you *feel* him?"

"He's enjoying himself immensely with his numerous friends," she replied at once. "He grows on one rather. He's a dear, I think." She looked at him, then turned away again. "Don't you, Tom?"

"Oh, rather. I've always thought so. I told you first long ago, didn't I?" He made no reference to the exaggeration about the friends. "And I think it's wonderful how well we—what a perfect trio we are."

"Yes, isn't it?"

They both became thoughtful then. There fell a pause between them, when Tom broke in abruptly once again: "But—what do *you* feel? Because *I* think he's half in love with you, if you want to know." He leaned over and whispered in her ear. The words tumbled out as though they were in a hurry. "It pleases me immensely, Lettice; it makes me feel so proud of you and happy. It'll do him a world of good, too, if he loves a woman like you. You'll teach him something." She smiled shyly and said, "I wonder, Tom. Do you really think so? He certainly seems fond of me, but I hadn't thought quite that. You think everybody must fall in love with me." She pushed him away with a gentle yet impatient pressure of her arm, indicating the Arab coachman with a nod of her head. "Take care of him, Lettice: he's a dear fellow; don't let him break his heart."

Tom began to flirt outrageously; his arm crept round her, he leaned over and stole a kiss—and to his amazement she did not try to stop him. She did not seem to notice it. She sat very still—a stone statue in the moonlight.

Then, suddenly, he realized that she had not replied to his question. He promptly repeated it therefore. "You put me off with what *he* feels, but I want to know what *you* feel," he said with emphasis.

"But, Tom, I'm not putting you off, as you call it—with anything," and there was a touch of annoyance in her tone and manner.

"Tell me, Lettice; it interests me. You're such a puzzle, d'you know—? out here." His tone unconsciously grew more earnest as he spoke.

Madame Jaretzka broke into a little laugh. "You boy!" she exclaimed teasingly, "you're trying to heighten his value so as to increase your own by contrast. The more people you can find in love with me, the more you'll be able to flatter yourself."

Tom laughed with her, though he did not quite understand. He had never heard her say such a thing before. He accepted the cleverness she gave him credit for, however. "Of course, and why shouldn't I?" And he was just going to put his original question in another form, had already begun it, in fact, when she interrupted him, putting her hand playfully over his mouth for a second: "I do think Tony's a happy entertaining sort of man," she told him, "even fascinating in a certain kind of way. He's very stimulating to me. And I feel—don't you, Tom?"—a slight change—was it softness?—crept into her tone—"a sort of beauty in him somewhere?"

"Yes, p'raps I do," he assented briefly, "but, I say, Lettice darling, you mischievous Egyptian princess."

"Be quiet, Tom, and take your arm away. Here's the hotel in sight." And yet, somehow, he fancied that she preferred his action to the talk.

"Tell me this first," he went on, obeying her peremptory tone: "do you think it's true that we three have been together before like that—as Tony said, I mean? It's a funny thing, but I swear it sounded true when he said it." His tone was earnest again. "It gave me the creeps a bit, and, d'you know, you looked so queer, so wonderful in the moonlight—you looked un-English, foreign—like one of those Egyptian figures come to life. That's what made me cold, I think." His laughter died away. He was grave suddenly. He sighed a little and moved closer to her. "That's—what made me get up and leave you," he added abruptly.

"Oh, he's always saying that kind of thing," she answered quickly, moving the rugs for him to get out as the carriage slowed up before the brilliantly lit hotel. She made no reference to his other words. "There's a lot of poetry in Tony too—out here."

"Said it before, has he?" exclaimed Tom with genuine astonishment. "All three of us or—or just you and him? Am *I* in the business too?" He was now bubbling over with laughter again for some reason; it all seemed comical, almost. Yet it was a sudden, an emotional laughter. His emotion—his excitement surprised him even at the time.

"All three of us—I think," she said, as he held her hand a moment, saying good-by. "Yes, all three of us, of course. Now good-night, you inquisitive and impertinent boy, and if you have to stay in bed to-morrow we'll come over and nurse you all day long." He answered that he would certainly stay in bed in that case—and watched her waving her hand over the back of the carriage as she drove away into the moonlight like a fading dream of stars and mystery and beauty. Then he took his telegrams and letters from the Arab porter with the face of expressionless bronze, and went up to bed.

"What a strange and wonderful woman!" he thought as the lift rushed him up: "out here she seems another being, and a thousand times more fascinating." He felt almost that he would like to win her all over again from the beginning. "She's different to what she was in England. Tony's different too. And so am I, I do believe!" he exclaimed in his bedroom, looking at his sunburned face in the glass a moment. "We're all different!" He felt singularly happy, hilarious, stimulated—a deep and curious excitement was in him. Above all there was high pride that she belonged to him so absolutely. And the analysis he had indulged in England vanished here. He forgot it all.... He was in Egypt with her ... now.

He read his letters and telegrams, only half realizing at first that they called him back to Assouan. "What a bore," he thought, "I simply shan't go. A week's delay won't matter. I can telephone."

He laid them down upon the table beside him and walked out on to his balcony. Responsibility seemed less in him. He felt a little reckless. His position was quite secure. He was his own master. He meant to enjoy himself.... But another, deeper voice was sounding in him too. He heard it, but at first refused to recognize it. It whispered. One word it whispered: "Stay...!"

There was no sleep in him; with an overcoat thrown across his shoulders he watched the calm Egyptian night, the soft army of the stars, the river gleaming in a broad band of silver. Hitherto Lettice had monopolized his energies, he had neglected Egypt, whose indecipherable meaning now came floating in upon him with a strange insistence. Lettice came with it too. The two beauties were indistinguishable....

A flock of boats lay motionless, their black masts hanging in mid-air; all was still and silent, no voices, no footsteps, no movements anywhere. In the distance the desolate rocky hills rolled like a solid wave along the horizon. Gaunt and mysterious, they loomed upon the night. They were pierced by myriad tombs, those solemn hills; the stately dead lay there in hundreds; he imagined them looking forth a moment like himself across the peace and silence of the moonlit desert. They focussed upon Thebes, upon the white hotel, upon a modern world they could not recognize— upon his very windows. It seemed to him for a moment that their ancient eyes met his own across the sand, across the silvery river, and, as they met, a shadowy gleam of recognition passed between them and himself. At the same time he also saw the eyes he loved. They gazed through half-closed eyelids... the eastern eyes of his early boyhood's dream. He remembered again the strange emotion of the day he first arrived in Egypt, weeks ago....

And then he suddenly thought of Tony, and of Tony's careless remark as they sat in ruined Karnak together: "I feel as if we three had all been here before."

Why it returned to him just now he did not know: for some reason unexplained the phrase revived in him. Perhaps he felt an instinctive sympathy towards the poet's idea that he and *she* were lovers of such long standing, of such ancient lineage. It flattered his pride, while at the same time it disturbed him. A sense of vague disquiet grew stronger in him. In any case, he did not dismiss it and forget—his natural way of treating fancies. "Perhaps," he murmured, "the bodies she and I once occupied lie there now—lie under the very stars their eyes—*our* own—once looked upon."

It was strange the fancy took such root in him.... He stood a long time gazing at the vast, lonely necropolis among the mountains. There was an extraordinary stillness over that western bank, where the dead lay in their ancient tombs. The silence was eloquent, but the whole sky whispered to his soul. And again he felt that Egypt welcomed him; he was curiously at home here. It moved the deeps in him, brought him out; it changed him; it brought out Lettice too—brought out a certain power in her. She was more of a woman here, a woman of the world. She was more wilful, and more human. Values had subtly altered. Tony himself was altered.... Egypt affected them all three....

The vague uneasiness persisted. His mood changed a little, the excitement gradually subsided; thought shifted to a minor key, subdued by the beauty of the southern night. The world lay in a mysterious glow, the hush was exquisite. Yet there was expectancy: that glow, that hush were ready to burst into flame and language. They covered secrets. Something was watching him. He was dimly aware of a thousand old, forgotten things....

He no longer thought, but felt. The calm, the peace, the silence laid soothing fingers against the running of his blood; the turbulent condition settled down. Then, through the quieting surface of his reverie, stole up a yet deeper mood that seemed evoked partly by the mysterious glamour of the scene, yet partly by his will to let it come. It had been a long time in him; he now let it up to breathe. It came, moreover, with ease, and quickly.

For a gentle sadness rose upon him, a sadness deeply hidden that he suddenly laid bare as of set deliberation. The recent play and laughter, above all his own excitement, had purposely concealed it—from others possibly, but certainly from himself. The excitement had been a mask assumed by something deeper in him he had wished—and tried—to hide. Gently, it came at first, this sadness, then with increasing authority and speed. It rose about him like a cloud that hid the stars and dimmed the sinking moon. It spread a veil between him and the rocky cemetery on those mournful hills beyond the Nile. In a sense it seemed, indeed, to issue thence. It emanated from their silence and their ancient tombs. It sank into him. It was penetrating—it was familiar—it was deathless.

But it was no mood of common sadness, there lay no physical tinge in it; but rather a deep, unfathomable sadness of the spirit: an inner loneliness. From his inmost soul it issued outwards, meeting half-way some sense of similar loneliness that breathed towards him from these tragic Theban hills.

And Tom, not understanding it, tried to shake himself free again; he called up cheerful things to balance it; he thought of his firm position in the world, of his proud partnership, of his security with her he loved, of his zest in life, of the happy prospect immediately in front of him. But, in spite of all, the mood crept upwards like a rising wave, swamping his best resistance, drowning all appeal to joy and confidence. He recognized an unwelcome revival of that earlier nightmare dread connected with his boyhood, things he had decided to forget, and had forgotten as he thought. The mood took him gravely, with the deepest melancholy he had ever known. It had begun so delicately; it became in a little while so determined; it threatened to overmaster him. He turned then and faced it, so to speak. He looked hard at it and asked of himself its meaning. Thought and emotion in him shuffled with their shadowy feet.

And then he realized that, in germ at any rate, the mood had lain actually a long time in him, deeply concealed—the surface excitement merely froth. He had hidden it from himself. It had been accumulating, gaining strength and impetus, pausing upon direction only. All the hours just spent at Karnak it had been there, drawing nearer to the surface, this very night, but a little while ago, during the drive home as well, before that even, during all the talks and outdoor meals and expeditions: he traced its existence suddenly, and with tiny darts of piercing, unintelligible pain, as far back as Alexandria and the day of his arrival. It seemed to justify the vivid emotions that had marked his entry into Egypt. It became sharply clear now— this had been in him subconsciously since the moment when he read the little letter of welcome Lettice sent to meet him at the steamer, a letter he discovered afterwards was curiously empty. This disappointment, this underlying sadness he had kept hidden from himself: he now laid it bare and recognized it. He faced it. With a further flash he traced it finally to the journey in the train when he had read over the Warsaw and the Egyptian letters.

And he felt startled: something at the roots of his life was trembling. He tried to think. But Tom was slow; he could feel, but he could not dissect and analyze. Introspection, with him, invariably darkened vision, led to distortion and bewilderment. The effort to examine closely confused him. Instead of dissipating the emotion, he intensified it. The sense of loneliness grew inexplicably—a great, deep loneliness, a loneliness of the spirit, a loneliness, moreover, that it seemed to him he had experienced before, though when, under what conditions, he could not anywhere remember.

His former happiness was gone, the false excitement with it. This freezing loneliness stole in and took their places. Its explanation lay hopelessly beyond him, though he felt sure it had to do with this haunted and mysterious land where he now found himself, and in a measure with her, even with Tony too....

The hint Egypt dropped into him upon his arrival was a true one—he had slipped over an edge, slipped into something underneath, below him—something past. But slipped *with her*. She had come back to fetch him. They had come back to fetch—each other... through pain....

And a shadow from those somber Theban mountains crept, as it were, upon his life. He knew a sinking of the heart, a solemn, dark presentiment that murmured in his blood the syllables of "tragedy." To his complete amazement—at first he refused to believe it indeed— there came a lump into his throat, as though tears must follow to relieve the strain; and a moment later there was moisture, a perceptible moisture, in his eyes. The sadness had so swiftly passed into foreboding, with a sense of menacing tragedy that oppressed him without cause or explanation. Joy and confidence collapsed before it like a paper platform beneath the pressure of a wind. His feet and hands were cold. He shivered....

Then, gradually, as he stood there watching the calm procession of the stars, he felt the ominous emotion draw down again, retreat. Deep down inside him whence it came, it retired into a kind of interior remoteness that lay beyond his reach. It was incredible and strange. The intensity had made it seem so real.... For, while it lasted, he had felt himself bereft, lonely beyond all telling, outcast, lost, forgotten, wrapped in a cold and desolate misery that frightened him past all belief. The hand that lit his pipe still trembled. But the mood had passed as mysteriously as it came. It left him curiously shaken in his heart. "Perhaps this too," thought murmured from some depth in him he could neither control nor understand, "perhaps this too is—Egypt."

He went to bed, emotion all smoothed out again, yet wondering a good deal at himself. For the odd upheaval was a new experience. Such an attack had never come to him before; he laughed at it, called it hysteria, and decided that its cause was physical; he persuaded himself that it had a very banal cause—a chill, even a violent chill, incipient fever and over-fatigue at the back of it. He smiled at himself, while obeying the loving orders he had received, and brewing the comforting hot mixture with his spirit lamp.

Then, drinking it, he looked round the room with satisfaction at the various evidences of precious, motherly care. This mother-love restored his happiness by degrees. His more normal, stolid, unimaginative self climbed back into its place again—yet with a touch of awkwardness and difficulty. Something in him was changed, or changing; he had surprised it in the act.

The nature of the change escaped him, however. It seemed, perhaps—this was the nearest he could get to it,—that something in him had weakened, some sense of security, of confidence, of self-complacency, given way a little. Only it was not his certainty of the mother-love in her: that remained safe from all possible attack. A tinge of uneasiness still lay like a shadow on his mind—until the fiery spirit chased it away, and a heavy sleep came over him that lasted without a break until he woke two hours after sunrise.

CHAPTER XVII

He sprang from his bed, went to the open window and thrust his head out into the crystal atmosphere. It was impossible to credit the afflicting nightmare of a few hours ago. Gold lay upon the world, and the face of Egypt wore her great Osirian look.

In the air was that tang of mountain-tops that stimulated like wine. Everything sparkled, the river blazed, the desert was a sheet of burnished bronze. Light, heat, and radiance pervaded the whole glad morning, bathing even his bare feet on the warm, soft carpet. It was good to be alive. How could he not feel happy and unafraid?

The change, perhaps, was sudden; it certainly was complete.... These vivid alternations seemed characteristic of his whole Egyptian winter. Another self thrust up, sank out of sight, then rose again. The confusion seemed almost due to a pair of competing selves, each gaining the upper hand in turn—sometimes he lived both at once.... The uneasy mood, at any rate, had vanished with the darkness, for nothing sad or heavy-footed could endure amid this dancing exhilaration of the morning. Born of the brooding night and mournful hills, his recent pain was forgotten.

He dressed in flannels, and went his way to the house upon the Nile soon after nine o'clock; he certainly had no chill; there was only singing in his heart. The curious change in Lettice, it seemed, no longer troubled him. And, finding Tony already in the garden, they sat in the shade and smoked together while waiting for their hostess. Light-hearted as himself, Tony outlined various projects, to which the other readily assented. He persuaded himself easily, if recklessly; the work could wait. "We simply must see it all together," Tony urged, "You can go back to Assouan next week. You'll find everything all right. Why hurry off?"... How his cousin had improved, Tom was thinking; his tact was perfect; he asked no awkward questions; showed no inquisitiveness. He just assumed that his companions had a right to be fond of each other, while taking his own inclusion in the collective friendship for granted as natural too.

And when Lettice came out to join them, radiant in white, with her broad sun-hat and long blue veil and pretty gauntlet gloves, Tony explained with enthusiasm at the beauty of the picture: "She's come into her own out here with a vengeance," he declared. "She ought to live in Egypt always. It suits her down to the ground." Whereupon Tom, pleased by the spontaneous admiration, whispered proudly to himself, "And she is mine—all mine!" Tony's praise seemed to double her value in his eyes at once. So Tony, too, was aware that she had changed; had noted the subtle alteration, the enhancement of her beauty, the soft Egyptian transformation!

"You'd hardly take her for European, I swear—at a distance—now, would you?"

"N-no," Tom agreed, "perhaps you wouldn't—" at which moment precisely the subject of their remarks came up and threw her long blue veil across them both with the command that it was time to start.

The following days were one long dream of happiness and wonder spent between the sunlight and the stars. They were never weary of the beauty, the marvel, and the mystery of all they saw. The appeal of temple, tomb, and desert was so intimate—it seemed instinctive. The burning sun, the scented winds, great sunsets and great dawns, these with the palms, the river, and the sand seemed a perfect frame about a perfect picture. They knew a kind of secret pleasure that was satisfying. Egypt harmonized all three of them. And if Tom did not notice the change increasing upon one of them, it was doubtless because he was too much involved in the general happiness to see it separate.

There came a temporary interruption, however, in due course—his conscience pricked him. "I really must take a run up to Assouan," he decided. "I've been rather neglecting things perhaps. A week at most will do it— and then for another ten days' holiday again!"

The rhythm broke, as it were, with a certain suddenness. A rift came in the collective dream. He saw details again—saw them separate. And the day before he left a trifling thing occurred that forced him to notice the growth of the change in Lettice. He focussed it. It startled him a little.

The others had not sought to change his judgment. But they planned an all-night bivouac in the desert for his return; they would sleep with blankets on the sand, cook their supper upon an open fire, and see the dawn. "It's an exquisite experience," said Tony. "The stars fade quickly, there's a puff of warmer wind, and the sun comes up with a rush. It's marvelous. I'll get de Lorne and his sister to join us; he can tell stories round the fire, and perhaps she will get inspiration at last for her awful pictures." Madame Jaretzka laughed. "Then we must have Lady Sybil too," she added; "de Lorne may find courage to propose to her fortune at last." Tom looked up at her with a momentary surprise. "I declare, Lettice, you've grown quite worldly; that's a very cynical remark and point of view."

He said it teasingly, but it was this innocent remark that served to focus the change in her he had been aware of vaguely for a long time. She was more worldly here, the ordinary "woman" in her was more in evidence: and while he rather liked it—it brought her more within his reach, as it were, yet without lowering her—he felt also puzzled. Several times of late he had surprised this wholesome sign of sex in things she said and did, as though the woman-side, as he called it, was touched into activity at last. It added to her charm; at the same time it increased his burning desire to possess her absolutely for himself. What he felt as the impersonal—almost spiritually elusive—aspect of her he had first known, was certainly less in evidence. Another part of her was rising into view, if not already in the ascendant. The burning sun, the sensuous color and beauty of the Egyptian climate, he had heard, could have this physiological effect. He wondered.

"Sybil has been waiting for him to ask her ever since I came out," he heard her saying with a gesture almost of impatience. "Only he thinks he oughtn't to speak because he's poor. The result is she's getting bolder in proportion as he gets more shy."

They all laughingly agreed to help matters to a climax when Tom, looking up suddenly, saw Madame Jaretzka smiling at his cousin with her eyelids half closed in the way he once disliked but now adored. He wondered suddenly how much Tony liked her; the improvement in him was assuredly due to her, he felt; Tony had less and less time now for his other friends. It occurred to him for a second that the change in her was greater than he quite knew, perhaps. He watched them together for some moments. It gave him a proud sense of pleasure to feel that her influence was making a man out of the medley of talent and irresponsibility that was Tony. Tony was learning at last to "find himself." It must be quite a new experience for him to know and like a woman of her sort, almost a discovery. But with a flash—too swift and fleeting to be a definite thought—Tom was conscious of another thing as well—and for the first time: "How she would put him in his place if he attempted any liberties with her!"

The same second he was ashamed that such a notion could ever have occurred to him: it was mean towards Tony, ungenerous toward her; and yet—he was aware of a distinct emotion, a touch of personal triumph in it somewhere....

His thoughts were interrupted by a sudden tumult; there was a scurry; Tony flung a stone, Madame Jaretzka leaped upon a boulder, gathering her skirts together hurriedly, with a little scream. "Kill it, Tony! Quick!" he heard her cry. And he saw then a very large and hairy spider crawling swiftly across the white paper that had wrapped their fruit and sandwiches, an ugly and distressing sight. "It's a tarantula," she screamed, half laughing, half alarmed, showing neat ankles as she balanced precariously upon her boulder, "and it's coming at me. Quick, Tony, another stone," as he missed it for the second time, "it's making for me! Oh, kill it, kill it!" Tony, still aiming badly, assured her it was not a tarantula, nor poisonous even; he knew the species well. "It's quite harmless," he cried, "there's no need to kill it. It's not in a house—" and he flung another useless stone at it.

What followed happened very quickly, in a second or two at most. Tom saw it with sharp surprise, a curious distaste, almost with a shudder. It certainly astonished him, and in another sense it shocked him. He had done nothing himself because Lettice, he thought, was half in fun, making a diversion out of nothing. Only much later did it occur to him that she had turned instinctively to Tony for protection, rather than to himself. What caused him the unpleasant sensation, however, was that she deliberately stepped down from her perch of safety and kicked at the advancing horror. Probably her intention was merely to drive it away—she was certainly excited but the result was that she set her foot upon the creature and crushed its life out with an instant's pressure of her dainty boot. "There!" she cried. "Oh, but I didn't mean to kill it! How frightful of me!"

He heard Tony say, "Bravo, you *are* a brave woman! Such creatures have no right to live!" as he hid the disfigured piece of paper beneath some stones... and, after a few minutes' chatter, the donkey-boys had packed up the luncheon things and they were all on their way towards the next object of their expedition, as though nothing had happened. The entire incident had occupied a moment and a half at most. Madame Jaretzka was laughing and talking as before, gay as a child and pretty as a dream.

In Tom's mind, however, it went on happening—over and over again. He could not at once clean his mind of a disagreeable impression that remained. Another woman, any woman for that matter, might have done what she did without leaving a trace in him of anything but a certain admiration. It was a perfectly natural thing. The creature probably was poisonous as well as hideous; Tony merely said the contrary to calm her; moreover, he gave no help, and the insect was certainly making hurriedly towards her—she had to save and protect herself. There was nothing in the incident beyond an ugliness, a passing second of distress; and yet—this was what remained with him—it was not a natural thing for "Lettice" to have done. Her intention, no doubt, was otherwise; there was miscalculation as well. She had only meant to frighten the scurrying creature. Yet at the same time the instinctive act issued, he felt, from another aspect, another part of her, a part that in London, in Montreux, lay unexpressed and unawakened. And it issued deliberately too. The exquisite tenderness that could not have put a fly to death was less in her. Egypt had changed her oddly. He was aware of something that made him shrink, though he did not use the phrase even to himself in thought; or something hard and almost cruel, though both adjectives lay far from clothing the faint sensation in his mind with definite words.

Tom watched her instinctively from that moment, unconsciously, that is; less with his eyes than with a little pair of glasses in his heart. There was certainly a change in her that he could not quite account for; the notion came to him once or twice that some influence was upon her, some power that was outside herself, modifying the sharp outlines of her first peculiar tenderness. These dear outlines blurred a trifle in the fierce sunlight of this desert air. He knew not how to express it even to himself, for it was too tenuous to seize in actual words.

He arrived at this partial conclusion anyhow: that he was aware of what he called the "woman" in her, but a very human woman—a certain wilfulness that was half wildness in it. There was a hint of the earthly, too, as opposed to spiritual, though in a sense that was wholesome, good, entirely right. Yet it was rather, perhaps, primitive than earthly in any vulgar meaning.... It had been absent or dormant hitherto. She needed it; something— was it Egypt? Was it sex?—had stirred it into life. And its first expression— surprising herself as much as it surprised him—had an aspect of exaggeration almost.

The way she raced their donkeys in her sand-cart on the way home, by no means sparing the whip, was extremely human, but unless he had witnessed it he could never have pictured it as possible—so utterly unlike the gentle, gracious, almost fastidious being he had known first. There was a hint of a darker, stronger color in the pattern of her being now, partly of careless and abundant spirits, partly of this new primitive savagery. He noticed it more and more, it was both repellant and curiously attractive; yet, while he adored it in her, he also shrank. He detected a touch even of barbaric vanity, and this singular touch of the barbaric veiled the tenderness. He almost felt in her the power to inflict pain without flinching—upon another....

The following day their time of gaiety was to end, awaiting only his return later from Assouan. Tony was going down to Cairo with some other friends ; Tom would be away at least a week, and tried hard to persuade his cousin to come with him instead, but Tony had given his word, and could not change. Moreover, he was dining with his friends that very night and must hurry off at once. He said his good-bys and went.

"We're very rarely alone now, are we, Lettice?" Tom began abruptly the instant they were together. At the back of his mind rose something he did not understand that forced more significance into his tone than he intended. He felt very full—an accumulation that must have expression. He blurted it out without reflection. "Hardly once since I arrived two weeks ago, now I come to think of it." He looked at her half playfully, half reproachfully.

"'We're always three,'" he added with the frank pathos of a boy. And while one part of him felt ashamed, another part urged him onward and was glad.

But the way she answered startled him.

"Tom dear, don't scold me now. I *am* so tired." It was the tone that took his breath away. For the first time in their acquaintance he noticed something like exasperation. "I've been doing too much," she went on more gently, smiling up into his face: "I feel it. And that dreadful thing—that insect—" she shuddered a little—"I never meant to hurt it. It's upset me. All this daily excitement and the sun, and the jolting of that rickety sand-cart—there, Tom, come and sit beside me a moment and let's talk before you go. I'm really too done up to drive you to the station to-night. You'll understand and forgive me, won't you?" Her voice was very soft. She was excited, too, talking at random rather. Her being seemed confused.

He took his place on a sturdy cushion at her feet, full of an exaggerated remorse. She looked pale, though her eyes were very sparkling. His heart condemned him. He said nothing about the "dreadful incident."

"Lettice, dearest girl, I didn't mean anything. You have been doing far too much, and it's my fault; you've done it all for me—to give me pleasure. It's been too wonderful." He took her hand, while her other stroked his head. "You must rest while I'm away."

"Yes," she murmured, "so as to be quite fresh when you come back. You won't be *very* long, will you?" He said he would risk his whole career to get back within the week. "But, you know, I have neglected things rather—up there." He smiled fondly as he said "up there." She looked down tenderly into his eyes. "And I have neglected you—down here," she said. "That's what you mean, boy, isn't it?" And for the first time he did not like the old mode of address he once thought perfect. There seemed a flavor of pity in it. "It *would* be nice to be alone sometimes, wouldn't it, Lettice? Quite alone, I mean," he said with meaning.

"We shall be, we will be—later, Tom," she whispered; "*quite* alone together." She paused, then added louder, "the truth is, Egypt—the air and climate—stimulates me too much; it makes me restless. It excites me in a way I can't quite understand. I can't sit still and talk and be idle as one does in sleepy, solemn England."

He was explaining with laborious logic that it was the dryness of the air that exhausted the nerves a bit, when she straightened herself up and took her hand away. "Oh, yes, Tom, I know, I know. That's perfectly true, and everybody says that—I mean, everybody feels it, don't they?" She said it quickly, almost impatiently.

The old uneasiness flashed through him at that moment: it occurred to him, "I'm dull, I'm boring her." She was over-tired he remembered then, her nerves on edge a trifle; it was natural enough; he would just kiss her and leave her to rest quietly. Yet a tiny sense of resentment, even of chill crept over him. This impatience in her was new to him. He wondered an instant, then crushed back the words that tried to rise. He said good-by, taking her in his arms for a moment with an over- mastering impulse he could not check. Deep love and tenderness were in his heart and eyes. He yearned to protect and guide her—keep her safe from harm. He felt his older years, his steadier strength; he was a man, she but a little, gentle woman. And the elemental powers of life were very strong. With a sudden impulsive gesture, then, that surprised him, she returned the embrace with a kind of vehemence, pressing him closely to her heart and kissing him repeatedly on the cheeks and eyes.

Tom had expected her to resist and chide him. He was bewildered and delighted; he was also puzzled—for the first second only. "You darling woman," he cried, forgetting utterly the suspicion, the uneasiness, the passing cold of a moment before. He marveled that his heart could have let such fancies come to birth. Surely he had changed for such a thing to be possible at all!... Various impulses and emotions that clamored in him he kept back with an effort. He was aware of clashing contradictions. Confidence was less in him. He felt curiously unsure of himself—also, in a cruel, subtle way—of her. There was a new thing in her—rising. Was it against himself somewhere? The tangle in his heart and mind seemed inextricable: he wanted to seize her and carry her away... struggling but captured, and at the same time—singular contradiction—to entreat her humbly, though passionately, to love him more, and to *show* more that she loved him. Surely there were two selves in him.

He moved over to the door. "Cataract Hotel, remember, finds me." He stood still, looking back at her.

She smiled, repeating the words after him. "And Lettice, you *will* write?" She blew a kiss to him by way of answer. Then, charged to the brim with a thousand things he ached to say, yet would not, almost dared not say, he added playfully—a child must have noticed that his voice was too deep for banter and his breath came oddly:

"And mind you don't let Tony lose his head *too* much. He's pretty far gone, you know, already."

The same instant he could have bitten his tongue off to recall the words. Somewhere he had been untrue to himself, almost betrayed himself.

She rose suddenly from her sofa and came quickly towards him across the floor; he felt his heart sink a moment, then start hammering irregularly against his ribs. Something frightened him. For he caught in her face an expression he could not understand—the struggle of many strong emotions—anxiety and passion, fear and love; the eyes were shining, though the lids remained half closed; she made a curious gesture: she moved swiftly. He braced himself as against attack. He shrank. Her power over him was greater than he knew.

For he saw her in that instant as another person, another woman, foreign—almost eastern; the barbaric primitive thing flamed out of her, but with something regal, queenly, added to it; she looked Egyptian; the Princess, as he called her sometimes, had come to life. And the same moment in himself this curious sense of helplessness appeared—he raged against it inwardly—as though he were in her power somehow, as though her little foot could crush him—too—into the yellow sand....

A spasm of acute and aching pain shot through him: he winced; he wanted to turn and fly, yet was held rooted to the floor. He could not escape. It had to be. For oddly, mysteriously, he felt pain in her quick approach: she was coming to do him injury and hurt. The incident of the afternoon flashed again upon his mind—with the idea of cruelty in it somewhere, but a deep surge of strange emotion that flung wild sentences into his mind at the same instant. He tightly shut his lips, lest a hundred thoughts that had lain in him of late might burst into words he would later regret intensely. He must not avoid, delay an inevitable thing. To resist was somehow to be untrue to the deepest in him—to something painful he deserved, and, paradoxically, desired too. What could it all mean ?... He shivered as he waited—watching her come nearer.

She reached his side and her arms were stretched towards him. To his amazement, she folded him in closely against her breast and held him as though she never could let him go again. He stood there helpless; the revulsion of feeling took his strength away. He heard her breathless, yearning whisper as she kissed him: "My Tom, my precious boy, I couldn't see a hair of your dear head injured—I couldn't see you hurt! Take care of yourself and come back quickly—do, *do* take care of yourself. I shall count the days—" she broke off, held his face between her hands, gazed into his astonished eyes, and kissed him with the utmost tenderness again, the tenderness of a mother who is forced to be separated from the boy she loves better than herself.

Tom stood there trembling before her, and no speech came to help him. The thing passed like a dream: the dread, the emotion left him; the nightmare touch was gone. Her self-betrayal his simple nature did not at once discern. He felt only her divine tenderness pour over him. A spring of joy rose bubbling in him that no words could tell. Also he felt afraid. But the fear was no longer for himself. In some perplexing, singular way, he felt afraid for her.

Then, as a sentence came struggling to his lips, a step was heard upon the landing. There was time to resume conventional attitudes of good-by when Mrs. Haughstone appeared on the staircase leading to the hall. Tom said his farewells hurriedly to both of them, making his escape as naturally as possible. "I've just time to pack and catch the train," he shouted, and was gone.

And what remained with him afterwards of the curious little scene was the absolute joy and confidence those last tender embraces had restored to him, side by side with another thing that he was equally sure about, yet refused to dwell upon because he dared not—yet. For, as she came across the floor of the sunny room towards him, he realized two things in her, two persons almost. Another influence, he was convinced, worked in her strangely—some older, long-buried presentment of her interpenetrating, even piercing through, the modern self. She was divided against herself in some extraordinary fashion, one half struggling fiercely, yet struggling bravely, honestly, against the other. And the relationship between himself and her, though the evidence was so negligibly slight as yet, he knew had definitely changed....

It came to him as the Mother and the Woman in her. The Mother belonged unchangeably to him: the Woman, he felt, was troubled, tempted, and afraid.

CHAPTER XVIII

Afterwards, months, years afterwards, looking back upon these strange weeks of his brief Egyptian winter, Tom marveled at himself; he looked back, as it were, upon the thoughts and emotions of another man he could not recognize. This illusion involved his two companions also, Madame Jaretzka supremely, Tony slightly less, all three, however, together affected, all three changed.

As regards himself, however, there was always a part, it seemed, that remained unaffected. It looked on, it compared, it judged. He called it the Onlooker....

Explanation lay beyond his reach; he termed it enchantment: and there he left it. Insight seemed only to operate with regard to himself: of *their* feelings, thoughts, or point of view he was uninformed. They offered no explanations, and he sought none.... The man honest with himself is more rare than a January swallow. He alone is honest who can state a case without that bias of exaggeration favorable to himself which is almost lying. Try as he may, his statement leans one way or the other. The spirit-level of absolute honesty is hard to find, and, of course, Tom was no exception.... Occasionally he recalled the "spiral theory," which once, at least, had been in the minds of all three—the notion that their three souls lived over a former episode together, but from a higher point, and with the bird's-eye view which brought in understanding. But if this offered a hint of that winter's inner spiritual structure, Tom certainly did not claim it as a true solution. The whole thing began so stealthily, and progressed so slowly yet so surely....

He could only marvel at himself: he was so singularly changed—imagination so active, judgment alternately so positive and so faltering, every emotion so amazingly intensified. All the weakest and least admirable in him, the very dregs, seemed dragged up side by side with what was noblest, highest, and flung together in the rush and smother of the breaking Wave.

Events, in the dramatic meaning of the word, and outwardly, there were few perhaps, and those few meager and unsensational. No one was shot or drowned, no one was hanged and quartered: the police were not called in; to outsiders there seemed no air or attitude of drama anywhere; but in three human hearts, thrown together as by chance currents of normal life, there came to pass changes of a spiritual kind, conflict between essential, primitive forces of the soul, battlings, temptings, aspirations, sacrifice, that are the truest drama always, because the inmost being, whether glorified or degraded, is thereby—changed.

In this fierce intensification of his own being, and in the events experienced, Tom recognized the rising of his childhood Wave towards the breaking point. The early premonition that had seemed causeless to his learned father, that stirred in his mother the deep instinct to protect, and that ever, more or less, hung poised above the horizon of his passing years, had its origin in the bed-rock of his nature. It was associated with memory and instinct; the native tendencies and forces of his being had dramatized their inevitable fulfilment in a dream. He recognized intuitively what was coming—and he welcomed it. The body shrank from pain; the soul held out her hands to it....

Thus, looking back, he saw it mapped below him from a higher curve in life's ascending spiral. In the glare of a drenching sunshine that seemed hauntingly familiar, in the stupendous blaze of Egypt that knew and favored it, the action lay spread out: but in darkness, too, an oppressive, suffocating darkness as of the grave, as of the bottom of the sea. The map was streaked with this alternate light and gloom of elemental kind. It passed swiftly, he went swiftly with it. A few short crowded weeks of the intensest pain and happiness he had ever known,—and the Wave, its crest reflected in its origin, fell with a drowning crash. He merged into his background, yet he did not drown: in due course he again—emerged.

The sense of rushing that accompanied it all was in himself apparently: heightened by the contrast of the divine stillness which is Egypt—the golden, hanging days, the nights of cool, soft moonlight, the sighing winds with perfume in their breath, the mournful palms that fringed the peaceful river, the calm of multitudinous stars. The grim Theban hills looked on; the ruined Temples watched and knew; there were listening ears within a thousand tombs.... And there was the Desert—the endless emptiness where everything had already happened, the place where, therefore, everything could happen again without affronting time and space—the Desert seemed the infinite background whence the Wave tossed up three little specks of passionate human action and reaction. It was the "sea," a sea of dust. Yet out of the dust wild roses blossomed eventually with a sweetness of beauty unknown to any cultivated gardens....

And while he and his two companions made their moves upon this ancient chessboard of half-forgotten, half-remembered life, all natural things as well seemed raised to their most significant expression, sharing the joy and sadness, the beauty and the terror of his own experience. For the very scenery borrowed of his intensity, the familiar details urged a fraction beyond the normal, as though any moment they must break down into their elemental and essential nakedness. The pungent odor of the universal sand, the dust, the minute golden particles suspended in the flaming air, the marvelous dawns and sunsets, the mighty, awful pylons and the heat—all these contributed their quota of wonder and mystery to what happened. Egypt inspired it, and was satisfied.

The sediment of his nature was drawn up, the rubbish floated before his eyes, he saw himself through the curtains of suspended dust—until the flood, retiring, left him high upon the shore, no longer shuffling with his earthly, physical feet.

In the train to Assouan, Tom still felt the clinging arms about his neck, still heard the loving voice, eager with tenderness for his welfare and his quick return. She needed him: he was everything to her. He knew it, oh he was sure of it. He thought of his work, and knew some slight anxiety that he had neglected it. He would devote all his energies to the interests of his firm: there should be no shirking anywhere; his ten days' holiday was over. His mind fixed itself deliberately, though not too easily, on this alone.

He knew his own capacity, however, and that by concentration he could accomplish in a short time what other men might ask weeks to complete. Provided all was going well, he saw no reason why he could not be free again in a week at most. He knew quite well his value to the firm, but he knew also that he must continue to justify it. He was complacent, but, he hoped, not carelessly complacent. Tom felt very sure of himself again.

To his great relief he found things running smoothly. He examined every detail, interviewed all and sundry, supervised, decided, gave instructions. There was a letter from the London office conveying the formal satisfaction of the Board with results so far, praising especially certain reductions in cost he had judiciously effected; another letter from the older partner, referred confidently to greater profits than they had dared to anticipate; also there was a brief note from Sir William, the Chairman, now at Salonica, saying he might run over a little later and see for himself how the work was getting along.

Tom was supremely happy with it all. There was really very little for him to do; his engineers were highly competent: they could summon him at a day's notice from Luxor if anything went wrong. "But there's no sign of difficulty, sir," was their verdict; "everything's going like clockwork; the men working splendidly: it's only a matter of time."

It was the evening of the second day that Tom decided to go back to Luxor. He was eager for the promised bivouac they had arranged together. He had written once to say that all was well, but no word had yet come from her; she was resting, he was glad to think: Tony was away at Cairo with his friends; there might be a letter for him in the morning, but that could be sent after him. Joy and impatience urged him. He chuckled happily over his boyish plan; he would not announce himself; he would surprise her. He caught a train that would get him in for dinner.

And during his journey of six hours, he rehearsed this pleasure of surprising her. She was lonely without him. He visualized her delight and happiness. He would creep up to the window, to the edge of the verandah where she sat reading, Mrs. Haughstone knitting in a chair opposite. He would call her name "Lettice...." Her eyes would lighten, her manner change. That new spontaneous joy would show itself....

The sun was setting when the train got in, but by the time he had changed into flannels at his hotel the short dusk was falling. The entire western sky was gold and crimson, the air was sharp, the light dry desert wind blew shrewdly down the street. Behind the eastern hills rose a huge full moon, still pale with daylight, peering wisely over the enormous spread of luminous desert... He drove to her house, leaving the *arabyieh* at the gates. He walked quickly up the drive. The heavy foliage covered him with shadows, and he easily reached the verandah unobserved: no one seemed about; there was no sound of voices: the thick creepers up the wooden pillars screened him admirably. There was a movement of a chair, his heart began to thump, he climbed up softly, and at the other end of the verandah saw—Mrs. Haughstone knitting. But there was no sign of Lettice—and the blood rushed from his heart.

He had not been noticed, but his game was spoilt. He came round to the front steps and wished her politely a good-evening. Her surprise once over, and explanations made, she asked him, cordially enough, to stay to dinner. "Lettice, I know, would like it. You must be tired out. She did not expect you back so soon; but she would never forgive me if I let you go after them."

Tom heard the words as in a dream, and answered also in a dream—a dream of astonishment, vexation, disappointment, none of them concealed. His uneasiness returned in an acute, intensified form. For he learnt that they were bivouacking on the Nile to see the sunrise. Tony had, after all, not gone to Cairo; de Lorne and Lady Sybil accompanied them. It was the picnic they had planned together against his return. "Lettice wrote," Mrs. Haughstone mentioned, "but the letter must have missed you. I warned her you'd be disappointed—if you knew."

"So Tony didn't go to Cairo after all?" Tom asked again. His voice sounded thin, less volume in it than usual. That "if you knew" dropped something of sudden anguish in his heart.

"His friends put him off at the last moment—illness, he said, or something." Mrs. Haughstone repeated the invitation to dine and make himself at home. "I'm positive my cousin would like you to," she added with a certain emphasis.

Tom thanked her. He had the impression there was something on her mind. "I think I'll go after them," he repeated, "if you'll tell me exactly where they've gone." He stammered a little. "It would be rather a lark, I thought, to surprise them." What foolish, what inadequate words!

"Just as you like, of course. But I'm sure she's quite safe," was the bland reply. "Mr. Winslowe will look after her."

"Oh, rather," replied Tom; "but it would be good fun—rather a joke, you know—to creep upon them unawares,"—and then was surprised and sorry that he said it. "Have they gone very far?" he asked, fumbling for his cigarettes.

He learned that they had left after luncheon, taking with them all necessary paraphernalia for the night. There were feelings in him that he could not understand quite as he heard it. But only one thing was clear to him— he wished to be quickly, instantly, where Lettice was. It was comprehensible. Mrs. Haughstone understood and helped him. "I'll send Mohammed to get you a boatman, as you seem quite determined," she said, ringing the bell: "you can get there in an hour's ride. I couldn't go," she added, "I really felt too tired. Mr. Winslowe was here for lunch, and he exhausted us all with laughing so that I felt I'd had enough. Besides, the sun—"

"They all lunched here too?" asked Tom.

"Mr. Winslowe only," she mentioned, "but he was a host in himself. It quite exhausted me—"

"Tony can be frightfully amusing, can't he, when he likes," said Tom. Her repetition of "exhausted" annoyed him furiously for some reason.

He saw her hesitate then: she began to speak, but stopped herself; there was a curious expression in her face, almost of anxiety, he fancied. He felt the kindness in her. She was distressed. And an impulse, whence he knew not, rose in him to make her talk, but before he could find a suitable way of beginning, she said with a kind of relief in her tone and manner: "I'm glad you're back again, Mr. Kelverdon." She looked significantly at him. "Your influence is so steadying, if you don't mind my saying so." She gave an awkward little laugh, half of apology, half of shyness, or of what passed with her for shyness. "This climate—upsets some of us. It does something to the blood, I'm sure—"

"You feel anxious about—anything in particular?" Tom asked, with a sinking heart. At any other time he would have laughed.

Mrs. Haughstone shrugged her shoulders and sighed. She spoke with an effort apparently, as though doubtful how much she ought to say. "My cousin, after all, is—in a sense, at least—a married woman," was the reply, while Tom remembered that she had said the same thing once before. "And all men are not as careful for her reputation, perhaps, as you are." She mentioned the names of various people in Luxor, and left the impression that there was considerable gossip in the air. Tom disliked exceedingly the things she said and the way she said them, but felt unable to prevent her. He was angry with himself for listening, yet felt it beyond him to change the conversation. He both longed to hear every word, and at the same time dreaded it unspeakably. If only the boat would give him quickly an excuse.... He therefore heard her to the end, concerning the unwisdom of Madame Jaretzka in her careless refusal to be more circumspect, even— Mrs. Haughstone feared—to the point of compromising herself. With whom? Why, with Mr. Winslowe, of course. Hadn't he noticed it? No! Well, of course there was no harm in it, but was a mistake, she felt, to be seen about always with the same man. He called, too, at such unusual hours....

And each word she uttered seemed to Tom exactly what he had expected her to utter, entering his mind as a keenly poisoned shaft. Something already prepared in him leaped swiftly to understanding; only too well he grasped her meaning. The excitement in him passed into a feverishness that was painful.

For a long time he merely stood and listened, gazing across the river, but seeing nothing. He said no word. His impatience was difficult to conceal, yet he concealed it.

"Couldn't you give her a hint perhaps?" continued the other, as they waited on the steps together, watching the preparations for the boat below. She spoke with an assumed carelessness that was really a disguised emphasis. "She would take it from *you*, I'm sure. She means no harm; there is no harm. We all know that. She told me herself it was only a boy and girl affair. Still—"

"*She* said that?" asked Tom. His tone was calm, even to indifference, but his eyes, had she looked round, must certainly have betrayed him. Luckily she kept her gaze upon the moon-lit river. She drew her knitted shawl more closely round her. The cold air from the desert touched them both. Tom shivered.

"Oh, before you came out, that was," she mentioned; and each word was a separate stab in the center of his heart. After a pause she went on: "So you might say a little word to be more careful, if you saw your way. Mr. Winslowe, you see, is a poor guide just now: he has so completely lost his head. He's very impressionable—and very selfish—*I* think."

Tom was aware that he braced himself. Various emotions clashed within him. He knew a dozen different pains, all equally piercing. It angered him, besides, to hear Lettice spoken of in this slighting manner, for the inference was unavoidable. But there hid below his anger a deep, dull bitterness that tried angrily to raise its head. Something very ugly, very fierce moved with it. He crushed it back.... A feeling of hot shame flamed to his cheeks.

"I should feel it an impertinence, Mrs. Haughstone," he stammered at length, yet confident that he concealed his inner turmoil. "Your cousin— I mean, all that she does is quite beyond reproach."

Her answer staggered him like a blow between the eyes.

"Mr. Kelverdon—on the contrary. My cousin doesn't realize quite, I'm sure—that she may cause *him* suffering. She won't listen to me, but you could do it. *You* touch the mother in her."

It was a merciless, keen shaft—these last six words. The sudden truth of them turned him into ice. He touched only the mother in her: the woman— but the thought plunged out of sight, smothered instantly as by a granite slab he set upon it. The actual thought was smothered, yes, but the feeling struggled horribly for breath; and another inference, more deadly than the first, stole with a freezing touch upon his soul.

He turned round quietly and looked at his companion. "By jove," he said, with a laugh he believed was admirably natural, "I believe you're right. I'll give her a little hint,—for Tony's sake." He moved down the steps. "Tony is so—I mean he so easily loses his head. It's quite absurd."

But Mrs. Haughstone did not laugh. "Think it over," she rejoined. "You have excellent judgment. You may prevent a little disaster." She smiled and shook a warning finger. And Tom, feigning amusement as best he might, murmured something in agreement and raised his helmet with a playful flourish.

Mohammed, soft of voice and moving like a shadow, called that the boat was ready, and Tom prepared to go. Mrs. Haughstone accompanied him half-way down the steps.

"You won't startle them, will you, Mr. Kelverdon?" she said. "Lettice, is rather easily frightened." And she laughed a little. "It's Egypt—the dry air—one's nerves—"

Tom was already in the boat, where the Arab stood waiting in the moonlight like a ghost.

"Of course not," he called up to her through the still air. But, none the less, he meant to surprise her if he could. Only in his thought the pronoun insisted, somehow, on the plural form.

CHAPTER XIX

The boat swung out into mid-stream. Behind him the figure of Mrs. Haughstone faded away against the bourgainvillæa on the wall; in front, Mohammed's head and shoulders merged with the opposite bank; beyond, the spectral palms and the shadowy fields of clover slipped into the great body of the moon-fed desert. The desert itself sank down into a hollow that seemed to fling those dark Theban hills upwards—towards the stars.

Everything, as it were, went into its background. Everything, animate and inanimate, rose out of a common ultimate—the Sea. Yet for a moment only. There was this sense of preliminary withdrawal backwards, as for a leap that was to come....

He, too, felt merged with his own background. In his soul he knew the trouble and tumult of the Wave—gathering for a surging rise to follow....

For some minutes the sense of his own identity passed from him, and he wondered who he was. "Who am I?" would have been a quite natural question. "Let me see; I'm Kelverdon, Tom Kelverdon." Of course! Yet he felt that he was another person too. He lost his grip upon his normal modern self a moment, lost hold of the steady, confident personality that was familiar... The voice of Mohammed broke the singular spell. "Shicago, vair' good donkey. Yis, bes' donkey in Luxor—" and Tom remembered that he had a ride of an hour or so before he could reach the Temple of Deir El-Bahri where his friends were bivouacking. He tipped Mohammed as he landed, mounted "Chicago," and started off impatiently, then ran against little Mohammed coming back for a forgotten—kettle! He laughed. Every third Arab seemed called Mohammed. But he learned exactly where the party was. He sent his own donkey-boy home, and rode on alone across the moon-lit plain.

The wonder of the exquisite night took hold of him, searching his heart beyond all power of language—the strange Egyptian beauty. The ancient wilderness, so calm beneath the stars; the mournful hills that leaped to touch the smoking moon; the perfumed air, the deep old river—each, and all together, exhaled their innermost, essential magic. Over every separate boulder split the flood of silver. There were troops of shadows. Among these shadows, beyond the boulders, Isis herself, it seemed, went by with audible footfall on the sand, secretly guiding his advance; Horus, dignified and solemn, with hawk-wings hovering, and fierce, deathless eyes—Horus, too, watched him lest he stumble....

On all sides he seemed aware of the powerful Egyptian gods, their protective help, their familiar guidance. The deeps within him opened. He had done this thing before.... Even the little details brought the same lost message back to him, as the hoofs of his donkey shuffled through the sand or struck a loose stone aside with metallic clatter. He heard the lizards whistling....

There were other vaster emblems too, quite close. To the south, a little, the shoulders of the Colossi domed awfully above the flat expanse, and soon he passed the Ramesseum, the moon just entering the stupendous aisles. He saw the silvery shafts beneath the huge square pylons. On all sides lay the welter of prodigious ruins, steeped in a power and beauty that seemed borrowed from the scale of the immeasurable heavens. Egypt laid a great hand upon him, her cold wind brushed his cheeks. He was aware of awfulness, of splendor, of all the immensities. He was in Eternity; life was continuous throughout the ages; there was no death....

He felt huge wings, and a hawk, disturbed by his passing, flapped silently away to another broken pillar just beyond. He seemed swept forward, the plaything of greater forces than he knew. There was no question of direction, of resistance: the Wave rushed on and he rushed with it. His normal simplicity disappeared in a complexity that bewildered him. Very clear, however, was one thing—courage; that courage due to abandonment of self. He would face whatever came. He needed it. It was inevitable. Yes—this time he would face it without shuffling or disaster.... For he recognized disaster—and was aware of blood....

Questions asked themselves in long, long whispers, but found no answers. They emerged from that mothering background and returned into it again.... Sometimes he rode alone, but sometimes Lettice rode beside him: Tony joined them.... He felt them driven forward, all three together, obedient to the lift of the same rising wave, urged onwards towards a climax that was lost to sight, and yet familiar. He knew both joy and shrinking, a delicious welcome that it was going to happen, yet a dread of searing pain involved. A great fact lay everywhere about him in the night, but a fact he could not seize completely. All his faculties settled on it, but in vain—they settled on a fragment, while the rest lay free, beyond his reach. Pain, which was a pain at nothing, filled his heart; joy, which was joy without a reason, sang in him. The Wave rose higher, higher... the breath came with difficulty... wind was icy... there was choking in his throat.

He noticed the same high excitement in him he had experienced a few nights ago beneath the Karnak pylons—it ended later, he remembered, in the menace of an unutterable loneliness. This excitement was wild with an irresponsible hilarity that had no justification. He felt *exalté*. The wave, he swinging in the crest of it, was going to break, and he knew the awful thrill upon him before the dizzy, smothering plunge.

The complex of emotions made clear thought impossible. To put two and two together was beyond him. He felt the power that bore him along immensely greater than himself. And one of the smaller, self-asking questions issued from it: "Was this what *she* felt? Was Tony also feeling this? Were all three of them being swept along towards an inevitable climax?"... This singular notion that none of them could help themselves passed into him....

And then he realized from the slower pace of the animal beneath him that the path was going uphill. He collected his thoughts and looked about him. The forbidding cliffs that guard the grim Valley of the Kings, the haunted Theban hills, stood up pale yellow against the stars. The big moon, no longer smoking in the earthbound haze, had risen into the clear dominion of the upper sky. And he saw the terraces and columns of the Deir El-Bahri Temple facing him at the level of his eyes.

Nothing bore clearer testimony to the half-unconscious method by which the drama developed itself, to the deliberate yet uncalculated attitude of the actors towards some inevitable fulfilment, than the little scene which Tom's surprise arrival then discovered. According to the mood of the beholder it could mean much or little, everything or nothing. It was so nicely contrived between concealment and disclosure, and, like much else that happened, seemed balanced exquisitely, if painfully, between guilt and innocence. The point of view of the onlooker could alone decide. At the same time it provided a perfect frame for another picture that later took the stage. The stage seemed set for it exactly. The later picture broke in and used it too. That is to say, two separate pictures, distinct yet interfused, occupied the stage at once.

For Tom, dismounting, and leaving his animal with the donkey-boys some hundred yards away, approached stealthily over the sand and came upon the picnic group before he knew it. He watched them a moment before he announced himself. The scene was some feet below him. He looked down.

Two minutes sooner, he might conceivably have found the party quite differently grouped. Instead, however, his moment of arrival was exactly timed as though to witness a scene set cleverly by the invisible Stage Manager to frame two similar and yet different incidents.

Tom leaned against a broken column, staring.

Young de Lorne and Lady Sybil, he saw, were carefully admiring the moonlight on the yellow cliffs. Miss de Lorne stooped busily over rugs and basket packages. Her back was turned to Tony and Madame Jaretzka, who were intimately engaged, their faces very close together, in the half-prosaic, half-poetic act of blowing up a gipsy fire of scanty sticks and crumpled paper. The entire picture seemed arranged as though intended to convey a "situation." And to Tom a situation most certainly was conveyed successfully, though a situation of which the two chief actors—who shall say otherwise?—were possibly unconscious. For in that first moment as he leaned against the column, gazing fixedly, the smoking sticks between them burst into a flare of sudden flame, setting the two faces in a frame of bright red light, and Tom, gazing upon them from a distance of perhaps some twenty yards saw them clearly, yet somehow did not—recognize them. Another picture thrust itself between: he watched a scene that lay deep below him. Through the soft blaze of that Egyptian moonlight, across the silence of that pale Egyptian desert, beneath those old Egyptian stars, there stole upon him some magic which is deathless, though its outer covenants have vanished from the world.... Down, down he sank into the forgotten scenes whence it arose. Smothered in sand, it seemed, he heard the centuries roar past him...

He saw two other persons kneeling above that fire on the desert floor, two persons familiar to him, yet whom he could not wholly recognize. In that amazing second, while his heart stopped beating, it seemed as if thought in anguish cried aloud: "So, there you are! I have the proof!" while yet all verification of the tragic "you" remained just out of reach and undisclosed.

He did not recognize two persons whom he knew, while yet some portion of him keenly, fiercely searching, dived back into the limbo of unremembered time.... A thin blue smoke rose before his face, and to his nostrils stole a delicate perfume as of ambra. It was a picnic fire no longer. It was an eastern woman he saw lean forward across the gleam of a golden brazier and yield a kiss to the lips of a man who claimed it passionately. He saw her small hands folded and clinging about his neck. The face of the man he could not see, the head and shoulders being turned away, but hers he saw clearly—the dark, lustrous eyes that shone between half-closed eyelids. They were highly placed in life, these two, for their aspect as their garments told it; the man, indeed, had gold about him somewhere and the woman, in her mien, wore royalty. Yet, though he but saw their hands and heads alone, he knew instinctively that, if not regal, they were semi-regal, and set beyond his reach in power natural to them both. They were high-born, the favored of the world. Inferiority was his who watched them, the helpless inferiority of subordinate position. That, too, he knew... for a gasp of terror, though quickly smothered terror, rose vividly behind an anger that could gladly—kill.

There was a flash of fiery and intolerable pain within him....

The next second he saw merely—Lettice!—blowing the smoke from her face and eyes, with an impatient little gesture of both hands, while in front of her knelt Tony—fanning a reluctant fire of sticks and paper with his old felt hat.

He had been gazing at a colored bubble, the bubble had burst into air and vanished, the entire mood and picture vanished with it—so swiftly, so instantaneously, moreover, that Tom was ready to deny the entire experience.

Indeed, he did deny it. He refused to credit it. It had been, surely, a feeling rather than a sight. But the feeling having utterly vanished, he discredited the sight as well. The fiery pain had vanished too. He found himself watching the semi-comical picture of de Lorne and Lady Sybil flirting in dumb action, and Tony and Lettice trying to make a fire without the instinct or ability to succeed. And, incontinently, he burst out laughing audibly.

Yet, apparently, his laughter was not heard; he had made no actual sound. There was, instead, a little scream, a sudden movement, a scurrying of feet among the sand and stones, and Lettice and Tony rose upon one single impulse, as once before he had seen them rise in Karnak weeks ago. They stood up like one person. They looked about them into the surrounding shadows, disturbed, afflicted, yet as though they were not certain they had heard... and then, abruptly, the figure of Tony went out ... it disappeared. How, precisely, was not clear, but it was gone into the darkness....

And another picture—or another aspect of the first—dropped into place. There was an outline of a shadowy tent. The flap was stirring lightly, as though behind it some one hid—and watched. He could not tell. A deep confusion, as of two pictures interfused, was in him. For somehow he transferred his own self—was it physical desire? was it spiritual yearning? was it love?—projected his own self into the figure that had kissed her, taking her own passionate kiss in return. He actually experienced it. He did this thing. He had done it—once before! Knowing himself beside her, he both did it and saw himself doing it. He was both actor and onlooker....

There poured back upon him then, sweet and poignant, his love of an Egyptian woman, the fragrance of remembered tresses, the perfume of fair limbs that clung and of arms that lingered round his neck—yet that in the last moment slipped from his full possession. He was on his knees before her; he gazed up into her ardent eyes, set in a glowing face above his own; the face bent lower; he raised two slender hands, the fingers henna-stained, and pressed them to his lips. He felt their silken texture, the fragile pressure, her breath upon his face—yet all sharply withdrawn again before he captured them completely. There was the odor of long-forgotten unguents, sweet with a tang that sharpened them towards desire in days that knew a fiercer sunlight.... His brain went reeling. The effort to keep one picture separate from the other broke them both. He could not disentangle, could not distinguish. They intermingled. He was both the figure hidden behind the tent and the figure who held the woman in his arms. What his heart desired became, it seemed, that which happened....

And then the flap of the tent flung open, and out rushed a violent, leaping outline—the figure of a man. Another—it seemed himself—rushed to meet him. There was a gleam, a long deep cry.... A woman, with arms outstretched, knelt close beside the struggling figures on the sand. He saw two huge, dark, muscular hands about a bent and yielding neck, blood oozing thickly between the gripping fingers, staining them... then sudden darkness that blacked out the entire scene, and a choking effort to find breath.... But it was his own breath that failed, choked as by blood and fire that broke into his own throat.... Smothered in sand, the centuries roared past him, died away into the distance, sank back into the interminable desert.... He found his voice this time. He shouted.

He saw again—Lettice, blowing the smoke from her face and eyes with an impatient little gesture of both hands, while Tony knelt in front of her and fanned a reluctant fire with his old felt hat. The picture—the second picture—had been instantaneous. It had not lasted a fraction of a second even.

He shouted. And this time his voice was audible. Lettice and Tony stood up, as though a single person rose. Both turned in the direction of the sound. Then Tony moved off quickly. Tom's vision had interpenetrated this very action even while it was actually taking place—the first time.

"Why—I do declare—if it isn't—Tom!" he heard in a startled woman's voice.

He came down towards her slowly. Something of the "pictures" still swam in between what was next said and done. It seemed in the atmosphere, pervading the three of them. But it was weakening, passing away quickly. For one moment, however, before it passed, it became overpowering again.

"But, Tom—is this a joke, or what? You frightened me"—she gave a horrid gasp—"nearly to death! You've come back!"

"It's a surprise," he cried, trying to laugh, though his lips were dry and refused the effort. "I have surprised you. I've come back!"

He heard the gasp prolonged. Breathing seemed difficult. Some deep distress was in her. Yet, in place of pity, exultation caught him oddly. The next instant he felt suddenly afraid. There was confusion in his soul. For it was *he and she*, it seemed, who had been "surprised and caught." And her voice called shrilly:

"Tony! Tony...!"

There was amazement in the sound of it—terror, relief, and passion too. The thin note of fear and anguish broke through the natural call. Then, as Tony came running up, a few sticks in his big hands—she screamed, yet with failing breath:

"Oh, oh...! Who *are* you...?"

For the man she summoned came, but came too swiftly. Moving with uncertain gait, he yet came rapidly—terribly, somehow, and with violence. Instantaneously, it seemed he covered the intervening space. In the calm, sweet moonlight, beneath the blaze of the steady stars, he suddenly was—there, upon that patch of ancient desert sand. He looked half unearthly. The big hands he held outspread before him glistened a little in the shimmer of the moon. Yet they were dark, and they seemed menacing. They threatened— as with some power he meant to use, because it was his right. But the gleam upon them was not of swarthy skin alone. The gleam, the darkness, were of blood.... There was a cry again—a sound of anguish almost intolerable....

And the same instant Tom felt the clasp of his cousin's hand upon his own, and heard his jolly voice with easy, natural laughter in it: "But, Tom, old chap, how ripping! You're really back! This *is* a grand surprise! It's splendid!"

There was nothing that called upon either his courage or control. They were overjoyed to see him, the surprise he provided proved indeed the success of the evening.

"I thought at first you were Mohammed with the kettle," exclaimed Madame Jaretzka, coming close to make quite sure, and murmuring quickly—nervously as well, he thought—"Oh, Tom, I *am* so glad," beneath her breath. "You're just in time—we all wanted you so."

Explanations followed; Tony's friends had postponed the Cairo trip at the last moment; the picnic had been planned as a rehearsal for the real one that was to follow later. Tom's adroitness in finding them was praised; he became the unwilling hero of the piece, and as such had to make the fire a success and prove himself generally the *clou* of the party that hitherto was missing. He became at once the life and center of the little group, gay and in the highest spirits, the emotion accumulated in him discharging itself in the entirely unexpected direction of hilarious fun and gaiety.

The sense of tragedy he had gathered on his journey, if it muttered at all, muttered out of sight. He looked back upon his feelings of an hour before with amazement, dismay, distress—then utterly forgot them. The picture itself—the vision—was as though it had not been at all. What, in the name of common sense, had possessed him that he could ever have admitted such preposterous uneasiness? He thought of Mrs. Haughstone's absurd warnings with a sharp contempt, and felt his spirits only rise higher than before. She was meanly suspicious about nothing. Of course he would give Lettice a hint: why not, indeed? He would give it then and there before them all and hear them laugh about it till they cried. And he would have done so, doubtless, but that he realized the woman's jealousy was a sordid topic to introduce into so gay a party.

"You arrived in the nick of time, Tom," Lettice told him. "We were beginning to feel the solemnity of these surroundings, the awful Tombs of the Kings and Priests and people. Those cliffs are too oppressive for a picnic."

"A fact," cried Tony. "It feels like sacrilege. They resent us being here." He glanced at Madame Jaretzka as he said it. "If you hadn't come, Tom, I'm sure there'd have been a disaster somewhere. Anyhow, one must feel superstitious to enjoy a place like this. It's the proper atmosphere!"

Lettice looked up at Tom, and added, "You've really saved us. The least we can do is to worship the sun the moment he gets up. We'll adore old Amon-Ra. It's obvious. We must!"

They made themselves merry over a rather sandy meal. She arranged a place for him close beside her, and her genuine pleasure at his unexpected return filled him with a joy that crowded out even the memory of other emotions. The mixture called Tom Kelverdon asserted itself: he felt ashamed; he heartily despised his moods, wondering whence they came so strangely. Tony himself was quiet and affectionate. If anything was lacking, Tom's high spirits carried him too boisterously to notice it. Otherwise he might possibly have thought that she spoke a little sharply once or twice to Tony, neglecting him in a way that was not quite her normal way, and that to himself, even before the others, she was unusually—almost too emphatically—dear and tender. Indeed, she seemed so pleased he had come that a cynical observer, cursed with an acute, experienced mind, might almost have thought she showed something not far from positive relief. But Tom, too happy to be sensitive to shades of feminine conduct, was aware chiefly, if not solely, of his own joy and welcome.

"You didn't get my letter, then, before you left?" she asked him once; and he replied, "The answer, as in Parliament, is in the negative. But it will be forwarded all right." He would get it the following night. "Ah, but you mustn't read it *now*," she said. "You must tear it up unread," and made him promise faithfully he would obey. "*I* wrote to you too," mentioned

Tony, as though determined to be left out of nothing. "You'll get it at the same time. But you mustn't tear mine up, remember. It's full of advice and wisdom you badly need." And Tom promised that faithfully as well. The reply was in the affirmative.

The bivouac was a complete success; all looked back upon it as an unforgettable experience. They declared, of course, they had not slept a wink, yet all had snored quite audibly beneath the wheeling stars. They were fresh and lively enough, certainly, when the sun poured his delicious warmth across the cloudless sky, while Tom and Tony made the fire and set the coffee on for breakfast.

Of the marvelous beauty that preceded the actual sunrise no one spoke; it left them breathless rather; they watched the sky beyond the hills change color; great shafts of gold transfixed the violet heavens; the Nile shone faintly; then, with a sudden drive, the stars rushed backwards in a shower, and the amazing sun came up as with a shout. Perfumes that have no name rose from the desert and the fields along the distant river banks. The silence deepened, for no birds sang. Light took the world—and it was morning.

And when the donkey-boys arrived at eight o'clock, the party were slow in starting: it was so pleasant to lie and bask in the sumptuous bath of heat and light that drenched them. The night had been chilly enough. They were a tired party. Once home again, all retired with one accord to sleep, remaining invisible until the sun was slanting over Persia and the Indian Ocean, gilding the horizon probably above the starry skies of far Cathay.

But as Tom dozed off behind the shuttered windows in the hotel towards eleven o'clock, having bathed and breakfasted a second time, he thought vaguely of what Mrs. Haughstone had said to him a few hours before. It seemed days ago already. He was too drowsy to hold the thought more than a moment in his mind, much less to reflect upon it. "It may be just as well to give a hint," occurred to him. "Tony *is* a bit too fond of her— too fond for his happiness, perhaps." Nothing had happened at the picnic to revive the notion; it just struck him as he fell asleep, then vanished; it was a moment's instinct. The vision—it had been an instantaneous flash after all and nothing more—had left his mind completely for the time.

But Tom looked back afterwards upon the all-night bivouac as an occasion marked specially in memory's calendar yet for a reason that was unlike the reasons his companions knew. He remembered it with mingled joy and pain, also with a wonder that he could have been so blind—the last night of happiness in his brief Egyptian Winter.

CHAPTER XX

He slept through the hot hours of the afternoon. In the cool of the evening, as he strolled along the river bank, he read the few lines Lettice had written to him at Assouan. For the porter had handed him half-a-dozen letters as he left the hotel. Tony's he put for the moment aside; the one from Lettice was all he cared about, quite forgetting he had promised to tear it up unread. It was short but tender—anxious about his comfort and well-being in a strange hotel "when I am not there to take care of you." It ended on a complaint that she was "tired rather and spending my time at full length on a deck-chair in the garden." She promised to write "at greater length to-morrow."

"Instead of which," thought Tom with a boy's delight, "I surprised her and we talked face to face." But for the Arab touts who ran beside him, offering glass beads made in Birmingham, he could have kissed the letter there and then.

The resplendent gold on the river blinded him, he was glad to enter the darker street and shake off the children who pestered him for bakshish. Passing the Savoy Hotel, he hesitated a moment, then went on. "No, I won't call in for Tony, I'll find her alone, and we'll have a cozy little talk together before the others come." He quickened his pace, entered the shady garden, discovered her instantly, and threw himself down upon the cushions beside her deck-chair. "Just what I hoped," he said, with pleasure and admiration in his eyes, "alone at last. That is good luck—isn't it, Lettice?"

"Of course," she agreed, and smiled lazily, though some might have thought indifferently, as she watched him arranging the cushions.

He flung himself back and gazed at her. She wore a dress of palest yellow, and the broad-brimmed hat with the little roses. She seemed part of the flaming sunset and the tawny desert.

"Well," he grumbled playfully, "it is true, isn't it? Our not being alone often, I mean?" He watched her without knowing that he did so.

"In a way—yes," she said. "But we can't have everything at once, can we, Tom?" Her voice was colorless perhaps. A tiny frown settled for an instant between her eyes, then vanished. Tom did not notice it. She sighed. "You baby, Tom. I spoil you dreadfully, and you know I do."

He liked her in this quiet, teasing mood; it was often the prelude to more delightful spoiling. He was in high spirits. "You look as fresh as a girl of sixteen, Lettice," he declared. "I believe you're only this instant out of your bath and bed. D'you know, I slept like a baby too—the whole afternoon—"

He interrupted himself, for at that moment a cigarette case on the sand beside him caught his eye. He picked it up—he recognized it. "Yes—I wish you'd smoke," she said the same instant, brushing a fly quickly from her cheek.

"Tony's," he exclaimed, examining the case.

He noticed at the same time several burnt matches between his cushions and her chair.

"But he'd love you to smoke them: I'll take the responsibility." She laughed quietly. "I'm sure they're good—better than yours; he's wickedly extravagant." She watched him as he took one out, examining the label critically, then lighting it slowly and inhaling the smoke to taste it. There was a faint perfume that clung to the case and its contents.

"Ambra," said Lettice, a kind of watchful amusement in her eyes. "You don't like it!"

Tom looked up sharply.

"Is that it? I didn't know."

She nodded. "It's Tony's smell, haven't you noticed it? He always has it about him. No, no," she laughed, noticing his expression of disapproval, "he doesn't use it. It's just in his atmosphere, I mean."

"Oh, is it?" said Tom.

"I rather like it," she went on idly, "but I never can make out where it comes from. We call it ambra—the fragrance that hangs about the bazaars: I believe they used it for the mummies; but the desert perfume is in it too. It's rather wonderful—it suits him—don't you think? Penetrating, and so delicate."

What a lot she had to say about it! He made no reply. He was looking down to see what caused him that sudden, inexplicable pain—and discovered that the lighted match had burned his fingers. The next minute he looked up again—straight into her eyes.

But, somehow, he did not say exactly what he meant to say. He said, in fact, something that occurred to him on the spur of the moment. His mind was simple, possibly, yet imps occasionally made use of it. An imp just then reminded him: "Her letter made no mention of the picnic, of Tony's sudden change of plan, yet it was written yesterday morning when both were being arranged."

So Tom did not refer to the ambra perfume, nor to the fact that Tony had spent the afternoon with her. He said quite another thing—said it rather bluntly too: "I've just got your letter from Assouan, Lettice, and I clean forgot my promise that I wouldn't read it." He paused a second. "You said nothing about the picnic in it."

"I thought you'd be disappointed if you knew," she replied at once. "That's why I didn't want you to read it." And she fell to scolding him in the way he usually loved,—but at the moment found less stimulating for some reason. He smoked his stolen cigarette with energy for a measurable period.

"You're the spoilt child, not I," he said at length, still looking at her. "You said you were tired and meant to rest, and then you go for an exhausting expedition instead."

The tiny frown reappeared between her eyes, lingered a trifle longer than before, and vanished. She made a quick gesture. "You're in a very nagging mood, Tom: bivouacs don't agree with you." She spoke lightly, easily, in excellent good temper really. "It was Tony persuaded me, if you want to know the truth. He found himself free unexpectedly; he was so persistent; it's impossible to resist him when he's like that—the only thing is to give in and go."

"Of course." Tom's face was like a mask. He thought so, at least, as he laughed and agreed with her, saying Tony was an unscrupulous rascal at the best of times. Apparently there was a struggle in him; he seemed in two minds. "Was he here this afternoon?" he asked. He learned that Tony had come at four o'clock and had tea with her alone. "We didn't telephone because he said it would only spoil your sleep, and that a man who works as well as plays must sleep—longer than a younger man." Then, as Tom said nothing, she added, "Tony *is* such a boy, isn't he?"

There were several emotions in Tom just then. He hardly knew which was the true, or at least, the dominant one. He was thinking of several things at once too: of her letter, of that faint peculiar odor, of Tony's coming to tea, but chiefly, perhaps, of the fact that Lettice had not mentioned it,—but that he had found it out.... His heart sank. It struck him suddenly that the mother in her sought to protect him from the pain the woman gave.

"Is he—yes," he said absent-mindedly. And she repeated quietly, "Oh, I think so."

The brief eastern twilight had meanwhile fallen, and the rapidly cooling air sighed through the foliage. It grew darker in their shady corner. The western sky was still a blaze of riotous color, however, that filtered through the trees and shed a luminous glow upon their faces. It was a bewitching light—there was something bewitching about Lettice as she lay there. Tom himself felt a touch of that deep Egyptian enchantment. It stole in among his thoughts and feelings, coloring motives, lifting into view, as from far away, moods that he hardly understood and yet obeyed because they were familiar.

This evasive sense of familiarity, both welcome and unwelcome, swept in, dropped a fleeting whisper, and was gone again. He felt himself for an instant—some one else: one Tom felt and spoke, while another Tom looked on and watched, a calm outside spectator. And upon his heart came a touch of that strange, rich pain that was never very far away in Egypt.

"I say, Lettice," he began suddenly, as though he came to an abrupt decision. "This is an awful place for talk—these Luxor hotels—" He stuck. "Isn't it? You know what I mean." His laborious manner betrayed intensity, yet he meant to speak lightly, easily, and thought his voice was merely natural. He stared hard at the glowing tip of his cigarette.

Lettice looked across at him without speaking for a moment. Her eyelids were half closed. He felt her gaze and raised his own. He saw the smile steal down towards her lips.

"Tom, why are you glaring at me?"

He started. He tried to smile, but there was no smile in him.

"Was I, Lettice? Forgive me." The talk that was coming would hurt him, yet somehow he desired it. He would give his little warning and take the consequences. "I was devouring your beauty, as the *Family Herald* says." He heard himself utter a dry and unconvincing laugh. Something was rising through him; it was beyond control; it had to come. He felt stupid, awkward, and was angry with himself for being so. For, somehow, he felt powerless too.

She came to the point with a directness that disconcerted him. "Who has been talking about me?" she enquired, her voice hardening a little; "and what does it matter if they have?"

Tom swallowed. There was something about her beauty in that moment that set him on fire from head to foot. He knew a fierce desire to seize her in his arms, hold her for ever and ever—lest she should escape him.

But he was unable to give expression in any way to what was in him. All he did was to shift his cushions slightly further from her side.

"It's always wiser—safer—not to be seen about too much with the same man—alone," he fumbled, recalling Mrs. Haughstone's words, "in a place like this, I mean," he qualified it. It sounded foolish, but he could evolve no cleverer way of phrasing it. He went on quicker, a touch of nervousness in his voice he tried to smother: "No one can mistake *our* relationship, or think there's anything wrong in it." He stopped a second, as she gazed at him in silence, waiting for him to finish. "But Tony," he concluded, with a gulp he prayed she did not notice, "Tony is a little—"

"Well?" she helped him, "a little what—?"

"A little different, isn't he?"

Tom realized that he was producing the reverse of what he intended. Somehow the choice of words seemed forced upon him. He was aware of his own helplessness; he felt almost like a boy scolding his own wise, affectionate mother. The thought stung him into pain, and with the pain rose, too, a first distant hint of anger. The turmoils of feeling confused him. He was aware—by her silence chiefly—of the new distance between them, a distance the mention of Tony had emphasized. Instinctively he tried to hide both pain and anger—it could only increase this distance that was already there. At the same time he saw red.... Her answer, then, so gently given, baffled him absurdly. He felt out of his depth.

"I'll be more careful, Tom, dear—you wise, experienced chaperone."

The words, the manner, stung him. Another emotion, wounded vanity, came into play. To laugh at himself was natural and right, but to be laughed at by a woman, a woman whom he loved, whom he regarded as exclusively his own, against whom, moreover, he had an accumulating grievance—it hurt him acutely, although he seemed powerless to prevent it. He felt his own stupidity increase.

"It's just as well, I think, Lettice." It was the wrong, the hopeless thing to say, but the words seemed, in a sense, pushed quickly out of his mouth lest he should find better ones. He anticipated, too, her exasperation before her answer proved it: "But, really, Tom, you know, I can look after myself rather well as a rule—don't you think?"

He interrupted her then, a mixture of several feelings in him—shame, the pain of frustrate yearning, perplexity too. For, in spite of himself, he wanted to hear how she would speak of Tony. He meant to punish himself by hearing her praise him. He, too, meant to speak well of his cousin.

"He's a bit careless, though," he blurted, "irresponsible, in a way—where women are concerned. I'm sure he means no harm, of course, but—" He paused in confusion, he was no longer afraid that harm might come to Tony; he was afraid for her, but now also for himself as well.

"Tom, I do believe you're jealous!"

He laughed boisterously when he heard it. It was really comical, awfully comical, of course. It sounded, too, the way she said it—ugly, mean, contemptible. The touch of shame came back.

"Lettice! But what an idea!" He gasped, turning round upon his other elbow, closer to her. But the sinking of his heart increased; he felt an inner cold. And a moment of deep silence followed the empty laughter. The rustle of the foliage alone was audible.

Lettice looked down sideways at him through half-closed eyelids; propped on his cushions beside her, this was natural: yet he felt it mental as well as physical. There was pity in her attitude, a concealed exasperation, almost contempt. At the same time he realized that she had never seemed so adorably lovely, so exquisite, so out of his reach. He had never felt her so seductively desirable. He made an impetuous gesture towards her before he knew it.

"Don't, Tom; you'll upset my papers and everything," she said calmly, yet with the merest suspicion of annoyance in her tone. She was very gentle, she was also very cold—cold as ice, he felt her, while he was burning as with fire. He was aware of this unbridgeable distance between his passion and her indifference; and a dreadful thought leaped up in him with stabbing pain: "Her answer to Tony would have been quite otherwise."

"I'm sorry, Lettice—so sorry," he said bruskly, to hide his mortification. "I'm awfully clumsy." She was putting her papers tidy again with calm fingers, while his own were almost cramped with the energy of suppressed desire. "But, seriously," he went on, refusing the rebuff by pretending it was play on his part, "it isn't very wise to be seen about so much alone with Tony. Believe me, it isn't." For the first time, he noticed, it was difficult to use the familiar and affectionate name. But for a sense of humor he could have said "Anthony."

"I do believe you, Tom. I'll be more careful." Her eyes were very soft, her manner quiet, her gentle tone untinged with any emotion. Yet Tom detected, he felt sure, a certain eagerness behind the show of apparent indifference. She liked to talk—to go on talking—about Tony. "Do you *really* think so, really mean it?" he heard her asking, and thus knew his thought confirmed. She invited more. And, with open eyes, with a curious welcome even to the pain involved, Tom deliberately stepped into the cruel little trap. But he almost felt that something pushed him in. He talked exactly like a boy: "He—he's got a peculiar power with women," he said. "I can't make it out quite. He's not good-looking—exactly—is he?" It was impossible to conceal his eagerness to know exactly what she did feel.

"There's a touch of genius in him," she answered. "I don't think looks matter so much—I mean, with women." She spoke with a certain restraint, not deliberately saying less than she thought, but yet keeping back the entire truth. He suddenly realized a relationship between her and Tony into which he was not admitted. The distance between them increased visibly before his very eyes.

And again, out of a hundred things he wanted to say, he said—as though compelled to—another thing.

"Rather!" he burst out honestly. "I should hate it if—you hadn't liked him." But a week ago he would have phrased this differently—"If *he* had not liked you."

There were perceptible pauses between their sentences now, pauses that for him seemed breaking with a suspense that was painful, almost cruel. He knew worse was coming. He both longed for it yet dreaded it. He felt at her mercy, in her power somehow.

"It's odd," she went on slowly, "but in England I thought him stupid rather, whereas out here he's changed into another person."

"I think we've all changed—somehow," Tom filled the pause, and was going to say more when she interrupted. She kept the conversation upon Tony.

"I shall never forget the day he walked in here first. It was the week I arrived. You'll laugh, Tom, when I tell you—" She hesitated—almost it seemed on purpose.

"How was it? How did he look?" The forced indifference of the tone betrayed his anxiety.

"Well, he's not impressive exactly—is he?—as a rule. That little stoop—and so on. But I saw his figure coming up the path before I recognized who it was, and I thought suddenly of an Egyptian, almost an old Pharaoh, walking."

She broke off with that little significant laugh Tom knew so well. But, comical though the picture might have been—Tony walking like a king—Tom did not laugh. It was not ludicrous, for it was somewhere true. He remembered the singular inner mental picture he had seen above the desert fire, and the pain within him seemed the forerunner of some tragedy that watched too close upon his life. But, for another and more obvious reason, he could not laugh; for he heard the admiration in her voice, and it was upon that his mind fastened instantly. His observation was so mercilessly sharp. He hated it. Where was his usual slowness gone? Why was his blood so quickly apprehensive?

She kept her eyes fixed steadily on his, saying what followed gently, calmly, yet as though another woman spoke the words. She stabbed him, noting the effect upon him with a detached interest that seemed indifferent to his pain. Something remote and ancient stirred in her, something that was not of herself To-day, something half primitive, half barbaric.

"It may have been the blazing light," she went on, "the half-savage effect of these amazing sunsets—I cannot say—but I saw him in a sheet of gold. There was gold about him, I mean, as though he wore it—and when he came close there was that odd, faint perfume, half of the open desert and half of ambra, as we call it—" Again she broke off and hesitated, leaving the impression there was more to tell, but that she could not say it. She kept back much. Into the distance now established between them Tom felt a creeping sense of cold, as of the chill desert wind that follows hard upon the sunset. Her eyes still held him steadily. He seemed more and more aware of something merciless in her.

He sat and gazed at her—at a woman he loved, a woman who loved him, but a woman who now caused him pain deliberately because something beyond herself compelled. Her tenderness lay inactive, though surely not forgotten. She, too, felt the pain. Yet with her it was in some odd way—impersonal.... Tom, hopelessly out of his depth, swept onward by this mighty wave behind all three of them, sat still and watched her—fascinated, even terrified. Her eyelids were half closed again. Another look stole up into her face, driving away the modern beauty, replacing its softness, tenderness with another expression he could not fathom. Yet this new expression was somehow, too, half recognizable. It was difficult to describe—a little sterner, a little wilder, a faint emphasis of the barbaric peering through it. It was darker. She looked eastern. Almost, he saw her visibly change—here in the twilight of the little Luxor garden by his side. Distance increased remorselessly between them. She was far away, yet ever close at the same time. He could not tell whether she was going away from him or coming nearer. The shadow of tragedy fell on him from the empty sky....

In his bewilderment he tried to hold steady and watch, but the soul in him rushed backwards. He felt, but could not think. The wave surged under him. Various impulses urged him into a pouring flood of words; yet he gave expression to none of them. He laughed a little dry, short laugh. He heard himself saying lightly, though with apparent lack of interest: "How curious, Lettice, how very odd! What made him look like that?"

But he knew her answer would mean pain. It came just as he expected:

"He is wonderful—out here—quite different—" Another minute and she would have added "I'm different, too." But Tom interrupted hurriedly:

"Do you always see him—like that—now? In a sheet of gold—with beauty?" His tongue was so hot and dry against his lips that he almost stammered.

She nodded, her eyelids still half closed. She lay very quiet, peering down at him. "It lasts?" he insisted, turning the knife himself.

"You'll laugh when I tell you something more," she went on, making a slight gesture of assent, "but I felt such joy in myself—so wild and reckless—that when I got to my room that night I danced—danced alone with all my clothes off."

"Lettice!"

"The spontaneous happiness was like a child's—a sort of freedom feeling. I *had* to shake my clothes off simply. I wanted to shake off the walls and ceiling too, and get out into the open desert. Tom—I felt out of myself in a way—as though I'd escaped—into—into quite different conditions—"

She gave details of the singular mood that had come upon her with the arrival of Tony, but Tom hardly heard her. Only too well he knew the explanation. The touch of ecstasy was no new thing, although its manifestation may have been peculiar. He had known it himself in his own lesser love affairs. But that she could calmly tell him about it, that she could deliberately describe this effect upon her of another man—! It baffled him beyond all thoughts or words.... Was the self-revelation an unconscious one? Did she realize the meaning of what she told him? The Lettice he had known could surely not say this thing. In her he felt again, more distinctly than before, another person—division, conflict. Her hesitations, her face, her gestures, her very language proved it. He shrank, as from some one who inflicted pain as a child, unwittingly, to see what the effect would be... He remembered the incident of the insect in the sand....

"And I feel—even now—I could do it again," her voice pierced in across his moment of hidden anguish. The knife she had thrust again into his breast was twisted then.

It was time that he said something, and a sentence offered itself in time to save him. The desire to hide his pain from her was too strong to be disobeyed. He wanted to know, yet not, somehow, to prevent. He seized upon the sentence, keeping his voice steady with an effort that cut his very flesh: "There's nothing impersonal exactly in *that*, Lettice—!" he exclaimed with an exaggerated lightness.

"Oh no," she agreed. "But it's only in England, perhaps, that I'm impersonal, as you call it. I suppose, out here, I've changed. The beauty, the mystery,—this fierce sunshine or something stir—" She hesitated for a fraction of a second.

"The woman in you," he put in, turning the knife this time with his own fingers deliberately. The words seemed driven out by their own impetus; he did not choose them. A faint ghastly hope was in him—that she would shake her head and contradict him.

She waited a moment, then turned her eyes aside. "Perhaps, Tom. I wonder...!"

And as she said it, Tom knew suddenly another thing as well. It stood out clearly, as with big printed letters that violent advertisements use upon the hoardings. Her new joy and excitement, her gaiety and zest for life—all had been caused, not by himself, but by another. Heavens! how blind he had been! He understood at last, and a flood of freezing water drenched him. His heart stopped beating for a moment. He gasped. He could not get his breath. His accumulating doubts hitherto unexpressed, almost unacknowledged even, were now confirmed.

He got up stiffly, awkwardly, from his cushions, and moved a few steps towards the house, for there stole upon her altered face just then the very expression of excitement, of radiant and spontaneous joy, he had believed until this moment was caused by himself. Tony was coming up the darkened drive. He was exactly in her line of sight. And a severe, embittered struggle then took place in a heart that seemed strangely divided against itself. He felt as though a second Tom, yet still himself, battled against the first, exchanging thrusts of indescribable torture. The complexity of emotions in his heart was devastating beyond anything he had ever known in his thirty-five years of satisfied, self-centered life. Two voices spoke in clear, sharp sentences, one against the other:

"Your suspicions are unworthy, shameful. Trust her. She's as loyal and true and faithful as yourself!" cried the first.

And the second:

"Blind! Can't you see what's going on between them? It has happened to other men, why not to you?" She is playing with you; she has outgrown your love. It was the older voice that used the words.

"Impossible, ridiculous!" the first voice cried. "There's something wrong with me that I can have such wretched thoughts. It's merely innocence and joy of life. No one can take *my* place."

To which, again, the second Tom made bitter answer. "You are too old for her, too dull, too ordinary! You hold the loving mother still, but a younger man has waked the woman in her. And you must let it come. You dare not blame. Nor have you the right to interfere."

So acute, so violent was the perplexity in him that he knew not what to say or do at first. Unable to come to decision, he stood there, waving his hand to Tony with a cry of welcome. His first vehement desire to be alone, to make an excuse, to get to his room and think, had passed: a second, a maturer attitude conquered it: to take whatever came, to face it, in a word to know the worst.... And the extraordinary pain he hid by an exuberance of high spirits that surprised himself. It was, of course, the suppressed emotional energy finding another outlet. A similar state had occurred that "Karnak night" of a long ten days ago, though he had not understood it then. Behind it lay the misery of loneliness that he knew in his very bones was coming.

"Tony! So it is. I was afraid he'd change his mind and leave us in the lurch."

Tom heard the laugh of happiness as she said it; he heard the voice distinctly—the change of tone in it, the softness, the half-caressing tenderness that crept unconsciously in—the faint thrill of womanly passion. Unconsciously, yes! he was sure, at least, of that. She did not know quite yet, she did not realize what had happened. Honest to the core, he felt her. His love surged up tumultuously. He could face pain, loss, death—or, as he put it, "almost anything," if it meant happiness to her. The thought, at any rate, came to him thus.... And Tom believed it.

At the same moment he heard her voice, close behind him this time. She had left her chair, meaning to go indoors and prepare for supper before Tony actually arrived. "Tom, dear boy," her hand upon his shoulder a moment as she passed, "you're tired or something. I can see it. I believe you're worrying. There's something you haven't told me—isn't there now?" She gave him a loving glance that was of purest gold. "You shall tell me all about it when we're alone. You must tell me everything."

The pain and joy in him were equal then. He was a boy of eighteen, aching over his first love affair; and she was divinely mothering him. It was extraordinary; it was past belief; another minute, had they been alone, he could almost have laid his head upon her breast, complaining in anguish to the mother in her that the woman he loved was gone. "I feel you're slipping from me! I'm losing you …!"

Instead he stammered some commonplace unreality about his work at Assouan and heard her agree with him that he certainly must not neglect it—and she was gone into the house. The swinging curtains of dried grasses hid her a few feet beyond, but between them, he felt, stretched five thousand years and half a dozen continents as well.

"Tom, old chap, did you get my letter? You promised to read it. Is it all right, I mean? I wouldn't for all the world let anything—"

Tom stopped him abruptly. He wished to read the letter for himself without foreknowledge of its contents.

"Eh? No—that is, I got it," he said confusedly, "but I haven't read it yet. I slept all the afternoon."

An expression of anxiety in Tony's face came and vanished. "You can tell me to-morrow—frank as you like, mind," he replied, to which Tom said quite eagerly, "Rather, Tony: of course. I'll read your old letter the moment I get back to-night." And Tony, merry as a sandboy, changed the subject, declaring that he had only one desire in life just then, and that was—food.

CHAPTER XXI

The conflict in Tom's puzzled heart sharpened that evening into dreadful edges that cut him mercilessly whichever way he turned. One minute he felt sure of Lettice, the next the opposite was clear. Between these two certainties he balanced in secret torture, one factor alone constant—that his sense of security was shaken to the foundations.

Belief in his own value had never been thus assailed before; that he was indispensable had been an ultimate assurance. His vanity and self-esteem now toppled ominously. A sense of inferiority crept over him, as on the first day of his arrival at Alexandria. There seemed the flavor of some strange authority in her that baffled all approach to the former intimacy. He hardly recognized himself, for, the foundations being shaken, all that was built upon them trembled too.

The insecurity showed in the smallest trifles—he expressed himself hesitatingly; he felt awkward, clumsy, ineffective; his conversation became stupid for all the false high spirits that inflated it, his very manners gauche; he said and did the wrong things; he was boring. Being ill at ease and out of harmony with himself, he found it impossible to play his part in the trio as of old; the trio, indeed, had now divided itself—one against two.

That is, keenly, and in spite of himself, he watched the other two; he watched them as a detective does, for evidence. He became uncannily observant. And since Tony was especially amusing that evening, Lettice, moreover, apparently absorbed in his stimulating talk, Tom's alternate gaucheries and silence passed unnoticed, certainly uncommented. In schoolboy phraseology, Tom felt out of it. His presence was tolerated—as by favor. The two enjoyed a mutual understanding from which he was excluded, a private intimacy that was spiritual, mental,—physical.

He even found it in him for the first time to marvel that Lettice had ever cared for him at all. Beside Tony's brilliance he felt himself cheaper, almost insignificant. He felt old.... His pain, moreover, was twofold: his own selfish sense of personal loss produced one kind of anguish, but the possibility that *she* was playing false produced another. The first was manageable: the second beyond words appalling.

Against this background of emotional disturbance he watched the evening pass. It developed as the hours moved. Tony, he noticed, though so full of life, betrayed a certain malaise towards himself and avoided that direct meeting of the eye that was his characteristic. More and more, especially when Mrs. Haughstone had betaken herself to bed, and the trio sat in the cooler garden alone, Tom became aware of a subtle intimacy between his companions that resented all his efforts to include him too. It was, moreover—his heart warned him now,—an affectionate, a natural intimacy, built upon many an hour of intercourse while he was yet in England, and, worst of all, that it was secret. But more—he realized that the missing part of her was now astir, touched into life by another, and a younger, man. It was ardent and untamed. It had awakened from its slumber. He even fancied that something of challenge flashed from her, though without definite words or gesture.

With a degree of acute perception wholly new to him, he watched the evidence of inner proximity, yet watched it automatically and certainly not meanly nor with slyness. The evidence that was sheer anguish thrust itself upon him. His eyes had opened; he could not help himself.

But he watched himself as well. Only at moments was he aware of this— a kind of higher Self, detached from shifting moods, looked on calmly and took note. This Self, placed high above the stage, looked down. It was a self that never acted, never wept or suffered, never changed. It was secure, superb, it was divine. Its very existence in him hitherto had been unknown. He was now vividly aware of it. It was the Onlooker.

The explanation of his mysterious earlier moods offered itself with a clarity that was ghastly. Watching the happiness of these two, he recalled a hundred subconscious hints he had disregarded: the empty letter at Alexandria, her dislike of being alone with him, the increasing admiration for his cousin, a thousand things she had left unsaid, above all, the exuberance and radiant joy that Tony's presence woke in her. The gradual but significant change, the singular vision in the desert, his own foretaste of misery as he watched the Theban Hills from the balcony of his bedroom—all, all returned upon him, arranged in a phalanx of neglected proofs that the new Tom offered cruelly to the old. But it was her slight exasperation, her evasion when he questioned her, that capped the damning list. And her silence was the culminating proof.

Then, inexplicably, he shifted to the other side that the old, the normal Tom presented generously to the new. While this reaction lasted he laughed away the evidence, and honestly believed he was exaggerating trifles. The new zest that Egypt woke in her—God bless her sweetness and simplicity— was only natural; if Tony stimulated the intellectual side of her, he could feel only pleasure that her happiness was thus increased. She was innocent. He could not possibly doubt or question, and shame flooded him till he felt himself the meanest man alive. Suspicion was no normal part of him. He crushed it out of sight, scotched as he thought to death. To lose belief in her would mean to lose belief in everybody. It was inconceivable. Every instinct in him repelled the vile suggestion. And while this reaction lasted his security returned.

Only it did *not* last; it merged invariably into its opposite again; and the alternating confidence and doubt produced a state of confused emotion that contained the nightmare touch in its most essential form. The Wave hung, poised above him—but would not fall—quite yet.

It was later in the evening that the singular intensity introduced itself into all they said and did, hanging above them like a cloud. It came curiously, was suddenly there —without hint or warning. Tom had the feeling that they moved amid invisible dangers, almost as though explosives lay hidden near them, ready any moment to bring destruction with a sudden crash—final destruction of the happy preexisting conditions. The menace of a thundercloud approached as in his childhood's dream; disaster lurked behind the quiet outer show. The Wave was rising almost audibly.

For upon their earlier mood of lighter kind that had preceded Mrs. Haughstone's exit, and then upon the more serious talk that followed in the garden, there descended abruptly this uncanny quiet that one and all obeyed. The contrast was most marked. Tom remembered how their voices hushed upon a given moment, how they looked about them during the brief silence following, peering into the luminous darkness as though some one watched them—and how Madame Jaretzka, remarking on the chilly air, then rose suddenly and led the way into the house. Both she and Tony, he remembered, had been restless for some little time. "It's chilly. We shall be cozier indoors," she said lightly, and moved away, followed by his cousin.

Tom lingered a few minutes, watching them pass along the verandah to the room beyond. He did not like the change. In the open air, the intimacy he dreaded was less suggested than in the friendly familiarity of a room, her room; out of doors it was more diffused; he preferred the remoteness that the garden lent. At the same time he was glad of a moment by himself—though a moment only. He wanted to collect his thoughts and face things as they were. There should be no "shuffling," if he possibly could prevent it.

He lingered with his cigarette behind the others. A red moon hung above the mournful hills, and the stars shone in their myriads. Both lay reflected in the quiet river. The night was very peaceful. No wind stirred.... And he strove to force the exquisite Egyptian silence upon the turmoil that was in his soul—to gain that inner silence through which the voice of truth might whisper clearly to him. The poise he craved lay all about him in the solemn stillness, in stars and moon and desert; the temple columns had it, the steadfast, huge Colossi waiting for the sun, the bleak stone hills, the very Nile herself. Something of their immemorial resolution and resistance he might even borrow for his little tortured self... before he followed his companions. For it came to him that within the four walls of her room all that he dreaded must reveal itself in such concentrated, visible form that he no longer would-be able to deny it: the established intimacy, the sweetness, the desire, and—the love.

He made this effort, be it recorded in his favor, and made it bravely; while every minute that he left his companions undisturbed was a long-drawn torment in his heart. For he plainly recognized now a danger he knew not how he might adequately meet. Here was the strangeness of it: that he did *not* distrust Lettice, nor felt resentment against Tony. Why this was so, or what the meaning was, he could not fathom. He felt vaguely that Lettice, like himself, was the plaything of greater forces than she knew, and that her perplexing conduct was based upon disharmony in herself beyond her possible control. Some part of her, long hidden, had emerged in Egypt, brought out by the deep mystery and passion of the climate, by its burning, sensuous splendor: its magic drove her along unconsciously. There were two persons in her.

It may have been absurd to divide the woman and the mother as he did; probably it was false psychology as well; where love is, mother and woman blend divinely into one. He did not know: it seemed, as yet, they had not blended. He was positive only that, while part of her was going from him, if not already gone, the rest, and the major part, was true and loyal, loving and marvelously tender. The conflict of these certainties left hopeless disorder in every corner of his being....

Tossing away his cigarette, he moved slowly up the verandah steps. The Wave was never more sensibly behind, beneath him, than in that moment. He rose upon it, it was under him, he felt its lift and irresistible momentum; almost it bore him up the steps. For he meant to face whatever came; deliberately he welcomed the hurt; it had to come; beyond the suffering beckoned some marvelous joy, pure as the dawn beyond the cruel desert. There was in him that rich, sweet pain he knew of old. It beckoned and allured him even while he shrank. Alone the supreme Self in him looked calmly on, seeming to lessen the part that trembled and knew fear.

Then, as he neared the room, a sound of music floated out to meet him— Tony was singing to his own accompaniment. Lettice, upon a sofa in the corner, looked up and placed a finger on her lips, then closed her eyes again, listening to the song. And Tom was glad she closed her eyes, glad also that Tony's back was towards him, for as he crossed the threshold a singular impulse took possession of his legs and he was only just able to stop a ridiculous movement of shuffling with his feet upon the matting. Quickly he gained a sofa by the window and dropped down upon it, watching, listening. Tony was singing softly, yet with deep expression half suppressed:

We were young, we were merry, we were very very wise,
    And the door stood open at our feast,
When there passed us a woman with the West in her eyes,
    And a man with his back to the East.

O, still grew the hearts that were beating so fast,
    The loudest voice was still.
The jest died away on our lips as they passed,
    And the rays of July struck chill.

He sang the words with an odd, emphatic slowness, turning to look at Lettice between the phrases. He was not yet aware that Tom had entered. The tune held all the pathos and tragedy of the world in it. "Both going the same way together," he said in a suggestive undertone, his hands playing a soft running chord. "The man and the woman," he again leaned in her direction. "It's a pregnant opening, don't you think? The music I found in the very depths of me somewhere. Lettice, I believe you're asleep!" he whispered tenderly after a second's pause.

She opened her eyes then and looked meaningly at him. Tom made no sound, no movement. He saw only her eyes fixed steadily on Tony, whose last sentence, using the Christian name so softly, rang on inside him like the clanging of a prison bell.

"Sing another verse first," said Madame Jaretzka quietly, "and we'll pass judgment afterwards. But I wasn't asleep, was I, Tom?" And, following the direction of her eyes, Tony started, and turned round. "I shut my eyes to listen better," she added, almost impatiently. "Now, please go on; we want to hear the rest."

"Of course," said Tom, in as natural a tone as possible. "Of course we do. What is it?" he asked.

"Mary Coleridge—the words," replied Tony, turning to the piano again. "In a moment of aberration I thought I could write the music for it—" The softness and passion had left his voice completely.

"Oh, the tune is yours?"

His cousin nodded. There was a little frown between the watching eyes upon the sofa. "Tom, you mustn't interrupt; it spoils the mood—the rhythm," and she again asked Tony to go on. The difference in the two tones she used was too obvious to be missed by any man who heard them—the veiled exasperation and—the tenderness.

Tony obeyed at once. Striking a preliminary chord as the stool swung round, he said for Tom's benefit, "To me there's tragedy in the words, real tragedy, so I tried to make the music fit it. Madame Jaretzka doesn't agree." He glanced towards her; her eyes were closed again, her face, Tom thought, was like a mask. Tony did not this time use the little name.

The next verse began, then suddenly broke off. The voice seemed to fail the singer. "I don't like this one," he exclaimed, a suspicion of trembling in his tone. "It's rather too awful. Death comes in, the bread at the feast turns black, the hound falls down—and so on. There's general disaster. It's too tragic, rather. I'll sing the last verse instead."

"I want to hear it, Tony. I insist," came the command from the sofa. "I want the tragic part."

To Tom it seemed precisely as though the voice had said, "I want to see Tom suffer. He knows the meaning of it. It's right, it's good, it's necessary for him."

Tony obeyed. He sang both verses:

The cups of red wine turned pale on the board,
   The white bread black as soot.
The hound forgot the hand of his lord,
   She fell down at his foot.

Low let me lie, where the dead dog lies,
   Ere I sit me down again at a feast,
When there passes a woman with the West in her eyes,
   And a man with his back to the East.

The song stopped abruptly, the music died away, there was an interval of silence no one broke. Tom had listened spellbound. He was no judge of poetry or music; he did not understand the meaning of the words exactly; he knew only that both words and music expressed the shadow of tragedy in the air as though they focussed it into a tangible presence. A woman and a man were going in the same direction; there was an onlooker... A spontaneous quality in the words, moreover, proved that they came burning from the writer's heart, and in Tony's music, whether good or bad, there was this same proof of genuine feeling. Judge or no judge, Tom was positive of that. He felt himself the looker-on, an intruder, almost a trespasser.

This sense of exclusion grew upon him as he listened; it passed without warning into the consciousness of a mournful, freezing isolation. These two, sitting in the room, and separated from him by a few feet of colored Persian rug, were actually separated from him by unbridgeable distance, wrapped in an intimacy that kept him inexorably outside—because he did not understand. He almost knew an objective hallucination—that the sofa and the piano drew slightly nearer to one another, whereas his own chair remained fixed to the floor, immovable—outside.

The intensity of his sensations seemed inexplicable, unless some reality, some truth, lay behind them. The bread at the feast turned black before his very eyes. But another line rang on with a sound of ominous and poignant defeat in his heart, now lonely and bereft: "Low let me lie, where the dead dog lies..." To the onlooker the passing of the pair meant death....

Then, through his confusion, flashed clearly this bitter certitude: Tom suddenly realized that after all he knew nothing of her real, her inner life; he knew her only through himself and in himself—knew himself in her. Tony, less self-centered, less rigidly contained, had penetrated her by an understanding sympathy greater than his own. She was unintelligible to him, but not to Tony. Tony had the key.... He had touched in her what hitherto had slept.

As the music wailed its dying cadences into this fateful silence, Tom met her eyes across the room. They were strong, and dark with beauty. He met them with no outer quailing, though with a sense of drenching tears within. They seemed to him the eyes of the angel gazing through the gate. He was outside...

He was the first to break a silence that had grown unnatural, oppressive.

"What was it?" he asked again abruptly. "Has it got a name, I mean?" His voice had the cry of a wounded creature in it.

Tony struck an idle chord from the piano as he turned on his stool, "Oh, yes, it's got a name. It's called 'Unwelcome.'" And Tom, aware that he winced, was also aware that something in his life congealed and stopped its normal flow.

"Tony, you *are* a genius," broke in quickly the voice from the other side of the room; "I always said so. Do you know, that's the most perfect accompaniment I ever heard." She spoke with feeling, her tone full of admiration.

Tony made no reply. He strummed softly, swaying to the rhythm of what he played.

"I meant the setting," explained Lettice, "the music. It expresses the emotion of the words too, too exactly. It's wonderful!"

"I didn't know you composed," put in Tom stupidly. He had to say something. He saw them exchange a glance. She smiled. "When did you do it?"

"Oh, the other day in a sudden fit," said Tony, without turning. "While you were at Assouan, I think."

"And the words, Tom; don't you think they're wonderful, too, and strange?" asked Lettice. "I find them really haunting."

"Y-es," he agreed, without looking at her. He realized that the lyric, though new to him, was not new to them; they had discussed it together already; they felt the same emotion about it; it had moved and stirred them before, moved Tony so deeply that he had found the music for it in the depths of himself. It was an enigmatical poem, it now became symbolic. It embodied the present situation somehow for him. Tom did not understand its meaning as they did; to him it was a foreign language. But they knew the language easily. It betrayed their deep emotional intimacy.

"You didn't hear the first part?" said Tony.

"Not quite. You had just started—when I came in." Tom easily read the meaning in the question. And in his heart the name of the poem repeated itself with significant insistence: *Unwelcome!* It had come like a blow in the face when Tony mentioned it, bruising him internally. He was bleeding.... He watched the big, dark hands upon the keys as they moved up and down. It suddenly seemed they moved towards himself. There was power, menace in them—there was death. He felt as if they seized—choked him.... They grew stained....

The voices of his companions came to him across great distance; there was a gulf between them, they on that side, he on this: he was aware of antagonism between himself and Tony, and between himself and Lettice. It was very dreadful; his feet and hands were cold; he shivered. But he gave no outer sign that he was suffering, and a desperate pride—though he knew it was but a sham, a temporary pride—came to his assistance. Yet at the same time—he saw red. He felt like a boy at school again.

In imagination, then, he visualized swiftly a definite scene:

"Tony," he heard himself say, "you're coming between us. It means all the world to me, to you it means only a passing game. If it means more, it's time for you to say so plainly—and let *her* decide."

The situation seemed all cleared up; the clouds of tragedy dissipated, the dreadful accumulation of emotion, suspense, and hidden pain, too long suppressed, too intense to be borne another minute, discharged itself in an immense relief. Lettice at last spoke freely and explained: Tony expressed regret, laughing it all away with his accustomed brilliance and irresponsibility.

Then, horribly, he heard Tony give a different answer that was far more possible and likely:

"I knew you were great friends, but I did not guess there was anything more between you. You never told me. I'm afraid I—I *am* desperately fond of her, and she of me. We must leave it—yes, to her. There is no other way."

He was lounging on his sofa by the window, his eyes closed, while these thoughts flashed through him. He had never known such insecurity before; he felt sure of nothing; the foundations of his being seemed sliding into space.... For it came to him suddenly that he was a slave and that she was set upon a throne far, far beyond his reach....

Across the room, lit only by a single lamp upon the piano, the voices of his companions floated to him, low pitched, a ceaseless murmuring stream. He had been listening even while busy with his own reflections, intently listening. They were still talking of the poem and the music, exchanging intimate thoughts in the language he could not understand. They had passed on to music and poetry at large—dangerous subjects by whose means innocent words, donning an easy mask, may reveal passionate states of mental and physical kind—and so to personal revelations and confessions the apparently innocent words interpreted. He heard and understood, yet could not wholly follow because the key was missing. He could not take part, much less object. It was all too subtle for his mind. He listened....

The moonlight fell upon his stretched-out figure, but left his face in shadow; opening his eyes, he could see the others clearly; the intent expression upon *her* face fascinated him as he watched. Yet before his eyes had opened, the feeling again came to him that they had changed their positions somehow, and the verification of this feeling was the first detail he then noticed. Tony's stool was nearer to the bass keys of the piano, while the sofa Lettice lay upon had certainly been drawn up towards him. And Tony leaned over as he talked, bringing their lips within whispering distance. It was all done with that open innocence which increased the cruelty of it. Tom saw and heard and felt all over his body. He lay very still. He half closed his eyes again.

"I do believe Tom's dropped asleep," said Lettice presently. "No, don't wake him," as Tony half turned round, "he's tired, poor boy!"

But Tom could not willingly listen to a private conversation.

"I'm not asleep," he exclaimed, "not a bit of it," and noticed that they both were startled by the suddenness and volume of his voice. "But I *am* tired rather," and he got up, lit a cigarette, wandered about the room a minute, and then leaned out of the open window. "I think I shall slip off to bed soon—if you'll forgive me, Lettice."

He said it on impulse; he did not really mean to go; to leave them alone together was beyond his strength. She merely nodded. The woman he had felt so proudly would put Tony in his place—nodded consent!

"I must be going too in a moment," Tony murmured. He meant it even less than Tom did. He shifted his stool towards the middle of the piano and began to strum again.

"Sing something more first, Tony; I love your ridiculous voice."

Tom heard it behind his back; it was said half in banter, half in earnest; yet the tone pierced him. She used the private language she and Tony understood. The little sentence was a paraphrase that, being interpreted, said plainly: "He'll go off presently; then we can talk again of the things we love together—the things he doesn't understand."

With his face thrust into the cold night air Tom felt the blood go throbbing in his temples. He watched the moonlight on the sandy garden paths. The leaves were motionless, the river crept past without a murmur, the dark hills rose out of the distant desert like a wave. There was faint fragrance as of wild flowers, very tiny, very soft. But he kept his eyes upon the gliding river, rather than on those dark hills, crowded with their ancient dead. For he felt as if some one watched him from their dim recesses. It almost seemed that from those bleak, lonely uplands, silent amid the stream of hurrying life to-day, came his pain, his agony. He could not understand it; the strange, sinister mood he had known already once before, stole out from the desolate Theban hills and mastered him again. Any moment, if he looked up, he would meet eves—eyes that gazed with dim, yet definite recognition into his own across the night. They would gaze up at him, for somehow he was placed above them.... He had known all this before, this very situation, these very actors—he now looked down upon it all, a scene mapped out below him. There were two pictures that yet were one.

"What shall it be?" the voice of Tony floated past him through the open window.

"The gold and ambra one—I like best of all," her voice followed like a sigh across the air. "But only once—it makes me cry."

To Tom, as he heard it, came the shattering conviction that the words were not in English, and that it was neither Lettice nor his cousin who had used them. Reality melted; he felt himself—brain, heart, and body—dropping down through empty space as though towards the speakers. This was another language that they spoke together. *He* had forgotten it.... They were themselves, yet different. Amazement seized him. A familiarity, intense with breaking pain, came with it. Where, O where...?

He heard the music steal past him towards these Theban hills.

His heart was no longer beating; it was still. Life paused, as it were, to let the voice insert itself into another setting, out of due place, yet at the same time true and natural. An intolerable sweetness in the music swept him. But there was anguish too. The pain and pleasure were but one sensation... All the melancholy blue and gold of Egypt's beauty passed in that singing before his soul, and something of transcendent value he had lost, something ancient it seemed, as those mournful Theban hills, rose with it. It was offered to him again. He saw it rise within his reach—once more. Upon this tide of blue and of gold it floated to his hand, could he but seize it.... Emotion then blocked itself through sheer excess; the tide receded, the vision dimmed, the gold turned dull and faded, the music and the singing ceased. Yet an instant, above the pain, Tom had caught a flush of inexplicable happiness. Beyond the anguish he felt joy breaking upon him like the dawn....

"Joy cometh in the morning," he remembered, with a feeling as of some modern self and sanity returning. He had been some one else; he now was Tom again. The pain belonged to that "some one else." It must be faced, for the final outcome would be joy....

He turned round into the room now filled with tense silence only.

"Tony," he asked, "what on earth was it?" His voice was low, but did not tremble. The atmosphere seemed drawn taut before him as though it must any instant split open upon a sound of crying. He saw Lettice on her sofa, the lamplight in her wide-open eyes that shone with moisture. She looked at Tony, not at him. There was no decipherable expression on her face. That elusive eastern touch hung mysteriously about her. It was all half fabulous.

Without turning Tony answered shortly: "Oh, just a little native Egyptian song—very old—dug up somewhere, I believe," and he strummed softly to himself, as though he did not wish to talk more about it.

Lettice watched him for several minutes, then fixed her eyes on Tom; they stared at each other across the room; her expression was enigmatical, yet he read resolution into it, a desire and a purpose. He returned her gaze with a baffled yearning, thinking how mysteriously beautiful she looked, frail, elusive, infinitely desirable, yet hopelessly beyond his reach.... And then he saw the eyelids lower slightly, and a shadowy darkness like a veil fall over her. A smile stole down towards the lips. Terror and fascination caught him; he turned away lest she should reach his secret and communicate her own. She looked right through him. Words, too, were spoken, ordinary modern words, though he did not hear them properly: "You're tired out... you know. There's no need to be formal where I'm concerned..." or something similar. He listened, but he did not hear; they were remote, unreal, not audible quite; they were far away in space. He was only aware that the voice was tender and the tone was very soft....

He made no answer. The pain in her leaped forth to clasp his own, it seemed. For in that instant he knew that the joy divined a little while before was *her*, but also that he must wade through intolerable pain to reach it.

The spell was broken. The balance of the evening, a short half hour at the most, was uninspired, even awkward. There was strain in the atmosphere, cross-purposes, these purposes unfulfilled; each word and action charged with emotion that was unable to express itself. A desultory talk between Tony and his hostess seemed to struggle through clipped sentences that hung in the air as though afraid to complete themselves. The unfinished phrases floated, but dared not come to earth; they gathered but remained undelivered. Tom had divined the deep, essential intimacy at last, and his companions knew it.

He lay silent on his sofa by the window, or nearly silent. The moonlight had left him, he lay in shadow. Occasionally he threw in words, asked a question, ventured upon a criticism; but Lettice either did not hear or did not feel sufficient interest to respond. She ignored his very presence, though readily, eagerly forthcoming to the smallest sign from Tony. She hid herself with Tony behind the shadowy screen of words and phrases.

Tony himself was different too, however. There was acute disharmony in the room, where a little time before there had been at least an outward show of harmony. A heaviness as of unguessed tragedy lay upon all three, not only upon Tom. Spontaneous gaiety was gone out of his cousin, whose attempts to be his normal self became forced and unsuccessful. He sought relief by hiding himself behind his music, and his choice, though natural enough, seemed half audacious and half challenging—the choice of a devious soul that shirked fair open fight and felt at home in subterfuge. From Grieg's *Ich liebe Dich* he passed to other tender, passionate fragments Tom did not recognize by name yet understood too well, realizing that sense of ghastly comedy, and almost of the ludicrous, which ever mocks the tragic.

For Tony certainly acknowledged by his attitude the same threatening sense of doom that lay so heavy upon his cousin's heart. There was presentiment and menace in every minute of that brief half-hour. Never had Tom seen his gay and careless cousin in such guise: he was restless, silent, intense and inarticulate. "He gives her what I cannot give," Tom faced the situation. "They understand one another... It's not *her* fault... I'm old, I'm dull. She's found a stronger interest.... The bigger claim at last has come!"

They brewed their cocoa on the spirit-lamp, they munched their biscuits, they said good-night at length, and Tom walked on a few paces ahead, impatient to be gone. He did not want to go home with Tony, while yet he could not leave him there. He longed to be alone and think. Tony's hotel was but a hundred yards away. He turned and called to him. He saw them saying goodnight at the foot of the verandah steps. Lettice was looking up into his cousin's face....

They went off together. "Night, night," cried Tony, as he presently turned up the path to his own hotel. "See you in the morning."

And Tom walked down the silent street alone. On his skin he still felt her fingers he had clasped two minutes before. But his eyes saw only—her face and figure as she stood beside his cousin on the steps. For he saw her looking up into his eyes as once before on the lawn of her English bungalow four months ago. And Tony's two great hands were laid upon her arm.

"Lettice, poor child...!" he murmured strangely to himself. For he knew that her suffering and her deep perplexity were somewhere, somehow almost equal to his own.

CHAPTER XXII

He walked down the silent street alone.... How like a theater scene it was! Supers dressed as Arabs passed him without a word or sign; the Nile was a painted hack-cloth; the columns of the Luxor Temple hung on canvas. The memory of a London theater flitted through his mind.... He was playing a part upon the stage, but for the second time, and this second performance was better than the first, different too, a finer interpretation as it were. He could not manage it quite, but he must play it out in order to know joy and triumph at the other end.

This sense of the theater was over everything. How still and calm the night was, the very stars were painted on the sky, the lights were low, there lay a hush upon the audience. In his heart, like a weight of metal, there was sadness, deep misgiving, sense of loss. His life was fading visibly; it threatened to go out in darkness. Yet, like Ra, great deity of this ancient land, it would suffer only a temporary eclipse, then rise again triumphant and rejuvenated as Osiris....

He walked up the sweep of sandy drive to the hotel and went through the big glass doors. The huge, brilliant building swallowed him. Crowds of people moved to and fro, chattering and laughing, the women gaily, fashionably dressed; the band played with that extravagant abandon hotels demanded. The contrast between the dark, quiet street and this busy modern scene made him feel it was early in the evening, instead of close on midnight.

He was whirled up to his lofty room above the world. He flung himself upon his bed; no definite thought was in him; he was utterly exhausted. There was a vicious aching in his nerves, his muscles were flaccid and unstrung; a numbness was in his brain as well. But in the heart there was vital energy. For his heart seemed alternately full and empty; all the life he had was centered there.

And, lying on his bed in the darkened room, he sighed, as though he struggled for breath. The recent strain had been even more tense than he had guessed—the suppressed emotion, the prolonged and difficult effort at self-control, the passionate yearning that was denied relief in words and action. His entire being now relaxed itself; and his physical system found relief in long, deep sighs.

For a long time he lay motionless, trying vainly not to feel. He would have welcomed instantaneous sleep—ten hours of refreshing, dreamless sleep. If only he could prevent himself thinking, he might drop into blissful unconsciousness. It was chiefly forgetfulness he craved. A few minutes, and he would perhaps have slipped across the border—when something startled him into sudden life again. He became acutely wakeful. His nerves tingled, the blood rushed back into the brain. He remembered Tony's letter—returned from Assouan. A moment later he had turned the light on, and was reading it. It was, of course, several days old already:

SAVOY HOTEL,
LUXOR.

DEAR OLD Tom—What I am going to say may annoy you, but I think it best that it should he said, and if I am all wrong you must tell me. I have seldom liked any one as much as I like you, and I want to preserve our affection to the end.

The trouble is this:—I can't help feeling—I felt it at the Bungalow, in London too, and even heard it *said* by some one whom, possibly, you may guess—that you were very fond of her, and that she was of you. Various little things said, and various small signs, have strengthened this feeling. Now, instinctively, I have a feeling also that she and I have certain things in common, and I think it quite possible that I might have a bad effect on her.

I do not suppose for one moment that she would ever care for me, but, from one or two signs in her, I do see possibilities of a sort of playing with fire between us. One *feels* these things without apparent cause; and all I can say is that, absurd as it may sound, I scent danger. To put it quite frankly, I can imagine myself becoming sufficiently excited by her to lose my head a little, and to introduce an element of sex into our friendship which might have some slight effect on us both. I don't mean anything serious, but, given the circumstances, I can imagine myself playing the fool; and the only serious thing is that I can picture myself growing so fond of her that I would not think it playing the fool at the time.

Now, if I am right in thinking that you love her, it is obvious that I must put the matter before you, Tom, as I am here doing. I would rather have your friendship than her possible excitement—and I repeat that, absurd as it may seem, I do scent the danger of my getting worked up, and, to some extent, infecting her. You see, I know myself and know the wildness of my nature. I don't fool about with women at all, but I have had affairs in my life and can judge of the utter madness of which I am capable, madness which, to my mind, *must* affect and stimulate the person towards whom it is directed.

On my word of honor, Tom, I am not in love with her now at all, and it will not be a bit hard for me to clear out if you want me to. So tell me quite straight: shall I make an excuse, as, for example, that I want to avoid her for fear of growing too fond of her, and go? Or can we meet as friends? What I want you to do is to be with us if we are together, so that we may try to make a real trinity of our friendship. I enjoy talking to her; and I prefer you to be with me when I am with her, really, believe me, I do.

Words make things sound so absurd, but I am writing like this because I feel the presence of clouds, almost of tragedy, and I can't for the life of me think why. I want her friendship and "motherly" care badly. I want your affection and friendship exceedingly; but I feel as though I were unconsciously about to trouble your life and hers: and I can only suppose it is that hardworking subconsciousness of mine which sees the possibility of my suddenly becoming attracted to her, suddenly losing control, and suddenly being a false friend to you both.

Now, Tom, old chap, you must prevent that—either by asking me to keep away, or else by making yourself a definite part of my friendship with her.

I want you to say no word to her about this letter, and to keep it absolutely between ourselves; and I am very hopeful I feel sure in fact—that we shall make the jolliest trio in the world.—Yours ever,

Tony

Tom, having read it through without a single stop, laid it down upon his table and walked round the room. In doing so, he passed the door. He locked it, then paused for a moment, listening. "Why did I lock it? What am I listening for?" he asked himself. He hesitated. "Oh, I know," he went on, "I don't want to be disturbed. Tony knows I shall read this letter to-night. He might possibly come up—" He walked back to the table again slowly. "I couldn't *see* him," he realized: "it would be impossible!" If any one knocked, he would pretend to be asleep. His face, had he seen it in the glass, was white and set, but there was a curious shining in his eyes, and a smile was on the lips, though a smile his stolid features had never known before. "*I* knew it," said the Smile, "I knew it long ago."

His hand stretched out and picked the letter up again. But at first he did not look at it. He looked round the room instead, as though he felt that he was being watched, as though somebody were hiding— And then he said aloud with clear distinctness:

"Light-blue eyes, by God! *The* light-blue eyes!"

The sound startled him a little. He repeated the sentence in a whisper, varying the words. The voice sounded like a phonograph:

"Tony's got light-blue eyes!"

He sat down, then got up again:

"I never, never thought of it! I never noticed. God! I'm as blind as a bat!"

For some minutes he stood motionless, then turned and read the letter through a second time, lingering on certain phrases, and making curious, unregulated gestures as he did so. He clenched his fists, he bit his lower lip. The feeling that he was acting on a stage had left him now. This was reality.

He walked over to the balcony, and drew the cold night air into his lungs. He remembered standing once before on this very spot, that foreboding of coming loneliness so strangely in his heart. "It's come," he said dully to himself. "It's justified. I understand at last." And then he repeated with a deep, deep sigh: "God—how blind I've been! He's taken her from me! It's all confirmed. He's wakened the woman in her!"

It seemed, then, he sought a mitigation, an excuse—for the man who wrote it, his pal, his cousin, Tony. He wanted to exonerate, if it were possible. But the generous impulse remained frustrate. The plea escaped him—because it was not there. The falseness and insincerity were too obvious to admit of any explanation in the world but one. He dropped into a chair, shocked into temporary numbness.

Gradually, then, isolated phrases blazed into prominence in his mind, clearest of all—that what Tony pretended might happen in the future had already happened long ago. "I can picture myself growing too fond of her," meant "I am already too fond of her." That he might lose his head and "introduce an element of sex" was conscience confessing that it had been already introduced. He "scented danger... tragedy" because both were in the present—now.

Tony hedged like any other coward. He had already gone too far, he felt shamed and awkward, he had to put himself right, as far as might be, with his trusting, stupid cousin, so he warned him that what had already taken place in the past *might* take place—he was careful to mention that he had no self-control—in the future. He begged the man he had injured to assist him; and the method he proposed was that old, well-proved one of assuring the love of a hesitating woman—"I'll tell her I'm too fond of her, and go!"

The letter was a sham and a pretense. Its assurance, too, was unmistakable: Tony felt certain of his own position. "I'm sorry, old chap, but we love each other. Though I've sometimes wondered, you never definitely told me that *you* did."

He read once again the cruelest phrase of all: "From one or two signs in her, I do see possibilities of a sort of playing with fire between us." It was cleverly put, yet also vilely; he laid half the burden of his treachery on her. The "introduction of sex" was gently mentioned three lines lower down. Tony already had an understanding with her—which meant that she had encouraged him. The thought rubbed like a jagged file against his heart. Yet Tom neither thought this, nor definitely said it to himself. He felt it; but it was only later that he knew he felt it.

And his mind, so heavily bruised, limped badly. The same thoughts rose again and again. He had no notion what he meant to do. There was an odd, half-boyish astonishment in him that the accumulated warnings of these recent days had not shown him the truth before. How could he have known the Eyes of his Dream for months, have lived with them daily for three weeks—the light-blue eyes—yet have failed to recognize them? It passed understanding. Even the wavy feeling that had accompanied Tony's arrival in the Carpathians—the Sound heard in his bedroom the same night—had left him unseeing and unaware. It seemed as if the recognition had been hidden purposely; for, had he recognized them, he would have been prepared; he might even have prevented. It now dawned upon him slowly that the inevitable may not be prevented. And the cunning of it baffled him afresh: it was all planned consummately.

Tom sat for a long time before the open window in a state of half stupor, staring at the pictures his mind offered automatically. A deep, vicious aching gnawed without ceasing at his heart: each time a new picture rose a fiery pang rose with it, as though a nerve were bared....

He drew his chair closer into the comforting darkness of the night. All was silent as the grave. The stars wheeled overhead with their accustomed majesty; he could just distinguish the dim river in its ancient bed; the desert lay watchful for the sun; the air was sharp with perfume. Countless human emotions had these witnessed in the vanished ages, countless pains and innumerable aching terrors; the emotions had passed away, yet the witnesses remained, steadfast, unchanged, indifferent. Moreover, his particular emotion *now* seemed known to them—known to these very stars, this desert, this immemorial river; they witnessed now its singular repetition. He was to experience it unto the bitter end again—yet somehow otherwise. He must face it all. Only in this way could the joy at the end of it be reached.... He must somehow accept and understand... This confused, unjustifiable assurance strengthened in him.

Yet this last feeling was so delicate that he scarcely recognized its intense vitality. The cruder sensations blinded him as with thick, bitter smoke. He was certain of one thing only—that the fire of jealousy burned him with its atrocious anguish... an anguish he had somewhere known before.

Then presently there was a change. This change had begun soon after he drew his chair to the balcony, but he had not noticed it. The effect upon him, nevertheless, had been gradually increasing.

The psychological effects of sound, it would seem, are singular. Even when heard unconsciously, the result continues; and Tom, hearing this sound unconsciously, did not realize at first that another mood was stealing over him. Then hearing became conscious hearing—listening. The sound rose to his ears from just below his balcony. He listened. He rose, leaned over the rail, and stared. The crests of three tall palms immediately below him waved slightly in the rising wind. But the fronds of a palm tree in the wind produce a noise that is unlike the rustle of any other foliage in the world. It was a curious, sharp rattling that he heard. It was *the* Sound.

His entire being was at last involved—the Self that used the separate senses. His thoughts swooped in another direction—he suddenly fixed his attention upon Lettice. But it was an inner attention of a wholesale kind:—not of the separate mind alone. And this entire Self included regions he did not understand. Mind was the least part of it. The "whole" of him that now dealt with Lettice was far above all minor and partial means of knowing. For it did not judge, it only saw. It was, perhaps, the soul.

For it seemed the pain bore him upwards to an unaccustomed height. He stood for a moment upon that level where she dwelt, even as now he stood on this balcony, looking down upon the dim Egyptian scene. She was beside him; he gazed into her eyes, even as now he gazed across to the dark Theban necropolis among the hills. But also, in some odd way, he stood outside himself. He swam with her upon the summit of the breaking Wave, lifted upon its crest, swept onward irresistibly.... No halt was possible... the inevitable crash must come. Yet she was with him. They were involved together.... The sea!...

The first bitterness passed a little; the sullen aching with it. He was aware of high excitement, of a new reckless courage; a touch of the impersonal came with it all, one Tom playing the part of a spectator to another Tom—an onlooker at his own discomfiture, at his own suffering, at his own defeat.

This new, exalted state was very marvelous; for while it lasted he welcomed all that was to come. "It's right and necessary for me," he recognized; "I need it, and I'll face it. If I refuse it I prove myself a failure—again. Besides... *she needs it too!*"

For the entire matter then turned over in his mind, so that he saw it from a new angle suddenly. He looked at it through a keyhole, as it were—the extent was large yet detailed, the picture distant yet very clearly focused. It lay framed within his thoughts, isolated from the rest of life, isolated somehow even from the immediate present. There was perspective in it. This keyhole was, perhaps, his deep, unalterable love, but cleansed and purified.

It came to him that she, and even Tony, too, in lesser fashion, were, like himself, the playthings of great spiritual forces that made alone for good. The Wave swept all three along. The attitude of his youth returned: the pain was necessary, yet would bring inevitable joy as its result. There had been cruel misunderstanding on his part somewhere: that misunderstanding must be burnt away. He saw Lettice and his cousin helping towards this exquisite deliverance somehow. It was like a moment of clear vision from a pinnacle. He looked down upon it....

Lettice smiled into his eyes through half-closed eyelids. Her smile was strangely distant, strangely precious: she was love and tenderness incarnate; her little hands held both of his.... Through these very eyes, this smile, these little hands, his pain would come; she would herself inflict it—because she could not help herself; she played her inevitable rôle as he did. Yet he kissed the eyes, the hands, with an absolute self-surrender he did not understand, willing and glad that they should do their worst. He had somewhere dreadfully misjudged her: he must, he would atone. This passion burned within him, a passion of sacrifice, of resignation, of free, big acceptance. He felt joy at the end of it all—the joy of perfect understanding... and forgiveness... on both sides....

And the moment of clear vision left its visible traces in him after it had passed. If he felt contempt for his cousin, he felt for Lettice a deep and searching pity—she was divided against herself, she was playing a part she had to play. The usual human emotions were used, of course, to convey the situation, yet in some way he was unable to explain, she was—*being* driven. In spite of herself she must inflict this pain.... It was a mystery he could not solve....

His exaltation, naturally, was of brief duration. The inevitable reaction followed it. He saw the situation again as an ordinary man of the world must see it.... The fires of jealousy were alight and spreading. Already they were eating away the foundations of every generous feeling he had ever known.... It was not, he argued, that he did not trust her. He did. But he feared the insidious power of infatuation, he feared the burning glamour of this land of passionate mirages, he feared the deluding forces of sex which his cousin had deliberately awakened in her blood—and other nameless things he feared as well, though he knew not exactly what they were. For it seemed to him that they were old as dreams, old as the river and the menace of these solemn hills.... From childhood up, his own trust in her truth and loyalty had remained unalterably fixed, ingrained in the very essence of his being. It was more than his relations with a woman he loved that were in danger: it was his belief and trust in Woman, focused in herself symbolically, that were threatened.... It was his belief in Life.

With Lettice, however, he felt himself in some way powerless to deal; he could watch her, but he could not judge... least of all, did he dare prevent.... *Her* attitude he could not know nor understand....

There was a pink glow upon the desert before he realized that a reply to Tony's letter was necessary; and that pink was a burning gold when he knew his answer must be of such a kind that Tony felt free to pursue his course unchecked. Tom held to his strange belief to "Let it all come," he would not try to prevent; he would neither shirk nor dodge. He doubted whether it lay in his power now to hinder anything, but in any case he would not seek to do so. Rather than block coming events, he must encourage their swift development. It was the best, the only way; it was the right way too. He belonged to his destination. He went into his own background...

The sky was alight from zenith to horizon, the Nile aflame with sunrise, by the time the letter was written. He read it over, then hurriedly undressed, and plunged into bed. A long, dreamless sleep took instant charge of him, for he was exhausted to a state of utter depletion.

DEAR TONY—I have read your letter with the greatest sympathy —it was forwarded from Assouan. It cost you a good deal, I know, to say what you did, and I'm sure you mean it for the best. I feel it like that too—for the best. I'm sorry you've been upset.

But it is easier for you to write than for me to answer. Her position, of course, is an awfully delicate one; and I feel—no doubt you feel too—that her standard of conduct is higher than that of ordinary women, and that any issue between us—if there is an issue at all!— should be left to her to decide.

Nothing can touch my friendship with her; you needn't worry about *that*. But if you can bring any added happiness into her life, it can only be welcomed by all three of us. So go ahead, Tony, and make her as happy as you can. The important things are not in our hands to decide in any case; and, whatever happens, we both agree on one thing: that her happiness is the important thing.—Yours ever,

Tom.

CHAPTER XXIII

He was wakened by the white-robed Arab housemaid with his breakfast. He felt hungry, but still tired; sleep had not rested him. On the tray an envelope caught his eye—sent by hand evidently, since it bore no stamp. The familiar writing made the blood race in his veins, and the instant the man was gone, he tore it open. There was burning in his eyes as he read the penciled words. He devoured it whole with a kind of visual gulp—a flash: the entire meaning first, then lines, then separate words:

> Come for lunch, or earlier. My cousin is invited out, and Tony has suddenly left for Cairo with his friends. I shall be lonely. How beautiful and precious you were last night. I long for you to comfort me. But don't efface yourself again—it gave me a horrid strange presentiment—as if I were losing you—almost as if you no longer trusted me. And don't forget that I love you with all my heart and soul. I had such queer, long dreams last night—terrible rather. I must tell you. *Do* come.—Yours, L.
>
> P. S. Telephone if you can't.

Sweetness and pain rose in him, then numbness. For his mind flung itself with violence upon two sentences: he was "beautiful and precious"; she longed for him to comfort her. Why, he asked himself, was his conduct beautiful and precious? And why did she need his comfort? The words were like vitriol in the eyes.

Long before reason found the answer, instinct—swift, merciless interpreter—told him plainly. While the brain fumbled, the heart already understood. He was stabbed before he knew what stabbed him.

And hope sank extinguished. The last faint doubt was taken from him. It was not possible to deceive himself an instant longer, for the naked truth lay staring into his eyes.

He swallowed his breakfast without appetite... and went downstairs. He sighed, but something wept inaudibly. A wall blocked every step he took. The devastating commonplace was upon him—it was so ordinary. Other men... oh, how often he had heard the familiar tale! He tried to grip himself. "Others... of course... but *me!*" It seemed impossible.

In a dream he crossed the crowded hall, avoiding various acquaintances with unconscious cunning. He found the letter-box and—posted his letter to Tony. "That's gone, at any rate!" he realized. He told the porter to telephone that he would come to lunch. "That's settled too!" Then, hardly knowing what blind instinct prompted, he ordered a carriage... and presently found himself driving down the hot, familiar road to—Karnak. For some faultless impulse guided him. He turned to the gigantic temple, with its towering, immense proportions—as though its grandeur might somehow protect and mother him.

In those dim aisles and mighty halls brooded a Presence that he knew could soothe and comfort. The immensities hung still about the fabulous ruin. He would lose his tortured self in something bigger—that beauty and majesty which are Karnak. Before he faced Lettice, he must forget a moment—forget his fears, his hopes, his ceaseless torment of belief and doubt. It was, in the last resort, religious—a cry for help, a prayer. But also it was an inarticulate yearning to find that state of safety where he and she dwelt secure from separation—in the "sea." For Karnak is a spiritual experience, or it is nothing. There, amid the deep silence of the listening centuries, he would find peace: forgetting himself a moment, he might find—strength.

Then reason parsed the sentences that instinct already understood complete. For Lettice—the tender woman of his first acquaintance—had obviously experienced a moment of reaction. She realized he was wounded at her hands. She felt shame and pity. She craved comfort and forgiveness—his comfort, his forgiveness. Conscience whispered. As against the pain she inflicted, he had been generous, long-suffering—therefore his conduct was "beautiful and precious." Tony, moreover, had hidden himself until his letter should be answered—and she was "lonely."

With difficulty Tom suppressed the rising bitterness of contempt and anger in him. His cousin's obliquity was a sordid touch. He forgot a moment the loftier point of view. But for a short time only. The contempt merged again in something infinitely greater. The anger disappeared. *Her* attitude occupied him exclusively. The two phrases rang on with insistent meaning in his heart, as with the clang of a fateful sentence of exile, execution—death:

"How beautiful you were last night, and precious... I long for you to comfort me...."

While the carriage crawled along the sun-baked sand, he watched the Arab children with their blue-black hair, who ran beside it, screaming for backsheesh. The little faces shone like polished bronze, they held their hands out, their bare feet pattered in the sand. He tossed small coins among them. And their cries and movements fell into the rhythm of the song, whose haunting refrain pulsed ever in his blood: "We were young, we were merry, we were very very wise...."

They were soon out-distanced, the palm trees fell away, the soaring temple loomed against the blazing sky. He left the *arabyieh* at the Western entrance and went on foot down the avenue of headless rams. The huge Khonsu gateway dropped its shadow over him. Passing through the Court with its graceful colonnades, and the Chapel, flanked by cool, dark chambers, where the Sacred Boat floated on its tideless sea beyond the world, he moved on across the sandy waste of broken stone again, and reached in a few minutes the towering gray and reddish sandstone that was Amon's Temple.

This was the goal of his little pilgrimage. Sublimity closed round him. The gigantic pylon, its shoulders breaking the sky four-square far overhead, seemed the prodigious portal of another world. Slowly he passed within, crossed the Great Court where the figures of ancient Theban deities peered at him between the forest of broken monoliths and lovely Osiris pillars, then, moving softly beneath the second enormous pylon, found himself on the threshold of the Great Hypostyle Hall itself.

He caught his breath, he paused, then stepped within on tiptoe, and the hush of four thousand years closed after him. Awe stole upon him; he felt himself included in the great ideal of this older day. The stupendous aisles lent him their vast shelter; the fierce sunlight could not burn his flesh; the air was cool and sweet in these dim recesses of unremembered time. He passed his hand with reverence over the drum-shaped blocks that built up the majestic columns, as they reared towards the massive, threatening roof. The countless inscriptions and reliefs showered upon his sight bewilderingly.

And he forgot his lesser self in this crowded atmosphere of ancient divinities and old-world splendor. He was aware of kings and queens, of princes and princesses, of stately priests, of hosts and conquests; forgotten gods and goddesses trooped past his listening soul; his heart remembered olden wars, and the royalty of golden days came back to him. He steeped himself in the long, long silence in which an earlier day lay listening with ears of stone. There was color; there was spendthrift grandeur, half savage, half divine. His imagination, wakened by Egypt, plunged backwards with a sense of strange familiarity. Tom easily found the mightier scale his aching heart so hungrily desired. It soothed his personal anguish with a sense of individual insignificance which was comfort....

The peace was marvelous, an unearthly peace; the strength unwearied, inexhaustible. The power that was Amon lingered still behind the tossed and fabulous ruin. Those soaring columns held up the very sky, and their foundations made the earth itself swing true. The silence, profound, unalterable, was the silence in the soul that lies behind all passion and distress. And these steadfast qualities Tom absorbed unconsciously through his very skin.... The Wave might fall indeed, but it would fall into the mothering sea where levels must be restored again, secure upon unshakable foundations.... And as he paced these solemn aisles, his soul drank in their peace and stillness, their strength of calm resistance. Though built upon the sand, they still endured, and would continue to endure. They pointed to the stars.

And the effect produced upon him, though the adjective was not his, seemed spiritual. There was a power in the mighty ruin that lifted him to an unaccustomed level from which he looked down upon the inner drama being played. He reached a height; the bird's-eye view was his; he saw and realized, yet he did not judge. The vast structure, by its harmony, its power, its overmastering beauty, made him feel ashamed and mortified. A sense of humiliation crept into him, melting certain stubborn elements of self that, grown out of proportion, blocked his soul's clear vision. That he must stand aside had never occurred to him before with such stern authority: it occurred to him now. The idea of sacrifice stole over him with a sweetness that was deep and marvelous. It seemed that Isis touched him. He looked into the eyes of great Osiris.... and that part of him that ever watched— the great Onlooker—smiled.

His being, as a whole, remained inarticulate as usual; no words came to his assistance. It was rather that he attained—as once before, in another moment of deeper insight—that attitude towards himself which is best described as impersonal. Who was *he*, indeed, that he should claim the right to thwart another's happiness, hinder another's best self-realization? By what right, in virtue of what exceptional personal value, could he, Tom Kelverdon, lay down the law to this other, and say, "Me only shall you love... because I happen to love you...?"

And, as though to test what of strength and honesty might lie in this sudden exaltation of resolve, he recognized just then the very pylon against whose vast bulk they had rested together that moonlit night a few short weeks before... when he saw two rise up like one person... as he left them and stole away into the shadows.

"So I knew it even then—subconsciously," he realized. "The truth was in me even then, a few days after my arrival.... And they knew it too. She was already going from me, if not already gone...!"

He leaned against that same stone column, thinking, searching in his mind, feeling acutely. Reactions caught at him in quick succession. Doubt, suspicion, anger clouded vision; pain routed the impersonal conception. Loneliness came over him with the cool wind that stirred the sand between the columns; the patches of glaring sunshine took on a ghastly whiteness;

he shivered.... But it was not that he lost belief in his moment of clear vision, nor that the impersonal attitude became untrue. It was another thing he realized: that the power of attainment was not yet in him... quite. He could renounce, but not with complete acceptance....

As he drove back along the sandy lanes of blazing heat a little later, it seemed to him that he had been through some strenuous battle that had taxed his final source of strength. If his position was somewhat vague, this was due to his inability to analyze such deep interior turmoil. He was sure, at least, of one thing—that, before he could know this final joy awaiting him, he must first find in himself the strength for what seemed just then an impossible, an ultimate sacrifice. He must forget himself—if such forgetfulness involved the happiness of another. He must slip out. The strength to do it would come presently. And his heart was full of this indeterminate, half-formed resolve as he entered the shady garden and saw Lettice lying in her deck-chair beneath the trees, awaiting him.

CHAPTER XXIV

Events, however slight, which involve the soul are drama; for once the soul takes a hand in them their effects are permanent and reproductive. Not alone the relationships between individuals are determined this way or that, but the relationships of these individuals towards the universe are changed upon a scale of geometrical progression. The results are of the eternal order. Since that which persists—the soul—is radically affected, they are of ultimate importance.

Had the strange tie between Tom and Lettice been due to physical causes only, to mental affinity, or to mere sympathetic admiration of each other's outward strength and beauty, a rupture between them could have been of a passing character merely. A pang, a bitterness that lasted for a day or for a year—and the gap would be filled again by some one else. They had idealized; they would get over it; they were not indispensable to one another; there were other fish in the sea, and so forth.

But with Tom, at any rate, there was something transcendental in their intimate union. Loss, where she was concerned, involved a permanent and irremediable bereavement—no substitute was conceivable. With him, this relationship seemed foreordained, almost prenatal—it had come to him at the very dawn of life; it had lasted through years of lonely waiting; no other woman had ever threatened its fixed security; and the sudden meeting in Switzerland had seemed to him reunion rather than discovery. Moreover he had transferred his own sense of security to her; had always credited her with similar feelings; and the suspicion, now, that he had deceived himself in this made life tremble to the foundations. It was a terrible thought that robbed him of every atom of self-confidence. It affected his attitude to the entire universe.

The intensity of this drama, however, being interior, caused little outward disturbance that casual onlookers need have noticed. He waved his hat as he walked towards the corner where she lay, greeting her with a smile and careless word, as though no shadow stood between them. A barrier, nevertheless, was there, he knew. He *felt* it almost sensibly. Also—it had grown higher. And at once he was aware that the Lettice who returned his smile with a colorless "Good-morning, Tom, I'm so glad you could come," was not the Lettice who had known a moment's reaction a little while before. He told by her very attitude that now there was lassitude, even weariness in her. Her eyes betrayed none of the excitement and delight that another could wake in her. His own presence certainly no longer brought the thrill, the interest that once it did. She was both bored and lonely.

And, while an exquisite pain ran through him, he made a prodigious effort to draw upon the strength he had felt in Karnak a short half-hour ago. He struggled bravely to forget himself. "So Tony's gone!" he said lightly, "run off and left us without so much as a word of warning or good-by. A rascally proceeding, I call it! Rather sudden, too, wasn't it?"

He sat down beside her and began to smoke. She need not answer unless she wanted to. She did answer, however, and at once. She did not look at him; her eyes were on the golden distance. It had to be said; she said it. "He's only gone for two or three days. His friends suddenly changed their minds, and he couldn't get out of it. He said he didn't want to go—a bit."

How did she know it, Tom wondered, glancing up over his cigarette? And how had she read his mind so easily?

"He just popped in to tell me," she added, "and to say good-by. He asked me to tell you." She spoke without a tremor, as if Tom had no right to disapprove.

"Pretty early, wasn't it?" It was not the first time either. "He comes at such unusual hours"—he remembered Mrs. Haughstone's words.

"I was only just up. But there was time to give him coffee before the train."

She offered no further comment; Tom made none; he sat smoking there beside her, outwardly calm and peaceful as though no feeling of any kind was in him. He felt numb perhaps. In his mind he saw the picture of the breakfast-table beneath the trees. The plan had been arranged, of course, beforehand.

"Miss de Lorne's coming to lunch," she mentioned presently. "She's to bring her pictures—the Deir-el-Bahri ones. You must help me criticize them."

So they were not to be alone even was Tom's instant thought. Aloud he said merely, "I hope they're good." She flicked the flies away with her horse-hair whisk and sighed. He caught the sigh. The day felt empty, uninspired, the boredom of cruel disillusion in it somewhere. But it was the sigh that made him realize it. Avoiding the subject of Tony's abrupt departure, he asked what she would like to do that afternoon; he made various proposals. She listened without interest. "D'you know, Tom, I don't feel inclined to do anything much, but just lie and rest."

There was no energy in her, no zest for life; expeditions had lost their interest; she was listless, tired. He felt impatience in him, sharp disappointment too; but there was an alert receptiveness in his mind that noted trifles done or left undone. She made no reference, for instance, to the fact that they might be frequently alone together now. A faint hope that had been in him vanished quickly.... He wondered when she was going to speak of her letter, of his conduct the night before that was "beautiful and precious," of the comfort she had needed, or even of the dreams that she had mentioned. But, though he waited, giving various openings, nothing was forthcoming. That side of her, once intimately precious and familiar, seemed buried, hidden away, perhaps forgotten. This was not Lettice—it was some one else.

"You had dreams that frightened you?" he inquired at length. "You said you'd tell them to me." He moved nearer so that he could watch her face.

She looked puzzled for a second. "Did I?" she replied. She thought a moment. "Oh yes, of course I did. But they weren't much really. I'd forgotten. It was about water or something. Oh yes, I remember now—we were drowning, and you saved us." She gave a little unmeaning laugh as she said it.

"Who were drowning?"

"All of us—me and you, I think it was—and Tony—"

"Oh, of course."

She looked up. "Tom, why do you say 'Of course' like that?"

"It was your old idea of the river and the floating faces, I meant," he answered. "I had the feeling."

"You said it so sharply."

"Did I!" He shrugged his shoulders slightly. "I didn't mean to." He noticed the beauty of her ear, the delicate line of the nostrils, the long eyelashes. The graceful neck, with the firm, slim line of the breast below, was exquisite. The fairy curve of her ankle was just visible. He could have knelt and covered it with kisses. Her coolness, the touch of contempt in her voice made him wild.... But he understood his rôle; and—he remembered Karnak.

A little pause followed. Lettice made one of her curious gestures, half impatience, half weariness. She stretched; the other ankle appeared. Tom, as he saw it, felt something in him burst into flame. He came perilously near to saying impetuously a hundred things he had determined that he must not say. He felt the indifference in her, the coolness, almost the cruelty. Her negative attitude towards him goaded, tantalized. He was full of burning love, from head to foot, while she lay there within two feet of him, calm, listless, unresponsive, passionless. The bitter pain of promises unfulfilled assailed him acutely, poignantly. Yet in ordinary life the situation was so commonplace. The "strong man" would face her with it, have it out plainly; he would be masterful, forcing a climax of one kind or another, behaving as men do in novels or on the stage.

Yet Tom remained tongue-tied and restrained; he seemed unable to take the lead; an inner voice cried sternly No to all such natural promptings. It would be a gross mistake. He must let things take their course. He must not force a premature disclosure. With a tremendous effort, he controlled himself and smothered the rising fires that struggled towards speech and action. He would not even ask a single question. Somehow, in any case, it was impossible.

The subject dropped; Lettice made no further reference to the letter.

"When you feel like going anywhere, or doing anything, you'll let me know," he suggested presently. "We've been too energetic lately. It's best for you to rest. You're tired." The words hurt and stung him as though he were telling lies. He felt untrue to himself. The blood boiled in his veins.

She answered him with a touch of impatience again, almost of exasperation. He noticed the emphasis she used so needlessly.

"Tom, I'm *not* tired—not in the way *you* mean. It's just that I feel like being quiet for a bit. *Really* it's not so remarkable! Can't you understand?"

"Perfectly," he rejoined calmly, lighting another cigarette. "We'll have a program ready for later—when Tony gets back." The blood rushed from his heart as he said it.

Her face brightened instantly, as he had expected—dreaded; there was no attempt at concealment anywhere; she showed interest as frankly as a child. "It was stupid of him to go, just when we were enjoying everything so," she said again. "I wonder how long he'll stay—"

"I'll write and tell him to hurry up," suggested Tom. He twirled his fly-whisk energetically.

"Tell him we can't get on without our *dragoman*," she added eagerly with her first attempt at gaiety; and then went on to mention other things he was to say, till her pleasure in talking about Tony was so obvious that Tom yielded to temptation suddenly. It was more than he could bear. "I strongly suspect a pretty girl in the party somewhere," he observed carelessly.

"There is," came the puzzling reply, "but he doesn't care for her a bit.

He told me all about her. It's curious, isn't it, how he fascinates them all? There's something very remarkable about Tony—I can't quite make it out."

Tom leaned forward, bringing his face in front of her own, and closer to it. He looked hard into her eyes a moment. In the depths of her steady gaze he saw shadows, far away, behind the open expression. There was trouble in her, but it was deep, deep down and out of sight. The eyes of some one else, it seemed, looked through her into his. An older world came whispering across the sunlight and the sand.

"Lettice," he said quietly, "there's something new come into your life these last few weeks—isn't there?" His voice grated—like machinery started with violent effort against resistance. "Some new, big force, I mean? You seem so changed, so different." He had not meant to speak like this. It was forced out. He expressed himself badly too. He raged inwardly.

She smiled, but only with her lips. The shadows from behind her eyes drew nearer to the surface. But the eyes themselves held steady. That other look peered out of them. He was aware of power, of something strangely bewitching, yet at the same time fierce, inflexible in her... and a kind of helplessness came over him, as though he was suddenly out of his depth, without sure footing. The Wave roared in his ears and blood.

"Egypt probably—old Egypt," she said gently, making a small gesture with one hand towards the river and the sky. "It must be that." The gesture, it seemed to him, had royalty in it somewhere. There was stateliness and dignity—an air of authority about her. It was magnificent. He felt worship in him. The slave that lies in worship stirred. He could yield his life, suffer torture for days to give her a moment's happiness.

"I meant something personal, rather," he prevaricated.

"You meant Tony. I know it. Didn't you, Tom?"

His breath caught inwardly. In spite of himself, and in spite of his decision, she drew his secret out. Enchantment touched him deliciously, an actual torture in it.

"Yes," he said honestly, "perhaps I did." He said it shame-facedly rather, to his keen vexation. "For it *has* to do with Tony somehow."

He got up abruptly, tossed his cigarette over the wall into the river, then sat down again. "There's something about it—strange and big. I can't make it out a bit." He faltered, stammered over the words. "It's a long way off—then all at once it's close." He had the feeling that he had put a match to something. "I've done it now," he said to himself like a boy, as though he expected that something dramatic must happen instantly.

But nothing happened. The river flowed on silently, the heat blazed down, the leaves hung motionless as before, and far away the lime-stone hills lay sweltering in the glare. But those hills had glided nearer. He was aware of them,—the Valley of the Kings,—the desolate Theban Hills with their myriad secrets and their deathless tombs.

Lettice gave her low, significant little laugh. "It's odd you should say that, Tom—very odd. Because I've felt it too. It's awfully remote and quite near at the same time—"

"And Tony's brought it," he interrupted eagerly, half passionately. "It's got to do with him, I mean."

It seemed to him that the barrier between them had lowered a little. The Lettice he knew first peered over it at him.

"No," she corrected, "I don't feel that he's brought it. He's *in* it somehow, I admit, but he has not brought it exactly." She hesitated a moment. "I think the truth is he can't help himself—any more than we—you or I— can."

There was a caressing tenderness in her voice as she said it, but whether for himself or for another he could not tell. In his heart rose a frantic impulse just then to ask—to blurt it out: "Do you love Tony? Has he taken you from me? Tell me the truth and I can bear it. Only, for heaven's sake, don't hide it!" But, instead of saying this absurd, theatrical thing, he looked at her through the drifting cigarette smoke a moment without speaking, trying to read the expression in her face. "Last night, for instance," he exclaimed abruptly; "in the music room, I mean. Did you feel *that?*—the intensity—a kind of ominous feeling?"

Her expression was enigmatical; there were signs of struggle in it, he thought. It was as if two persons fought within her which should answer. Apparently the dear Lettice of his first acquaintance won—for the moment.

"You noticed it too!" she exclaimed with astonishment. "I thought I was the only one."

"We all—all three of us—felt it," he said in a lower tone. "Tony certainly did—"

Lettice raised herself suddenly on her elbow and looked down at him with earnestness. Something of the old eagerness was in her. The barrier between them lowered perceptibly again, and Tom felt a momentary return of the confidence he had lost. His heart beat quickly. He made a half impetuous gesture towards her—"What is it? What does it all mean, Lettice?" he exclaimed. "D'you feel what *I* feel in it—danger somewhere—danger for *us?*" There was a yearning, almost a cry for mercy in his voice.

She drew back again. "You amaze me, Tom," she said, as she lay among her cushions. "I had no idea you were so observant." She paused, putting her hand across her eyes a moment. "N-no—I don't feel danger exactly," she went on in a lower tone, speaking half to herself and half to him; "I feel—" She broke off with a little sigh; her hand still covered her eyes. "I feel," she went on slowly, with pauses between the words, "a deep, deep something—from very far away—that comes over me at times—only at times, yes. It's remote, enormously remote—but it has to be. I've never given you all that I ought to give. We have to go through with it—"

"You and I?" he whispered. He was listening intently. The beats of his heart were most audible.

She sighed. "All three of us—somehow," she replied equally low, and speaking again more to herself than to him. "Ah! Now my dream comes back a little. It was *the* river—my river with the floating faces. And the thing I feel comes—from its source, far, far away—its tiny source among the hills—" She sighed again, more deeply than before. Her breast heaved slightly. "We must go through it—yes. It's necessary for us—necessary for you—and me—"

"Lettice, my precious, my wonderful!" Tom whispered as though the breath choked and strangled hull. "But we stay together through it? We stay together *afterwards?* You love me still?" He leaned across and took her other hand. It lay unresistingly in his. It was very cold—without a sign of response.

Her reply half staggered him: "We are always, always together, you and I. Even if you married, I should still be yours. He will go out—"

Fear clashed with hope in his heart as he heard these words he could not understand. He groped and plunged after their meaning. He was bewildered by the reference to marriage—his marriage! Was she, then, already aware that she might lose him?... But there was confession in them too, the confession that she *had* been away from him. That he felt clearly. Now that the dividing influence was removed, she was coming back perhaps! If Tony stayed away she would come back entirely; only then the thing that had to happen would be prevented—which was not to be thought of for a moment.... "Poor Lettice...." He felt pity, love, protection that he burned to give; he felt a savage pain and anger as well. In the depths of him love and murder sat side by side.

"Oh, Lettice, tell me everything. Do share with me—share it and we'll meet it together." He drew her cold hand towards him, putting it inside his coat. "Don't hide it from me. You're my whole world. *My* love can never change.... Only don't hide anything!" The words poured out of him with passionate entreaty. The barrier had melted, vanished. He had found her again, the Lettice of his childhood, of his dream, the true and faithful Woman he had known first. His inexpressible love rose like a wave upon him. Regardless of where they were he bent over to take her in his arms— when she suddenly withdrew her hand from his. She removed the other from her eyes. He saw her face. And he realized in an instant that his words had been all wrong. He had said precisely again what he ought not to have said. The moment in her had passed.

The sudden change had a freezing effect upon him.

"Tom, I don't understand quite," she said coldly, her eyes fixed on his almost with resentment in them. "I'm not *hiding* anything from you. Why do you say such things? I'm true—true to myself."

The barrier was up again in an instant, of granite this time, with jagged edges of cut glass upon it, so that he could not approach it even. It was not Lettice that spoke then:

"I don't know what's come over you out here," she went on, each word she uttered increasing the distance between them; "you misunderstand everything I say and criticize all I do. You suspect my tenderest instincts. Even a friendship that brings me happiness you object to and—and exaggerate."

He listened till she ceased; it was as if he had received a blow in the face; he felt disconcerted, keenly aware of his own stupidity, helpless. Something froze in him. He had seen her for a second, then lost her utterly.

"No, no, Lettice," he stammered, "you read all that into me—really, you do. I only want your happiness."

Her eyes softened a little. She sighed wearily and turned her face away.

"We were only talking of this curious, big feeling that's come—" he went on.

"You were speaking of Tony—that's what you really meant, Tom," she interrupted. "You know it perfectly well. It only makes it harder—for *me*."

He felt suddenly she was masquerading, playing with him again, playing with his very heart and soul. The devil tempted him. All the things he had decided he would not say rose to the tip of his tongue. The worst of them—those that hurt him most—he managed to force down. But even the one he did suffer to escape gave him atrocious pain:

"Well, Lettice, to tell the truth, I do think Tony has a bad—a curious influence on you. I do feel he has come between us rather. And I do think that if you would only share with me—"

The sudden way she turned upon him, rising from her chair and standing over him, was so startling that he got up too. They faced each other, he in the blazing sunshine, she in the shade. She looked so different that he was utterly taken aback. She wore that singular Eastern appearance he now knew so well. Expression, attitude, gesture, all betrayed it. That inflexible, cruel thing shone in her eyes.

"Tom, dear," she said, but with a touch of frigid exasperation that for a moment paralyzed thought and utterance in him, "whatever happens, you must realize this —that I am myself and that I can never allow my freedom to be taken from me. If you're determined to misjudge, the fault is yours, and if our love, our friendship cannot understand *that*, there's something wrong with it."

The word "friendship" was like a sword-thrust. It went right through him. "I trust you," he faltered, "I trust you wholly. I know you're true." But the words, it seemed, gave expression to an intense desire, a fading hope. He did not say it with conviction. She gazed at him for a moment through half-closed eyelids.

"*Do* you, Tom?" she whispered.

"Lettice...!"

"Then believe at least—" her voice wavered suddenly, there came a little break in it—"that I am true to you, Tom, as I am to myself. Believe in that... and—Oh! for the love of heaven—help me!"

Before he could respond, before he could act upon the hope and passion her last unexpected words set loose in him—she turned away to go into the house. Voices were audible behind them, and Miss de Lorne was coming up the sandy drive with Mrs. Haughstone. Tom watched her go. She moved with a certain gliding, swaying walk as she passed along the verandah and disappeared behind the curtains of dried grass. It almost seemed—though this must certainly have been a trick of light and shadow—that she was swathed from head to foot in a clinging garment not of modern kind, and that he caught the gleam of gold upon the flesh of dusky arms that were bare above the elbow. Two persons were visible in her very physical appearance, as two persons had just been audible in her words. Thence came the conflict and the contradictions.

CHAPTER XXV

A few minutes later Lettice was presiding over her luncheon table as though life were simple as the sunlight in the street outside, and no clouds could ever fleck the procession of the years. She was quiet and yet betrayed excitement. Tom, at the opposite end of the table, watched her girlish figure, her graceful gestures. Her eyes were very bright, no shadows in their depths; she returned his gaze with untroubled frankness. Yet the set of her little mouth had self-mastery in it somewhere; there was no wavering or uncertainty; her self-possession was complete. But above his head the sword of Damocles hung. He saw the thread, taut and gleaming in the glare of the Egyptian sunlight.... He waited upon his cousin's return as men once waited for the sign thumbs up, thumbs down...

"Molly has sent me her album," mentioned Mrs. Haughstone when the four of them were lounging in the garden chairs; "she wonders if you would write your name in it. It's her passion—to fill it with distinguished names." And when the page was found, she pointed to the quotation against his birthday date with the remark, in a lowered voice: "It's quite appropriate, isn't it? For a man, I mean," she added, "because when a man's unhappy he's more easily tempted to suspicion than a woman is."

"What is the quotation?" asked Lettice, glancing up from her deck chair.

Tom was carefully inscribing his "distinguished" name in the child's album, as Mrs. Haughstone read the words aloud over his shoulder:

"'Whatever the circumstances, there is no man so miserable that he need not be true.' It's anonymous," she added, "but it's by some one very wise."

"A woman, probably," Miss de Lorne put in with a laugh.

They discussed it, while Tom laboriously wrote his name against it with a fountain pen. His writing was a little shaky, for his sight was blurred and ice was in his veins.

"There's no need for you to hurry, is there?" said Lettice presently. "Won't you stay and read to me a bit? Or would you rather look in—after dinner—and smoke?" The two selves spoke in that. It was as if the earlier, loving Lettice tried to assert itself, but was instantly driven back again. How differently she would have said it a few months ago.... He made excuses, saying he would drop in after dinner if he might. She did not press him further.

"I *am* tired a little," she said gently. "I'll sleep and rest and write letters too, then."

She was invariably tired now, Tom soon discovered—until Tony returned from Cairo....

And that evening he escaped the invitations to play bridge, and made his way back, as in a dream, to the little house upon the Nile. He found her bending over the table so that the lamp shone on her abundant coils of hair, and as he entered softly he saw the address on the envelope beside her writing pad, several pages of which were already covered with her small, fine writing. He read the name before he could turn his eyes away.

"I was writing to Tony," she said, looking up with an untroubled smile, "but I can finish later. And you've come just in time to take my part. Ettie's been scolding me severely again."

She blotted the lines and put the paper on one side, then turned with a challenging expression at her cousin who was knitting by the open window. The little name sounded so incongruous; it did not suit the big gaunt woman who had almost a touch of the monstrous in her. Tom stared a moment without speaking. The playful challenge had reality in it. Lettice intended to define her position openly. She meant that Tom should support her too.

He smiled as he watched them. But no words came to him. Then, remembering all at once that he had not kept his promise, he said quietly: "I must send a line as well. I quite forgot."

"You can write it now," suggested Lettice, "and I'll enclose it in mine." And she pointed to the envelopes and paper before him on the table.

There was a moment of acute and painful struggle in him; pride and love fought the old pitched battle, but on a field of her own bold choosing! Tom knew murder in his heart, but he knew also that strange rich pain of sacrifice. It was theatrical: he stood upon the stage, an audience watching him with intent expectancy, wondering upon his decision. Mrs. Haughstone, Lettice and another part of himself that was Onlooker were the audience; Mrs. Haughstone had ceased knitting, Lettice leaned back in her chair, a smile in the eyes, but the lips set very firmly together. The man in him, with scorn and anger, seemed to clench his fists, while that other self—as with a spirit's voice from very far away—whispered behind his pain: "Obey. You must. It has to be, so why not help it forward!"

To play the game, but to play it better than before, flashed through him.... Half amazed at himself, yet half contented, he sat down mechanically and scribbled a few lines of urgent entreaty to his cousin to come back soon.... "We want you here, it's dull, we can't get on without you..." knowing that he traced the sentences of his own death-warrant. He folded it and passed it across to Lettice, who slipped it unread into her envelope. That ought to bring him, you think?" she observed, a happy light in her eyes, yet with a faint sigh half suppressed as though she did a thing which hurt her too.

"I hope so," replied Tom. "I think so."

He knew not what she had written to Tony; but whatever it was, his own note would appear to endorse it. He had perhaps placed in her hand the weapon that should hasten his own defeat, stretch him bleeding on the sand. And yet he trusted her; she was loyal and true throughout. The quicker the climax came, the sooner would he know the marvelous joy that lay beyond the pain. In some way, moreover, she knew this too. Actually they were working together, hand in hand, to hasten its inevitable arrival. They merely used such instruments as fate offered, however trivial, however clumsy. They were *being* driven. They could neither choose nor resist. He found a germ of subtle comfort in the thought. The Wave was under them. Upon its tumultuous volume they swept forward, side by side... striking out wildly.

"And will you also post it for me when you go?" he heard. "I'll just add a line to finish up with." Tom watched her open the writing-block again and trace a hurried sentence or two; she did it openly; he saw the neat, small words flow from the nib; he saw the signature: "Lettice."

"Fasten it down for me, Tom, will you? It's such an ugly thing for a woman to do. It's absurd that science can't invent a better way of closing an envelope, isn't it?" He was oddly helpless; she forced him to obey out of some greater knowledge. And while he did the ungraceful act, their eyes met across the table. It was the other person in her—the remote, barbaric, eastern woman, set somehow in power over him—who watched him seal his own discomfiture, and smiled to know his obedience had to be. It was, indeed, as though she tortured him deliberately.

For a passing second Tom felt this—then the strange exaggeration vanished. They played a game together. All this had been before. They looked back upon it, looked down from a point above it.... Tom could not read her heart, but he could read his own.

In a few minutes at most all this happened. He put the letter in his pocket, and Lettice turned to her cousin, challenge in her manner, an air of victory as well. And Tom felt he shared that victory somehow too. It was a curious moment, charged with a subtle perplexity of emotions none of them quite understood. It held such singular contradictions.

"There, Ettie!" she exclaimed, as much as to say "Now you can't scold me any more. You see how little Mr. Kelverdon minds!"

While she flitted into the next room to fetch a stamp, Mrs. Haughstone, her needles arrested in mid-air, looked steadily at Tom. Her face was white. She had watched the little scene intently.

"The only thing I cannot understand, Mr. Kelverdon," she said in a low tone, her voice both indignant and sympathetic, "is how my cousin can give pain to a man like you. It's the most heartless thing I've ever seen."

"Me!" gasped Tom. "But I don't understand you!"

"And for a creature like that!" she went on quickly, as Lettice was heard in the passage; "a libertine"—she almost hissed the word out—"who thinks every pretty woman is made for his amusement—and false into the bargain—"

Tom put the stamp on. A few minutes later he was again walking along the narrow little Luxor street, the sentences just heard still filling the silent air about him, emotions charging wildly, each detail of the familiar little journey associated already with present pain and with prophecies of pain to come. The bewilderment and confusion in him were beyond all quieting. One moment he saw the picture of a slender foot that deliberately crushed life into the dust, the next he gazed into gentle, loving eyes that would brim with tears if a single hair of his head were injured.

A cold and mournful wind blew down the street, ruffling the darkened river. The black line of hills he could not see. Mystery, enchantment hung in the very air. The long dry fingers of the palm trees rattled overhead, and looking up, he saw the divine light of the starry heavens.... Surely among those comforting stars he saw her radiant eyes as well....

A voice, asking in ridiculous English the direction to a certain house, broke his reverie, and, turning round, he saw the sheeted figure of an Arab boy, the bright eyes gleaming in the mischievous little face of bronze. He pointed out the gateway, and the boy slipped off into the darkness, his bare feet soundless and mysterious on the sand. He disappeared up the driveway to the house—her house. Tom knew quite well from whom the telegram came. Tony had telegraphed to let her know of his safe arrival. So even that was necessary! "And to-morrow morning," he thought, "he'll get my letter too. He'll come posting back again the very next day." He clenched his teeth a moment; he shuddered. Then he added: "So much the better!" and walked on quickly up the street. He posted *her* letter at the corner.

He went up to his bedroom. His sleepless nights had begun now....

What was the use of thinking, he asked himself as the hours passed? What good did it do to put the same questions over and over again, to pass from doubt to certainty, only to be flung back again from certainty to doubt? Was there no discoverable center where the pendulum ceased from swinging? How could she be at the same time both cruel and tender, both true and false, frank and secretive, spiritual and sensual? Each of these pairs, he realized, was really a single state of which the adjectives represented the extremes at either end. They were ripples. The central personality traveled in one or other direction according to circumstances, according to the pull or push of forces—the main momentum of the parent wave. But there was a point where the heart felt neither one nor other, neither cruel nor tender, false nor true. Where, on the thermometer, did heat begin and cold come to an end? Love and hate, similarly, were extremes of one and the same emotion. Love, he well knew, could turn to virulent hatred—if something checked and forced it back upon the line of natural advance. Could, then, *her* tenderness be thus reversed, turning into cruelty.... Or was this cruelty but the awakening in her of another thing?...

Possibly. Yet at the center, that undiscovered center at present beyond his reach, Lettice, he knew, remained unalterably steadfast. There he felt the absolute assurance she was his exclusively. His center, moreover, coincided with her own. They were in the "sea" together. But to get back into the sea, the Wave now rolling under them must first break and fall....

The sooner, then, the better! They would swing back with it together eventually.

He chose, that is—without knowing it—a higher way of molding destiny. It was the spiritual way, whose method and secret lie in that subtle paradox: Yield to conquer.

CHAPTER XXVI

Yes, she was always "tired" now, though the "always" meant but three days at most. It was the starving sense of loneliness, the aching sense of loss, the yearning and the vain desire that made it seem so long. Lettice evaded him with laughter in her eyes, or with a tired smile. But the laughter was for another. It was merciless and terrible—so slightly, faintly indicated, yet so overwhelmingly convincing.

The talk between them rarely touched reality, as though a barrier deadened their very voices. Even her mothering became exasperating; it was so unforced and natural; it seemed still so right that she should show solicitude for his physical welfare. And therein lay the anguish and the poignancy. Yet, while he resented fiercely, knowing this was all she had to offer now, he struggled at the same time to accept. One moment he resisted, the next accepted. One hour he believed in her, the next he disbelieved. Hope and fear alternately made tragic sport of him.

Two personalities fought for possession of his soul, and he could not always keep back the lower of the two. They interpenetrated—as, at Dehrel-Bahri, two scenes had interpenetrated, something very very old projected upon a modern screen.

Lettice too—he was convinced of it—was undergoing a similar experience in herself. Only in her case just now it was the lower, the primitive, the physical aspect that was uppermost. She clung to Tony, yet struggled to keep Tom. She could not help herself. And he himself, knowing he must shortly go, still clung and hesitated, hoping against hope. More and more now, until the end, he was aware that he stood outside his present-day self, and above it. He looked back—looked down—upon former emotions and activities; and hence the confusing alternating of jealousy and forgiveness.

There were revealing little incidents from time to time. On the following afternoon he found her, for instance, radiant with that exuberant happiness he had learned now to distrust. And for a moment he half believed again that the menace had lifted and the happiness was for him. She held out both hands towards him, while she described a plan for going to Edfu and Abou Simbel. His heart beat wildly for a second.

"But Tony?" he asked, almost before he knew it. "We can't leave him out!"

"Oh, but I've had a letter." And as she said it his eye caught sight of a bulky envelope lying in the sand beside her chair.

"Good," he said quietly, "and when is he coming back? I haven't heard from him." The solid ground moved beneath his feet. He shivered, even in the blazing heat.

"To-morrow. He sends you all sorts of messages and says that something you wrote made him very happy. I wonder what it was, Tom?"

Behind her voice he heard the north wind rattling in the palms; he heard the soft rustle of the acacia leaves as well; there was the crashing of little waves upon the river; but a deep, deep shadow fell upon the sky and blotted out the sunshine. The glory vanished from the day, leaving in its place a painful glare that hurt the eyes. The soul in him was darkened.

"Ah!" he exclaimed with assumed playfulness, "but that's my secret!" Men do smile, he remembered, as they are led to execution.

She laughed excitedly. "I shall find it out—"

"You will," he burst out significantly, "in the end."

Then, as she passed him to go into the house, he lost control a moment. He whispered suddenly:

"Love has no secrets, Lettice, anywhere. We're in the Sea together. I shall *never* let you go." The intensity in his manner betrayed him; he adored her; he could not hide it.

She turned an instant, standing two steps above him; the sidelong downward glance lent to her face a touch of royalty, half pitying, half imperious. Her exquisite, frail beauty held a strength that mocked the worship in his eyes and voice. Almost—she challenged him:

"Soothsayer!" she whispered back contemptuously. "Do your worst!"— and was gone into the house.

Desire surged wildly in him at that moment; impatience, scorn, fury even, raised their heads; he felt a savage impulse to seize her with violence, force her to confess, to have it out and end it one way or the other. He loathed himself for submitting to her cruelty, for it was intentional cruelty—she made him writhe and suffer of set purpose. And something barbaric in his blood leaped up in answer to the savagery in her own... when at that instant he heard her calling softly:

"Tom! Come indoors a moment; I want to show you something!"

But with it another sentence sprang across him and was gone. Like a meteor it streaked the screen of memory. Seize it he could not. It had to do with death—his death. There was a thought of blood. Outwardly what he heard, however, was the playful little sentence of to-day. "Come, I want to show you something."

At the sound of her voice so softly calling all violence was forgotten; love poured back in a flood upon him; he would go through fire and water to possess her in the end. In this strange drama she played her inevitable part, even as he did; there must be no loss of self-control that might frustrate the coming climax. There must be no thwarting. If he felt jealousy, he must hide it; anger, scorn, desire must veil their faces.

He crossed the passage and stood before her in the darkened room, afraid and humble, full of a burning love that the centuries had not lessened, and that no conceivable cruelty of pain could ever change. Almost he knelt before her. Even if terrible, she was utterly adorable.

For he believed she was about to make a disclosure that would lay him bleeding in the dust; singularly at her mercy he felt, his heart laid bare to receive the final thrust that should make him outcast. Her little foot would crush him....

The long green blinds kept out the glare of the sunshine; and at first he saw the room but dimly. Then, slowly, the white form emerged, the broad-brimmed hat, the hanging violet veil, the yellow jacket of soft, clinging silk, the long white gauntlet gloves. He saw her small face peering through the dimness at him, the eyes burning like two dark precious stones. A table stood between them. There was a square white object on it. A moment's bewilderment stole over him. Why had she called him in? What was she going to say? Why did she choose this moment? Was it the threat of Tony's near arrival that made her confession—and his dismissal—at last inevitable?

Then, suddenly, that night in the London theater flashed back across his mind—her strange absorption in the play, the look of pain in her face, the little conversation, the sense of familiarity that hung about it all. He remembered Tony's words later: that another actor was expected with whose entry the piece would turn more real—turn tragic.

He waited. The dimness of the room was like the dimness of that theater. The lights were lowered. They played their little parts. The audience watched and listened.

"Tom, dear," her voice came floating tenderly across the air. "I didn't like to give it you before the others. They wouldn't understand—they'd laugh at us."

He did not understand. Surely he had heard indistinctly. He waited, saying nothing. The tenderness in her voice amazed him. He had expected very different words. Yet this was surely Lettice speaking, the Lettice of his spring-time in the mountains beside the calm blue lake. He stared hard. For the voice *was* Lettice's, but the eyes and figure were another's. He was again aware of two persons there—of perplexing and bewildering struggle. But Lettice, for the moment, dominated as it seemed.

"So I put it here," she went on in a low gentle tone, "here, Tommy, on the table for you. And all my love is in it—my first, deep, fond love—our childhood love." She leaned down and forward, her face in her hands, her elbows on the dark cloth; she pushed the square, white packet across to him. "God bless you," floated to him with her breath.

The struggle in her seemed very patent then. Yet in spite of that other, older self within her, it was still the voice of Lettice....

There was a moment's silence while her whisper hung, as it were, upon the air. His entire body seemed a single heart. Exactly what he felt he hardly knew. There was a simultaneous collapse of several huge emotions in him.... But he trusted her.... He clung to that beloved voice. For she called him "Tommy"; she was his mother; love, tenderness, and pity emanated from her like a cloud of perfume. He heard the faint rustle of her dress as she bent forward, but outside he heard the dry, harsh rattle of the palm trees in the northern wind. And in that—was terror.

"What—what is it, Lettice?" The voice sounded like a boy's. It was outrageous. He swallowed—with an effort.

"Tommy, you—don't mind? You *will* take it, won't you?" And it was as if he heard her saying "Help..." once again, "Trust me as I trust you...."

Mechanically he put his hand out and drew the object towards him. He knew then what it was and what was in it. He was glad of the darkness, for there was a ridiculous moisture in his eyes now. A lump *was* in his throat!

"I've been neglecting you. You haven't had a thing for ages. You'll take it, Tommy, won't you—dear?"

The little foolish words, so sweetly commonplace, fell like balm upon an open wound. He already held the small white packet in his hand. He looked up at her. God alone knows the strain upon his will in that moment. Somehow he mastered himself. It seemed as if he swallowed blood. For behind the mothering words lurked, he knew, the other self that any minute would return.

"Thank you, Lettice, very much," he said with a strange calmness, and his voice was firm. Whatever happened he must not prevent the delivery of what had to be. Above all, that was clear. The pain must come in full before the promised joy.

Was it, perhaps, this strength in him that drew her? Was it his moment of iron self-mastery that brought her with outstretched, clinging arms towards him? Was it the unshakable love in him that threatened the temporary ascendency of that other in her who gladly tortured him that joy might come in a morning yet to break?

For she stood beside him, though he had not seen her move. She was close against his shoulder, nestling as of old. It was surely a stage effect. A trapdoor had opened in the floor of his consciousness; his first, early love sheltered in his aching heart again. The entire structure of the drama they played together threatened to collapse.

"Tom... you love me less?"

He held her to him, but he did not kiss the face she turned up to his. Nor did he speak.

"You've changed somewhere?" she whispered. "You, too, have changed?"

There was a pause before he found words that he could utter. He dared not yield. To do so would be vain in any case.

"N—no, Lettice. But I can't say what it is. There is pain.... It has turned some part of me numb... killed something, brought something else to life. You will come back to me... but not quite yet."

In spite of the darkness, he saw her face clearly then. For a moment—it seemed so easy—he could have caught her in his arms, kissed her, known the end of his present agony of heart and mind. She would have come back to him, Tony's claim obliterated from her life. The driving power that forced an older self upon her had weakened before the steadfast love he bore her. She was ready to capitulate. The little, childish present in his hands was offered as of old.... Tears rose behind his eyes.

How he resisted, he never understood. Some thoroughness in him triumphed. If he shirked the pain today, it would have to be faced to-morrow—that alone was clear in his breaking heart. To be worthy of the greater love, the completer joy to follow, they must accept the present pain and see it through—experience it—exhaust it once for all. To refuse it now was only to postpone it. She must go her way, while he went his....

Gently he pushed her from him, released his hold; the little face slipped from his shoulder as though it sank into the sea. He felt that she understood. He heard himself speaking, though how he chose the words he never knew. Out of new depths in himself the phrases rose—a regenerated Tom uprising, though not yet sure of himself:

"You are not wholly mine. I must first—oh, Lettice!—learn to do without you. It is you who say it."

Her voice, as she answered, seemed already changed, a shade of something harder, and less yielding in it:

"That which you can do without is added to you."

"A new thing... beginning," he whispered, feeling it both belief and prophecy. His whisper broke in spite of himself. He saw her across the room, the table between them again. Already she looked different, "Lettice" fading from her eyes and mouth.

She said a marvelous, sweet thing before that other self usurped her then:

"One day, Tom, we shall find each other in a crowd...."

There was a yearning cry in him he did not utter. It seemed she faded from the atmosphere as the dimness closed about her. He saw a darker figure with burning eyes upon a darker face; there was a gleam of gold; a faint perfume as of ambra hung about the air, and outside the palm leaves rattled in the northern wind. He had heard awful words, it seemed, that sealed his fate. He was forsaken, lonely, outcast. It was a sentence of death, for she was set in power over him....

A flood of dazzling sunshine poured into the room from a lifted blind, as the others looked in from the verandah to say that they were going and wanted to say good-by. A moment later all were discussing plans in the garden, Tom as loudly and eagerly as any of them. He held his square white packet. But he did not open it till he reached his room a little later, and then arranged the different articles in a row upon his table: the favorite cigarettes, the soap, the pair of white tennis socks with his initial neatly sewn on, the tie in the shade of blue that suited him best... the writing-pad and the dates!

A letter from Tony next caught his eye and he opened it, slowly, calmly, almost without interest, knowing exactly what it would say:

"... I was delighted, old chap, to get your note," he read. "I felt sure it would be all right, for I felt somehow that I *had* exaggerated your feeling towards her. As you say, what one has to think of with a woman in so delicate a position is her happiness more than one's own. But I wouldn't do anything to offend you or cause you pain for worlds, and I'm awfully glad to know the way is clear. To tell you the truth, I went away on purpose, for I felt uneasy. I wanted to be quite sure first that I was not trespassing. She made me feel I was doing you no wrong, but I wanted your assurance too...."

There was a good deal more in similar vein—he laid the burden upon *her*—ending with a word to say he was coming back to Luxor immediately. He would arrive the following day.

As a matter of fact Tony was already then in the train that left Cairo that evening and reached Luxor at eight o'clock next morning. Tom, who had counted upon another twenty-four hours' respite, did not know this; nor did he know till later that another telegram had been carried by a ghostly little Arab boy, with the result that Tony and Lettice enjoyed their hot rolls and coffee alone together in the shady garden where the cool northern wind rattled among the palm trees. Mrs. Haughstone mentioned it in due course, however, having watched the *tête-à-tête* from her bedroom window, unobserved.

CHAPTER XXVII

And next day there was one more revealing incident that helped, yet also hindered him, as he moved along his *via dolorosa*. For every step he took away from her seemed also to bring him nearer. They followed opposing curves of a circle. They separated ever more widely, back to back, yet were approaching each other at the same time. They would meet face to face....

He found her at the piano, practising the song that now ran ever in his blood; the score, he noticed, was in Tony's writing.

"Unwelcome!" he exclaimed, reading out the title over her shoulder.

"Tom! How you startled me! I was trying to learn it." She turned to him; her eyes were shining. He was aware of a singular impression—struggle, effort barely manageable. Her beauty seemed fresh made; he thought of a wild-rose washed by the dew and sparkling in the sunlight.

"I thought you knew it already," he observed.

She laughed significantly, looking up into his face so close he could have kissed her lips by merely bending his head a few inches. "Not quite—yet," she answered. "Will you give me a lesson, Tom?"

"Unpaid?" he asked.

She looked reproachfully at him. "The best services are unpaid always."

"I'm afraid I have neither the patience nor the knowledge," he replied.

Her next words stirred happiness in him for a moment; the divine trust he fought to keep stole from his heart into his eyes: "But you would never, never give up, Tom, no matter how difficult and obstinate the pupil. You would always understand. *That* I know."

He moved away. Such double-edged talk, even in play, was dangerous. A deep weariness was in him, weakening self-control. Sensitive to the slightest touch just then, he dared not let her torture him too much. He felt in her a strength far, far beyond his own; he was powerless before her. Had Tony been present he could not have played his part at all. Somehow he had a curious feeling, moreover, that his cousin was not very far away.

"Tony will be here later, I think," she said, as she followed him outside. "But, if not, he's sure to come to dinner."

"Good," he replied, thinking that the train arrived in time to dress, and in no way surprised that she divined his thoughts. "We can decide our plans then." He added that he might be obliged to go back to Assouan, but she made no comment. Speech died away between them, as they sat down in the old familiar corner above the Nile. Tom, for the life of him, could think of nothing to say. Lettice, on the other hand, wanted to say nothing. He felt that she *had* nothing to say. Behind, below the numbness in him, meanwhile, her silence stabbed him without ceasing. The intense yearning in his heart threatened any minute to burst forth in vehement speech, almost in action. It lay accumulating in him dangerously, ready to leap out at the least sign—the pin-prick of a look, a word, a gesture on her part, and he would smash the barrier down between them and—ruin all. The sight of Tony, for instance, just then must have been as a red rag to a bull.

He traced figures in the sand with his heel, he listened to the wind above them, he never ceased to watch her motionless, indifferent figure stretched above him on the long deck-chair. A book peeped out from behind the cushion where her head rested. Tom put his hand across and took it suddenly, partly for something to do, partly from curiosity as well. She made a quick, restraining gesture, then changed her mind. And again he was conscious of battle in her, as if two beings fought.

"The Mary Coleridge Poems," she said carelessly. "Tony gave it me. You'll find the song he put to music."

Tom vigorously turned the leaves. He had already glanced at the title-page with the small inscription in one corner: "To L. J., from A. W." There was a pencil-mark against a poem half-way through.

"He's going to write music for some of the others too," she added, watching him; "the ones he has marked." Her voice, he fancied, wavered slightly.

Tom nodded his head. "I see," he murmured, noticing a cross in pencil. A sullen defiance rose in his blood, but he forced it out of sight. He read the words in a low voice to himself. It was astonishing how the powers behind the scenes forced a contribution from the commonest incidents:

> The sum of loss I have not reckoned yet,
>   I cannot tell.
> For ever it was morning when we met,
>   Night when we bade farewell.

Perhaps the words let loose the emotion, though of different kinds, pent up behind their silence. The strain, at any rate, between them tightened first, then seemed to split. He kept his eyes upon the page before him; Lettice, too, remained still as before; only her lips moved as she spoke:

"Tom...." The voice plunged into his heart like iron.

"Yes," he said quietly, without looking up.

"Tom," she repeated, "what are you thinking about so hard?"

He found no answer.

"And all to yourself?"

The blood rushed to his face; her voice was so soft. He met her eyes and smiled. "The same as usual, I suppose," he said.

For a moment she made no reply, then, glancing at the book lying in his hand, she said in a lower voice: "That woman had suffered deeply. There's truth and passion in every word she writes; there's a marvelous restraint as well. Tom," she added, gazing hard at him, "you feel it, don't you? You understand her?" For an instant she knit her brows as if in perplexity or misgiving.

"The truth, yes," he replied after a moment's hesitation; "the restraint as well."

"And the passion?"

He nodded curtly by way of agreement. He turned the pages over very rapidly. His fingers were as thick and clumsy as rigid bits of wood. He fumbled.

"Will you read it once again?" she asked. He did so... in a low voice. With difficulty he reached the end. There was a mist before his eyes and his voice seemed confused. He dared not look up.

"There's a deep spiritual beauty," he went on slowly, making an enormous effort, "that's what I feel strongest, I think. There's renunciation, sacrifice—"

He was going to say more, for he felt the words surge up in his throat. This talk, he knew, was a mere safety valve to both of them; they used words as people attacked by laughter out of due season seize upon anything, however far-fetched, that may furnish excuse for it. The flood of language and emotion too long suppressed, again rose to his very lips—when a slight sound stopped his utterance. He turned. Amazement caught him. Her frozen immobility, her dead indifference, her boredom possibly—all these, passing suddenly, had melted in a flood of tears. Her face was covered by her hands. She lay there sobbing within a foot of his hungry arms, sobbing as though her heart must break. He saw the drops between her little fingers, trickling.

It was so sudden, so unexpected, that Tom felt unable to speak or act at first. Numbness seized him. His faculties were arrested. He watched her, saw the little body heave down its entire length, noted the small convulsive movements of it. He saw all this, yet he could not do the natural thing. It was very ghastly.... He could not move a muscle, he could not say a single word, he could not comfort her—because he knew those tears were the tears of pity only. It was for himself she sobbed. The tenderness in her—in "Lettice"—broke down before his weight of pain, the weight of pain she herself laid upon him. Nothing that *he* might do or say could comfort her. Divining what the immediate future held in store for him, she wept these burning tears of pity. In that poignant moment of self-revelation Tom's cumbersome machinery of intuition did not fail him. He understood. It was a confession—the last perhaps. He saw ahead with vivid and merciless clar-

ity of vision. Only another could comfort her.... Yet he could help. Yes—
he could help—by going. There was no other way. He must slip out.

And, as if prophetically just then, she murmured between her tight-
pressed fingers: "Leave me, Tom, for a moment... please go away... I'm so
mortified... this idiotic scene.... Leave me a little, then come back. I shall
be myself again presently.... It's Egypt—this awful Egypt...."

Tom obeyed. He got up and left her, moving without feeling in his legs,
as though he walked in his sleep, as though he dreamed, as though he
were—dead. He did not notice the direction. He walked mechanically. It
felt to him that he simply walked clean out of her life into a world of emptiness and ice and shadows....

The river lay below him in a flood of light. He saw the Theban Hills
rolling their dark, menacing wave along the far horizon. In the blistering
heat the desert lay sun-drenched, basking, silent. Its faint sweet perfume
reached him in the northern wind, that pungent odor of the sand, which
is the odor of this sun-baked land etherealized.

A fiery intensity of light lay over it, as though any moment it must burst
into sheets of flame. So intense was the light that it seemed to let sight
through to—to what? To a more distant vision, infinitely remote. It was
not a mirror, but a transparency. The eyes slipped through it marvelously.

He stood on the steps of worn-out sandstone, listening, staring, feeling
nothing... and then a little song came floating across the air towards him,
sung by a boatman in mid-stream. It was a native melody, but it had the
strange, monotonous lilt of Tony's old-Egyptian melody.... And feeling stole
back upon him, alternately burning and freezing the currents of his blood.
The childhood nightmare touch crept into him: he saw the wavelike outline of the gloomy hills, he heard the wind rattling in the leaves behind him,
to his nostrils came the strange, penetrating perfume of the tawny desert
that encircles ancient Thebes, and in the air before him hung two pairs of
eyes, dark, faithful eyes, cruel and at the same time tender, true yet merciless, and the others—treacherous, false, light blue in color.... He began
to shuffle furiously with his feet.... The soul in him went under.... He turned
to face the menace coming up behind... the falling Wave.

"Tom!" he heard—and turned back towards her. And when he reached
her side, she had so entirely regained composure that he could hardly believe it was the same person. Fresh and radiant she looked once more, no
sign of tears, no traces of her recent emotion anywhere. Perhaps the interval
had been longer than he guessed, but, in any case, the change was swift
and half unaccountable. In himself, equally, was a calmness that seemed
unnatural. He heard himself speaking in an even tone about the view, the
river, the gold of the coming sunset. He wished to spare her, he talked as
though nothing had happened, he mentioned the deep purple color of the

hills—when she broke out with sudden vehemence.

"Oh, don't speak of those hills, those awful hills," she cried. "I dread the sight of them. Last night I dreamed again—they crushed me down into the sand. I felt buried beneath them, deep, deep down—*buried.*" She whispered the last word as though to herself.

The words amazed him. He caught the passing shiver in her voice.

"'Again'?" he asked. "You've dreamed of them before?" He stood close, looking down at her. The sense of his own identity returned slowly, yet he still felt two persons in him.

"Often and often," she said in a lowered tone, "since Tony came. I dream that we all three lie buried somewhere in that forbidding valley. It terrifies me more and more each time."

"Strange," he said. "For they draw me too. I feel them somehow known—familiar." He paused. "I believe Tony was right, you know, when he said that we three—"

How she stopped him he never quite understood. At first he thought the curious movement on her face portended tears again, but the next second he saw that instead of tears a slow strange smile was stealing upon her— upwards from the mouth. It lay upon her features for a second only, but long enough to alter them. A thin, diaphanous mask, transparent, swiftly fleeting, passed over her, and through it another woman, yet herself, peered up at him with a penetrating yet somehow distant gaze. A shudder ran down his spine; there was a sensation of inner cold against his heart; he trembled, but he could not look away.... He saw in that brief instant the face of the woman who tortured him. The same second, so swiftly was it gone again, he saw Lettice watching him through half-closed eyelids. He heard her saying something. She was completing the sentence that had interrupted him:

"We're too imaginative, Tom. Believe me, Egypt is no place to let imagination loose, and I don't like it." She sighed: there was exhaustion in her. "It's stimulating enough without *our* help. Besides—" she used a curious adjective—"it's dangerous too."

Tom willingly let the subject drop; his own desire was to appear natural, to protect her, to save her pain. He thought no longer of himself. Drawing upon all his strength, forcing himself almost to breaking-point, he talked quietly of obvious things, while longing secretly to get away to his own room where he could be alone. He craved to hide himself; like a stricken animal his instinct was to withdraw from observation.

The arrival of the tea-tray helped him, and, while they drank, the sky let down the emblazoned curtain of a hundred colors lest Night should bring her diamonds unnoticed, unannounced. There is no dusk in Egypt; the sun draws on his opal hood; there is a rush of soft white stars: the desert cools,

and the wind turns icy. Night, high on her spangled throne, watches the
sun dip down behind the Lybian sands.

Tom felt this coming of Night as he sat there, so close to Lettice that he
could touch her fingers, feel her breath, catch the lightest rustle of her thin
white dress. He felt night creeping in upon his heart. Swiftly the shadows
piled. His soul seemed draped in blackness, drained of its shining gold, hidden below the horizon of the years. It sank out of sight, cold, lost, forgotten.
His day was past and over....

They had been sitting silent for some minutes when a voice became audible, singing in the distance. It came nearer. Tom recognized the tune "We
were young, we were merry, we were very, very wise"; and Lettice sat up
suddenly to listen. But Tom then thought of one thing only—that it was
beyond his power just now to meet his cousin. He knew his control was
not equal to the task; he would betray himself; the rôle was too exacting.
He rose abruptly.

"That must be Tony coming," Lettice said. "His tea will be all cold!"
Each word was a caress, each syllable alive with interest, sympathy, excited
anticipation. She had become suddenly alive. Tom saw her eyes shining as
she gazed past him down the darkening drive. He made his absurd excuse.
"I'm going home to rest a bit, Lettice. I played tennis too hard. The sun's
given me a headache. We'll meet later. You'll keep Tony for dinner?" His
mind had begun to work, too; the evening train from Cairo, he remembered, was not due for an hour or more yet. A hideous suspicion rushed
like fire through him.

But he asked no question. He knew they wished to be alone together. Yet
also he had a wild, secret hope that she would be disappointed. He was
speedily undeceived.

"All right, Tom," she answered, hardly looking at him. "And mind you're
not late. Eight o'clock sharp. I'll make Tony stay."

He was gone. He chose the path along the river bank instead of going
by the drive. He did not look back once. It was when he entered the road
a little later that he met Mrs. Haughstone coming home from a visit to
some friends in his hotel. It was then she told him....

"What a surprise you must have had," Tom believes he said in reply. He
said something, at any rate, that he hoped sounded natural and right.

"Oh, no," Mrs. Haughstone explained. "We were quite prepared. Lettice had a telegram, you see, to let her know."

She told him other things as well....

Part IV

CHAPTER XXVIII

Tony had come back. The Play turned very real.

The situation *à trois* thenceforward became, for Tom, an acutely afflicting one. He found no permanent resting-place for heart or mind. He analyzed, asked himself questions without end, but a final decisive judgment evaded him. He wrote letters and tore them up again. He hid himself in Assouan with belief for a companion, he came back and found that companion had been but a masquerader—dis-belief. Suspicion grew confirmed into conviction. Vanity persuaded him against the weight of evidence, then left him naked with his facts. He wanted to kill, first others, then himself. He laughed, but the same minute he could have cried. Such complicated tangles of emotion were beyond his solving—it amazed him; such prolonged and incessant torture, so delicately applied—he marveled that a human heart could bear it without breaking. For the affection and sympathy he felt for his cousin refused to die, while his worship and passion towards an unresponsive woman increasingly consumed him.

He no longer recognized himself, his cousin, Lettice; all three, indeed, were singularly changed. Each duplicated into a double rôle. Towards their former selves he kept his former attitude—of affection, love, belief; towards the usurping selves he felt—he knew not what. Therefore he drifted... Strange, mysterious, tender, unfathomable Woman! Vain, primitive, self-sufficing, confident Man! In him the masculine tried to reason and analyze to the very end; in her the feminine interpreted intuitively: the male and female attitudes, that is, held true throughout. The Wave swept him forward irresistibly, his very soul, it seemed, went shuffling to find solid ground....

Meanwhile, however, no one broke the rules—rules that apparently had made themselves subtle and delicate, it took place mostly out of sight, as it were, inside the heart. Below the mask of ordinary surface-conduct all agreed to wear, the deeper, inevitable intercourse proceeded, a Play within a Play, a tragedy concealed thinly by general consent under the most commonplace comedy imaginable. All acted out their parts, rehearsed, it seemed, of long ago. For, more and more, it came to Tom that the one thing he must never lose, whatever happened, was his trust in her. He must cling to that though it cost him all—trust in her love and truth and constancy. This singular burden seemed laid upon his soul. If he lost that trust and that belief, the Wave could never break, she could never justify that trust and that belief.

This "enchantment" that tortured him, straining his whole being, was somehow a test indeed of his final worthiness to win her. Somehow, somewhence, he owed her this.... He dared not fail. For if he failed the Wave that should sweep her back into the "sea" with him would not break—he would merely go on shuffling his feet to the end of life. Tony and Lettice conquered him till he lay bleeding in the sand; Tom played the role of loss—obediently almost; the feeling that they were set in power over him persisted strangely. It dominated, at any rate, the resistance he would otherwise have offered. He must learn to do without her in order that she might in the end be added to him. Thus, and thus alone, could he find himself, and reach the level where she lived. He took his fate from her gentle, merciless hands, well knowing that it had to be. In some marvelous, sweet way the sacrifice would bring her back again at last, but bring her back completed—and to a Tom worthy of her love. The self-centered, confident man in him that deemed itself indispensable must crumble. To find regeneration he must risk destruction.

Events—yet always inner events—moved with such rapidity then that he lost count of time. The barrier never lowered again. He played his ghastly part in silence—always inner silence. Out of sight, below the surface, the deep wordless Play continued. With Tony's return the drama hurried. The actor all had been waiting for came on, and took the center of the stage, and stayed until the curtain fell—a few weeks, all told, of their short Egyptian winter.

In the crowded rush of action Tom felt the Wave—bend, break, and smash him. At its highest moment he saw the stars, at its lowest the crunch of shifting gravel filled his ears, the mud blinded sight, the rubbish choked his breath. Yet he had seen those distant stars.... Into the mothering sea, as he sank back, the memory of the light went with him. It was a kind of incredible performance, half on earth and half in the air: it rushed with such impetuous momentum.

Amid the intensity of his human emotions, meanwhile, he lost sight of any subtler hints, if indeed they offered: he saw no veiled eastern visions any more, divined no psychic warnings. His agony of blinding pain, alternating with briefest intervals of shining hope when he recovered belief in her and called himself the worst names he could think of—this seething warfare of cruder feelings left no part of him sensitive to the delicate promptings of finer forces, least of all to the tracery of fancied memories. He only gasped for breath—sufficient to keep himself afloat and cry, as he had promised he would cry, even to the bitter end: "I'll face it... I'll stick it out... I'll trust...!"

The setting of the Play was perfect; in Egypt alone was its production possible. The brilliant lighting, the fathomless, soft shadows, deep covering of blue by day, clear stars by night, the solemn hills, and the slow, eternal river—all these, against the huge background of the Desert, silent, golden, lonely, formed the adequate and true environment. In no other country, in England least of all, could the presentation have been real. Tony, himself, and Lettice belonged, one and all, it seemed, to Egypt—yet, somehow, not wholly to the Egypt of the tourist hordes and dragoman, and big hotels. The Onlooker in him, who stood aloof and held a watching brief, looked down upon an ancient land unvexed by railways, graciously clothed and colored gorgeously, mapped burningly mid fiercer passions, eager for life, contemptuous of death. He did not understand, but that it was thus, not otherwise, he knew....

Her beauty, too, both physical and spiritual, became for him strangely heightened. He shifted between moods of worship that were alternately physical and spiritual. In the former he pictured her with darker coloring, half barbaric, eastern, her slender figure flitting through a grove of palms beyond a river too wide for him to cross; gold bands gleamed upon her arms, bare to the shoulder; he could not reach her; she was with another— it was torturing; she and that other disappeared into the covering shadows.... In the latter, however, there was no unworthy thought, no faintest desire of the blood; he saw her high among the little stars, gazing with tender, pitying eyes upon him, calling softly, praying for him, loving him, yet remote in some spiritual isolation where she must wait until he soared to join her.

Both physically and spiritually, that is, he idealized her—saw her divinely naked. She did not move. She hung there like a star, waiting for him, while he was carried past her, swept along helplessly by a tide, a flood, a wave, though a wave that was somehow rising up to where she dwelt above him....

It was a marvelous experience. In the physical moods he felt the fires of jealousy burn his flesh away to the bare nerves—resentment, rage, a bitterness that could kill; in the alternate state he felt the uplifting joy and comfort of ultimate sacrifice, sweet as heaven, the bliss of complete renunciation—for her happiness. If she loved another who could give her greater joy, he had no right to interfere.

It was this last that gradually increased in strength, the first that slowly, surely died. Unsatisfied yearnings hunted his soul across the empty desert that now seemed life. The self he had been so pleased with, had admired so proudly with calm complacence, thinking it indispensable—this was tortured, stabbed and mercilessly starved to death by slow degrees, while something else appeared shyly, gently, as yet unaware of itself, but already clearer and stronger. In the depths of his being, below an immense horizon, shone joy, luring him onward and brightening as it did so.

Love, he realized, was independent of the will—no one can will to love: she was not anywhere to blame, a stronger claim had come into life and changed her. She could not live untruth, pretending otherwise. He, rather, was to blame if he sought to hold her to a smaller love she had outgrown. She had the inalienable right to obey the bigger claim, if such it proved to be. Personal freedom was the basis of their contract. It would have been easier for him if she could have told him frankly, shared it with him; but, since that seemed beyond her, then it was for him to slip away. He must subtract himself from an inharmonious three, leaving a perfect two. He must make it easier for *her.*

The days of golden sunshine passed along their appointed way as before, leaving him still without a final decision. Outwardly the little party *à trois* seemed harmonious, a coherent unit, while inwardly the accumulation of suppressed emotion crept nearer and nearer to the final breaking point. They lived upon a crater, playing their comedy within sight and hearing of destruction: even Mrs. Haughstone, ever waiting in the wings for her cue, came on effectively and filled her rôle, insignificant yet necessary. Its meanness was its truth.

"Mr. Winslowe excites my cousin too much; I'm sure it isn't good for her—in England, yes, but not out here in this strong, dangerous climate."

Tom understood, but invariably opposed her:

"If it makes her happy for a little while, I see no harm in it; life has not been too kind to her, remember."

Sometimes, however, the hint was barbed as well: "Your cousin *is* a delightful being, but he can talk nonsense when he wants to. He's actually been trying to persuade me that you're jealous of him. He said you were only waiting a suitable moment to catch him alone in the Desert and shoot him!"

Tom countered her with an assumption of portentous gravity: "Sound travels too easily in this still air," he reminded her; "the Nile would be the simplest way." After which, confused by ridicule, she renounced the hint direct, indulging instead in facial expression, glances, and innuendo conveyed by gesture.

That there was some truth, however, behind this betrayal of her hostess and her fellow-guest, Tom felt certain; it lied more by exaggeration than by sheer invention: he listened while he hated it; ashamed of himself, he yet invited the ever-ready warnings, though he invariably defended the object of them—and himself.

Alternating thus, he knew no minute of happiness; a single day, a single hour contained both moods, trust ousted suspicion, and suspicion turned out trust. Lettice led him on, then abruptly turned to ice. In the morning he was first and Tony nowhere, the same afternoon this was reversed precisely—yet the balance growing steadily in his cousin's favor, the evidence accumulating against himself. It was not purposely contrived, it was in automatic obedience to deeper impulses than she knew. Tom never lost sight of this amazing duality in her, the struggle of one self against another older self to which cruelty was no stranger—or, as he put it, the newly awakened Woman against the Mother in her.

He could not fail to note the different effects he and his cousin produced in her—the ghastly difference. With himself she was captious, easily exasperated; her relations with Tony, above all, a sensitive spot on which she could bear no slightest pressure without annoyance; while behind this attitude, hid always the faithful motherly care that could not see him in distress. That touch of comedy lay in it dreadfully:—wet feet, cold, hungry, tired, and she flew to his consoling! Towards Tony this side of her remained unresponsive; he might drink unfiltered water for all she cared, tire himself to death, or sit in a draught for hours. It could have been comic almost but for its significance: that from Tony she *received*, instead of gave. The woman in her asked, claimed even—of the man in him. The pain for Tom lay there.

His cousin amused, stimulated her beyond anything Tom could offer; she sought protection from him, leant upon him. In his presence she blossomed out, her eyes shone the moment he arrived, her voice altered, her spirits became exuberant. The wholesome physical was awakened by him. He could not hope to equal Tony's address, his fascination. He never forgot that she once danced for happiness.... Helplessness grew upon him—he had no right to feel angry even, he could not justly blame herself or his cousin. The woman in her was open to capture by another; so far it had never belonged to him. In vain he argued that the mother was the larger part; it was the woman that he wanted with it. Flaying separated the two aspects of her in this way, the division, once made, remained.

And every day that passed this difference in her towards himself and Tony grew more mercilessly marked. The woman in her responded to another touch than his. Though neither lust nor passion, he knew, dwelt in her pure being anywhere, there were yet a thousand and delicate unconscious ways by which a woman betrayed her attraction to a being of the opposite sex; they could not be challenged, but equally they could not be misinterpreted. Like the color and perfume of a rose, they emanated from her inmost being.... In this sense, she was sexually indifferent to Tom, and while passion consumed his soul, he felt her, dearly mothering, yet cold as ice. The soft winds of Egypt bent the full-blossomed rose into another's hand, towards another's lips…. Tony had entered the garden of her secret life.

CHAPTER XXIX

And so the fires of jealousy burned him. He struggled hard, smothering all outward expression of his pain, with the sole result that the suppression increased the fury of the heat within. For every day the tiniest details fed its fierceness. It was inextinguishable. He lost his appetite, his sleep, he lost all sense of what is called proportion. There was no rest in him, day and night he lived in the consuming flame.

His cousin's irresponsibility now assumed a sinister form that shocked him. He recognized the libertine in his careless play with members of the other sex who had pleased him for moments, then been tossed aside. He became aware of grossness in his eyes and lips and bearing. He understood, above all, his—hands.

Against the fiery screen of his emotions jealousy threw violent pictures which he mistook for thought... and there burst through this screen, then, scattering all lesser feelings, the flame of a vindictive anger that he believed was the protective righteous anger of an outraged man. "If Tony did her wrong," he told himself, "I would kill him."

Always, at this extravagant moment, however, he reached a climax, then calmed down again. A sense of humor rose incongruously to check loss of self-restraint. The memory of her daily tenderness swept over him; and shame sent a blush into his cheeks. He felt mortified, ungenerous, a foolish figure even. While the reaction lasted he forgave, felt her above reproach, cursed his wretched thoughts that had tried to soil her, and lost the violent vindictiveness that had betrayed him. His affection for his cousin, always real, and the sympathy between them, always genuine, returned to complete his own discomfiture. His mood swayed back to the first, happy days when the three of them had laughed and played together.

And to punish himself while this reaction lasted, he would seek her out and see that she inflicted the punishment itself. He would hear from her own lips how fond she was of Tony, fighting to convince himself, while he listened, that she was above suspicion, and that his pain was due solely to unworthy jealousy. He would be specially nice to Tony, making things easier for him, even urging him, as it were, into her very arms.

These moments of generous reaction, however, seemed to puzzle her. The exalted state of emotion was confined, perhaps, to himself. At any rate, he produced results the very reverse of what he intended; Tony became more cautious, Lettice looked at himself with half-questioning eyes.... There was falseness in his attitude, something unnatural. It was not the part he was cast for in the Play. He could not keep it up. He fell back once more to watching, listening, playing his proper rôle of a slave who was forced to observe the happiness of others set somehow over him, while suffering in silence. The inner fires were fed anew thereby. He knew himself flung back, bruised and bleeding, upon his original fear and jealousy, convinced more than ever before that this cruelty and torture had to be, and that his pain was justified. To resist was only to delay the perfect dawn.

> The sum of loss I have not reckoned yet,
>   I cannot tell.
> For ever it was morning when we met,
>   Night when we bade farewell.

He changed the pronouns in the last two lines, for always it was morning when *they* met, night when *they* bade farewell.

Mrs. Haughstone, meanwhile, neglected no opportunity of dotting the vowel for his benefit; she crossed each *t* that the writing of the stars dropped fluttering across her path. "Mr. Winslowe has emotions," she mentioned once, "but he has no heart. If he ever marries and settles down, his wife will find it out."

"My cousin is not the kind to marry," Tom replied. "He's too changeable, and he knows it."

"He's young," she said, "he hasn't found the right woman yet. He will improve—a woman older than himself with the mother strong in her might hold him. He needs the mother too. Most men do, I think; they're all children really."

Tom laughed. "Tony as father of a family—I can't imagine it."

"Once he had children of his own," she suggested, "he would steady wonderfully. Those men often make the best husbands—don't you think?"

"Perhaps," Tom replied briefly. "Provided there's real heart beneath."

"In the woman, yes," returned the other quietly. "Too much heart in the man can so easily cloy. A real man is always half a savage; that's why the woman likes him. It's the woman who guards the family."

Tom, knowing that her words veiled other meanings, pretended not to notice. He no longer rose to the bait she offered. He detected the nonsense, the insincerity as well, but he could not argue successfully, and generalizations were equally beyond him. Too polite to strike back, he always waited till she had talked herself out; besides he often acquired information thus, information he both longed for yet disliked intensely. Such information rarely failed: it was, indeed, the desire to impart it with an air of naturalness that caused the conversation almost invariably. It appeared now. It was pregnant information, too. She conveyed it in a lowered tone:

there was news from Warsaw. The end, it seemed, was expected by the doctors; a few months at most. Lettice had been warned, however, that her appearance could do no good; the sufferer mistook her for a relative who came to persecute him. Her presence would only hasten the end. She had cabled, none the less, to say that she would come. This was a week ago; the answer was expected in a day or two.

And Tom had not been informed of this.

"Mr. Winslowe thinks she ought to go at once. I'm sure his advice is wise. Even if her presence can do no good, it might be an unceasing regret if she was not there...."

"Your cousin alone can judge," he interrupted coldly. "I'd rather not discuss it, if you don't mind," he added, noticing her eagerness to continue the conversation.

"Oh, certainly, Mr. Kelverdon—just as you feel. But in case she asks your advice as well—I only thought you'd like to know—to be prepared, I mean."

Only long afterwards did it occur to him that Tony's informant was possibly this jealous parasite herself, who now deliberately put the matter in another light, hoping to sow discord to her own eventual benefit. All he realized at the moment was the intolerable pain that Lettice should tell him nothing. She looked to Tony for help, advice, possibly for consolation too.

There were moments of another kind, however, when it seemed quite easy to talk plainly. His position was absurd, undignified, unmanly. It was for him to state his case and abide by the result. Hearts rarely break in two, for all that poets and women might protest.

These moments, however, he did not use. It was not that he shrank from hearing his sentence plainly spoken, nor that he decided he must not prevent something that had to be. The reason lay deeper still:—it was impossible. In her presence he became tongue-tied, helpless. His own stupidity overwhelmed him. Silence took him. He felt at a hopeless disadvantage, ashamed even. No words of his could reach her through the distance, across the barrier, that lay between them now. He made no single attempt. His aching heart, filled with an immeasurable love, remained without the relief of utterance. He had lost her. But he loved now something in her place beyond the possibility of loss—an indestructible ideal.

Words, therefore, were not only impossible, they were vain. And when the final moment came they were still more useless. He could go, but he could not tell her he was going. Before that moment came, however, another searching experience was his: he saw Tony jealous—jealous of himself! He actually came to feel sympathy with his cousin who was his rival! It was his faithful love that made that possible too.

He realized this suddenly one day at Assouan.

He had been thinking about the long conversations Tony and Lettice enjoyed together, wondering what they found to discuss at such interminable length. From that his mind slipped easily into another question—how she could be so insensible to the pain she caused him?—when, all in a flash, he realized the distance she had traveled from him on the road of love towards Tony. The moment of perspective made it abruptly clear. She now talked with Tony as once, at Montreux and elsewhere, she had talked with himself. He saw his former place completely occupied. As an accomplished fact he saw it.

The belief that Tony's influence would weaken deserted him from that instant. It had been but a false hope created by desire and yearning.

There was a crash. He reached the bottom of despair. That same evening, on returning to his hotel from the works, he found a telegram. It had been arranged that Lettice, Tony, Miss de Lorne and her brother should join him in Assouan. The telegram stated briefly that it was not possible after all:— she sent an excuse.

The sleepless night was no new thing to him, but the acuteness of new suffering was a revelation. Jealousy unmasked her amazing powers of poisonous and devastating energy.... He visualized in detail. He saw Lettice and his cousin together in the very situations he had hitherto reserved imaginatively for himself, both sweets hoped for and delights experienced, but raised now a hundredfold in actuality. Like pictures of flame they rose before his inner eye; they seared and scorched him; his blood turned acid; the dregs of agony were his to drink. The happiness he had planned for himself, down to the smallest minutiæ of each precious incident, he now saw transferred in this appalling way—to another. Not deliberately summoned, not morbidly evoked—the pictures rose of their own accord against the background of his mind, yet so instinct with actuality, that it seemed he had surely lived them, too, himself with her, somewhere, somehow... before. There was that same haunting touch of familiarity about them.

In the long hours of this particular night he reached, perhaps, the acme of his pain; imagination, whipped by jealousy, stoked the furnace to a heat he had not known as yet. He had been clinging to a visionary hope. "I've lost her... lost her... lost her," he repeated to himself, as though with each repetition the meaning of the phrase grew clearer. Numbness followed upon misery; there were long intervals when he felt nothing at all, periods when he thought he hated her, when pride and anger whispered he could do without her.... A state of negative insensibility followed.... On the heels of it came a red and violent vindictiveness; next—resignation, complete acceptance, almost peace. Then acute sensitiveness returned again— he felt the whole series of emotions over and over without one omission.

This numbness and sensitiveness alternated with a kind of rhythmic succession.... He reviewed the entire episode from beginning to end, recalled every word she had uttered, traced the gradual influence of Tony on her, from its first faint origin to its present climax. He saw her struggles and her tears... the mysterious duality working to possess her soul. It was all plain as daylight. No justification for any further hope was left to him. He must go.... It was the thunder, surely, of the falling Wave.

For Tony, he realized at last, had not merely usurped his own place, but had discovered a new Lettice to herself, and setting her thus in a new, a larger world, had taught her a new relationship. He had achieved—perhaps innocently enough so far as his conscience was concerned?—a new result, and a bigger one than Tom, with his lesser powers, could possibly have effected.

There was no falseness, no duplicity in her. "She still loves me as before, the mother still gives me what she always gave," Tom put it to himself, "but Tony has plowed deeper—reached the woman in her. He loves a Lettice I have never realized. It is this new Lettice that loves him in return.... What right have I, with my smaller claim, to stand in her way a single moment?... I must slip out."

He had lost the dream that Tony but tended a blossom, the fruit of which would come sweetly to his plucking afterwards. The intense suffering concealed all prophecy, as the jealousy killed all hope. He spent that final night of awful pain on his balcony, remembering how weeks before in Luxor the first menacing presentiment had come to him. He stared out into the Egyptian wonder of outer darkness. The stillness held a final menace as of death. He recalled a Polish proverb.... "In the still marshes there are devils." The world spread dark and empty like his life; the Theban Hills seemed to have crept after him, here to Assouan; the stars, incredibly distant, had no warmth or comfort in them; the river roared with a dull and lonely sound; he heard the palm trees rattling in the wind. The pain in him was almost physical....

Dawn found him in the same position—yet with a change. Perhaps the prolonged agony had killed the ache of ceaseless personal craving, or perhaps the fierceness of the fire had burned it out. Tom could not say; nor did he ask the questions. A change was there, and that was all he knew. He had come at last to a decision, made a final choice. He had somehow fought his battle out with a courage he did not know was courage. Here at Assouan, he turned upon the Wave and faced it. He saw *her* happiness only, fixed all his hope and energy on that. A new and loftier strength woke in him. There was no shuffling now.

He would give her up. In his heart she would always remain his dream and his ideal—but outwardly he would no longer need her. He would do without her. He forgave—if there was anything to forgive—forgave them both....

Something in him had broken.

He could not explain it, though he felt it: Yet it was not her that he had given up—it was himself.

The first effect of this, however, was to think that life lay in ruins round him, that, literally, the life in him was smothered by the breaking wave....

And yet he did not break—he did not drown.

For, as though to show that his decision was the right, inevitable one, small outward details came to his assistance. Fate evidently approved. For Fate just then furnished relief by providing another outlet for his energies: the Works went seriously wrong: Tom could think of nothing else but how he could put things right again. Reflection, introspection, brooding over mental and spiritual pain became impossible.

The lieutenants he trusted had played him false; sub-contracts of an outrageous kind, flavored by bribery, had been entered into; the cost of certain necessaries had been raised absurdly, with the result that the profits of the entire undertaking to the Firm must be lowered correspondingly. And the blame, the responsibility was his own; he had unwisely delegated his powers to underlings whose ambitions for money exceeded their sense of honor. But Tom's honor was involved as well. He had delegated his powers in writing. He now had to pay the price of his prolonged neglect of duty.

The position was irremediable; Tom's neglect and inefficiency were established beyond question. He had failed in a position of high trust. And to make the situation still less pleasant, Sir William, the Chairman of the Company—Tom's chief, the man to whom he owed his partnership and post of trust—telegraphed that he was on the way at last from Salonika. One way alone offered—to break the disastrous contracts by payments made down without delay. Tom made these payments out of his own pocket; they were large; his private resources disappeared in a single day.... But, even so, the delay and bungling at the Works were not to be concealed. Sir William, shrewd, experienced man of business, stern of heart as well as hard of head, could not be deceived. Within half an hour of his arrival, Tom Kelverdon's glaring incompetency—worse, his unreliability, to use no harsher word—were all laid bare. His position in the Firm, even his partnership, perhaps, became untenable. Resignation stared him in the face.

He saw his life go down in ruins before his very eyes; the roof had fallen long ago. The pillars now collapsed. The Wave, indeed, had turned him upside down; its smothering crash left no corner of his being above water; heart, mind, and character were flung in a broken tangle against the cruel bottom as it fell to earth.

But, at any rate, the new outlet for his immediate energies was offered. He seized it vigorously. He gave up his room at Luxor, and sent a man down to bring his luggage up. He did not write to Lettice. He faced the practical situation with a courage and thoroughness which, though too late, were admirable. Moreover, he found a curious relief in the new disaster, a certain comfort even. There was compensation in it somewhere. Everything was going to smash—the sooner, then, the better! This recklessness was in him. He had lost Lettice, so what else mattered? His attitude was somewhat devil-may-care, his grip on life itself seemed slipping.

This mood could not last, however, with a character like his. It seized him, but retained no hold. It was the last cry of despair when he touched bottom, the moment when weaker temperaments think of the emergency exit, realize their final worthlessness—proving themselves worthless, indeed, thereby.

Tom met the blow in other fashion. He saw himself unworthy, but by no means worthless. Suicide, whether of death or of final collapse, did not enter his mind even. He faced the Wave, he did not shuffle now. He sent a telegram to Lettice to say he was detained; he wrote to Tony that he had given up his room in the Luxor hotel, an affectionate, generous note, telling him to take good care of Lettice. It was only right and fair that Tony should think the path for himself was clear. Since he had decided to "slip out" this attitude towards his cousin was necessarily involved. It must not appear that he had retired, beaten and unhappy. He must do no single thing that might offer resistance to the inevitable fate, least of all leave Tony with the sense of having injured him. True sacrifice forbade; renunciation, if real, was also silent—the smiling face, the cheerful, natural manner!

Tom, therefore, fixed his heart more firmly than ever upon one single point: her happiness. He fought to think of that alone. If he knew her happy, he could live. He found life in her joy. He lived in that. By "slipping out," no word of reproach, complaint, or censure uttered, he would actually contribute to her happiness. Thus, vicariously, he almost helped to cause it. In this faint, self-excluding bliss, he could live—even live on—until the end. That was true forgiveness.

Meanwhile, not easily nor immediately, did he defy the anguish that, day and night, kept gnawing at his heart. His one desire was to hide it, and— if the huge achievement might lie within his powers—to change it sweetly into a source of strength that should redeem him. The "sum of loss," indeed, he had not "reckoned yet," but he was beginning to add the figures up. Full measurement lay in the long, long awful years ahead. He had this strange comfort, however—that he now loved something he could never lose because it could not change. He loved an ideal. In that sense, he and Lettice were in the "sea" together. His belief and trust in her were not lost, but heightened. And a hint of mothering contentment stole sweetly over him behind this shadowy yet genuine consolation.

The childhood nightmare was both presentiment and memory. The crest of the falling Wave was reflected in its base.

CHAPTER XXX

Tom took his passage home; he also told Sir William that his resignation, whether the Board accepted it or not, was final. His reputation, so far as the firm was concerned, he knew was lost. His own self-respect had dwindled dangerously too. He had the feeling that he wanted to begin all over again from the very bottom. It seemed the only way. The prospect, at his age, was daunting. He faced it.

At the very moment in life when he had fancied himself most secure, most satisfied mentally, spiritually, materially—the entire structure on which self-confidence rested had given way. Even the means of material support had vanished too. The crash was absolute. This brief Egyptian winter had, indeed, proved the winter of his loss. The Wave had fallen at last.

During the interval at Assouan—ten days that seemed a month!—he heard occasionally from Lettice. "To-day I miss you," one letter opened. Another said: "We wonder when you will return. We *all* miss you very much: it's not the same here without you, Tom." And all were signed "Your ever loving Lettice." But if hope for some strange reason refused to die completely, he did not allow himself to be deceived. His task—no easy one— was to transmute emotion into the higher, selfless, ideal love that was now—oh, he knew it well enough—his only hope and safety. In the desolate emptiness of desert that yawned ahead, he saw this single tree that blossomed, and offered shade. Beauty and comfort both were there. He believed in her truth and somehow in her faithfulness as well.

Tom sent his heavy luggage to Port Said, and took the train to Luxor. He had decided to keep his sailing secret. He could mention honestly that he was going to Cairo. He would write a line from there or, better still, from the steamer itself.

And the instinct that led to this decision was sound and wise. The act was not as boyish as it seemed. For he feared a reaction on her part that yet could be momentary only. His leaving so suddenly would be a shock, it might summon the earlier Lettice to the surface, there might be a painful scene for both of them. She would realize, to some extent at any rate, the immediate sense of loss; for she would surely divine that he was going, not to England merely, but out of her life. And she would suffer; she might even try to keep him—the only result being a revival of pain already almost conquered, and of distress for her.

For such reaction, he divined, could not be permanent. The Play was over; it must not, could not be prolonged. He must go out. There must be no lingering when the curtain fell. A curtain that halts in its descent upon the actors endangers the effect of the entire Play.

He wired to Cairo for a room. He wired to her too: "Arrive to-morrow, *en route* Cairo. Leave same night." He braced himself. The strain would be cruelly exacting, but the worst had been lived out already; the jealousy was dead; the new love was established beyond all reach of change. These last few hours should be natural, careless, gay, no hint betraying him, flying no signals of distress. He could just hold out. The strength was in him. And there was time before he caught the evening train for a reply to come: "All delighted; expect you breakfast. Arranging picnic expedition.—LETTICE."

And that one word "all" helped him unexpectedly to greater steadiness. It eliminated the personal touch even in a telegram.

In the train he slept but little; the heat was suffocating, there was a Khamsin blowing and the fine sand crept in everywhere. At Luxor, however, the wind remained so high up that the lower regions of the sky were calm and still. The sand hung in fog-like clouds shrouding the sun, dimming the usual brilliance. But the heat was intense, and the occasional stray puffs of air that touched the creeping Nile or passed along the sweltering street, seemed to issue from the mouth of some vast furnace in the heavens. They dropped, then ceased abruptly; there was no relief in them. The natives sat listlessly in their doorways, the tourists kept their rooms or idled complainingly in the hotel halls and corridors. The ominous touch was everywhere. He felt it in his heart as well—the heart he thought broken beyond repair.

Tom bathed and changed his clothes, then drove down to the shady garden beside the river as of old. He felt the gritty sand between his teeth, it was in his mouth and eyes, it was on his tongue.... He met Lettice without a tremor, astonished at his own coolness and self-control; he watched her beauty as the beauty of a picture, something that was no longer his, yet watched it without envy and, in an odd sense, almost without pain. He loved the fairness of it for itself, for her, and for another who was not himself. Almost he loved their happiness to come—for her sake. Her eyes, too, followed him, he fancied, like a picture's eyes. She looked young and fresh, yet something mysterious in the following eyes. The usual excited happiness was less obvious, he thought, than usual, the mercurial gaiety wholly absent. He fancied a cloud upon her spirit somewhere. He imagined tiny, uncertain signs of questioning distress. He wondered.... This torture of a last uncertainty was also his.

Yet, obviously, she was glad to see him; her welcome was genuine; she came down the drive to meet him, both hands extended. Apparently, too, she was alone, Mrs. Haughstone still asleep, and Tony not yet arrived. It was still early morning.

"Well, and how did you get on without me—all of you?" he asked, adding the last three words with emphasis.

"I thought you were never coming back, Tom; I had the feeling you were bored here at Luxor and meant to leave us." She looked him up and down with a curious look—of admiration almost, an admiration he believed he had now learned to do without. "How lean and brown and well you look!" she exclaimed, "but thin, Tom. You've grown thinner." She shook her finger at him. Her voice was perilously soft and kind, a sweet tenderness in her manner, too. "You've been over-working and not eating enough. You've not had me to look after you."

He flushed. "I'm awfully fit," he said, smiling a little shyly. "I may be thinner. That's the heat, I suppose. Assouan's a blazing place—you feel you're in Africa—." He said the banal thing as usual.

"But was there no one there to look after you?" She gave him a quick glance. "No one at all?"

Tom noticed the repeated question, wondering a little. But there was no play in him; in place of it was something stern, unyielding as iron, though not tested yet.

"The Chairman of my Company, nine hundred noisy tourists, and about a thousand Arabs at the Works," he told her. "There was hardly a soul I knew besides."

She said no more; she gave a scarcely audible sigh; she seemed unsatisfied somewhere. To his surprise, then, he noticed that the familiar little table was only laid for two.

"Where's Tony?" he asked. "And, by the by, how is he?"

He thought she hesitated a moment. "Tony's not coming till later," she told him. "He guessed we should have a lot to talk about together, so he stayed away. Nice of him, wasn't it?"

Behind the commonplace sentences, the hidden wordless Play also drew on towards its Curtain.

"Well, it is my turn rather for a chat, perhaps," he returned presently with a laugh, taking his cup of steaming coffee from her hand. "I can see him later in the day. You've arranged something, I'm sure. Your wire spoke of a picnic, but perhaps this heat—this beastly Khamsin—"

"It's passing," she mentioned. "They say it blows for three days, for six days, or for nine, but as a matter of fact, it does nothing of the sort. It's going to clear. I thought we might take our tea into the Desert."

She went on talking rapidly, almost nervously, it seemed to Tom. Her mind was upon something else. Thoughts of another kind lay unexpressed behind her speech. His own mind was busy too—Tony, Warsaw, the long, long interval he had been away, what had happened during his absence, and so forth? Had no cable come? What would she feel this time to-morrow when she knew?—these and a hundred others seethed below his quiet manner and careless talk. He noticed then that she was exquisitely dressed; she wore, in fact, the very things he most admired—and wore them purposely: the orange-colored jacket, the violet veil, the hat with the little roses on the brim. It was his turn to look her up and down.

She caught his eye. Uncannily, she caught his thought as well. Tom steeled himself.

"I put these on especially for you, you truant boy," she said deliciously across the table at him. "I hope you're sensible of the honor done you."

"Rather, Lettice! I should think I am, indeed!"

"I got up half an hour earlier on purpose too. Think what that means to a woman like me." She handed him a grape-fruit she had opened and prepared herself.

"My favorite hat, and my favorite fruit! I wish I were worthy of them!" He stammered slightly as he said the stupid thing: the blood rushed up to his very forehead, but she gave no sign of noticing either words or blush. The strong sunburn hid the latter doubtless. There was a desperate shyness in him that he could not manage quite. He wished to heaven the talk would shift into another key. He could not keep this up for long; it was too dangerous. Her attitude, it seemed, had gone back to that of weeks ago; there was more than the mother in it, he felt: it was almost the earlier Lettice—and yet not quite. Something was added, but something too was missing. He wondered more and more... he asked himself odd questions.... It seemed to him suddenly that her mood was assumed, not wholly natural. The flash came to him that disappointment lay behind it, yet that the disappointment was not with—himself. Another caused it.

"You're wearing a new tie, Tom," her voice broke in upon his moment's reverie. "That's not the one *I* gave you."

It was so unexpected, so absurd. It startled him. He laughed with genuine amusement, explaining that he had bought it in Assouan in a moment of extravagance—"the nearest shade I could find to the blue you gave me. How observant you are!" Lettice laughed with him. "I always notice little things like that," she said. "It's what you call the mother in me, I suppose." She examined the tie across the table, while they smoked their cigarettes. He looked aside. "I hope it was admired. It suits you." She fingered it. Her hand touched his chin.

"Does it? It's your taste, you know."

"But *was* it admired?" she insisted almost sharply.

"That's really more than I can say, Lettice. You see I didn't ask Sir William what he thought, and the natives are poor judges because they don't wear ties." He was about to say more, talking the first nonsense that came into his head, when she did a thing that took his breath away, and made him tremble where he sat. Regardless of lurking Arab servants, careless of Mrs. Haughstone's windows not far behind them, she rose suddenly, tripped round the little table, kissed him on his cheek—and was back again in her chair, smoking as innocently as before. It was a repetition of an earlier act, yet with a difference somewhere.

The world seemed unreal just then; things like this did not happen in real life, at least not quite like this; nor did two persons in their respective positions talk exactly thus, using such banal language, such insignificant phrases half of banter, half of surface foolishness. The kiss amazed him— for a moment. Tom felt in a dream. And yet this very sense of dream, this idle exchange of trivial conversation cloaked something that was a cruel, an indubitable reality. It was not a dream shot through with reality, it was a reality shot through with dream. But the dream itself, though old as the desert, dim as those grim Theban Hills now draped with flying sand, was also true and actual.

The hidden Play had broken through, merging for an instant with the upper surface life. He was almost persuaded that this last, strange action had not happened, that Lettice had never really left her chair. So still and silent she sat there now. She had not stirred from her place. It was the burning wind that touched his cheek, a waft of heated atmosphere, lightly moving, that left the disquieting trail of perfume in the air. The glowing heavens, luminous athwart the clouds of fine, suspended sand, laid this ominous hint of dream upon the entire day.... The recent act became a mere picture in the mind.

Yet some little cell of innermost memory, stirring out of sleep, had surely given up its dead.... For a second it seemed to him this heavy, darkened air was in the recesses of the earth, beneath the burden of massive cliffs the centuries had piled. It was underground. In some cavern of those mournful Theban Hills, some one—had kissed him! For over his head shone painted stars against a painted blue, and in his nostrils hung a faint sweetness as of ambra....

He recovered his balance quickly. They resumed their curious masquerade, the screen of idle talk between significance and emptiness, like sounds of reality between dream and waking.

And the rest of that long day of stifling heat was similarly a dream shot through with incongruous touches of reality, yet also a reality shot through with the glamour of some incredible ancient dream. Not till he stood later upon the steamer deck, the sea-wind in his face and the salt spray on his lips, did he awake fully and distinguish the dream from the reality—or the reality from the dream. Nor even then was the deep, strange confusion wholly dissipated. To the end of life, indeed, it remained an unsolved mystery, labeled a Premonition Fulfilled, without adequate explanation....

The time passed listlessly enough, to the accompaniment of similar idle talk, careless, it seemed to Tom, with the ghastly sense of the final minutes slipping remorselessly away, so swiftly, so poignantly unused. For each moment was gigantic, brimmed full with the distilled essence, as it were, of intensest value, value that yet was not his to seize. He never lost the point of view that he watched a picture that belonged to some one else. His own position was clear; he had already leaped from a height; he counted, as he fell, the blades of grass, the pebbles far below; slipping over Niagara's awful edge, he noted the bubbles in the whirlpools underneath. They talked of the weather...

"It's clearing," said Lettice. "There'll be sand in our tea and thin bread and butter. But anything's better than sitting and stifling here."

Tom readily agreed. "You and I and Tony, then?"

"I thought so. We don't want too many, do we?"

"Not for our la—not for a day like this." He corrected himself just in time. "Tony will be here for lunch?" he asked.

She nodded. "He said so, at any rate, only one never quite knows with Tony." And though Tom plainly heard, he made no comment. He was puzzled.

Most of the morning they remained alone together. Tom had never felt so close to her before; it seemed to him their spirits touched; there was no barrier now. But there was distance. He could not explain the paradox. A vague sweet feeling was in him that the distance was not of height, as formerly. He had risen somehow; he felt higher than before; he saw over the barrier that had been there. Pain and sacrifice, perhaps, had lifted him, raised him to the level where she dwelt; and in that way he was closer. A new strength was in him. At the same time, behind her outer quietness, and her calm, he divined struggle still. In her atmosphere was a hint of strain, disharmony. He was positive of this. From time to time he caught trouble in her eyes. Could she, perhaps, discern—foreknow—the shadow of the dropping Curtain? He wondered. He detected something in her that was new.

If any weakening of resolve were in himself, it disappeared long before Tony's arrival on the scene. A few private words from Mrs. Haughstone later banished it effectually. "Your telegram, Mr. Kelverdon, came as a great surprise. We had planned a three-day trip to the Sphinx and Pyramids. Mr. Winslowe had written to you; he hoped to persuade you to join us. Again you left Assouan before the letter arrived. It's a habit with you!"

"Apparently."

The poison no longer fevered him; he was immune. "Mr. Winslowe—I had better warn you before he comes—was disappointed."

"I'm sorry I spoilt the trip. It was most inconsiderate of me. But you can make it later when I'm gone—to Cairo, can't you?"

Mrs. Haughstone watched him somewhat keenly. Did she discover anything, he wondered. Was she aware that he was no longer within reach of her little shafts?

"It's all for the best, I think," she went on in a casual tone. "Lettice was too easily persuaded—she didn't really want to go without you. She said so. And Mr. Winslowe soon gets over his sulks—"

Tom interrupted her, turning sharply round. "Oh," he laughed, "was that why he wouldn't come to breakfast, then?" And whether it was pain or pleasure that he felt he did not know. The moment's anguish—he verily believed it—was for Lettice. And for Tony? Something akin to sympathy perhaps! If Tony should ever suffer pain like his—even temporarily...!

The other shrugged her angular shoulders a little. "It's all passed now," she observed; "he's forgotten it, I'm sure. You needn't notice anything, by the way," she added, "if—if he seems ungracious."

"Not for worlds," replied Tom, throwing stones into the sullen river below. "I'm far too tactful."

Mrs. Haughstone looked away. There was a moment's expression of admiration on her face. "You're big, Mr. Kelverdon, very big. I wish all men were as generous." She spoke hurriedly below her breath. "I saw this coming before you arrived. I wish I could have saved you. You've got the hero in you."

Tom changed the subject, and presently moved away: it was time for lunch for one thing, and for another he wanted to hide his face from her too peering eyes. He was not quite sure of himself just then; his lips trembled a little; he could not altogether control his facial muscles. Tony jealous! Lettice piqued! Was this the explanation of her new sweetness towards himself! The position tried him sorely, testing his new strength from such amazing and unexpected angles. It was all beyond him somehow, the reversal of rôles so afflicting, tears and laughter so oddly mingled. Yet the sheet-anchor—his selfless love—held fast and true. There was no dragging, no shuffling where he stood.

Nor was there any weakening of resolution in him, any dimming of the new dawn within his heart. He felt sure of something that he did not understand, aware of a radiant promise some one whispered marvelously in his ear. He was alone, yet not alone, outcast yet companioned sweetly, bereft of all the world holds valuable, yet possessor of riches that the world passed by. He felt a conqueror. The pain seemed somehow turning into joy. He seemed above the earth. Only one thing mattered—that his ideal love should have no stain upon it.

The lunch he dreaded passed smoothly and without alarm. Tony was gay, light-hearted as usual, belying Mrs. Haughstone's ominous prediction. They smoked together afterwards, walking up and down the garden arm in arm, Tony eagerly discussing expeditions, picnics, birds, anything and everything that offered, with keen interest as of old; he even once suggested coming back to Assouan with his cousin—*alone!*... Tom made no comment on the adverb. Nor was his sympathy mere acting; he genuinely felt it; the affection for Tony somehow was not dead.... The joy in him grew, meanwhile, brighter, clearer, higher. It was alive. Some courage of the sun was in him. There seemed a great understanding with it, and a greater forgiveness.

Of one thing only did he feel uncertain. He caught himself sharply wondering more than once. For he had the impression—the conviction almost—that something had happened during his absence at Assouan—that there was a change in her attitude to Tony. It was a subtle change; it was beginning merely; but it was there. Her behavior at breakfast was not due to pique, not solely due to pique, at any rate. It had a deeper origin. Almost he detected signs of friction between herself and Tony. Very slight they were indeed, if not imagined altogether. His perception was still exceptionally alert, its acuteness left over, apparently, from the earlier days of pain and jealousy. Yet the result upon him was confusing chiefly.

In very trivial ways the change betrayed itself. The talk between the three of them remained incongruously upon the surface always. The play and chatter went on independently of the Play beneath, almost ignoring it. In that Wordless Play, however, the change was registered.

"Tom, you've got the straightest back of any man I ever saw," she exclaimed once, eyeing them critically with an amused smile as they came back towards her chair. "I've just been watching you both."

They laughed, while Tony turned it wittily into fun. "It's always safer to look a person in the face," he observed. If he felt the comparison was made to his disadvantage he did not show it. Tom, wondering what she meant and why she said it, felt that the remark annoyed him. For there was disparagement of Tony in it.

"I can read your soul from your back alone," she added.

"And mine!" cried Tony, laughing: "What about my back too? Or have I got no soul misplaced between my shoulder-blades?"

Tom laid his hand between those slightly-rounded shoulders then—and rather suddenly.

"It's bent from too much creeping after birds," he exclaimed. "In your next life you'll be on all fours if you're not careful."

The Arab appeared to say the donkeys and sand-cart were waiting in the road, and Tony went indoors to get cameras and other paraphernalia essential to a Desert picnic. Lettice continued talking idly to Tom, who stood beside her, smoking.... The feeling of dream and reality were very strong in him at the moment. He hardly realized what the nonsense was he had said to his cousin. There was a slight sense of discomfort in him. The little, playful conversation just over had meaning in it. He missed that meaning. Somehow the comparison in his favor was disagreeable—he preferred to hear his cousin praised, but certainly not belittled. Perhaps vanity was wounded there—that his successful rival woke contempt in her was unendurable.... And he thought of his train for the first time with a vague relief.

"Birds," she was saying, half to herself, the eyes beneath the big sun-hat looking beyond him, "that reminds me, Tom—a dream I had. A little bird left its nest and hopped about to try all the other branches, because it thought it ought to explore them—had to, in a way. And it got into all sorts of danger, and ran fearful risks, and couldn't fly or use its wings properly,— till finally—"

She stopped, and her eyes turned full upon his own. The love in his face was plain to read, though he was not conscious of it. He waited in silence:

"Till finally it crept back up into its own nest again," she went on, "and found its wings lying there all the time. It had forgotten them! And it got in, felt warm and safe and cozy—and fell asleep."

"Whereupon you woke and found it was all a dream," said Tom. His tone, though matter-of-fact, was lower than usual, but it was firm. No sign of emotion now was visible in his face. The eyes were steady, the lips betrayed no hint. Her little dream, the way of telling it rather, perplexed him.

"No," she said, "but I found somehow that the bird was me." She sighed a little.

It flashed upon him suddenly that she was exhausted, wearied out; that her heart was beating with some interior stress and struggle. She seemed on the point of giving up, some long long battle in her ended. There was something she wished to say to him—he got this impression too—something she could not bring herself to say, unless he helped her, unless he asked for it. The duality was ending, perhaps fused into unity again?... The intense and burning desire to help her rose upon him, the desire to protect. And the word "Warsaw" fled across his mind... as though it fell through the heated air into his mind... from hers.

"Tony declares," she was saying, "that our memories are packed away under pressure like steam in a boiler, and the dream is their safety-valve...

I wonder.... He read it somewhere. It's not his own, of course. But Tony never explains—because he doesn't really know. He's flashy—not the depth we thought—the truth... *Tom!*"

She called his name with emphasis, as if annoyed that he showed so little interest. There was an instant's cloud upon her face; the eyes wavered, then looked away; he felt again there was disappointment somewhere in her with himself or with Tony, he did not know.... He kept silent. He could think of nothing by way of answer—nothing appropriate, nothing safe.

She waited, keeping silent too. The Curtain was lowering, its shadow growing on the air.

"I dream so little," he stammered at length. "I can't say." It enraged him that he faltered. He turned away.... Tony at that moment arrived. The cart and animals were ready, everything was collected. He announced it loudly, urging them with a certain impatience, as though they caused the delay. He stared keenly at them a moment.... They started.

CHAPTER XXXI

How trivial, yet how significant of the tension of interior forces—the careless words, the foolish little dream, the playful allusion to one man's stoop and to another's upright carriage, how easy to read, how obvious! Yet Tom, too intensely preoccupied, perhaps, with keeping his own balance, was unaware of revelation. His mind perceived the delicate change, yet attached a wrong direction to it. Perplexity and discomfort in him deepened. He was relieved when Tony interrupted; he felt glad. The shifting of values was disturbing to him. It was as though the falling Curtain halted...

The hours left to him were few; they both rushed and lingered. The afternoon seemed gone so quickly, while yet the moments dragged, each separate instant too intense with feeling to yield up its being willingly. The minutes lingered; it was the hours that rushed.

Subconsciously, it seemed, Tom counted them in his heart.... Subconsciously, too, he stated the position, as though to do so steadied him: Three persons, three friends, were off upon a picnic. At a certain moment they would turn back; at a certain moment two of them would say good-by; at a certain moment a final train would start—his eyes would no longer see her.... It seemed impossible, unreal; it could not happen.... He could so easily prevent it. No question had been asked about his going to Cairo; it was taken for granted that he went on business and would return. He could cancel his steamer-berth, no explanation necessary, nor any asked.

But having weighed the sacrifice against the joy he was not wanting.

They mounted their lusty donkeys; Lettice climbed into her sand-cart; the boys came clattering after them down the street of Thebes with the tea-things and the bundles of clover for the animals. Across the belt of brilliant emerald green, past clover-fields and groves of palms, they followed the ancient track towards the desert. They were on the eastern bank, the Theban Hills far behind them on the horizon. Towards the Red Sea they headed, though Tom had no notion of their direction, aware only that while they went further and further from those hills, the hills themselves somehow came ever nearer. The gaunt outline followed them; each time he looked back the shadow cast was closer than before, almost upon their heels. But for the assurance of his senses he could have believed they headed towards these yellow cliffs instead of the reverse. He could not shake off the singular impression that their weight was on his back; he felt the oppression of those ancient tombs, those crowded corridors, that hidden subterranean world. No mummy, he remembered, but believed it would one day unwind again when the soul, cleansed and justified, came back to claim it. Regeneration was inevitable. A glorious faith secure in ultimate joy!

They hurried vainly; the distance between them, instead of increasing, lessened. The hills would not let them go.

The burning atmosphere, the motionless air caused doubtless the optical illusion. The glare was blinding. Tom did not draw attention to it. He tugged his obstinate donkey into line with the slower sand-cart, riding for several minutes in silence, close beside Lettice, aware of her perfume, her flying veil almost across his eyes from time to time. Tony was some way ahead.

"Tom," he heard suddenly, "must you really go to Cairo to-night?"

"I'm afraid so. It's important." But after a pause he added "Why?" He said it because his sentence sounded otherwise suspiciously incomplete. Above all, he must seem natural. "Why do you ask?"

The answer made him regret that extra word: "There's something I want to tell you."

"*Very* important?" He asked it laughingly, busy with the reins apparently.

"Far more important than your going to Cairo. I want your advice and help."

"I must," he said slowly. "Won't it keep?" He tugged violently at the reins, though the donkey was behaving admirably.

"How long will you stay?" she asked.

"One night only, Lettice. Not longer."

They were on soft and yellow sand by now; the desert shone with a luminous glow; Tom could not hear the sound of his donkey's hoofs, nor the crunching of the sand-cart. He heard nothing but a voice singing beside him in the burning air. But the air had grown radiant. He realized that he was beating the donkey without the slightest reason.

"When you come back, then—I'll tell you when you come back," he heard.

And a sudden inspiration came to his assistance. "Couldn't you write it?" he asked calmly. "The Semiramis Hotel will find me—in case anything happened. I should have time to think it over—I like that best if it's really so important. My mind, you know, works slowly."

Her reply had a curious effect upon him. She needed help—his help. "Perhaps, Tom. But one can depend so upon your judgment."

He knew that she was watching his face. With an effort he turned to meet her gaze. He saw her against the background of the hills, whose following mass towered menacingly above her little outline. And as he looked he was suddenly transfixed, he dropped his reins, he stared without a word. Two pairs of eyes, two smiles, two human physiognomies once again met his arrested gaze. He knew them, of course, well enough by now, but never before had he caught the two expressions so vividly revealed, so distinctly marked; clear as a composite picture, one face painted in upon another that lay beneath it. There was the darker face—and there was Lettice; and each struggled for complete possession of her features. There was conflict, sharp and dreadful; one second, the gleam of cruelty flashed out, a yellow of amber in it, as though gold shone reflected faintly—the next, an anguish of tenderness, as though love brimmed her eyes with the moisture of divine compassion. The conflict was desperate, amazing, painful beyond words. Then the darker aspect slowly waned, withdrawing backwards, melting away into the shadows of the hills behind—as though it first had issued thence—as though almost it belonged there. Alive and true, yet vanquished, it faded out.... He saw at last the dear, innocent eyes of—Lettice only. It was this Lettice who had spoken.

His donkey stumbled—it was natural enough, seeing that the reins hung loose and his feet had somehow left the stirrups. Tom pitched forward heavily, saving himself and his animal from an ignominious accident just in the nick of time. There were cries and laughter. The sand-cart swerved aside at the same moment, and Tony, from a distance, came galloping back towards them.

Tom recovered his balance and told his donkey in honest English what he thought of it. "But it was your fault, you careless boy," cried Lettice; "you let go the reins and whacked it at the same time. Your eyes were popping out of your head. I thought you'd seen a ghost."

Tom glanced at her. "I was nearly off," he said. "Another second and it would have been a case of 'Low let me lie where the dead dog—'"

She interrupted him with surprising vehemence: "Don't, don't, Tom. I hate it! I hate the words and the tune and everything. I won't hear it...!"

Tony came clattering up and the incident was over, ended as abruptly as begun. But, as Tom well realized, another hitch had occurred in the lowering of the Curtain. The actors, for a moment, had stood there in their normal fashion, betrayed, caught in the act, a little foolish even. It was the hand of a *woman* this time that delayed it.

"Did you hurt yourself anywhere, Tom?" Her question rang in his head like music for the next mile or two. He kept beside the sand-cart until they reached their destination. It was absurd—yet he could not ride in front with Tony lest some one driving behind them should notice—yes, that was the half-comical truth—notice that Tony was round-shouldered—oh, very, very slightly so—whereas his own back was straight! It was ridiculously foolish, yet pathetic. At the same time, it was poignantly dramatic....

And their destination was a deep bay of yellow sand, soft and tawny, ribbed with a series of lesser troughs the wind had scooped out to look like a shore some withdrawing ocean had left exposed below the westering sun. A solitary palm tree stood behind upon a dune.

The afternoon, the beating hotness of the air, the clouds of high, suspended sand, the stupendous sunset—as if the world caught fire and burned along the whole horizon—it was all unforgettable. The yellow sand about them blazed and shone, scorching their bare hands; the Desert was empty, silent, lonely. Only the western heavens, where the sun sank in a red mass of ominous splendor, was alive with energy. Colored shafts mapped the vault from horizon to zenith like the spokes of a prodigious wheel of fire. Any minute the air and the sand it pressed upon might burst into a sea of flame. The furnace where the Khamsin brewed in distant Nubia sent its warnings in advance; it was slowly traveling northward. And hence, possibly, arose the disquieting sensation that something was gathering, something that might take them unawares. The sand lay listening, waiting, watching. There was whispering among the very grains....

It was half way through tea when the first stray puffs of wind came dropping abruptly, sighing away in tiny eddies of dust beyond the circle. Three human atoms upon the huge yellow carpet, that ere long would shake itself across five hundred miles and rise, whirling, driving, suffocating all life within its folds—three human beings noted the puffs of heated air and reacted variously to the little change. Each felt, it seemed, a slight uneasiness, as though of trouble coming that was yet not entirely atmospherical. Nerves tingled. They looked into each other's faces. They looked back.

"We mustn't stay too late," said Tony, filling a basket for the donkey-boys in their dune two hundred yards away. "We've a long way to go." He examined the portentous sky. "It won't come till night," he added, "still—they're a bit awkward, these sandstorms, and one never knows."

"And I've got a train to catch," Tom mentioned, "absurd as it sounds in a place like this." He was scraping his lips with a handkerchief. "I've eaten enough bread-and-sand to last me till dinner, anyhow." He helped his cousin with the Arabs' food. "They probably don't mind it, they're used to it." He straightened up from his stooping posture. Lettice, he saw, was lying with a cigarette against the bank of sloping sand that curved above them. She was intently watching them. She had not spoken for some time; she looked almost drowsy; the eyelids were half closed; the cigarette smoke rose in a steady little thread that did not waver.... There was perhaps ten yards between them, but he caught the direction of her gaze, and throwing his own eyes into the same line of sight, he saw what she saw. Instinctively, he took a quick step forward—hiding Tony from her immediate view.

It was certainly curious, this desire to screen his cousin, to prevent his appearing at a disadvantage. He was impelled, at all costs and in the smallest details, to help the man she admired, to increase his value, to minimize his disabilities, however trivial. It pained him to see Tony even at a physical disadvantage; Tony must show always at his very best; and at this moment, bending over the baskets, the attitude of the shoulders was disagreeably emphasized.

Tom did not laugh, he did not even smile. Gravely, as though it were of importance, he moved forward so that Lettice should not see the detail of the rounded shoulders that, he knew, compared unfavorably with his own straighter carriage. Yet almost the next minute, when he looked back again, he saw that the cigarette had fallen from her fingers, the eyes were closed, her body had slipped into a more recumbent angle, she seemed actually asleep.

"Give a shout, Tom, and the boys will come to fetch it," said Tony, when at length the basket was ready. He put his hands to his own mouth to co-ee across the dunes. Tom stopped him at once. "Hush! Lettice has dropped off," he explained; "you'll wake her. It's the heat. I'll carry the things over to them." He noticed Tony's hands as he held them to his lips. And again he felt a touch of sympathy, almost pity. Had she, so observant, so discerning in her fastidious taste—had *she* failed to notice the small detail too?

"No, let me take it," Tony was saying, seizing the hamper from his cousin. Tom suggested carrying it between them. They tried it, laughing and struggling together with the awkward burden, but keeping their voices low. They lost the direction too; for all the sand-dunes were alike, and the boys were hidden in a hollow. It ended in Tony going off in triumph with the basket under one arm, guided at length by the faint neighing of a donkey in the distance.

Some little time had passed, perhaps five minutes, perhaps longer, and Tom went back to the tea-place across the soft sand, stepping cautiously so as not to disturb the sleeper. And another five minutes, perhaps another ten, had slipped by before Tony's head reappeared above a neighboring dune. A boy had come to meet him, shortening his journey.

But Fate calculated to a nicety, wasting no seconds one way or the other. There had been time—just time before Tony's return—for Tom to have stretched himself at her feet, to have lit a cigarette, and to have smoked sufficient of it for the first ash to fall. He was very careful to make no sound, even lighting the match softly inside his hat. But his hand was trembling. For Lettice slept, and in her sleep made little sounds of pain. No words were audible.... He watched her. There was a tiny frown between the eyebrows, the lips twitched from time to time, she moved uneasily upon the bank of sliding sand; and, as she made these little broken sounds of pain, from beneath the closed eyelids two small tears crept out upon her cheeks.

Tom watched, making no sound or movement. The tears rolled down and fell into the sand. The suffering in the face made his heart beat irregularly. Something transfixed him. She wore the expression he had seen in the London theater. For a moment he felt terror—a terror of something coming, something going to happen. He stared, trembling, holding his breath. She was dreaming, as a person even in a three-minute sleep can dream—deeply, vividly. He waited. He had the amazing sensation that he knew what she was dreaming—that he took part in it with her almost.... Unable, finally, to restrain himself another instant, he moved—and the noise wakened her. She sighed. The eyes opened of their own accord. She stared at him in a dazed way for a moment. Then she looked over his shoulder across the desert.

"You've been asleep, Lettice," he whispered, "and actually dreaming—all in five minutes."

She rubbed her eyes slowly, as though sand was in them. She stared into his face a moment before she spoke.

"Yes, I dreamed," she answered with a little frightened sigh. "I dreamed of you— There was a tent—the flap lifted suddenly—oh, it was so vivid! Then there was a crowd and awful drums were beating—and my river with the floating faces was there and I plunged in to save one—it was yours, *Tom,* yours—"

She paused for a fraction of a second, while his heart went thumping against his ribs. He did not speak. He waited.

"Then somehow you were taken from me," she went on; "you left me, Tom." Her voice sank. "And it broke my heart in two."

"Lettice...!"

He made a sudden movement in the sand—at which movement, precisely, Tony's head appeared above the neighboring dune, the rest of his body following it immediately.

And it seemed to Tom that his cousin came upon them out of the heart of a dream, out of the earth, out of a sandy tomb. His very existence, for those minutes, had been utterly forgotten, obliterated. He rose from the dead and came towards them over the hot, yellow desert. The distant hills—the Theban Hills above the Valley of the Kings—disgorged him. And, as once before, he looked dreadful, threatening, his great hands held out in front of him. He came gliding down the yielding slope. He caught them!

In that second—it was but the fraction of a second actually—the impression upon Tom's mind was acute and terrible. Speech and movement were not in him anywhere; he could only sit and stare, both terrified and fascinated. Between himself and Lettice stretched an interval of six feet certainly, and into this very gap, the figure of his cousin, followed and preceded by heaps of moving sand, descended now. It was towards Lettice that Tony came so swiftly gliding.

It was his cousin surely...?

He saw the big hands outspread, he saw the slightly stooping shoulders, he saw the face and eyes, the light blue eyes. But also he saw strange, unaccustomed raiment, he saw a sheet of gold, he smelt the soft breath of ambra.... And the face was dark and menacing. There were words, too, careless, playful words, uttered undoubtedly by Tony's familiar voice: "Caught you both asleep! Well, I declare! You *are* a couple...!" followed by something else about its being "time to pack up and go because the sand was coming...." Tom heard the words distinctly, but far away, tiny with curious distance; they were half smothered, half submerged, it seemed, behind an acute inner hearing that caught another set of words he could not understand—in a language he both remembered and forgot. And the deep sense of dread passed swiftly then into a blinding jealous rage; he saw red; a fury of wrath that could kill and stab and strangle rushed over him in a flood of passionate emotion. He lost control. He rushed headlong.

Seconds dragged out incredibly into minutes, as though time halted.... An intense, murderous hatred blazed in his heart.

From where he sat, both figures were above him, sheltered half way up the long sliding slope. At the base of the yellow dune he crouched; he looked up at them. His eyes perhaps were blinded by the red tempest in his heart; or perhaps the tiny particles of flying sand drove against his eyeballs. He saw, at any rate, the two figures close together, as if the man came gliding straight into her arms.

At the same moment a draught of sudden, violent wind broke with a pouring rush across the desert, and the entire crest of the undulating dune behind them rose to meet it in a single whirling eddy. As a gust of sea-wind tosses the spray into the air, this burst of scorching desert-wind drew the ridge up after it, then flung it in a blinding swirl against his face and skin.

The dune rose in a Wave of glittering yellow sand, drowning them from head to foot. He saw the glint and shimmer of the myriad particles in the sunset; he saw them drifting by the thousand, by the million through the whirling mass of it; he saw the two figures side by side above him, caught beneath the toppling crest of this bending billow that curved and broke against the fiery sky; he smelt the faint perfume of the desert underneath the hollow arch; he heard the thin, metallic grating of the countless grains in friction; he heard the palm leaves rattling; he saw two pairs of eyes... his feet went shuffling. It was The Wave—of sand....

And the nightmare clutch laid hold upon his heart with giant pincers. The fiery red of insensate anger burst into flames, filled his throat to choking, set his paralyzed muscles free with uncontrollable energy. This savage lust of murder caught him. The shuffling went faster, faster.... He turned and faced the eyes. He would kill—rather than see her touched by those great hands. It seemed he made the leap of a wild animal upon its prey....

Fire flashed... then passed, before he knew it, from red to shining amber, from sullen crimson into purest gold, from gold to the sheen of dazzling whiteness. The change was instantaneous. His leap was arrested in midair. The red wrath passed amazingly, forgotten or transmuted. With a miraculous swiftness he was aware of understanding, of sympathy, of forgiveness.... The red light melted into white—the white of glory. The murder faded from his heart, replaced by a deep, deep glow of peace, of love, of infinite trust, of complete comprehension.... He accepted something marvelously. He forgot—himself....

The eyes faded, the gold, the raiment, the perfume vanished, the sound died away. He no longer shuffled upon yielding sand. There was solid ground beneath his feet.... He was standing alert and upright, his arms outstretched to save—Tony from collapse upon the sliding dune. And the sandy wind drove blindingly against his face and skin.

The three of them stood side by side, holding to each other, laughing, choking, spluttering, heads bent and eyes closed tightly. Tom found his cousin's hand in his own, clutching it firmly to keep his balance, while behind himself—against his "straight back," he realized, even while he choked and laughed—Lettice clung for shelter. Tom, therefore, actually *had* leaped forward—but to protect and not to kill. He protected both of them. This time, however, it was to himself that Lettice clung, instead of to another.

The violent gust passed on its way, the flying cloud of sand subsided, settling down on everything. For a moment they stood there rubbing their eyes, shaking their clothing free; then raising their heads cautiously, they looked about them. The air was still and calm again, but in the distance, already a mile away and swiftly traveling across the luminous waste, they saw the miniature whirlwind driving furiously, leaping from ridge to ridge. It swept over the innumerable dunes, lifting the series, one crest after another, into upright waves upon a yellow shimmering sea, then scattering them in a cloud that shone and glinted against the fiery sunset. Its track was easily marked. They watched it....

Tony was the first to recover breath.

"Whew!" he cried, still spluttering, "but that was sudden! It took me clean off my feet for a moment. I got your hand, Tom, only just in time to save myself!" He shook himself, the sand was down his back and in his hair, his shoes were full of it. "There'll be another any minute now—another whirlwind—we'd better be starting." He began packing up busily, shouting as he did so to the donkey-boys. "By jove!" he cried the next second, "look what's happened to our dune!"

Tom, who was on his knees, helping Lettice shake her skirts free, rose to look. The high, curving bank of sand where they had sheltered had indeed changed its shape; the entire ridge had been flattened by the wind; the crest had been lifted and carried away, scattered in all directions. The wave-outline of two minutes before no longer existed, it had broken, fallen over, melted back into the surrounding sea of desert whence it rose....

"It's disappeared!" exclaimed Tom and Lettice in the same breath.

The boys arrived with the animals and sand-cart; the baskets were quickly arranged, Tony mounted, Tom helped Lettice in. She leaned heavily on his arm and shoulder. It was in this moment's pause before the actual start that Lettice turned her head suddenly as though listening. The air, motionless again, extraordinarily heated, hung in a dull and yet transparent curtain between them and the sinking sun. The entire heavens seemed to form a sounding-board, the least vibration resonant beneath its stretch.

"Listen!" she exclaimed. She had uttered no word till now. She looked down at Tom, then looked away again.

They turned their heads in the direction where she pointed, and Tom caught a faint, distant sound as of little strokes that fell thudding on the heavy air. Tony declared he heard nothing. The sound repeated itself rapidly, but at rhythmic intervals; it was unpleasant somewhere, a hint of alarm and menace in the throbbing note—ominous as though it warned. In the pulse of the blood it seemed, like the beating of the heart, Tom thought. It came to him almost through the pressure of her hand upon his shoulder, although his ear told him it came from the horizon where the Theban Hills loomed through the coming dusk, just visible, but shadowy. The muttering died away, then ceased, but not before he suddenly recalled an early morning hour beside a mountain lake, when months ago the thud of invisible paddle-wheels had stolen upon him through the quiet air....

"A drum," he heard Lettice murmur. "It's a native drum in Thebes. My little dream! How the sound travels too! And how it multiplies!" She peered at Tom through half-closed eyelids. "It must be at least a dozen miles away...!" She smiled faintly, then dropped her eyes quickly.

"Or a dozen centuries," he replied, not knowing quite why he said it. "And more like a thousand drums than only one!" He smiled too. For another part of him, beyond capture somehow, knew what he meant, knew also why he smiled—knew also that *she* knew.

"It frightens me! It's horrible. It sounds like death!" And though she whispered the words, more to herself than to the others, Tom heard each syllable.

The sound died away into the distance, and then ceased.

Then Tony, watching them both, but, unable to hear anything himself, called out again impatiently that it was time to start, that Tom had a train to catch, that any minute the real, big wind might be upon them. The hand slowly, half lingeringly, left Tom's shoulder. They started rapidly with a kind of flourish. In a thin, black line the small procession crept across the immense darkening desert, like a strip of life that drifted upon a shoreless ocean....

The sun sank down below the Lybian sands. But no awful wind descended. They reached home safely, exhausted and rather silent. The two hours seemed to Tom to have passed with a dream-like swiftness. The stars were shining as they clattered down the little Luxor street. In a dream, too, he went to the hotel to change, and fetch his bag; in a dream he stood upon the platform, held Tony's hand, held the soft hand of Lettice, said good-by ... and watched the station lights glide past as he left them standing there together.

CHAPTER XXXII

One incident, however,—trivial, yet pregnant with significant revelation,—remained vividly outside the dream. The Play behind broke through, as it were; an actor forgot his rôle, and involved another actor; for an instant the masquerade tripped up, and merged with the commonplace reality of daily life. Explicit disclosure lay in the trifling matter.

There was a touch of comedy, but of rather ghastly comedy, ludicrous and at the same time painful—those smart, new yellow gloves that Tony put on when he climbed into the sand-cart and took the reins. His donkey had gone lame, he abandoned it to the boys behind, he climbed in to drive with Lettice. Tom, riding beside the cart, witnessed the entire incident; he laughed as heartily as either of the others; he felt it, however, as she felt it—a new sudden spiritual proximity to her proved this to him. Both shrank—from something disagreeable and afflicting. The hands looked somehow dreadful.

For the first time Tom realized the physiognomy of hands—that hands, rather than faces, should be photographed; not merely that they seemed now so large, so spread, so ugly, but that somehow the glaring canary yellow subtly emphasized another aspect that was distasteful and unpleasant—an undesirable aspect in their owner. The cotton was atrocious. So obvious was it to Tom that he felt pity before he felt disgust. The obnoxious revelation was so palpable. He was aware that he felt ashamed—for Lettice. He stared for a moment, unable to move his eyes away. The next second, lifting his glance, he saw that she, too, had noticed it. With a flash of keen relief, he was aware that she, like himself, shrank visibly from the distressing half-sinister revelation that was betrayal.

The hands, cased in their ridiculous yellow cotton, had physiognomy. Upon the pair of them, just then, was an expression not to be denied: of furtiveness, of something sly and unreliable, a quality not to be depended on through thick and thin, able to grasp for themselves but not to hold—for others; eager to take, yet incompetent to give. The hands were selfish, mean and unprotective. It was a remarkable disclosure of innate duality hitherto concealed. Their physiognomy dropped a mask the face still wore. The hands looked straight at Lettice; they assumed a sensual leer; they grinned.

"One second," Tony cried, "the reins hurt my fingers,"—and had drawn from his pocket the gloves and quickly slipped them on—canary yellow—cotton!

"Oh, oh!" exclaimed Lettice, "but how can you! It's ghastly... for a man...!" She stared a moment, as though fascinated, then turned her eyes away, flicking the whip in the air and laughing—a trifle boisterously.

Why the innocent, if vulgar, scraps of clothing should have been so revealing was hard to say. That they were incongruous and out of place in the Desert was surely an inconsiderable thing, that they were possibly in bad taste was of even less account. It was something more than that. It came in a second of vivid intuition—so, at least, it seemed to Tom, and therefore perhaps to Lettice too—that he saw his cousin's soul behind the foolish detail. Tony had put his soul upon his hands—and the hands were somewhere cheap and worthless.

So difficult was it to catch the elusive thought in language, that Tom certainly used none of the adjectives that flashed unbidden across his mind; he assuredly thought neither of "coarse," "untrustworthy," nor of "false" or "nasty"—yet the last named came probably nearest to expressing the disquieting sensation that laid its instant pressure upon his nerves, then went its way again. It was disturbing in a very searching way; he felt uneasy for *her* sake. How could he leave her with the owner of those hands, the wearer of those appalling yellow cotton gloves! The laughter in him was subtle mockery. For, of course, he laughed at himself for such an absurd conclusion.... Yet, somehow, those gloves revealed the man, betrayed him mercilessly! The hands themselves were stained and they were—naked.

It was just then that her exclamation of disapproval interrupted Tom's curious sensations. It came with welcome. "Thank Heavens!" a voice cried inside him.... "She feels it too!"

"But my sister sent them to me," Tony defended himself, "sent them from London. They're the latest thing at home!" He was laughing at himself. At the same time he was shifting the responsibility as usual.

Lettice laughed with him then, though her laughter held another note that was not merriment. He felt disgust, resentment in her. There was no pity there. Tony had missed a cue—the entire Play was blocked. The "hero" stirred contempt in place of admiration. But more—the incident confirmed, it seemed, much else that had preceded it. Her eyes were opened.

The conflict of pain and joy in Tom was most acute. His entire sacrifice—for an instant—trembled in a hair-like balance. For the capital rôle stood gravely endangered in her eyes.

"Take them off, Tony! Put them away! Hide them! I couldn't trust you to drive me with such things on your hands. A man in yellow canary cotton!"

All three laughed together, and Tom, watching the trivial incident, as he rode beside them, saw her seize one hand and pull the glove off by the fingers. It seemed she tore a mask from one side of his face—the face beneath was disfigured. The glove fell into the bottom of the cart, then caught the loose rein and was jerked out upon the sand. The next second, something of covert fury in the gesture, Tony had taken off the other and tossed it to keep company with the first. Both hands showed naked: the entire face was bare. Tom looked away.

"They *are* hideous rather, I admit," exclaimed Tony. "The donkey boys can pick them up and wear them." And there was mortification in his tone and manner; almost—he was found out.

It was the memory of this pregnant little incident that held persistently before Tom's mind now, as the train bore him the long night through between the desert and the river that were Egypt. The bigger crowding pictures, scenes and sentences, thronged panorama of the recent weeks, lay in hiding underneath; but it was the incident of those yellow gloves that memory tossed up for ever before his eyes. He clung to it in spite of himself. Imagination played its impish pranks. What did it portend? Removing gloves was the first act in undressing, it struck him. Tony had dressed up for the Play, the Play was over, he must put off, piece by piece, the glamour he had worn so successfully for his passionate rôle. Once off the stage, the enchantment of the limelight, the scenery, the raiment of gold that left a perfume of ambra in the air—all the assumed allurements he had borrowed must be discarded. The Tony of the dream withdrew, the real Tony stood discovered, undressed—by no means admirable. No longer on the boards, walking like a king, with the regal fascination of an older day, he would pass along the busy street unnoticed, unadorned, bereft of the high distinction that imagination, so strangely stirred, had laid upon him for a little space.... The yellow gloves lay now upon the desert sand; perhaps the whirling tempest tossed them to and fro, perhaps it buried them; perhaps the Arab boys, proud of the tinsel they mistook for gold, now wore them in their sleep, lying on beds of rushes beneath the flat-roofed houses of sun-baked clay....

This vivid detail kept the heavier memories back at first; somehow the long review of his brief Egyptian winter blocked each time against a pair of stooping shoulders and a pair of yellow cotton gloves.

During the voyage of four days, however, followed then the inevitable cruel aftermath of doubt, suspicion, jealousy he had fancied long since overthrown. A hundred incidents and details forced themselves upon him from the past—glances, gestures, phrases, such little things and yet so pregnant with delayed or undelivered meaning. The meanings rose remorselessly to the surface now.

All belonged to the first days in Egypt before he noticed anything; the mind worked backwards to their gleaning. They had escaped his attention at the time, yet the mind had registered them none the less. He did not seek their recovery, but the series offered itself, compelling him to examine one and all, demanding that he should pass judgment. He forced them back, they leaped up again on springs; the resilience was due to their life, their truth; they were not to be denied.

All pointed to the same conclusion: the month spent alone with Tony had worked the mischief before his own arrival—by the time he came upon the scene the new relationship was in full swing beyond her power to stop it. Heavens, he had been blind! Ceaselessly, endlessly, he made the circle of alternate pain and joy, of hope and despair, of doubt and confidences— yet the ideal in him safe beyond assault. He believed in her, he trusted, and he—hoped.

The most poignant test, however, came when port was reached and the scented land-wind met his nostrils with the—Spring. He saw the harbor with its white houses shining in the early April sunshine; the blue sea recalled a wide-shored lake among the mountains: he saw the seagulls, heard the lapping of the waves against the shipping....

He took the train to a little town along the coast, meaning to stay there a day or two before facing London, where the dismantling of the Brown Flat, and the search for work awaited him. And there the full-blooded spring of this southern climate took him by the throat. The haze, the sweet moist air, the luscious fields, the woods and flowery roads, above all the singing birds—this biting contrast with the dry, blazing desert skies of tawny Egypt was dislocating. The fierce glare of perpetual summer seemed a nightmare he had left behind; he came back to the sweet companionship of friendly life in field and tree and flower.

The first soft shower of rain, the first long twilight, the singing of the thrushes after dark, the light in the little homestead windows—he felt such intimate kindness in it all that the tears rose to his eyes. He longed to share it with her... there was no joy in life without her.... Egypt lay behind him with its awful loneliness, its stern, forbidding emptiness, its nightmare sunsets, its cruel desert, its appalling vastness in which everything had already happened. Thebes was a single, enormous tomb; his past lay buried there; from the solemn, mournful, desolate hills he had escaped.... He emerged into a smiling land of running streams and flowers. His new life was beginning like the Spring. It gushed everywhere, reminding him of another Spring he had known among the mountains.... The "sum of loss" he counted minute by minute, hour by hour, day by day. He began the long, long reckoning...

He felt intolerably alone. The hunger and yearning in his heart seemed more than he could bear. This beauty... without her beside him, without her to share the sweet companionship of the earth... was too much to bear. For one minute with her beside him in the meadows, picking flowers, listening to the birds, her blue veil flying in the wet mountain wind—he would have given all his life, his past, his future, everything that mind and heart held precious.... In the middle of which and at its darkest moment came the certain knowledge with a joy that broke in light and rapture on his soul—that she was beside him because she was within him.... He approached the impersonal, selfless attitude to which the attainment of an ideal alone is possible. She had been added to him....

CHAPTER XXXIII

The silence, meanwhile, was like the silence that death brings. He clung tenaciously to his ideal, yet he thought of her daily, nightly, hourly. She was really never absent from his thoughts. He starved, yet perhaps he did not know he starved.... The days grew into weeks with a grinding, dreadful slowness. He had written from the steamer, explaining briefly that he was called to England. He had written a similar line to Tony too. No answers came.

Yet the silence was full of questions. The mystery of her Egyptian infatuation remained the biggest one of all perhaps. But there were others, equally insistent. Did he really possess her in a way that made earthly companionship unnecessary? Had he lasting joy in this ideal possession? Was it true that an ideal once attained, its prototype becomes unsatisfying? Did he deceive himself? And had not her strange experience after all but ripened and completed her nature, provided something she had lacked before, and blended the Mother and the Woman into the perfect mate his dream foretold and his deep heart's instinct prophesied?

He heard many answers to these questions; his heart made one, his reason made another. It was the soft and urgent Spring, however, with its perfumed winds, its singing birds, its happy message breaking with tumultuous life—it was the Spring on those wooded Mediterranean shores that whispered the compelling truth. He needed her, he yearned. An ideal, on this earth, to retain its upward lure, must remain—an ideal. Attainment in the literal sense destroys it. His arms were hungry and his heart was desolate. Then one day he knew the happy yet unhappy feeling that she suffered too. He felt her thoughts about him like soft birds....

And he wrote to her: "I should just like to know that you are well—and happy." He addressed it to the Bungalow. The same day, chance had it, he received word from her, forwarded from the Semiramis Hotel in Cairo. She wrote two lines only: "Tom, the thing I had to tell you about was—Warsaw. It is over. As you said, it is better written, perhaps, than told. Yours, L."

Egypt came flooding through the open window as he laid the letter down; the silence, the desert spaces, the perfume and the spell. He saw one thing clearly in that second, for he saw it in a flash. The secret of her trouble that last day in Luxor was laid bare—the knowledge that within a few hours she would be free. To Tom she could not easily tell it; delicacy, modesty, pride forbade. Her long, painful duty, faithfully fulfilled these many years, was over. Her world had altered, opened out. Values, of course, had instantly altered too; she saw what was real and what ephemeral; she looked at Tony and she looked at—himself. She could speak to Tony—it was easier, it did not matter—but she could not so easily speak to Tom. The yellow gloves of cotton!... His heart leaped within him....

He stared out of the window across the blue Mediterranean with its dancing, white-capped waves; he saw the white houses by the harbor; he watched the whirling sea-gulls and tasted the fresh, salt air. How familiar it all was! Of her whereabouts at that moment he had no knowledge; she might be on the steamer, gazing at the same dancing waves; she might be in Warsaw or in London even; she might pass by the windows of the Brown Flat....

He turned aside, closing the window. Egypt withdrew, the glamour waned, the ancient spell seemed lifted. He thought of those Theban Hills without emotion. Yet something in him trembled; he yearned, he ached, he longed with all the longing of the Spring. He wavered—oh, deliciously...! He was glad, radiantly glad, that she had written. Only—he dared not, he could not answer....

Yet big issues are decided sometimes by paltry and ignoble influences when sturdier considerations produce no effect. It is the contrast that furnishes the magic. It was contrast, doubtless, that swayed Tom's judgment in the very direction he had decided was prohibited. His surroundings at the moment supplied the contrast, for these surroundings were petty and ignoble—they drove him by the distress of sheer disgust into the world of larger values he had known with her. Probably, he did not discover this consciously for himself: the result, in any case, was logical and obvious. Values changed suddenly for him, too, both in his outlook and his judgment.

For he was spending a few days with his widowed sister, she who had been playmate to Lettice years ago; and the conditions of her life and mind distressed him. He had seen her name in a hotel list of Mentone; he surprised her with a visit; he was received with inexplicable coldness. His tie with her was slight, her husband, a clergyman, little to his liking; he had not been near them for several years. The frigid reception, however, had a deeper cause he felt; his curiosity was piqued.

His sister's chart of existence, indeed, was too remote from his own for true sympathy to be possible, and her married life had not improved her. They had drifted apart without openly acknowledging it. There was no quarrel, but there was a certain bitterness between them. She had a marked *faiblesse*, strange in one securely born, for those nominally in high places that, while disingenuous enough, jarred painfully always on her brother. God was unknown to her, although her husband preached most familiarly concerning Him. She had never seen the deity, but an Earl was a living reality, and often very useful. This banal weakness, he now found, had increased in widowhood. Tom hid his extreme distaste—and learned the astonishing reason for her coldness. It was Mrs. Haughstone. It took his breath away. He was too amazed to speak.

How clearly he understood her conduct now in Egypt! For Mrs. Haughstone had spread stories of the Bungalow, pernicious stories of an incredible kind, yet with just sufficient basis of apparent truth to render them plausible—plausible, that is, to any who were glad of an excuse to believe them against himself. These stories by a roundabout way, gathering in circumstantial detail as they traveled, had reached his sister. She wished to believe them, and she did. Certain relatives, moreover, of meager intelligence but highly placed in the social world, and consequently of great importance in her life, were remotely affected by the lurid tales. A report in full is unnecessary, but Mary held that the family honor was stained. It was an incredible imbroglio. Tom was so overwhelmed by this revelation of the jealous woman's guile, and the light it threw upon her rôle in Egypt, that he did not even trouble to defend himself. He merely felt sorry that his sister could believe such tales—and forgave her without a single word. He saw in it all another scrap of evidence that the Wave had indeed fallen, that his life everywhere, and from the most unlikely directions, was threatened, that all the most solid in the structure he had hitherto built up and leaned upon, was crumbling—and must crumble utterly—in order that it might rise secure upon fresh foundations.

He faced it, but faced it silently. He washed his hands of all concerned; he had learned their values too; he now looked forward instead of behind; that is, he forgot, and at the same time utterly—forgave.

But the effect upon him was curious. The stagnant ditch his sister lived in had the result of flinging him headlong back into the larger stream he had just left behind him; in that larger world things happened indeed, things unpleasant, cruel, mysterious, amazing—but yet not little things. The scale was vaster, horizons wider, beauty and wonder walked hand in hand with love and death. The contrast shook him; the trivial blow had this immense effect, that he yearned with redoubled passion for the nobler region in which ideals with their prototypes, however broken, existed side by side.

This yearning, and the change involved, remained subtly concealed, however. He was not properly conscious of it. Other very practical considerations, moreover, influenced him; his money was getting low; he had luckily sublet the flat, but the question of work was becoming insistent. There was much to be faced.... A month had slipped by, it was five weeks since he had left Egypt. He decided to go to London. He telegraphed to the Club for his letters—he expected important ones—to be sent to Paris, and it was in a small high room on the top floor of a second-rate hotel across the Seine, that he found them waiting for him. It was here, in this dingy room, that he read the wondrous words. The letter had lain at his Club three days, it was dated Switzerland and the postmark was Montreux. It was in pencil, without beginning and without end; his name, her signature did not appear:

Your little letter has come—yes, I am well, but happy I am not. I went to the Semiramis and found that you had sailed, sailed without even a good-by. I have come here, here to familiar little Montreux by the blue lake, where we first knew the Spring together. I can't say anything, I can't explain anything. You must never ask me to explain; Egypt changed me—brought out something in me I was helpless to resist. It was something perhaps I needed. I struggled—perhaps you can guess how I struggled, perhaps you can't. I have suffered these past weeks, I believe that I have expiated something. The power that drove me is exhausted, and that is all I know. I have worked it out. I have come back. There is no blame for others—for any one; I can't explain. Your little letter has come, and so I write. Help me, oh, help me in years to find my respect again, and try to love the woman you once knew—knew here in Montreux beside the lake, long ago in our childhood days, further back still, perhaps, though where I do not know. And, Tom—tell me how you are. I must know that. Please write and tell me that. I can bear it no longer. If anything happened to you I should just turn over and die. You have been true and very big, oh, so true and big. I see it now....

Tom did not answer. He took the night train. He was just in time to catch the Simplon Express from the Gare de Lyon. He reached Montreux at seven o'clock, when the June sun was already high above the Dent du Midi and the lake a sheet of sparkling blue. He went to his old hotel. He saw the swans floating like bundles of dry paper, he saw the whirling sea-gulls, he obtained his former room. And spring was just melting into full-blown summer upon the encircling mountains.

It was still early when he had bathed and breakfasted, too early for visitors to be abroad, too early to search.... He could settle to nothing; he filled the time as best he could; he smoked and read an English newspaper that was several days old at least. His eyes took in the lines, but his mind did not take in the sense—until a familiar name caught his attention and made him keenly alert. The name was Anthony Winslowe. He remembered suddenly that Tony had never replied to his letter.... The paragraph concerning his cousin, however, dealt with another matter that sent the blood flaming to his cheeks. He was defendant in the breach of promise suit brought by a notorious London actress, then playing in a popular revue. The case had opened; the letters were already produced in court—and read. The print danced before his eyes. The letters were dated last October and November, just before Tony had come out to Egypt, and with crimson face Tom read them. It was more than distressing, it was afflicting—the letters tore an established reputation into a thousand pieces. He could not finish the report; he only prayed that another had not seen it....

It was eleven o'clock when he went out and joined the throng of people sunning themselves on the walk beside the lake. The air was sweet and fresh, there were sailing-boats upon the water, the blue mountains lifted their dazzling snow far, far into the summer sky. He leaned over the rail and watched the myriads of tiny fishes, he watched the swans, he saw the dim line of the Jura hills in the hazy distance, he heard the muffled beat of a steamer's paddle-wheels a long way off. And then, abruptly, he was aware that some one touched him; a hand in a long white glove was on his arm; there was a subtle perfume; two dark eyes looked into his; and he heard a low familiar voice:

"One day we shall find each other in a crowd."

Tom was amazingly inarticulate. He just turned and looked down at her, moving a few inches closer as he did so. She wore a black boa; the fur touched his cheek.

"You have come back," he said.

There was a new wonder in her face, a soft new beauty. The woman in her glowed.... He saw the suffering plainly too.

"We have both found out," she said very low, "found out what we are to one another."

Tom's supply of words failed completely then. He looked at her—looked all the language in the world. And she understood. She lowered her eyes. "I feel shy," he thought he heard. It was murmured only. The next minute she raised her eyes again to his. He saw them dark and beautiful, tender as his mother's, true and faithful, as in his boyhood's dream of years ago. But they were now a woman's eyes.

"I never really left you, Tom..." she said with absolute conviction. "I never could. I went aside... to fetch something—to give to you. That was all!"

THE END